*This book is dedicated with love to
three of the Gallaher musketeers:*

Joyce Rucker
Suzie Bissell
and
Robert W. Gallaher

A thing of beauty is a joy forever:
Its loveliness increases; it will never
Pass into nothingness; but still will keep
A bower quiet for us, and a sleep
Full of sweet dreams, and health, and
   quiet breathing.

—JOHN KEATS, *Endymion*, Bk. I

ACKNOWLEDGMENTS

The author gratefully acknowledges the kind help of Terry Root, proprietor of The Orchid Zone in Moss Landing, California, for the personal tour of his extraordinary facility and the tidbits he passed along to me from his vast store-house of knowledge about orchids. Any mistakes regarding orchids are my own. And, as always, thanks are due to Nancy Austin and Bill Cawley for their countless kindnesses, not least of which was introducing me to the wonders of Santa Cruz County, California.

Time To Say Goodbye

The End as the Beginning
Early Fall 2000

The weather was peculiar for this time of year. Perhaps, the man thought, it was in deference to the occasion. The sun was virtually obscured in the overcast autumn sky, only the palest milky specter breaking through the cloud cover. The fog shrouded the landscape amid its moist swirls, making even the majestic redwoods appear to be ghostly apparitions.

A small shell-encrusted vase had been made especially for the occasion. Filled with the remains.

A whole lifetime reduced to a handful of ashes, he thought.

The man turned to his companion. His handsome features did not conceal the unbearable loss and pain that he felt, hard as he tried to mask them, but he straightened his shoulders and they began the short walk to their car. He opened the door for her, then walked around and slid in on the driver's side, carefully placing the vase on the seat next to him. He started the car, backed out, and began the drive over to the coast, then south, down to Big Sur.

The drive was silent but for the occasional sigh or a choked sob from the passenger seat, a sound that barely registered on the man's consciousness, absorbed as he was with his loss and the task at hand. As if to cloak his sorrow, the fog obscured the beauty of the wildly dramatic coastline, offering only an occasional view of the precipitous headlands and narrow canyons, the rocky outcrops and marine terraces. It wreathed the pines and cypresses, enveloped the heights of the gnarled live oaks and ancient redwoods, and congealed the coast's special light into a pearlescent gray.

Nearing their destination, he slowed the car, searching for the turnoff. It was not well marked and all but invisible in the fog. Then, suddenly, there it was to the right. Sycamore Canyon Road. He hit the brakes and swerved onto the road, jogging her out of her reverie, but she swallowed her fright, maintaining the silence.

He pressed the button to roll down his window, and the car was filled with the relentless roar of the surf crashing on the rocky shore. *This is a place that begs for tragedy*, he thought, *despite its great beauty or perhaps because of it*. He slowed to a snail's pace, suddenly reluctant to do what he had come here to do. He

2

parked, turned the ignition off, then stared straight ahead into the swirling fog. After a few moments he turned to her.

'I won't be long,' he said. Without waiting for a response, he got out of the car and reached back in to retrieve the shell-encrusted vase. Then he began the lonely walk to the beach, his precious cargo in the crook of his arm.

His long strides brought him to the edge of a granite and sandstone outcrop. He stopped and looked around to get his bearings. Through the vaporous tendrils of fog, he could make out the familiar path down through the rocks, and in the distance the deep indigo of the sea.

This is a truly magical place, he thought, *all crashing waves, sea caves, and arches. A place of grandeur and mystery and aching beauty.*

And now it is to be her final resting place.

With that thought, he took a deep breath, the salty sea air filling his lungs. The path, he knew, was narrow and steep, dangerous in places. With his lips set in a line of grim determination and the vase clutched securely against his chest, he began his descent, carefully picking his way over the barren rocks, down to the sea. His muscular body was constrained by the suit he'd worn to the memorial service, but he didn't think of it. The numbness that had carried him through the last few days saw him down the path toward the sea and his inevitable duty.

When he finally reached the shore, he saw that no one else was about. He was alone with her. He planted his feet in the sand and glanced out at an invisible horizon, then north, south, and back up at the rocky outcrop down which he had just climbed. Shifting his gaze back to the south, he began walking. It was only about fifty yards or so to the spot she had chosen, the spot that he knew so well in his mind's eye, as she had. The wind whipped against his jacket and tie, blew salty spume in his eyes, and danced madly in his hair, but he ignored it, concentrating on his destination.

Reaching the place, he looked about him again, then nodded with satisfaction.

This is it, he thought.

He waded out into the water, not caring about the shock of its icy chill. He shifted the vase from the crook of his arm to his hands and looked down at it.

How do you say good-bye to someone who was so full of life? Who found life endlessly curious and amusing, sometimes mysterious, but always interesting? Someone who had never tired of taking chances with him, of risking her all for him? Someone with whom he had shared so much passion? So much love?

Her life had been stolen away and now she was but ashes. Tears began to form in his eyes, and as he removed the lid from the vase, they slid unchecked down his cheeks.

He lifted the vase up, up to the heavens, letting the wind pick up the ashes – *her ashes* – and scatter them hither and yon.

'Good-bye, my love,' he whispered. 'Good-bye.'

At that moment the sun broke through the clouds

and shone down, bathing him and the sea in an ethereal light, and he imagined that he saw her ashes swirl heavenward, toward that golden light above this magical place. Suddenly blinded, he lowered the vase to his waist. Then he took it in one powerful bronzed hand, and drawing his arm back, heaved it in an arch to the sea, where it splashed in the water, bobbing only a moment before disappearing. It would disintegrate along with her ashes.

He walked back onto the sandy shore, looking up at the rocky outcrop. The climb back up would be a chore, not the joyous trip that it had always been with her, but he strode toward it on soaked feet.

How do I go on living? he wondered.

When he reached the top of the rocky outcrop, he stopped to catch his breath. He shrugged out of his jacket, soaked with sweat from his exertions and the heat of the sun, and threw it across his shoulder. Turning, he looked back out to sea. The fog had completely rolled away, and the sun burned bright and hot. A thin line of haze demarcated the horizon in the far distance, and close in to the shore, he could see happily frolicking sea otters in the water.

She loved them so much, he thought, remembering her delight when they'd stop to watch the otters that splashed all along the coast here. But today he took no pleasure in watching them, unable as he was to share the joy with her.

How do I go on living? he wondered anew, feeling a sadness such as he had never known. But the sea, usually

5

a source of pleasure, of solace, of healing even, held no answers for him. It continued its eternal rise and fall on the sandy shoreline.

He trudged on down the road, alone in the unbearable silence.

BOOK ONE

Joanna and Josh
Spring and Summer 2000

1

Joanna Cameron Lawrence applied the brakes and slowed her elderly but immaculate Mercedes convertible to a crawl, carefully turning onto the narrow, twisting road that led up into the Santa Cruz Mountains. She'd been on the road before, but it had been a long time. Not long enough for her to forget that it was exceedingly dangerous, however, like the road to her own house in Aptos, nearby in the mountains.

Although it had two narrow lanes – in theory at least – in many places part of the road was washed out due to the inevitable mud slides during the heavy winter rains. Because the slides often left a mere sliver of blacktop, stop signs announced impending washouts so that traffic hopefully could come and go on the single remaining lane without major collisions.

She inhaled the cool, eucalyptus-scented air. To her left the mountain rose straight up from the road, its side adorned with houses that clung to it perilously. To her right, a ravine – a small canyon really – plunged dramatically, in places a hundred feet or more deep, to a creek that rose and fell with the seasons. Cypress trees, towering redwoods, eucalyptus, and pines created a canopy that permitted the sun to enter only at intervals.

Across the ravine, perched like commodious bird-houses on the mountainside opposite, she spotted occasional houses, rustic cottages most of them. They were isolated from one another, placed on large, almost vertical pieces of property. Most of them were reached by footbridges, some of which had been washed out in the winter floods – or dislodged by the periodic earthquake – and hung limply into the ravine. The inhabitants of these magical cottages had to park somewhere on this side of the ravine, then walk across the bridges to their homes.

They must be an intrepid breed, she decided, and she liked that about them. They dared to be different, to deal with all sorts of inconveniences to live in this dramatic setting.

She looked at the house numbers on the roadside mailboxes and saw that she was nearing her destination. The woman she was going to see had told her there was room to park – just – near her footbridge.

On the right she saw a big old rusty cream Jeep

Wagoneer, parked on the narrow shoulder off the road. It was the car the woman had told her to look for. Joanna slowed down and eased over onto the shoulder behind the Wagoneer, creeping as close to it as possible. She put on her parking brake and killed the engine.

Looking into the rearview mirror, she grabbed a brush from her big leather and canvas carryall and quickly ran it through her wind-tousled hair. There, that's good enough, she thought, inspecting it in the mirror once again. Then, grabbing her carryall, she threw her car keys into it, slung it across her shoulder, and slid out of the silver sports car.

I'll leave the top down, she decided. It's not going to rain, and it's nice and shady here so the interior won't get too hot. Plus, it ought to be safe.

She walked around the Wagoneer to the footbridge, and stood staring at it for long moments. It was about sixty feet across to the other side, and if there was anything in the world Joanna Lawrence feared, it was heights.

Oh, jeez, Joanna, she thought, cringing inside, *you've done it now, old girl. You have to walk across this thing. High up in the air over that deep, deep ravine. Nothing below your feet but a few puny-looking old boards.*

Taking a deep breath, she slowly put her right foot out onto the bridge, and at the same time she grabbed hold of the rustic wooden railing with all her might. She followed suit with her left foot, then stood still for a moment, exhaling. She could feel the bridge move slightly under her weight. She could also hear it creak.

Oh, Lord, she prayed, *protect me now!*

She remembered that someone had once told her to stare straight ahead under such circumstances – don't look down whatever you do! – and proceed slowly and steadily. Easier said than done.

She took another deep breath, looked firmly at the adorable cottage on the other side, and moved one foot in front of the other, slowly at first, then faster, faster, holding her breath and white-knuckling it all the way.

Reaching the other side, she stopped and shivered with relief. The short – but oh, so long! – trip was over. She turned slightly and looked back at the ravine. *Harmless,* she told herself. She hated this irrational fear, any kind of fear, but had never learned to conquer it. Straightening her shoulders, she glanced over at the cottage.

Like the footbridge, it was a gingerbread structure of batten board, weathered the color of the bark on the pines around it, with dark green shutters. Window boxes held cheerful red geraniums. The cedar-shingled roof was weathered a silvery brown, and the stone chimney and foundation were covered with moss and lichen. Fretwork decorated the eaves and the screened-in front porch, and vines grew all over the little house. A narrow stone path, which led to the front door, was bordered by all kinds of shade-loving shrubbery.

What a lovely, romantic place, Joanna thought.

She walked up the stone path to the front door. There was no doorbell, so she lifted the door knocker, a shiny brass pineapple that denoted hospitality, and knocked twice.

The door was opened almost immediately by a tall, slim woman about her own age, early thirties. She had sandy, shoulder-length hair and bright, alert eyes the color of tortoiseshell, a rich brown shot through with a golden yellow and amber. High cheekbones, beautifully arched eyebrows, a straight nose, and full, sensual lips were set off by healthy, very lightly tanned skin.

'Mrs Lawrence?' she asked with a friendly smile. Her lively eyes took in Joanna's crisp oyster linen blouse, matching trousers, and espadrilles. Casual but elegant.

'Joanna, please,' the visitor said.

'And I'm April Woodward,' the woman said. 'Come on in.'

She held the door wide, and Joanna stepped into the cottage. In the tiny entrance foyer, she noticed a wrought-iron stand, filled with assorted umbrellas, some with amusing animal heads as handles, and walking sticks of various lengths. A small pine console, over which a simple pine mirror hung, held a Staffordshire bowl with keys. On the floor was a kilim rug, old, faded, and multicolored.

'Joanna,' April asked, 'would you like something to drink? There's green tea, and I have some mineral water.'

'Oh, I love green tea,' Joanna replied. 'If it's no trouble.'

April shook her head. 'None at all,' she said. 'Sugar? Honey? Sweetener?'

'A touch of honey would be perfect,' Joanna said.

'Make yourself comfortable,' April said. 'I'll be right back.'

Joanna watched her stroll out of the room, noticing that April wore no-nonsense khakis, a pinstriped shirt, and loafers. Joanna headed for the big, comfortable-looking sofa in front of the stone fireplace, and sank into its deep cushions. She liked the feel of its slipcover fabric, which looked like natural linen.

She placed her carryall on the floor and glanced around the small room. It was paneled in knotty pine with built-in bookshelves that were filled to bursting with all sorts of books, well read from the looks of them. The big stone fireplace dominated one wall. It was a warm, cozy, and inviting room, to her mind in the best of taste. *Charming, simple, and unpretentious,* she thought. *Like April herself appears to be. A wonderfully romantic cottage, but not cloyingly sweet or overdone. Not extravagantly expensive either.*

April appeared with a small tray. On it were a teapot, cups, saucers, and a pot of honey. She sat it on the coffee table, then took a seat on the stone hearth.

'You didn't have to go to so much trouble,' Joanna protested.

'It's no trouble,' April replied. 'I enjoy doing it.' She poured their tea, put a small dollop of honey in each, and handed Joanna hers.

'Thanks, April,' she said.

'You're welcome.' April smiled and took a sip of the tea. 'Now, then,' she said. 'Let me get this straight. You told me you're interested in doing a sort of grotto?' She looked at Joanna with curiosity.

Joanna nodded. 'Yes,' she said. 'I've brought some pictures with me. I tore some of them out of magazines, and some of them are color Xeroxes from books I've got. They'll give you an idea of the sort of thing I have in mind.'

She set her tea down on the table and reached into her carryall, pulling out a large manila envelope. 'I guess it sounds a little crazy,' she went on as she opened the envelope and extracted the pictures, 'but I think you'll see what I mean.'

She handed the pictures to April, who slowly looked through them, one by one. When she was finished, she put the pictures down on the coffee table and smiled.

'These are fabulous,' she said excitedly, her tortoise-shell eyes sparkling. She tapped the pictures with a hand. 'And you're really serious about this?'

'Absolutely,' Joanna said, returning her smile. She was gratified that the pictures had excited April. 'I saw the fountain and garden walls you did at Ingrid and Ronald Wilson's house, and I loved them. They have such a sense of fantasy about them.'

'Thanks a lot,' April said.

'Anyway, something told me that you could do this,' Joanna said.

'Amazing,' April said. 'Nobody does this sort of thing anymore.'

'*I* do,' Joanna said, laughing. 'At least I want to. Even if it is a little crazy. There's this old stone building on

15

our property that used to be a stable. It's not too big, but it has a great view of the mountains.'

'A grotto's usually a cave, isn't it?' April said. 'Or like a cave.'

Joanna nodded. 'Yes, in the strictest sense. But I want this to be a sort of garden pavilion, not a real grotto. I guess I call it that because I want the whole room encrusted with seashells and pebbles. Walls, floor, and ceiling. With murals and architectural detail. Like the rooms you see in these pictures.'

April clapped her hands and laughed again. 'This is wonderful,' she enthused.

Joanna smiled. 'But I don't want to copy the pictures,' she said. 'I want us to come up with a plan of our own.' She paused and looked over at April. 'Hear that? I've already got you saying yes to the project, don't I?' she continued.

April smiled.

'Anyway, I have a few ideas. My husband and I are in the orchid business, and I want the murals to reflect that. You know, orchid murals made out of seashells and pebbles, that sort of thing?' She looked at April questioningly.

April took a sip of her tea, then set it down. 'Why don't I show you my portfolio?' she said matter-of-factly. 'I think you ought to have an idea of the kind of things I've done.'

'That would be great,' Joanna said.

'Excuse me just a minute,' April said. 'I'll just run and get it.'

As she left the room, Joanna noticed small water-colors on the walls that she hadn't seen before, and got up to look at them. There were several beach scenes, the dunes and sea, and some landscapes, featuring the local mountains.

April came back into the living room, carrying a large leather folder. 'Oh, I see you've discovered my little hobby,' she said. 'Or one of them.'

'They're lovely,' Joanna said. 'Really lovely.'

'Thanks,' April said, looking at them with a maternal eye. 'I'm working on botanicals now. Local flora. I'll show them to you before you leave if you like.'

'I'd love to see them,' Joanna replied. 'I love botanicals. In fact, I have a few in the car that I'm getting framed.'

'Really?' April said. 'Well, anyhow, in the meantime, let me show you some of the work I've done with shells and stones.'

They sat back down, both of them on the sofa, and April put the big portfolio down on the coffee table. She opened it and began flipping pages, showing Joanna photographs and drawings of various projects she'd worked on.

'This is fantastic,' Joanna said, pointing to a garden path created entirely of little pebbles set in elaborate patterns.

'Ummm . . . thanks,' April murmured. 'As you can see I haven't done a great deal, at least not with seashells, and most of it has been outdoors. Terraces, walls, paths, fountains, and such. But a lot of this work is along the same lines as what you're thinking about. Creating a formal layout, then designing the patterns to fill it in. Sometimes with tile and stone. Whatever people want.' She looked at Joanna. 'I'm sure I could do the same thing with seashells and stone. I have done one room sort of like you're talking about, but I don't have pictures.'

'Why's that?' Joanna asked.

'The client was this enormously rich man in Los Angeles,' she said, 'and he didn't want any photos taken. He didn't want them "leaked," as he put it. He was a little paranoid, I think.'

'You must deal with all sorts of people,' Joanna said.

'Oh, yes,' April replied.

Joanna nodded, then looked back down at the portfolio again. 'I see that some of your work is neoclassical, some of it's baroque or rococo.'

'Whatever the client wants,' April said with a smile. 'But I do try to put as much of myself into the work as possible. Making suggestions and such.'

'Well,' Joanna said, looking back up, 'I like what I see very much, April. The work is truly beautiful. I could go on all day about it, but I know you've heard it all before.'

She paused and took a sip of her tea. 'Do you think you'd be interested in my grotto?' she asked.

April nodded. 'Definitely,' she said, 'but I would like to have a look at the building first.'

'Great,' Joanna said enthusiastically. 'I just know it'll work out.'

She ran a hand through her hair, looking thoughtfully off into the distance. Then she turned her gaze to April. 'I've been collecting shells and pebbles for years. I have boxes and boxes and . . . well, you wouldn't believe!'

She laughed, her violet eyes dancing with light. 'You'll probably think I'm crazy when you see. Anyway, I've got catalogues from wholesalers, so I could order whatever we don't have that we need.'

'From the sound of it,' April said, 'the catalogues will come in handy, because this project is going to take a lot. Probably more than you realize. But, of course, I need to see the building first to get a better idea.'

'Well,' Joanna said, 'you can see it anytime that's convenient with you. How about tomorrow? I'd like to get started as soon as possible. That is, if you agree to take it on.'

'Let me check my appointment book,' April said. She rose to her feet. 'Why don't you come on back to the studio with me? You can look at those botanicals I was talking about.'

'Great,' Joanna said. She got up and followed April down a short hallway and into a small, high-ceilinged room that Joanna thought was probably added on to the cottage as a conservatory or garden room. It had windows on three sides, with French doors allowing access to the garden, and the ceiling was almost entirely skylights. It had been designed to allow as much natural light as possible. The room was dominated by a large worktable covered with jars filled with artist's tools: brushes, pencils, pens, charcoal, and such. Watercolor paper in various sizes lay helter-skelter all over it, and books were piled all around. Rolled-up blueprints filled tall urns, and little vases of flowers were everywhere. An enormous easel had a small watercolor in progress clipped to it. Some sort of flower, Joanna noticed.

'What a wonderful room,' she said.

'The heart of the house,' April replied, picking up her leather appointment book and flipping to the correct page. She studied it for a moment, then looked over at Joanna. 'Tomorrow's fine,' she said. 'Anytime you like.'

'How about around noontime, then?' Joanna asked. 'We could look over the building and have a bite of lunch?'

'Lunch?' April hesitated a moment, then smiled. 'Sure,' she said, 'why not?'

'About twelve-thirty, one-ish, then?' Joanna said.

'Okay,' she said. 'I'll be there.'

'Is this one of your botanicals?' Joanna asked, indicating the watercolor on the easel.

'Oh, yes,' April replied. 'Obviously not finished. This is a type of verbena. I've got the correct name written down.'

'I love the detail,' Joanna said, looking at it closely. 'Oh, and I love the little bugs you've put on it. How clever!'

April blushed slightly. 'Thanks,' she said. 'Let me show you some finished ones.' She opened a large leather portfolio on the table and started flipping pages.

Joanna drew up to the table beside her and looked

through it. 'They're really lovely,' she said. 'My favorite thing, though, is your imagination. Doing the flowers so correctly, then adding the little bugs and dewdrops and things.'

'Doing the flowers right is the easy part,' April said. 'It's making them interesting that's the difficult part. Hence my little additions.'

Joanna smiled. 'I'm so glad to see you enjoy doing these,' she said. 'Especially since I want to incorporate some of our orchids into the grotto.'

'It's a brilliant idea,' April said.

'I hope so,' Joanna said in a self-deprecating voice. 'Sometimes my ideas don't work out very well, but Ingrid Wilson assured me that you would at least understand me.'

'I don't think that'll be a problem,' April said.

'I don't either,' Joanna said. 'I can see by the way that you live – I mean, the way you've decorated your cottage and all – that we have very similar ideas and tastes. I meet very few people like that.'

'Surprised?' April asked with a little laugh.

'Sort of,' Joanna said honestly. 'And Ingrid told me you'd been married to Roger Woodward, that famous actor. So I guess I expected somebody more . . . oh, I don't know . . .'

'More glamorous?' April supplied, smiling. 'Somebody more Hollywood and with it?'

Joanna reddened slightly, then nodded. 'I guess you're right,' she said. 'Isn't that awful of me?'

'No,' April said. 'It happens a lot . . . when people

21

find out I was married to Roger.' She looked at Joanna with a serious expression. 'But that was another world, a lifetime ago. Now I have a life that's entirely of my own making, and I like it very much.'

'That's wonderful,' Joanna said. 'I don't think many people can say that.' She paused, then said: 'I guess I'd better get on my way. It's been wonderful to meet you, and to see your house. It's so charming.'

'I look forward to tomorrow,' April said, smiling somewhat shyly.

'I'll just get my bag,' Joanna said, turning toward the hallway.

In the living room, Joanna picked up her carryall and slung it over her shoulder. 'Would you like to keep the pictures to study?' she asked. 'Or should I take them home with me?'

'If you could leave them, that'd be great,' April said.

'That's fine,' Joanna said, and went to the front door. She turned to April. 'See you tomorrow.'

April opened the door. 'Yes, see you then,' she said.

''Bye, April, and thanks,' Joanna said, starting down the little stone path to the footbridge.

''Bye,' April said. She closed the door, then glanced out a window, watching Joanna approach the bridge and cautiously step onto it, holding on to the railing for dear life.

What a lovely, lovely but odd *woman Joanna Lawrence is*, April thought. *And what an exciting but odd project she's come up with.*

Odd and wonderful, she thought, shaking her head.

22

Little did April know that her life was about to be changed forever by Joanna Lawrence.

Joanna reached her Mercedes and, leaning over, heaved her carryall onto the passenger seat. Then she opened the door and slid in. She threw her head back and took several deep breaths, trying to calm her racing heart. She could feel her pulse beating against her ear.

The trip back across the rustic footbridge had been no less frightening than the first time, and now, added to her adrenaline-generated fear, was the spark of excitement that coursed throughout her body.

After a few minutes her breathing began to slow and her heartbeat gradually returned to normal. She tested her hands on the steering wheel. They didn't shake, although they felt somehow electrified. She strapped on her seat belt, then extricated her sunglasses from her carryall and put them on.

She started the car, its powerful motor purring expensively. Then she carefully backed up on the thin shoulder and, after looking both ways, turned around on the narrow road.

She drove slowly, the wind whipping her hair about her face, the cool, scented air refreshing, stabilizing, although she still felt the excitement of her discovery coursing through her. The mountain's almost sheer side rose to her right, and the ravine, like a gigantic scar in the earth, lay on her left. She gradually picked up speed as she felt more confident of her driving. She had been negotiating these roads all of her life and had never had an accident.

Today won't be any different, she told herself, but then she remembered that so much had been different lately, that, in fact, her whole life had irrevocably changed.

Suddenly she laughed into the wind, tapping the steering wheel lightly with her hand. *You never know what fate has in store for you.* She shivered with excitement. She was watching the road ahead, but all she could see was the face and long, lean body of April Woodward shimmering before her in the dappled sunlight like some sort of chimera, enticing, alluring, and seductive, those tortoiseshell eyes of hers like a siren's call.

I think I've found her, she told herself. *At long last.*

She abruptly realized that she had reached the bottom of the mountain and would be back in lots of traffic, not far from the road that would take her back up into the mountains, back up to her own mountaintop aerie. But she wasn't going home yet. No, not now. She would go on down to Capitola, to a little custom framing shop she had used before, and finally get those botanicals properly matted and framed.

She headed north on the expressway, then took the Capitola exit, cruising slowly down into the little beachside village, chock-a-block with its lovely pastel Victorian cottages. She spotted the framing shop on the little main street and pulled over and parked. Reaching behind her seat, she retrieved the heavy folder that she'd stored the botanicals in.

A bell tinkled when she opened the door to the little shop. But, looking around, she didn't see Woody. She began looking at the hundreds of framing choices, many of them mounted on the walls, others glued to heavy board on large revolving racks. She bent over to look at an interesting piece of molding in a stack propped against the wall, and suddenly felt as if someone were watching her. She jerked up and looked around.

A young man stood regarding her, his darkly tanned muscular arms folded across his chest. His dark eyes traveled up and down her body, and Joanna felt herself blush under the weight of his assessing gaze.

He's undressing me, she thought, *or he sure seems to be.* He had done this on the several other occasions she had come, and she supposed she should feel flattered, but it made her uncomfortable. At least he knew his business.

'Oh, hello,' she said. 'I didn't see you when I came in.'

'I was in the back,' Woody said, maintaining his pose.

'I've got some botanical prints,' Joanna said, indicating her big folder. 'Six of them, and I want them matted and framed identically.'

Woody's demeanor changed to one more appropriate to a shopkeeper. 'Let's have a look. Over here.' He turned and walked over to a large, well-lit table.

Joanna followed him to the table and began pulling the prints out of the folder. She spread them out, then looked over at him.

'Nice,' he said, nodding his shaggy black curls. He came around to her side of the table to get a better look. 'Yeah, real nice.'

'We're in the orchid business, you see,' she said, 'and these are hand-colored prints from about 1815. I'd like to put them in my husband's—'

Suddenly she felt the heat and weight of his body press against hers and the light but definite brush of his hand across her buttocks.

Joanna turned steely eyes on him, and said, 'Stop that. Please.'

There was a smirk on his face. 'Hey,' he said, spreading his hands wide in a 'Who me?' gesture. 'Don't get the wrong idea. I didn't mean anything.'

She quickly gathered her prints and placed them in the folder, then turned to leave. 'I think I'll have somebody else do these,' she said, and headed toward the door.

'You do that,' the young man said in a snarl as she opened the door.

As she stepped out, she heard him add: 'Bitch.'

Joanna hurried to her car and got in, stowing the folder behind her seat. *What a bastard!* she thought, ignoring the Victorian charms of the little village as she headed back toward the expressway. He wasn't like that before.

But as she sped homeward, toward Aptos, her thoughts turned from the unpleasantness of the encounter to April Woodward.

April, she thought, *is the right physical type.* Tall, slim, and elegant, but not hard or brittle-looking. She wasn't a fashion victim striving too hard for chic. She simply had *it.* Her sandy hair, probably once blond, was well-cut, and those tortoiseshell eyes of hers were beguiling. Her features, while not traditionally pretty or beautiful, were striking. And her bearing, her attitudes and interests! They couldn't have been more perfect. She was extremely creative, but down to earth – a very important quality in the young woman she'd been looking for.

Still, Joanna thought, *there's no way to predict what will happen, whether or not she's actually perfect for my plan.* But something told her she wouldn't be disappointed. *April Woodward seems like the perfect young woman for what I have in mind.*

J oshua Lawrence was in the Stud Room, a small
enclosure inside the greenhouse. Perched on a high
metal stool, hunched over a wooden table, his sun-
bleached hair falling forward into his ultramarine eyes,
he was completely lost to the rest of the world, all of
his powers of concentration on the task at hand.

The end of a toothpick projected from his mouth,
rotating slowly as he maneuvered it around, gathering
as much of his saliva as he could. After a few moments
he extracted the toothpick from his mouth and held
it up to the light with one latex-gloved hand. The
toothpick gleamed in the light with a thick coat of
his saliva.

'Ah, good,' he said aloud, although there was no one

around to hear him. His sensuous lips parted in a smile, and he nodded with satisfaction.

On the table where he worked were two rare and beautiful orchid plants, one of them a prize *Paphiopedilum* Screaming Eagle, the other a *Paphiopedilum* of a different sort. Quickly but delicately he began using the saliva-wet toothpick to pick up and transfer minuscule pollen capsules from one *Paphiopedilum* parent plant to the other.

Sex, he thought with wry amusement. *There's nothing quite like it.* For, in principle, that is what was happening. He was fertilizing one plant with the pollen of another.

It was a somewhat tedious process, the old-fashioned pollination process, requiring great patience and a skilled hand. But it was the only way to pollinate *Paphiopedilums*. They couldn't be propagated by tissue culture, a quick method that worked for many orchids. However, this old-fashioned, tedious work and the long wait for results – anywhere from six to eighteen years for the finished flower – was well worth the trouble. At least to Joshua Lawrence and a select clientele.

He had created some of the most extravagant orchids ever seen. With their waxy, glistening sacs, striking top sepal, and bizarre markings and colors, they had become much sought after by collectors the world over. While there were many other hybridizers, his hybrids were considered among the best, with large flowers, flattened petals, luscious folds, erect columns, hairs, warts, spots, and veins – all in extraordinary color combinations from the purest whites to near black.

He put the toothpick back in his mouth, working more saliva onto it. He wanted to make certain that he got plenty of pollen on the plant. Glancing idly at his watch, he noticed that it was lunchtime, and Joanna hadn't called him on the intercom they used here at home.

Strange, he thought. *She should have called by now, and she's usually so prompt, so efficient. Besides, she likes to hang out and watch me mate the plants.*

He was working in the small greenhouse in back of their mountaintop home, and usually ate lunch with Joanna when he was working there. This was a special greenhouse, distinct from the vast commercial ones they owned down in the valley. For it was here, close to home, that they kept some of the rarest, and therefore most expensive, of their orchid plants. They were protected by an elaborate alarm system, under constant lock and key, with video cameras and lasers trained on the precious stock night and day. The security might have seemed excessive to the casual observer, but some of the plants were worth a fortune. Several were valued at twenty-five thousand dollars apiece, and the parent stock was virtually priceless.

He reached over and punched the intercom button, calling to her. Once. Twice. Three times.

No response.

What the hell?

Turning his attention back to the orchids, he repeated

the process, meticulously applying the pollen from the parent Screaming Eagle to the other parent *Paphiopedilum*. After a few minutes, he sat back up, satisfied. He stretched his back and powerful, sunbronzed arms.

Reaching over, he tried the intercom again.

Still no response.

Shit! Not even Connie's picking up.

He shoved the pollinated orchid to the back of the table and pulled another one forward. He would be repeating the pollination process with several of the *Paphiopedilums*. Taking a fresh toothpick from the little box on the table, he stuck it in his mouth, still wondering where Joanna could be.

She hasn't been herself lately, he thought, maneuvering the fresh toothpick around in his mouth. *She's been distant and withdrawn. Maybe even a little secretive. Gone for hours at a time without any explanations for her time away. Not leaving word with Connie or me. She's even been short-tempered with Connie.*

That sudden realization was the clue that something must be very wrong indeed. Joanna Lawrence would never abuse Connie Cespedes, no matter how upset, angry, or harried she might be. Connie was like a member of the family, and Joanna admired her, believing that it was the ambitious struggles of people like Connie who had made this country the great place that it is.

He examined the new toothpick in the light, and began the pollination process again, trying to concentrate, but distracted by disturbing thoughts of his wife.

What could be wrong? he wondered.

Was it simply that her irritating older sister, Christina, had recently swept in unannounced for a brief but, well, a highly irritating visit? He doubted that. Even though he and Joanna both were left exhausted by Christina, the aftereffects of her drama-filled visitations were usually short-lived, and besides, Joanna's uncharacteristic behavior had started long before Christina's latest sojourn.

Could it be financial worries? he wondered. They lived extremely well, but the business did have its ups and downs. Lately, they'd been under pressure from the Rossi brothers, their chief competitors, to sell out. They wanted their land and greenhouses badly.

He heaved another sigh. *Maybe it's something really simple,* he told himself. *Like she needs a new project to work on.* She always had to be busy working on some kind of project, never content to run the house and help with the business. She'd done a beautiful book on orchids that had been well received, but that had been finished months ago. Maybe, then, it was simply the lack of a new project?

He put the toothpick back in his mouth, slowly shaking his head. *No,* he thought. *That's not it. No way. It's not that simple.* Lately . . . just the last two or three months . . . if truth be told, lately she hadn't seemed very interested in him. She hadn't snapped at him like she had at Connie, but she hadn't *wanted* him either. Not like she used to, that's for sure.

He took the toothpick back out of his mouth and, like the others, examined it in the light. Satisfied, he began pollinating again. *Could it be that she's grown tired of me?* he asked himself. *Could it be something like the seven-year itch? Or did that only happen to men? Besides, they'd been married for ten years now. The ten-year itch?*

He didn't know, but he was becoming convinced that something was very, very wrong. He heaved a sigh, moving the pollinated orchid out of the way, then began the procedure on another one. *Maybe,* he thought, *maybe it's because we still don't have any children. Maybe that's it.* They both wanted children, but they'd waited a long time to try. Then when they'd stopped using birth control, just a couple of years ago, nothing happened. Finally, they'd both gone to the doctor and gotten clean bills of health. Still nothing. At least so far. And now. Well, now, she didn't seem to be interested in even trying!

Suddenly, like a poisonous snake, an evil thought crept into his consciousness. *Joanna has found someone else.* He slumped forward, putting his head in his latex-covered hands, thinking about their years of bliss together. From the moment he had laid eyes on her, he had wanted her, beautiful, fanciful, yet practical creature that she was. And the same had been true for Joanna. Or so she'd always said. And their love, he'd thought, had only grown with the mounting years. They were lovers, partners, and friends.

What the hell was happening?

At that moment the telephone rang, jarring the quiet of the greenhouse.

Josh reached over to answer it. 'Hello?' he said.

'Josh,' the Hispanic-accented voice said, 'it's Carl.'

An involuntary tremor of nervousness ran up Josh's spine. Carl never bothered him at home unless it was extremely important. 'What is it, Carl?'

'I think you'd better get down here fast,' he replied.

'What *is* it?' Josh repeated.

'Something with the misters,' he said. 'I don't know if it's the computer or what.'

'Ah, shit!' Josh swore. Without another word he replaced the receiver on the telephone, threw down his latex gloves, and ran for the car.

3

Christina Cameron von Leydon luxuriated on the cool cotton Pratesi sheets, a champagne silk duvet thrown tantalizingly across her ample breasts and curving down between her firm tan thighs. She gazed across her vast bedroom's Carrara marble floor with its pale ivory and pink Aubusson carpet to the bathroom door. It stood slightly ajar.

She smiled to herself with satisfaction.

He was in there, and she could hardly wait for him to come back out again.

A Dunhill cigarette in one hand, and a vodka tonic in the other, she sipped the drink, then set it down on the draped table next to her bed. She puffed on the Dunhill, patting her expensively streaked silver and blond hair

– 'A dozen different shades, at least!' she would tell those who asked – normally a perfect helmet that defied destruction, now a tousled mess. Her makeup, which had gradually become more elaborate as she had aged, was in need of repair.

But it didn't matter. No, indeed. Not today. For he was responsible for her mussed hair and messy makeup. He and his ravenous appetite for her body. A sigh of pleasure escaped her lips.

All that yoga, the personal trainers, the two face-lifts, the breast implants – and subsequent reduction – the endless miles on the treadmill and stationary bike, to say nothing of the perpetual dieting – all of it had paid off for her. In her mid-thirties, her body was still youthful and tempting.

Even to a stud like Peter Rossi, she thought.

He came out of the bathroom, and she gloried at the sight of his body – all that thick, hard muscle, tall and suntanned, that fabulous toy between his powerful legs. With his dark eyes glittering in anticipation and a cocky smile on his sensuous lips, he strode to the bed and stood over her, taking pleasure in her obvious enjoyment of his body.

Christina quickly stubbed her cigarette out in an ashtray and reached over and brushed his hardening shaft with her hand. Then, sitting up and sliding her legs over the side of the bed, she encircled his hips with her arms and stroked his hard buttocks with her hands.

'Oooo, yeah, baby,' he crooned. 'That feels so good.' He took her breasts in his big hands, stroking them hard and squeezing her nipples between thumb and forefinger.

Christina moaned with pleasure, her tongue darting out to caress his heavy balls, then lick the length and breadth of his thick shaft. It throbbed with anticipation, and she was certainly not one to disappoint. Opening her mouth wide, she took as much of it as she could, licking and sucking, licking and sucking.

Peter groaned and put his hands on her head, moving his big thighs against her mouth harder and faster, harder and faster, until he suddenly stopped, his body tensing all over. 'Wo-ow!' he gasped. 'I'm getting too close, baby. Too damn close.'

He eased out of her mouth, then reached down, one huge arm under each of hers, and lifted her up off the bed to face him. 'You're too goddamn much, Christina,' he said, smiling. 'Too goddamn much.'

He pulled her hard against him then, kissing her hungrily, his tongue delving between her lips, exploring her mouth, his hands on her breasts again, stroking and squeezing, then moving over her buttocks and between her thighs.

Christina relished his body against hers, his hands all over her, the hardness of his cock against her, and gave herself up to him utterly. She could feel her own wetness between her thighs, and ground herself against him lasciviously.

Peter pulled back for a moment, both of them breathing hard, then eased her down onto the bed, where she lay on her back, already aching for his touch again.

Smiling down at her, he crouched over her on his knees, spreading her legs wider apart, his eyes devouring her hungry mound. He leaned down and slowly began to lick her thighs, his hands on her buttocks lifting her to him. Christina's moans of pleasure urged him on and on and on, until his tongue found her most magical of places and plunged lustily inside her, ravenous for her juices.

She gasped aloud and ground herself against him, her hands entwined in his raven-black hair, her body writhing from side to side, lost in an ecstasy of carnal delight.

He suddenly stopped, withdrawing from her, breathing heavily, and she groaned at the loss of him there. But she was not to be disappointed for long because he came up on his knees, spreading her legs wide again, and she saw his engorged manhood only for a moment before he plunged inside her, farther than she thought possible, and began to pump away at her like a man possessed.

In a rapture of desire, the fires of her lust inflamed by his need for her, she instantly responded to him, matching his rhythm, her body working with his, until in a mad writhing and pumping they reached orgasm at the same time, Peter bellowing with release and Christina screaming as wave after wave of ecstasy engulfed her body in shudders. Finally, he collapsed atop her, and they both gasped for air, utterly spent, their heaving bodies coated in a sheen of sweat.

'Oh, my God!' she rasped throatily. 'Oh, my God! That ... that was so ... so fantastic, Peter!'

He hugged her tightly, rolling onto his side and bringing her with him, staying inside her. He held her buttocks tightly, peppering her face with kisses, still catching his breath.

'Jesus ... Christina,' he finally gasped. 'I didn't think ... I didn't think it could get any better ... any better ... than the last time.'

She laughed lightly, as thrilled with his pleasure in her as she was in her own satisfaction. 'Me either,' she said.

He kissed her on the lips, slowly easing out of her, then sat up slightly, an arm around her shoulders, and looked into her eyes. 'You're one hell of a woman,' he said.

'And you, Peter Rossi,' she said, 'are one hell of a man.'

He reached over and took her cigarettes and lighter off the bedside table, then lit one and handed it to her.

'Thanks,' she said.

He lit one for himself and blew a streamer of smoke toward the ceiling. 'Your ex-husband must be crazy,' he said. 'Why the hell would your husband go looking for another woman?'

Christina shrugged. 'You tell me,' she replied. 'I don't know.' She took a drag off her cigarette, exhaled through her nostrils, then went on. 'But I do know that he was a prick just like all the others, and I hope he's happy with his trashy little whore because she's costing him a fortune.'

41

Peter barked a laugh. 'You took him to the cleaners, huh?'

'Bet your ass,' Christina said. 'Just like the two bastards before him.'

Peter laughed again. 'Serves 'em right,' he said, stroking her arm.

Christina looked into his eyes. 'I'm sure glad we ran into each other when I was up at Joanna's this past weekend,' she said.

'Yeah, me too,' he said, returning her gaze. He crushed his cigarette into the ashtray. 'I could get used to this.' He cupped a breast with a beefy hand and began fondling it. 'I think we make a real good team.'

Christina nodded. 'Yes, but we've got to keep this our little secret, don't we?' she said, leaning over and brushing her lips across his massive chest.

'For more reasons than one,' he said.

One of her hands crept down his chest and on down his stomach to come to rest at the base of his thick, instantly responsive cock.

'Whoa,' he said. 'We better not get started again. Don't forget, I've got to get to that meeting in Santa Barbara, and a bunch of business calls to make.'

'Oh, I know,' Christina said somewhat testily, removing her hand, then putting out her cigarette.

'Don't worry, babe,' he said. 'I'll come back tonight after it's over . . . if you still want me to.' He grinned over at her.

She socked him playfully in the chest. 'You'd better be back tonight,' she said.

*   *   *

Christina had soaked in a hot, scented bath and carefully applied fresh makeup, then slipped into a long silk dressing gown. She'd made herself a fresh vodka and tonic, then stood in the living room of her splendid neoclassical mansion, slowly sipping her drink, looking out the French doors, beyond the yards upon yards of shimmering silk draperies that decorated them, toward the misty Pacific Ocean in the distance. It lay far beyond the acres of elegant, well-tended gardens with their statuary and the huge swimming pool with its columned pool house. The beautiful, expensive view offered by her hilltop setting in exclusive Montecito gave her pleasure today, despite the wounds of her latest divorce. The reason, of course, being Peter Rossi.

What serendipity, she thought. That he'd been coming to Santa Barbara on business and could help her lick her wounds. *And how!*

Today the divorce decree had been handed down by the courts, and it was all official: Christina was free – again. Husband number three was history, and like she'd told Peter, she'd taken the son of a bitch to the cleaners. But good.

Sighing expansively, she turned and padded over to the downy comfort of an ecru, silk-covered chaise longue. Shoving a pillow covered with a fragment of scratchy antique tapestry out of her way, she made herself comfortable. She took a generous sip of her vodka tonic, then set the crystal glass down on the bronze and glass Giacometti table at her side. She noticed the orchid plant sitting there, resplendent in its exotic beauty. Joanna had sent it down to cheer her up.

Well, this time around, she didn't need her sister's cheering up. No, siree. This time she'd lucked out. Ordinarily, she would be suffering from the excruciating loneliness and boredom that divorce brought on, from the terrible sense of loss and defeat that seemed to engulf her in the aftermath of a marriage gone wrong. But not this time, thank God. Peter Rossi had come along just in time.

She could feel her pulse begin to race at the mere thought of him. So tall – at least six-three or -four – and with a thick, hard, muscular body – the beefy body of the football player he'd once been. Black hair. Dark brown eyes. A very young near-forty. She knew that he'd come from the wrong side of the tracks, but she also knew that he was a ruthless businessman, very ambitious, very powerful, very rich. And unscrupulous. Oh, yes, she knew that too, and with a certainty. He had a mean streak a mile long. But she found the combination – the money and power and ruthlessness – a potent aphrodisiac, irresistible and compelling.

To top it all off, she thought with an almost guilty pleasure, Peter Rossi was her sister and brother-in-law's chief competitor. They loathed and feared him. And well they should. He and his brothers had built up a huge nursery empire, starting virtually from scratch, and now they wanted Joanna and Josh's business as well.

She smiled to herself. Peter Rossi was truly forbidden fruit – and nothing could be tastier to her hungry lips.

Picking up her drink, she glanced at the orchid. A *Paphiopedilum lowii*. *How like Joanna*, she thought. *To send the orchid.*

She reached over and plucked a bloom off the orchid. It was in full flower, its showy pink and green blossoms striated in some places, freckled with darkest purple in others. *Sweet*, she thought, even though Joanna knew she wasn't really crazy about orchids. They always made her think of her youth, the compost stench of greenhouses, and their father's twin obsessions, with orchids and the land.

She shivered, revolted by the thought.

How different my sister and I are! she thought. Joanna actually shared their father's interests and took great pleasure in these repulsive plants. She was content to live in what was a provincial backwater compared with the relative sophistication of Christina's world, content to live in their father's home, to carry on his business.

Joanna, she thought. *Joanna, who's always had everything. Everything any woman could ever want. She's strikingly beautiful and supremely healthy. She has plenty of money, even if she's not enormously rich like me. She has a beautiful home, even if it's not a spectacular showplace like mine. And, most of all, she's got Josh.*

Oh, yes! Joshua Lawrence, of the tall, muscular body, the sun-bleached hair, the blue, blue eyes, the strong, masculine good looks. And the perfect disposition to go with it. His was a confident masculinity, not a swaggering macho pose.

She lay back against the down-filled lounge, her

gaze directed at the orchid but not really seeing it. She'd always secretly envied her sister her happiness with him.

Well, she thought, *I'm not so sure I envy little sister anymore. No, indeed. Josh Lawrence seems somehow like a second-stringer compared with Peter Rossi. Josh might have more class, but class isn't everything. It certainly isn't the turn-on that money and power are. Or that mean streak, either.*

She idly continued picking at the orchid, thinking about Joanna and Josh, their land and business – the land and business that used to belong to *her* father. *I think I may have gotten a raw deal when Dad died,* she decided. *Just getting money while Joanna got everything else. It seemed fair at the time, but now . . . now I'm not so sure. I think I deserved more. Yes, I should have gotten some of that land, some of the business, too.*

Christina looked over at the orchid plant Joanna had sent. Its beautiful, exotic blossoms lay in a scrunched-up pile on the table and spilled over onto the floor. She had completely deflowered it.

Yes, she decided. *It's time for me to have some of the things Joanna's always had. Starting with the right man, then . . . well, we'll see, won't we?*

The atmosphere in the enormous greenhouse was like that of a tropical rainforest: warm, breezy, and humid. The smell of compost, to which Josh was all but inured, permeated the air with its ripe pungency. Something was missing, however, and the lack of that one essential ingredient could destroy hundreds of thousands of dollars' worth of orchids.

Mist, Josh thought with a scowl. *There's no goddamn mist.*

The computer-operated misters that bathed the plants in a tropical rain and created the humidity necessary for their survival had malfunctioned – or been tinkered with – and they didn't know when. It might have been anytime over the weekend, from Friday afternoon to

Monday morning. And that period of time can make the difference between life and death in a fragile tropical atmosphere.

Josh stalked through the big greenhouse, looking from side to side, examining the orchid plants, surveying them for damage.

'Christina was here the past few days so I didn't drop by over the weekend. *Damn!* One of the few weekends that ever goes by that I didn't drop by here.' He looked at his manager. 'I guess we lucked out, Carl,' he said.

'Yeah,' Carl Cespedes grunted in reply. The nursery manager, an unusually tall and broad Peruvian with Indio features, followed closely on Josh's footsteps. His face, normally a mask of passivity no matter what the situation, wore a worried expression. He treated the nursery as if it were his own, and he seemed as puzzled as Josh by the recent turn of events.

They had already examined the misting equipment for mechanical problems and had found nothing amiss. Then they'd reset the computer controls, and the misting system had kicked in perfectly. The problem obviously lay in the computer. Either it had malfunctioned for some unknown reason, or someone had reset it in a deliberate attempt to let the orchids dry out.

'Thank God the shades were working,' Josh said, 'or there might have been major damage already.'

Carl grunted again, looking overhead at the automatically controlled shades that ran the length of the greenhouse. They compensated for the shadows of passing clouds, and had they malfunctioned, the plants would have received either too much or too little light.

'One big catastrophe could practically wipe us out,' Josh continued. 'And that's just what the Rossi brothers would like to see happen. So they could come in and pick up the pieces.'

Carl looked at him. 'They still trying to get you to sell?'

Josh nodded. 'Yeah,' he said, walking on. 'They won't give up. This is the only direction they can expand in.' Then he abruptly stopped in his tracks and turned to Carl. 'I still don't understand how anybody could've gotten in,' he said, looking into Carl's dark eyes. '*If* somebody did. Miguel didn't hear or see *anything*?'

'No,' Carl said, shaking his head. 'I called him at home when I saw that the misters weren't working. He said he didn't hear or see anything last night. Nothing or nobody.'

Josh scratched his head. 'Damn!' he swore. 'I just can't figure it out. We're going to have to get the people in who installed that mister, and we're going to have to call the cops.'

'The cops?' Carl said.

'Absolutely,' Josh said. 'We've looked for signs of forced entry and didn't come up with anything, but maybe they will. You know, maybe they'll see something we didn't.'

'I guess so,' Carl said, not really believing it. He didn't think most of the police he'd run across would be able to find anything he hadn't, even if they tried.

'And call Miguel,' Josh said. 'Tell him I want to talk to him.'

'I already did. He's waiting for you in the office,' Carl said.

Josh looked surprised for a moment, then smiled and said, 'Thanks, Carl, you're thinking ahead of me.' He turned and started for the greenhouse door practically at a trot, then turned and called out: 'If anybody needs me, I'll be in the office. Making phone calls and talking to Miguel.'

Carl nodded.

Josh sprinted to the big Victorian house rising in the flat, dun-colored fields, surrounded by greenhouses. The immaculate white house looked incongruous here, a nineteenth-century piece of clapboard wedding cake, decorated with all the froufrou a skilled carpenter could conjure up, now hemmed in on all sides by high-tech twentieth-century greenhouses.

Joanna's paternal family, the Camerons, had built the house before the turn of the century and had lived there, farming the hundreds of acres surrounding it. Brussels sprouts and strawberries, then later on artichokes, had been their primary produce, as it still was for many of the farmers in this area. But Mitchell Cameron, Joanna's father, had different ideas.

Mitch had been bitten by the orchid bug, was in fact a true victim of orchidelirium, a not uncommon obsession in Victorian England. He was also a dreamer and a romantic, who had begun buying orchid stock as a teenager, built a small greenhouse, and started hybridizing, creating new orchids. After inheriting the farm from his father, he had eventually shut down the farming operation and turned exclusively to orchid growing, and after a few years, money like manna had begun to pour in.

That was when he asked the beautiful Julia Lenoir to marry him. Her family had long owned the farm adjoining his nursery, and they had known each other since they were tots. Julia had accepted with alacrity, and he had commenced on the building of their dream house, a huge shingle-style mansion in the manner of McKim, Mead, and White. But the house wasn't here in the valley, it was high in the Santa Cruz Mountains, with its cooler breezes and fantastic vistas, away from the air laden with the smells of compost, fertilizer, insecticides, and the crops themselves.

Joanna and Josh lived in that house now, and as Mitchell Cameron had done before them, they used the old Victorian homestead as an office and for storage.

Josh dashed up the wooden steps to the porch, pushed through one of the double doors, and went into the airy hallway of the house. Luna, Carl's wife, sat behind a desk, typing at a computer keyboard, a telephone held at one ear by her shoulder. Josh wondered how she did it with her long, eggplant-colored fingernails. Half-Venezuelan and half-American, Luna had been born in the States and was legal. Carl's marriage to the fiery, tempestuous virago had gotten him a green card. They had fought like cats and dogs since the day they'd met, and were deeply in love.

'Hey, boss,' she said, looking up, her heavily painted lips, also eggplant, parted in a smile that revealed dazzling white teeth.

'Hey, Luna,' he replied, 'and quit calling me boss.' He looked at her, returning her wide smile. 'Please?'

'Sure, boss,' she said, ignoring him as always. She nodded her head toward his office, her long jet-black hair swinging with the motion. 'Miguel's in there,' she said, 'waiting for you.'

'Thanks, Luna.' He turned and walked to the glass-paned French doors that led to what had once been a parlor. Opening one, he went in and saw Miguel sitting in a chair. He was engrossed, playing with Lucy, the gray and white cat that lived in the house.

Josh took a seat behind his desk and looked over at Miguel. He was a short, wiry Mexican in his thirties. He was probably mentally retarded – Josh wasn't really sure – but he was very slow on the uptake in any case. The child of migrant laborers, he'd been given work by Josh when no one else would hire him. Miguel was harmless, even childlike, Josh told himself, and he was devoted to Josh and the nursery.

Miguel looked over the desk at him, grinning from ear to ear. 'Lucy, she like me,' he said. 'She play with me.'

'I know, Miguel,' Josh said. 'I've noticed how she really likes you.' He cleared his throat: 'Miguel, I need to talk to you about last night.'

Suddenly Miguel's face contorted in fear. His dark eyes widened, and for a moment he looked as if he might burst into tears.

'Don't worry, Miguel,' Josh reassured him. 'It's not serious. I just need to find out what you know.'

Miguel jerked his head from side to side, almost spastically. 'I don't see nothing,' he said. 'Nothing, nothing, nothing. I don't see nothing.'

Josh looked at him steadily for a moment, wondering about the wisdom of having a nightwatchman impaired as Miguel was. 'Are you absolutely certain?' he asked. 'You didn't see anything? Anything at all?'

Miguel jerked his head from side to side again, even more violently. 'No, I don't see nothing.'

'Did you hear anything?' Josh asked. 'Any little thing that you can remember? Maybe something that was different? Unusual?'

'No, no, no! Nothing!' Miguel continued to shake his head, closing his eyes, the troubled expression on his face fixed there.

He seemed to be in genuine anguish, Josh thought, and he hated to ask him any more questions. *What have I got to gain anyway?* he asked himself. But he felt like he had to know the answer to one more question.

'Do you think you might have . . . accidentally, I mean . . . fallen asleep, Miguel? I know the nights are long and lonely and—'

Miguel burst into tears, and Lucy tore out of his lap. 'No, no, no!' he cried. 'Never! I never fall asleep on the job. Never!'

Tears ran in rivulets down his dusty cheeks, and Josh felt like kicking himself. He got up and went around the desk to Miguel's chair. He put his hands on Miguel's shoulders and patted him. 'It's okay, Miguel,' he said soothingly. 'It's okay. Here.' He reached over to the desk and took a Kleenex out of a box there. 'Blow your nose and wipe your eyes,' he said, handing the tissue to him. 'It's okay now. No more questions. I promise.'

Miguel blew his nose, then wiped away his tears with his dirty hands. He looked up at Josh with pitiful eyes. 'Lucy, she run away from me,' he said.

'She'll come back,' Josh said. Then he suddenly had a thought, a brilliant idea, in fact. Or so he assumed. 'Hey, Miguel,' he said. 'What if I get a dog to keep you company at night? You'd like that, wouldn't you? A trained guard dog—'

Miguel shrank back from him in horror, his eyes widening again. Looking at Josh as if he were the devil incarnate, he began to tremble. 'I . . . I . . . I . . . scared of dogs!' he stuttered. 'Sc . . . sc . . . scared of dogs!'

Ah, Jesus! Josh thought. *Some days I just can't win.*

'Forget it, Miguel,' he said hurriedly, patting his shoulders again. 'Never mind. Forget I said it. We won't do anything to scare you. Here, look, Miguel, Lucy's come back. See?'

Thank God! he thought. *Just in time.* He reached down and picked up the cat and held her out to Miguel. 'Look, Miguel,' he said. 'She wants you to hold her again. See.'

Miguel looked up at the cat, and instantly he grinned. He took Lucy from Josh's hands, set her in his lap, and began stroking her, humming to himself softly.

Josh returned to his desk chair, sat down, and

thought: *No good deed goes unpunished.* He sighed. *Oh, well, what the hell? What's the harm?* He reached over and picked up the telephone receiver, then put it back down again.

'Miguel?' he said.

Miguel looked over at him.

'Why don't you take Lucy outside with you, and then get one of the boys to give you a lift back home? You've got to get some sleep so you'll be ready for work tonight. Okay?'

Miguel nodded. 'Okay,' he readily agreed. He got up and left the office, closing the door behind him carefully.

When he was out of earshot, Josh picked up the telephone and punched the number for the greenhouse. When Carl picked up, he said: 'Carl, get one of the boys to take Miguel home. Fast. I don't want him around when the cops get here. They'll scare him half to death, asking questions.'

Carl grunted. 'You got it,' he said, and hung up.

Josh then dialed the number for the company that had installed the computer-controlled misters. He'd call them before the police. Idly tapping a pencil against the desktop, he waited for someone to pick up, thinking: *I hope to God they'll check out the system and tell me it's malfunctioned, but somehow I don't think that's what they're going to say.*

Later, Josh sat in the office with Carl. The company that maintained the computer-controlled equipment had come and gone. They had discovered nothing amiss with the equipment, and had told Josh that the only way the malfunction could have occurred was human error.

'In other words,' he'd said, 'someone tampered with the equipment.'

'Exactly,' the two technos had responded, nodding.

The police had arrived soon after and had done a thorough search of the perimeter and the greenhouses themselves. They turned up empty-handed.

'You sure nobody else has beepers to unlock the gates?' they'd asked him.

'No,' he'd said. 'Just Carl, me, and my wife. That's it.'

When he'd walked them to the car, one of the cops had turned to Josh and said: 'I think you'd better keep a close watch on your men, Mr Lawrence. Looks like an inside job to me.'

Josh had nodded his assent and thanked them politely, but deep down inside, he refused to believe that anybody who worked for him could have had anything to do with the malfunction.

It's got to be something else, he told himself. *We're practically like a family here.*

He looked over at Carl, sitting across the desk from him. 'I hate to do it,' he said, 'but I think we're going to have to get a guard dog.' He heaved a sigh. 'Maybe you can help Miguel get to know it, take him through it. If he just can't handle it, maybe I'll install video security or we'll just have to hire somebody new and put Miguel on something else.'

Carl nodded and rose to his feet. 'I'll try,' he said, 'but you know Miguel.'

'Yes, I know Miguel,' Josh said. 'Anyhow, I'll see you in the morning.'

'Okay,' Carl said, and turned and left the office.

Josh started to pick up the telephone to call Joanna, but it rang at that moment.

'Hello?' he said.

'Mr Lawrence?' the male voice said.

'Yes,' Josh replied, straining to hear. The caller was apparently on a cell phone and there was a lot of static.

'This is Peter Rossi.'

'Hello, Mr Rossi,' Josh said. 'Can you speak up? I'm having trouble hearing you.'

'I'm on the road,' Rossi said in a louder voice.

'What can I do for you, Mr Rossi?' he asked.

'I was just wondering, Mr Lawrence,' the man said, 'if you might have changed your mind about selling us your company. So many things can go wrong in this business. All those greenhouses and all that land are such responsibilities, don't you agree?'

Josh flushed red, and had to make an effort to control the anger he felt. 'No, Mr Rossi,' he replied. 'I don't agree. On the contrary, I've always welcomed the responsibility.'

And with that, he slammed the receiver down onto its cradle.

'Shit,' he said aloud. 'Shit, shit, *shit!*'

5

April poured herself a glass of wine, a relatively inexpensive but delicious Alexander Valley chardonnay that she'd discovered recently, and stirred the pasta sauce that was on the stove. Inhaling its aroma, she smiled to herself.

Woody will love it, she thought.

She'd sauteed some garlic in butter, put in a filet of cod, added some of her rich homemade tomato sauce, tossed in lots of capers and green olives with a little of their juices, and then sprinkled in salt and pepper with a couple of bay leaves.

Roger, her ex-husband, had always said she was a peasant at heart, and nothing reflected that more than her taste in food. She'd always preferred relatively simple, uncomplicated food, with seasonal, fresh ingredients, if possible, and the only complicated cooking she'd ever done was to satisfy Roger's taste for the baroque in all things. His motto had been the fancier the better – or embellish, embellish, embellish.

She turned around to the old pine kitchen table, placing her glass of wine on its well-worn surface, and then gave the salad a few more tosses. *Done*, she decided. She took a sip of her wine and then turned to check on the pasta sauce. *Perfect*. She turned it off. It would heat up in a minute, when she and Woody were ready to eat. Looking at her watch, she wondered where he was. He usually came early and stayed late. She sat back down, and began flipping idly through a garden magazine, thinking about Woody.

He nearly always brought a smile to her face. He was part Peter Pan, part teddy bear, part eternal surfer, part businessman. He was thirty-three, a year older than she was, and going on sixteen. He'd been a friend of Roger's growing up and now had a framing shop in Capitola. With his shoulder-length mop of curls, perpetually tanned muscles, and gleaming white smile, she'd thought he had come on to her in a major way. But he'd quickly backed off when he saw that she wasn't interested or wasn't ready, and he'd done it in the most gracious manner. Maybe that was in part because he'd been a friend of Roger's and had some sort of special respect for her. She didn't really know, but she was grateful there hadn't been any of the snarling backlash typical of the accomplished and cocky Casanova, none of the whimpering or pleading of the rebuffed suitor.

No, Woody had gradually become a pal – without the complications of a sexual relationship. While she suspected he wanted more, he was content to give her the space she needed without making demands.

She took a sip of her wine and flipped the magazine closed. *Where is he?* she wondered, looking at her watch again.

As if he were psychically attuned to her thoughts, she heard the living room door open and Woody's familiar voice.

'April?' his deep baritone called. 'Hey, kiddo, where are you?'

'In here, Woody,' she answered. 'The kitchen.'

He came rambling in, hands in his worn Levi's, a loud Hawaiian shirt hanging loose, making a production of twitching his nose in the air. 'I smell heaven,' he said, his dark eyes flashing mischievously. He kissed her forehead.

April laughed. 'Have some wine,' she said, starting to get up to get a glass for him.

'Sit,' he said. 'I'll get it.' He got a wineglass out of a cabinet, filled it, then sat down opposite her. 'Cheers,' he said, holding up his glass.

'Cheers to you, too,' April said, lifting hers and clinking it lightly against his.

'Did you have a busy day?' she asked after she'd taken another sip.

'Yeah.' He nodded his shaggy head and began tapping the table with the fingers of both hands, using it as a drum. 'Filled some old orders. Took a lot of new orders. Did some paperwork. You know. Same-old. Same-old.' He finished drumming with a flourish and looked over at her with a smile. 'You?'

'It was . . . different,' she said.

'Yeah?' he said. 'How different?'

'Well, I had an appointment with a lady who wants to do a grotto . . . sort of,' she replied.

'A grotto?' he asked, his dark eyebrows lifting quizzically.

'She has an old stone stable on her property,' April said. 'She wants the inside completely covered in seashells and stones. With murals.'

'No shit?' he said. 'Sounds like a huge job to me.'

April nodded. 'It would be.'

'You gonna do it?' he asked.

'I'm not sure yet,' she replied. 'I'm going over there tomorrow to look at the building and talk more about exactly what she wants.' She paused for a moment to take another sip of wine, then looked at him levelly. 'But if she wants what I think she wants, I hope it works out, because it would be really exciting. My biggest job to date.'

'Wow,' he said. 'Sounds cool.'

'Cool it would be, Woody,' she said. 'Murals of orchids and—'

'Orchids?' he said, his face screwed up questioningly.

'Orchids,' she repeated. 'They're in the orchid business.'

Woody suddenly sat up straight and looked at her with a serious expression. 'Who is she?' he asked.

'Joanna Lawrence,' she replied. 'She's—'

'I *know* who she is,' Woody said darkly.

'You do?' April said with surprise.

'Yeah,' he said. 'I've done some business for her.' He took a large sip of his wine and set the glass back down. 'She's like a lot of rich women, you know? Spoiled and arrogant.'

'She seemed like a very nice lady to me,' April said. 'A terrific lady, in fact.'

He finished off his glass, then poured himself another. 'Yeah,' he said in a sarcastic tone of voice. 'She *seems* like a terrific lady. But if you ask me, she's just another rich, smug *asshole*. You don't come from around here like I do, so you don't know. She comes from a really old family, big-shot father and all. Her older sister's some socialite tramp. You know. Makes the party circuit from San Francisco to L.A. and points in between. Wherever rich trash gathers.'

April looked at him. 'You sound a little resentful,' she said. 'And that doesn't sound like you, Woody.'

'Well, yeah. It's not important.' He heaved another sigh, then gave her a meaningful look. 'But I'm warning you, April.' He pointed a finger at her. 'You better watch your back. People like her are real bloodsuckers.'

April took a sip of her wine, looking at her friend across the table. She had seen Woody worked up before. He thrived on drama and created it where it was missing. But somehow this seemed different.

April nodded. 'I'm glad you told me,' she said. 'Most of the time I don't know what I'm walking into with clients. And some of them can be really screwy. In fact, I guess the richer they are, the screwier they are. Even if they're friends of friends. Anyway, Mr Pearlman!' She looked over at him and smiled. 'Are you hungry tonight?'

'You bet,' he said, smiling back, his gleaming teeth such a contrast to his darkly tanned skin.

'Then why don't you set the table,' she said, 'and I'll finish the food off and serve.'

'You got it,' Woody said, getting up and going to a kitchen cabinet to get out the dishes.

Later, after they'd finished the meal, they sprawled on the living room sofas, sipping coffee. Woody had built a small fire in the big stone fireplace to take the chill off the cool spring evening, and its light danced across their features as they talked, facing each other across the big coffee table.

'Guess who I saw last weekend?' Woody asked.

'Who?' April replied.

'David Jarman,' he said with a giggle.

'Arrrrgggghhhh,' April groaned between gritted teeth. 'And you just had to mention it,' she added.

'I thought you'd be interested,' Woody said, his eyes gleaming with a mischievous light. 'He was with a real Barbie doll. You know. Bleached blond hair, big blue eyes, perfect bod – biiig bozooms. Skin-tight leather mini.' He laughed helplessly.

April laughed, too. 'Sounds like he's found the perfect woman,' she said.

Woody nodded his shaggy-haired head vigorously. 'He's gonna marry the bimbo!' He laughed again.

'Marry her!' she said. 'Well, it's just what he deserves. But then, she may be a very smart, very nice person for all we know.'

'Oh, sure, April,' Woody said sardonically. 'Sure.'

April smiled. 'And I was just certain that he was waiting for *me*,' she said with amusement. She sighed dramatically. 'But those Silicon Valley millionaires are all in a hurry, aren't they? Don't have much time to shop around, they're so busy making all that dough.' She frowned then. 'To think I ever dated that ... that big bag of testosterone! And you!' She pointed a finger at Woody. 'You introduced us!'

'Yeah,' he countered, 'but I didn't know the jerk was going to ask you out.'

'I bet,' April said.

'No,' Woody said, sitting up. 'I really didn't, April. When those loaded Silicon Valley types descend to the beach on the weekends, nine out of ten of them are looking for one thing, and one thing only.'

She nodded. 'All the more reason I wonder why you introduced us,' she said.

'How could I know he'd actually want to go out with you?' he said defensively. 'It wasn't like I was trying to set you up, you know?'

'Okay, Woody,' she said. 'Okay. But in the future, don't do me any more favors like that one. I didn't

think I'd ever get the aggressive creep out of my hair.'
She paused and sipped her coffee.

'It was interesting, though,' she said thoughtfully.
'He proved you don't have to be a controlling, ego-
obsessed actor in Hollywood to be controlling and
ego-obsessed. You can be a techno wizard that's made
millions of dollars in Silicon Valley and be just as
controlling and ego-obsessed.' She laughed. 'Just as
big a shit.'

'We're not all like that, April,' Woody said.

'No,' she said. 'I'm sure you're not. At least I don't
think you are. I guess I just haven't met the right one.'
She looked at Woody. 'I'm thirty-two years old now.
What are my chances?'

Woody got up from the sofa and came around to
hers. He sat down next to her and gave her a chaste
kiss on the forehead. 'You've always got me, April,' he
said, his dark eyes serious.

She looked up at him. 'Thanks, Woody,' she said,
squeezing his thick surfer's arm. 'You're sweet.'

Then she wondered seriously: *What are my chances?
I've dated lots of men since I was in high school. I've been
married. I keep meeting men that I guess a lot of women
would jump at the chance to go out with, even marry.
Why don't I seem to find the right fit? Is it me? And will
I always be alone?*

Suddenly she felt weird, being thirty-two and alone
in the world. No family except for distant cousins. No
real prospects in the husband category, if she excluded
Woody. But then, she reminded herself, she'd wanted

this independent life, and now she'd simply have to live with the consequences.

Deep down inside, however, something instinctual told her that her life was about to change, for better or worse, and that she had no control over it.

J osh cruised into the pea-gravel courtyard in front of their mountaintop house and brought his ancient yellow Toyota Land Cruiser FJ40 to a halt. He didn't see Joanna's Mercedes in the courtyard, and the garage bay where she kept it was empty, its door yawning wide open.

Well, he thought, killing the engine and jumping out of the big SUV, *Connie'll know where she is.* He saw that her old Plymouth Voyager was parked in its corner of the courtyard. Climbing the stone steps to the front door, he smelled the heady fragrance of the wisteria, then noticed that it was beginning to bloom. It draped in luscious-looking purple clusters from the pergola that ran the length of the house.

69

He started to go through the front door, then looked down at his boots. 'Crap,' he said. They were caked with muck from the nursery, as usual, and the door mat would never clean it all off. Turning to his left, he walked down the length of the pergola and opened the gate that led down a path through the garden to the little mud room around the side of the house. Opening the French door that led into it, he called out for Connie. No answer.

Sitting down on the old pine bench near the door, he quickly unlaced his boots, pulled off his socks, and wiggled his toes. Then he bounded down the hallway to the kitchen, where he was sure Connie would be.

'Connie,' he called again. Still no answer.

In the kitchen, he looked around and saw that no one was there. 'Well, hell,' he murmured. Then he spotted Connie through a window, outside on the terrace in the back, talking on the remote phone. He grinned. Connie, like her sister-in-law, Luna, loved talking on the phone. To whom and what about, he had no idea. As much Spanish as he knew, her rapid-fire conversations were completely lost on him. He didn't want to disturb her, so he backed away from the window.

He looked at the little blackboard near the refrigerator, checking to see if there was a note from Joanna. Nada. The big Sub-Zero refrigerator beckoned, and he opened it and took out a chilled bottle of white wine. It would be good, he decided, after a rotten day at the nursery. He poured himself a glass, then approached the window again, having already forgotten about Connie.

She glimpsed him from where she stood near a teak table, and he saw that she immediately punched the Off button on the telephone, then started toward the house with a smile.

When she came through the French doors to the kitchen, Josh said: 'Connie, you know you didn't have to get off the telephone because of me.'

'I know,' she said in her lightly accented English, 'but I was finished anyway. Just talking to my friend.' With her tiny fingers, she loosened her black hair from the rubber band that held it in a ponytail, then shook it and ran the fingers of one hand through it. She looked up at him. 'So, how are you, Josh?' she asked.

'Okay, Connie,' he replied, then added: 'Well, sort of.'

'What's wrong?' she asked, her pretty features suddenly lined with concern.

He looked at her and smiled grimly. 'You want a glass of wine or are you in a hurry?'

'You know I'm not in a hurry if you need to talk to me,' she said. 'I'll have a glass of wine.' She went to the refrigerator, got out the bottle, and poured herself a glass.

'You want to take it outside?' he asked.

'Sure,' she said. 'Let's go.'

She walked ahead of him, her petite, youthful body a vision in black. Simple black knit top with black jeans tucked into black cowboy boots. She looked like anything but a maid, he thought for the thousandth time, and she was wise beyond her years.

They walked out to the weathered teak table and chairs and sat down under the big market umbrella. The stone terrace was large, accessible from nearly every first-floor room in the horseshoe-shaped house. At its open end, across a bridge, was the swimming pool, its turquoise water barely rippling in the light wind. Beyond it, the dramatic peaks and canyons of the Santa Cruz Mountains were covered with spring's verdancy.

'What's bothering you, Josh?' she asked, after taking a sip of her wine.

He sighed. 'I . . . I just wondered if you'd noticed Joanna acting . . . well . . . sort of strange lately?'

Connie's dark eyes flickered in the afternoon light, then she looked away. 'Weeelll . . .,' she began, clicking pink-painted fingernails on the weathered teak, 'I don't know.'

He knew that she was holding back. 'Come on, Connie,' he said, cajoling her. He thought that once he got her started talking, she wouldn't be able to stop. Connie loved to conspire, whether with Joanna or him, but only in a very positive way. It was never conspiring *against* one or the other of them.

Connie took a sip of her wine, then set the glass down. 'Maybe the only thing that's been bothering Joanna is that bitchy sister of hers, huh?' She laughed and looked at him mischievously.

Josh couldn't help but laugh. 'Yeah, well, there is that,' he conceded, but then his expression became serious. 'But that's not it, Connie. I'm really getting worried,' he continued, 'and I need to know what you think.

Nobody knows Joanna better than you do, and I know the two of you don't have any secrets from each other.'

She took another sip of her wine, then set the glass down and looked at him. 'Well, Josh,' she said hesitantly, 'I guess so. You know.' She looked away. 'She has been gone a lot, and she's always thinking about something else. You know what I mean?'

He nodded. 'I know exactly what you mean,' he said. *Good*, he thought. *I've got her hooked.*

'It's like she's always on another planet,' Connie said. 'And she never tells me where she's going anymore.' She looked at him meaningfully.

'Me, either,' he said. He looked out at the swimming pool, then returned his gaze to Connie. 'Do you have any idea what might be going on?' he asked.

'Nooo,' Connie replied slowly. 'She doesn't tell me anything. I've started to wonder if maybe she's hiding something, you know?'

'Do you think she's worried about something?' he persisted.

Connie heaved a sigh. 'I don't know,' she said. 'I just know she's been . . .' She looked at Josh and laughed. 'She's been a *bitch*, Josh,' she said. 'Sometimes, anyway. Over little things.'

Josh smiled. He knew that Connie loved Joanna like a sister and he took no offense at her remark.

'Yeah,' he said, 'and that's another thing that's worried me. It's not like her. Not one bit.'

Connie shook her head. 'No, it's not,' she agreed. She drummed her pink fingernails on the tabletop again. '*Misterioso*,' she said darkly, looking off into the distance.

'Do you think—' he began before he was interrupted by a very cheerful voice in the distance.

'Hello, you two!' Joanna called from a doorway. She set down several shopping bags and breezed out onto the terrace, all smiles.

Josh rose to his feet and planted a kiss on her cheek. 'Hi, beautiful,' he said. 'We're just having a glass of wine. You want one?'

'You bet,' she said.

He dashed off toward the kitchen.

Joanna brushed Connie's cheek with a kiss, then sat down. 'Did I interrupt a good gossip session?' she asked, her eyes glinting with amusement.

'Nooo,' Connie said. 'We were just, you know, enjoying the breezes.'

Joanna laughed. 'Since when have you ever stopped long enough to enjoy a breeze, Connie?' she asked, looking her in the eye.

Connie shrugged. 'Oooh, since now,' she said. Then they both laughed. She knew, of course, that Joanna guessed they'd been discussing her, and she also knew that Joanna wouldn't try to pump her for information, happy to let them enjoy their conspiracy.

Josh returned with Joanna's wine and handed it to her, then sat back down.

'Thanks,' she said, taking a sip. 'Ummm. That tastes so good.' She set the glass down and looked at Josh. 'How was your day?'

He frowned. She was in such a cheerful mood that he hated to tell her what had happened at the nursery, but he had to. 'I was working here in the Stud Room,' he said, 'and Carl called from the nursery. So I went out there. Either the computer-controlled misting system malfunctioned or somebody tinkered with it.'

'What!' Joanna exclaimed, her eyebrows rising with alarm. 'Oh, my God! Was there any damage?' *Oh, Lord,* she thought. *Why this on top of everything else that's happened to me lately?*

'Hardly any,' he said. 'We got lucky this time, but it could've been a disaster. We don't know how long it was off. It could've been out since last Friday afternoon. With Christina's visit, none of us were down there all weekend.' He looked at Connie. 'Your brother discovered it, so we have him to thank for saving the day.'

Connie, sipping her wine, simply nodded.

He looked back at his wife. 'Several people were in and out of that greenhouse, but Carl is the only one who noticed that the misters weren't functioning.'

'Oh, Josh.' Joanna paused for a moment, looking at him. 'And do you think that somebody might have deliberately fooled around with the system?' she asked.

He nodded. 'Maybe,' he said grimly. 'But the police didn't find any sign of forced entry. Nothing suspicious. The outfit that sold me the equipment has sent somebody out, and they say the computer didn't malfunction.'

'Excuse me,' Connie said, scooting her chair back and getting to her feet. 'I'd better get going.'

Joanna looked up at her. 'You won't have another glass of wine?' she asked.

'No, thanks. I really have a lot to do,' Connie said. She kissed Joanna on the cheek. 'See you in the morning.'

Josh stood up. ''Bye,' he said, winking at her. 'See you tomorrow.'

Connie wiggled her tiny fingers, turned, and quickly disappeared into the house.

Josh sat back down, and Joanna looked at him thoughtfully. 'Did you tell the police about the Rossi brothers wanting to buy us out?'

'No,' he said. 'I thought that might sound a little paranoid. Besides, they didn't find anything, so what was the point?'

'I guess you're right,' Joanna said, 'but something tells me that they might have had something to do with this.'

'I certainly wouldn't put it past them,' Josh agreed. He took a sip of wine. 'Peter Rossi called me at the office. Wanted to know if I'd changed my mind about selling out.'

'What!' she exclaimed. 'God, they've got a lot of nerve.'

'You bet they do,' he replied. 'From what I hear, when they bought the old Giglio place, they didn't want the buildings. They were just in the way. So instead of spending the money to tear them down, they paid somebody to drop a match, then collected the fire insurance.'

'I think these people are really dangerous, Josh,' she said. 'Capable of anything.'

'Well,' he said, 'I don't think it's anything I can't handle. Anyway, enough about my day,' he said, setting his glass back down. 'What've you been up to?' he asked, wondering if she would be forthcoming. Although he'd seen the shopping bags, he knew that she hadn't spent the entire day in the shops.

Joanna's expression immediately changed from one of concern and worry to a radiant smile. 'Oh, Josh, you wouldn't believe it!' she said excitedly. 'I've met the most wonderful lady!'

Josh looked over at her, gratified to see her smiling. 'Who?' he asked. 'Who is this wonderful lady you met?'

'You know the garden walls and fountain at Ingrid and Ronald Wilson's that you loved so much?' she asked.

'Sure,' he said. 'They were spectacular.'

'Well, I called Ingrid and found out who did them,' Joanna said.

'Was it somebody around here?' Josh asked.

'Yes,' Joanna replied. 'April Woodward's her name, and she lives nearby. Here in the mountains. So I made an appointment and went over to see her today.' She smiled and looked at him playfully, then took a sip of her wine.

'And?' Josh asked.

'And she's coming over here tomorrow to look at the old stone stable,' Joanna said. 'I think she's excited about my ideas for it.'

'That's great, honey,' Josh said, 'but are you sure you

really want to go through with this? I mean, I loved the Wilsons' place, but it's a lot of work and—'

'Oh, Josh, I've *got* to do it!' Joanna said, clapping her hands together. 'I'm so glad you mentioned the Wilsons' because it started me thinking. You know how I've been collecting all those seashells and pebbles for years and years and always dreamed of doing a sort of grotto.'

Josh laughed. 'Oh, God, Joanna, do I ever,' he said. He reached across the table and took one of her hands in his. He hadn't seen her this animated in a long time, and it reassured him that all was right with the world.

'You know,' he said, 'collecting all those shells and stuff is the only thing you've ever done that I thought bordered on an obsession.'

'I know,' she said, 'but I can't help it. Anyway, I took a bunch of pictures I've saved over to April's. You know, all those fabulous rooms made out of shells and tiles and things. And we talked about it.' She looked into Josh's bright ultramarine eyes. 'And you know what?'

'What?' he asked, smiling.

'She didn't think I was crazy!' Joanna laughed, and he laughed with her.

'I think she really understood what I want to do,' she said.

'Well, that's pretty amazing,' Josh said teasingly. 'Maybe she's crazy, too.'

'You devil.' Joanna squeezed his hand affectionately.

'No, really. She's even done something similar for somebody in Los Angeles,' she went on. 'Just not quite on this scale. So.' She paused and sat back in her chair. 'Tomorrow we'll see how it goes.'

'I hope it works out,' he said, 'but are you sure you want to start a project this big? I mean, it's—'

'I told you,' Joanna interjected. 'I have to. It's like ... well, it's like a kind of legacy. Like the orchid book I did.' She gave him a look that was at once both serious and wistful. 'Something with a little piece of me in it. It's something that I can leave behind in this world, Josh. Something that will be here when I'm ... gone.'

He looked at her with relief. He knew that he needn't have worried so much about her behavior recently. 'You're so much like your father,' he said.

'How do you mean?' she asked, knowing exactly what he meant, but wanting to hear it said.

'You're a dreamer and a builder,' he said. 'You have a creative impulse that's a bit different and that's got to be expressed. And, by God, you've got to leave your stamp on the world.'

Joanna looked down at the table, flushed slightly from the wine and his words. When she looked back up, she said, 'I guess we all want to contribute something, don't we? We want to give something back, to do something more than simply pass through this life, don't we? To make it a better place?'

'You know what?' Josh said.

'What?'

'I love you, Joanna,' he said in a near whisper. 'Truly and deeply.'

A smile trembled on her lips and unbidden tears sprang into her eyes. 'And I love you, Joshua Lawrence,' she said. 'More than you'll ever know.'

7

April maneuvered her trusty old Jeep Wagoneer up the dangerously narrow and curvy mountain roads with ease, slowing down to look for the road signs at turnoffs that Joanna had written down for her. It was a road very much like her own, beautiful and lethal at once, overhung with a sun-filtering canopy of fir trees, cypress, redwoods, eucalyptus, and live oak, complete with washouts where the road suddenly became a single narrow lane.

She wasn't quite prepared, however, for what awaited her after she made the last turn on Joanna's instruction sheet and climbed steadily uphill. Reaching a small plateau on the mountaintop, she slowed to a crawl, craning her neck both left and right, trying to take in the sheer magnificence that surrounded her on all sides: peaks and canyons of awesome heights and depths, all dressed in the fresh greens of spring dotted with vibrantly colored wildflowers. It was truly stunning, this mountaintop perch.

Ahead, she saw the driveway that led up to Joanna's house. She slowly turned onto it, taking in the old apple trees that lined both sides of the road. The short drive led to two massive stone gateposts, topped by copper lanterns with a verdigris patina. Heavy black iron gates were open wide, and looked as if they were always thus, ready to welcome visitors. The same iron was used in fencing that extended from either side of the gateposts, encompassing what appeared to be gardens surrounding the house.

Between the stone pillars she went, slowly pulling in to a large courtyard. On her left rose a large gray-shingled house with snowy white trim and shutters. A pergola, dripping with purplish wisteria, ran its entire length. Straight ahead was a four-bay garage, connected to the house by the pergola. On her right was another pergola, this one covered with old-fashioned-looking roses of the palest pink, thousands of them in riotous bloom. The whole had about it an air of solid, old-money affluence combined with loving and lavish care.

Pulling her big shoulder bag out of the Jeep after her, April walked up the stone steps to the front door. It was painted the darkest green, a green with a lot of blue in it. She rang the bell and waited.

The door opened and an extremely pretty petite young woman with jet-black hair and dark eyes greeted her.

'Hello,' she said cheerfully. 'You must be April, right?'

April nodded. 'Right,' she said, smiling.

'I'm Connie,' the woman said, opening the door wide. 'Come in. Joanna's waiting for you outside.'

April trailed after her, looking about. The loveliness of the exterior of the house hadn't prepared her for the immensity and old-fashioned grandeur of the interior. The spacious entrance hall was centered with a large round Regency table, over which hung a sparkling crystal chandelier, and an elegantly curving staircase led to the second floor. Following Connie, who was fast on her feet, April barely glimpsed rooms to the right and left, but the impression was one of burnished woods, polished silver and brass, and richly glowing fabrics and rugs.

Straight ahead, she could see that French doors at the back of the house framed a view across a stone terrace and verdant greenery to distant mountain peaks. She had been in many homes in this area, some of them belonging to very wealthy people, but April didn't think she'd ever been in one that exuded such luxurious tranquility. She wanted to reach out and brush fabrics between her fingertips, to stroke highly polished woods, to indulge her eyes in the visual feast that she sensed all around her; but Connie, who'd already reached the French doors, was standing there, an impatient smile on her face, awaiting her.

'Out here,' Connie said, opening the door.

'Thanks, Connie,' April said.

She saw Joanna seated at a big teak table under a market umbrella. Stacks of books and magazines were piled on the stone terrace and on the table. When Joanna saw her, she took off her sunglasses and rose to her feet.

'Hi,' she called. 'Welcome.'

'Thanks,' April said. 'It's so beautiful here, Joanna! I had no idea. I can't believe that after living here all this time, I've never been up this road before.' She looked out over the bridge toward the pool and beyond to the mountains and canyons. 'It's heaven!'

'It really is, isn't it,' Joanna said, reaching out a hand.

April took it, and Joanna didn't so much shake it as squeeze it affectionately. 'Here,' she said, 'have a seat and tell me what you'd like to drink. There's tea and soda and mineral water, whatever you'd like.'

April sat down and looked at Joanna's glass. 'What are you having?' she asked.

'Some iced green tea,' Joanna said.

'Oh, great,' April said. 'I'll have the same.'

Joanna turned to Connie, who stood waiting. 'Connie, why don't you bring a pitcher out?' she said.

'Sure,' Connie said, then turned toward the house.

Joanna sat down and looked at the young woman across from her. She was every bit as lovely today as she'd remembered.

'After you've had a drink, I'll show you around,' she said. 'Is that okay?'

'Yes,' April replied, looking about her, trying to take in all the plants, flowers, shrubbery, and trees. She breathed deeply, enjoying the mixed bouquet carried on the light breeze. 'I really can't get over this place,' she enthused. 'It's spectacular and . . . voluptuous, in a way. A quiet way.'

Joanna looked surprised. 'You've hit the nail on the head, I think,' she said. 'A quiet voluptuousness.'

'Have you lived here a long time?' April asked.

Joanna nodded. 'I've never really lived anywhere else,' she said. 'My father built the place when he and my mother married, so I grew up here. Then right after Josh and I got married, my father died and left it to us.' She paused and smiled. 'We were living in this little place down at the beach that Dad had given us as a wedding present. In the middle of nowhere near Pajaro Dunes. A beach shack really, but wonderful.'

'Well, this place certainly is,' April said. 'It's so un-Californian. I mean, the house and everything seem to have been here forever. You know what I mean? To have real *roots* here.'

Joanna laughed. 'Not like a lot of California. Covered up with vinyl-sided boxes that were built yesterday or the day before.'

Connie returned with a tray loaded down with a pitcher of tea and glasses, which she set on the table. 'There's real sugar, Sweet 'n Low, and honey,' she said, pouring a glass of iced tea for April.

'Thanks, Connie,' April said. 'I can do the rest.'

'Sure,' Connie said. 'I'll go finish lunch now, okay?'

'Yes,' Joanna said. 'We'll be ready in about half an hour or so.'

'Okay.' Connie rushed off, back to the kitchen.

'She's so pretty,' April said, 'and seems so energetic and happy.'

'She's a wonder,' Joanna said. 'Before Dad died, he practically adopted Connie and Carl, her brother. They were Consuelo and Carlos then, and had just moved here with their mother from Peru. Living in a little trailer in one of those horrible migrant labor places. Connie came to work here, and Carl works at the nursery.'

'They changed their names?' April asked, sipping her tea.

'Yes,' Joanna said with a nod. 'They wanted to be as American as possible. Still do.'

'Oh, so they're not legal,' April said.

'Carl is,' Joanna said. 'He married Luna Garber, a half-Venezeulan, half-Jewish American. She works at the nursery, too, running the office. But Connie ... well, it's so complicated.' Joanna laughed lightly.

'What?' April said, intrigued.

'Well, Connie found somebody to marry. You know, just a marriage of convenience. So we loaned her the five thousand dollars to pay the guy—'

'Five thousand dollars!' April interjected.

Joanna nodded. 'Seems to be the going rate. Anyway, they married, then when they had interviews at immigration, she didn't pass.'

'What?' April asked. 'But how's that possible?'

'The interviewer was probably having a bad day,' Joanna said. 'Anyway, he certainly smelled something fishy, because they couldn't answer all sorts of personal questions about each other. It was obvious that they hardly even knew each other, much less lived together as man and wife. So she didn't get her green card.'

'So what happened?' April asked.

'The way things stand right now,' Joanna said, 'is that we've hired a very expensive lawyer who specializes in these cases to help her out. He has a good track record, so we'll see. In the meantime, the fellow she married has disappeared with his cash.' She laughed again. 'There's always a little drama around here.'

'Sounds like it,' April said. 'It also sounds like you've been very generous with her.'

'Well,' Joanna said, 'Connie's worked here since she was about eighteen, and she's really like family. I'm as close to her as I am to my sister, Christina. She's been absolutely wonderful. She *is* wonderful. And smart and ambitious.'

'She's so pretty,' April said, 'I'm surprised somebody legal didn't sweep her off her feet right away.'

'It does seem odd, doesn't it?' Joanna replied. 'She dates some, but Connie is extremely particular. I mean, fussy beyond belief. A real snob when it comes to men. What they look like, what they do for a living. She's determined to get as far away as she can from that childhood of poverty in Peru. Plus, I don't think she's really fallen for anybody yet.'

'That does count for something, doesn't it,' April said with a laugh.

'Yes,' Joanna agreed. 'At least I think it does.' She saw that April had finished her iced tea. 'You ready to see the old stable?' she asked.

'Yes,' April said. 'I can hardly wait.'

'Well, follow me,' Joanna said, scraping her chair back from the table and getting to her feet.

She led the way across the stone terrace and over a little wooden bridge that brought them to the pool area.

'I love the bridge and the landscaping,' April said with enthusiasm. 'It's all so perfect.'

'Dad started it,' Joanna replied, 'but Josh and I have done a lot more over the years.'

They walked past the pool and on through lushly landscaped grounds until April could see the old stable about a hundred feet away, set on sloping ground surrounded with apple trees. From here the view of the peaks and canyons was even more dramatic than from the terrace.

'Oh, wow, Joanna!' she said. 'This spot is so beautiful.'

'I know,' Joanna said. 'That's one reason I think it would make a great place to entertain or just to meditate. You know, read, get away from the activity in the house. I discovered when I was working on the orchid book that as big as the house is, I could've used a separate place – a separate building – to get away to.'

They arrived at the stable and stood before it. Joanna

watched April's face for signs of what she might be thinking, but her expression was inscrutable.

Without saying anything, April slowly began walking the circumference of the small building, with Joanna trailing behind her. Then she stepped inside from the front, looking around her. Finally, arms akimbo and feet planted widely on the ground, she looked Joanna in the eye. Her expression was thoughtful.

'You know what I think?' she said in an even tone.

'What?' Joanna asked, a little worried that she might think the building unsuitable for what she had in mind.

April smiled widely. 'I think it's perfect,' she said. 'It's just right for what you want to do.'

Joanna felt a sense of relief rush through her. *Thank God!* she thought. *She'll take on the project.*

'Great,' she said. 'I'm glad you feel that way. I was afraid you'd think I was crazy wanting to fix this place up at all, much less do something elaborate with it.'

April shook her head. 'No, no,' she said. 'I really mean it. I think it's absolutely right.' She turned to what had once been stable doors leading to individual stalls. 'Look,' she said. Her speech became more rapid with her excitement. 'These openings are perfect for French doors. They're begging for French doors. They'd give a view of the mountains on this one side. Then,' she went on, 'the other three sides would be as they are. No doors or windows. Totally closed in.' She turned and looked at Joanna again. 'You'd be totally surrounded by architectural motifs and murals made of seashells and pebbles.'

Joanna's eyes brightened. 'You really do love the idea, don't you?'

'Oh, yes,' April said, nodding. 'It can be really fabulous, a real fantasy.' Then she added quietly, 'It can have real magic.'

Just the words I wanted to hear, Joanna thought. 'So you'll take on the project?'

'Well . . . we should talk about scheduling, terms, and so forth,' April said. 'But, yes.' She smiled. 'I'd love to take on the project.'

'That's wonderful, April,' Joanna said. 'I'm so excited.' She reached over and hugged April's shoulders, then kissed her cheek.

It was completely spontaneous and so unlike anything she would normally do with someone she barely knew that Joanna drew back and laughed nervously. 'I'm sorry,' she said. 'I . . . I know I hardly know you, but I'm just so excited.'

April blushed slightly. 'That's perfectly all right,' she said. 'I'm excited, too, and I . . . I already feel like I've known you for a long time.'

'I feel exactly the same way,' Joanna said. 'Like you're an old friend.' She paused thoughtfully. 'I guess we think a lot alike,' she said. 'We're both rather practical, I think, but we like a bit of fantasy, a bit of humor and whimsy in our lives.'

'Yes,' April agreed. 'I think we like the same things.'

Joanna took her arm. 'There's one more thing I want to show you, then we'll have lunch. Okay?'

'Sure,' April said.

'Over here,' Joanna said, indicating a corner of the stable.

April followed her to a corner where huge sheets of plastic hid whatever was underneath. Joanna pulled off the plastic sheets, and April saw that there must be at least a hundred or more neatly stacked boxes and storage bins. They towered from the floor nearly to the ceiling.

Joanna opened one of the plastic ones and turned to April. 'Look,' she said.

April drew closer and looked in. Her eyes widened in surprise at the sight of the colorful seashells packed inside the bin. Then she inhaled deeply. 'It's as if you've brought the ocean home with you. And they're beautiful,' she said.

'Yes,' Joanna said, 'there are thousands of them. All boxed by type.'

'Incredible!' April exclaimed.

'Anyway, I hope we can incorporate the ones I've collected,' Joanna said.

'That should be a priority,' April replied.

Joanna closed the plastic bin. 'Well, let's go have lunch now. That is, if you've seen enough.'

'Yes,' April said. 'For now anyway.'

Joanna led her up the slight incline, through the apple trees, back onto the lushly landscaped grounds, and on toward the pool and stone terraces.

'Connie is a great cook,' she said as they walked. 'She makes several Peruvian specialties. With her own added twist, of course. And they are delicious. The only problem is that most of them are very rich. And hard to say no to.'

April laughed. 'Like so many good things in life.'

Reaching the table, she could see that it had been elegantly set with beautiful china and sparkling silver and crystal. There was even a white linen tablecloth with matching crisp white linen napkins. In the center of the table was a small pot of delicate-looking pale lilac orchids, so beautiful they themselves appeared edible.

'Everything's so beautiful,' April said. 'You shouldn't have gone to so much trouble.'

'Doing things beautifully is never too much trouble,' Joanna said.

April looked at her and realized that she meant it. This was a woman who would spare no effort to see that her world was as beautiful as she could make it.

'I've never seen lilac orchids quite like these,' April said.

'They're *Cattleya skinneri*,' Joanna said. 'Not rare or difficult, but a very pretty color, I think. Here,' she said, 'you sit over here.' She indicated a chair. 'And I'll sit here.'

They sat down, and as if by magic, Connie appeared from the kitchen, carrying a tray toward them.

The remains of the lunch lay colorfully on the exquisite china, testimony to Connie's skills in the kitchen. Bowls still pink from the creamy, rich shrimp soup that was perfumed with cilantro. Plates a mixture of greens, whites, and browns from a hearty *calsa*, a casserole of chicken breast, creamed potatoes, and avocado. The contents of the salad plates had merely been nibbled at, but the dessert plates looked as if they'd hardly been used, eaten clean of the delicious flan that Connie had made.

'That was out of this world,' April said, folding her napkin.

'Connie never fails,' Joanna said. 'You know, I've had people call from everywhere, even Europe, after they've eaten here. All of them want to know her recipe for shrimp soup.'

'Does she give it out?' April asked.

'Almost never.' Joanna laughed. 'There was one time when a great lady, a very rich orchid collector in France, called, and I begged Connie to give it to her. She's such a good customer, you see.'

'Did she?' April grinned.

'Well, she gave her a *version* of the recipe,' Joanna said. 'I've forgotten what she left out, but she did leave out something.'

They both laughed.

April caught herself brushing the orchid plant on the table with her fingertips. 'Oh, I'm sorry,' she apologized. 'It makes you want to touch it.'

'That's okay,' Joanna said. 'Like I said, these aren't rare or difficult. Why don't you take it home with you?'

'Really?' April's eyebrows drew up in surprise.

'Of course,' Joanna said. 'It's easy to take care of. I'll give you an instruction sheet before you go. We have them for customers at the nursery. Would you like to see the little greenhouse before you go?'

'Yes,' April said. 'I'd love to. If I do work on this project, then I'm going to have to get on friendly terms with orchids.'

'Come on, I'll show you.'

April followed her across the little bridge to the pool area, then they followed a path around the pool house, which led to a small greenhouse a few feet away.

'You'd never know it was here,' April said. 'At least not from the house.'

'That was part of the idea of putting it here,' Joanna replied. 'These are really special orchids, for the most part. Rare and expensive. And Josh has his Stud Room here.'

'His what?' April asked with a quizzical expression. She almost snorted with laughter.

Joanna looked at her and smiled. 'You heard correctly. Stud Room. It's called that because that's where he pollinates the orchid plants. Manually. Some of them are very difficult. He's working on creating hybrids. That's one of the mainstays of the orchid business. *Our* orchid business, at any rate. Creating hybrids. Coming up with something new and different that will generate a lot of interest and *sell*. It's a long process, and you can't be absolutely sure what you'll get when you cross plants.'

She pulled a beeper from the pocket of her loose-fitting, sand-colored silk trousers. She punched in a code, aiming it at the greenhouse. There was a click, then Joanna opened the door.

'We have to have a security system here because the orchids are so valuable.'

As April followed Joanna in, her mouth almost fell open. 'Oh, this is like nothing else in the world,' she said in awe, looking about her at the riot of exotic blossoms and colors. Reds, pinks, purples, white, yellows, greens, near-blacks – every color of the rainbow and some she didn't think she'd ever seen before. The plants themselves, with their variable foliage and roots, were sights to behold, from tiny, potted orchids with strange foliage to orchids almost the size of trees.

'Wait till you see the nursery,' Joanna said. She could see where Josh had been pollinating the *Paphiopedilum lowii*. 'Do you like this one?' she asked.

April studied the plant. 'It's extraordinary,' she said. 'The greens and pinks and purples. Really beautiful.'

'Josh is trying to hybridize it with something else, I'm not sure what. Maybe several other orchids. To see what he'll come up with.'

'Did I hear my name being tossed about?' a deep male voice from behind them asked.

'Oh!' Joanna exclaimed. 'I didn't realize you were here.'

He took her in his arms, giving her a kiss on the lips. April watched, surprised by their unembarrassed display of affection for one another in front of someone else. They were so natural together, she thought, with such an easy familiarity.

'Josh,' Joanna said, 'this is my friend, April Woodward. And April, my husband, Josh.'

Josh leaned forward and took April's hand in his, and she shook it firmly, looking into his eyes.

Such eyes, she thought. *I've never seen such eyes before. They are almost mesmerizing in the depths of their blueness. And his smile! Those white, white teeth contrasting with his tanned body. And his hair!*

Suddenly she realized that she'd been staring at him, that she'd held his hand longer than she should have. She quickly let go and looked down at the ground for a moment, then back up at him. 'It's a pleasure to meet you,' she said. 'Joanna was just showing me some of your work.'

'The tip of the iceberg,' he said with a smile. 'What do you think of her project, April? Or have you had time to think about it?'

'I'm very excited about it,' she said, 'and I think we can work something out.'

'We've already been down to the stable,' Joanna said, 'and April really liked it.'

'Good,' Josh said. 'A lot of people don't really understand my wife's wonderful ideas, I'm afraid.' He took Joanna's hand and squeezed it. 'I guess that's one of the things I love about her.'

'Oh, Josh,' Joanna said, 'I think you've thought some of them were pretty crazy, too.'

He laughed. 'Yeah, that's true.'

'Listen,' Joanna said, 'how about you showing April the greenhouse while I run up to the house and get some things ready for her to take home with her? Is that okay with the two of you?'

April nodded. 'It's fine with me.'

'You sure you won't be bored to death?' Josh asked.

'Oh, no,' April said. 'Not with all these fantastic flowers.'

'I'll see you at the house, then,' Joanna said, and turned and left the greenhouse.

'So what did Joanna show you?' Josh asked, looking at April.

His eyes are like magnets, she thought. *I've got to stop looking at them. And his hair! I hadn't noticed before how sun-bleached it is, how streaked with gold.*

'Well,' April said, recovering herself, 'she was showing me something you're trying to pollinate over there.' She pointed to the *Paphiopedilum lowii*.

'Are you really interested?' he asked.

'Oh, yes,' she said, nodding.

He could see that she was serious, and he appreciated that. A lot of people were interested in the end product – a beautiful, exotic flower – but few had any enthusiasm for how it got to be that way.

He showed her how the sunshades and the computer-controlled misting system worked. Then he put on latex gloves and demonstrated how he used toothpicks to take pollen from one plant and pollinate another.

She watched with fascination as he took a saliva-coated toothpick from his mouth and swirled it around in one orchid, then transferred the toothpick, now laden with pollen, to the next orchid.

'Does this disgust you?' he asked, looking up at her.

'Oh, no,' she said, shaking her head. 'I think it's fascinating. You're more or less making them have sex.'

He grinned. 'That's exactly right.'

Afterward, they walked around the small facility, and he showed her various types of orchids, discussed their characteristics, areas of origin, and a thousand other details about them that became a confusing swirl in April's head.

Josh turned and saw the look on her face and laughed. 'I'm going too fast,' he said. 'And trying to cover too much ground for someone who doesn't know much about all this.'

'Yes,' April said honestly, 'but it's fascinating, and I can see that you have a real passion for it.'

'Uh-huh,' he said. 'I got it from Mitch Cameron, Joanna's father. He had the disease – orchid fever – and transmitted it to me. I've had it ever since.' He paused and looked at her. 'I came to work part-time at the nursery one summer while I was in college.' He paused and laughed. 'And I never left.'

'Really?' she asked. 'Just like that?'

'Yes.' He nodded and flashed a smile.

That *smile*, she thought.

'I fell in love with orchids, Mitch Cameron, *and* his daughter.'

'What an amazing coincidence,' she said. 'To fall into all this. It's such a . . . such a different life.'

'But then, so is yours,' he said. 'At least from what Joanna's told me.'

She looked at him. 'I . . . I guess you're right,' she said. 'There aren't many people who're interested in what I do, much less people who actually do it.'

'Do you love it?' he asked. 'I mean, really love your work, with a passion?'

He studied her face closely, and suddenly found that he had been ignoring her tall, slender body, her brown and golden amber eyes and sandy hair, and her strikingly beautiful features. Now that he had taken notice of her – real notice – he found it impossible to believe that he was actually noticing her for the first time. He'd been concentrating all of his attentions on Joanna when he'd first come in and had failed to realize that such an exquisite creature had been here all along.

'Yes,' she said, looking him in the eye. 'I do have a passion for my work. Whether it's working with shells or tiles or stone or simply doing my watercolors, I put everything I've got into it. I really do love it. It's what keeps me . . . I hate to use the word *centered* . . . but I guess that describes it.'

She paused and smiled ruefully. 'I guess if the rest of the world seems crazy and uncontrollable . . .' She sighed and shrugged.

'If the rest of the world is crazy and out of your control,' Josh finished for her, 'at least you have your work. And it's something you *can* control to some extent. You can decide where to put that piece of tile or shell, or how you want that watercolor to look. You can actually find peace in it.'

'That's it exactly,' she said, nodding.

How strange, he thought, *she seems to think just like Joanna. And me. And she has that remarkable self-possession, poise, and ease, that Joanna has about her. She also seems to be purposeful and practical like Joanna, despite her imagination. No wonder they are hitting it off.*

'I guess I'd better get up to the house,' Josh said. 'I left some paperwork here and have to get back out to the nursery.'

'Thanks a lot for the tour and all the information,' April said.

'I hope I didn't scare you off,' Josh said with a grin.

'No,' April said. 'Not at all.'

They left the greenhouse and walked back toward the house. On the terrace in the distance, Joanna was sitting at the table watching them, a hint of a smile on her lips.

They look so good together, she thought. *So perfect for one another. And I bet they're already finding it easy to talk to each other, to get to know each other.*

She lifted an arm and waved to them, and they both waved back. She could see that they were laughing together, sharing something humorous.

Perfect! she thought again.

When they reached the table, Josh leaned down and kissed Joanna's cheek. 'I've got to get some paperwork in my office. Then I'm going back out to the nursery.'

'You have to leave again?' she asked.

'Yes,' he said. 'All kinds of business to tend to.'

'Okay, darling,' Joanna said, 'I'll see you later, then.'

Josh turned to April. 'It was a pleasure to meet you,' he said. 'And I hope everything works out on the project.'

'It was nice to meet you, too,' April replied. 'And I'm sure the project will work out very well.'

As he walked toward the house, Joanna said to April, 'Have a seat for a minute and then I'll let you go.'

April pulled out a chair and sat down across from Joanna. 'Your husband's a very nice man.'

'He's pure gold,' she replied. 'In fact, he's like Fort Knox.' She and April laughed together.

'How lucky you are,' April said.

Joanna nodded and smiled dreamily. 'Oh, yes,' she said, her violet eyes looking off into the distance. 'Yes, indeed. And I don't mean to seem smug about it, but I'm the luckiest woman alive.'

April thought that she detected a certain wistfulness, possibly even sadness, in Joanna's eyes. She wondered what in the world could make this woman sad, but then decided she was imagining what she'd seen.

'Well,' Joanna said, looking back at April. 'I have some things for you to take home, and I think we should discuss some specifics now. If that's okay with you.'

'Sure,' April said. 'Fire away.'

'I don't know how you usually go about this,' Joanna said, 'but I was wondering if you could give me a rough sketch of what you propose to do and an estimate. I know that I'll have to choose orchids that I want you

101

to use, but at least you can give me rough outlines of what you think would work.'

'When would you want this?' April asked.

'A week from today.'

'A week!' April almost gasped. 'That's awfully fast, Joanna.'

'I'm in a hurry,' Joanna said simply.

April looked at her and saw that she was serious. 'Well, okay then. I'll have to drop everything else, but I can do it.'

'Good,' Joanna said. 'Next week it is.' She paused, with a thoughtful expression on her face. 'Now then,' she began again, 'as for completion.'

April looked at her. She had the distinct impression that Joanna wanted this huge project finished yesterday.

'I would like to see the entire project finished within the next six months,' she said. 'At the latest. Four would please me even more, but I'll allow six.'

April gritted her teeth and grimaced. 'Ouch,' she said. 'Next week is one thing, but six months to finish? Joanna, that would be a tremendous challenge.'

'And I bet you love a challenge,' Joanna said.

'No, really,' April said. 'It would mean dropping or delaying practically everything else I have lined up.' She paused, biting on the end of a fingernail, then looked over at Joanna, seeming to have come to some sort of decision.

'Okay,' she said at last. 'Six months guaranteed. Four months, practically impossible, and I can't make any promises, but I'd be willing to give it a try.'

Joanna smiled. 'That's what I wanted to hear,' she said. She reached across the table and took one of April's hands. 'This will be a fabulous project, April,' she said. 'Believe me, you won't regret it.'

'I'm sure I won't,' April said, but she wondered if she wasn't already regretting it a little.

'Now,' Joanna said. 'I've got two shopping bags here for you to take home. In one is the orchid that was on the table, with instructions for its care.'

'Oh, thank you, Joanna,' April said. 'It's so lovely.'

'And,' Joanna continued, 'there's a copy of the orchid book I did a couple of years back. You can pick out some of your favorites, then next week the two of us will decide together which to incorporate into the murals. How's that?'

'Fine,' April said. 'And thanks so much. You've really been so generous.'

'Oh, you'll be paying me back,' Joanna said. 'So don't worry about it.'

'Well, I'd better get going,' April said. 'I've got tons of work to do between now and next week.'

'Should I give you an advance on this week's work?' Joanna asked.

'No, that won't be necessary,' April said. 'We'll see about it next week.'

They walked to the house, where the shopping bags were waiting for April at the front door. They exchanged kisses like old friends, and April left.

Joanna watched her pull out of the courtyard, then leaned back against the closed door, breathing a sigh of relief. I have *found her!* she thought. *Oh, yes, indeed, Josh. I've found the perfect woman!*

April slowly cruised down the dangerous mountain, her mind swirling with thoughts of the beautiful and decidedly different Joanna Lawrence. *What a woman she is*, she thought. *What a unique mind and what unique interests.*

And her world! April thought. So beautiful, so perfect! It was as if her universe were enchanted. Her magnificent mountaintop abode was lavishly elegant yet warm and inviting. The attention to detail was incredible, from the vine-laden pergolas to the way the table was set.

April stopped at one of the signs that indicated a washout, looked cautiously ahead, then proceeded on down the mountain.

I've got to concentrate on the road, she thought.

But inevitably her mind wandered back to the earthly paradise of Joanna Lawrence. There was, of course, the perfect completion to this heavenly picture: Josh Lawrence. Almost unearthly handsome with his sun-bleached hair and tanned skin, his Roman nose and square jaw, he was also possessed of a great charm and seemed to be gentle and patient, with a passion for life. His handsomeness, she decided, was particularly appealing because he seemed totally oblivious to it. Oh, yes, his was an easily worn masculinity, relaxed and comfortable.

Joanna and Josh Lawrence: What a couple! She could

only envy their easy affection for one another, and the picture-perfect life they had created together.

Turning onto the highway, heading south, toward her own humble but charming mountainside cottage, she ran a hand through her hair.

Yet, she thought, *yet . . . there is something decidedly off kilter about the two of them and their blissful world. No,* she corrected herself, *it's more to do with Joanna. Yes, Joanna. There's something definitely . . . well, not fishy exactly, but something that didn't ring exactly true.*

But what? she asked herself. *And why do I feel this way? Am I just looking for a bug in the ointment? Am I so skeptical that I refuse to accept what the surface appears to be? Can't a marriage, a world, like theirs appears to be, exist?*

Slowing down for her exit off the highway, she wondered if the feeling she had couldn't be the result of some instinct gone awry. Sometimes she didn't think she could trust her own instincts, these gut-level feelings that she had. Still, the feeling that something was amiss with the picture that the Lawrences presented to the world wouldn't go away. She couldn't put her finger on it, but something was telling her to be on her guard.

8

The sun in a last spectacular display of orange had gone down behind the mountains, and the evening air was beginning to cool. The landscape lighting dramatically lit carefully chosen trees and paths. The pool's lights rendered the water's blue a quieter shade of turquoise than the natural light of day. Big scented candles, all a refined honeysuckle aroma, burned in crystal hurricane holders placed on tables, on garden walls, and even around the pool itself.

It was Joanna's favorite time to swim. She had finished her nightly laps, and now lay on a float, staring up at the sky. She loved the early morning too, but if required to choose, her choice would definitely be for nighttime swims under the stars.

Ancient Japanese koto music wafted on the air from hidden speakers. Joanna found the music immensely relaxing – a quirk, she supposed, because it was unanimously vilified by her friends. Josh sometimes enjoyed it, but sometimes even he had to change the music.

Tonight she had the pool to herself, however, and the combination of the light, the water, the scented air, and the music was working its magic. Her mind and body – all of her senses – felt they had been afforded a particularly luxurious kind of massage, and the result was nothing less than a feeling of utter peace within.

Ah, yes, she thought, *tranquility reigns. For the moment at least.*

It's just what the doctor ordered, she decided, smiling ruefully. For she desperately needed these private moments – increasingly of late – to recharge. Sometimes she thought that, if not for these moments, she would go mad.

Tonight, she had managed to keep those feelings at bay, to enjoy this moment for what it was, and not worry about yesterday or tomorrow or next week or next month. No. She wouldn't worry about the trouble at the nursery tonight or Josh and all the responsibilities he had . . . and was going to have.

No. Tonight, she felt that she could count her blessings. And she had, literally ticking them off in her mind one by one, thanking her lucky stars – whatever powers that be – that she had been afforded a life of such abundance and joy and such love.

She rolled off the float and swam to the steps at

the shallow end of the pool, climbing up them and out of the water. She took a sip of the white wine spritzer on the table at poolside, then picked up a big, fluffy beach towel off a chair and began patting herself dry.

Suddenly, she felt powerful arms encircle her waist and a rush of warm breath on her neck. She was momentarily startled, but almost instantly recognized Josh's intoxicatingly masculine aroma.

'You look so beautiful,' he whispered, kissing her neck.

'And you feel so wonderful,' she responded. 'Even if you nearly scared me half to death.'

'Did I?' he asked, nibbling her ear.

'It's okay,' she said. 'I'll forgive you just this once.'

She turned to face him, and he kissed the tip of her nose.

'You're going to get soaking wet from me,' she said, kissing his chin.

'I don't care,' Josh said, smiling. 'You can get me wet anytime you want to.'

Joanna laughed. 'Are you as hungry as I am?' she asked.

'I could eat,' he said. 'In fact, I'm starved.'

'Good,' she said. 'Then you can help me prepare a simple feast.'

'What?' he asked, his eyebrows arching questioningly.

'Steaks,' she said. 'Juicy rib eyes. Some roasted potatoes with rosemary that I just have to warm up in the microwave, and a salad.'

'Sounds yummy,' he said. 'And let me guess what I have to do.'

'You got it,' she said. 'Grill the steaks while I get the salad ready.'

'It's a deal,' he said.

'Good.' She hugged him tightly, then let go. 'Let me get out of this bikini, and I'll be right back.'

'How about I mix up some killer martinis in the meantime?' he asked.

'Heaven,' she said, already walking across the terrace to the French doors that led into the house.

Josh followed, heading into the kitchen, where he got a bottle of chilled Stolichnaya out of the refrigerator, the vermouth from a liquor cabinet, and got busy mixing their drinks, gently stirring a mere whisper of vermouth into the vodka.

He had hardly finished before Joanna appeared in the kitchen, her hair still somewhat wet, wearing nothing but a short caftan made of a white gauzy crinkled muslin. The bodice was cut in a deep V, revealing lightly tanned cleavage.

'Ready?' she asked.

Josh gave the pitcher of martinis another stir, then flourished the glass stirrer in the air. 'Voilà,' he said with a grin. He filled their martini glasses nearly to the brim and handed her one.

'What, no olive? No twist?' Joanna joked.

'We wouldn't want to adulterate the pure and sublime taste of the alcohol, would we?' Josh replied, raising his glass to hers.

Joanna laughed. 'Not if you say so.'

They clinked glasses and took sips of their drinks.

'Whoa! That's powerful!' Joanna exclaimed.

'The better to render you powerless, my dear,' Josh said with amusement.

'Thought so,' she said. She set her glass down and went to the refrigerator, where she pulled out a plate with two steaks. 'These are for you,' she said. 'I'll pop the potatoes in the microwave and do the salad.'

'Rare as usual?' Josh asked.

'Charred on the outside, hardly cooked on the inside,' Joanna replied.

'At your service,' Josh said and picked up the plate of steaks, the pitcher of martinis, and his drink, placed them on a tray, and went back out to the terrace.

Within minutes, Joanna had tossed a salad of several different greens and fresh ripe tomatoes and dressed it with garlic, olive oil, and balsamic vinegar. The microwave *bing*ed and she took the rosemary-scented potatoes out. Placing everything on a tray, she joined Josh on the terrace, where the table had been set earlier. She sat down and sipped her drink.

'About done?' she asked.

'Soon,' he said. He sat down next to her and took a sip of his martini, looking over at his wife. 'You look a little tired,' he said. 'Is it getting ready for this new project?'

Joanna shook her head. 'No, no,' she said emphatically. 'I feel fine, and I think the project is going to work out wonderfully.' She paused and looked over at Josh. 'What did you think of April?' she asked.

'Well,' he began, 'I . . . I guess she seemed okay.'

Joanna laughed. 'You can surely do better than that, Josh.'

He grinned. 'Well, she seemed capable and enthusiastic and . . . well, I don't know.'

'Oh, come on,' she cajoled. 'Say it.'

'Say what?' he asked defensively.

'Her looks and attitude knock your socks off. Right?' Joanna watched him.

Josh reddened slightly.

Joanna felt a mixture of feelings begin to stir within her. *He really did like April,* she thought. *He really was affected by her. Otherwise he wouldn't be reacting this way.* She was glad, but at the same time, she felt a little . . . a little . . . jealousy? *Oh, God!* She hated to think she could be that way.

'Maybe I better scrap this project,' Joanna teased. 'I think you took a cotton to her.'

Josh reached over and took her hands in his, drawing her closer to him. He kissed her lips, then drew back, looking into her eyes.

'You know very well,' he said in a near whisper, 'that nobody else on earth could make me as happy as you.'

Joanna nodded slightly.

Without another word, Josh rose to his feet, pulling her up with him. He took her in his well-muscled arms and kissed her lips tenderly. 'Oh, I do love you so much,' he whispered. Then his lips traveled to her forehead, her eyes, her nose, her cheeks, her ears and neck. He began to kiss her more passionately, with more urgency, his hands moving down to her firm, rounded buttocks and pushing her against him.

Joanna responded at once, relishing the feel of him against her, his desire for her serving to increase her own. She ran her hands over his powerful back and shoulders, then suddenly gasped when she felt his hard manhood pressing firmly against her.

She drew back, looking into his eyes. 'Quick,' she said breathlessly, 'turn the grill off.'

Josh reached around behind him and switched the gas off, then took her in his arms again. *Oh, yes,* he thought. *Food can definitely wait.*

He kissed her lips again, then took one of her hands in his. 'Let's go to the bedroom,' he said. 'Okay?'

'Oh, yes,' she said.

Together, they walked inside and upstairs to their bedroom, where they quickly disrobed, leaving their clothes in a pile on the floor. Josh lit candles at the bedside, then stood relishing the sight of her body, splendid in the candlelight. Her pert breasts with their small rosy nipples beckoned to him from above a long, slender torso that culminated in the sweetness between her firm thighs.

Joanna went to him, her desire heightened by the sight of his tanned body, its classical proportions and hard muscularity accentuated by his leanness. His manhood, magnificent in arousal, brushed against her as she slid her arms around his thickly muscled neck, offering her lips to him.

Josh took her in his powerful arms, running them up and down her back and across her shapely buttocks, kissing her passionately, deeply, his tongue exploring her mouth. Then drawing back slightly, he led her to the bed, and she spread out on her back, looking up at him. He moved atop her, his knees between her thighs, his hands running up her thighs to her torso and on up to her breasts, caressing her tenderly. Then, leaning down, he took a breast in his mouth, kissing and licking it, while massaging the other with his hand.

Joanna moaned with pleasure and reached down, down between his strong thighs, and took his throbbing cock in her hand, squeezing it slightly. Josh tensed momentarily and groaned, then spread his thighs and let her lightly feather his testicles with her fingertips.

Aroused to a feverish pitch, he ran his tongue from her breasts down her torso, licking and kissing her flesh with urgent need, until he reached the mound between her thighs. He sat up and brushed the darkness there with his fingers, enjoying the look of carnal desire on her face, guiding her hand back to his cock again. Slowly and gently he inserted a finger between her swollen lips, playfully exploring her wetness as she stroked his manhood.

Joanna moaned again, her need overwhelming. 'Oh, Josh,' she whispered. 'Please, please. I can't wait.'

He withdrew his fingers and took her hand away from his cock, then spread her legs apart slightly. Leaning down, he buried his mouth between her thighs, licking and kissing her ravenously, teasing her unmercifully with his tongue.

Joanna writhed from side to side, moans of ecstatic pleasure escaping her parted lips. She didn't think she could hold back another instant, so close to climax was she, but he suddenly withdrew and then covered her body with his in one swift motion. His mouth hungrily sought out hers as he lifted his buttocks and plunged into her, all the way to the hilt.

Joanna gasped aloud and threw her arms around his back, opening herself to him, welcoming his need. They began to move together, their rhythm increasing in speed almost instantaneously. It seemed only moments before she cried aloud as wave after wave of heavenly contractions consumed her, engulfing her in a climactic ecstasy that only this man had ever given her.

'Oh, Josh,' she cried. 'Oh, my God. Oh, yes. Yes, yes, *yes!*'

With the sound of her cry, Josh let himself go, thrusting with all his might, not holding back any longer. When he came, he groaned with pleasure, his entire body tensing, then quivering, as his love for Joanna burst forth, filling her to overflowing.

He collapsed atop her then, his mouth peppering her face with kisses. 'Oh, Joanna,' he rasped. 'Oh, my God, that was wonderful.'

'Oh, yes,' she gasped between breaths, squeezing him to her. 'Oh, yes.'

He rolled off her, and they lay face to face in

the candlelight, kissing one another tenderly, stroking gently as their breathing slowly returned to normal.

At last Josh, his hands cradling her face, looked into her eyes. 'I love you so much,' he said. 'I don't think you'll ever know how much.'

'And I love you, Josh,' she said.

There was a hint of sadness in her voice and in her eyes that Josh didn't detect because a cool, powerful breeze caught the draperies at the open French doors, and they billowed out into the room like banners. The candles at the bedside sputtered and nearly went out.

Joanna shivered involuntarily, then laughed. 'Maybe we'd better bring the food inside,' she said. 'What do you think?'

Josh squeezed her gently and smiled. 'Maybe that's a good idea,' he replied. 'If the wind hasn't blown it away.'

In the breakfast room, Joanna laid down her knife and fork, then wiped her lips with a napkin.

Josh looked over at her and smiled. 'Are you quitting already?' he asked. 'I know the steak is terrible, it's so overdone, but it *is* edible.'

'It's okay,' Joanna replied. 'I've had plenty.'

Josh looked at her worriedly. It wasn't like her not to eat. She usually relished her food even if she did watch her portions and calories. But, he reasoned, there was probably nothing amiss. After all, the salad was now limp, the potatoes were overdone from two trips to the microwave, and the steak tasted like it had been boiled.

'It's not too great, is it?' he said with a grin.

Joanna smiled. 'Not exactly what I'd planned,' she said, taking a sip of her wine.

'Well, who cares?' Josh replied. He touched his fingers to his lips, then pressed them to her cheek. 'I'd rather have you for dinner anytime.'

Joanna smiled again. 'You bet,' she said, pressing his fingers with her hand. 'Maybe that's why I'm so full.'

She watched Josh finish eating, reflecting on the evening. Her swim had been wonderfully relaxing and invigorating, and their lovemaking had been nothing less than perfection. Nevertheless, the evening's magic was already beginning to dissipate, and she was beginning to feel uncomfortably edgy.

Oh, why, she asked herself, *do I feel this awful sort of darkness descending? Why do I feel as if I'm merely marking time here, with my beloved Josh?* But she knew the answer. She simply couldn't verbalize it yet, as if refusing to discuss it would keep its grim reality at bay.

No, she wouldn't give the awful truth credence. Not now. Not yet.

9

The sun had already burned off the morning's mist and was quickly warming up the day. Josh walked into the breakfast room, stretching his powerful arms and shaking his luxuriant head of hair.

'Good morning, everyone,' he announced.

He leaned down and nuzzled Joanna vigorously with his clean-shaven face, peppering her with an inordinate number of kisses.

Joanna looked up at him, smiling. He was like a kid, she thought. He beamed with the pride and satisfaction of a boy who'd discovered one of life's greatest secrets the night before.

Connie, who was busy in the kitchen shelling shrimp, looked through the arched doorway with a bemused expression. 'You're awfully cheery this morning, Josh.'

Josh winked at her. 'Had an exceptional night, Connie. An exceptional night!' He grinned. 'Slept like a bear, too.'

Connie laughed and shook an accusatory finger at him. 'You better behave yourself.'

'I always do, Connie,' he replied. 'Always do.' He sat down and picked up the newspaper that was laid next to his place at the table and started flipping through it.

The telephone rang, and Connie answered it in the kitchen.

'It's for you, Josh,' she called. 'Carl.'

He picked up an extension in the breakfast room. 'Carl?' He listened for a few minutes, grunting replies, then hung up the receiver.

'Anything important?' Joanna asked.

'No, not really,' he replied, going back to his newspaper.

Joanna pretended to be interested in the latest *Vogue*, idly flipping through it, nursing a cup of coffee. Despite the great sex, she had hardly slept at all, had tossed and turned all night. And when she'd finally dozed off, terribly realistic nightmares had haunted her in such a frightening way that she'd gladly relinquished them for an unhappy wakefulness.

Josh began heartily putting away the pancakes with strawberries and cream that Connie had brought to him, washing it down with hot black coffee. He looked over at Joanna. 'You've already eaten?' he asked.

'Yes,' she said, looking up from the magazine. 'I was up with the birds and went ahead.'

'What've you got planned for today?' he asked.

'I've got ten million errands to run,' she said, 'and a lot of telephone calls to make. The usual.'

'Home for lunch?' he asked.

She nodded. 'If you'll be here, I'll be here.'

'Good,' he said with a smile. 'I'll be here for sure.'

He finished eating quickly, then rose to his feet, and leaning down, kissed her on the cheek. 'I've got to run, but I'll be back from the nursery somewhere around twelve-thirty.'

Josh raced out of the house, and in the distance they could hear him fire up his ancient Land Cruiser. After he was out of earshot, Joanna put the *Vogue* down and headed for the bedroom. She shrugged off her bathrobe and quickly changed into khaki slacks, a lightweight cashmere pullover, and comfortable Gucci flats. Grabbing a straw sun hat and her shoulder bag, she went back out to the kitchen.

'I'll be out for a while, Connie.'

'Errands?' Connie asked, still peeling shrimp.

Joanna nodded. 'Yes.'

Connie looked at her with a puzzled expression but didn't say anything. Normally, Joanna would tell her exactly where she was going and how long she expected to be gone. Not today. She worried, like Josh, that something was truly wrong.

Joanna went out to the entrance hall, where she took her car keys from an Imari bowl set atop an

121

Irish Georgian console. She took her sunglasses out of her shoulder bag, slid them out of their case, and put them on. Finally, she put on the straw hat and looked at herself in the large gilt-framed mirror over the console.

'You'll do,' she told her reflection. She stepped out the front door and opened the garage door with her electronic beeper. Her old Mercedes convertible, a gift from her father years ago, appeared in its bay, and she hurried to it and slid in. The top was already down. She adjusted the chin strap on her hat to keep it from flying off, then fired the car up and drove out of the courtyard in a flash.

As she left the house behind and began the curvy descent down the mountain, she breathed a sigh of relief. *Thank God*, she thought. *I can get away from the house, from Connie, from Josh, the telephone.* From all the responsibilities, the decisions, that running the household entailed.

She had a million things to do, but she simply couldn't cope with any of that today. Shopping could wait, the grotto project could wait, the various orchid societies could wait, all of her charitable activities could wait. And her friends with their gossip, their problems, their little triumphs and defeats could wait, too!

I have to be alone, she thought. *Alone to think.*

Reaching the freeway ramps, she made a spur-of-the-moment decision to head south. South to – where? She didn't know, but she had to drive. Speeding along in the freeway's light morning traffic, she finally began to breathe easier. She let up on the gas, slowing her pace a little. She didn't want to be stopped by the highway patrol, and she could see that they were out in full force, as usual.

She gradually became aware of the sun's warmth on her body, of the wind whipping at her hat, of the terrain around her. She caught occasional glimpses of the Pacific off in the distance to her right, the sun glinting off it brightly.

On she drove, mindless of where she might end up, almost unaware of the fact that she exited the freeway somewhere in Watsonville and started driving down meandering streets but, inevitably it seemed, gradually climbing back up into those very same mountains she'd just left.

The road became a series of twists and turns with washouts and stop signs, almost indistinguishable from the one that wound up the mountain to her house.

Slowing down, she suddenly realized where she was. *My God*, she thought. *I must've been on automatic pilot or something.* It was as if some force greater than herself, some mysterious kind of magnet, had drawn her here. She had discovered that in this magical place the terrible headaches that had begun six months ago often dissipated, their pain blanketed for a while at least.

Approaching the turnoff on her left, she became excited. *I hope no one's here*, she thought, looking about.

She made the turn and slowly drove up the steep,

curving drive to the small parking area. She was pleased to see that there wasn't another car there. She looked over at the garden's high fence. It was lushly overladen with several different varieties of climbing roses, many of them huge, old plants. She strolled over, stopping to sniff Dainty Bess, a fragrant pale pinkish one, then found the familiar wooden gate and let herself in, careful to latch it closed against the deer.

She looked about her.

No one. Not another soul.

She smiled and took a deep breath. The air was heady with the perfume of thousands of rose blooms. She began slowly negotiating the garden paths, looking at the little markers to familiarize herself once again with the names of the roses that grew here. Many of them were of the old-fashioned variety, dating from the 1800s, and they were much more fragrant than most of the modern hybrid teas which had become so popular.

Kneeling down, she took a huge Comte de Chambord in hand and smelled its fragrance, noting that, according to its marker, it was from 1860. She walked on, smiling at the names. Duchess d'Brantes, Marchioness of Lorne, Lady Hillingdon, Bishop Darlington, Honorine de Brabant, Gruss an Coberg, Gruss an Aachen, Jacques Cartier, Louise Odier.

The beds were laid out in a haphazard manner, lined with old boards, and the paths were either dirt, blacktop, or gravel. The fencing varied, too, from weathered wood to rusty wire. There was a guiding principle in this garden, however, Joanna thought, and that was beauty. The sheer beauty of the colors and the fragrances made up for the garden's apparent lack of formal structure and its rundown condition.

Certainly, she thought, *love has been lavished on this magical little clearing here in the midst of the redwoods.*

She strolled on, passing the small area devoted to potted roses that were for sale and stopped to look at the wooden stall that served as an office. The garden operated on the honor system, and there was a box with a slot in which to deposit checks or cash for roses. Joanna was always gratified that the system seemed to work and had for as long as she could remember.

Ahead she saw a wooden bench, weathered silver by time and weather. It offered a shady seat under a rickety wooden arbor, a venerable pink Cécile Brünner climbing up the arbor, then cascading down it dramatically. Sitting, she inhaled deeply again, savoring the mixture of perfumes, the warmth of the sun on her legs, the cool of the shade on her face. She closed her eyes for a few minutes, enjoying the peaceful quiet, as her mind, without the distractions of home, began to focus on the problem that she had to sort out.

I've got to talk to somebody about this, she decided. *And soon. I simply can't carry this terrible secret alone anymore.*

She had thought for some time now that she could bravely soldier along, bottling her problems up inside, not burdening anyone else. *I guess I'm not as brave as I thought,* she reflected. *Because I have to talk to somebody.*

I see that now. I have to share this terrible pain, this dreadful sense of loss, and the overwhelming fear.

Josh, of course, was the obvious choice. After all, he was her husband and her closest friend. *I must tell Josh first. It's only fair that I share this burden with him, despite the pain and suffering that he'll have to endure.*

Now she felt immensely pleased, with this place and herself. She felt some of the tremendous weight that lay so heavily on her shoulders lift. Perhaps now, she thought, some of the darkness that pervaded her nights and days would dissipate, too. After all, it was becoming increasingly difficult to hide the truth from him.

Yes, she thought. *I'll tell my sweet Josh. He deserves to know the truth.*

She lingered a while longer, ambling along the garden's paths, then decided to leave, but not before she'd said a prayer of thanks to this beautiful, magical place for the solace that it had afforded her, for the truths that it inevitably seemed to make evident to her.

Josh sat alone at the big dining table on the terrace, finishing the last of the two tuna fish sandwiches that Connie had made him. He always loved the flavor of cilantro that she put in it, but lately he'd come to the conclusion she was putting cilantro in everything.

Or maybe I'm just grumpy, he thought.

He looked over at the remains of the artichoke salad that had tasted so great. Did it have cilantro in it too?

He took a sip of the iced tea, then set the glass down and wiped his mouth with a crisp linen napkin. He looked across the table at the place that had been set for Joanna. *Great*, he thought. *Only there's no Joanna.* And that, he knew, was why he was in such a bad mood. She had done another of her disappearing acts.

In all the years of their marriage, they had dined together whenever possible, and few were the times when either of them hadn't been able to make it. Perhaps, he thought, he expected too much of her. After all, how many couples did he know who managed to live the way they did? Or wanted to, for that matter?

He realized that most of the couples they knew wouldn't *want* to live and work as closely as they did. He and Joanna, however, had found that this way of life suited them. They had been a team from the very beginning, and he couldn't conceive of their being any other way. He guessed it was because he was as in love with her now, after ten years of marriage, as he had been all those years ago when they'd first met.

Maybe that's the problem, he thought. *I'm still in love with her and she's—*

'Josh!' Joanna's unmistakably cheerful voice rang in his ears, interrupting his thoughts.

He turned and saw her rushing across the terrace to the table, all smiles. He slid his chair back and got to his feet. When she reached him, he kissed her breathless lips and hugged her to him.

'I'm . . . sorry I'm . . . late,' she said breathily.

'Where've you been?' he asked.

She sat down, dropping her shoulder bag to the

127

terrace beside her. Josh sat down too, taking another sip of his tea.

Connie appeared with a tray of sandwiches and salad for Joanna and began pouring tea for her.

'Thanks, Connie,' Joanna said. Then she looked at Josh. 'Oh ... I ... I had a lot of errands to run,' she replied.

He knew immediately that she was being vague. He hated to pursue the subject, playing the inquisitor, but he couldn't help himself. 'What kind of errands?' he asked, trying to sound as casual as possible.

'Oh, you know,' she said, taking her napkin and placing it in her lap. 'Little things. Dumb things like taking some clothes to the cleaners. You know, nothing important.'

Connie's heavy-lidded eyes narrowed to suspicious slits. She knew that Joanna had left empty-handed, and she also knew that she hadn't come back home with any shopping. She didn't say anything, however.

Josh gazed across the table at his wife with curiosity. He remembered the decision he'd come to out in the greenhouse, about having a serious talk with her. Now he felt compelled to continue questioning her, to probe further into her recent penchant for being aloof.

But then the memory of last night's wonderful intimacy swept aside any doubts he might have had about Joanna's behavior. She had been herself then, he thought. Loving, caring, and attentive, and the lingering sense of well-being and joy that their sex had left him with, that had made his morning so extraordinarily cheerful, reassured him that there was nothing really wrong.

Still, he thought, *maybe I should just mention her aloofness lately. Just ask her if there's something going on that I should know about, without making a big deal out of it.*

But before he could say anything the telephone bleeped, and Connie, who was putting his empty plates on a tray, picked up the remote that lay on the table.

'Hello?' she said, then listened for a moment.

She held the remote out to Josh. 'It's Carl,' she said.

Josh took the receiver from her. 'Thanks, Connie,' he said.

'What's going on, Carl?' he asked.

Joanna, munching on her tuna fish sandwich, watched him from across the table. She could see that he'd become visibly excited and wondered what Carl could be calling about.

The instant Josh punched the off button on the remote, she asked, 'What is it?'

Josh just looked at her and grinned like a Cheshire cat.

'What?' she repeated, really intrigued now.

'Guess who's coming in to the nursery?' Josh asked her teasingly.

'Who?' she asked, becoming exasperated, but enjoying his game.

'Guess.'

'Oh, Josh, stop it!' she cried. 'Who is it?'

'Mr Hara,' he said.

'Oh, heaven!' she exclaimed. 'This is heaven!' She jumped up from her seat and dashed to him, throwing her arms around his neck and planting a kiss on the top of his head.

'He called from his car,' he went on. 'He's on his way down from San Jose and will only be here today. So I'd better get moving.'

Joanna kissed his head again, then let him get to his feet. 'Do you want me to come with you?' she asked.

'No, you don't have to,' he said. 'I will happily deal with this.'

'Okay,' she said. 'I was going to go through some books to get more material together for April, but if you need me—'

'No,' he said. 'Do your thing.' He gave her a quick kiss. 'But how about helping me load up a few prize specimens from the greenhouse here to take down with me.'

'Let's go,' she said.

Holding hands, they headed toward the greenhouse, set aside the specimens Josh wanted, and made four trips to his Land Cruiser to load them up. When he left, Joanna was blowing kisses from the courtyard. Josh returned her kisses and waved out the window.

On his way to the nursery, he knew that he should be counting his lucky stars. Mr Hara was one of the world's richest and most important collectors of rare orchids, and just to have an orchid in his collection was deemed an honor among orchid growers and fanciers. He would spend as much as fifteen or twenty thousand dollars for a seedling in bloom, and Josh wouldn't be surprised if he spent a hundred thousand dollars or more today.

His enthusiasm was tempered, however, by a niggling awareness that had crept into his consciousness and refused to go away. It was an annoying feeling that something important had been left unsaid, that there was definitely something amiss on the home front.

I've got to have that talk with Joanna, he reminded himself. *Got to.*

10

Spring was turning to summer with a vengeance, and April cruised down the road in her old Jeep Wagoneer with all the windows open. The breeze filled the car with the overpowering aroma of Brussels sprouts. Some would call it a stench, she reflected, but she didn't mind it at all. There were acres and acres of them on both sides of the road here, in fields as flat as her kitchen table. On her right, they spread out as far as the eye could see toward the mountains, and on her left they swept straight up to the dunes that bordered the Pacific. She'd always marveled that such potentially expensive real estate would be used for growing vegetables.

She drove at a brisk pace, but kept her eyes peeled for the turnoff to Lawrence Nursery. She'd been down this road a thousand times on her way south to Monterey and points beyond, but she'd never noticed the sign for the nursery.

When Joanna had called yesterday and asked to meet her here, she'd assumed she was phoning to see if the preliminary sketches were finished. They were due tomorrow, and April thought that Joanna, like so many clients, might be getting anxious, perhaps even a little pushy. Instead, she'd been pleasantly surprised to be invited to meet her at the nursery today, without a single mention of the sketches.

She'd been glad to hear from her in any case. After being cooped up in the cottage like a hermit for the past week, working for hours a day drawing, erasing, and redrawing, she was more than ready for an outing. Woody had tried to cajole her into dinner, but she'd refused, so intent was she on meeting Joanna's deadline. When she hadn't been actually sketching, she'd been thumbing through all the books and pictures Joanna had lent her, searching for ideas, inspiration – anything to set her imagination on fire. And set on fire it had become, working feverishly, supplying her with more ideas than she could realistically use.

Now she felt as if her preliminary plans were more or less final, but she wanted to spend some more time with them tonight.

On her left, she spotted the sign that announced Lawrence Nursery. She'd never been to an orchid nursery before, and looked forward to the grand tour.

Joanna thought she should see as many orchid specimens as possible to get ideas for the grotto.

A quarter of a mile or so down the road, she saw the nursery on her right. Turning off, April pulled into the gravel parking lot. Grabbing her carryall, she slid out of the car and stood looking around.

Shielding her eyes from the sun with her hand, she gazed at the big Victorian house with its gingerbread trim, incongruously surrounded by greenhouses. It was immaculately kept, imposing even, but still, it looked oddly out of place.

She didn't see Joanna's Mercedes in the parking lot, but she followed the sign to a gate and a little walkway to the house. The fenced-in yard was tiny, with a few trees and shrubs, beautifully tended, but disproportionately small for the size of the house. She walked up the steps to the porch and opened one of the double doors into the cool of the office.

The reception area had obviously once been the entrance hall, an oddly shaped room, almost but not quite round. In the center was a desk, behind which sat a strikingly beautiful woman with jet-black hair and large dark eyes and too much makeup. She was talking on the telephone in rapid-fire Spanish.

When she looked over and saw April, she smiled slightly and pointed to a chair with her long carmine-lacquered fingernail, but didn't miss a beat in her telephone conversation. The torrent of Spanish continued at a furious pace, her eyes glittering, her free hand gesticulating wildly.

April sat down in the indicated chair and watched the woman with fascination. She could see that her lips were the brightest cerise, lined with a darker shade of red, and the heavy eye shadow above her dark brown eyes was a purplish brown. Her lashes were thick with mascara, and rouge highlighted her prominent cheekbones. Her perfect white teeth shone dazzlingly against her painted lips.

Suddenly the woman burst into a series of high-pitched giggles, said 'Ciao,' then replaced the receiver in its cradle. She looked over at April. 'Sorry,' she said in lightly accented English. 'A loco customer. Loco, loco, *loco!*'

'No problem,' April said, smiling. 'I'm supposed to meet Joanna Lawrence here.'

The young woman's eyebrows lifted. 'Joanna? Ah! Just a minute, please.' She pressed a button on the telephone and picked up the receiver, then looked at April again. 'What's your name?' she asked.

'April Woodward,' she replied.

'April,' the woman said, as if practicing. Then speaking into the receiver: 'There's a lady here. April Woodward. She's supposed to meet Joanna, but Joanna's not here.'

She listened for a moment, then hung up. 'Josh, Mr Lawrence, will be right out,' she said.

'Thanks,' April said.

The curtained French doors to her left opened, and Josh Lawrence stepped out of his office, beaming, his teeth no less dazzling against his darkly tanned skin than the secretary's. Dressed in khaki cargo shorts, khaki shirt, and work boots, he looked like the nurseryman he was. *He also looks drop-dead handsome,* she thought.

'April,' he said, holding out his hand for a shake. 'Welcome to our little operation.'

April rose to her feet and shook his hand. 'I hope I'm not imposing,' she said, looking into his blue eyes. 'Joanna asked me to meet her here. She's supposed to give me the grand tour.'

'No trouble at all,' he said. 'She's probably just running a little late. Did you meet Luna?' He indicated the secretary/receptionist.

'No,' she said, turning and extending a hand to Luna. 'Not formally.'

Luna stood up and shook hands across her desk. 'It's nice to meet you,' she said. She looked at Josh and let out another giggle. 'I was ... I was on the telephone when she came in,' she said.

Josh grinned. 'As usual,' he said good-naturedly. He turned to April. 'Come on in, I'll see if I can get Joanna on the telephone.'

April walked into his office and looked around. *Must have been the parlor,* she thought. Facing her was a large Victorian desk centered in front of a bay window. The desk chair was on the window side, and on her side were two comfortable-looking leather-upholstered chairs.

'Have a seat,' Josh said, walking in behind her and closing the French door. 'I'll try to get Joanna.'

'Thanks,' April said, sitting in one of the chairs.

She watched as Josh sat on the edge of the desk and dialed a number, then she quickly averted her gaze. *Why do I feel as if I'm staring?* she wondered. *Trying to better see his blue eyes, his sun-bleached hair, those white-white teeth, and that wonderful tanned body?*

'Hey, Connie,' he said, 'is Joanna around, or has she left for here?'

He listened a moment, then said, 'Thanks, Connie, see you later.'

He hung up the receiver and turned to April. 'She's on her way,' he said. 'She refuses to get a cell phone, or I'd see how long she's going to be.' He smiled apologetically. 'I hope Luna didn't keep you waiting.'

'It's okay,' April assured him. 'I've got time.' Suddenly she felt slightly uncomfortable being alone in his presence. *How silly,* she thought. *He's Joanna's husband and a perfectly nice, perfectly harmless man.* Nevertheless, she found herself nervous as she tried to make conversation.

'Luna seems to be quite a lady,' she said.

He laughed. 'Luna's a little bit of a maniac,' he said. 'But she can juggle eight or ten phone calls at a time and get blood out of a turnip. Meaning,' he said, looking at her with amusement, 'she can get slow-paying customers to cough up cash. And fast.'

April smiled. 'Sounds like what every office needs.'

'She's great,' he said. 'Her husband's our manager. Carl. You'll meet him today. He's Connie's brother.'

'Oh,' she said, 'so you've got the whole family on the payroll.'

'Just about,' he replied, standing up. 'What do you say we go ahead and start the tour without Joanna? Is that okay with you?'

138

'That's fine,' April said, 'if I'm not taking too much of your time.'

'No,' he said, 'I can always spare time to get out of the office.'

April rose to her feet, and Josh ushered her out.

'Luna, we'll be looking around the greenhouses,' he said. 'Send Joanna on out when she gets here.'

Luna, her ear attached to the telephone receiver, nodded.

They went back out into the tiny front yard and through the gate, then turned onto a path leading to the greenhouses.

'This place is fascinating,' April said.

'Joanna's family built it in the eighteen hundreds,' Josh said. 'They were farmers. Then her father started the nursery, and it grew and grew. So he built the house we live in now and moved out of this place. But Mitch, her dad, always wanted to keep the house as office space. So we've kept up the tradition.'

They came to a high chain-link fence that surrounded the greenhouse area. The gates were open, and they walked on toward an enormous greenhouse.

'Good Lord,' April said, 'I've never seen a greenhouse this big before.'

'There are seven in all,' Josh said. 'They cover over eighty thousand square feet.'

'Eighty thousand!' April exclaimed.

'Uh-huh,' he said. 'Our business is almost totally wholesale. We ship thousands of relatively inexpensive, easy-to-grow orchids to nurseries all over the country.

We also supply a lot of the nurseries that sell through catalogues. Our specialty, though, is dealing in the rarities – they set us apart from other nurseries.'

He opened the door to the greenhouse and held it wide for her.

April stepped in and almost gasped at the sheer size of the space and what must have been thousands of orchid plants. As at the little greenhouse at their house, the air smelled of compost and was damp with humidity.

'It looks like you've got every orchid on earth here,' she said.

'Hardly,' Josh said. 'There're over twenty thousand species of orchids, and there're over a hundred thousand hybrid crosses registered so far.'

'I had no idea,' she said.

They started walking down a path between tables. 'This is one of what I call our bread-and-butter areas. All these are *Phalaenopsis*,' he said. 'What a lot of people call the Moth Orchid. It's one of the biggest sellers because they're relatively inexpensive and easy to grow at home. We have thousands of these. *Paphiopedilums* and *Cattleyas*, too, for the same reason. But we're getting so much competition from the Taiwanese with these varieties that it's a good thing we've always relied on our rarities for the really major money. That and our reputation for having the best stock available.'

'The Taiwanese?' she said. 'But how can they compete with you here?'

'Our government allows them to ship in orchid plants if they're bare roots, not in dirt,' he said. 'They've flooded the market with some varieties shipped in bare root, then potted here. Now what the Taiwanese have started doing is buying up land and building greenhouses all the way from Vancouver down to San Diego. They grow vast quantities without any regard to quality.'

'That's ... unbelievable,' she said.

'Believe it,' he said. 'Luckily, we have rarities and are known for extraordinary quality. That's what's kept us going while a lot of others have been wiped out.'

On they walked, through greenhouse after greenhouse, stopping here to admire a particularly flamboyant specimen, there to discuss native habitats. He patiently explained the computer-operated misters that periodically bathed the plants, and answered her questions about the automatic overhead screens that opened and closed to compensate for the shadows of passing clouds. He explained that conditions in the different greenhouses varied, depending on the orchids housed there, in an effort to reproduce their natural habitats.

'We have orchids from places as diverse as the temples at Machu Picchu, the Himalayas, and the most tropical parts of Brazil,' he told her. 'So we have to re-create their environments.'

Josh could see that she was truly interested in the nursery, even the technical aspects, and was gratified by her constant stream of questions. He met lots of orchid lovers, but very few people who were really interested in anything much beyond the beauty of their exotic blooms and where they came from.

'You know what?' she said after they'd been touring for quite some time, 'I've been so absorbed in all this that I completely forgot to make notes.'

'Make notes?' he asked. 'For what?'

'For the grotto room, of course,' she said. 'I wanted to pick out some of the orchids that would especially lend themselves to being re-created with shells and pebbles.'

'So you've definitely decided to take on the project?' he asked.

'Oh, yes,' April said enthusiastically. 'Definitely. I've become so wrapped up in it the last week that I couldn't say no.'

From behind them came an unmistakable voice. 'That's the first *I've* heard of it!'

Startled, April and Josh turned to look behind them and saw Joanna, arms akimbo, eyebrows knotted in a frown. For a moment April didn't know what to think of Joanna's posture, but then Joanna burst into gales of laughter and rushed forward to hug April and pepper her cheeks with kisses.

'I'm so thrilled!' she cried. 'I was afraid you might say no.'

Josh watched the two of them with a smile on his face. It was so wonderful to see Joanna this enthused by a project, and she'd obviously found the perfect person for it. *Yes*, he thought, *April is really . . . special.*

'I almost did say no,' April said. 'Because of the tight schedule and having to give up other projects, but after spending the last few days doing sketches, and now, seeing this place' – she shrugged eloquently – 'I guess I've sort of caught the bug.'

Josh's eyes widened with surprise, and he looked at her intently. 'You mean the orchid bug?' he asked.

'Well . . .' April began, 'I . . . I guess it's a combination of the grotto project with the shells and pebbles *and* the orchids. All mixed up together, it's a sort of rare and . . . well, seductive proposition.'

'I knew it,' Joanna said. 'I knew I'd discovered just the person.'

'Welcome to the family,' Josh said.

April looked up at him and smiled tentatively. 'Thanks,' she managed to say, not certain what she should make of his statement.

'Have you spotted some candidates for the grotto?' Joanna asked.

'I was just telling Josh that I'd completely forgotten to take notes,' April replied. 'But I've definitely seen some excellent choices.'

'Why don't I leave you two alone to do your work?' Josh said, 'and I'll get back to mine.'

'That's fine,' Joanna said. 'We'll be here for a bit, then we're going back up to the house.'

They kissed and he turned to April. 'See you later,' he said.

'Thanks a million for all your trouble, Josh,' she said. 'I really do appreciate it.'

He nodded and left.

'Now,' Joanna said, 'did you see everything?'

'I think so,' April replied, 'but I'm not really sure.'

'Well, what if we do a quick run-through,' she proposed, 'and I'll show you plants I've thought would be good to use. And you can show me the ones you like. We can make a list and then pare it down.'

The neoclassical conservatory at Joanna and Josh's had well-worn floors of old French limestone. It was filled with various kinds of palms, ferns, and, of course, orchids. In the center was a huge *pietra dura* table, its various marbles fitted together to create beautiful patterns, centered with doves in trees. Over the table hung a magnificent crystal chandelier with sixteen lights. It was the ideal place to work, Joanna and April decided, and it was there that April spread out her preliminary sketches.

After poring over them intently for several minutes, shuffling them this way and that, Joanna looked up at April, who had been watching like a slightly nervous mother hen for her reactions to them.

'They're beautiful,' Joanna said simply. 'And exactly what I had in mind.'

April let out a sigh of relief. 'Good,' she said. 'I've really done my homework this week, and was hoping you'd be pleased.'

'Just one or two things,' Joanna said in a take-command voice.

Oh, no, April thought with a sinking heart. *Now she's probably going to act like some clients and change everything I've done.*

Joanna saw the obvious look of consternation on

April's face, and her voice and demeanor immediately softened.

'Oh, dear,' she said. 'I've alarmed you, haven't I?'

'It's okay,' April said. 'Go ahead and say what it is that displeases you.'

'April!' Joanna turned and placed her hands on April's shoulders and looked her in the eye. 'It's nothing,' she said. 'I *love* your plans, but I want to make a couple of suggestions. That's all. Now look happy.'

April couldn't help but smile.

'That's better,' Joanna said, and she turned back to the plans, shuffling them around again, until she found what she wanted. It was a sketch of an interior wall, complete with a dado, niches, and other architectural elements, all made of shells and pebbles.

'Look at this, for example,' Joanna said.

April leaned down over the drawing with Joanna. She had worked so hard on these drawings that she couldn't believe anybody would want to change anything.

'This is a perfect interpretation of a wall in a neoclassical room,' Joanna said. 'I love it. And there's only *one* little change I want you to execute.'

April looked at her, and Joanna smiled.

'Blur the boundaries,' Joanna said.

'What do you mean?' April asked.

'Pretend this is a plan for a formal garden, if you will,' Joanna said.

'Okay,' April said, nodding.

'Now,' Joanna went on, 'pretend this garden is

planted, everything very neatly placed, as it is here. Every shell and pebble in its proper place.'

April nodded again.

'Now,' Joanna said, looking at her, 'let the plants get a little overgrown. Let them run a little rampant.' Then, carefully enunciating each word, she said: 'Let the formal lines blur. Allow a shell to creep over a line, or a pebble to do the same.'

April looked at her with dawning comprehension. 'I . . . I see what you mean,' she said.

'I thought you would,' Joanna said, smiling.

'I could get a little baroque around the edges,' April said, looking back at her plan.

'*Yes!*' Joanna said. 'Put the line there, then super-impose a curve on it. That sort of thing.'

'And that'll be a snap with the shells,' April said. 'Oh, you're a genius, Joanna!' she said.

Joanna laughed. 'No,' she said, 'I've just thought about it a lot. I can see masses of coral used as pediments over doors—'

'Coral?' April exclaimed.

'Why, yes,' Joanna said. 'What's wrong?'

'Joanna,' April said, 'coral is endangered. You are not, I repeat, *not* going to use coral in this grotto.'

Joanna looked at her and saw that she was quite serious. 'Well,' she said, 'I have tons of it that I've collected over the years, just waiting to be used. Why let it go to waste?'

'Because when people see what you've done here, some of them will want to try to copy it,' April said.

'They'll go out and buy coral wherever they can find it, and that'll only encourage shops to keep selling it. It's like a vicious cycle.'

'But—'

'No buts,' April said, shaking her head. 'Besides, there are substitutes. Things that aren't endangered that will work just as well.'

Joanna took a deep breath and sighed. *This is one gutsy lady,* she thought. *Sticking to her guns like this. She has real backbone, real principles.*

'You win,' she finally said with a smile. 'I have to admit I feel a little embarrassed because I knew that coral was endangered, but I wanted to use it anyway. But I see what you mean.'

'You know, there are going to be so many options,' April said, 'that I don't think you'll miss the coral.'

'Oh, I know,' Joanna said. 'Oh, by the way ...' She walked over to a long built-in bookshelf under one of the windows and started rummaging around, then pulled out a large stack of books and catalogues. 'Look what I've got,' she said, returning to the table and putting down her load.

'What?' April asked.

'You'll see,' Joanna said. She took a catalogue off the top of the stack and handed it to April.

April started flipping through it, and her eyes widened with amazement. 'This is fabulous,' she said excitedly. 'Oh, Joanna, how did you ever come by this?'

'I bought some shells in a shop in Monterey,' she said. 'There were so many that the lady packed them in a box from her wholesaler. So I called the whole-saler up in Oregon, pretended to be an artist who worked with seashells, and they sent me the cata-logue.'

April looked at her, and they both laughed.

'It was one of the hardest things I ever did,' Joanna said. 'I mean actually telling the lady I was an *artist*. Not only an artist, but one who worked with *seashells*. It felt so ... goofy ... and phony. But she bought it hook, line, and sinker. So did several others. Because I started going into shops and making little purchases and telling shopkeepers the same thing to get the name of their wholesalers.'

'You are *so* clever,' April said. 'We're certainly not going to have a problem getting enough shells or the types that we need. We'll pool our resources. I've used a couple of wholesalers in the past.'

'Plus,' Joanna said, 'we've still got the thousands I've collected, and I want to use them first, if possible. They have a lot of sentimental value for me.'

'I can see why,' April said, 'and I think that's a wonderful idea.

'Another thing we'd better discuss right away – well, two actually. One is the orchids, and the other is my estimate. I hadn't intended to give it to you until the meeting we'd planned tomorrow, but I have it with me and might as well go ahead and give it to you before we go any further.'

'Why don't we discuss the orchids first?' Joanna said with a laugh.

April smiled. 'I want to sketch a few of the ones here and photograph them, and some of those we saw today at the nursery.'

'That's fine,' Joanna said.

'But,' April said, 'I don't want to take them home with me to do the work. I don't want to be responsible for any valuable ones.'

'I understand,' Joanna said. She tapped her lips with a finger for a moment, thinking, then looked back at April. 'You're welcome to work on them here, if you like,' she said. 'You could use this room. The light's wonderful. What do you think of that?'

'I wouldn't be in the way?' April asked.

'Not at all,' Joanna said. 'Besides, you're going to have to be here a lot of the time anyway. So what's the difference?'

'Okay,' April said, 'if you really think so. I could use this as a base until the construction work is finished on the stable. Then I could move down there.'

'Perfect,' Joanna said.

'Now,' April said. 'My estimate.' She reached for her shoulder bag, which sat on a chair next to her, and took a folder out. She opened the folder and slid out her typed-up estimate. 'Here,' she said, 'study this and see if you have any questions. I've broken all the costs down as closely as possible.'

Joanna took the estimate from her and looked at it for a long time. April stepped away and looked out the windows toward the swimming pool, trying to give Joanna a degree of privacy.

'I see you've already priced the plumbing and carpentry and everything,' Joanna said.

April turned and nodded.

'I think it's fine,' Joanna said. 'I'll ask Josh to look at it when he comes in tonight, but I don't think there'll be a problem.'

'Okay,' April said, relieved once again. The cost of the project was huge, she knew, but it was going to take the next few months out of her life and require a lot of work.

Joanna approached her and gave her another hug, then drew back and looked at her. 'It'll be fine,' she said. 'So don't worry.'

She turned then and walked back to the big table and picked up a list she'd made. 'Now, let me see,' she said. 'Just a couple of things I've made a note to tell you. I'm going to give you a beeper for the gates out front. They're usually open, but you might find them closed sometime. Oh, and I'll have to give you a beeper for the greenhouse, so you can take plants back and forth anytime you need to.'

'That would be great,' April said.

'And, listen, April,' Joanna continued, 'don't hesitate to ask Connie for anything in the kitchen. Food or drink. Anytime. There's always too much of everything, so that would only be a help to us.'

April laughed. 'That's awfully nice,' she said, 'but I'll probably do like I usually do and bring my lunch.'

'Whatever suits you,' Joanna said.

'Right now,' April said, 'I'd like to go down to the

stable and do some more measurements and do some careful remeasuring. Plus, I might sketch some down there. Is that okay?'

'Sure,' Joanna replied.

'I'll probably be quite a while,' she said.

'Then why don't you stay for dinner?' Joanna said.

'Oh, no,' April said. 'I really shouldn't. I mean . . .'

'I won't take no for an answer,' Joanna said. 'We can have a little champagne to celebrate the beginning of my grotto.'

'In that case,' April said with a laugh, 'I can't say no, can I?'

'No,' Joanna said, shaking her head. 'Absolutely not.'

'Okay,' April said. She started gathering up drawing materials and shouldered her big bag. 'I'll see you later, then.'

'We'll probably eat about seven-thirty or eight,' Joanna said. 'And have that champagne before. Come on back up anytime, or I'll come and get you.'

'Fine,' April said, already heading out through the French doors toward the stable.

From the windows, Joanna watched her walk across the terrace, the little bridge to the pool area, and make her way around the pool until she was out of sight. She squeezed herself with delight.

This is so wonderful, she thought. *It's going to work out better than I had imagined.*

The light was beginning to dim inside the old stable, and April realized that it was later than she'd thought.

She had been so absorbed in her work that time had flown by. She gathered up her measurements, slipped them into a folder, and put it in her shoulder bag. Then she began gathering the few sketches she'd made. They were much more detailed than those she'd shown Joanna, and they also incorporated Joanna's advice about 'blurring the lines.'

She smiled to herself. *Normally*, April thought, *I'm as stubborn as a mule, determined to have it the way I want it.* Today, however, Joanna had taught her a valuable lesson. She could stick to the rules and use the formal structures she knew so well, but then she could play with them – just as she did in her botanical drawings – and actually improve them.

Packed up at last, she left the stable and started back up through the apple trees toward the pool area. The evening was beautiful, the air refreshing, and she felt a wonderful sense of accomplishment from the day's work.

As she crested the rise to the pool area, she heard laughter and water splashing. She came to a standstill when she got within sight of the pool. Candles in hurricane lanterns were all around the pool, set on tables and on walls. The setting was so romantically beautiful, April almost gasped.

Josh was in the pool splashing water up at Joanna, who was sitting on the stone terrace convulsed in laughter.

'That's what you get for dunking me!' he laughed, splashing her once again.

Joanna screeched with delight. 'Stop it!' she cried. 'I'll have to go change clothes now.' She stood up, surveying the damage to her slacks and blouse.

'Serves you right,' he said, his voice full of amusement. He climbed out of the pool and threw his soaking arms around his wife, planting a kiss on her lips.

Joanna squealed with delight again. 'Oh, now you've really done it, Josh,' she said. But she didn't try to struggle out of his arms.

April felt slightly embarrassed watching this sweet domestic scene, but she couldn't take her eyes off them. The picture was so perfect, everything she'd ever imagined a couple to be, everything she'd ever imagined having with a man.

And what a man he is, she mused. *So tall and strong and handsome, yet so tender, gentle, and playful.*

She felt the ache of a longing somewhere deep down inside. It was not the first time she'd ever felt that longing, but it had been a long time. It was almost as if desire were reawakening in her after having been extinguished by her unhappy marriage.

'There you are!' Josh shouted, and to her embarrassment, April realized that he had seen her.

She came completely into view, trying to appear as if she'd just reached the pool area. 'Hi,' she called back.

'Spying on us!' he said playfully.

'No,' she said. Then she laughed. 'But I did see you kiss.'

Joanna and Josh both laughed. 'Come have a glass of

champagne,' Joanna said. 'We were waiting for you to open the bottle.'

'That's so nice of you,' April said. 'But only if Josh promises not to splash water all over me.'

'I promise,' he said with a smile. He picked up a lightweight robe and tied it around himself, then started opening the champagne that rested in a bucket on the table.

April set her shoulder bag down on the terrace next to a chair and watched him.

'I'll be right back,' Joanna said. 'I've got to put on something dry.'

'Hurry,' Josh said, calling after her. 'We might drink it all while you're gone.' Then he looked at April. 'Take a seat,' he said. 'Make yourself comfortable.'

'Thanks, Josh,' she said, sitting down. 'It's so beautiful out here with the candles,' she said.

'It is, isn't it,' he agreed. 'You know, you're welcome to use the pool anytime you want to while you're working here.'

'Thanks,' she said. 'That's awfully generous.'

'Well, it's right here,' he said, 'so why not?' With a loud *pop!* the cork came free from the bottle and April watched a tendril of vapor escape into the air.

'Voilà!' Josh said. He poured champagne into three crystal flutes set on a silver tray. After putting the bottle back in its silver bucket, he handed a glass to April.

'Thanks,' she said, 'but don't you think we should wait for Joanna to have a toast?'

'Yes,' he said. 'You're right. I'm just a greedy pig.'

They both laughed.

'So I'll have a tiny sip, and she won't notice that it's missing from my glass,' he said. He paused and set his glass back down. 'But you will,' he continued. 'So I'd better wait on Joanna.'

April smiled.

'By the way,' he said, 'Joanna showed me your estimate, and I think it's fine. You did a very professional job of it.'

'Thanks,' April said. 'It's a big project so it wasn't easy to do. The construction and all isn't much of a problem, but figuring my own time wasn't easy.'

'I'm sure it'll work out,' Josh said, 'and I'm really glad because it makes Joanna so happy. She's so much like Mitch, her father, always having to be working on something a little creative. She fixed up the old shack at the beach practically by herself. She did her orchid book, and she's always doing something around here. Adding to the garden or redecorating a room, or just changing a color or something.'

'I think that's great,' April said. 'She could be spending all of her time shopping, like some women I know.'

He laughed. 'Thank God I'm spared that.'

'I'm back,' Joanna called. She walked over to the table and sat down. 'How nice,' she said. 'You waited for me.' She turned to April. 'Here,' she said, 'I brought you a shawl in case you get cool in the night air. We'll have dinner in about thirty minutes.'

'Oh, thanks, Joanna,' April said. She took the proffered shawl and wrapped it around her shoulders. It was a luxuriously soft pashmina and a beautiful shade of doeskin that looked good on her.

She noticed that Joanna had changed into a beige silk blouse with matching trousers. A white cashmere sweater was looped around her neck. It was a very casual look that April knew was not easy to achieve. *Like everything else about her*, April thought. She put a lot of hard work into making everything appear to be easy.

'Okay,' Josh said, picking up his champagne flute, 'I'm going to make a toast.'

Joanna and April followed suit, picking up their glasses.

'To the shell grotto,' Josh said, smiling. 'A cockamamie project I never thought Joanna would see to fruition.'

I only hope I do, Joanna thought.

But she laughed with them, clinking glasses and taking sips of the champagne.

April loved the way it was bubbly on her tongue and its smooth taste. She hadn't had expensive champagne for a long time. Or anything to celebrate, for that matter.

'Oh,' Josh said, raising his glass again. 'One more toast.'

'What?' Joanna asked, lifting her glass.

'To April,' he said, his swimming pool eyes shifting to April's, 'the only woman I've ever met who's listened to Joanna and actually heard what she was saying.'

'Hear, hear,' Joanna cried, watching the look that her husband was giving April. She felt a shiver of excitement, seeing that the two of them were slowly developing an easy familiarity, and possibly more.

April sipped her champagne along with them, and felt that little ache of longing swell up within her once again. It was comforting, thrilling even, to be a part of this couple's lives, but she worried that that aching little feeling might be more than that – more than a longing to be a part of something so warm and welcoming, that it might center more directly on Josh Lawrence himself.

11

Full-fledged summer was now upon them as work progressed on the stable. The French doors had been installed, but hadn't been satisfactory until Joanna had hunted down and purchased – at great expense – just the right hardware. The simple brass door handles that had been installed were replaced with gilded bronze handles in – what else? – a shell motif.

April had assumed that once the work began, Joanna would, like so many of her clients, do a disappearing act, checking in only occasionally to review progress. She'd been surprised when she discovered that Joanna took very much a hands-on approach. With some clients this might have posed a problem. Joanna, however, had proved herself indispensable, offering advice and helping make crucial decisions.

She had rejected the small fountain that was to be placed in the center of the room as too ornate, for example.

'But I thought it would appeal to your sense of fantasy,' April had said.

'The fountain itself is only a base to work on,' Joanna had replied. 'It has to be very simple. The ornateness will come with the shells and pebbles that embellish it. Remember? Establish a rather severe line, then blur it.'

April had looked at her and laughed. She wouldn't forget again.

When the appropriate fountain was finally installed, Joanna had been right there alongside the plumbers, making certain that they adjusted the jets to the proper height and that each one was aimed in precisely the correct direction.

On the other hand, Joanna learned from April's experience. She noticed that April worked alongside the various tradesmen, cajoling them to do their best. When a piece of molding was 'almost level,' it was April who talked them into making it 'level,' extricating the little bit of extra time and work required for perfection.

The days flew by in such a whirlwind of work that when basic construction was actually finished and the time had arrived for April to begin working her own personal magic – embellishing the old stable-cum-grotto with shells and pebbles – she and Joanna were both surprised.

They had gradually become friends over the last few weeks, April often reflected, and one Friday morning in early June, while they were cooling off in the swimming pool together, April wasn't surprised when Joanna started talking about her sister, Christina.

'Christina's four years older, and she could be very bossy and very mean,' she said. 'But sometimes she was also very protective and motherly. We had some wonderful times together. She taught me about clothes and makeup and told me about the birds and the bees, and we had great talks about boys. Without a mother around, I can't imagine what it would've been like without her.'

'Are you still close to her?' April asked.

'Well,' Joanna began thoughtfully, 'we do have a history together, and we visit each other occasionally. I go down to Montecito a couple of times a year, and Christina . . . well, she might be here once a year or ten times. She's unpredictable.' She laughed. 'She was here a few weeks ago. But we are just so different.'

'Really?' April said. 'How?'

'In so many ways,' Joanna replied. 'Christina was always very ambitious, socially I mean. And money crazy. And man crazy like you wouldn't believe.' She looked at April. 'Maybe I should say crazy for men with money and power. Usually social standing too.'

They both laughed.

'I guess a lot of women are,' April said.

'Christina is, for sure,' she said. 'She's thirty-six and been married three times. All of them filthy rich, very

161

powerful, and very important socially. She runs around with a crowd that's strictly Montecito, Palm Beach, like that. Rich and idle. They follow the sun and maybe the horses. Polo crowd, some of them. Most of them have big trust funds and have never worked.'

'That doesn't sound like you at all,' April said.

Joanna shook her head. 'No way,' she said. 'And you know, the strange thing is, a lot of these people are really miserable. I don't mean all rich people are, but Christina always seems to fall in with a crowd that's bored and restless and really unhappy.'

'No goals or ambitions,' April said.

'Exactly,' Joanna said. 'They obsess on their problems all the time. You know, like their hair, their clothes. Their face-lifts and jewelry. Their latest lover. All that vital stuff that can really be a problem.' She smiled.

April returned her smile. 'People like that need to get outside themselves,' she said. 'I think that's the best therapy when you're feeling blue. Try to do something for somebody else.' She looked at Joanna. 'Does that sound corny?'

'That sounds exactly like something I would say,' Joanna said with a laugh. 'I've said it a million times. What Christina needs to do is some hands-on charity work. Get involved outside of herself with something, just like you said.'

'You said you're close,' April said. 'Do you get along well? Being so different, I mean?'

Joanna shrugged. 'Okay,' she said. 'I guess you could say we've agreed to disagree about things. And be friends, regardless. Before Dad died he asked us how we wanted to break up the estate. It was going to be either land and business or money. Christina immediately jumped for all the money, and I was really happy because I wanted the land and business.'

She paused for a moment, looking off into the distance, then continued. 'It's worked out beautifully, I think, even though it was really an uneven split. This house and the beach shack and the business and land weren't worth nearly as much as the stock portfolio and cash that Christina got.'

'That's pretty amazing,' April said. 'That the *worth* of one sister could be so much more and not create bad blood.'

Joanna nodded. 'It is, isn't it? But we've never feuded about it at all. I told you. We're completely different. I didn't really care about the money, and Christina couldn't have cared less about the business.' She paused, a thoughtful expression on her face. 'Or at least she didn't used to.'

'What do you mean?' April asked. 'She does now?'

Joanna frowned and shook her head. 'I don't know,' she said. 'I don't guess so, but she's been asking all kinds of questions about the nursery lately. Stuff she usually doesn't give a hoot about. It's odd.' She laughed. 'Maybe it's because she's just bored between husbands or she's suddenly getting sentimental about family and the business.' She shook her head. 'I don't know. Oh, anyhow,' she said smiling, 'suffice it to say that we've grown apart, no doubt about that. Taken *very* different paths in life, but in some ways she mothered me when I was little, and I'll always appreciate it. I'll never forget it.'

'What happened to your mother?' April asked. A few weeks earlier she wouldn't have felt comfortable asking this question, but she and Joanna had reached such a stage of intimacy that she didn't think twice about it now.

'Right after I was born,' Joanna said, 'she drowned.'

'Oh, my God,' April said. 'I had no idea.'

'It happened in Monterey Bay, down near the beach shack. Dad had a sailboat, and the two of them were out sailing alone. A squall came up suddenly and a pea-soup fog rolled in with it. There were big swells, and they were rushing to get back to shore. Anyway, they'd both had a few drinks, and she wasn't wearing her safety harness. She fell overboard and drowned before Dad could save her. He searched for a long time and radioed for help, but it was useless. She washed up on shore the next day, almost in front of the beach shack.' She looked at April with huge sad eyes.

'How terrible for you,' April said. 'I always wondered about your mother because I've heard you and Josh both talk so much about your father.'

'It wasn't really so terrible for me,' Joanna replied. 'After all, I was a baby. I don't remember her at all. Christina barely remembers her, and sometimes thinks she doesn't really remember her at all but just thinks she does from the pictures of her or the stories about her.'

'And your father never remarried?' April asked.

Joanna shook her head. 'No,' she said. 'I don't think he ever even looked at another woman.' She coughed a little. 'He was a wonderful madman. After Mother drowned, he set the boat on fire and watched it sink, then he quit drinking. He never had another drop.'

'Did he always blame himself?' April asked.

'I think so,' Joanna said. 'And he tried to make it up to us. He devoted himself to Christina and me, lavished us with love. Sometimes I think he waited until we were both married, then – and only then – allowed himself to get cancer and die. He knew that we were taken care of and he could call it quits.'

'That's extraordinary,' April said. 'You were really lucky to have him, weren't you?'

'Oh, yes,' Joanna said with a nod of her head. 'He was the best father – and man – imaginable. I always thought that it was so unfair – so *cruel* – that he died such a horrible death. So slow and painful. He suffered so much at the end, after living such a decent, generous life.'

She paused, then looked at April with a serious expression. 'I guess I lost any faith I had in any kind of benevolent God then, and I don't know whether I've ever regained it or not. I'm still trying to come to terms with the unfairness, with the cruelty, that life can dole out.'

She laughed lightly. 'I didn't mean to get so serious,' she said. 'I can tell you this. Christina and I were blessed. No two girls were ever loved so much, or spoiled, I guess.'

'Well, you don't seem spoiled to me,' April said. 'You seem to know what you have and appreciate it.'

'Thanks, April,' Joanna said. 'Anyhow, I'm keeping you from your work.'

'Speaking of which,' April said, 'I've got Woody coming over to help me for a while today.'

'Is he the one you told me about?' Joanna asked. 'The one with the shop?'

'Yes,' April replied. 'He's worked for me before on big jobs. He helps me when I use quick-setting cement to do some of the shell and pebble placement. If it has to be done really fast, I get somebody to help me. It saves a lot of time, and he's good at doing quick simple background stuff. I won't let him do anything elaborate.'

'What does he do about his shop?' Joanna asked.

'He has somebody running it for him, you know,' April said. 'Then he sacrifices some of his surfing time to catch up on the shop work.'

Joanna didn't want to tell April that she knew Woody Pearlman, at least not yet. She certainly hadn't forgotten her trip to his shop and the pass he'd made at her. Still, he'd done good work the two earlier times. Maybe, she told herself, he'd just been having a bad day.

'He must like you an awful lot to drop everything and help out,' Joanna said. 'Is he by any chance in love with you?'

'No,' April said. 'Well . . . not exactly . . . love. Oh, hell, Joanna. I don't know.'

'How do you feel about him?' Joanna asked.

166

April smiled, then laughed. 'I'm not in love with him. At least I don't think so. We've been like pals for a while. He was a friend of my ex-husband's, so we've known each other for years, but it's more like a brother-sister thing. At least I think it is. I've certainly never had any weak-in-the-knees, heart-fluttering moments with Woody, at any rate. Woody's the kind of guy I go to the movies with. You know, for company.'

Joanna felt relieved to hear this news but didn't say anything to April. *Woody Pearlman isn't worthy of April*, she thought. *I'm sure of it.* She knew that she would have mixed feelings about any man April was seeing, that she had proprietary feelings about her. But remembering her own brief encounter, she was certain that Woody was a heart-breaking Casanova of the first order. *He's after one thing and one thing only, that man.*

How, then, she asked herself, could you explain their friendship, which was obviously pretty close? She was certain that after he got enough of what he wanted, Woody would move on to the next woman. April would no longer be a challenge.

April climbed up out of the pool. 'I'm going to change and watch out for Woody,' she said.

'Okay,' Joanna said. 'I'll see you at lunch.'

'You're sure I'm not wearing out my welcome, Joanna?' April said.

'Don't be silly,' Joanna replied. 'Besides, today's special. The construction's finished and the real work begins. So it's time to celebrate.'

'We already did,' April said. 'Remember?'

'One can't have too many celebrations in this life,' Joanna laughed.

'Well, I'll be there,' April said. She turned and walked off toward the pool house to change, guiltily wondering if Josh would be at lunch today.

Woody stood with his hands in his pockets, eyeballing the stable with curiosity. Finally, he shook his shaggy head of black hair and whistled.

'I gotta say, April,' he said with admiration in his voice, 'this is gonna be one cool room.'

'Well,' April replied, 'it was Joanna's idea, not mine.'

'Yeah, but you did all the design work,' Woody said, 'and now you're doing the shell work.' He turned and looked at her. His dark eyes glittered with intensity. 'Give yourself some credit, you know.'

'Thanks, Woody,' April said. 'Anyhow, now you've seen the layout and what's got to be done. Are you sure you can spare the time to help? I'll only need you for the fast work.'

'Yeah,' he said. 'I can make the time for you, April.' He looked around again. 'What's gonna be the fast work anyway?'

April laughed. 'Large spaces filled in with mostly identical shells or pebbles. No intricate designs. Look.' She motioned for him to come over to the work-table she'd set up in the room. Plans were spread out all over it.

'Look at the design for that wall,' she said, indicating the south wall with a hand. 'See these large areas between moldings? Areas like that can be done with quick-setting cement. They call for identical shells or pebbles.'

'I understand,' Woody said. 'It's the simple, boring stuff any idiot can do.'

'Exactly,' April said. 'I've saved the hard, more stimulating stuff for myself.'

Woody laughed. 'You're the boss.'

April looked at her watch. 'Listen,' she said, 'I'm going up to the house for lunch, so I've got to run. You can find your way back out?'

'Sure,' Woody said. 'No problem. Mind if I stay a while, though? I'd like to study these plans to see how much of that simple, boring stuff there is.'

'That's fine, Woody,' she replied. She was surprised that he was taking such an interest. She knew that he worked very well, quickly and efficiently, because of his help in the past, but she'd always thought he was simply passing the time, not really caring much about the work.

'That way,' he said, 'when we get started Monday, I'll have a good idea of exactly what areas I'm going to be working on. I can set little goals.'

'Oh, Woody,' April said with a laugh, 'you're so funny.' She gave him a kiss on the cheek. 'I'd better run. I'll see you tonight. Okay?'

'Later,' he said. 'Have fun.'

She turned and left the grotto, walking up to the pool area. Woody's eagle eyes followed her until she was out of sight.

*   *   *

'No, keep your seat,' Joanna insisted. 'I've got this under control, and I don't need any help.'

'If you're sure,' April said.

'Believe me, she's sure,' Josh said with a grin.

Joanna headed on into the house carrying a tray laden with dirty dishes. They had finished lunch – all but dessert – and she was going to get coffee and the simple dessert she'd made herself.

'Is Connie off today?' April asked.

'Yes,' Josh said. 'I don't know what she's up to. She takes off every now and then without any warning, but it's not a problem. Anyhow, Joanna loves going it solo in the kitchen when Connie's gone. I think she likes it so much because it's like this rare treat.'

April laughed. 'Makes sense,' she said. 'I enjoy the kitchen a lot more if I'm doing something special for my friends.'

'That's the way I am,' Josh said. 'Sometimes it's fun to cook a special meal for Joanna and myself, or maybe make something special to contribute to a dinner party. If it were routine, well, I don't think I'd like it so much.'

'Growing up,' April said, 'sometimes I'd make a big deal out of making myself a sandwich or something. Make it really special. Like put chocolate sauce on peanut butter.'

Josh laughed. 'I did exactly the same thing!' he said. 'I'd make a sandwich out of sardines and then pour ketchup all over it. Or put ketchup in a can of soup.'

'Ugh! It sounds so awful now,' April said, 'but when you're little and alone, you do crazy things to entertain yourself.'

'You sure do,' Josh said with a thoughtful expression. 'We do really nutty things to make life ... better.'

'Yes,' she agreed.

'You seem to have made a very good life for yourself,' he said. 'You've got your storybook cottage Joanna told me about, and your work. And you seem like a pretty happy camper to me.'

April nodded. 'You're right, Josh,' she agreed. 'I'm a pretty happy camper. It's not always heaven, but it's a hell of a lot better than it used to be. And projects like this with you and Joanna help make it that way. Speaking of which, where *is* Joanna?'

'If I know Joanna, she's in the kitchen putting the finishing touches on dessert,' he said, 'which could mean quite some time.' He looked at her and smiled again. 'She's trying to do whatever it is perfectly, needless to say. And I'm sure you know something about that.'

From the conservatory windows, Joanna had been watching the two of them. The dessert was ready to serve, the coffee was made, but she hadn't been able to tear her eyes away from the scene she had seen unfold before her.

Tears of both sadness and joy, and relief, had rolled down her cheeks. Simply observing the friendly camaraderie that was developing between Josh and April – the camaraderie she had prayed for – had churned up

171

a cauldron of conflicting emotions within her that she had never expected.

Now, torn between a glorious sense of elation and a terrible sense of loss, she had to recommit herself to the dangerously tricky path she had set out upon. This was unchartered territory, for an intimacy was developing between all three of them, a potentially destructive intimacy, and she began to doubt the wisdom of her decision.

Who do I think I am that I can play God? she asked herself.

But then she reminded herself that she *must* take this bold gamble, that she *must* see to fruition the plot that she had hatched.

After all, what have I really got to lose? she asked. *Absolutely nothing.*

And what have they got to gain?

She knew the answer to that, too: *Everything.*

Woody turned out the lights in the grotto and began weaving his way through the apple trees up toward the pool area. On the wind, he could hear the sound of soft voices engrossed in conversation, almost as if they were whispering, punctuated by an occasional tinkle of ice in a glass.

When he came within view of the terrace, he stopped and stood, unseen, in the shadow of one of the old apple trees. Josh Lawrence. Big, bright, rich Josh Lawrence, one of his hands on one of April's. And April. Eating it up. Obviously.

Woody would have liked to spit on the spot. He scowled maliciously, then turned on his heel and quietly backtracked, going around the terrace so as not to be seen.

How could she do this? he wondered. *How could she let herself be taken in by that rich bitch's handsome stud?* She was practically drooling over the son of a bitch, from the looks of things.

Why won't she give me what I want? he wondered. *Why that lousy bastard?*

When he reached the courtyard, he took out his car keys and started toward his van. He saw Josh Lawrence's old Toyota Land Cruiser sitting there. *Really old*, he thought. *Really perfect condition.* He took his car key and, walking along the side of the big RV, he firmly held the key against the fading canary yellow paint, slicing a thin line of paint from the metal, all the way from the back to the front.

Serves the prick right, he thought, getting into his van and starting the engine. Spewing gravel, he spun out of the courtyard and started down the hill, feeling little satisfaction from his wanton act of destruction. Wondering what he could do to really get even.

12

Christina walked up the concrete steps to the board-walk, her expensive Gucci stiletto heels clicking loudly, and grimaced with distaste, wishing herself invisible. She had tried to get Peter Rossi to meet her somewhere else, but he had insisted on this dreary place – some shop at the southern end of the Santa Cruz boardwalk. He was in a hurry and had some business to do at a place here, he'd said, and it wasn't especially busy on an early evening in the summer, so no one they knew would see them here.

Not likely, Christina thought. *God knows, nobody I know would be caught dead here.*

Besides, Peter had told her, there were dozens of places close by where they could spend a couple of hours together. Still, she wondered if he wasn't testing her, just to see what sort of mettle she had, to see if perhaps she was too grand to mix it up with a guy that had come from the wrong side of the tracks.

In this case, Christina thought with a smile, *he could be from Mars and it wouldn't pose a problem.*

The piping of cheerless calliope music filled the air, but was almost overcome by the roar of the Giant Dipper roller coaster, its constant din punctuated by the shrieks of fear and shouts of laughter that erupted from the evening revelers. The smell of corn dogs and cotton candy, underlaid with beer, suntan oil, and sweat, permeated the air. It was a stench in her nostrils.

God! she thought. *I feel so out of place here.*

She felt nothing but contempt for the particular stripe of humanity that was attracted to the amusement rides, cheap food, and the countless tacky souvenir shops that sold T-shirts, seashells, jewelry, and other trinkets. She glanced at a group of filthy, leather-clad bikers and their dingy girlfriends with barely concealed disgust, then noticed that the boardwalk police in their khaki shorts were circling their bicycles near the group, making their presence felt.

She looked away, smiling to herself. The cops might not look so tough on their bicycles, but she knew they were.

She strolled up the boardwalk, ignoring the rides and the beach on her left, staying closer to the well-lighted shops on her right, looking for the one that he'd named.

Finally she glimpsed it just ahead: Poseidon's Garden. Just one slightly shabby trinket shop like so many others. She slowed her pace, seeing if she could spot him through the glass double doors, but her view was blocked by a peroxide-blond, muscle-bound couple, she in a tiny orange bikini that left little to the imagination, he in an almost nonexistent flesh-colored posing strap that left even less to wonder about. Their bronzed bodies, pumped up from steroids and weightlifting, filled both doors as they edged their way out, laden with shopping bags.

The fools must be freezing, she thought, for the early evening air was cool.

She watched them leave, noticing that their slow, deliberate movements seemed to emphasize every ripple and flex of their muscles.

She looked back through the shop doors, craning her neck to try to see Peter. There he was. So tall and handsome. So big and strong. She could swear she felt her heart skip a beat. He was standing between shelves of – what? Seashells? She couldn't tell from here. She took a deep, calming breath and pushed her way in. He didn't turn around and look to see who'd come in, but a clerk at the counter near the door looked over at her with a blank expression.

'Help you?' the clerk asked in a zombie's voice, looking as if the last thing she wanted to do was make a sale. She was slumped on the counter, chin in hands, two fingers alternately twirling the blond skunk stripes in her pitch-black hair and the rings in her nose, lips, and eyebrows. Tattoos decorated her skinny arms.

'I'm just looking, thanks,' Christina said, trying not to cringe.

She started toward the back of the store, and could feel her pulse quicken as she approached Peter, who still hadn't seen her. 'Hello,' she said, sidling up to him.

He turned to her and smiled. 'Hey, there,' he replied.

'What are you so engrossed in?' she asked.

'Just looking at these postcards,' he said.

She noticed that he was holding cards that depicted huge sharks, caught and laid out on a pier for show, a horrendous bloodbath surrounding them.

'Pretty,' she said sarcastically.

He replaced the cards in the rack without replying and picked up a seahorse in a box of shells nearby. 'Bizarre, aren't they?' he said, looking at her.

She looked at him and nodded. 'Yes,' she agreed, 'but very beautiful.'

'Fragile, too,' he said. 'You can snap them in two between your fingers.' He smiled a shark's smile.

She stared mutely at his handsome face, not quite sure what to make of his comment. Was it some sort of less than subtle threat? But then, why would he threaten her? She wasn't certain, but she knew he was a ... a dangerous man. And that really turned her on.

'Let's get out of here,' he said. He took her arm and quickly led her back outside onto the boardwalk, then south a few feet and down a flight of concrete stairs to the street.

'I've got us a room in a motel down the block,' he said, his powerful arm around her shoulders now, rushing her along beside him.

No asking, she thought. *Just telling.* She liked that. She liked that a lot.

It was all she could do to keep up with his pace in her high heels, but she did, excited by his rush, by her own aroused sexuality, and the secrecy of their meeting.

They crossed the street and entered the courtyard of a small, nondescript motel. It was pink stucco with a garish neon sign: *The Seabre ze*, it flashed in red.

At the entrance to room number 9, Peter took the key out of his trouser pocket and unlocked the door. He held it open for her, and she stepped inside, looking around. *Thank God*, she thought. *At least it looks clean.*

He closed the door behind them, then turned to her, taking her in his massive arms roughly, kissing her hard on the lips, his powerful body almost slamming her against the closed door.

She felt a thrill rush through her entire body, and gasped as he began pushing her skirt up, running his huge hands up her thighs and around to her firm buttocks, then pulling her even harder against him. She could feel his tumescence and almost swooned with desire.

'Glad to see me, babe?' he whispered.

'Oh, God, yes,' she breathed, her legs quivering, damp already between her thighs.

Without another word, he began unceremoniously

pulling her clothes off, then quickly undressed himself
and led her to the bed. He mounted her like an animal,
tearing into her with a merciless and selfish abandon,
pounding away at her savagely, relentless in pursuit of
his own satisfaction.

She loved it, her body almost instantly responding to his brutal thrusts by contraction after ecstatic
contraction, her juices flowing freely as with a bellow he rammed himself into her with a final mighty
thrust and released a flood that filled her to overflowing.

It was over almost before it started, so excited were
they both, and they panted feverishly, a glistening sheen
of sweat coating their bodies as they lay entwined,
letting their breathing return to normal. Neither of
them spoke, but they steadily looked into one another's
eyes as their hands slowly began stroking, exploring,
discovering.

It was only moments before they were devouring
each other again, ravenously but this time a little less
fiendishly, taking the time to savor their bodies, to thrill
one another in various ways, until they finally climaxed
in a spent heap of shining flesh.

Only when they'd caught their breath did Peter light
cigarettes for them both.

'Glad you could come up here and meet me, babe,'
he said, kissing her on the cheek and slapping her fanny
playfully. He handed her a cigarette.

Christina took it and inhaled a long drag. 'Oh, God,
me too,' she said, appreciating the fact that he'd said

that, imagining that Peter Rossi rarely told anyone he was glad to see them.

'Your sister and brother-in-law don't know you're here, do they?' he asked.

Christina coughed a laugh, cigarette smoke sputtering out of her mouth. 'No way!' she said. Then she looked at him with a sly smile. 'But I'm not worried about it, Peter. If somebody happens to see the Rolls or me, I'll tell Joanna I've been to see friends in San Francisco or something. Just passing through.'

He smiled. 'You got balls,' he said, playfully slapping her fanny once again.

'Why do you say that?' she asked, relishing his attention. 'Because I'm sleeping with the enemy?'

'That's right, babe,' he said, taking a drag off his cigarette. 'Maybe even helping out the enemy a little bit, huh?'

They both laughed. 'I'm going to humiliate that fucking brother-in-law of yours till I have my way,' he said. 'Down the road, they're going to beg me to buy them out.'

She could hear the amusement in his voice, and couldn't help but share the joy he took in his wicked intentions. She knew that their secrecy and the pure evil of their actions only served to heighten the ardor of their sexual encounters – heightened it, in fact, to levels Christina had never before experienced.

And, she thought smugly, *I have experienced a great deal.*

'Well, from what I hear,' she said, looking over at

him, 'they're beefing up security.' She blew a streamer of smoke out her nostrils. 'So it might be harder to do anything.'

'We'll see,' he said. 'You can keep me posted.'

She nodded. 'I'll find out what I can from Joanna without showing too much interest,' she said. 'I certainly don't want her to get the idea that I'm *too* interested in what's going on, if you know what I mean.'

She looked over at him. 'You see? They could suspect *me*. I'll be taking risks for you, Peter.' Her voice was almost petulant. She looked at him again, expecting some sort of show of support.

Peter Rossi's eyes seemed to harden, becoming glints of obsidian that bored through her. He stubbed out his cigarette and then slowly smiled. 'You can handle it, babe,' he said mildly, still looking into her eyes. He pulled her naked body to his, squeezing her. 'For us, huh?'

'For us,' she echoed. Then she smiled. 'Hmmm,' she said, putting out her cigarette. 'I think I can do it.'

'Yeah,' he nodded. 'I thought so.' He leaned down and kissed her again, on the lips this time, lingering there, his tongue parting her lips, exploring her slowly, almost tenderly. Then he pulled back, reluctantly and just as slowly, and smiled.

'You want to know what we're going to do next?' he asked.

She looked at him questioningly and nodded but didn't say anything.

He cupped one of her breasts in a hand, fondling it

gently, then leaned over to her ear, his tongue brushing it teasingly, before whispering into it, telling her what she had to do next.

When he'd finished, he began kissing her again, harder, more passionately, and his hand brushed lightly down her stomach, trailing on down to her mound. He teased her there, inserting a finger, then drawing it out.

'Oh, Peter,' she moaned quietly. 'Oh ... oh ... oh, my God.' She began to move her hips against his hand, delighted that her body was once again responding to this man. But he suddenly removed his hand and his lips, pulling away from her.

'What—?' she gasped, looking at him.

'Give you something to remember me by, babe,' he said. 'Till the next time, you know?' He smiled his shark's smile.

She was sorely disappointed, but knew that she would get hot just thinking about the next time, just thinking about the unfinished business they had in bed.

'Okay,' she said with a sigh.

'Now,' he said, 'I'd better get out of here. Get my ass back home.'

He got out of bed and began to get dressed. She lay there watching him, hating to see him go but enjoying the sight of him dressing, watching the movement of his tanned muscles against his expensive clothing.

When he was finished, he went over to her, leaning down and kissing her deeply for long moments. Then he drew himself back up to his full height and smiled. 'I'll be in touch,' he said.

She nodded. 'Can't wait,' she said, meaning it.

Then she watched as he went to the door, tossing the room key onto a dresser on his way. He turned at the door, blew her a kiss, then was gone.

She began dressing then, slowly, savoring the tiredness of her body, the feeling of utter satiation that engulfed her in a pleasant contentedness. Despite the complications of their seeing each other, she couldn't wait until the next time.

She both loved and hated these clandestine meetings, but they were a necessity. They must not let anyone see them together. For one thing, he was in the process of divorcing his wife, and he had to look like an angel until it was final. And for the other, she was a traitor.

Yes, I'm a traitor, she thought. *Sleeping with the enemy. Betraying Joanna and Josh. Helping him ruin their business in any little way I can. Giving him information. And oh, oh, oh! they have another little surprise waiting for them soon at the nursery. But I don't care*, she decided. *Joanna and Josh have always had everything. Everything! And it's a small price to pay to have Peter Rossi. To have his power and money. And that sexy mean streak that turns me on so.*

Ah, yes, Christina thought again, *I'm a traitor. But for a very good cause*: me.

13

Josh picked up the telephone on his desk at the nursery. 'Hello?' he said.

'Mr Lawrence?' the deep voice asked.

Despite himself, Josh felt a chill run up his spine. He knew the voice and it gave him the creeps, but after a moment anger replaced his initial reaction. Trying to sound as matter-of-fact as possible, he said, 'Yes, Mr Rossi.'

'I was wondering,' Peter Rossi said, 'if you'd had a change of heart about selling out.'

Josh could hear amusement in the thug's suave voice, and it only infuriated him more. He couldn't keep a lid on his anger any longer.

'No!' he shouted. 'I am *not* selling out. Not to you. Not to *anybody*!'

He slammed the receiver down in its cradle, then put his head in his hands. *The fucker*, he thought. *The goddamn lowlife motherfucker.* He took a few deep breaths, trying to compose himself, his mind racing around in circles.

I should call the police right now, he thought. *But for what? What am I going to tell them? That every time we have trouble here at the nursery Peter Rossi calls me afterward wanting to buy me out?*

He got to his feet and went out to the reception area, slamming the office door behind him.

'Luna,' he said, without glancing at her. 'I'm headed home. Take any messages.'

'Sure, boss,' she said, her eyes wide as she watched him slam the front door behind him.

Josh let the mud room door slam and sat down on the old pine bench with a loud *thunk!* He slowly unlaced his boots, kicked them off, then pulled off his sweaty socks and threw them on the floor.

'Joanna!' he called out with a scowl on his face. 'Joanna!'

There was no answer. He stood up and kicked one of his boots, sending it sailing across the floor to bounce off a table leg.

'Joanna!' he cried again. 'Joanna!' He started toward the kitchen, determined to find his wife.

Where the hell is she this *time?* he asked himself. He was getting sick and tired of not being able to get hold of her. Nobody had picked up the telephone here all afternoon, and the damn woman wouldn't have a cell phone.

Her refusal hadn't bothered him at first, but now it was making him crazy. It was as if there were a plot against him.

He looked around the kitchen. No Joanna. No Connie. No note. He walked through the downstairs rooms calling. No Joanna. He dashed up the stairs to the second floor, calling. No answer.

Where is she when I really need her?

He tromped back downstairs and retraced his steps to the mud room, where he slipped into a pair of Top-Siders. Then, walking out onto the terrace, he looked toward the pool.

Nobody in sight.

He crossed the little bridge to the pool area and looked around the plateau that the pool was built on.

Nothing. Nobody. Shit!

He stomped toward the old apple orchard, heading in the direction of the grotto, and almost bumped into April, coming from between the trees.

'Whoa,' she said. 'What's the hurry?' Then she saw the look on his face. 'What's wrong, Josh?'

'Joanna,' he said between gritted teeth. 'Joanna is what's wrong. I mean, something is going on and I'm getting pissed off.'

'Ooooh,' she said, 'you really *are* upset.'

'I'm sorry,' he said. 'I'm just . . .'

'You're at your wit's end,' she finished for him. 'And it's okay. You want to talk about it?'

187

'No,' he said. 'Well, I don't know. Maybe . . .'

She took his elbow and steered him uphill toward the pool area. 'Come on,' she cajoled. 'Let's go sit down. I think you need to cool your heels.'

They sat at one of the tables that was situated poolside. Although it was hot and humid, there was a slight breeze, and April thought that just looking at the pool helped cool her off.

April saw the look of sad defeat on Josh's face and felt disturbed by it. *He's always so genial, so happy-go-lucky,* she thought, *but he's not unflappable, after all.* She decided to let him do the talking, if he wanted to, because she certainly didn't want to pry, even though he had given her an opening.

'Did you see her at lunch?' he asked, looking at her questioningly.

April shook her head. 'No,' she said, 'I haven't seen her all day. She was already gone when I got here this morning.'

'That's weird,' he said. He looked more perplexed than ever.

'She's probably just running errands, Josh,' April said with a smile, trying to pacify him, but not really believing her own words. Who ran errands at eight o'clock in the morning? Besides, she knew that it was unlike Joanna not to be home for lunch.

Josh looked at her steadily across the table. 'Maybe,' he said, 'but I somehow doubt it.'

'Didn't she leave a note like she always does?' April asked.

He shook his head. 'No,' he replied, 'and it really has me worried.'

'Oh, come on, Josh,' April said. 'She's nearly always here for you, isn't she? Morning, noon, and night.'

He heaved a sigh. 'Yes,' he conceded. 'I guess she is, but lately . . . I don't know. It seems like something's going on.'

'I think maybe you've just had a rough day,' April said. 'Maybe you're overreacting a little bit.'

He nodded. 'Yeah, it's been a rough day, all right.' He stretched his arms. 'And that's putting it mildly. It was the *worst*, April.'

'What?' she said. 'Mr Hara didn't stop by and drop another hundred grand in your pocket?' She was making an effort to lighten the atmosphere for him, but it didn't work.

Josh grimaced. 'No,' he said. 'I wish.' He slumped in his chair. 'But this is really serious. I think somebody's been trying to sabotage the nursery.'

'Are you serious?' she asked, surprised.

'Dead serious,' he said.

'But how do you know?' she asked.

He sat straight up. 'Let's have a glass of wine, okay?' he asked.

'Oh, Josh,' April said, 'I really shouldn't. I ought to get going in a few minutes.'

'Just a glass?' he said.

She could hear the plea in his voice, and knew that he needed to talk to somebody. 'Well . . . okay,' she said, 'but just one glass.'

'I'll run get a bottle and glasses,' he said. 'Be right back.'

April watched him hurry toward the kitchen, wondering what could be going on at the nursery that was upsetting him so much. Maybe it's not really that serious after all, she thought. Maybe that and Joanna's errand-running or whatever, maybe the two together, make it all seem much worse than it really is.

Her reverie was interrupted by Woody, who suddenly appeared at her side.

'Oh, my God, Woody!' she said. 'You scared me half to death.'

'You're crazy,' he said in a near whisper, his glittering dark eyes riveted to hers.

'What?' she said.

'You're playing with fire, April,' he said in the same barely audible voice. Then he turned and stomped off, back toward the orchard, skirting the terrace area, leaving work for the day.

Jesus, April thought, *what's his problem? I'm going to have to have another little talk with him.* She wondered now about the wisdom of hiring Woody to help her with this job, never suspecting that he would behave this way. But then, she realized, on past jobs, when Woody had helped out, she hadn't been involved with the clients like she was here.

Josh returned with a bottle of chilled white wine. 'Here we go,' he said, pouring them each a glass. He handed April hers, then sat back down.

April took a sip of the cool wine. 'Okay,' she said.

'Tell me about this nursery business. You really think it's sabotage?'

'Definitely,' Josh replied. 'It started a few weeks ago. The computer-operated misting system malfunctioned. If Carl hadn't been paying attention, a lot of orchids could've been lost. Either soaked to death or dried out.'

'I remember Joanna told me about it,' April said. 'But I thought it was just a computer problem.'

'The technicians that came out didn't think so,' Josh replied. 'They think that somebody had tinkered with the system.'

'Could they have been trying to cover their own asses?' April asked. 'So their ·system wouldn't look bad.'

'I doubt it,' Josh said. 'They've got a great reputation in this area.'

'But if it was sabotage,' April asked, 'who could it have been? And why?'

Josh looked at her steadily. 'I have a good guess,' he replied. 'The Rossi brothers have been trying to buy us out. They're a huge operation with land on both sides of us, and they want to expand.'

'And you've refused to sell,' April guessed.

'Yes.' Josh took a sip of his wine and set the glass back down. 'We could get enough to retire if we wanted to or go into something else, but Joanna's father really treasured that land. And the business. He spent his whole life building it up. And Joanna feels very strongly about it, too.'

April looked at him. 'And so do you,' she said. 'You've got the orchid bug, and you're devoted to that business.'

Josh nodded in agreement. 'Yeah,' he said, smiling, 'You're right about that.' He fell silent, lost in thought.

'So you think it might be these Rossi brothers who're trying to sabotage you,' she said.

'Yes,' Josh said. 'After the computer mister episode, Peter Rossi actually called me to make another offer.'

'What?' April said. 'You're serious?'

'Yep,' he said. 'It's almost like they're playing with me.'

She looked at him with a stunned expression. 'Did you tell the police that?'

'Yes,' he said. 'For what it's worth. There's nothing they can do. Nothing they can act on.'

'I can see that,' she replied. 'And now something else has happened?'

Josh sighed. 'There's been an outbreak of some kind of fungal disease in one of the greenhouses. *Phytophthora*, I believe. It's a black rot fungus that's attacked some of the *Phalaenopsis*.'

'Oh, Lord, no,' April exclaimed. 'Is it serious?'

'I don't know yet,' he said. 'It's contained to that one greenhouse. All *Phalaenopsis*. We're having the bacteria analyzed to see exactly what it is, but it doesn't really matter. It's good-bye to some of the plants, and a long period of nursing for the ones we can save. A lot of them were due to be shipped, so we have to buy more stock or lose orders.'

'That's horrible!' April said.

'The weird thing is, the environment for those orchids was perfect. Exactly as it should be. Air, temperature, humidity, spacing between plants, all of it perfect. The fungus should never have appeared.'

'Did you call the police again?' April asked.

'Yes,' he replied, 'and like the last time they couldn't find any sign of forced entry. Nothing. And like the last time, Miguel, the night watchman, saw and heard nothing out of the ordinary. And he says that the watchdog we got hasn't raised any alarms, either.'

He paused and took another sip of wine. 'Of course,' he continued, 'this being a fungus, somebody could've come in like a customer during regular hours and deposited it in the *Phalaenopsis* greenhouse. But I don't think so, because we have very few walk-ins and they're usually with a salesperson.'

'Oh, Lord,' April said. 'It gets more and more difficult to pin down.' She flicked a bug away from her wine. 'Did you get a telephone call this time?' she asked.

'Yep,' he said. 'That too.' His eyes locked on to hers. 'See what I mean about being played with?'

'Oh, God, this is creepy,' she said. 'Was it the same guy, uh, Peter—'

'Peter Rossi.' He nodded. 'I'm beginning to think it's getting a little creepy, too. These people have a reputation for being ruthless and unscrupulous, but jeez, I can't believe the gall he has to call like this. I mean . . . he seems to have no fear whatsoever.'

'So what are you going to do?' she asked.

'I don't know, April,' he said. 'I really don't know. That's one reason I was so angry about Joanna not being here. I need to talk to her about this.'

April sat staring at him. He had slumped in his chair again and looked defeated. She wished she could make him feel better, but she knew that she couldn't.

'I'm sure Joanna will be here soon,' she finally said. 'She's probably been shopping or something and just paid no attention to the time. You know how she gets distracted.'

He looked up at her then. 'Thanks for listening,' he said, 'and trying to cheer me up.' He smiled. 'You're really . . . special.'

April felt that peculiar uncomfortable feeling again, that longing that he seemed to arouse in her, and knew that she was blushing slightly.

'Thanks, Josh,' she said. 'You and Joanna are very special, too.' She took the last sip of her wine and set the glass back down. 'I'd really better get going now,' she said. 'I've got a lot to do at home.'

He sat up. 'I'm sorry,' he said. 'You've been stuck here working all day, and I've kept you way over-time.'

'It's okay,' she said, smiling. She rose to her feet and reached down, picking up her carryall. 'I don't mind at all. That's what friends are for.'

Josh, on his feet too, picked up their glasses and the

bottle of wine. 'Well, thanks a lot anyhow.' He looked at her. 'And I'm glad you can call us friends.'

'Me, too,' she said, already walking toward the house. 'Me, too.'

The beach stretched before her, an almost entirely deserted expanse ranging from dark gray, where waves lapped at the shore, to beige, to a dry white at the dunes. Driftwood lay beached like prehistoric sea creatures, and kelp, rubbery and tubelike, was strewn in generous clumps across the sand. To the south, she could see a lone fisherman casting a line, and far beyond him the towering stacks of the power plant near Moss Landing.

She turned and looked north, the wind whipping her hair across her face. Using both hands, she swept it out of her eyes. She could barely make out what she knew to be Santa Cruz, although the fog, which was rolling in off the ocean in great pearly clouds, would soon render visibility nil. In the near distance, she could see Joe Camel, her name for the huge upright piece of driftwood with its camel's head that marked the path in the dunes leading to the old beach shack.

She had walked for miles and miles and lost all track of time, even though the position of the sun and its relative intensity were a reminder that time was fleeting. She should have been home hours ago.

Today, she had decided, would be different. She had left for the beach immediately after Josh went to work, not leaving a note, not letting anyone know what she was doing. It was a luxury, this willful, self-centered escape, but she had no apologies. She wanted to be alone here at her father's old shack, on the beach that she had loved with all her heart, all her life. No place had ever meant more to her than the simple, rustic cabin where she had spent weekends and holidays with her father and sister, and where she and Josh had spent the first exquisite months of their marriage.

As she neared the camel's head, her legs and arms suddenly became weary. She eased herself onto the sand, carefully setting down the heavy plastic bags of shells she'd collected. There were hundreds, she supposed, a few of them perfect specimens, the vast majority broken. But they would have their use, she told herself. Every last one of them. Whole or incomplete, beautifully colored or uninterestingly dull, it didn't matter.

She faced the horizon, which was gradually disappearing in the encroaching fog, and saw that the sun was beginning to set. The end of the day, she thought. The end of the day. Tears came into her eyes, and she let them flow silently down her face. Normally, she would have tried to hide them, but now she let them stream unchecked, down onto her sweater, wherever they might fall. Sobs began to wrench her body, and she put her arms across her stomach. Despite the roar of the wind, she could hear her own choking wails of agony, could hear them as they became louder and louder shrieks alternating with barely discernible mewls of pain.

Her screams were answered only by the roar of the

wind and surf, the screeches of birds, the sounds of her plastic bags whipped by the wind.

When her fury was finally spent, her body aching with exhaustion, she collapsed on the sand, her chest heaving, the salty sand sticking to her wet face. She rested there for a long time, catching her breath, murmuring and sighing, gradually becoming conscious of her surroundings.

When at last she sat back up, she could see that dark was fast approaching. She stood up, brushing the sand off her clothes, off her face, fatigue almost overwhelming her. Picking up the bags of shells, she trudged through the dry sand, slowly making her way over the dunes to the sea shack. She passed the outdoor shower at the foot of the steps leading up to the big screened-in front porch, but she ignored it. She didn't care about tracking sand throughout the house.

Inside, she laid her shells on a chair, then flipped on a light. She padded across the worn wooden floor to the bathroom and, flipping on a light there, looked at herself in the mirror. 'What a mess you are, old girl,' she murmured to her reflection. She started to laugh, but quickly checked the impulse. She didn't want to cry anymore. She washed her face, then brushed her hair in long, even strokes. That done, she flipped off the light, then went back out to the living room.

I should straighten up the bedroom, she thought. *And put away the wine and glasses and—*

'Forget it,' she said aloud. *Nobody much comes here*

anymore but me, she thought, *and what difference does it make anyway?*

She gathered up her bags of shells, closed up the house, and went out to the car. For a few minutes, she sat silently, taking deep breaths of air, then she started the car, feeling finally that she could go home and play the good wife.

Josh turned off the hot shower and stepped out onto the cool marble floor. Taking a big, fluffy white towel, he started drying off, humming tunelessly to himself. When he heard the car in the courtyard, he threw the towel down and grabbed his terrycloth bathrobe off the brass door hook. He went through the bedroom and down the hallway in the direction of the stairs.

Finally, he thought, sailing down the steps. *Now, let's see what Joanna's been up to – or says she's been up to.*

He reached the bottom of the stairs just as the front door was opening, and Joanna started edging her way in, her arms loaded down with heavy plastic bags.

'Hi,' she chirped, smiling, radiantly cheerful.

Josh felt a sense of relief surge through him, coupled with that familiar joy that her sparkling presence never failed to evoke.

'Wait a minute, honey,' he said. 'Let me help you.'

He rushed over and held the door wide, at the same time trying to extricate some of the plastic bags from her hands, an impossible task as they were entwined with her fingers.

'Ouch!' she said. 'My hands are trapped!'

'Just drop them,' he said.

'But they're filthy, Josh!' she exclaimed. 'Covered up with sand and who knows what else.'

'Never mind the dirt, just drop them,' he said.

Joanna eased the heavy bags down onto the hallway's marble floor, then drew herself back up and planted a kiss on his lips. 'Hi, handsome,' she said. 'I'm glad you were here to help. I didn't realize these were so heavy.'

He immediately detected the smell of alcohol on her breath and was surprised. Joanna, who always smelled of an exotic citrus and vetiver perfume, had come in reeking like a Bowery bum. Then he noticed that her hair was a mess and her clothes were too.

'What've you got here?' he asked. 'Smells like the fish market.'

'Oh, you wouldn't believe!' Joanna said excitedly. 'I've been shelling, and I got oodles of all kinds of things!'

He smiled, swept up in his wife's charm and innocent excitement.

'Look,' she said, rummaging around in one of the bags. 'A whole bagful of little bits of mother-of-pearl! Great for filling in background in the grotto.'

'Yeah,' he said, 'looks like quite a haul you got for yourself. I'll get some garbage bags in the kitchen to stick these into, so just leave them here.'

'Clever,' she said. 'You're so clever.'

She followed him out to the kitchen. Opening the refrigerator door, she said, 'A nice chilled white. Just what the doctor ordered after lugging all that weight.'

'I put a couple of bottles in earlier, so they should be chilled,' Josh said, taking some garbage bags from a box.

'You too?' she asked. 'Want some vino?'

'Sure,' he replied. 'I'll be right back.' He started out of the kitchen, then turned back to her. 'Do you want me to put these in the laundry room so we can start soaking them?'

'That'd be great, Josh.'

He went back out to the entrance hall while Joanna opened the bottle of wine, retrieved two crystal glasses from a cabinet, then took the bottle and glasses out to the terrace table.

She sat down under the big umbrella and looked out toward the swimming pool. Fog, in cottony wisps, was swirling all around, and it would be a beautiful time to relax in the pool. She'd missed her swim this evening, but she decided she was too tired to go near the pool. In the distance, she could see huge fog banks enshrouding the mountainsides.

Josh approached from behind her and put his powerful hands on her shoulders, massaging her lightly.

'Oh, that feels so good,' she said, looking up at him and smiling dreamily. She closed her eyes and gave herself up to the sensuous feel of his hands on her.

'Aren't you hungry?' Josh asked. 'It's past dinnertime, and Connie's got tons of stuff in the fridge ready for us.'

'Dinnertime,' she said, sitting up. 'Is it that late?'

'Uh-huh,' Josh said.

'Oh, my gosh,' she said. 'I had no idea.'

'Have you by any chance been drinking?' he asked lightly. 'It's not like you to forget dinner.'

'Yes,' she exclaimed. 'It was wonderful, too. I stopped off at Umberto's and had some wine and watched the sunset from their terrace.'

'Umberto's?' he asked. 'You hate that place.'

'It was perfect just this once,' she said. 'For the sunset. I didn't even notice all the plastic flowers and furniture.'

Josh laughed. 'You are in a mood, aren't you?' He gave her shoulders a final pat, then sat down next to her at the table. 'Alone?' he asked as casually as possible.

She nodded sleepily. 'Um-hm,' she said. 'Just me and my lonesome.'

Josh didn't know whether to believe what she was saying or not, but he had the distinct feeling that she was lying. Obviously she'd been shelling and obviously she'd been drinking, but Umberto's? With all those kids and surfer types and tourists?

He wanted to know what she'd really been up to, but he looked at her sleepy eyes and knew that he wouldn't pry any further. *I wish I could talk to her*, he thought. *And I need to tell her about the problems at the nursery today. But now is definitely not the time. Not when she's high from drinking.*

'April was here when I got home,' he said, changing the subject.

'How was she?' Joanna asked, taking a sip of her wine. 'I missed her today.'

'She was fine,' he said, 'but I think she had some questions to ask you. Wanted your approval on some things.'

'There's always tomorrow,' Joanna said. 'Besides, I trust her implicitly.' She leaned back in her chair and closed her eyes again.

'Oh,' Josh said, 'I almost forgot. Christina called. Just a little while ago.'

Joanna sat back up and opened her eyes. 'And what does my precious sister want?' she asked.

'She wants to know if you're coming down to visit like you said you would,' Josh replied.

'Oh, God,' Joanna said. 'I'd forgotten all about it. With this project going on and all.'

'I told her I didn't know,' Josh said. 'I didn't even know you'd called her and told her you were going down there.'

Joanna averted her gaze, looking off into the distance. 'Well, I thought she could use the company,' she said. 'I know she's very unhappy after the divorce.' She returned her gaze to Josh. 'I've been terribly neglectful,' she said. 'Christina's really suffering and I just . . .'

He reached over and took one of her hands in his. 'Don't worry about it now, Joanna,' he said gently. 'Come on.' He rose to his feet, bringing her hand with him. 'I'll whip up something to eat, and we'll put something in that empty stomach of yours.'

Joanna let him pull her to her feet, then stood there next to him. He drew her closer, against his nearly naked body, and kissed her tenderly.

She felt his warmth and inhaled his clean masculine aroma and realized that he was aroused. *Oh, Lord*, she thought. *I hate to disappoint Josh, of all people, but I'm just so very, very tired.*

She looked up into his eyes. 'Josh,' she whispered. 'I'm . . . I'm really exhausted. I think I ought to take a quick shower and go straight to bed.'

'You're sure?' he asked, not wanting to take no for an answer.

She nodded. 'I'm exhausted.'

'Okay,' he said, the lusty excitement in his eyes dimming. 'I'll be in a little later.' He let his arms fall from around her.

''Night,' Joanna said. She gave him a quick kiss on the lips and walked off toward the French doors leading into the kitchen. He supposed he should be angry with her, but he just couldn't summon up those feelings. She'd looked so happy when she came in and had looked somehow so . . . fragile just now.

Josh watched her disappear into the house, then sat back down and took a sip of his wine. He felt more mystified than ever, and couldn't make any sense of her behavior. *She's gone all day and comes home a little high on wine*, he thought. *Says she's been to a café she detests. Forgot she'd promised her sister she'd be down for a visit. She won't eat.*

But worst of all, he told himself, *is that she doesn't want to make love.* He couldn't remember when she'd last refused him. In all the years of their marriage, it had happened only a handful of times. She'd either been really sick or really upset about something. But now? He didn't think she'd ever said she was too tired.

Doesn't she want me anymore? he wondered. He told himself that thinking that way was ridiculous. Just plain paranoid. Hadn't they made love several times lately? And hadn't it been as great as always? *Then what the hell's going on?*

14

Josh sat on a stool in the marble bathroom, staring down at the package in his hand. His eyes were filled with tears, and he had the look of a wounded animal.

Why didn't I take the time to have that talk with her? he asked himself once again. But he knew why, of course. At the nursery, the last few days had flown by in a haze of relentless work, everyone working overtime, getting orders out, isolating and nursing the fungal-infected plants, acquiring more stock.

And all the while, his home life – his relationship with his wife – was becoming a nightmare.

Staring down at the package, he felt as if Joanna had become someone else altogether, someone devious, uncaring, and unloving. *Or*, he thought, *maybe I never really knew her at all.*

He was going to turn in early because he was exhausted. He had been looking for her to kiss her good night. She'd been in her little office earlier, doing something on the computer, so he'd gone there first. But the computer had been turned off, and she wasn't there. He'd looked in the bathroom next to it to see if she was there, and saw instead the offensive package on the marble counter. In plain view.

He'd been stunned at first. Then the pain came, a hurt so intense that he didn't yet feel the rage that he was certain must come. He'd sat down on this stool and tried to figure out what to do next.

I have to confront her about this. And right now, he decided. *No more putting off a talk. No more being too busy. No more excuses. This does it.*

He snatched up the package and headed downstairs for the kitchen. She'd probably be in there or in the sunroom. When he reached the kitchen, he saw that she was pouring herself a glass of wine.

She saw him out of the corner of her eye. 'Would you like some?' she asked. She topped her glass, then turned to face him.

Josh planted himself in front of her and held out the offensive package. 'Why?' he asked, his voice an anguished plea.

Joanna saw the package in his hand, and her face went a ghostly white. She let the wineglass slip from her fingers, and it crashed onto the Mexican tile floor, glass and wine flying everywhere.

'Why, Joanna?' Josh repeated. As much as he loved

her, at this moment he wanted to hit her, something he had never done. Something he could never have even imagined wanting to do before tonight.

'I . . . I . . .' Joanna stuttered. Suddenly she emitted an animal wail of anguish, tears coming into her eyes, and she rushed over the splinters of glass, ignoring them, past him, and out of the kitchen.

Josh stood glancing down at the shattered glass and wine for a moment. Then he opened the cabinet with the garbage bins and tossed the package of birth control pills in. He slammed the cabinet door shut with all his might, then turned and headed back upstairs to the bedroom. He was determined to have that talk with her. And tonight.

He tried to open the bedroom door, but it was locked. 'Joanna,' he called, 'please, honey, open the door. We've got to talk.'

There was no response, and he pounded on the door with his fists. 'Joanna,' he cried, 'we've got to talk about this. *Now.* Open up.'

He put his ear to the door, but not a sound could be heard from the other side. He raised his fists and started to bang again, but dropped them, feeling suddenly ridiculous.

She is already miserable, he thought. *I don't want to compound that.*

He went down the hall to a guest room and, heading toward the bed, noticed the bar setup for guests. There were several bottles of liquor and glasses on a large silver tray. The ice bucket was empty, but it didn't matter. He poured himself a large dollop of scotch, then threw off his bathrobe and spread out on the bed, staring up at the ceiling, sipping the scotch. He'd never slept in this room before, and it felt strange not to have Joanna at his side. He wondered if he would be able to fall asleep. His mind was still such a whirlwind of mixed emotions that he doubted he'd get a wink. He looked at the glass of scotch, but decided he didn't want a fuzzy head on top of everything else in the morning.

But no matter what, he decided, *tomorrow is D day. We're going to discuss this come hell or high water.* Then, so exhausted was he, he fell into a deep undisturbed sleep.

Josh came awake with a start. He instantly knew that he wasn't in his own bed and, eyes open, scanned the room quickly. Even in his slightly disoriented state, he knew where he was. Then he remembered last night, and what had happened.

He sat up slowly and glanced at the clock on the bedside table. Nearly seven. Looking toward the windows, he could tell from a chink in the curtains that the light was a uniform gray. The fog hadn't burned off yet, probably wouldn't for a few hours yet.

He slid his legs around and put his feet on the floor, then noticed his bathrobe where he'd thrown it off last night. He slipped it on, then rose to his feet. He stretched his arms and rolled his head around, yawning loudly.

'I've got to go find Joanna now,' he said aloud. 'This

very minute.' He knew that he had to act fast before the chance slipped away. Joanna might dash off somewhere before he could talk to her.

He padded out into the hallway toward their bedroom. The door was ajar, but he listened at it for a moment before going on into the room. Silence. And then he heard her in the bathroom.

She's crying, he thought miserably.

He rushed through the bedroom and opened the door into Joanna's big marble bathroom. She was sitting at her vanity table, her head in her hands.

'Joanna!' he said. 'Joanna, what is it? What's wrong?' He flew to her, gently putting his arms around her, trying to comfort her.

When at last her sobbing stopped, she turned and looked up at him with a pained expression. Her tear-streaked face was flushed, and her eyes were puffy and red. She let her head drop against his robed shoulder.

'Joanna, darling, Joanna. Please tell me what's wrong,' he said in an anguished voice, hugging her closer.

She remained silent, then got up and went to the sink, where she turned on the cold water tap. She quickly splashed her face several times with the icy water, then patted it dry with a thick white towel.

When she was done, she turned back to him, looking up into his blue eyes. As long as she had put off the inevitable, she realized that she had to tell him the truth now. He had discovered the birth control pills, and her disease was progressing at such a rate that she couldn't hide it from him much longer.

'We have to talk,' she finally said, hugging herself with her arms.

'What *is* it, Joanna?' he asked, going to her and wrapping his arms around her.

She could see the panic in his eyes and could only think of the torture this wonderful man was going to be put through because of the terrible words she was going to utter.

She reached out and took one of his hands in hers. 'First, why don't we grab some coffee downstairs and take it outside on the terrace?' she said. 'Is that okay?'

'Sure,' he said, squeezing her hand in his.

Together they went down to the kitchen and went through the early-morning ritual of making coffee as if nothing were amiss. As they stepped outside, the morning fog floated around the terrace in endlessly shifting swirls. They sat under the big umbrella, still in their bathrobes, sipping hot coffee.

Josh reached across the space between them and took her hand again. He didn't know why he was so unnerved, but he didn't remember ever feeling such fear before.

'I ... I've known that something was wrong for a while, but if this is because of my anger last night, finding the pills—'

She shook her head vigorously. 'No, no, Josh,' she said. 'Don't even think about blaming yourself for anything.'

She looked down into her coffee, as if searching its depths for the right words, the most painless way to tell him what she must. But, she decided, there was only the simple truth.

She looked back up into his handsome eyes. She could see the fear there and wished she could dispel it. 'I'm going to die,' she said calmly.

She felt his hand jerk in hers. It was as if he had been bitten by a snake. She held it more fiercely in her own. She saw his sad eyes widen, and his mouth open as if to speak.

'I didn't want to tell you,' she continued, 'but I don't have any choice now, Josh. I'm going to die.'

'Die?' he finally whispered.

She nodded. 'Yes. The disease is progressing—'

'What disease?' Josh said, almost angrily. 'What in God's name is wrong with you, Joanna?'

'It's cancer, Josh,' she said. 'Brain cancer. And it's terminal.'

For a moment he looked at her as if she'd gone mad. Then he got out of his chair and, getting down on his knees, put his arms around her waist, his head on her bosom, and held her tight.

'Are you certain about this, Joanna?' he asked, his voice almost a whisper.

'Yes,' she said, nodding. She stroked his hair with her fingers, tenderly, lovingly. 'Absolutely, Josh.'

'But . . . but . . . there must be something we can do!' he cried. 'We'll stop at nothing. You'll see all the best doctors. The best doctors in the—'

'Josh!' she said with firm authority. 'You must listen to me.' She paused, then continued. 'Doctors might be able to prolong my life by a few months at the most. Using horrible invasive procedures and radiation and chemotherapy.'

'Then—' he began.

'No!' she cried. 'Listen to me. I am *not* going to try to gain a few months that will only be misery for me and everyone else.' She took his shoulders in her hands and squeezed them hard. 'I am not going to die like my father. Suffering on and on and on. In constant pain. I am going to die my way, Josh. With dignity.'

'But ... but—' he began again.

'No, there are no buts,' Joanna said softly. 'Don't you see? The symptoms have already started. Some headaches and nausea. And now they're getting worse. There's even been some blurred vision—'

'But how did you find out?' he asked. 'When did you go to the doctor?'

'Last January when I went to San Francisco on that shopping trip, I saw a doctor at Stanford. Because of the headaches.'

'But you never said a thing,' he accused. 'You hardly even mentioned having headaches.'

She nodded. 'I know,' she said in a matter-of-fact voice. 'I wanted things to be as normal as possible. For as long as possible. And I still do. Besides, the doctor's given me some medication that helps with the headaches. It's just that you have to be aware of the symptoms now, and the decisions I've come to.'

'What decisions?' he asked.

'That I die with dignity,' she said. 'Here at home. I

don't want to go to the hospital, and I don't want any treatment that will only prolong my life.'

'But—'

'I've already told you, Josh. No buts. And don't try to change my mind. It's made up.' She paused and hugged him fiercely. 'We've had a wonderful life together, darling. We've had the greatest gift there is – our love for one another. I can die in peace knowing that. Don't you see?'

He nodded, but he wasn't certain that he did see. His eyes had filled with tears, and he fought to hold them back. Nothing of what she'd said had truly sunk in yet. It all seemed so unreal, as if their lives had suddenly become someone else's, as if this were a movie.

'Josh?' she said, taking both his hands in hers. 'Josh?'

'Yes?' he said, looking into her eyes.

'I want to ask a very important favor.'

'Anything,' he said, tears spilling from his eyes.

'I meant it when I said that I want our lives to go on as normally as possible,' she said. 'As if this didn't exist. I know that's going to be difficult, but that's the way I want it. And I don't want anybody to know that doesn't have to. The one thing in the world that would make me happiest is to go on as usual.'

He nodded, not trusting himself to speak. Tears streamed from his eyes unchecked.

'I want you to go to work as usual,' she went on, 'and I'll carry on here as usual. I know that's not going to be easy, but that's what I want.'

'Who . . . who's your doctor?' he managed to say.

'I've made a list for you,' she said. 'It's in the top right-hand drawer of the desk in my office. All the doctors and their telephone numbers are there. There's also a couple of articles about the particular kind of cancer I have. They'll help you understand it better.'

He put his head in her lap, and she stroked his hair again, running her fingers through it gently, savoring the feel of his warm breath on her.

Funny, she thought. *I thought I would cry when I finally told him. I thought I would hardly be able to get it all out. But . . . having him here, holding me . . . our being together, has made it easy.*

He abruptly looked up at her. 'This is why you took the birth control pills, isn't it?'

She nodded. 'I found out about the cancer right after we started to try to have a baby, so I decided I'd better not. I might not have lived till full term. There could've been all sorts of complications.' She didn't tell him that she wanted him to have a child with someone else, that she hoped he would father a child that would have both its parents. No, she would wait to tell him that. And a lot more.

'Oh, Joanna, you're so brave,' he said. 'To have held this inside for all these months. I wish you'd told me before, so you wouldn't have felt so alone with it. It makes me . . . it makes me angry, I guess, that you haven't included me.'

'I've had to come to terms with it myself,' she said. 'And I didn't want to talk about it until then, Josh. I didn't want to leave you out, but I simply couldn't tell you till I was ready.'

'I'm glad you did,' he said.

'I am too, Josh,' she said. She paused, then ruffled his hair. 'Now, I want you to get up and go get ready for work. Let's have a normal day. Remember? April will be coming soon and so will Connie. There's a lot to do.'

'You're crazy, Joanna!' he said. 'A normal day after this?'

'I'm not crazy,' she said evenly. 'And yes, I want us to have a normal day. As normal as possible.'

'You really mean it?' he asked in disbelief.

'Oh, yes,' she said. 'And I'll be upset if you don't go right now and get ready. Please try to do this for me, Josh. I know it's hard, but it's really what I want. It'll make it so much easier for *me*.'

He stood up then, and looked down at her. She thought she detected a look of determination in his eyes. *Good*, she thought. *He's going to try to be brave.* But then, she wouldn't have thought otherwise of him.

'Go,' she said. 'And then come down and kiss me good-bye before you leave. If you can, come home for lunch as usual.'

He stood there, immobile, reluctant to move.

'Go, Josh,' she said again, very quietly.

Finally he walked off toward the house, and she watched him, trying to fix in her mind his every footstep, every subtle twist in his shoulders, the slight movement in his arms. For a moment she thought that her love for him would overwhelm her, but she was determined to remain dry-eyed, to be calm and in control.

Nevertheless, she had to finger a tear from her eye. *Josh, Josh, Josh*, she thought. *I will miss you. Miss you so very much.*

Then she straightened her shoulders and took a sip of coffee.

I may be dying, she thought, *but my work in this life isn't finished yet. Not by a long shot. I've got a lot to do before I go.*

BOOK TWO

April and Josh
Fall and Winter 2000

15

April sat at the big table in her kitchen, sipping coffee and nibbling on toast with butter and jam, blackcurrant on one slice and orange marmalade on the other. The morning newspaper was spread out on the table, and she eyed it while eating. When the telephone rang, she reached over to get it, her eyes still on the paper.

'Hello,' she said distractedly.

'April?'

Josh?

She instantly put down the paper, her antennae on full alert. Why on earth would he be calling her?

'Hi, Josh,' she said. 'What's going on?'

'I ... I need to talk to you,' he said hesitantly. 'If ... if you don't mind.'

What's wrong? she wondered, her curiosity piqued. His voice held none of its customary cheer, she thought. In fact, it was downright grave.

'Of course I don't mind,' she replied lightly. 'I'm all ears, Josh. What is it?' When he didn't answer immediately, she added: 'You don't sound like yourself.'

'I'm not,' he said. 'I . . . well . . . I'd rather discuss this in person, if you don't mind. It's . . . it's something very important, April. I hate to bother you, but I really need to talk to somebody. It's . . . it's really important.'

'Sure, Josh,' she said. 'That's fine. Do you want me to come up there?'

'No,' he said. 'I don't think so.' He paused, then asked, 'Do you mind if we meet someplace? I really need to discuss this in absolute privacy.'

My God, she thought, *he sounds so . . . desperate.*

'Why don't you come on over here, Josh?' she offered. 'I'll put on a fresh pot of coffee. How's that?'

'That'd be great, April,' he said, sounding somewhat relieved. 'I'll come straight on over, if that's okay.'

'That's fine, Josh,' she said. 'Do you know how to get here?'

'Yes,' he replied. 'Joanna's told me all about it. I don't think I could miss it.'

She could hear a hint of familiar amusement return to his voice and felt relieved. Perhaps whatever he had to discuss wasn't so serious after all.

'I'll see you in a half hour or so,' he said. 'Okay?'

'Perfect,' she said.

'See you in a bit.'

''Bye.' April hung up the telephone and sat staring off into space for a few minutes, then turned her attention back to the newspaper, but she couldn't seem to read the print, much less concentrate. Finally, she folded it up and laid it aside, then got to her feet to make a fresh pot of coffee.

What the devil could be going on up there? she wondered. *Josh Lawrence wouldn't be calling me unless it was important. And he certainly wouldn't be asking to meet me in private unless it was very important. But* what? *Had they suddenly decided they didn't like her work? Could they have decided to call off the project for some reason?*

Dumping the old coffee grounds in the garbage, she missed the can and grounds went flying in wet clumps.

'Damn!' she exclaimed. When she went to the sink and dampened some paper towels to clean up the mess, she realized that her hands were shaking.

Why am I so nervous? she asked herself. But deep down inside, she knew the answer to that question. Despite her efforts to suppress her feelings for Josh Lawrence, they had only grown more powerful. And they were not the feelings of a sister for a brother. No, indeed.

And now this! she thought. *Whatever* this *might be.*

Cleaning up the mess on the floor, she promised herself anew that no matter what Josh might have on his mind, she would put the skids on her own volatile emotions for Joanna's sake. For Joanna had come to be the sister she'd never had, and she wouldn't want anything – nothing in the world, especially not her feelings for Josh – to get in their way now.

Cruising up the mountain road, Joanna eyed the small package in its burnt orange box with the brown bow. It lay on the Mercedes passenger seat next to her. She smiled with delight just thinking about it. When she'd seen the beautiful Hermès scarf with its fanciful shell motif, she'd known immediately that she must get one for April.

Now, freshly coiffed, she'd decided to swing by April's house on her way home and surprise her with it. She'd been waiting for just the right time to give it to her, and something told her this morning that she should take the package with her to the beauty parlor, then drop by April's.

She braked at one of the stop signs on this treacherous stretch of the road and waited for an oncoming car to negotiate the narrow pass before continuing on ahead. She glanced over at the cottages across the ravine on her right. Some of them were barely discernible in the junglelike growth around them, but that was part of their charm, she thought.

She slowed down because she knew that April's cottage was just ahead, around the next corner. She hoped she'd be able to park behind April's car, but as she slowly rounded the corner she saw that the narrow shoulder behind the old Wagoneer was already occupied.

By Josh's ancient Land Cruiser. Unmistakably Josh's.

Joanna put on the brakes, her mind racing, her heart pounding. Then she swiftly stepped on the gas and sped on up the mountain road. Though she thought it doubtful they would, she didn't want them to see her car passing from across the ravine.

When she reached a crossroads, she made a left and pulled over to the side of the road. There was a wide shoulder here, and she put the car in park and sat staring through the window. Her heart was still racing, and she could feel a pulse in her ear.

My God, she thought. *Even my hands are shaking.*

She took a few deep breaths, trying to steady her nerves and clear her mind. After a few minutes, she looked over at the beautiful package on the seat next to her. The gift she'd so excitedly bought for April. Suddenly she began to laugh, a barely audible sound at first, but gradually increasing in intensity until her entire body shook with hilarity and the car was filled with the sound.

I've done it now, she thought. *Oh, yes, I've accomplished almost everything I set out to do. Only I didn't expect to feel quite so . . . jealous! Quite so . . . left out and . . . betrayed by it all!*

Her laughter quickly dissolved into tears, and she quietly cried, hating herself for her own jealousy – a feeling that she despised owning up to – and at the same time hating Josh and April for the bond that she

223

could see had developed between them. A bond that she had helped create, that she had nourished like a mother hen.

Of course he would come straight to her, she thought. *And it's only natural that he should. I should count my lucky stars and be grateful that Josh has her to talk to. God knows, he needs somebody.*

When her tears at last subsided, she took off her sunglasses and wiped her eyes with a Kleenex. Then she suddenly began laughing again, less raucously this time, but helplessly laughing nevertheless.

The irony of it all, she thought. *I've gotten exactly what I wanted. So I should be thrilled.*

But now she realized that she would have to grow accustomed to the success of her project. *How stupid of me,* she thought. *Not to have had the foresight to realize that I would be so powerfully affected by Josh's attraction to someone else. Even if it was someone of my own choosing.*

She finally put the car in drive and eased back onto the road. She would take an alternate route back down the mountain, then go on home, she decided. As she drove, she gradually began to feel a little less anxious, and reflected back on the history of her illness.

When she'd first learned that she was sick, Joanna had immediately decided that she must find another woman as her replacement in Josh's affections. She knew that despite his good looks, charming personality, and a strong masculine presence, he needed the support of a partner. Physically, emotionally, and spiritually. But then, she supposed, didn't everybody?

It was her love for Josh that drove her to search for someone to replace her when she was gone. First, there had been the up-and-coming interior decorator Julie Gillette. Joanna had hired her to help with ordering wallpaper and fabrics that were available only through decorators, and had become intrigued by her. Initially, she had seemed as if she might be the perfect second wife for Josh. But after only a matter of days Joanna discovered that Julie, for all her good qualities – and they were many – was too aggressively upwardly mobile and obsessed with being a friend of the very rich and very social. There was nothing wrong with that in and of itself, Joanna thought, but Julie's relentless social ambitions simply didn't fit with Josh's idea of a way to live. They wouldn't have made it past first base, she decided.

Next, there had been Rachel Lewis, a photographer. Joanna had met her when she was working on her orchid book. At the time she'd thought that photographs of the flowers would accompany the text – rather than the drawings she later decided on – and she'd interviewed several photographers, examining their work. She'd met Rachel, who was both a great photographer and a great beauty. Over the course of their discussions, she discovered that although Rachel was indeed a wonderful woman, she lacked one essential ingredient: She was emotionally weak and lacked an inner strength that Josh could rely on. Rachel, it seemed, could barely keep her own fitful demons at bay, much less lend moral support to someone else.

There had been others that she'd briefly considered pursuing as candidates. Frieda, the beautiful, divorced bookshop proprietor, who she soon discovered would be ideal but for the fact that she was a lesbian. Then there'd been Laura, the young, wealthy horsewoman who was extremely poised, strong of character, and as well-bred as one of her Arabian horses. Unfortunately, she was also both unintelligent and ill-educated, though she'd been to the very 'best' schools.

Joanna sighed with relief as she zipped along the highway, headed back toward home. All of those defeats were in the past, she thought happily. After giving up the search and reconciling herself to the fact that Josh would have to make his own way in the world, April had fallen into her lap. *Their* laps, she reminded herself. April, the perfect mate for Josh. April, whose inner strength and character were more than enough to lend Josh the support he needed. April, who gladly gave of herself and would happily receive.

Joanna smiled to herself, her fears and conflicted feelings conquered – for the moment at least. She could hardly wait until Monday, when she could give April the beautiful scarf with its colorful shells. She could hardly wait to see the look of delight that she knew would cross her lovely features when she opened the package. *She will love it,* she thought with satisfaction. *They will both love it.*

*   *   *

'And she just told you about it?' April asked, her face etched with concern.

Josh nodded. 'She wouldn't even have told me today if I hadn't discovered that she was taking birth control pills.' He paused and looked into those compassionate eyes of hers.

'You see, April, we'd waited a long time to try to have a baby. Then we finally decided the time was right. So she stopped taking the pill. A year later, she was diagnosed.' He paused again, shaking his head. 'So, she immediately started taking the pill again. She didn't know if she could carry a baby to term, and she didn't want to endanger an unborn child.'

April sat staring at him, her mind a maelstrom of conflicting thoughts and emotions. She felt as if she were in shock, so stunned was she by the news. It didn't seem real somehow. Not yet, at least.

'Oh, my God, Josh,' April said, making an effort not to cry. 'I don't know what to say except that I'll do everything humanly possible to help. Just say the word. Anything at all, and you know that I mean it.'

Josh looked into her eyes. They were huge and sorrowful, but she hadn't shed a tear. The tears would come later, of that he was certain. He looked down at the mug of coffee on the kitchen table in front of him, then looked back up at her.

'Thanks, April,' he said. 'I . . . I know that you love Joanna or I wouldn't have told you. I felt like I *had* to tell you. Not just to unburden myself, but because

I thought you should know. I thought you had a right to know.'

April reached across the space between them, and placed a hand on his. 'I'm so glad you told me, Josh,' she said. 'I'm really honored that you did. And you're right, of course. I love Joanna dearly. She's so wonderful, so ... I don't know. Like no one else I've ever known. And I've said it a dozen times, but she's been like the sister I always wanted.'

Her voice choked, and she paused a moment until she trusted herself to speak. 'I ... I love you both, Josh,' she finally said, looking directly into his sad blue eyes. Her face suddenly burned brightly with this admission, but she continued. 'And I'll be there for you both. Whatever it takes.'

Josh swallowed hard and squeezed her hand in his. Oh, my God, he thought. *I wish I was brave enough to tell her that I feel the same way. That we both love her, too. That I love her.* But he felt as if it would be a betrayal of his love for Joanna to say the words. Even thinking them felt like a betrayal.

'I knew I could rely on you,' he finally said with a tight smile. 'You've been so great to us both, April, that we feel like you're family. I hope you understand that. I think you do.'

She nodded. 'Yes,' she said simply. She looked out through the windows at the luxuriant foliage that surrounded the cottage, then shifted her gaze back to him. 'One thing, Josh,' she said.

'What's that?' he asked.

'I don't think I should tell Joanna that you've told me,' she said. 'I think I should wait for her to tell me herself.'

He nodded silently.

She removed her hand from his and ran her fingers through her hair nervously. 'I'm sure that she will, and I hope it's soon.'

'I think it probably will be,' he replied hoarsely. He cleared his throat before continuing. 'She ... she's beginning to have more problematic symptoms. More frequent headaches and some blurring of vision. Medicine takes care of some of it, but she's going to have to confide in you soon, I'm sure. You know ... to explain what's going on.'

April nodded. 'Well,' she said with quiet confidence, 'I'll be there.'

'Thanks again, April,' he said. He shifted in his chair uncomfortably. 'I guess I'd better get going. I don't know when Joanna will be back home, and I want to be there. I'm a little afraid for her to be alone, even if she wants things to be normal.'

'It's that bad, you think?' April asked.

'Getting there,' he answered. He rose to his feet, and April followed suit.

'If there's anything I can do between now and Monday morning,' she said, 'let me know. Call me anytime, Josh. And I mean it. Anytime. I'll be here puttering around all weekend.'

'Thanks,' Josh said. He smiled sadly. 'We'll just have to play it by ear, you know?'

'Yes,' April said. 'I guess so.'

She walked him to the front door, then to the foot-bridge. 'Remember,' she said, turning and looking up into his eyes, 'don't hesitate to call if you need me.'

Josh returned her gaze. 'I will,' he promised. He wanted desperately to reach out and embrace her, to thank her, to feel the warmth and support of her body against his.

At that moment April, as if sensing his need, put her arms around him and hugged him to her. 'We have to be strong for Joanna,' she whispered.

'Yes,' he said, returning her embrace. Then he drew back and started across the bridge to his car.

April watched until he'd pulled out, waving as he left. Then she turned and went back into the house. She closed the door behind her, and leaned back against it, her feelings more confused than ever. The tears she'd so long delayed for his sake began to flow. She wept and wept. Tears for Joanna, for Josh, and for herself.

Josh drove into the courtyard and was relieved to see Joanna's Mercedes there. He parked and leapt out, heading toward the mud room, anxious to see her. His visit with April had, he reflected, made him feel stronger. He didn't know why exactly, but supposed it was just the knowledge that he would have her moral support in dealing with Joanna's illness.

He also realized that after sharing his secret, he felt a new and more powerful bond with April. It was a wondrous feeling, but at the same time it made him feel a little guilty. He had really enjoyed being with her, had enjoyed being in her little cottage – with its feeling of warmth and charm and coziness, of beauty tinged with a sense of fantasy.

The same kind of feeling that Joanna creates in her surroundings, he thought.

In the mud room, he realized that he was wearing spiffy-clean Top-Siders and didn't need to take off dirty work boots. He headed toward the kitchen, but Joanna wasn't there or on the terrace outside. In the entrance hall, he shouted upstairs, but there was no answer. On an impulse, he turned and walked back to the kitchen and out the French doors to the terrace, over the little bridge to the pool area, and down through the apple trees to the grotto.

He saw her before she realized that he was there. Standing outside the doors, he watched her. She was idly walking about the room, brushing her hands across the shell-encrusted surfaces, then standing back and studying them with a critical eye. Then she would step closer again and touch them anew.

He stepped into the room. 'Joanna?' he said in a soft voice.

She turned to him, not at all startled. He was surprised to see a beautiful smile on her face. She appeared to be calm, serene and happy even. 'It's becoming truly beautiful, isn't it?' she said, taking one of his hands in hers.

'Yes,' he nodded, giving her hand a gentle squeeze.

'It'll have a bit of me in it, don't you think?' she asked, looking up at him.

'It's pure Joanna,' he replied. 'Your ideas, your imagination at work.' Tears suddenly formed in his eyes.

Joanna reached up and brushed them away with a fingertip. 'None of that,' she said. 'Remember? We have to be strong, and you have to go on for me. Keep building what we've started together. Always building, making everything more beautiful.' She paused, then kissed his lips lightly. 'And not on your own,' she said.

Early the next morning, Joanna woke with a start. Something was definitely wrong, but she wasn't certain what it was. She reached over for Josh, but didn't feel his familiar warmth next to her.

That's it, she thought with relief. *Josh isn't in bed. He's already up and about. Funny, how we become so accustomed to sleeping with someone that their absence can set off alarms.*

She slid out of bed and slipped into her bathrobe, then padded into the bathroom on bare feet and took the first pill of the day, a preventative painkiller. She washed her face and brushed her teeth, then ran a brush through her hair, looking at her reflection in the mirror.

Odd, she thought. *I don't look sick at all. In fact, I look pretty damn good.* She smiled and flipped off the light. *Now to find my husband.*

She started down the hall to the stairs, but passing

by his office, she saw that the door was ajar and the lights were on. Peeking in, she saw Josh at his desk, the computer screen bright with words or figures she couldn't read from here. Piled up on the desk next to him were several stacks of paper, some of them she guessed to be the articles and notes she'd told him about, some of them apparently printouts that he'd run recently.

She tapped lightly on the door, then went on into the office. 'Josh?' she asked.

He jerked up and turned around. She saw at once that his eyes were bloodshot and weary-looking, with dark circles. His hair was a tousled mess, and his clothes were rumpled. The room was airless and smelled stale.

'You look exhausted,' Joanna said worriedly.

He nodded and smiled grimly. 'I am,' he said.

She went to him and put her arms around his shoulders, then ran her fingers through his hair affectionately. She didn't have to ask what he'd been doing because she was certain she knew, but she did anyway.

'What've you been up to?' she asked.

'I . . . I've been surfing the Net,' he said hoarsely. 'I . . . I've been trying to find out as much as I can about your . . . your—' He looked up at her with wounded, sorrowful eyes.

'You can say it, Josh,' Joanna said quietly, looking into his eyes. 'It's not a disgrace, you know. *Cancer*. See? It's just a word.'

'I . . . I'm sorry, Joanna,' he said. 'I still . . . I still find it hard to believe.' She could see that he was fighting back tears.

She hugged his head to her closely, then leaned down and kissed it tenderly. *I've got to be brave*, she told herself, holding back her own tears. She loved him so much and knew she was breaking his heart by being sick.

'You'll come to terms with it eventually, my darling,' she said. She forced cheer into her voice, and once again tousled his hair. 'Now, tell me what you've been doing.'

'I was finding out as much as I can,' he said calmly. 'The American Brain Tumor Association, the Brain Tumor Society, the National Cancer Institute, the National Brain Tumor Foundation. On and on and on. I've been up all night going from one website to another, seeing what I can find out. I called Dr Saltzman in Palo Alto yesterday, and he filled me in on everything and answered all my questions. But I thought maybe I could learn something else.'

'No wonder you're exhausted,' she said. 'Come on, let's go down and get some coffee. Or do you want to shower and go to bed?'

'No,' he said. 'I'm too wound up to sleep. Let's go get that coffee.'

They walked hand in hand to the kitchen, where Joanna ground beans and put on the coffee while Josh made toast, poured fresh-squeezed orange juice, and set the table out on the terrace. When they finally sat down to eat, the warm morning sun was already burning off the fog.

'I saw that your doctor is listed on Best Doctors, Inc., website,' Josh said, after sipping his coffee.

'I know,' Joanna said. 'That's not where I found out about him, but I think I've probably visited every website there is that deals with my form of cancer.'

Josh set down his coffee cup and looked at her, his eyes burning with an unfamiliar intensity. 'Joanna,' he said, 'you know that there're a lot of new techniques out there that make treatment for brain cancer a lot more effective than it used to be. And there're a lot—'

'Josh,' she said firmly, looking him in the eye. 'I know *all* about them, believe me. I've studied the literature, and I've talked to umpteen-million doctors about my case.' She took a sip of coffee and set her cup back down. 'And they all say virtually the same thing. They can only buy me time. And not much of that.'

'But what about some of the experimental studies, Joanna,' he persisted. 'You know—'

Joanna slammed her hand down on the table. 'No!' she cried. 'Stop it! Right now! I don't want to hear any more!' Her voice broke and tears came into her eyes.

Josh quickly jumped out of his chair and, kneeling down beside her, put his arms around her. 'Oh, Joanna,' he cried, 'I'm sorry. I just ... I just don't want to see you give up so easily. I keep thinking there might be something, some miracle that will make you well. It just can't ... end ... this ... way.'

'Look at me, Josh,' she said calmly.

He looked up into her eyes and saw a resolute determination shining there that he knew no one could defeat.

'I've told you before,' she said. 'I don't want to die like Dad did. I don't want all that pain and misery. The terrible lingering. And I will not be a guinea pig. Don't you see, Josh? I might be alive, but I wouldn't be living. I've made up my mind about this, once and for all, and I hope that you can respect that.'

After a moment of silence, he slowly nodded his head, knowing that nothing he could say would change her mind, and yet he couldn't quite fathom what seemed to him her acceptance of this awful death sentence.

'Joanna,' he said, 'aren't you angry? Don't you hate this?'

Her eyes flickered briefly with recognition, then she nodded. 'Yes,' she said. 'I've been angry, Josh, and I've cursed God and the world and everybody in it. At first, anyway.' She took a deep breath, then continued. 'But now,' she said, 'now I've reconciled myself to it. To its inevitability. To my ... my powerlessness over it.'

She looked at him and smiled, not with amusement, he thought, but a little sadly. 'I've come to a kind of peace, Josh,' she said finally, 'and I hope you will, too.'

She leaned down and kissed him, and he hugged her tightly. 'Now,' she said, 'let's finish breakfast, because I've got a busy day.'

'What?' he said, rising to his feet and sitting back down in his chair.

'I've got to start packing,' she said. 'I'm going down to Christina's for a little visit. I hate to leave you here alone, but you'll be busy at work. Anyway, I want to tell her what's going on. And in person, not over the phone.'

He looked at her almost with astonishment, marveling at her composure. 'Do you think you really ought to take a trip like that?'

'I told you,' she said. 'We've got to carry on as usual, and I meant it.' She laughed. 'It's not so much that I'm anxious to go down to Christina's, but it's only fair, Josh.'

He nodded as if in agreement, but he still didn't *feel* it. Not really.

'Are you going to the nursery today?' she asked.

He shook his head. 'No,' he said. 'I don't have any appointments this weekend, so Carl can handle everything. I thought I'd stay here and get some work done in the Stud Room.'

'Why don't you try to get some sleep first?' she said. 'You're exhausted.'

'I'll try,' he said.

'Promise?'

He nodded. 'Yes,' he said with a smile. But he knew he wouldn't. He couldn't. Not yet.

16

April was up on the scaffolding, lying flat on her back, the ceiling only two feet above her. She was embedding circular scallop shells, in shades ranging from off-pink to orange, in the quick-drying cement. She was carefully following the lines she had sketched out because making a mistake and having to redo was painstaking and time-consuming.

Argopecten circularis, she thought with wry amusement. *I'm learning more about shells than I ever dreamed I would. Or wanted to, for that matter.*

She had been at it all day, with a short lunch break. Woody had left, and she was working late. She was doing as much overtime as she possibly could in light of Josh's revelation. Plus she wanted to surprise Joanna with the progress she'd made when she returned from Montecito.

In her fantasies the ceiling would be completely finished, and although that wouldn't really happen, she would nearly be finished. The ceiling was the hardest part by far, due to the simple fact that she had to do it flat on her back, up in the air. Despite the fans they'd set up, the heat was still suffocating, and the work was dirty.

Placing the last of the scallop shells at the end of the line she'd marked out, she breathed a sigh of relief. *This is going to be it for the day*, she said. *And I mean it.* She'd told herself that several times, only to keep going, trying to get a little closer to completion of this section of the ceiling.

'Hello up there,' Josh called from one of the French doors.

'Hi,' April called down.

'It's getting late. Don't you think it's time you quit for the day?'

'I'm just finishing up,' she replied. 'This *is* the last one for the day.'

Josh stepped into the room and stood looking up at the ceiling. He could see from the work so far that it was going to be a spectacularly beautiful and exotic room, unlike anything he had ever seen. The difference between the sketches and the reality was startling. But then, he told himself, so was the enormous time and patience the work required.

April scooted over to the edge of the boards she lay

on, then eased herself down to the next level of the scaffolding. When she finally reached the floor, she pulled off the latex gloves she wore, then stretched her arms and shoulders and rolled her head around.

'This kills your arms and shoulders.' She laughed. 'I don't know how Michelangelo ever did it. I don't know how any of those guys did it. They must've all died cripples.'

Josh laughed. 'It's paying off, though, isn't it?'

It was good to hear him laugh, April thought. There had certainly been little laughter since Joanna had left. She looked up at the ceiling and then looked at him with a pleased expression. 'I think so,' she said. 'I think it's really going to be terrific.'

'Listen,' he said. 'You want to stay for dinner? Connie's made something, and I hate to eat alone again. Besides, I'd say you deserve a good meal after what you've put in today.'

April looked at him and for a moment didn't know what to say. Then she decided she was being silly. She wanted to stay for dinner, so why not? Besides, it might do Josh some good should he want to talk.

'That'd be great,' she said. 'But ... oh, my Lord! Look at me. I'm filthy. Covered up with cement dust and stuff.'

'That's okay,' Josh said. 'You can wash off if you want to or take a shower.'

'I'll just wash off,' April said, untying the big painter's smock she wore. 'That is, if I won't offend you looking so ... well ...'

241

'Like a working artist,' Josh said. 'There's nothing wrong with that.'

'I'll just straighten up my things here,' April said, 'then come on up. How's that?'

'Great,' Josh said. 'You can come up to the house and clean up in a guest bath or use a pool house bath if you want to.'

'The pool house bath is fine,' April said. 'I'm getting to know it quite well.'

Josh laughed. 'Okay,' he said. 'See you up on the terrace.'

After he left, she quickly straightened up the room, getting ready for the next morning, and gathered up her tools that needed washing. She placed them in a bucket as she did every day, picked up her carryall, flipped off the light, and left, closing the French door behind her. In one of the pool house's two bathrooms she cleaned her tools and dried them off.

She looked in the bathroom mirror. 'Hopeless,' she said to her reflection. She washed her hands and arms, scrubbing them clean of cement and dust, then washed her face and neck. Toweling off, she looked in the mirror again.

'My hair!' she cried. Cement dust coated it in a thin white layer. 'I look like an actress in a high school play. Trying to age her appearance. And failing miserably.'

She grabbed her hairbrush and started brushing, brushing, brushing. 'Hopeless,' she repeated. 'Hopeless.' Finally, she put the brush down and sighed. 'Screw it,' she said. 'I'll just have to be me. And Josh'll have to like it.'

She flicked white dust off her shoulders, her arms, her bust, then picked up her carryall and headed out toward the pool, then across the little bridge to the terrace that adjoined the house.

The area had been transformed while she'd been in the bathroom. Candles burned in hurricane lamps all around, and the table had been beautifully set, as always, with a crisp linen cloth and napkins. Provençal plates, shiny silver, and crystal wine goblets. A potted orchid sat in the middle of the table, its abundance of small, delicate blooms cascading down onto the table. She walked over to take a closer look. The flowers made her want to reach out and stroke them.

'They're real beauties, aren't they?'

She turned and saw Josh, approaching from the house, a bottle of wine in hand.

'They're gorgeous,' she said. 'So fragile-looking.'

'*Barkeria spectabilis*,' he said. 'One of the *Cattleya* Alliance.' He pulled a chair out for her. 'Here, take a seat. Connie's bringing the food in just a minute.'

April sat down in the proffered chair. 'Thanks, Josh,' she said.

He sat down opposite her and filled her glass with wine, then poured some for himself. 'To ... to you, Michelangelo,' he said, lifting his glass. 'I guess that's Michelangel*a*,' he amended, 'and the crazy, beautiful grotto ceiling.'

April smiled and lifted her glass to his. 'And to you,' she replied, 'and beautiful, beautiful orchids.'

They sipped their wine, and Connie came with a tray of food. 'I'm going to let you serve yourselves,' she said, setting the tray on the table, 'because I've got to get going.'

'That's fine, Connie,' Josh said. 'And thanks for sticking around to do all this.'

'That's okay,' she said, smiling at Josh. 'You know that.' With a barely perceptible lift of her chin, she gazed at April, her eyes sleepy-looking, as if they veiled a deep dark secret. 'Have a nice dinner.'

'Thanks, Connie,' April said.

Connie turned and hurried back into the house.

When she was out of earshot, April said, 'Sometimes I think she doesn't really like me very much.'

Josh's eyebrows lifted in surprise. 'Why would you say that?' he asked. He began to serve them from the tray, putting salad on their plates, then chicken, roasted new potatoes, and green beans.

'Thanks,' April said. 'This looks delicious.'

'And it'll taste better than it looks,' Josh said. 'The way she spices things. Anyhow, tell me why you think she doesn't like you.'

'Oh, I don't know,' April replied. 'Just little things. I mean, she's friendly, but a little guarded. I get the feeling she doesn't like our being friends.'

'You mean, you and me?' he asked.

'No, that's not what I mean,' April said. 'Well, maybe that, too.' She laughed lightly. 'I don't think she likes my being friends with Joanna, either. Maybe she feels as if I'm encroaching on her territory or something. I know she and Joanna are very close.'

'Oh, yes,' Josh said. 'You can bet on that. But Joanna has other friends, and Connie doesn't seem to mind.' He began chewing on a piece of fried chicken.

'Well, maybe I'm wrong,' April said with a shrug, 'but I get that feeling. Maybe it's because I'm around nearly all the time, and Joanna and I spend a lot of time together. Time that she might normally spend with Connie.'

Josh stopped eating and looked at her. 'I hadn't really thought about it,' he said, 'but you might have something there. Joanna's always confided in Connie. Connie's always been like a member of the family.'

'I know,' April said. 'And I don't want to ... well ... interfere with that. Especially not now.' She tasted the potatoes. 'Oh, these are fabulous.'

'I told you so,' Josh said with a grin. 'But listen, April,' he said. 'Seriously, I want you to know that you're not interfering in anything. It's only natural that Joanna's been confiding in you. She's taken to you like a fish to water. You know that, and vice versa, I know.'

April nodded. 'Oh, yes,' she agreed.

'That's what I mean,' Josh said. 'So don't worry about it. Believe you me, Connie can handle it. She may be petite, but she's got really thick hide. It's just that Joanna has found a sort of sister in you, and I'm truly grateful for that.'

April smiled. 'I am, too,' she said. 'I haven't had a friend like her since ... well, I don't think ever in my life.

Not like Joanna.' She paused and took a deep breath. She felt tears threaten, and she certainly didn't want to cry. Not in front of Josh. She quickly picked up her glass and sipped her wine, aware of Josh watching her from across the table.

Joanna decided to check her makeup one last time before the dinner party. She flipped on the light in the luxurious marble and mirror bathroom and was startled as always by the multitude of reflections that bounced back at her. All of herself. The scent of gardenias was cloying, from the three bushes that decorated the enormous length of the vanity. Edging up to the mirror over one of the twin gold sinks, she looked closely at herself.

Not bad, she thought, leaning back again. *No, not bad at all. I do seem to have a glow about me.* She smiled ruefully. *A glow of life and health? Ha!*

She leaned in closer to the mirror again. *But . . . I could use just a tad more blusher.* She reached over for her little compact and lightly brushed another hint of Givenchy's Sunset onto her cheekbones.

She stood back and looked again. *That's fine*, she decided. *There'll be bronzed flesh all around me tonight, so I'll fit in a bit better.* Christina and her friends constantly globe-trotted, worshiping the sun all over the planet, and were generally very darkly tanned the year round. *Too dark*, she thought, *for their own good.* A lot of them paid doctors a fortune to repair the sun damage, then went right back out and did the same thing again.

She snapped the compact closed and stood back, looking at herself full length. She did a quick twirl in front of the mirrors, then stopped. The outfit was beautiful, she thought. It had a big, flowing, golden silk mousseline blouse with long sleeves, worn with a shawl that was made of yards of the same silk. The lightweight wool jersey pants were the same color. All by Chanel. And very much her cup of tea. She knew that she looked elegant, but casually so, as if no effort had been expended in achieving the look.

If they only knew the time it takes to look as if you've spent no time putting yourself together.

She flipped one of her drop earrings with a fingernail and watched it glint in the light. She loved these earrings because Josh, who couldn't really afford them at the time, had somehow scraped together the money and given them to her for a wedding present. They were gold drops, set with small rubies and diamonds. Later, on their first anniversary, he'd given her a matching necklace. She didn't wear them often, but welcomed the chance. Tonight, she'd made a special effort for Christina because her sister always did if she was coming up to one of Josh and Joanna's rare parties, and besides, she wanted to look her best when she gave Christina her news.

She went back out into her bedroom, inhaling the sweet aroma of the beautiful arrangements of fresh flowers. *Christina has tried to make everything perfect,* she thought. She leaned over and stuck her nose in an enormous pink rose. 'Luscious,' she said aloud. The bed had been made with the finest pure linen, and the latest books and magazines had been neatly stacked on a table. There was a mini-fridge, well stocked with all sorts of drinks, a bar, and fresh fruit. The bathroom had been supplied with the gardenias and a host of luxurious toiletries. Christina knew how to pamper guests.

Joanna sat on the edge of the bed and slipped into her high-heeled Manolo Blahnik sandals. She looked at them admiringly, sticking her legs out in front of her and wiggling her toes. They matched her outfit beautifully, and she adored the tiny crystal posies at the toes.

I guess I'm silly, she thought. *To be so concerned about such frivolous things at a time like this, but at least they're . . . distracting.*

She wasn't really looking forward to a dinner party, not tonight, but had decided to be a good sport for her sister. She'd come down to Montecito to tell Christina her news in person – she'd thought it was vital that she did so – and had hoped to have a sister-to-sister tête-à-tête. She'd also reasoned that Christina could use the company since her divorce and, gruesome as her own news was, had hoped that it would distract Christina from her own woes.

Christina had surprised her, however, by being in a cheerful, even expansive, mood. She'd not once mentioned Rudi, her ex-husband, or the loneliness that invariably accompanied the periods between husbands.

What's going on? Joanna wondered idly. She knew her sister well enough to know that something big was percolating in Christina's mind. What else could explain the joie de vivre that had so uncharacteristically taken hold of her sister?

She picked up her handbag at the bedside. Rummaging through it, she took out a small bottle of pills, took off the lid, and jiggled two out. Then she reached for the glass of mineral water on the bedside table and took the pills. *Just a precaution,* she told herself. *In case I feel one of those terrible headaches coming on.*

But I'm fine, she reassured herself. *Really. Only I'd better talk to Christina. And tonight.*

She'd been putting it off ever since she'd gotten here, telling herself that there was plenty of time. But the time had flown by, and now she had to be getting back home. And still she hadn't broached the subject. They'd been so busy doing a thousand things, and besides, Christina had seemed so happy and excited that Joanna didn't want to upset her.

There was a soft knock at the bedroom door, and Joanna walked over and opened it.

'Are you ready, darling?' Christina asked, looking into the room with wide, worried eyes.

'Yes,' Joanna said. 'I'm ready.'

'Oh, you look beautiful!' Christina exclaimed, coming into the bedroom. 'Absolutely beautiful! I don't know how you do it. Without even half trying. Not like me, spending hours and hours, working myself half to death, just trying to look presentable.'

Joanna rolled her eyes. 'Christina,' she said mildly, 'you look fabulous and you know it. But if you're fishing for compliments, you've come to the right place. You really do look wonderful, and that dress looks like it was made for you.'

'It was,' Christina exclaimed. 'By Josephus Thimister, in Paris. It took four – not the usual three, darling, but four – fittings.' She swirled around in the exquisite floor-length gown, then stood looking at Joanna. 'Divine, isn't it?'

'Breathtaking,' Joanna said. And she really meant it. The dress was an artful blend of tatters, made of silk and tulle in palest pink, almost flesh-toned. Christina had gilded the lily with huge diamond earrings, a diamond necklace, and diamond bracelets and rings.

'Well,' Christina said, tossing her many-shaded blond tresses, 'let's go in, shall we? We can have a little drinkie before the hordes arrive.'

Leading the way, Christina left the bedroom with Joanna following, and they went out to the huge marble living room to await the guests.

The dinner was over and the guests had left. Joanna and Christina were seated in Christina's opulent sunroom, a vast neo-classical space that faced the beautifully lit gardens, the pool, and a cascade of water that fell down the hillside as far as the eye could see.

Joanna thought the room was slightly eerie because of the many marble busts on plinths that lined the walls, and the plethora of statues and fragments of antiquity that were everywhere. *So much cold marble*, she thought. *So many long-dead people. So many body parts.*

Christina looked over at her and could tell that she was anxious to talk. She took a drag off her cigarette. 'Did you enjoy yourself tonight?' she asked, exhaling a plume of smoke.

'Yes,' Joanna said. 'It was amusing, and very different from the dinners I usually go to.'

Christina stared at her for a moment. 'Amusing?' She coughed a laugh. 'Well, I guess *that's* the death knell. You didn't have a good time, did you?'

'I did, Christina,' Joanna exclaimed. 'I just . . . I guess I was just a little distracted, that's all.'

Christina's expression turned serious. 'Don't tell me,' she said, 'you're having trouble with Josh.'

Joanna shook her head. 'No, it's nothing like that,' she said, laughing.

'You can tell me, Joanna,' Christina said, inching closer to her on the sofa. 'I know how men are and, believe me, sister dear, they're all *pigs*.' A thoughtful expression crossed her face momentarily. 'Well . . . most of them anyway,' she amended.

Joanna laughed again. 'No, no, *no!*' she cried merrily. 'You've got it all wrong, Christina. It's got nothing to do with Josh at all.'

'What, then?' Christina asked, exhaling another plume of smoke.

Joanna looked about her. 'Why don't we go out on the terrace?' she said. 'I don't want any of the help to hear me.'

'Seriously?' Christina asked. 'They're making so much noise in the kitchen they couldn't hear a gunshot.'

'This is a deep dark secret, Christina,' Joanna said. 'I would feel a lot more comfortable.'

Christina immediately rose to her feet and extended a hand to Joanna. 'Let's go,' she said. 'You've got me so excited about this secret, I'd walk from here to Santa Barbara to hear it.'

Joanna took her hand and got to her feet, then followed Christina out onto the terrace, where they spread out on adjoining chaise longues. There was a steady breeze, and Joanna relished the feel of it on her skin.

'All right,' Christina said, fighting the breeze to light another cigarette, 'tell me what's going on.'

Joanna looked into Christina's eyes steadily before she spoke. 'What I'm going to tell you must not go further,' she said. 'And I mean it, Christina. Do you promise?'

'You know you can trust me.'

'I mean you can't tell anybody,' Joanna said. 'This has to be like when we were little girls conspiring against Daddy. Only it's a lot more important.'

Christina's eyes went wide with wonder, but she didn't say a word.

'Still promise?' Joanna asked.

Christina nodded slowly. 'Yes,' she said. A sense of dread was coming over her because she'd never seen Joanna in a mood like this before.

Joanna looked into her sister's eyes. 'I'm going to die, Christina,' she said simply.

Christina's body heaved, almost as if she were going to be sick. 'Wh ... wh ... what do you *mean*?' she stammered, the whites of her eyes huge in the near darkness.

'Just what I said,' Joanna said calmly. 'It's brain cancer, and I have a few months at the most.'

Christina's features collapsed into a knot of disbelief, fear, and horror all at once. 'But ... but ... but,' she blubbered, tears beginning to form in her eyes. 'Joanna! You can't mean this!' Her voice was a dramatic, hoarse whisper.

'It's true,' Joanna said, 'and I wanted you to know. Because you're my sister and have a right to know what's going on.'

Christina jumped up from the chaise longue and sat down next to Joanna, pushing her over with her hip, then taking her by the shoulders with her hands. 'Tell me you're lying,' she cried. 'Tell me you're lying.'

Joanna gently took Christina's hands off her shoulders and held them in her own. 'I'm not lying, Christina. I've never been more serious in my life.' She looked up at her sister, who had begun to weep uncontrollably. 'I hate for you to have to know,' she said, 'but I had to tell you.'

Christina's hands jerked spastically within Joanna's, and she choked back her tears. 'But what about Josh?' she whispered. 'Does he know?'

Joanna nodded. 'Yes,' she said. 'And I'm going to tell you what I told him. I want everything to be as normal as possible till the end. Can you understand that?'

'Normal?' Christina burst out.

'Yes,' Joanna said, looking with steely eyes at her sister. 'As normal as possible. For my sake.'

Christina stared at her for a moment. 'I guess I understand,' she finally said.

'I'm asking us all to be very strong,' Joanna said, 'and I know it's difficult.'

Christina drew herself up and looked at her sister. Her eyes burned bright with tears. 'You know I can be strong!' she said. 'You know that no matter what comes along, no matter what a mess my life always is, deep down inside, I'm as strong as an ox! I'll do anything I can for you!'

Joanna pushed herself up and put an arm around Christina's shoulder, then planted a kiss on her cheek. 'I know you will,' she said. 'And I love you for it.'

Christina hugged her close to her. 'If you need any help, any help at all, Joanna, I'll be there,' she whispered.

As if the breeze had caught her words and then brought them back to her like an echo, Christina wondered whether or not she meant them. She squeezed her eyes shut and tried to clear her mind. *I don't know,* she thought with confusion. *I don't know what I feel anymore. I don't know what I really think. I have to think of myself . . . of Peter . . .*

Josh took a sip of his wine and looked across the table at April. 'I'm like you,' he said. 'I've never had a friend like Joanna, either.'

April heard the wistful note in his voice, and hoped that she hadn't steered the conversation in a painful direction.

'Joanna could've had almost anything or anybody, but—'

'*You* were for her,' April said, pointing a finger at him.

Josh smiled a little sadly. 'You bet,' he said. '*We* were for each other.' He looked off into the distance a moment, then returned his gaze to April.

'It was like a miracle,' he continued. 'When Joanna and I met, I didn't have a thing,' he said. 'Nothing but the job her father had given me. Maybe two dollars left over at the end of the week.' He laughed. 'But it didn't matter at all. Not to Joanna. She was beautiful and fun and imaginative and creative. And she believed in me. God, we've been happy.'

He stared off into the distance again, and April saw the anguish that came into his eyes.

'I've thought you were the luckiest couple I've ever met,' April said, trying to fill in the silence. 'Since the very first time I met you.'

He drew his gaze back in and looked at her. 'Did you?' he asked. 'Really?'

'Yes,' she said, noticing that his eyes were shining with unshed tears. 'You both seemed so good for each other. Still do. Like everything I ever wanted. Everything *most* people want.'

Josh looked into her eyes, and realized that she meant it. At the same time he understood that she was lonely, or if not exactly lonely, then hoping for someone special in her own life.

His heart went out to her, and he reached over and

touched her hand. 'I'm sure the same thing will happen to you, April,' he said. 'You'll end up with the greatest man in the world for you.'

She had almost jerked away when he touched her, but she quickly reminded herself they were friends, after all. Confidants even. And it was completely innocent. Nevertheless, she felt a familiar pinprick of guilt, knowing that she enjoyed the touch of his hand upon hers.

'A woman like you,' Josh went on, 'is bound to find someone. Just because the first time turned out lousy doesn't mean it won't happen.' His hand lingered on hers for another moment, until it occurred to him that he might have been a little forward. He told himself that it was merely a gesture of compassion and friendship, however, and April didn't seem to mind.

If it weren't for Joanna . . ., he thought. He quickly took his hand away, and a blush of guilt burned his ears. *I shouldn't even be thinking this way*, he told himself. *Especially not with the way things are now.*

'Thanks for the vote of confidence,' April said, forcing a smile. 'I need that sometimes. I guess I don't always feel as good about myself as I should.'

'What was he like?' Josh asked. 'I mean Roger Woodward. Or is that being nosy?'

'No, no,' April said quickly, 'not at all.' She paused, thinking. 'Roger was an adorable shit,' she finally said, her voice full of amusement. 'We were married for four years, but sometimes it seems like it was two weeks. Two fuzzy weeks in my memory.'

'Do you miss Hollywood and all that?' Josh asked.

'It must be so different here after being married to a movie star and all.'

'No,' April said emphatically. 'When we met, Roger was totally unknown and I was an architecture student.' She looked at Josh and shrugged. 'It's an old story. I quit school to support him while he took acting classes and went to auditions. With the promise that when he hit it big, I'd go back to school. But' – she paused and thrust a finger in the air – 'when Roger got the Big Break, he didn't want me out of his sight. Like a lot of actors, he was an egomaniac. Wanted me to be a slave to him and his career. I decided I didn't fit the bill. I wanted to have a career of my own.'

'So that's what caused the split,' he said.

'More or less,' she agreed. 'I started doing work for a friend, designing garden structures, working with tile and stone.' She looked at Josh and grinned. 'And shells.'

He laughed. 'And it's a good thing, too,' he said.

'Anyway, we finally agreed to a divorce,' she went on, 'and I bought the cottage up here with my teensy settlement.'

'Teensy?' he asked. 'Why?'

'Because I didn't want to feel like I owed anybody anything,' she said. 'Especially him. I wanted a life of my own. Anyway, I had a big commission up here, and I really loved it. So . . . the rest, as they say, is history.'

'And I know you're happy in your work,' he said.

She nodded. 'Oh, yes. I love it. There's nothing wrong with being a housewife, but it's not the only thing I want to do. I guess I want to have my cake and eat it too,' she said. 'Because someday I do want a family.' She looked at him. 'Kids and all.'

Josh's expression became sober. 'Yeah,' he said. 'Me too.' He was silent for a moment, his head hanging. Then he looked up at her with curiosity. 'Were you a happy kid?' he asked.

'I . . . I . . . well . . . a lot of the time, I guess,' April stammered. 'I was alone a lot. My mother was divorced and worked, and my father lived on the East Coast, so I almost never saw him.'

'Sounds familiar,' Josh said. 'My parents were divorced, too, and I almost never saw my dad. And my mom worked, so I was left to my own resources a lot.'

'And I bet you were very resourceful, too,' April joked.

He smiled. 'You bet I was,' he replied. 'Always up to something. I guess you'd say I had a very early education about the ways of the world.' He looked at her. 'You too?'

April shrugged. 'Well, yes and no,' she said. 'I had a lot of freedom, but I was always trying to . . . well, I guess you'd say I was always trying to make things *look* better than they were. To make myself better than . . . better than the situation I was living in.'

Josh detected a long-buried pain in her voice and saw it in her bright eyes and immediately identified with it. 'Things weren't so great at home, and you wanted to get away from there? To have a better life for yourself?'

April nodded. 'Yes,' she said. 'To be perfectly honest ...' She laughed and looked at him. 'I hate that expression,' she said, 'because I know I'm about to be lied to if somebody says it.'

Josh grinned. 'That one, or "to tell you the truth." You know you're going to be lied to.' He took a sip of wine and set his glass down. 'Come on,' he said, 'finish what you were saying. I want to know all about you.'

She could see that he really meant what he said, and felt a curious sort of thrill that he would really want to know about her. To know *her*. She looked down at her fingernails, as if studying them. 'Well, I was going to say that I ... I was ashamed of our ... our being poor ... our cheap clothes ... and our cheap little studio apartment in West Hollywood.'

She looked away then and cleared her throat. 'I feel a little guilty now, in retrospect. But I really was ashamed,' she continued. 'We lived so close to Beverly Hills, and most of the kids I knew had bigger houses and fancier cars and beautiful clothes. Sometimes brothers and sisters, too, and sometimes both parents.'

Josh sat staring at her mutely, his face suddenly burning bright red, his teeth clenched in his square jaw, his hand rigid on the glass he held.

April saw the effect her words had had on him and felt acutely embarrassed, as if she had been too personal. She felt a blush rising from the top of her chest, up her neck, and suffusing her face with its heat. She quickly took a sip of her wine, fumbling with the glass.

Oh, my God, she thought. *I've ruined everything*

259

now. This wonderful man was truly interested in me, and I've completely turned him off with my stupid, sad little story. Nobody, but nobody, wants to hear about my dreary past.

Then, through the pulse that beat a violent tattoo against her eardrum, she heard his gentle voice.

'April,' he was saying, 'I think we grew up in the same place.'

She turned and looked at him. All the tension had gone out of his body. Those mesmerizing ultramarine eyes of his bored into hers, and there was a hint of a smile quivering tentatively at the corners of his lips.

'What? . . . I'm . . . I'm sorry,' she stammered. 'What did you say?'

'I said, April,' he continued in a near whisper, 'that we grew up in the same place.'

He astonished her by reaching over and taking one of her hands in his. 'What I mean to say is, we both grew up in shame. We both grew up poor, surrounded by . . . well, what we thought were our betters.' He squeezed her hand again.

Tears, unbidden, sprang into April's eyes, threatening to spill over. She couldn't trust herself to speak.

'I knew there was a reason I took such an instant liking to you,' he said, 'or thought I did. It wasn't just that you and Joanna think so much alike and share the same interests. It was this, this past you carry around with you, that I recognized. Because I identify with it so strongly. I guess I somehow sensed it in you because it's something that's so much a part of me.'

260

'It . . . it is?' she finally uttered.

'You can bet on it,' he said. He picked up his napkin and, reaching across the table, tenderly brushed the tears from her eyes. 'There,' he said, 'that's better, isn't it?'

'Yes,' she said, wishing that she could give him a hug. 'Much better. I . . . I feel like such a fool, Josh,' she said. 'I'm sorry. I feel like I've made a scene and—'

'Hush,' he said quietly. 'You haven't made a scene at all. You simply told me something about yourself that's painful. And you happened to tell just the right person.' He beamed across the table, his perfect teeth dazzling in the candlelight. 'So cheer up,' he said. 'You're in good company.'

'Oh, Josh,' she said. 'Oh, thank you. I thought I'd made a terrible mistake, being too personal. It's just that you and Joanna have been so wonderful and warm and have shared yourselves with me so generously that I sort of got carried away, I guess.'

'You're allowed to be yourself with us, April,' he said. 'You're safe here, remember that.'

'Thanks, Josh,' she said. 'Oh, I feel like an idiot!' She laughed lightly.

'Because you've exposed a little of yourself,' he said. 'You've been honest. That's all. Now you can appreciate what it took out of me to confide in you about Joanna.'

They both laughed, delighting in their understanding of one another, this common ground that had proved to be a link between them.

261

'I guess one reason I was drawn to Joanna and her father,' he said seriously, 'was that their world was so different from mine, so beautiful, so ordered and calm. The orchids, too. A way to make the world more beautiful, and with my hybridizing maybe even create a new beautiful specimen.'

'I know what you mean,' she said. 'Absolutely. It's why I was drawn to architecture and design, and why I do my botanical drawings and my garden work. And now grotto work.' She smiled. 'I've been trying to make order out of chaos, trying in a way to make things more beautiful, and all the while—' She shrugged.

'You felt like an outsider sometimes?' he suggested.

April nodded again. 'Exactly. Like I don't really belong. Anywhere, really. Like the rest of the world is part of this club that I'm not part of. Sometimes I bridge the gap quite well.' She looked at him. 'Like when I met you and Joanna.'

Josh smiled. 'It's always been the same with me,' he said. 'And I think it goes right back to the shame and so on.'

April saw the wisdom of his words at once. 'I'd have to agree with you,' she said. 'So ... we make the best of it!' She looked at him with a bright-eyed expression.

Josh's eyes lingered on her for a long moment, then he abruptly clapped his hands together. 'Dessert!' he said. 'I hope you've got room for more.'

'More?' April said.

'Yep. Connie's special flan,' he said. 'And you keep

your seat while I run up to the house and get it, okay?'

April watched his tall, lithe body walk up to the house and at that precise moment knew that she had fallen in love with him. She couldn't deny it to herself, shameful though it made her feel.

I'm hopelessly in love with Josh Lawrence, she thought. *A new friend. And worse, my new best friend's husband. My sick—*

She couldn't finish the thought. Guilt washed over her. *I can't do this to Joanna,* she thought. *Or Josh. Or myself. I'll have to discourage any contact outside of work. Especially when Joanna isn't around.*

Suddenly she wished that Joanna hadn't gone to Montecito, as much as she relished her time with Josh. She quickly poured a splash of wine in her glass and took a large swallow. Its taste was no longer quite so delicious on her palate. Now it tasted of guilt and remorse, of a longing unfulfilled, of awful treachery and betrayal.

When Josh returned with their dessert, Connie's flan, she smiled, performing as best she could under the circumstances.

Josh looked at her with an almost wary expression for a moment, then returned her smile. He had experienced a frightening realization in the kitchen: He was falling in love with April Woodward. Now he would have to control the powerful urges that drove him toward her, that made him want her so desperately, despite the guilt that he was already experiencing.

Oh, my God! he thought. *How could I even think of*

such a thing? Especially considering Joanna's . . . condition.
Nevertheless, the feeling would not go away. It was
there, real, almost a tangible feeling that could not
be denied.

17

April had filled the popcorn maker and positioned the large metal pot under its spout, waiting for the big, fluffy kernels to come spewing out. Woody was standing at the stove, melting a lot of butter, she noticed, to pour over the top. The popcorn popper had a little metal cup for melting butter, but it didn't hold enough.

She laughed over the noise of the popper.

Woody looked over at her and grinned. 'What's so funny?' he asked.

'Has it ever occurred to you how silly it is to have this expensive air popper when we're just going to pour a ton of butter over the popcorn anyway?' she asked.

'Yeah,' he said, 'it's pretty silly. Except the popper's really great.'

'There is that,' she agreed. Popcorn had begun to shoot out of the spout like BBs, and April couldn't resist trying a few. Lousy, she decided, without all that yummy butter and salt.

When she'd come home from work, there'd been a message on her machine to please call Woody. She was still a little miffed with him because of his stupid comments that time he'd seen her talking to Josh, but she decided to let bygones be bygones. They'd worked together very efficiently, if a bit quietly, since then, and April thought it was time to clear the air. Besides, Woody's voice on the machine had been endearingly contrite and pleading. But, she told herself, she was definitely going to have to talk with him about his obnoxious behavior.

She'd called him, and he'd apologized, then he'd begged to take her out to dinner. April had said no, that she was going to have a quick nibble at home, take a bath, then pile up in bed and watch something on television. That was when Woody had proposed one of their popcorn-and-video nights, which he knew April found almost irresistible.

'You win,' she'd told him. 'Come on over in an hour or so. Just don't bring one of those videos with tons of blood and violence. And I mean it. I'm not in the mood to see one of those tonight. Not even for a goof, Woody.'

Now she was glad he was here – *and* his warm, sweet

self instead of the sneering macho creep she'd seen at Josh and Joanna's. And he'd brought *Ridicule*, a French movie she'd yet to see, but had heard had beautiful costumes. *He really does feel contrite*, she thought with amusement. *Otherwise, he'd never have shown up with this movie.*

The popper had spewed out its last popcorn, and she looked at the big pot, then turned to Woody. 'Do you think this is enough?' she asked.

Woody looked over at the pot and shook his shaggy black curls. 'No way, April,' he said, grinning. 'For two people? With a good movie to watch?'

She smiled. 'Thought so,' she said. She got out another big pot and filled the machine again to pop some more. 'You want to go ahead and butter and salt this while it's hot, Woody?'

'Yeah,' he said. 'Will do. Then I'll put on some more butter.' He got the pot, poured butter over it, dashed lots of salt on, then put the lid on and began shaking it, doing a sort of Carmen Miranda with castanets.

'You're so silly,' April said, laughing.

He finished his act and set the pot down. 'I know,' he said.

'What got into you, anyway?' April asked. 'Up at Joanna and Josh's that time? Making those stupid remarks.'

'Uh . . . I don't know, April,' he said, putting more butter on to melt. 'I just think those people are really snakes in the grass, you know?'

'That is ridiculous, Woody,' she said. The popper

began firing out popcorn, and she made certain the pot was in position. 'In fact, they are super-nice people.'

Woody shrugged. 'Have it your way, April,' he said, 'but I still wouldn't trust 'em. She's like this spoiled rich bitch, tooling around in her old Mercedes like she owns the world, and he's just like her. An arrogant bastard. Tooling around, flexing his muscles, teasing the local babes.'

April looked at him in amazement. It was as if they weren't even talking about the same people. 'You are demented, Woody,' she said. 'That's just plain crazy. I don't know whether they're rich or not. I guess they're well fixed, at least, but they don't act spoiled or arrogant. And Josh Lawrence wouldn't run around teasing the local babes, either. They're the most devoted couple I've ever seen.'

He slid her a look out of the corner of his eye. 'Like I said, have it your way, April,' he said off-handedly. 'But I know different.'

He turned the burner off and rolled the melted butter around in the pot, then looked over at her. 'I could tell you stories I've heard about her sister that'd make your hair stand on end,' he said.

April stared at him for a moment. 'Well, I don't know anything about her,' she said, 'but I do know them. And you're wrong about them, Woody.'

She could envision Joanna and thought of her extraordinary generosity of spirit, of her loving friendship, and of her illness, and she couldn't listen to another word of his stupid allegations.

'Woody,' she said, her eyes fiery, 'I don't want to discuss this again. Ever. And I don't want to hear another word against either one of them. Hear me?'

His expression changed to one of irritation. 'If I'm so wrong, April,' he said, 'then why was Josh Lawrence looking all goo-goo-eyed at you? Huh?'

'That's ridiculous,' she said defensively. 'He was telling me about some problems at work, that's all.'

'That's not the way it looked,' Woody said. 'And I'm not blind, April. You know? That guy's creaming over you.'

'Oh, *you*,' she said. 'I said I don't want to discuss it anymore, and I meant it. So let's forget it. You're not rational about them.'

'Okay,' he said. 'Okay. But you asked me my opinion, and I gave it to you.'

The popper shut off, the last few pieces of popcorn trickling out of the spout spastically. 'Here,' she said, 'more to salt and butter.'

They walked into the bedroom and piled up on her big bed with lots of pillows, putting the popcorn bowls between them. April idly watched as Woody fed the tape into the VCR, but her mind was elsewhere. Woody might be an overgrown boy in many ways, but he was not stupid, she reminded herself.

He was a fairly astute observer, as a matter of fact, and she worried about what he'd seen. The intimacy he'd detected between her and Josh when he'd seen them talking. If he'd sensed it, then wouldn't Connie? And wouldn't . . . Joanna?

April felt a sick feeling in the pit of her stomach, and reached into a bowl of popcorn and took a handful, then began chewing on it, but not really tasting it. She realized what her feelings for Josh Lawrence were – there was no denying them – but she hoped they weren't too obvious. As for the way Josh felt about her, could Woody be right? Did Josh really feel as strongly about her as Woody suspected?

She sensed that the bond between them was becoming more than friendship, and that he was enjoying it as much as she was. But she wasn't certain, and she didn't want to think about it right now. Deep down inside, she felt little warning bells going off. She was afraid that Woody might have sensed something that others could, something that could break Joanna's heart. That, April decided, she couldn't live with. No matter what.

'Ready?' Woody asked, snapping her out of her reverie.

She nodded. 'Ready,' she said. 'In fact, I have a head start on the popcorn.'

Later, as they lay together, Woody's eyes slid sideways, observing April, who was watching the movie as if hypnotized. She was eating it up, like the popcorn, enjoying every minute of it, he thought. He felt gratified, even though the movie didn't particularly appeal to him. He liked pleasing April, but then, he enjoyed pleasing any woman. Well, any woman he wanted, that is. Any woman he found desirable. And he thought April was one of the most desirable women he'd ever met. She was a challenge, too, and he liked that. His eyes moved down to her breasts, outlined against the T-shirt she was wearing. *She'll come around,* he thought. *I know she will. They all do for Woody Pearlman, don't they?*

18

Josh walked slowly through the greenhouse, Carl at his heels, looking from side to side, eyeballing the replacements for the fungal-infected *Phalaenopsis* that had been destroyed. They had finally arrived, at great expense, but they were of excellent stock. Unfortunately, when the fungus had attacked, there was enough damage that the plants couldn't be nursed back to health in time to fill the orders they had. They'd decided to purchase very expensive stock just so they wouldn't lose orders and potentially damage future business.

'I still think we need to spring for more security,' Carl said. 'Strategically placed video cameras.'

Josh shook his head. 'I don't think we'll need to, Carl,'

he said. 'We've got Miguel and the guard dog at night now. And during the daytime somebody on the staff has to be with anybody that comes in. Like an escort.'

'Yeah, but Josh,' Carl argued, 'we were requiring escorts when somebody planted the damn fungus. And I don't know how much good Miguel and a guard dog are going to be. Why are you being so stubborn about this?'

'I'm not being stubborn, Carl,' he replied testily. 'You know, we could've gotten some stock that had already been contaminated and just took a while to show up,' he went on. 'That's a real possibility. And besides, we didn't have *everybody* go through with an escort like we do now.'

'No,' Carl agreed, 'not everybody. But it's much more likely that this was done at night. You know what I think?'

'What?' Josh asked.

'I think you're still trying to deny that anybody would deliberately do this,' Carl said. 'And you're fooling yourself if you don't think that this is sabotage.'

Josh didn't want to tell Carl that he'd hardly given the problem any thought since Joanna's news. He'd found it difficult to concentrate on business.

'Josh! Josh!' It was Luna calling him from the other end of the greenhouse. He and Carl saw her running toward them, her large breasts heaving against her tight-fitting blouse, her stiletto-heeled shoes kicking up sawdust and gravel. Carl laughed, and Josh couldn't help but smile.

She reached them breathlessly.

'What is it, Luna?' Josh asked.

'Mr What . . . what's . . . his name,' she sputtered. 'He's . . . in the . . . office.'

'Who?' Josh asked. *Luna's information leaves something to be desired*, he thought with amusement.

'That . . . that Japanese man!' she blurted.

'Which one?' Josh asked, growing excited.

'You know,' she said. 'He has black hair and . . . oh, he's one of the really rich ones.'

'Why didn't you page me?' Josh asked. 'Or use the intercom?'

'I was too excited!' she said. 'He said he must see you *now*!'

'Thanks, Luna,' he said. *It has to be Mr Hara*, he thought. *Back to buy some more orchids. Or maybe even Mr Nakamura.* He took off at a fast pace, practically running, heading toward the office.

Josh leaned back in his desk chair, staring happily at the ceiling. *There may be a God after all*, he thought. Mr Nakamura had spent a small fortune, enough even to cover the costs of replacing the lost *Phalaenopsis* stock with a little bit left over. Visits like this were becoming more frequent occurrences as he and the nursery gained an international reputation for their stock, but Josh had still not grown used to it. He certainly hadn't been spoiled by it.

I've got to tell Joanna, he thought. *Right away*.

He swung forward in his chair and, picking up the

receiver, dialed the number. Connie picked up after three rings.

'Connie,' he said. 'Let me speak to Joanna, please.'

'She's not here, Josh,' Connie replied.

'Where is she?' he asked. 'I've got to chase her down.'

'I don't know,' Connie said.

'You don't know?' he said, bewildered. *Goddamn it,* he thought. *Joanna shouldn't be off alone without our knowing where she is. What if—*

'All I know,' Connie said in exasperation, 'is that she's acting really strange.'

'What do you mean?' Josh asked. He felt a chill run up his spine.

'Ooooh, I don't know.'

'Come on, Connie,' Josh cajoled. 'Tell me what you know.'

'Well, like when I went down to clean the beach place,' Connie said.

'What about it?' Josh asked.

'You wouldn't have believed it.'

'Why?' Josh asked. 'Come on, Connie. Tell me.'

'It was a *wreck*,' Connie spat, 'and I mean a *wreck*.'

'How do you mean, a wreck?' Josh asked, becoming increasingly distressed.

'Oh, you know,' she said. 'Empty wine bottles all over the place. Half-empty bottles sitting out uncorked. The bed looked like somebody had died in it. Sand and stuff all over the floor.' She paused, and when she spoke again her voice was angry. 'It took me hours to straighten up.'

Josh felt a knot twist in the pit of his stomach, and beads of sweat broke out on his forehead. He felt sick. He knew that Joanna must have been there sometime in the last few weeks, licking her wounds most likely. All alone. It was too terrible to contemplate.

When he found his voice, he said, 'I'm sorry about that, Connie. You should've told me.'

'I didn't want to worry you.'

'Anyhow, I'm coming on home,' he said. 'I'll see you there in a while.' He decided that it was probably time that they told Connie what was going on so that she would understand Joanna's unusual behavior.

'Okay,' she said, then hung up.

Josh sat at his desk, staring off into space. How a few minutes could change your mood, he thought. The elation over Mr Nakamura's visit had drained away completely, replaced by a looming sense of fate that threw everything else in shadow.

What difference does anything *make now?* he asked himself. *Except Joanna.*

He got to his feet and went out into the reception area. 'Luna,' he said. 'I'm leaving for the day. If anything comes up, you can get me at home.'

Luna, telephone receiver plastered to her ear as usual, put her hand over it for a moment. 'Okay, boss,' she said with a smile. 'Don't worry about anything here.' She removed her hand from the receiver and immediately began speaking in rapid-fire Spanish again.

Out in the parking lot, Josh hopped into his big Land Cruiser and headed out to the highway, toward home.

Rolling north in the heat, he glanced over at the Rossi brothers' property on his right.

'Goddamn,' he cursed aloud. He almost slammed on the brakes and pulled into their lot, but then thought better of it. He cruised on north, fresh worries plaguing his already overburdened mind. Carl's truck – unmistakably Carl's – had been parked right out in front of the Rossi offices.

What the hell is Carl doing there? he asked himself. *And if he has some legitimate business for going there – although I can't imagine what it could be – then why didn't he tell me about it?*

Shit! He slammed the steering wheel in anger, and only succeeded in hurting the palm of his hand. *Is the whole world turning against me?*

Josh pulled into the courtyard at home and parked the Land Cruiser. Joanna's car wasn't there, but he saw April's Jeep Wagoneer and Connie's van. He went in through the mud room, slipped out of his dirty boots and put on clean Top-Siders, then went to the kitchen.

Connie looked up at him from a kitchen counter, where she was busy making something. 'Hi,' she said. Her eyes held that sleepy expression that he knew indicated that she would not discuss anything further with him.

'Hey, Connie,' he replied. 'I guess you haven't heard from Joanna.'

'No,' she said, shrugging. 'She's still not here. Just

that April down at the stable and the man working with her.'

Josh heard the disdain in Connie's voice. He wondered why she didn't like April – was it jealousy? He still wasn't sure, but he wasn't going to pursue that right now.

He went out through the French doors and headed across the terrace and down through the apple orchard to the old stable. He poked his head through an open door and looked around. April was up on a scaffold, and her partner was working on the south-facing wall. Dozens of boxes of shells and pebbles, many of which he recognized, lined the north wall, some open, some shut.

'Hey,' he said. 'How's it going with you two?'

'Josh,' April said, pulling down her paper face mask. 'It's going great.' She hurried down from the scaffold and snapped off her latex gloves.

Woody looked over from the south wall, where he was fitting small pieces of mother-of-pearl into an area of background. He watched the two of them for a moment, then turned silently back to his work.

'Look,' April said excitedly. 'The ceiling's finally almost finished.'

Josh looked up and surveyed the finished work for the first time. He was stunned by the beauty of the design. The ceiling was a night sky complete with many of the constellations, all of it worked in seashells and pebbles.

'My God,' he said. 'It's really beautiful, April. I had

no idea it was going to be so intricate. And the colors are spectacular.'

'Thanks,' she said. 'It's really coming together now, isn't it?'

He shook his head. 'You can say that again.' He looked at her. 'Has Joanna seen this yet?' he asked.

'No,' April said. 'She saw it when she got back from Montecito, but not since then. I can't wait for her to get home. I think she's really going to be pleased.'

'I know she will be,' Josh replied. 'I've never seen anything like it. Abalone, trochus, scallops, mother-of-pearl, cowries, cones, spiders, turbos, cockles, even thorny oysters. You've worked in shells I would never have imagined.'

'I didn't know you knew so much about them,' she said.

'He's the one who got me so interested in sea-shells in the first place,' came Joanna's voice from behind them.

They both turned to see her standing just inside the doorway, smiling happily at the two of them. She was carrying shopping bags, which she eased down onto the floor, and walked over to them.

'Hello, darling,' she said, kissing Josh on the cheek.

'Hi, beautiful,' he said, glad to see her.

Joanna brushed April's cheek with a kiss and hugged her. Then she backed away and looked up at the ceiling for a long time.

'April,' she said, turning to her in almost a swoon of delight, 'you are nothing less than a magician! A sorceress! This is already so beautiful I want to move into the room. It's . . . heavenly!'

April laughed. 'Well, that's the idea with the ceiling.'

'You know what I mean,' Joanna said, smiling. 'It's really perfect. Now I long to see the rest of it finished.'

'We're working as fast as we can,' April said. 'Oh, by the way, Joanna, the plaster busts for the wall niches came today. They're over there, lined up with the boxes of shells, if you want to see them now.'

Joanna abruptly looked over at Josh. Her face was contorted in pain. 'I . . . I'm going to go lie down,' she said.

Without another word, she swept out of the room and disappeared, leaving her shopping bags behind.

Woody turned and watched her leave with a smirk. *Yeah, I bet she's got to lie down*, he thought. *Seeing the two of them together's put her to bed. Serves her right.*

April looked at Josh, whose face held a worried expression. 'I'd better check on her,' he said quietly.

'Tell her I hope she feels better,' April said, herself alarmed by Joanna's sudden departure. It wasn't like her, April thought. No, not at all.

Josh opened the bedroom door and saw that the room was in complete darkness. The curtains were shut, and all the lights were out. He could just make out Joanna, lying on top of the bed in a short silk bathrobe. He approached the bed quietly and sat down next to her.

'Are you all right?' he asked worriedly.

'Yes,' she said. 'I just need to rest.'

'You're sure?' he persisted.

'It's nothing,' she assured him. 'Don't worry, Josh, I
. . . I really just need to be alone and rest.'

'Okay,' he said, getting the message. 'I'll be here if
you need anything.'

'Thanks,' she murmured.

He left the darkened room and shut the door behind
him. Suddenly, he leaned against the wall in the hallway, his heart heaving in his chest. *Oh, God, he prayed.
Please don't make her suffer.*

Fear, like a palpable force, gripped him in its claws
and held him there, immobilized, for what seemed an
eternity. Finally, weak from its clutches, he went into
his study, where he poured himself a straight scotch
and spread out on the daybed, unable to concentrate,
exhausted by the terrible feeling that had begun to eat
away at him.

He felt so alone.

19

Joanna looked through the open doorway to the grotto and saw that April and Woody were busily working away, applying shells to cement. She didn't want to interfere, but just to watch them work for a while. There had been more and more days recently when she'd simply had to rest, reading in her bedroom or the conservatory, storing up her energy in order to perform only those tasks she really had to do. So she hadn't been down here for several days and was anxious to see the progress.

'April?' she asked.

'Oh, Joanna,' April cried, turning her head toward the door. 'Come on in, stranger. I didn't realize you were down here.' She was up on the scaffolding, working in a corner where wall met wall.

'Do you mind if I watch a little while?' Joanna asked. 'I promise to be quiet as a mouse. I would just love to watch it coming together a bit.'

'Of course, that's fine,' April said. 'Pull up a chair and get comfortable. Just keep a little distance so you don't get covered up with cement dust.'

'Thanks,' Joanna said. 'You won't even know I'm here.'

Woody glanced at her out of the corner of his eye, but didn't say anything. He continued filling in background space on a wall.

Joanna scraped a little bistro chair over to a corner and sat down, looking around her. Happily, the work on the grotto was progressing on schedule, and there were days when the dramatic effects of all the hard work put into it could easily be seen. Sometimes, though, days passed, even a week at a stretch, when the tedious and time-consuming work didn't seem to accomplish anything.

Today, Joanna was happy to discover, was one of those great days when she could see the work coming together. As she looked about the room, she felt a sense of joy and fulfillment, of a cherished ambition nearly realized. The ceiling with its constellations was a marvel to behold, and the niches, which would hold fanciful shell-encrusted busts on pedestals, were completely finished. Various kinds of shells had been used to create the effect of fantastic moldings all around the ceiling, the doors, and the niches. April had even created a dado with them, below which the walls appeared to be paneled in a dozen different kinds of precious stones.

She could see where blank spaces had been left. These, she knew, were to be filled in with shell orchids. Joanna had to bite her tongue to keep from enthusing about the work, but she could withhold her praise until lunchtime. April had promised to eat with her today, so she'd discuss it with her then.

April continued working silently, carefully positioning shells, but despite her concentration, she was constantly aware of Joanna's presence. For months Joanna had come and gone quite a bit, coaxing April into having lunch or dinner with her, but her visits had begun to become less frequent in the last two or three weeks. April knew why, of course, but did her best to act unconcerned, because she knew that that's the way Joanna wanted it to be.

She also realized that Joanna was becoming impatient, but realized, of course, what her anxiousness stemmed from: She feared that she wouldn't live to see the grotto complete. But there was nothing April could do to hurry the project along. She was working as hard as she could, working overtime, in fact, hoping against hope that she would finish in time.

She placed the last shell in her box into position, held it there a moment, then let go and sat back on her haunches to eye the line she'd created. It was fine, she decided. Straight as could be.

'Woody,' she said, 'would you be an angel and hand me another box of the leafy carditas, please?'

'Just a second, April,' he replied, carefully positioning a piece of mother-of-pearl in a background spot.

April looked down at him, where he sat in a lotus position facing the wall, working diligently, covered from head to toe with cement and fine white cement dust, like herself. She smiled at his comical appearance. They'd complained to one another about having to wash their hair every night, but they'd decided that was preferable to wearing a shower cap all day.

'Hey, Woody,' she said, 'those beautiful black curls of yours are getting gray before their time.'

He laughed. 'Yeah, well, I wouldn't talk if I were you. That blond hair of yours is looking pretty much like an old lady's,' he said. He shifted around and got to his feet, then found the box of leafy carditas and took them over to the scaffolding and handed them up to her.

'Thanks, Woody,' she said, placing the box on the boards where she sat.

'No problem,' he replied. He went back to his spot on the floor, assuming the lotus position again and getting back to work.

Joanna sat for a long time, watching them from the corner. They had an easy camaraderie that she'd noticed ever since Woody had first started helping April, and they worked together very well, so attuned to each other that they almost seemed to have a secret code between them.

Like the secret language of very close friends, she thought. *Or lovers.*

She had to admit that Woody was very attractive –

physically, at least – and she could see that he would have great appeal for a lot of women. Especially women who were looking for good sex with a few laughs, lots of muscles, and no commitment.

After watching the two of them for several weeks, she'd seen that he was extremely protective of April, and she sensed that he was even jealous of her relationships with other people. One thing was for sure, Joanna thought. If Woody wasn't in love with April, then he wanted desperately to add her to his list of conquests and, Joanna believed, he would play the big brother for a very long time just to try to get her in the sack.

In the course of her conversations with April, Joanna saw that April was almost convinced that Woody really was a big brother she liked to have around. She'd laughed at his antics with other women, not believing that she herself could be hurt by him. But Joanna was afraid that April would be deeply hurt by him, and wondered what to do about it. Plus, she told herself, she didn't want anything or anybody to interfere with April's friendship with her – or Josh.

'You've been so quiet,' April said, approaching Joanna from across the room.

Joanna almost jerked, so lost in thought she'd been. She laughed. 'I told you I'd be a little mouse,' she said. 'The work was going so beautifully I didn't want to interrupt.'

April looked around, smiling. 'It really *is* coming along wonderfully,' she said with pride in her voice.

'You're still having lunch with me?' Joanna asked.

'Yes,' April said. 'I'm just going to run up to the bathroom at the pool house and clean up a little bit.'

'Okay,' Joanna said. 'I'll meet you on the terrace. I think I'll sit here for a few more minutes and just soak up some of the atmosphere that's beginning to develop.'

'You're so funny,' April said with amusement, 'but I know exactly what you mean. See you in a few minutes.' She turned and started out the door, then turned around. 'Woody,' she said, 'I'll see you in an hour or so.'

'You got it,' he said. He stood across the room from Joanna, busily wiping his hands off on a rag.

Joanna watched him for a minute, then cleared her voice. 'Do you go home for lunch, Woody?' she asked. They were still playing the game that they'd never met each other before.

Woody continued cleaning his hands and didn't look up. 'Sometimes,' he replied. 'But usually I grab something close by here.'

'You'll have to stay for lunch one day,' Joanna said, more out of politeness than sincerity.

'Ah, I usually meet a friend for lunch,' Woody said. 'But thanks.' He threw down the rag. 'See ya,' he said, sauntering out the door.

You bet you will, Joanna thought, watching his cocky strut up the hill.

20

Christina arrived first, creeping through the thick fog into the lot and parking at the south end as Peter had instructed her to. Looking about, she saw only one or two other cars parked here.

She got out and slowly made her way through the thick swirls of fog over to the wooden ramp that led up the dunes to the cedar-shingled condominiums. Luckily, his was the southernmost, because she couldn't see where the buildings began and ended.

Jesus, she thought, *why does it always have to be like this? Meeting in such spooky places.* But of course she knew the answer to that question. They couldn't be seen together. Thus, today they were meeting in a condo he kept on the beach as a secret hideaway.

Huge eucalyptus trees and wind-tortured pines shivered loudly in the heavy breeze coming off the ocean, and sand, fine and gritty, blew up at her face, stinging it ferociously.

My God, she thought, pulling a silk scarf out of her handbag and holding it up in front of her face. *This is plain creepy.* But she didn't care. Not today. Because today she was going to meet Peter, and she could hardly wait.

She carefully started up the wooden ramp, holding on to the old railing for support, her high heels making the steep climb that much more difficult. *I should have worn flats*, she thought. But then she nixed that idea. *No, Peter likes to see me all dressed up. He thinks I look classy like that.* His word, *classy*. She almost giggled aloud, thinking that what they were doing was anything but.

At the top of the ramp, the fog was even thicker. She stood there, the scarf still held protectively up to her face, catching her breath, her eyes searching for the sign that would direct her to the correct condo.

I'll never find it in this fog. Then she made out a small wooden plaque with weathered brass numbers and arrows on it, almost right in front of her. The arrow pointed to her right for unit 803. She followed the arrow until she reached the sign indicating 803, at the top of a flight of wooden stairs.

Christina took a deep breath, then started up, her eyes on the aqua-painted door above. She reached the top and stopped, cursing the cigarettes she smoked and her thirty-six-year-old lungs. Then she went down the walkway and, standing on her tiptoes, reached up, her fingers searching the top of the light fixture next to the door for the key.

Yes, there it is, she thought. *The key to nirvana.*

She let herself in, taking the silk scarf away from her face at the same time, then closed the door behind her. Kicking off her murderous high-heeled shoes, she looked around her. Straight ahead, all the way through the dining area, the kitchen, and the living room, she could see a huge floor-to-ceiling window that looked out over the sea. Today the view was exclusively of the grays and whites of the fog.

She picked up her shoes and walked through to the living room. The condo was decorated entirely in shades of white and furnished with big comfortable modern sofas and chairs, also white, and inexpensive wooden tables. *Boring but serviceable*, she thought. Dropping her shoes in front of the sofa, she idly flung the silk scarf over a shoulder, then walked to the window and stood in front of it, trying to see if she could make out the sea at all.

The fog was almost mesmerizing, she thought. She stood there, all sense of time suspended, her eyes searching to no avail.

It occurred to her that the old beach shack that Joanna and Josh had fixed up so beautifully was just down this beach, one of the few surviving old-fashioned cottages that used to be sprinkled along the coast. Now huge developers and agribusinesses – owned by smart men like Peter – had swallowed up nearly all the land

291

hereabouts. *The old beach shack must be worth a fortune*, she thought, still looking toward the invisible sea.

She almost screamed aloud as she felt huge arms encircle her and the warmth of a large body press firmly against hers. She could feel his breath on her neck. Almost as quickly as he had crept up behind her, wrapping those powerful arms around her, she realized that it was Peter.

'Oh, my God,' she wailed, her knees suddenly weak, her body beginning to shake. 'You – you—!'

'Scare you, baby?' he asked quietly, his mouth going to the nape of her neck, his tongue licking the wind-driven salt and sand that coated her from head to toe.

'Oh . . . Jesus . . . Peter!' she gasped. 'Who wouldn't be? You could've been a . . . a crazy rapist or something. There's nobody around out here.'

He laughed, turning her roughly to face him, his obsidian eyes staring hard into hers. 'Yeah, but I wasn't, was I?' he said.

She looked up into his eyes and knew that he was enjoying her fear. 'I – I—'

He jerked her harder against his huge muscular body and kissed her on the mouth. Ravenously, fiendishly. Then pulled back, leaving her gasping, and whispered, 'You like it, don't you, baby?'

Christina felt her body begin to quiver again, but not from the shock this time. It was as if something in the deepest, darkest recesses of her being was responding to him of its own accord. And it was something over which she had no control. She could feel a wetness between her thighs, and her pulse had begun to race. She was breathy with desire now, and any reservations she might have had were gone, as if picked up by the fog swirling at the window behind her and carried away into some netherworld.

'Yes,' she whispered, 'I like it, Peter. Oh, yes. I like it.'

'Yeah, baby,' he said. 'I thought so.'

He pulled the silk scarf from over her shoulder and quickly whipped it into a long blindfold. She watched his adroit movement with fascination. Then, before she realized what he was doing, he had placed it around her head – tight and thick across her eyes – and tied it firmly at the back.

'Peter!' she gasped, her body trembling. 'I can't . . . I can't see a thing! I—'

'Shhh,' he breathed. He grabbed her hands in his and led her across the carpeting into a bedroom.

'What . . . what are you doing?' she almost whimpered.

'Shhh,' he breathed again. 'You're going to like it, babe.'

She felt him begin to take her clothes off, quickly and unceremoniously, anxious to get to her naked flesh. When he finished, she stood trembling before him, but she knew that the fear and sexual excitement held her in its thrall.

She heard him undressing himself and wished that she could watch, but sensed that she should remain still.

How she would love to see that magnificently powerful body, every inch of it, gradually exposed to her hungry eyes! How anxious she was to feel it against her again! On her! *In* her!

As if her thought was his command, she felt his hands on her again, running lightly over her breasts, then trailing down her torso to the soft damp mound between her thighs. Then brushing across her buttocks and up her back.

Christina thought she would go crazy with desire but continued to hold her tongue, stifling a gasp of utter pleasure, afraid to interfere with this scenario he had conjured up.

Now his hands were at her breasts again, squeezing them gently, then more firmly, thrumming away at her rosy nipples, lightly at first, then harder and harder, until she thought she couldn't stand the pleasure turning to pain another second. But he abruptly stopped, and she felt his hot, wet mouth on her right breast, his tongue licking it slowly, slowly, then more rapidly as his hand found her mound and stroked it gently before pushing a finger up into her mounting wetness, exploring, massaging, caressing.

'Ah . . . ah . . . ah!' Christina cried, unable to hold her tongue any longer. 'Ah, my God, Peter!' She reached out for his cock, but he grabbed her hands with one of his and held them behind her, at the base of her spine.

Then she felt his free hand on her shoulder, pushing her down, down onto her knees in front of him. He let go of her hands and pushed her head into his groin, rubbing her face against his loaded balls and rock-hard shaft.

Christina's tongue began licking him frantically, like a woman starved, and he finally guided her blindfolded face to his shaft. Her mouth took him, and she almost cried as she felt his enormous manhood within her. She worked her tongue around it, licking and licking, taking as much as she possibly could.

His hands forced her head harder against him, moving it back and forth on his shaft, until she couldn't possibly take any more. That's when he shoved the hardest, choking her for a long moment before finally relenting and jerking her head back off him.

'Yeah, baby,' he whispered. 'You really like that, don't you? Huh?'

Christina's eyes had filled with tears from the choking, but she was more enthralled than ever by his powerful, commanding body. 'Oh, yes,' she rasped.

He pulled her up and led her over to the bed, where he picked her up and practically threw her on it. 'Ah!' Christina gasped on an expulsion of air.

But before she could protest, before she knew what was coming next, he was on top of her, spreading her legs with his knees, then mounting her like a vicious beast, plunging into her up to the hilt of his shaft, filling her as she'd never been filled before.

For a moment she thought he had torn her apart, despite her wet readiness, but as he began his ruthless movements, ramming into her with merciless abandon, her body quickly responded, moving with his, welcoming his huge shaft, almost crying out for it when he pulled all the way out, only to ram it in again, harder yet, pinning her to the bed with it.

Stars burst before her blinded eyes, and her body began to writhe wildly as wave after wave of ecstatic orgasm convulsed through her, her body pumping madly against his. Peter rose up and rammed inside her one final time, then bellowed like a bull as his massive cock exploded, flooding her with his juices, his body convulsing atop hers. She let out a scream, unable to hold back any longer, and felt her body go completely rigid before she contracted a final, mighty time, her floodgates opening as never before.

They collapsed in a tangle of sweaty flesh, gasping for air, still holding on to one another, his throbbing cock still inside her. It was long moments before either of them could speak, and it was Christina who spoke first.

'Oh . . . Jesus . . . Peter,' she rasped. 'You . . . you can . . . blindfold . . . me anytime.'

They both laughed breathlessly, then he slapped her fanny in his playful way and rolled off her onto his side.

'You liked it, huh, babe?' he asked, a hint of pride in his voice.

'Oh, yes, I liked it, all right,' she said. She reached up, pulling at the silk scarf, but Peter pushed her hands out of the way and reached around and untied the scarf himself. He pulled it loose, then wrapped it around his fist, like a boxer's bandages, and began stroking circles on her belly with it.

Christina blinked and looked down at his hand on her stomach, then up into his eyes.

'We'll have to play with this some more,' he said, his obsidian eyes staring into hers. 'You know? Maybe get a few more. Make it more exciting.'

Returning his stare, she knew that he wasn't kidding, that he wanted to up the ante, so to speak. And while something deep down inside her found his suggestion weird, repugnant even, Christina decided she didn't really give a damn. She wanted this man, and she wanted to keep him. Besides, she'd never had such exciting sex. So why not?

She nodded then, still staring into his eyes.

With a smile he leaned down and kissed her on the lips, then drew back and sat up, reaching for the pack of cigarettes and lighter he'd put on the bedside cabinet when he'd undressed.

He lit a cigarette and handed it to her, then lit one for himself. Christina scooted up, leaning her head on his shoulder, and he wrapped a big arm around her shoulders.

'So what's up with your sister that we've got to talk about?' he asked, exhaling a plume of blue-gray smoke. 'They upset about their latest little problem?'

Christina wriggled even closer to him. 'You're not going to believe it,' she said.

'Try me,' he replied.

'It's a lot more than the latest little problem at the

nursery,' she said. 'Joanna's sick. She's going to die.' Her voice was emotionless, but she felt a twitch of discomfort in her stomach.

He looked at her with a quizzical expression, then his lips slowly formed a smile. 'You're shitting me,' he said.

'No,' Christina said, smoke curling out of her nostrils. 'She has a few months at most. Cancer.' She stubbed her cigarette out in an ashtray, then turned back to him. 'So,' she said, tracing a fingertip across his lips, 'if you just bide your time, the place will be yours. The whole kit and caboodle. Josh'll be glad to get rid of it.' She smiled. 'I'm sure of it.'

Staring at her, he put out his cigarette and took the finger she was brushing across his lips. He opened his mouth and began to lick it, running his hand down her arm, then over to her breast, his fingers latching on to her nipple.

Christina's breath caught in her throat, and her body eased down farther on the bed, her eyes still staring into his. In only moments he was riding her again, fast and hard, worshiping her body with his own as no one ever had, as if her information had served to feed the fires of his desire.

This is worth it, she thought ecstatically, her body beginning to writhe beneath his. *This is worth any price I have to pay.*

21

The big Morris Beige Rolls-Royce Corniche rolled majestically into the courtyard, its beige top down. Christina was in the driver's buttery-soft beige leather seat with its beige piping. The ubiquitous cigarette was between two of her bejeweled fingers, as if it were a fashion accessory.

Connie, who had heard the car, peeked out a window to see who it was and gasped aloud. 'Oh, shit, no!' she exclaimed to herself. 'The plastic bitch has flown in on her expensive broomstick.' She hated Christina with a passion that she could barely conceal – and sometimes didn't – and dreaded her visits. She went back to the kitchen, where April was helping her get a simple lunch ready to take down to the poolside.

April looked up and smiled when she came into the room. 'What's wrong, Connie?' she asked, seeing her look of distress.

Connie leaned against the doorjamb with a distasteful expression. 'Joanna's sister is here,' she spat.

April's eyes widened. 'Here? Uh, unexpectedly?'

'Yes,' Connie said. 'Out front in the courtyard. In the big broomstick she flew in on.'

April couldn't help but laugh. She knew about Connie's intense dislike of Christina – and all women of her ilk – and she knew that it was tolerated by Joanna and Josh, even gleefully so at times.

What none of them realized, however, was the depth of Connie's hatred. Nor did they understand that Connie ached to live exactly like Christina, to have everything Christina had. In short, they didn't fully understand that Connie's hatred was a result of a deep-seated envy.

'I'll go greet her, Connie,' she said. 'You can stay here if you want. And there's no need to go get Joanna and have her come all the way up here. I'll take her sister down to the pool.'

April put down the tray she'd loaded with dishes and cutlery, and rushed off toward the front door. She pulled it open and stared for a moment at the astonishing sight that greeted her eyes.

The much-talked-about Christina von Leydon was dressed as if for an afternoon stroll on the Via Condotti. She stood at the trunk of her enormous Rolls-Royce convertible, her hair wrapped in a brightly colored

Hermès scarf tied at the base of her neck, over which she wore a black gaucho hat, secured beneath her chin. Huge Jackie O-type sunglasses virtually hid her face. A white silk blouse was tied in a knot at her waist – and unbuttoned down to there. Beneath that were tight white silk capri pants and cherry-red stiletto-heeled sandals. On her arm was a shiny candy-apple red Vuitton carryall.

'Christina?' April called questioningly.

Christina turned around and pulled her sunglasses down her nose, the better to look at April. 'Yes?' she responded haughtily. 'Who are you?'

'Sorry,' April said, walking down the steps and approaching her. 'I'm April Woodward,' she offered, holding out a hand to shake. 'I'm doing some work for your sister.'

'I see,' Christina said, looking her up and down, but ignoring the proffered hand. 'It must be rather dirty work, huh?'

April looked down at remnants of the cement dust that she'd tried unsuccessfully to clean off her clothes before lunch. 'Well, yes, it is,' she said.

'Humpf,' Christina grunted.

'I don't believe Joanna is expecting you,' April said, unwilling to let this unpleasant woman intimidate her.

'No. This is a surprise visit, and it would hardly have been a surprise had I told her, would it?' Christina replied with undeniable logic. She looked over April's shoulder, toward the house.

Connie slowly descended the front steps, eyeing Christina suspiciously.

'Oh, Connie,' Christina cried. 'How nice to see you – and how convenient. Be a dear and take my luggage in.'

'Is there a lot?' April asked.

'Hardly a thing,' Christina said airily. 'Connie can handle it.'

'Good,' April said. 'If you want, you can come with me. Joanna's down at the grotto, and I know she'll want to see you.'

'Grotto?' Christina asked. 'What grotto? What the hell's going on?'

'You'll see,' April said mysteriously. 'It's something Joanna's been working on.' With April leading the way, they headed down to the grotto.

Connie looked into the big car's trunk, her features set in a glare. *Louis Vuitton luggage*, she thought. *Of course! And tons of it. Aren't I lucky?*

'You look marvelous,' Christina said, holding out her skinny, tanned arms.

Joanna, who'd been settled into a chaise longue relaxing, watching the progress, rose to her feet. She hugged Christina, and they exchanged air kisses. 'And you look . . . very glamorous,' Joanna said.

'Pish!' Christina exclaimed. 'I look every bit the face-lifted, liposuctioned harridan that I am.' Then she smiled, her expensively bonded teeth dazzling white. 'But that ain't so bad, is it?'

Joanna laughed. 'No, indeed it's not.'

'Now,' Christina said, 'what is this ... this grotto business?' She took notice of the room for the first time, and stood with her arms akimbo.

'Why, Joanna, it's beautiful!' she gasped as she looked around in the grotto.

'Well, you have this young woman to thank for that,' Joanna said, indicating April, who stood watching the two of them in fascination. 'Although you've more or less met, April, this is my sister, Christina, and Christina, this is the resident magician who's done all this work.'

April nodded. 'It's nice to meet you, Christina.'

'It's nice to meet you, too,' Christina said, eyeing her more critically.

'Oh, and this is her helper,' Joanna said, indicating Woody, who was cementing abalone in place. 'Woody, this is my sister, Christina.'

Woody looked up from his work, a frown on his face, and simply nodded his shaggy head and grunted.

'Lovely to meet you, too,' Christina said, her voice tinged with sarcasm. Then she looked at Joanna and winked. 'This really is an enormous project,' she said.

'Yes,' Joanna said. 'It's taking thousands and thousands of shells and a lot of work.'

'Well, it's absolutely marvelous,' Christina said, 'if a bit over the top. But I mean, why, Joanna? Especially now ...'

Christina realized her mistake the instant the words were out of her mouth and quickly blurted, 'I mean, it just seems a little over the top, if you know what I mean. You've done so much work on this old place.'

April tried not to cringe inside, but Christina, whose eagle eyes seldom missed anything, was certain that she detected a knowing look in April's eyes.

She knows about Joanna, Christina thought. She wondered why a stranger – a common worker – would be privy to such intimate information and made a mental note to ask about it later.

'I'm doing it because I want to,' Joanna said, knowing there was no way her sister could argue with such an answer. 'Anyway, we're just about to have lunch at the pool. You want to freshen up and join us?'

'That's heaven,' Christina said. 'And I do need to freshen up a bit first and see to my things.'

'I'll take you up to the house, then,' Joanna said. She turned to April. 'Lunch will be just a little late, April,' she said, rolling her eyes. 'We'll be back down shortly.'

April smiled and nodded.

Joanna led Christina toward the French doors and back outside, where they walked through the apple orchard up toward the pool, Christina carefully negotiating her way in her stiletto heels.

'Who *is* she?' Christina asked when they were out of earshot.

'April?' Joanna said. 'She's an absolute angel who works in shells and pebbles and such. We saw some garden work she did for Ingrid Wilson, and we both loved it, so we hired her to make a grotto out of the old stable. She's turned out to be a real joy to have around. A real friend.'

Christina, who had always been irrationally jealous of her younger sister's friends, did not like what she heard. 'And the guy?' she asked. 'Who's he?'

'That's Woody Pearlman, a friend of April's,' Joanna replied as they arrived at the pool area. 'He has a framing shop in Capitola but helps her out sometimes on big projects.'

'He's a real cutie,' Christina said, giggling almost girlishly. 'But he's awfully rude.'

'That's Woody,' Joanna said, not wanting to discuss him any further.

'Hmm,' Christina said. 'Too bad, really. He looked like he has a terrific bod under those work clothes. Bet he'd be a good roll in the hay.'

'Christina!' Joanna laughed. 'Sometimes I don't believe you.'

'Oh, I'm not serious,' Christina replied. 'But . . . well, he does look hot.'

'You are shameless,' Joanna said with amusement. They reached the house and went into the kitchen.

Connie had a loaded tray in her hands, and was getting ready to go down to the pool. 'Your luggage is in your usual guest room,' she said to Christina.

'Did you unpack everything?' Christina asked.

Connie looked at her with deceptively sleepy-looking eyes. 'Noooo,' she said. 'I thought your things are so special that only you would know what to do with them.'

Christina looked at Joanna, her face a mixture of amazement and anger.

Joanna shrugged helplessly. 'I'll help you unpack,' she said.

'No, no,' Christina said quickly. 'I can handle it myself. Besides, I'm sure you need to rest . . . or something . . . before lunch?'

'I'm fine,' Joanna said. 'We'll meet out by the pool in a few minutes.'

'Fine,' Christina said. She swept out of the kitchen and headed toward the entrance hall to the stairs.

Joanna turned to Connie. 'Connie,' she said, 'I know you don't like Christina, and I know she's a real pain. But couldn't you be a little bit more civilized?'

Connie looked at her with those same heavy-lidded eyes. 'What? You think I don't like her? I'm not nice to her?'

'I *know* you're not,' Joanna said. 'And *you* know I know.'

'I don't even give the plastic bitch a thought,' Connie said spitefully.

Joanna sighed, then went back out onto the terrace. She had almost laughed aloud at Connie's comment, but she didn't want to encourage her dislike of Christina. Her sister was enough of a handful without Connie complicating matters. She walked on out to the pool and sat down under one of the big market umbrellas.

She was tempted to call Josh at the nursery to tell him that Christina had arrived unannounced, but she decided not to bother him with the news.

Poor Josh, she thought. *He's having a hard enough time coping without Christina around.*

I should never have confided in her, she decided. Christina's intentions might be the best, but Joanna knew that her sister would drive her and Josh crazy in a matter of days, if not hours. She also realized that Christina was incapable of acting as if everything was normal, the way she wanted it to be.

Now what? she wondered.

She knew that Christina would try to be *too* helpful in all the wrong ways. And in the process, her manipulative and controlling behavior would completely alienate Connie, Josh, and April, at the very least. In other words, those closest to her.

I've got to do something to remedy the situation, she thought, *and I might as well start right now.*

She got up from the table and headed toward the grotto. She would start by asking April to dinner, even though she was already having lunch with them. Aside from the fact that Joanna wanted her there, April would act as a sort of buffer zone between herself and Christina. She knew that Christina wouldn't discuss her illness in front of someone she considered an outsider.

Lunch had gone smoothly, with Christina dominating the conversation, regaling Joanna and April with the latest antics of the rich and spoiled from San Francisco to Montecito. Now dinner was over, and Christina and Joanna were placing the last of the dishes on big trays to take to the kitchen. Connie had made excuses to leave rather than stay and help serve and clean up as she usually did when there was company. Joanna knew the reason, of course, but she hadn't objected to Connie's leaving.

'Please,' April asked for the second time, 'let me do something?'

'No,' Joanna said. 'You're a guest, and besides, Christina and I will have this done in no time.'

'And,' Christina chimed in, 'we want to have a nice sister-to-sister talk, don't we, Joanna?'

'Oh, yes,' Joanna said to humor her.

They finished loading the trays and headed off to the kitchen, leaving Josh and April alone at the dinner table on the terrace. Josh took a sip of his coffee and looked over at April with a smile. 'What do you think of big sister?' he asked.

April returned his smile. 'Weeeell,' she drawled, 'she's certainly larger than life. She's beautiful and intelligent and can be really sharp and funny, but . . .' She looked at him and shrugged.

'But what?' he asked.

'Well,' April ventured, 'she also seems bossy and sarcastic and supercilious and mean and . . .' She stopped and looked at Josh with a sheepish expression.

He laughed. 'Go on,' he encouraged her. 'Don't stop now. It was just getting interesting.'

'I . . . I'm sorry,' April apologized. 'I think I've overstepped my bounds here.'

'You know you shouldn't feel that way, April,' Josh said. 'You're like one of the family.' He laughed again. 'And like all families, we have our differences.'

'I didn't mean to be unkind,' April said. 'Or so judgmental. I mean, I hardly know the woman.'

'Well,' Josh said, amusement in his voice, 'I think you've hit the proverbial nail on the head.' He looked off into the distance. 'I wish she wasn't here, and I know Joanna feels the same way. I don't think Joanna really wants her here' – Josh paused and looked at her knowingly – 'not until the end. If then.'

Despite herself, April felt a quiver of fear rush through her. Joanna seemed so healthy most of the time, even though she did rest a lot, that her illness still seemed unreal somehow, and speaking of it made it seem all too real. It was, she thought, like acknowledging the existence of evil. She felt compelled to change the subject.

'How're things going down at the nursery?' she asked. 'Joanna hasn't mentioned anything to me lately.'

'Okay,' Josh replied. 'Knock on wood.' He tapped the table with a fist. 'I hope we don't have any more bad luck. We sure don't need it.' He looked at her and smiled. 'I don't have to ask you about how your work is going,' he said. 'Joanna is thrilled with it, and I am too.'

April felt herself blush and looked away. She loved to hear his praise, despite the twinges of guilt she felt. *Every time he says anything the least bit appreciative of me, I feel that I'm somehow betraying Joanna because I like it so much. But I want to hear even more! Oh, what am I going to do?*

*　　　*　　　*

Christina glanced out the library window as she settled down on the big leather Chesterfield sofa. She smiled tightly, then turned away, nervously fluffing her multicolored hair with long, Jezebel Red-lacquered fingernails. Heavy gold bracelets, set with small, glinting gemstones, clanked dully on her thin wrists. She took a large swallow of her brandy, then chased it with a long pull of her cigarette.

So, she thought, *the little gray wren from the grotto stays to dinner. And she's in like Flint with Josh, too. How cozy.*

Her features contorted into an ugly mask. *I don't give two hoots about Josh Lawrence, but I'll be damned if some meddling little nobody is going to come in here – to the house I grew up in – and take over. Acting like Miss Goody Two-shoes, when it's obvious she's nothing but a little tramp from nowhere. I'll break this up, and now!*

She smashed her cigarette out in an ashtray and got to her feet, heading for the terrace. Joanna almost collided with her, returning to the library from the powder room.

'Where are you going in such a hurry?' she asked Christina.

'I was just going out to the terrace,' Christina said. 'I see Josh and that April person out there looking awfully cozy.' She arched a brow at Joanna.

Joanna laughed. 'Sit back down and leave them alone,' she said. 'They're perfectly fine, and we can have that talk.'

Christina hesitated before finally sitting back down

on the big leather Chesterfield. 'What kind of a name is April, anyway?' she said in a nasty voice.

Joanna laughed again. 'You can be so mean, Christina, and April is the nicest person in the world.'

'I bet she is,' Christina said sarcastically. She lit a cigarette and looked over at Joanna, exhaling a long plume of smoke. 'Do you think she's making it with that hunky Woody person?'

'I don't have the faintest idea,' Joanna said, slightly exasperated. She didn't like this interest of Christina's in Woody.

She cringed inside. Christina was like all of her ex-husbands in that respect. While they'd all been promiscuous, invariably taking up with other, usually younger, women, Christina herself relished the occasional toy boy.

No, Joanna decided, she didn't like this one bit. She could see a potentially explosive dalliance in the making, and it was a complication she hadn't anticipated.

Then suddenly it came to her – what she must do. She had already formulated a plan that involved the sullen Mr Woody Pearlman. Now she would simply carry out her plan earlier than expected, and kill two birds with one stone. Pleased with herself, she gladly turned her full attention to her sister.

'Now then, Christina, darling,' she said, 'when did you say you were leaving?'

22

Josh rushed down the hallway toward the bedroom, almost out of breath. He had raced home from the nursery after April called him.

She was coming toward him, and before he could say anything, she put a finger to her lips. 'She's sleeping now,' she whispered.

'What . . . what is it?' he asked, gasping for air. 'What happened, April?'

He felt her hand on his shoulder, patting him lightly. 'Let's go downstairs,' she said, taking his hand for him to follow her. The gesture was so natural that neither of them was aware of it.

Together, they walked down the stairs and out to the terrace, where they sat down at the big teak table.

Josh looked over at her anxiously. 'Tell me what happened, April,' he said. He was making an effort to control the hysteria in his voice.

April gripped his hand in her own as if for strength. 'We were down at the grotto,' she said calmly, 'and Joanna started having a severe headache and some blurring of vision. So I called the doctor and had him paged.'

April took a deep breath before continuing. 'I've given her a very heavy dose of the pain medication, and sleeping pills, too, like the doctor told me to. She'll probably sleep for quite a while, then be okay when she wakes up.'

Josh's eyes never left April's face, and his fingers began stroking her hand. 'Thank God you were here,' he said. 'This is . . . well, it's going to be so difficult for all of us. Especially with her staying here at home. And you know you don't have to do these things. I can hire—'

'Stop right there, Josh,' April said in a firm voice. 'Don't even think about it. Joanna is fine most of the time, and I love having her down at the grotto with me. I can keep an eye on her that way. So . . . forget about a nurse or whatever.'

'I really appreciate that, April,' he said quietly.

'I told you I would be here for Joanna,' she said, 'and I meant it.'

Just then he noticed that she was in her work clothes, her hair a disheveled mess and a liberal sprinkling of cement dust all over her. 'You've had your work interrupted,' he said, indicating her clothes.

'Oh, this,' she said, laughing lightly. 'Well, that's not important, is it?'

He smiled. 'No, I don't think so under the circumstances.' Frowning, he asked, 'Where were Christina and Connie when all this was going on?'

April shrugged. 'I don't know,' she replied. 'I know that Christina went somewhere this morning because Joanna mentioned it. Shopping or something, I guess. Connie came in and did some cleaning, then left to go do some grocery shopping, I think.'

'She's still gone?' he said.

'Yes,' she nodded. 'I know she had a lot to do with Christina being here and so on. Joanna mentioned it. We were down at the grotto. You know, just chattering away about some of the shells to use and the best orchids to try to do in shells. Stuff like that.'

She paused and looked off toward the pool, her eyes beginning to tear. 'We were having such a good time, and that's when it happened.' Her voice broke, but she continued. 'Suddenly, with no warning.'

Josh took her hand again. 'You've been so brave, April,' he said.

She shrugged. 'Joanna's the brave one,' she said.

They sat in silence for a moment, then April looked at her watch. 'I'd better get back to work,' she said. 'I was going down to the nursery later to finally decide which orchids to use for the grotto, but Woody's not here today, and I've got a lot to do.'

'He couldn't come in?' Josh asked.

'I don't know,' April said. 'He was supposed to be

here, but he didn't show up. It's not like him to do this, so I don't know what's going on. Maybe he had a lot of work to catch up on.' She looked at Josh and smiled. 'I guess it's just a crazy day.'

'I guess so,' he said.

'But listen, Josh,' she said, 'don't worry about Joanna. If you need to get back to the nursery, I'll run up to the house every now and then and check on her. The doctor says she should be out for quite a while. So I can handle this end of things.'

'No,' he said. 'I appreciate the offer, but you can get back to work. I'll call Carl. He can handle whatever comes up at the nursery, and I'll stick around here. Maybe get some work done in the Stud Room.'

'Okay,' April said. 'But I'll still be running up to check on Joanna every now and then.'

He gave her hand a final squeeze. 'Okay,' he said. 'Between the two of us, we ought to be able to handle this.' He looked thoughtful for a moment. 'I wonder if Christina will come back expecting lunch,' he said.

'Well,' April said, 'if she does, she's a grown woman, and she knows where the refrigerator is, doesn't she?'

Josh's face actually lit up. 'That's the spirit,' he said with a laugh.

Christina lay spread-eagled on the big king-size bed, her wrists tied to the headboard and her ankles to the footboard. Her Hermès scarf that he had so efficiently wrapped and knotted around her eyes rendered her blind.

Her body quivered in a mixture of fear and anticipation. After three husbands and numerous lovers,
she'd never been this sexually aroused. Every fiber of
her being was concentrated on Peter Rossi and what
he would do to her next, how he would indulge her
insatiable appetite for him.

She had already feasted on his big, thick shaft, had
already made love to those huge balls of his, so heavy
with nectar, and he had ravished her entire body in
turn, his powerful hands and sensuous lips and tongue
torturing her with a thousand delights.

Now she could sense movement about the room,
could feel shifts in air currents, almost as if the fog
outside were curling around the room, undulating in
wisps that she felt ever so lightly on her body.

What is he doing? she wondered. Then she could sense
his presence near her, his tall, muscular body hovering
over her at the side of the bed, preparing to mount and
assault her mercilessly. Her thighs trembled anew, so
hungry was she for him, and when she felt his hand
suddenly clap onto her mound and his thick fingers
ruthlessly enter her, she cried out at once, a cry of both
alarm and ecstasy, relishing his control over her and her
own submission to his every desire. He explored her
brutally, and her body gave up its sweet juices as she
lay panting, whimpering, then almost screaming out,
begging for more, more, more.

As swiftly as his hand had entered, he withdrew it,
and he crawled onto the bed over her, poised, she was
certain, to enter her with his massive manhood. And

he did, savagely plunging into her, his hands under her buttocks, ramming her up against him with mighty thrusts.

She came at once, screaming as her body uncontrollably writhed and contracted around his cock, spasm after spasm engulfing her in a primal ecstasy she had never thought possible. When he exploded into her with the growl of a beast, she ached to fling her arms around him and sink her nails into him, pulling him ever closer, to savor every ounce of his hot, copious juice.

When it was over, they both lay panting like winded animals, their bodies covered with a fine sheen of sweat. The scents of their bodies commingled in the heady perfume of sex, of spent lust and desires fulfilled.

When her breathing had at last returned to normal, Christina merely cooed a long 'Hmmmmmm,' momentarily unable to find the words to describe her satisfaction, her utter satiation with this powerful man.

Without uttering a word, he rolled off her, then got off the bed.

What's he doing now? she wondered, her body still aching for his touch.

She heard him moving around. It sounded as if he was getting dressed. *Jesus,* she thought, *what does he think he's doing?*

She wriggled against the restraints that held her to the bed, growing alarmed by his continuing silence and the sound of his dressing.

'Peter?' she gasped at last. 'What – what are you doing?'

She heard the sound of the zipper on his pants, the sound of him cinching his belt closed, then the swish of fabric as he put on his jacket.

'Peter?' she said again, louder this time, irritation in her voice. 'What the hell are you doing?'

Still there was silence, and she wriggled against the restraints again, more frantically this time. 'Peter,' she almost shouted, 'let me go.'

Then she heard sibilant whispering.

Whispering?

Her mind spun in a thousand different directions, and she couldn't think. Fear, like a poisonous vice, was beginning to take her in its grip, and she broke out into a sweat that coated her body anew.

'Peter!' she screamed, wriggling frantically again. 'Let me go! *Now!*' She began to whimper like a child until—

Laughter?

But not his deep, masculine laughter.

No, it was the tinkle of a woman's laughter. Cruel, mocking laughter.

Christina thought for a moment that she would faint, and she began to jerk like a demon possessed at the restraints that held her so securely, her body lurching up off the bed. Then she began to scream and cry at once, begging him to let her go.

Suddenly she felt his weight on the bed and his hand clapped over her mouth, and she frantically gasped for breath.

'Cool it, babe,' he said calmly. 'Just cool it. I'm right here.'

She whimpered, still panicked, wondering what was going on.

'I'm going to take my hand off now,' he said, 'but I'll put it back on if you make one fucking sound. You got that?'

Christina nodded wildly. *Anything, anything,* she thought. *Just to get this over with.*

She felt his weight shift slightly, then he said, 'Go wait out at the car.'

There was another heave of laughter – *the woman's laughter!* – as if she were trying to control it, and then she heard footsteps, very light and quick, exit the room. She heard the condo's front door slam.

Christina felt her entire body begin to tremble uncontrollably, but it was with fear and exhaustion, not the delight of sexual anticipation.

She felt him get off the bed, but she didn't say anything, so shocked was she by the turn of events.

'I'm going to untie you now, babe,' he said. 'Then I'm going to go. Got that?'

She nodded again but didn't speak.

She felt him first free her right leg, then her left, as quickly and efficiently as he'd tied her down. She began moving her legs about, shaking them gingerly, to get the blood moving. Then he moved to the headboard, where he untied her left arm.

As fast as he had started, he stopped. 'Now I'm going to split, babe,' he said. 'You can untie your other arm, then go. Just close the door behind you.'

'What – who—' she began.

'Just do what I say,' he said, his voice menacing.

'But, Peter,' she whined miserably. 'Who – who was that? And what about – what about us? What—?'

'There is no *us*, babe,' he said nastily. 'I don't need you anymore. So forget about it, or you're dead. Understand?'

For a moment Christina couldn't believe her ears. Then her mind turned white-hot with an all-consuming rage. She wanted to lash out at him with her nails, her teeth, anything to tear him to pieces. But fear kept her silent.

'Ciao,' she heard him say lightly. Then she heard him leave the room and the front door close.

Frantically, she began wrenching the blindfold off with her free hand. It wasn't easy because he'd tied it securely. When she managed to yank it off at last, she opened her eyes and blinked several times, adjusting to the light. She looked around. There was no one in the room, of course. Quickly, she began untying the restraint that held her right arm, fumbling in her nervous hurry but finally succeeding. Her arm free at last, she shook it repeatedly and rubbed her wrist, trying to get the circulation going again.

She jumped to her feet and dashed to the front door of the condo. Edging the door open, she peeked out at the parking lot, but she could see nothing in the fog. Nothing and nobody. There was only the sound of the myriad sea birds, their cries a lonely plaint in her ears.

She went back to the bedroom and dressed. Only

when she was fully clothed did she sit down on the bed and begin to cry, heaving silently at first, her head in her hands, then gradually letting go, wailing aloud and slamming her fists into the bed as the tears flowed.

When she was finally exhausted, her body aching from convulsions, she rose to her feet, tottering on her heels, and went into the bathroom. She switched on the light and looked into the mirror. *What a pretty sight!* she thought. She snatched Kleenex from a box on the counter and quickly wiped away trailing mascara and the remainder of tears. Then, before fresh tears began to flow, she retrieved her handbag from the bedroom, returned to the bathroom, then fished around in it until she'd found all of her makeup.

Looking into the mirror again, she began applying fresh makeup to her face, trying to control her still shaky hand. When she had repaired the damage as best she could, she threw the makeup back into her handbag and started to switch off the light. Then on second thought, she fished around in her handbag again until she found her eyebrow pencil. Taking it out, she held it poised in front of the bathroom mirror for a moment.

No, this won't do, she thought. *Too easy to clean up.*

She went back into the bedroom, where she slipped out of her heels and climbed onto the bed. Removing the badly drawn seascape that hung above the bed, she threw it against the mirrored closet doors. The mirror cracked in a spider web, and the glass covering the drawing shattered.

Good, she thought, though there was no real joy for her in the destruction.

Taking eyebrow pencil in hand, she began to write on the wall, going over and over the letters to make them thick and bold. When she was finished, she eased down off the bed, slipped into her heels, grabbed her handbag, and walked to the bedroom door. She turned and looked at her handiwork: FUCK TRASH, it read. Centered beneath the first line, the second read: PIG. An arrow pointed down to the bed.

Pleased with her literary endeavors and the paint job that would be required to conceal it, she turned and left the apartment without looking back.

23

The sun had burned off the fog and streamed in through the breakfast room windows. Josh had left for work, and Connie was busy upstairs. April had said a quick hello, then gone on down to the grotto. She had been working alone for several days because Woody was catching up on work at his shop and wouldn't return until next week. Joanna and Christina sat alone at the table, sipping the last of their morning coffee.

'I feel great,' Joanna said, and she meant it. It had been a week since her last bout with the headaches and vision problems, and the episode, though frightening, seemed like a distant memory.

'Have you already called Vincent?' she asked.

'Oh, yes,' Christina said. 'But only after you told

me last night that you had appointments and would be tied up all day. So I was up with the little birdies, and got on the horn right away.' She drummed her long fingernails on the table with nervous energy.

'And Vincent was up and at it that early?' Joanna asked.

'Yes, indeed,' Christina said. 'Making his awful jokes about early birds getting the worms. In his case, a very different sort of worm, I should think.'

Joanna smiled. 'But your hair is perfect, Christina,' she said, noting that her sister was wearing full makeup. 'As good as they say Vincent is, I don't understand why you want to do anything to it.'

Christina patted her dozen shades of blond hair with a bejeweled hand. 'It's never perfect, darling,' she said. 'And Vincent, despite the fact that he's in this backwater of a place, is one of the best haircutters I've ever run across. He can do it without it looking like you've had a haircut, and that's what I like.'

'I see what you mean,' Joanna said, not really paying attention. She couldn't fathom the amount of time and money her sister spent on her looks. She would be bored out of her wits. But then, she supposed, boredom was what led Christina to obsess on her appearance anyway.

'Too bad you can't come with me,' Christina said, although she'd been certain Joanna would turn her down before she'd asked her. 'We could get Vincent to do something really exciting with your hair. It'd be fun.'

'No,' Joanna said. 'I've got several errands to run, and I can't spare the time. Anyway, I like the way Jonathan cuts my hair.'

'But you never change it!' Christina exclaimed.

'And I never will,' Joanna countered.

'Oh,' Christina said, 'what a bore!'

'Anyway,' Joanna said, 'I'll drop you off on my way, if you like. Unless you want to take your car.'

'I'll be quite a while,' Christina said. 'I might do some poking around in shops, too. Explore some of the new places. So maybe we ought to go our separate ways.' Then she paused and lowered her voice. 'Are you certain you're okay to be out on your own? I can always stay here or go with you.'

'Oh, no,' Joanna replied. 'Thanks for being so concerned, but I'm fine. Really. You go ahead.'

'If you say so,' Christina said. She rose to her feet and stretched. 'I'll get a jacket and get on my way, then. I don't want to keep Vincent waiting.' She leaned down and gave Joanna an air kiss. 'See you later, darling.'

''Bye,' Joanna said. 'Have fun.'

'Oh, I will,' Christina chirped as she left the room.

Joanna sat staring out the window. Christina had been behaving awfully strangely, she thought. She'd been somewhat tearful a time or two, until Joanna had chastised her for it, but for the most part she'd been uncharacteristically cheerful, busying herself out and about. The local shopping trips – let alone getting her hair cut here – and her dinners and lunches with friends Joanna didn't know she had: This was a new Christina, one that surprised Joanna.

Oh, well, she thought, *as long as she's happy.*

Then Joanna decided she'd better get busy with her errands. *Time's flying,* she thought, *and I don't want to waste a minute of it.*

Joanna drove out of the courtyard and started down the treacherous mountain road. She was at her bank within ten minutes, where she had to park and go inside. The business transaction she had in mind couldn't be done by machine or drive-in teller. After a considerable delay, she returned to the Mercedes, gratified that her shoulder bag had a big, fat envelope in it.

She headed toward the charming little village of Capitola. Within twenty minutes, she reached the ocean-side town with its brightly painted Victorian houses and its plethora of pricey boutiques, many of which featured the work of area craftspeople.

Being a weekday, it was easy to park, right in front of the shop, in fact. She got out of the car, hefting her shoulder bag. Then she walked straight to the shop.

Squaring her shoulders, she opened the door and looked around. A teenage girl piped up from behind a counter, 'May I help you?' She had long bleached hair and a dark, dark tan.

'I don't think so,' Joanna said. 'I need to speak to Mr Pearlman.'

'He's not here,' the girl said.

'Do you know if he's at home?' Joanna asked.

The girl hesitated before she answered. 'I . . . I really don't know,' she said. 'I can take a message.'

Joanna stared at her for a moment. The girl was lying, that much she was sure of. 'No,' she said, 'I'll stop in later.'

'Okay,' the girl said.

Joanna turned and walked out of the shop, then went around to the side of the building, where a wooden staircase led up to the second floor. She knew that he lived upstairs, and she knew about the staircase from April's mentioning it. Joanna had asked her about a limp, and April had told her about slipping on the wet staircase leading up to Woody's apartment the night before.

Joanna looked up the sun-bleached gray steps and took a deep breath. *Here goes*, she thought, and started climbing. At the top of the stairs, she opened the rusty screen door and knocked on the apartment's faded wooden one with her knuckles. No response. She knocked again, louder this time. Still no response.

Then she saw the little once-white buzzer button attached to the door frame. She put her finger on it, hoping it worked. And it did, because she could hear it buzzing loudly inside.

The door opened a crack, and Woody peeked out. His large dark eyes widened in surprise, but for a mere instant before his face assumed a casual, what-do-I-care demeanor.

'Hey,' he said. 'What ya need?'

'Could we speak in private?' Joanna asked.

'Uh, I'm really sorta busy right now,' he said.

'This is extremely important,' Joanna said. 'And I think you'd be a poorer man if you didn't hear me out.'

'Well, uh, give me just a minute,' he said. 'I gotta put something on.'

'Fine,' she said, noticing for the first time that he seemed to be holding a towel around his waist.

He disappeared from sight but left the door open a crack. Joanna patiently waited outside, dreading what she was about to do, but determined to go ahead.

Woody returned and opened the door. 'Come on in,' he said, cocking his thumb toward the room.

Joanna stepped into the apartment and looked around. She was surprised to see beautifully framed prints and paintings hung chock a block on all the walls, many she recognized as being by local artists. The furnishings were expensive but modern and austere. From down a hallway she could hear jazz, its sound muted by a closed door.

'I hope this won't take long,' he said, 'because I've got to get downstairs.'

'I'll only be a minute,' Joanna said, suddenly uncertain of how she would broach the subject.

'What's on your mind?' he asked, studying her from across the room. In nothing but a pair of baggy shorts, he looked bigger and more muscular than ever, his curly black hair seemed shaggier, and his dark eyes shone with intensity.

Joanna felt extremely uncomfortable, but she forged

ahead. 'I hate to be too personal,' she said, looking him in the eye, 'but it's very important for me to know something.'

'What?' Woody asked with a haughty stare. He was rocking on the balls of his feet slightly, his big arms folded across his chest. He seemed to enjoy her discomfort, although Joanna could tell that he was nervous. 'I don't have any secrets,' he added. 'Fire away.'

'Are you in love with April?' Joanna asked, her eyes staying riveted to his.

He stopped rocking and stood perfectly still. His eyes shifted from her to the floor, then back up again. He stroked his chin with one hand. 'I don't think that's any of your business,' he said at last.

'I thought you didn't have any secrets,' Joanna said in a quiet but firm voice.

'I don't,' he said angrily.

'Then what's—' Joanna began.

'I think you're being a little too personal,' he broke in, his voice and manner haughty again, 'but if you have to know, yeah, I think I may be in love with April.'

'You "think,"' Joanna said, echoing him. 'Then you aren't certain that you're in love with her?' she persisted, her heart sinking, hoping that he wouldn't say yes. She had come here convinced that Woody was an egotistical, testosterone-driven seducer who operated on the principle that no woman should be denied the vast pleasures that his body offered.

'Well. . .' Woody said, scratching his head, 'I've known April a long time, knew her ex and all, you know? She's really talented and smart and sexy and . . .'

He shrugged, and Joanna felt the knot of worry in her stomach dissipate, replaced by a stir of impending triumph.

'And how do you think she feels about you?' Joanna asked.

'Like a friend,' he said without hesitation. 'Sort of like a big brother, I guess.' He grinned. 'Except big brothers usually don't want to screw their little sisters.'

Joanna grimaced, but forged on ahead. 'From what April's told me, that hasn't happened.'

His grin disappeared, replaced by a frown. 'If you know so damn much,' he snarled, 'then what are you doing here?' He paused, folded his muscular arms across his chest again, and began rocking on his heels. 'Besides,' he went on, 'April might get to like it, you know? Every other woman does.'

His posturing didn't impress Joanna, nor did it frighten her. 'Would you consider leaving April alone?' she asked. 'What I mean is, making some excuse to her, then simply walking out of her life? Forever.'

He glared at her, his dark eyes shiny in the apartment's semi-gloom. 'What the fuck're you getting at?'

'I think you know,' Joanna said, her eyes remaining on his, despite the malevolence she saw there.

'What if I paid you off? Think you could handle that?'

'Paid me off?' he said, his thick brows knitted in a question.

'Well, could you?' Joanna persisted. 'Could you handle that?'

'You're crazy,' he said.

'Maybe,' Joanna said. 'But that doesn't answer my question. If I gave you, say, fifty thousand dollars, would you disappear from April's life? And I do mean forever.'

'Fifty thousand dollars?' he parroted.

Joanna nodded silently.

'You're ... serious?' he asked.

Joanna nodded again.

He continued his slow rock, then finally began to nod his head, hesitantly at first, his shaggy hair falling over his forehead, then more definitely. He quit rocking and looked at her. 'Yeah,' he said at last, 'I'd fuck off for fifty grand.'

'You'll call and make some excuse,' Joanna said, 'and really stay away?'

'Yeah,' he said. 'I'll call her tonight. Tell her I met Miss Right. Tell her to stay away, or she'll fuck up the picture. I'll disappear from her life for good.'

Joanna decided she believed him, even though he was a first-class creep. She reached into her shoulder bag and withdrew the fat manila envelope. 'Here,' she said, holding it out to him. 'I expect you to keep your word.'

Woody nodded and took the envelope from her. He didn't want to give her the pleasure of seeing him open it in front of her to have a look at the money, but he couldn't resist and tore it open immediately, satisfying himself that there was fifty thousand dollars in it.

'Not a word about this to anyone,' Joanna said. 'If you tell April about this, she'll drop you like a hot potato because she'll know about the bribe.'

Woody carelessly pitched the envelope onto a couch. Joanna's eyes followed it, then suddenly stopped, dumbstruck by what she saw. A pair of spike-heeled black leather Gucci sandals, identical to Christina's, lay on the floor in front of the couch. Tossed on the couch was a pony skin jacket, also from Gucci, also identical to Christina's. And resting atop the jacket was a black leather handbag. Needless to say, Gucci and identical to Christina's.

Joanna's heart began to pound. She was certain that she must have turned white as a sheet, and she took several deep breaths to steady herself.

Woody saw her staring at the couch, then saw the look on her face.

After a moment she looked back over at him with a grim smile on her face.

'What can I say?' he said. 'They all want me, you know?'

Joanna turned to leave, pausing at the door. 'Not April,' she said. Then she started down the stairs.

Woody stuck his head out the door and called after her, and Joanna turned to look at him.

'What if I hadn't ... gone along with you?' he asked.

Joanna smiled. 'I was certain you would.'

Then she continued down the stairs to her car. She started the engine, pulled out, and raced down the village street to get away from Woody and the sordid scene in his apartment. A scene she herself had engineered, only to discover that her precious sister had upped the sleaze factor considerably.

God, she thought, *I guess we're more alike than I ever wanted to admit.*

At the next light, she had to stop. Across the street in a parking lot, she spotted a Morris Beige Rolls-Royce Corniche.

Christina's, she thought. *It has to be. So she was there for certain.*

The light changed, and Joanna stomped on the gas, anxious to leave Capitola. The ugly scene had left her with the feeling that she needed to take a bath to wash the filthy memory of it away.

Well, I certainly have no right to be angry with Christina, she thought miserably. *I'm no better. I've never stooped so low. Bribery! And it's someone who, despite his flaws, April has come to rely on.*

But she wasn't sorry, she decided. Oh, no. For she had effectively removed him from April's life, paving the way for Josh to replace him. Of course, she hadn't factored in Christina.

What on earth would that come to? she wondered. But Joanna didn't know, and decided she really didn't care. Woody was out of April's life, and that's what mattered. Hadn't she seen the proof of Woody's true character firsthand?

No, Joanna thought. *Sinner that I am, I'm not one bit sorry that I've done this. It's for the better. I'm sure it is now.*

24

Joanna crossed the little bridge to the pool area and spied Christina spread out on a chaise longue, big straw hat shielding her face from the sun, huge sunglasses making reading possible. She was wearing an orange bikini and, as she'd always done, was letting all of her body tan while protecting her face from the worst of the sun's aging effects.

As she drew near to her sister, Christina looked up. 'You're up,' she said gaily, as if nothing were amiss. 'How do you feel today, darling?'

'Fine,' Joanna said.

'Are you sure?' Christina asked.

'Yes,' Joanna said, trying not to sound too exasperated.

'Why don't you have a seat?' Christina said. 'I'm having a look at the slicks. Italian *Vogue* right now. All the winter goodies coming up.'

'I don't think so,' Joanna replied. 'I'm going down to the grotto for a while to see April.'

'Oh,' Christina said. 'Well, I hope you won't wear yourself out down there in all that filthy cement dust. You could be relaxing here in the bright, clean sunshine.'

'Don't get too comfortable,' Joanna said, looking down at her sister's prone body, 'because I would like it very much if you left no later than tomorrow morning.'

Christina laid the magazine on her lap and slipped her glasses down her nose. 'What . . . do you mean?' she asked innocently.

'I think I made myself perfectly clear,' Joanna said. 'I would've told you yesterday, but I didn't see you since you came in so late last night.'

'Well,' Christina said, 'I . . . I—'

'Never mind, Christina,' Joanna said. 'Just be ready to leave after breakfast tomorrow. I have enough to deal with right now without dealing with you, too.'

'But—' Christina protested.

'Just go!' Joanna said from between clenched teeth. Then she went on past Christina and down the short trek to the grotto. She didn't want to discuss yesterday's events with Christina. She had no idea what Woody had told her, and she didn't really care. She just wanted Christina out of her sight.

When she entered the grotto, April was on a ladder, working alone. 'Hi,' she said, smiling at Joanna as she walked through the door. 'I'm so glad you're here. If you want to visit, I can get down in just a minute, and we can look over some orchid drawings I've done.'

'Wonderful,' Joanna said. She looked around the big room, smiling to herself. 'I know I've said it a thousand times, April, but it's turning out to be more fabulous than I ever expected.'

'Well, like I've said a thousand times, you've had a lot to do with it,' April replied. 'But thanks anyway.'

Joanna brushed off a chair seat with a clean paper towel and sat down. 'Where's Woody, by the way?' she asked casually. 'Isn't he helping out today?'

April started climbing down the ladder. 'I'll tell you about it in a second,' she said. When she reached the floor, she took off her dusty smock and draped it over a ladder rung, smacked off her hands, then rubbed them and her face on a clean towel kept on a hook just outside. When she was finished, she came back in and poured some mineral water into a glass.

'Do you want some?' she asked Joanna.

'Not now, April,' Joanna replied. 'But thanks.'

April took a big swallow of water, then scooted a little bistro chair over to where Joanna sat. She sank down onto the chair and heaved a sigh. 'You came at the perfect time for a break,' she said.

'Oh, good,' Joanna said. 'I really hate to interfere, but I love looking in on you and watching when it doesn't bother you.'

'It never bothers *me*,' April said, 'but I think it bothered Woody sometimes.'

'I see,' Joanna said. 'I don't think he's crazy about me.'

'Well, you won't have to worry about that anymore,' April said.

'What do you mean?' Joanna asked.

'He called me to tell me he's quit,' April said. 'He's too busy with his own work. But' – she held a finger up in the air – 'get this piece of news. Not only did he call to say he'd quit, but he told me that he's met somebody special. He says she's the one, Miss Right. So . . . he doesn't want to see me anymore.' She looked over at Joanna, a happy smile on her face.

'How do you feel about all this?' Joanna asked. 'Are you upset? I know you and Woody were friends and all.'

'To tell you the truth, it's an odd feeling right now,' April said. 'I haven't quite gotten used to it yet, but I'm sure I will. He'd come over if I felt blue. We'd go to a movie or out to dinner. Since I moved up here, he's always been there for me, you know? So I was never really lonely.'

'You've told me,' Joanna said, nodding.

April took a sip of her water, then laughed. 'The thing is, Joanna, I was beginning to get a little nervous about Woody. He was starting to get a little too close, a little too cloying, and I hated to give him the old heave-ho and hurt his feelings. Underneath all those muscles is a very insecure guy.'

'I'm sure he'd have gotten over it,' Joanna said.

April nodded. 'He'd have gotten over it pretty quickly, I imagine,' she said. She looked at Joanna and grinned. 'From what he's told me, he'd had oodles of women in the past, and I know from going out with him that he attracts them like flies.'

'I bet he does,' Joanna said.

'Anyway,' April continued, 'he was really becoming too dependent on me, I think. And too protective. At least for someone I considered just a friend. And vice versa, I suppose.' She laughed. 'Sometimes we're better off dealing with our loneliness alone, aren't we?'

Joanna nodded. 'I know what you mean,' she said. 'We have to learn to rely on ourselves, our inner resources, and if we depend on somebody else to distract us from ourselves, well . . .'

'In that case, we never really get to know ourselves, do we? We never learn to be alone with ourselves.' April looked thoughtfully into the distance for a moment. 'The long and short of it is, I'm relieved because he was pressuring me about sex – not aggressively, but I always felt it. And it just wouldn't have worked for me. Not with Woody.'

'I'm glad you don't feel hurt,' Joanna said. 'And I'm sure there'll be somebody to take his place.'

April chuckled. 'Yes, but who's going to help me out here? That's the million-dollar question. I've got to start looking for help.'

'Let me help you,' Joanna said.

April looked at her with astonishment. 'You? Help me? But, Joanna . . . I mean . . .'

'You mean in my present condition,' Joanna said. 'With my cancer.'

April stared at her with widened eyes, her face flushing red, but she didn't utter a word. She didn't know what to say.

'Yes, I know that you know,' Joanna said in a soft voice. 'And it's all right.'

April's eyes shifted to the French doors, and she unconsciously clenched her hands together before her gaze returned to Joanna. 'How . . . how did you know?' she finally asked.

'Oh, little things,' Joanna said. 'Little looks. Little concerns. Not to say that you weren't always concerned with me, but maybe a little more so than usual now. And I know that you picked up on Christina's silly faux pas when she came down to see the grotto.'

Then she laughed lightly. 'Of course, the clincher was seeing Josh's car at your place the very day I told him.' Joanna smiled mischievously. 'I'd come by to see you and didn't stop because I knew he was confiding in you.'

April looked at her with a stunned expression.

Joanna began to laugh again, and April finally joined in. 'I'm just glad Josh felt comfortable confiding in you,' Joanna said.

'And I'm glad he felt that way, too,' April said, almost sheepishly.

Joanna chucked her under the chin. 'Don't worry,

April,' she said quietly. 'About the confidences that you and Josh share. It ... it delights me more than you'll ever know.'

April looked at her with a mixture of wonder and love, not certain how to respond.

Joanna smiled ruefully. 'Anyway, I'm happy that you know, and happy that just because I'm dying, you don't think I should stop living. That I should just stop with this project. You know as well as I do that it's part of what I want to leave behind. For Josh. And you, too.'

April felt tears threaten, but she was determined not to cry. 'I think you're so brave,' she said, when she could trust herself to speak.

'I'm just doing what feels right and natural for me to do,' Joanna said. 'I think you and Josh are the brave ones,' she added. 'To be able to go on as you have, knowing what you do about me. I assumed that Josh would tell you because he needs all the support he can get.'

April nodded. 'Yes,' she said. 'He needed to talk to someone.'

'I'm pleased that he chose you,' Joanna said. 'He's very vulnerable, April, like you and me.'

'I know,' April said.

'We've been very much a team since we first met, Josh and I,' Joanna continued. 'And my one great sorrow is that part of the team will be missing when I die. I ... I want more than anything for Josh to be part of a team again ... after I'm gone.'

Her violet eyes looked piercingly into April's. 'Josh

has loved this life – the life we've had together – and not just because of me. The business and everything have meant so much to him, and I hope he'll go on with it. Keep fighting those Rossi brothers. But I know Josh, and I know he's better off with a partner in life, and that's one reason that I hope, desperately hope, that he'll marry again. The sooner after I die the better.'

Joanna turned the full wattage of her gaze on April, looking at her with an intensity April had never seen there before. 'It would mean more than anything else in the world to me,' Joanna went on. 'For him to have somebody to go on with, to continue to build on the beautiful life that we've had together.'

April held her gaze, but her entire being was caught up in a vortex of conflicting emotions. She was rendered speechless by Joanna's words, and was certain that she detected the message that lay behind them.

Suddenly, she felt almost faint with the significance of this moment, but she knew that she must be as strong as Joanna thought she was.

'Now,' Joanna said in a blithe tone of voice, 'you must show me where to begin.' She rose to her feet and placed a hand on April's shoulder, smiling. 'You've got to show me how to do Woody's job.'

The day had been more exhausting than usual, April reflected as she reached the courtyard where her old Wagoneer was parked. Added to her own painstaking work had been patiently teaching Joanna what to do.

Luckily, Joanna was both a quick study and a determined and motivated pupil, an excellent combination. By day's end, she was doing Woody's job as well as he had, although she hadn't yet built up his speed.

April knew that what had really exhausted her was the emotional toll that her conversation with Joanna had wrought. Joanna's intimate revelations had moved April to the very core of her being. She had wanted to weep but had kept her emotions in check all day long.

Now, she thought, climbing into her Wagoneer, *I feel like an old dishrag, and one that's been wrung out to dry at that.*

She was closing the door when she heard her name being called. Christina was approaching her from the house, and she waited to start the car, curious as to what she might want.

'Hi, Christina,' she said, when Joanna's sister reached the car. She noticed that Christina, as usual, was groomed to perfection and dressed luxuriously in a printed silk blouse and silk pants. Her jewelry glinted expensively in the evening's fading light.

'I'm *so* glad I caught you before you left,' Christina said in an ingratiating voice. 'Could I have a word with you for just a moment?'

'Sure,' April replied, wondering what on earth Christina could have to say to her. 'What is it?'

Christina couldn't help but eye April with a somewhat superior air, although she was making an effort to act sincere. 'You're such a nice person,' Christina said, 'that I'm sure you'll understand what I have to say.'

'Yes?' April said.

'Woody Pearlman, dear,' Christina continued, 'the young man who used to help you?'

'Yes,' April said. 'What about him?'

'I know you were friends and all,' Christina went on, 'for a long time, I gather. And anyway, I just wanted to let you know that he and I are seeing each other now. Quite seriously.'

April made a supreme effort not to show her surprise. 'I see.'

'So,' Christina continued, 'I hope you'll be the lady that Joanna thinks you are and keep your distance. From Woody, I mean.'

April stared at her for a moment, then said, 'I don't think that'll be a problem, Christina. Woody doesn't want to see me anymore.'

'Well,' she said, 'sometimes we have a change of heart, don't we? Even Woody might.' She lowered her voice and grabbed April by the upper arm, clenching it fiercely. 'So stay the fuck away from Woody, understand?'

'I understand perfectly,' April said. 'And I wouldn't think of interfering in your ... relationship ... in any way. I think you and Woody are absolutely perfect for each other.'

'Really?' Christina said enthusiastically.

'Yes,' April said. 'He's had nearly every woman in the country, and from what I'm told, you've had most of the men, so you'll make a great pair.'

With that said, April removed Christina's hand from

her arm, slammed the door shut, and fired up the engine. Christina backed away, her face a mask of fury.

Shoving the car in gear, April tore out of the court-yard as if leaving the scene of a particularly odious crime.

Christina glared after her, her face flushed red, her features twisted. 'You little fuck!' she spat under her breath. 'I'll get you!'

25

'You know, April,' Joanna said, 'this is the most fun I think I've had in years.'

'Seriously?' April replied, turning to look at her.

'Well . . .' Joanna demurred, 'maybe the most fun I've had except with Josh.'

They both laughed, then turned back to their work. They'd been working well together, chatting away all the while, discussing everything from life in general to just plain gossip. With Christina gone, it was as if the air had somehow become cleaner, and certainly less tense.

In the beginning, April had worried that their working together would interfere with their friendship. But now that she and Joanna had been more or less closeted together in the grotto for the last couple of weeks, their easy friendship had only grown that much stronger.

Familiarity, April decided, does not always breed contempt.

But one thing that worried April continuously, always in the back of her mind, was her encounter with Christina the night before she left. She had repeatedly asked herself if she should tell Joanna about it.

As if she had read her mind, Joanna resolved the problem for her. 'By the way, April,' she said, 'I've wanted to tell you something for the last few days, but I've been having trouble finding the right words to say it.'

April looked over at her with curiosity. 'That doesn't sound like you, Joanna,' she said. 'I can't imagine what you would find difficult to tell me.'

Joanna laid down her trowel and looked into April's eyes. 'I . . . I've been holding out,' she said seriously. 'I've wanted to tell you that, believe it or not, Christina and Woody have taken up with each other. It happened sometime after they met here, and I . . . I've just been sort of nervous about telling you.'

A smile slowly came to April's lips, and then she burst out into laughter.

Joanna looked at her in amazement. 'What – what's so funny?' she asked.

April's infectious laughter continued for a minute, and Joanna helplessly joined in.

'I – I've been doing the . . . the same thing!' April finally managed to say. 'I knew about it, and I've been agonizing about telling you!'

'No!' Joanna said. 'But . . . how? How did you know?'

'The night before Christina left,' April said, 'she came outside when I was leaving for the day. She told me in no uncertain terms to keep my hands off Woody.'

Joanna looked at her in amazement again. 'I don't believe it,' she said. 'But I do! It sounds just like Christina.'

April then told her about their conversation, and she and Joanna both laughed heartily. It was as if they were exorcizing the demon that was Christina and her troublemaking at last.

'She was on her strangest behavior the whole time she was here,' Joanna said. 'This time and the last. Disappearing to shop and go to lunches and dinners with friends I never heard of. Visiting the nursery even. And that is something she almost never does.'

She looked at April with a serious expression. 'I guess I never really knew my sister,' she said, 'at least not as well as I thought. She's still a sort of enigma to me, and I guess she always will be.' She paused, then gazed back at April. 'But you know what?' she asked, not waiting for an answer. 'It's not really important now. You're important, and Josh is important. Not much else matters, really.'

April reached over and touched her tenderly on the cheek, and Joanna took her hand and kissed it. They sat like that for a moment, then Joanna abruptly let go of April's hand.

'I – I've got to go rest,' she said. Suddenly a look of fear and panic came into her eyes, and she wobbled to her feet. April immediately jumped up and went to her side. 'Here, Joanna,' she said. 'Let me walk you to the house.'

Joanna simply nodded and took her arm.

Josh and April sat together out on the terrace as they had before, trying to comfort one another while Joanna slept in a heavily sedated state.

April didn't think that she'd ever felt as sad and fearful, but she had told Joanna and Josh that she would be here for them. And it felt right and natural, as Joanna might have said. She looked over at Josh. His face looked older, grayer somehow, with sorrow and anxiety. The cheerful, tanned boyishness was gone, for the time being at least.

He looked over at her and put a hand on top of her hands, patting them. He smiled sadly. 'I'm so glad you were with Joanna when this happened,' he said, almost in a whisper. 'I can't imagine what would've happened otherwise. Just thinking about it—'

April placed her hands on his shoulders. 'Listen, Josh,' she said firmly. 'I *was* here, and if I hadn't been, Connie could've handled it. So don't drive yourself crazy thinking about what-ifs. Somehow, we'll work this out so that Joanna can stay at home, like she wants to. Hell, I'll move in if I have to.'

He held her hand more tightly, fighting the urge to get up and hug her, to kiss her. 'I guess we can handle it together.'

April felt that familiar stirring within her, the one

that was such a thrill, even if guilt inevitably followed it. Josh had said 'we,' whether realizing it or not, and April couldn't help but feel a rush of warmth and pleasure.

'I'd better go check on her now,' April said, reluctantly removing her hands from his. 'I know she should be out for another couple of hours, but I just want to be sure.' She rose to her feet.

'I'll come, too,' Josh said, getting up.

Together, they walked up to her room. Joanna lay on the bed in semidarkness, her lovely face serene. Her breathing was calm and seemed normal. The dampness of her hair, however, gave evidence of the recent agony that she had endured.

Josh reached down and gently took one of her hands in his. He held it for long moments, stroking it tenderly, while April stood watching. 'Joanna,' he whispered. 'You're going to be all right.'

Joanna didn't move or acknowledge him in any way. Obviously the heavy sedation was still at work. Josh, nevertheless, continued to whisper to her, to stroke her hand, to encourage and comfort her with his words.

Tears formed in April's eyes, but she quickly brushed them away with her fingers. His love for Joanna touched her so deeply, stirred something deep down inside her so powerfully, that she was almost overcome by emotion. She didn't think that she would ever forget these few moments in this room with these two people.

After several minutes, Josh leaned down and brushed Joanna's forehead with his lips, then straightened back up and turned to April. His face was etched with anguish. 'We'll come back in a while,' he said.

April nodded and they left the room, returning to the terrace. They sat down, and April looked at her watch. 'It'll most likely be another hour or so before she wakes up. Do you want to get something to eat?' she asked. 'Connie's gone for the day, but I could rustle something up in the meantime.'

'Sure,' Josh said. 'I'll help, but first I'd better go call the nursery. Carl'll be leaving soon, and I'd better check in with him. I think I'll try Connie, too. I'm going to have to tell her what's going on and see if she can work some extra hours.'

'That's probably a good idea,' April said. 'Besides, I think it's only fair at this point that she knows the truth.'

Josh nodded. 'You're right,' he agreed.

They got up and went into the house.

'I'll be here in the kitchen,' April said, 'seeing what our options are.'

'Be back in a minute,' Josh said. He turned and went down the hallway to the library to make his telephone calls.

April started rifling through the refrigerator, and discovered that Connie had left tons of food already prepared. Her famous shrimp soup, for starters. Lots of fried chicken and her casserole of chicken with avocado and potatoes. *Bless her*, thought April. *She's been awfully busy making sure everybody eats – and well at that.*

She took out the container of shrimp soup, got out a

pot, and started heating it up. She thought that it would probably be all they would want tonight. Before it was even warm, Josh was back.

'All's well at the nursery,' he said.

'Good,' April replied. 'And Connie? Did you get her?'

'No,' he said. 'She must be out. I'll have to try her later tonight or talk to her in the morning.'

'Look,' April said. 'She's left a wealth of food, but I thought the shrimp soup would fit the bill. What do you think?'

'Perfect,' he said, smiling at her.

They finished eating and checked up on Joanna, who was still sleeping peacefully, and decided to sit out on the terrace, despite the chill night air.

'I was supposed to go down to the nursery tonight,' April said. 'To pick up the orchids we finally decided to use. Joanna gave me a beeper for the gate today.'

Josh couldn't help but grin. 'You mean you two finally made up your minds?'

April nodded. 'Finally,' she said. 'It's only taken us months. Anyway, I thought that I'd go on down there, if you don't mind, and pick them up. I could always come back here and spend the night if you want me to.'

Josh shook his head. 'No,' he said. 'You've done enough for one day, April. I'm sure everything here'll be okay. Just don't feel like you have to go all the way down there tonight.'

'I really want to,' April said. 'I need to take those

orchids home so I can draw them. And the sooner the better.' She looked over at him. 'I . . . well, I feel like time is of the essence. I know that Joanna said it was from the very beginning, but now I really feel it. More than ever.'

Josh nodded and looked down at the table.

April reached over and took his hand. 'I . . . I didn't mean to upset you, Josh,' she said.

'That's the last thing you could do,' he said, looking up at her. 'I don't know what I'd do without you.' He stared at her for a moment longer, then in a cheerful voice, said, 'Now, get on out of here and go get those damned orchids for Joanna.'

April drove down the freeway, careful to observe the speed limit. The highway patrol seemed to have a special affinity for this stretch of highway, and she didn't want a speeding ticket. The windows were rolled down, and the evening air felt good on her skin and in her hair, especially after the grueling day. In fact, she thought, the drive was almost therapeutic, and she looked forward to seeing all the orchids again.

The ones she was picking up weren't rare and expensive specimens, so she'd decided she could keep them around her house for several days to try to figure out the best way to render them in seashells. Sometimes, she'd discovered, she would get an idea about a particular way to render a flower or plant simply by living with it a few days, acquainting herself with it in different lights, at various angles.

She got off the freeway and breezed on down the road toward the nursery. She pulled into the parking lot and hopped out. She'd never been there at night before, and it was eerily quiet, with the exception of the cacophony of nocturnal insects. She followed the path out toward the greenhouses, and when she arrived at the main set of gates, she pressed the code into the beeper. The gates made a metallic clicking sound, then quietly parted. She went through on one side, then started down the path toward the *Phalaenopsis* house.

She saw no sign of Miguel and idly wondered where he and the guard dog were. *Probably catching a little shut-eye*, she thought. *And why not? If the dog was as good as they said, then there was nothing to worry about. He would alert Miguel to any intruder.*

She was continuing down the path toward the *Phalaenopsis* house when she suddenly felt a chill run up the nape of her neck.

I'm not alone, she thought, alarm bells ringing in her head.

She stopped in her tracks, pricking up her ears. She was certain she had heard something, but what? Come to think of it, why *hadn't* she heard the guard dog yet? He should have been barking like crazy by now, shouldn't he?

There! She heard it again. On the other side of the hedge that lined the path. A sort of gasping. And groans. *Oh, my God,* she thought, is somebody hurt? Could somebody have broken in and injured Miguel?

357

She dared not move yet and remained still as a statue, listening with all her might. *There, again.* But two distinctly different groans, she decided. *One male and one female.*

She took three quiet steps, practically on tiptoe, then stopped at the point where the hedge ended. She listened again, holding her breath. She could hear more clearly now and knew at once that she'd been right. It was two people, a man and a woman.

She cautiously peered around the hedge, trying not to make a sound and—

She almost gasped aloud at the sight that greeted her eyes, but she caught herself, quickly jerking her head back behind the cover of the hedge.

She felt a cold snake of fear and revulsion slither up her back and neck, then slip on over the top of her head. Beads of sweat broke out on her forehead, and she began to shiver involuntarily. At the same time she felt a bizarre urge to laugh aloud. She took several deep breaths, then as quickly as possible retraced her steps to her car.

When she got in, she started the engine and crept out of the parking lot, not turning on her lights until she was well clear of the nursery.

Only when she hit the main highway, headed back north, did she feel that she could breathe easy. Then she suddenly realized the absurdity of her fear and revulsion and, slapping the steering wheel, gave vent to the urge to laugh that she had tried so hard to control. Relief, sweet, sweet relief, immediately swept over her body, relaxing her tensed-up muscles and giving her a fresh perspective on what she'd seen.

Just wait till I tell Joanna and Josh, she thought. *Are they ever going to get a kick out of this.* Then just as suddenly as the laughter had come, it died in her throat.

Oh, my God! What a fool I am! This means ... almost certainly means ... that I've found out who's been causing the trouble at the nursery. And Joanna will be ... devastated. Josh, too, for that matter. She knew that she could be wrong, but she seriously doubted it.

She wondered about whether or not she should tell Joanna at all. Perhaps, she decided, she should go straight to Josh, tell him, then he could make the decision about whether or not Joanna should know.

I'd better wait until tomorrow, April decided. *Not bother him tonight. It was definitely not a good time to break the news. Not after today's events.* She could probably catch him alone in the morning. It all depended on how Joanna was doing.

April stepped on the gas, her mouth set in a grim line. *I don't like being the bearer of bad news,* she thought miserably. *But I don't have a choice, do I? No. I have to tell him what I saw. And the awful truth, painful as it may be, will be out in the open at last.*

26

April pulled into the courtyard earlier than usual, hoping to catch Josh the first thing. She parked next to Connie's Plymouth van and hopped out of her old Jeep, making a beeline for the kitchen.

'Hi, Connie,' she said cheerfully, her nose happily inhaling the smell of fresh, strong coffee.

Connie looked up from a counter where she was chopping vegetables. 'Good morning, April,' she said. 'You're early.'

'I need to talk to Josh for a minute,' April said. 'Is he around?'

Connie nodded and laughed. 'Look right in front of you,' she said. 'Out the door. They're on the terrace.'

April had been in such a hurry that she hadn't even

seen them. 'Oh!' she said. 'Stupid me. I guess I'm not awake yet.'

'Go on out,' Connie said. 'I'll bring you some coffee, okay?'

'That'd be great, Connie,' she said. She went on outside, waving at Joanna and Josh, who had seen her and were gaily beckoning her to them. She couldn't help but be astonished at the change in Joanna since last night.

'Good morning,' she said cheerfully as she approached the table. She leaned down and kissed Joanna on the cheek, then kissed Josh on the top of the head.

'You're early,' Joanna said, 'but I'm so glad.'

'How're you feeling this morning?' April asked, sitting down next to Joanna.

'Fabulous, now that you're here,' she said. 'Like a new person.'

'Honestly?' April asked, looking from her to Josh.

'It's incredible,' Joanna said. 'I don't feel any after-effects at all.'

'I'm so thrilled,' April said. Joanna really did look perfectly normal and, if not exactly lively, she was very much herself.

'April,' Joanna said, 'I . . . I know that my insisting on being at home is making things difficult for you. And everybody else, for that matter.'

'Don't say that,' April said. 'Don't even think that way, Joanna.'

'But it's true,' she said. 'And I just want to thank you for all you've done. I really want to be here.'

Josh put an arm around her shoulders and hugged her to him tenderly. 'You are, my love,' he said. 'And you will be. Make no mistake about that.'

Joanna patted his back. 'Thanks,' she said. 'Both of you. For indulging a crazy lady.'

'You're not crazy,' Josh said. Then he laughed shortly. 'Well, maybe a little.'

The three of them laughed together, but April couldn't get her mind off of the news that she had to tell Josh.

Connie came out onto the terrace then. 'Josh,' she said, 'telephone. It's Carl.'

Josh's laughter died away, and his expression changed to one of concern. 'I'll be right back,' he said, getting up. 'Better see what this is about.' He walked off toward the house.

When he was out of earshot, Joanna turned to April. 'There's some paperwork I need to take care of this morning,' she said, 'but I'll be down later to help. Okay?'

'Good Lord, Joanna,' April replied. 'You don't have to do a thing. Except take care of yourself. Maybe you should rest today. What do you think?'

Joanna shook her head. 'Seize the day and all that,' she said, smiling. 'Speaking of which, I wanted to tell you something . . . something that I guess sounds silly, but . . .'

'Go ahead,' April said. 'You've said silly things before.'

They both laughed, then Joanna looked at her seriously. 'I hope that after I'm gone,' she said, 'you won't let the memory of me . . . of our friendship . . . prevent you from living the fullest life possible. And sooner than later.'

April looked at her with a curious expression. 'What—?'

Joanna squeezed her hands. 'You should have a husband and children, April. You told me you want them. And I want them for you. I want you and Josh both to have full and rich lives once I'm gone.'

'But . . . ?' April began.

Joanna reached up and touched her fingertips to April's mouth. 'Shhhh,' she whispered. 'I love you both.'

April had been working alone in the grotto for about twenty minutes when Josh appeared in the doorway. She looked up and knew immediately that something was wrong. She quickly stood up and went to him. 'Josh?' she asked softly. 'Josh, what is it?'

His head was lowered. 'There's been damage to the lab,' he said. 'Some of my orchid crosses deliberately destroyed.' He shook his head. 'Just when they were beginning to grow.'

'Josh—' she broke in, but he continued.

'Which means,' he went on, 'a huge loss this time. At least in terms of my time. I *created* those little seedlings from crosses I made.' He sighed and looked up at her. 'There's just no winning, April.'

'Josh,' she said, 'you've got to listen to me. I got here early this morning because I had to talk to you about the nursery.'

'What're you talking about?' he asked.

'Last night,' April said, the words tumbling out in a rush, 'when I went down there, I heard these strange noises. I went to investigate, and I saw Miguel and Connie having sex—'

His eyes widened in surprise. 'What?' he exclaimed. 'You've got to be joking!'

She shook her head. 'They were just off the path that runs into the greenhouses. In fact, right behind the lab, back behind the hedge. I looked around and the watchdog was muzzled, chained up to a stake. Right next to them. It looked at me like it wanted to tear me to pieces.'

'Oh, Jesus,' Josh exclaimed.

'And Connie and Miguel were going at it like . . . well, like I don't know what,' April said.

Josh put an arm around her shoulder and drew her to him. 'April,' he said, 'I'm so sorry you had to see something like that.' He shook his head. 'I don't *believe* it!'

He suddenly removed his arm and started pacing the room, then stopped and looked at her. 'Connie's been practically like a sister to Joanna,' he said, 'and Carl's been like a brother. I just can't believe Connie could have anything to do with this.'

'If you say so,' April said. 'But I think you ought to seriously consider this. Joanna's told me herself how upwardly mobile Connie is. How she despises most of her own people. How she's so proud and snobbish and determined to get ahead.'

365

Josh was becoming increasingly disturbed by her words, but he let her continue.

'You've also told me,' April went on, 'that she only dates hot up-and-comers. *Anglo* up-and-comers, at that.' She looked Josh in the eyes. 'I know you don't like hearing this, or even thinking about it, but why would Connie be down there at the nursery making it with Miguel? He's a poor simpleton, like you said. Connie wouldn't give Miguel the time of day, Josh, and you know it.'

He hung his head. 'I've been such a fool,' he said, 'not wanting to believe what's right in front of my face. This is going to break Joanna's heart.'

'Maybe . . . maybe she doesn't have to know,' April said, although she thought that Joanna would definitely want to know, regardless of the awful betrayal involved.

'We'll see,' he said. 'But before I do anything else,' he said, 'I'll have to talk to Miguel and see what I can get out of him. Then I'll go from there.'

'Sounds like a good plan,' she said.

'I should get down to the nursery right now,' he said.

'Then go,' she said. 'I'll be here if Joanna needs anything.'

'It's amazing,' he said, looking at her. 'She's in her study doing some paperwork. Seems as content as can be. Says she's coming down here to help you.'

'Good,' April said. 'So we've got this front covered. You go on to the nursery.'

'I will,' he said. 'And I'm really sorry you saw what you did, April. I know it must have been a shock.'

She nodded. 'I'll get over it,' she said, smiling ruefully.

Then he hugged her and quickly let go. 'I'll see you in a while.'

He turned and left, and April's heart was pounding as never before. *Oh, Lord*, she thought. *Forgive me, but I . . . I really do love this man, and I think he loves me.*

Miguel shifted uncomfortably in the chair in front of Josh's desk. He didn't come into the office often, and he didn't like it. Luna always teased him, and usually when Josh wanted to see him here it was for something serious.

Josh looked over the desk at Miguel, dreading what he had to do. He cleared his throat. 'Miguel,' he said calmly, 'does anybody ever come to see you when you're here at night?'

Miguel shook his head violently from side to side, clenching his eyes shut. 'No, nobody,' he said quickly. 'I'm always by myself.'

'Are you sure about that, Miguel?' Josh asked.

Miguel didn't look at him. He clenched his eyes shut again and began to shake his head. 'Nobody, like I said,' he muttered. 'Never. Never, anybody.'

As he did all of the people who worked for him, Josh knew Miguel very well. Now, watching him across the desk, he knew without a shadow of a doubt that Miguel was lying to him. It saddened him, but he could hardly hold Miguel responsible for his actions. Miguel had the mind of a child, after all.

'Miguel,' he finally said, 'I think you've forgotten something.'

'Nooo, Mr Josh. I didn't forget nothing,' Miguel said, shaking his head more slowly this time.

'I believe you did, Miguel,' Josh said. 'Because I think Connie's been down here to visit you, hasn't she?'

'Connie?' Miguel repeated, his eyes widening.

'Yes,' Josh said, 'Connie. You've been seen together here . . . having a very good time together, I hear.' Josh forced himself to smile.

Miguel looked up at him and grinned hugely, forgetting himself. Almost as soon as he did, he realized his mistake and let out a yelp that sounded like a puppy's. Then the inevitable tears began to flow.

'I'm sorry, Mr Josh,' he sputtered. 'I'm sorry.'

Josh hated himself for making Miguel cry, but he had to get to the bottom of this. He got up from behind the desk and went around it to Miguel. Kneeling down, he put his hands on the boyman's powerful shoulders.

'It's okay, Miguel,' he said calmly, patting him softly. 'It's okay.'

Miguel choked and sobbed but wouldn't look Josh in the eye.

'Listen, Miguel,' Josh said. 'You've got to help me. You're the only person who can. Did you know that? The only person. Do you think you can quit crying and do that? Can you help me save the nursery?'

Miguel finally looked over at him. 'Me?' he said.

'Yes, you, Miguel,' Josh replied. 'You can do it. Just tell me if Connie did anything while she was here. Did she . . . tinker with anything?'

'Tinker?' Miguel looked perplexed.

'Did she mess with anything?' Josh persisted. 'Did she . . . go into any of the greenhouses or the lab?'

Miguel regarded him silently.

'Think, Miguel. It's very important. Remember, you can save the nursery,' Josh said. 'What did she do while she was here?'

'We just had fun,' Miguel replied.

'Where, Miguel?' Josh asked. 'Inside? Outside? Where?'

'Different places,' Miguel said. 'Sometimes in the greenhouses. Different ones. The lab. She . . . she made me open them.'

'And the last time it was the lab?' Josh ventured.

Miguel nodded. 'I think so,' he said. 'The one with all the shelves full of glasses.'

Josh gave Miguel's shoulders a squeeze, then sat back on his heels, letting go of him. He didn't want to believe what he'd heard, but there was no mistaking the truth. Connie was working for the Rossis. Had to be. Ever-faithful Connie, of all people, had betrayed them.

Josh felt a bitter wave of bile rise in his throat. The knowledge of her treachery almost made him physically ill, and at the same time he felt saddened and disgusted. It was as if his best friend had suddenly turned on him for no reason.

He slowly rose to his feet. 'Okay, Miguel,' he said. 'Let's go. I'll take you home now.'

Miguel got up, and Josh held the door open for him. In the reception area, Luna looked up from behind her desk, quickly put the telephone down, and smiled, her Hershey bar lipstick emphasizing the gleaming whiteness of her teeth.

'Miguel,' she cooed. 'You look so handsome today. I love those torn jeans. So sexy.'

Miguel made tracks out the front door, and Josh scowled at Luna. 'Lay off him,' Josh said.

Her smile immediately disappeared, and was replaced with big pouty lips.

'I'm going home,' Josh said. 'You and Carl hold down the fort.'

'You just got here,' Luna said in a petulant voice. 'But sure, boss,' she added. 'Whatever you say.'

She was picking the telephone back up as Josh left, hurrying after Miguel. Hurrying home.

Pulling into the courtyard, Josh saw Connie's old Plymouth van. He hopped out of his Land Cruiser and started to head into the house, but decided to check up on Joanna first. He skirted around the house to a gate that led down to the pool area, hoping that she would be down at the grotto with April.

As he approached, he was surprised to hear laughter. Joanna's laugh – unmistakably hers, musical, throaty, rich, and mirthful. He couldn't help but smile at the sound and stopped short of the grotto amid the apple trees to listen and watch.

Just inside one of the grotto's French doors,

Joanna sat on the floor, her legs crossed, covered from head to toe with cement dust. April and some young man – *who's he?* he wondered – were sitting on the floor near her. They were all drinking from iced tea glasses. It was obviously break time. When the laughter subsided, he could hear Joanna and April chattering away. It was as if they didn't have a care in the world.

He stood for a moment longer, reluctant to intrude upon their happy camaraderie, and finally decided to go back to the house and get his confrontation with Connie over with.

When he got to the house, she was in the kitchen, peeling potatoes, humming tunelessly to herself.

'Josh,' she said, smiling up at him. 'You're back so soon.'

'Yes, Connie,' he said. 'Actually . . . I came home because I need to talk to you about something.'

Connie continued peeling as if he hadn't said anything.

'It's pretty serious, Connie,' he said.

She shrugged and replied, 'Don't worry, Josh. I already know what you're going to say.'

'You do?' he said, surprised.

'Joanna told me all about her cancer,' Connie said. She shrugged again. 'I had to know because I would see her sick.'

Josh remained silent, digesting this news.

'I'm really sorry,' Connie continued, glancing at him out of the corner of her eye. 'I remember when it happened to my uncle. It was terrible. It can happen to anybody, even Joanna.'

Her voice was so matter-of-fact, so devoid of emotion that Josh was shocked. She had been so close to them for so long, had been like a member of the family. Was it simply a fatalistic attitude? he wondered. He wasn't sure, but he only had to remind himself of the reason he'd come to talk to her to understand that Connie was not the woman he'd once thought she was.

'I didn't come here to discuss Joanna,' he said.

'Oh?' Connie said, peeling away. 'Then what's on your mind, Josh?'

'You've been seeing Miguel, down at the nursery,' he said. 'Haven't you, Connie?'

Connie dropped the peeler and sputtered in laughter. 'Miguel!' she cried. Then she began to laugh hysterically, practically collapsing with laughter. Her face reddened, and she slapped her thighs with her hands.

Her dramatic response seemed forced to Josh, as if trying to make her lies seem convincing.

'Miguel?' she repeated. 'Did he tell you that?'

Josh nodded. 'Yes, Connie, he did.'

'Well, he's a *mongolito*, isn't he?' she said with a derisive laugh. 'So why do you believe him, Josh?'

She started peeling potatoes again, looking up at Josh, her pretty face alight with seeming amusement.

'You've been *seen* there with him, Connie,' he said.

The look of amusement disappeared, replaced by an angry glare. 'Who told you this?' she demanded, the peeler poised in her hand but not moving.

Josh didn't answer but stared at her sadly.

'Who?' she cried angrily. 'Who tells you this lie?'

'April,' Josh said.

'That's crazy,' Connie said. '*She's* crazy.'

'No, Connie,' he said. 'She's not crazy, and you know it. Why would she make it up? Huh? Why would she make up the fact that she saw you screwing Miguel outside the lab?'

The anger and defiance slowly ebbed from Connie's face, and she laid the potato peeler down carefully. She knew that any further denials on her part would be futile. The jig was up.

'Why, Connie?' Josh asked her quietly. 'Why would you do this to us? We've loved you so much and thought you loved us.' He paused, staring at her. 'Did the Rossi brothers pay you that much?'

'I don't know what you're talking about,' she said, angry again.

'I think you do,' he said. He sighed wearily. 'I hate to believe it,' he went on. 'You and Carl and Luna – all of you have been like family to Joanna and me. We've only tried to help you. Jesus, Connie, right now a lawyer is working away, trying to get you a green card. Because we love you enough to pay him to.'

Connie's face burned brightly, but she was still defiant. She slipped off her apron and flung it down on the granite kitchen counter. 'I don't have to listen to this,' she said arrogantly. 'And I don't need your help anymore. I don't need your fucking lawyer anymore.'

Her glaring eyes locked with his for a brief instant.

'Peter Rossi's going to marry me!' she spat. 'He likes me more than he likes Joanna's whore sister!'

'What – what are you talking about?' Josh asked her in amazement.

'Christina was screwing him while I was doing all the dirty work,' she cried, 'but I got him. Not her! And now I'll be richer than you are!'

Before Josh could respond, she turned and stormed out of the kitchen in triumph.

He stood and watched until she'd disappeared from his view, then sighed again.

It's like the end of an era, he thought. *A happier and more innocent era. And the future seems to promise nothing but bleak loneliness.*

He started to head back down to the grotto, but decided he didn't want to inflict his somber mood on the happy trio down there. Besides, he needed to talk to Carl right away. Yet another unpleasant task. He had to tell Carl that his sister was working for the Rossi brothers, causing the trouble at the nursery. Just then he remembered seeing Carl's truck parked at the Rossi brothers' nursery some time ago.

He can't be in on it, too? Can he?

He didn't know, but he decided he'd better find out fast. He rushed out of the kitchen to the courtyard, and tore down the road to the nursery once again.

The pool area was aglow with the flickering light from dozens of candles. They burned along the retaining walls, hung suspended in lanterns from the trees, graced the tables in big hurricane lamps, and even floated on the surface of the placid turquoise pool. The dining table was centered with a large orchid, a *Miltonia spectabilis* var. *moreliana*, its exotic blooms ranging from a dark fuschia to the most delicate pink, cascading down onto the table.

The dinner was delicious and hearty fare. Josh had grilled thick filet mignons on the terrace, baked potatoes, tossed a salad of mixed greens, and served it all with a very fine Château Latour he'd been saving for a special occasion.

'That was fabulous,' Joanna said, setting down her wineglass.

'I'll second that motion,' April chimed in.

'Thank you, ladies,' Josh replied with a nod. 'My pleasure.'

'And to what do we owe all your culinary endeavors?' Joanna asked.

'Oh, I was just in the mood,' Josh replied goodnaturedly.

'I see,' Joanna said. 'And where's Connie? I thought she was going to be staying late and helping out.'

Josh and April exchanged glances. He had briefed her earlier in the kitchen while Joanna was changing clothes for dinner. He knew that he was going to have to tell Joanna about Connie's treachery, but he'd wanted to delay it. He'd hoped tonight the three of them could have an enjoyable dinner without discussing the day's events, but he could see that was not to be.

'Come on, Josh,' Joanna said. 'Something's going on, and I want to know what it is.'

'Well . . .' he began hesitantly, 'Connie's left.'

'Left?' Joanna said with alarm. 'What do you mean "left"? She would never just leave.'

Josh hated to tell her the truth. 'Well,' he said, 'I noticed that all her things were gone when I came home this evening.'

Joanna stared at him for long moments, her eyes shining intensely. Finally she expelled a deep sigh. 'She betrayed us,' she said, 'didn't she?' It was a statement, not a question.

Josh looked over at her and nodded.

Joanna's face registered an immense sadness, but only for a fleeting moment. April, watching her closely, didn't think she would ever forget that look of sorrow. Brief as it was, it had such poignancy that it bespoke a profoundly abiding bond that had been cruelly severed.

'She caused the trouble at the nursery, didn't she?' Joanna said.

Josh nodded again but remained mute.

Joanna looked at him, his anguished features, before shifting her gaze to April, whose face was a solemn mask.

Suddenly she threw back her head and roared in throaty laughter, stunning both of them. She laughed deeply, barely able to contain her mirthful outburst.

April and Josh exchanged bemused glances. Joanna's laughter would normally have been infectious, but neither of them knew what to make of it.

When she finally calmed down, Joanna looked at them again. 'Wipe the solemn looks off your faces,' she exclaimed. 'You can only laugh at such a betrayal. That or you cry. And I, for one, would rather not do that.'

Nevertheless, they saw tears come into her eyes, which she deftly wiped away. 'All those years of trust and friendship,' she said wistfully. 'I hope they paid her awfully well.'

'At least now you know the source of the trouble,' April said. 'Not that it's much consolation.'

'That's my girl,' Joanna said. 'You've got the right attitude, looking on the bright side.'

April wasn't certain whether Joanna was being facetious or not. 'Are you serious?' she asked.

'I'm quite serious,' Joanna said. 'It's time to move on.' She looked at Josh. 'Did one of the Rossi brothers call as usual?' she asked.

Josh nodded. 'Yes,' he replied. 'Peter, as usual.'

'Well, finding out about Connie doesn't mean the Rossi brothers will stop trying to buy us out or force us out, but at least they don't have an insider working against us.' She paused and looked at Josh. 'They don't, do they?'

'I thought maybe they did,' he replied. 'But—'

'Who?' Joanna asked anxiously.

'Carl,' he said. 'But I was wrong, thank God. I'd seen his truck at the Rossi place and got worried, especially after finding out about Connie, but it turned out they'd asked him there for a legitimate job interview. Offered him a lot of money to leave us, in fact. But he wouldn't take it.'

'That's a mercy,' Joanna said. 'He restores a bit of my faith in people.'

'Not so quick,' Josh said. He decided he might as well tell her the rest of it, now that she been dealt the hardest blow.

'There's *more*?' Joanna asked, looking at him.

He shook his head. 'Apparently,' he said, 'Christina had been seeing Peter Rossi.'

'What!' Joanna looked at him in amazement.

'How did you find out about this?' April asked, as stunned as Joanna by the news.

'Connie,' he said. 'I don't know exactly what to believe, but from what she said, Christina had been fooling around with Peter Rossi. He was probably just getting information out of her. Now, at least from what Connie said, he dumped Christina, and he's going to marry Connie.'

Joanna was silent for a moment, then shook her head as if to clear it of the news. 'I guess I should be shocked,' she said, 'but I'm not. Not really. A little surprised, maybe.' Then she looked over at April. 'I guess she went running to Woody when Peter Rossi dumped her.'

'Poor Woody,' April said. 'But then I guess they deserve each other.'

She and Joanna laughed, and Josh finally joined in.

'So, we've been betrayed by Connie and Christina both,' Joanna said quietly. 'Not a good track record, I suppose, but' – she looked from Josh to April – 'we've

378

got each other, don't we?' She reached out and held hands with both of them.

'You bet,' Josh said.

'You bet,' April echoed, squeezing Joanna's hand lightly. Then her face became serious, and she looked at Josh. 'And the damage this time?' she asked, after their laughter had stopped. 'How bad is it?'

Josh groaned. 'I don't even like to think about it.'

'We've got to,' Joanna said. 'The sooner it's dealt with, the better.'

'Some of the cultures in the lab were destroyed,' Josh said. 'I'm not sure exactly which ones yet.'

Joanna groaned.

He turned to April. 'The cultures were from crosses that I've made – between orchid plants – so it's a big setback, no matter what. They'd just started to grow in the lab.'

'So what do you do about it?' April asked.

'It means starting over from scratch on whatever's been destroyed,' Josh said. 'It could only be worse if they decided to torch the place. First, I'll have to see exactly which cultures were destroyed. They're all numbered, so that'll be easy, just tedious. Then I'll have to try to replicate the destroyed ones. Very time-consuming.'

'I'll be glad to help in any way I can,' April offered. 'I know I'd have to learn, but I'd give it a try.'

'That's really thoughtful of you,' Josh replied, 'but I think you've got your hands full here. By the way, who was the guy helping out today?' he asked.

'Randy Jarvis,' April replied. 'He's worked with me

once or twice before, so I called to see if he could pick up the slack for Woody. Luckily, he was available and came on over.'

'That's great,' Josh said. 'Because I know you've got a lot to do.'

'You bet,' April said. Then she looked at Joanna. 'We've got a grotto to finish,' she said. 'Right?'

'Damn right, and fast!' Joanna said. Then she looked at April and smiled somewhat slyly. 'You can help out at the nursery later. In the future.'

They all laughed, but April felt as if she was being not so subtly pushed in a definite direction. She didn't mind. *No*, she told herself. *I don't mind at all. In fact, I like it very much.*

27

The days flew by in a whirlwind of activity, with April and Randy both working overtime to finish the grotto. Joanna often joined them, helping out, and sometimes she would spread out on a chaise and simply watch them, taking pleasure in the progress they made. But there were frequently days now when she retreated to the house, to rest alone in the privacy of her bedroom.

April never questioned her decisions, never made suggestions, or offered help. She knew that Joanna would ask for whatever help she needed, and she didn't want to intrude on her sense of self-reliance, of privacy, and of dignity. Nevertheless, she felt a deep-seated sorrow more powerful than any she had ever known before. It threatened to overwhelm her at times. But working on the grotto gave her a goal outside of herself. It was something to focus on, rather than giving in to the awful awareness of approaching death.

She knew that Joanna was slowly slipping away from them, but she knew that she was powerless over the outcome. Sometimes she could see a faraway look in Joanna's eyes, almost as if she had already left them or had glimpsed another, more desirable place and was only waiting patiently to go there.

April recognized the pain that Josh was suffering, but pleaded with him to go on as usual. He respected Joanna's wishes as much as possible, coming and going to work as if nothing were out of the ordinary, all the while aching inside.

It's no less than Joanna's doing, he often thought.

Work, fortunately, proved somewhat therapeutic. He lost himself in cataloguing the orchid crosses that had been destroyed and trying to re-create them. As winter approached, he also hoped that a special hybrid he'd created would be ready to show Joanna soon.

About a month after the last trouble at the lab, April went up to the house to have lunch. Joanna was feeling particularly well today, her eyes dancing, laughing and chatting away as if all were well.

Connie's replacement, a Peruvian cousin of Carl's named Elizabeth, had served dessert – a flan very much like Connie's – and Joanna and April sat at the table in the conservatory eating the last of it.

'That was delicious,' April said.

'It was, wasn't it?' Joanna agreed. 'We're so lucky

to have Elizabeth. She'll never be the confidante that Connie was, but ... well, maybe she'll be a little less treacherous.' She laughed lightly, and April couldn't help but laugh, too.

'Which reminds me,' Joanna said, picking up a local newspaper that lay on the chair next to her. 'I thought you might be interested in this.' She handed the newspaper to April.

April instantly recognized the woman in the photograph of a bride and groom. 'Oh, my God,' she uttered in disbelief. 'I ... I know what she told Josh, but still ... I can hardly believe it.'

CESPEDES-ROSSI VOWS EXCHANGED

Connie Louise Cespedes and Peter Anthony Rossi, both residents of Watsonville, were married Saturday by Judge Thomas Quinn in a civil ceremony in Watsonville. The groom is president of Rossi Brothers, Inc., an agribusiness that includes a wholesale nursery concern, and the bride is a vice president there.

April handed the newspaper back to Joanna. 'I guess they deserve each other.'

'Oh,' Joanna said mildly, 'I think they'll be very good for each other. They're both very aggressive and upwardly mobile. I hope Connie is happy with him, and I mean it. They do seem suited for each other. Just like Christina and Woody.'

April looked at her. 'Have you heard from her?' she asked.

Joanna nodded, then she smiled mischievously. 'She called this morning. I shouldn't gloat,' she said with amusement in her voice, 'because I know that Christina is in pain, but I can't help myself.' She paused for dramatic effect.

'What?' April asked. 'Oh, tell me, Joanna, before I explode.'

'My dear sister and Woody were married in Montecito,' she said.

'No!' April said.

'Yes,' Joanna said, laughing. 'And guess what?'

'What?' April asked.

'He's already fooling around on her,' Joanna replied. 'How do you like that for poetic justice?'

'It's a miserable state of affairs,' April said, 'but I can't say that it ruins my day.'

'Nor mine,' Joanna said. 'I've certainly told her how I feel about her carrying on with Peter Rossi – and Woody, for that matter – and I've forgiven her. But not before I gave her a piece of my mind.' She paused and looked at April. 'I think forgiveness is important,' she continued, 'because we can't carry around resentments. They only eat us up. The way I look at it now is that Christina will always be family, but not my family of choice. That's you and Josh.'

She reached over and took April's hand. 'Listen to me, April,' she said.

April nodded.

'I looked and looked,' she said, 'hoping to find the perfect partner for Josh when I'm gone. I suppose I was trying to play God.' Her violet eyes gleamed with happiness.

April felt lightheaded suddenly, as if none of this were real, as if Joanna couldn't possibly be uttering these words so calmly and clearly, but she listened without interrupting.

'Then fate brought you from out of the blue,' she continued. 'And you've made me so very happy. And Josh. Now I hope you'll both – you and Josh – honor my memory by going on living. Living life to the fullest.' She paused, a beatific smile on her lips. 'I won't say anything more. I think you . . . know what I mean.'

April didn't know what to say, but with tears in her eyes, she leaned over and kissed Joanna and hugged her tenderly.

'Now then,' Joanna said. 'I'm going to my room for a nap, and I'll be down later to inspect your work.' She rose to her feet and placed a hand on April's head, stroking it lightly. 'So get busy on our crazy grotto.'

She turned away, and April watched her leave the room, almost overwhelmed with emotion.

An hour later, glad that Joanna was asleep, April borrowed Randy's cell phone and stepped outside the grotto to make a call. She'd gotten the number from the telephone book when Joanna had gone upstairs to nap. She punched it into the cell phone now, and waited for an answer.

'Rossi Brothers, Inc.,' a woman answered on the third ring.

'Connie Rossi, please,' April said.

'Who may I say is calling?' the woman asked.

'April Woodward,' April said, hoping that using her name wouldn't end the call then and there.

'Just a moment, please.'

April waited patiently to see what would happen, then suddenly she heard Connie, unmistakably.

'April,' she said, her voice full of confidence, perhaps even cockiness. 'What do you want?'

'I just want to tell you that if Josh has any more trouble at the nursery,' April said, 'I'll go straight to the police. I'll gladly tell them that I saw you having sex with the night watchman to gain access to the lab and greenhouses, and I'll get Miguel to verify it. Not only that but Josh will tell them what you told him in the kitchen before you left here.'

Then she crossed her fingers and lied. 'Christina will also testify that Rossi pumped her for information about the nursery business.'

For a moment there was no response, then Connie said nastily, 'It's your word against mine.'

'No,' April said. 'It's my word, *plus* Miguel's word, *plus* Josh's word, *plus* Christina's.'

April crossed her fingers again. 'I think you should know, too, that we've already hired a lawyer in case anything else happens.' She took a breath. 'Finally, I'm very friendly with some newspaper people here, and you can be certain that there'll be a huge newspaper article about the whole thing – including you and Miguel – if anything else happens. I think your wedding photo would look really great with the article.'

She could hear Connie sigh heavily.

'So I suggest you convince your husband that he'd better lay off,' she said. 'You understand?'

'Yeah,' Connie said slowly. 'I understand. But I don't think you need to worry about trouble. Nobody wants that small-time operation anymore.'

She slammed the receiver in April's ear.

April pushed the End button, then sat down and sighed in relief. She could only hope that her call would make a difference. There was no guarantee, but she thought that Connie, for whom appearances were very important – especially since she was now the wife of Mr Peter Rossi, a rich Anglo – would do everything in her considerable powers to persuade Peter Rossi to back off.

She got up and went back to the grotto, returning Randy's cell phone to him. Then she got busy, working away, determined to finish this grotto, for herself, for Josh, and for Joanna.

Joanna looked down toward the grotto from her bedroom window. She couldn't see what was happening, of course, but she could picture it in her mind's eye. She smiled to herself happily. It would soon be finished, and it would be beautiful. A fantasy fulfilled. For herself. For April and Josh.

She turned and picked up her handbag, then walked

downstairs to the entrance hall. She took a quick glance around at the polished surfaces, the gleaming beauty that her father had started and that she and Josh had nourished. She slipped out the front door and rushed to her little Mercedes convertible. She put on her sunglasses, backed out of the garage, turned around in the courtyard, and glanced at the gracious, vine-laden house. Then she drove out between the stone pillars, past the open gates, looking straight ahead.

April looked at her watch.

Almost quitting time, she thought, *and Joanna still hasn't been down. I wonder what's up? Maybe . . . maybe she's slept through this afternoon. She was so lively and talkative at lunch that maybe she was worn out.*

'You about ready to leave, Randy?' she asked.

'I'm already cleaning up, April,' he replied tiredly. 'You've been so lost in thought you didn't even notice. Me, I can't do another ounce of work today. I'm bushed.'

'Well,' she said, 'get a good night's rest because there'll be more of the same tomorrow.' She smiled. 'I really appreciate the overtime.'

'And I really appreciate the opportunity,' he said, 'not to mention the money.'

They both laughed.

Randy finished laying out his tools for tomorrow, then picked up his jacket. 'See you in the morning,' he said.

When he was gone, she took off her smock, and

brushed off her clothes vigorously. Then she took her tools to the pool house bathroom and washed them, then dried them off. She brushed her hair and washed her face and hands as best she could, deciding that she'd go check on Joanna before leaving.

She walked up to the house and saw that Elizabeth was in the kitchen. 'Where's Joanna?' she asked.

'I don't know,' Elizabeth replied. 'I haven't seen her since lunch.'

'Thanks,' April said. 'I'm going to check on her.' She walked to the entrance hall, then climbed the stairs to the second floor and quietly tiptoed down the hallway to Joanna and Josh's bedroom.

The door was slightly ajar, so April pushed on it silently, peeking in. The bed was empty.

She must be in the bathroom, April thought. She stepped into the bedroom and called out. 'Joanna?'

There was no response. 'Joanna?' she called again, louder this time.

She saw that the bathroom door was wide open, and she walked in. No Joanna. She left the bedroom, walking back downstairs. She searched the first-floor rooms, but there was no sign of her.

What the devil? April wondered.

She went into the kitchen again. 'Are you sure you haven't seen her since lunch?' she asked Elizabeth.

'No,' Elizabeth replied. 'Why? Is something wrong?'

'She's not here,' April said worriedly. 'Or at least I can't find her.'

She heard a car in the courtyard and rushed to the

entrance hall, thinking that it might be Joanna. She swung open the front door and dashed outside. Josh was hopping out of his Land Cruiser.

'Where's Joanna?' he asked.

'I don't know,' April said. 'I was just looking for her.'

'You don't know?' he cried in alarm. 'Her Mercedes is gone.'

'What?' April exclaimed. 'Oh, Josh, I don't know what to think. We had lunch together, then she went up to rest. She said she was coming down to the grotto, but she didn't. I just came up to check on her, and couldn't find her.' She paused, looking about her wildly, as if Joanna might appear, walking in out of thin air. 'I didn't even think to look for her car.'

'What about Elizabeth?' he asked, putting an arm around her shoulders. 'Did she hear her leave? Or did Joanna leave a message?'

April shook her head. 'No,' she said. 'Elizabeth told me she hadn't seen her since lunch.' She looked up at him worriedly. 'Where – where do you think she's gone? What on earth could she be doing?'

With his arm across her shoulders, they walked together to the house, then on into the kitchen. Josh questioned Elizabeth again but received the same answers. Then he poured two glasses of wine.

'Here,' he said, handing her one, 'let's sit down in the library and think this through.'

In the library, they sat down on the big leather Chesterfield, sipping their wine.

'How was she at lunch?' Josh asked.

'Extraordinary,' April replied. 'That's the best way to put it. She was brilliant, as if nothing in the world were wrong. More alert and funny and chatty and . . .' Her voice trailed off and tears came into her eyes, but she quickly brushed them away.

Josh set his glass down and put his arms around April. Then his lips chastely brushed her forehead. 'Please don't cry,' he said. 'I couldn't stand to see you cry.'

April felt his arms around her and then his lips against hers, and her heart leapt in her throat despite the awfulness of the situation. She put her arms around him and hugged him to her, for a moment at least keeping guilt at bay.

They sat like that for a long time, then hesitantly parted. 'I didn't mean to . . .'

'Don't worry about it, Josh,' April said. 'I'm as guilty as you are. I . . . I . . . oh, let's not think about it right now. We've got to find Joanna.'

He nodded, but he was already staring at the floor thoughtfully, as if in another world. April could see that his mind was working feverishly.

At last he looked up at her. 'I know where she is,' he said quietly. 'She has to be.'

'Where?' April asked.

'Will you come with me?' he asked.

She nodded. 'Of course I will.'

He jumped to his feet. 'Grab a jacket and let's go,' he said, making tracks toward the entrance hall.

They were out in his Land Cruiser and on the road in a minute.

The sun had set before they reached the exit off the freeway that led to the lonely strip of beach at Pajaro, just north of Moss Landing, but the moon was full, washing the landscape in an eerie silver glow. Storm clouds had gathered earlier, threatening rain, but so far they hadn't fulfilled their promise.

As they raced west, headed toward the Pacific Ocean, they passed between perfectly flat acres of Brussels sprouts, strawberries, broccoli, and artichokes. There were no other cars on this lonely stretch, and Josh sped relentlessly ahead, his eyes fixed on the empty road, rigid in his seat.

April didn't ask any questions because she didn't want to intrude on his silence, but now she knew where they were going, although she had never been there before.

The old beach house, she thought. *It makes perfect sense.*

She knew that the ocean and the old house held great significance for Joanna. It was also here that she had come all alone, to suffer, to try to come to grips with her mortality, and to lick her wounds like a dying animal. As much as she could understand Joanna's love for this place, a chill went up April's spine at the thought of Joanna being here alone, of possibly . . . coming here to . . . die.

Josh swerved the big Land Cruiser off the pavement onto a track made of crushed shells and sand. It was very narrow, and vegetation crowded in on both sides, as if wanting to reclaim it. April saw a rusty old metal gate ahead, wide open. From the end of the gate dangled a much newer-looking chain of heavy links.

Josh slowed down and reached across and took her hand in his, squeezing it gently. She looked over at him and, sensing her gaze, he glanced at her.

'She's here,' he said. 'She must be, with the gate open.'

He drove slowly past the gate and around a slight bend in the road. He heaved a sigh and braked with a jerk. Straight ahead, the chrome of Joanna's Mercedes reflected his headlights.

He looked at April. 'Do you want to wait out here?' he asked, his voice almost expressionless.

April shook her head. 'No,' she said, 'I'm coming with you.'

He leaned over and kissed her cheek, chastely and tenderly. 'Thanks,' he said.

They got out of the Land Cruiser, and Josh came around to her side. Together, they started walking through the sand toward the house. They could see a dim light burning somewhere within.

Suddenly a flash of lightning rent the night sky and then a clap of thunder, so loud and ominous that April almost cried aloud. A torrential deluge instantly followed, soaking them both to the skin before they could reach the porch at the back of the house.

When they reached its protection, Josh looked down at her. 'Okay?' he asked.

April nodded. 'Fine,' she said.

He held his keys out, ready to unlock the back door, but they saw that it was open. He pulled the screen door wide, letting April go in ahead of him, then closed it and the inner door, too.

Straight ahead, even in the virtual darkness, April could see all the way to the front of the house with its huge window that gave onto the Pacific. Overhead, the storm raged loudly against the roof and skylights.

Josh took her by both arms and looked down at her. 'You can wait here,' he said. 'She must be there . . . in the front bedroom. That's where the light's coming from.'

April looked up into his eyes. 'No,' she said. 'I want to be with you.'

He hugged her a moment, and then together they walked to the front bedroom. The door was open, and they could see Joanna on the bed. She appeared to be sleeping peacefully, a beatific expression on her face. She was slightly propped up on pillows so that she could see out the floor-to-ceiling window that faced the ocean.

The light they had seen came from a single lamp at the bedside, and in its pool of light was a bag with shells spilling out. No doubt, April thought, the treasures she'd found on her last walk on the beach.

Together they walked to the bed and gazed down upon her. She was not breathing. They stared at her helplessly, their eyes beginning to tear.

She looks alive and as beautiful as she always did, April thought. *Only asleep.*

Josh leaned down close, taking one of Joanna's hands

in his. Then he put his head down on her chest, listening for a heartbeat that he already knew wasn't there.

April stood watching, fully understanding his gesture, despite its futility.

Josh sat down on the bed and took Joanna's lifeless body in his arms, cradling her, rocking her gently, weeping silently, his body heaving. As the storm continued to rage, April's tears began to flow freely, and she didn't think she'd ever before felt such a sense of loss or such agonizing pain. She wondered if a pain this great, this soul-wrenching, would ever completely go away.

At long last, Josh gently laid Joanna back down. He leaned over and kissed her tenderly, then looked up at April.

She had seen sorrow and anguish on his face before but never like this, never of this intensity, she thought. Reaching down, she offered him her hand, and he took it, rising to his feet. Together they stood looking down at her, saying good-bye.

The End as the Beginning
Winter 2000–2001

Despite their grief, the rain-chilled days of winter passed swiftly for April and Josh. Now, though spring's rebirth was only faintly discernible, April could sense its impending arrival. She stood alone in the spectacular fantasy of the grotto, surveying the months of effort she had put in. The work, she reflected, had been awesome, painstaking, but it was Joanna's initial vision that was responsible for this exquisite creation. Without her vision, April reflected, none of it would have been possible.

Josh hadn't once ventured down to the grotto since Joanna's death, even though April had finished. It had simply been too difficult for him emotionally. April had dealt with her own sorrow by struggling to complete the grotto – and it had been a struggle – wanting to see the vision that she and Joanna had shared fully realized. She had also lent a hand at the nursery so that Josh could devote himself to hybridizing – creating the all-important new orchids that the future of the business depended upon.

Now, months later, the two of them had overcome their grief enough to consider a christening of the grotto. Tonight, she and Josh would celebrate Joanna's legacy at last.

April looked around the room with wonder, despite the fact that she had spent the better part of her time here for months. Every surface was covered with shells or pebbles. On the ceiling was the resplendent sky with many of its constellations, and on the walls were now fantastic 'paintings' of rare orchids, executed entirely in colorful shells.

In niches, set on neoclassical plinths, were plaster busts of men and women, once merely famous, now bizarre and fantastic creatures from another world, entirely encrusted with shells. The windows and doors were surrounded with garlands of shells that emulated the intricate and brilliant carvings of Grinling Gibbons.

In the center of the room was a small fountain, a simple birdbath-type affair set in a small circular pool. April had used pebbles here, in many shapes and sizes and textures, to give the effect of mosaics. She had done the same with the floor, creating a mosaic of sea creatures, some of them entwined in 'kelp' that resembled garlands of orchids. Two chandeliers, which hung on either side of the fountain, were encrusted with shells, and beneath them were silver-leafed Venetian tables and chairs, all carved in a shell motif. Each table held crystal hurricane candle holders, which April now lit.

On one of the tables she had placed a silver wine cooler, in which rested a bottle of Louis Roderer Cristal champagne. Two crystal champagne flutes, Russian antiques that April treasured, stood waiting to be filled.

Finally, she turned her attention to a central wall panel that until today had been covered with a large canvas drop cloth. She smiled to herself. She'd told no one what was behind the canvas.

It was a surprise that she had secretly worked out for several weeks. April looked at it with pride and satisfaction: a shimmering pearl-white orchid made almost entirely of abalone. Below it, its name was spelled out in a mosaic of sea-smoothed pebbles: *Phalaenopsis* Joanna. On one of the Venetian tables was an example of the orchid itself. A hybrid that Josh had secretly bred and named for Joanna, it was of the purest white and, like its shell counterpart, seemed to shimmer when the light struck it.

He had let April in on his secret, but she had saved her rendering of the orchid as a special surprise for him. She could hardly wait to see the look on Josh's face when he saw the shell mural of the orchid for the first time.

She stood back and surveyed the scene once more.

'Oh, yes,' she said aloud, 'we can finally have that champagne tonight. To celebrate the grotto's completion.'

It was, she decided, more a work of art than mere craftsmanship. She looked from individual shell to individual shell: *Laliotis ruber, Lischkea imperialis, Spondylas princeps,* and *Wrightianus, Babelomurex spinosus, Ocinebra erinaceus,* the provocatively named *Purpura patual.*

My Lord, she thought, I've learned so much doing this. Not just about the shells themselves, but about design and execution. And possibilities. Oh, yes, she thought, most important of all about possibilities. Joanna had helped her to see the infinite creative potential in these humble, if beautiful, materials.

She switched off the chandeliers and started out of the grotto, on her way to get Josh, but turned once more and peered into the room. *And friendship and love,* she reflected. *I've learned more about friendship and love than I ever thought possible.*

April went into the grotto first and made certain the candles were still burning, then turned on the chandeliers and dimmed them to a romantic glow. She turned on the fountain, which began its singsong tinkle and splash. The effect of the whole was enchantingly breathtaking. Satisfied that everything was perfect, she stepped back outside to tell Josh that he could come in now.

'You sure it's finally ready?' he teased, hesitating to cross the threshold.

'Finito,' April said with a smile.

'Then let's christen it!' he said, stepping into the room.

His blue eyes swept around the room slowly, taking in its many splendors, and as they did, an expression of awe began to replace the amusement that had been on his face.

April watched the transformation with a growing sense of pride and accomplishment. Yet at the same time she was unnerved by his silence, a silence that stretched on and on as he continued to survey the scene. She desperately wanted him to be as pleased as she knew Joanna would have been, and she needn't have worried.

Finally his eyes came to rest on her. For a moment he was distracted by the beautiful Hermès scarf she was wearing. It was the one with the seashell motif that Joanna had given her. Then those handsome blue eyes gazed directly into hers.

'Well,' he said, 'you've done exactly what she wanted. Only more.' He paused for a moment, then smiled. 'It's exquisite, April, and I love it.'

April breathed a sigh of relief, and Josh, hearing it, put his arms around her and hugged tightly. 'You couldn't possibly think that I wouldn't be crazy about it, could you?'

'I hoped,' April said.

He laughed, then chucked her under her chin and kissed her lips. 'Now,' he said, 'let's have that champagne.'

He uncorked the Cristal, filled the two flutes, and handed one to April.

'I want to propose a toast,' he said.

April held her glass aloft, next to his.

'To life,' he said. 'And to our future,' he added.

'And to our future,' April echoed as she clinked glasses with him.

Unbidden, her heart surged in her chest, and despite the anguish of the last few months, she felt an excitement, a need and desire, that propelled her forward to *him*.

Josh put down his glass, and April followed suit. He put his hands on her shoulders and looked down into her eyes. She gazed up at him, an expectant look on her face.

On his handsome features, she could clearly see the toll that the last few months had taken. She had seen it in the mirror. Nevertheless, the bone weariness that had dwelled in his eyes for so long was disappearing, and the immeasurable sadness had slowly begun to ebb.

The grief that had enveloped them both was gradually being replaced by a renewed interest in life, in each other, and in love.

She stroked his lean, tanned face with a slender finger. He took her hand, squeezing it gently in his own. She hadn't wanted to disturb his quietude, to interrupt the thoughts that she knew must be coursing through his mind, as they were through her own.

'This is exactly how she would have wanted it,' he said simply, extending an arm as if to encompass the grotto. Then his eyes looked deeply into hers again, and he stroked her cheek tenderly. 'And so is this.' A hint of a smile spread across his lips. 'This is all part of her legacy. The grotto . . . and our love.'

April nodded and returned his smile, holding his gaze. His sunbleached hair had fallen into his eyes, and she reached up and pushed it away, then tenderly kissed his cheek.

'Yes,' she said softly. 'It's all part of Joanna's legacy. It's a new world, a new life, and her love for you – and me – paved the way for it.'

He embraced her, tightly enfolding her in his powerful arms, and together they began a celebration of their new life, of their love for one another.

A Moment in Time

To the memory of the late Marilyn Kimball Austin of Palo Alto, California, a wife, a mother, an animal lover, a reader, an inspiration, besides much more, and a lady in the best sense of the word.

To Dr. Anina la Cour, of the Chathams Small Animal Hospital in North Chatham, New York, a wonder among women, whose devotion to the care of animals is exemplary and who, I believe, truly has a magic touch.

To Marion Bienes of Amsterdam, the Netherlands, whose heroic, courageous, fearless, and untiring hands-on work on behalf of animals should serve as an inspiration for us all.

ACKNOWLEDGMENTS

The author wishes to thank the Bilinskis and everyone else at the Chathams Small Animal Hospital, North Chatham, New York, for their useful information and good cheer, and for their loving care of the late Happy and the very much alive Mina, Billy, and Jeffrey. In particular, I feel a debt of gratitude to Dr. Anina la Cour, who helped Happy go in peace and who has graciously shared bits of her considerable knowledge with me.

Please note that any mistakes regarding veterinary medicine, animal behavior, or animal care are the author's own, and are not the result of information I have been given by any of the above.

The models for all of the animals in this novel are pets of friends and have served as springboards for characters; thankfully, they are all in the best of health.

Beauty and terror are inseparable.
They come from the same place.

—Herbert Muschamp
The New York Times

BOOK ONE

The Beauty

Chapter One

South Chatham, New York

Valerie looked out across the gray stone terrace toward the hills in the distance, watching as the last sliver of the summer's blood-orange sun slipped from view. The clouds were tinged with beautiful violets and pinks, the palest mauve and deepest orange. Valerie smiled to herself. The sunsets from Apple Hill were nearly always spectacular, and tonight's seemed even more so than usual.

She shifted slightly on the weathered teak chaise longue and idly stretched a hand down to Elvis, her Heinz 57 Variety mutt, who lay half asleep at her side on the terrace. His wide white collar set with aurora borealis rhinestones, a gift from Tami, her secretary, gleamed in the fading light. She stroked his jet-black coat, which was still wet from the swimming pool, and his tail swished sideways once, then came to rest again.

"Hey, gorgeous," a man's deep baritone from behind her asked, "what're you thinking about?"

Valerie felt Teddy's hands on her bare shoulders, but her gaze remained on the distant hills. "I'm not thinking about anything," she said. "I've just been watching the sunset. It was so beautiful."

He squeezed her shoulders softly, then leaned down and brushed her cheek with a kiss. "Just like you," he said. "In fact, I arranged it for you." His voice was a croon, full of promise and possibilities for the night that lay ahead.

"I wouldn't doubt that one little bit," Valerie said. And, she reflected, it was true. She sometimes thought that Teddy de Mornay was capable of anything once he set his mind to it. Aside from the fact that he was terribly handsome and had money to burn, he was personable, charming, and extremely popular. There didn't seem to be a man—or woman—for miles around that didn't admire Teddy de Mornay.

She turned to look up at him. "Where've you been?" she asked, noticing that, although he had dried off, he was still in his bathing trunks, his bronzed body tall, its musculature well-defined throughout his lean physique. His blond hair was lighter than usual, sun-bleached almost white in places, and his pale blue eyes gleamed against his tan.

"I was in the kitchen," he said, "mixing us some drinks. Hattie's almost done with dinner."

"I guess we'd better get changed, then," Valerie said, reluctant to move from the comfort of the chaise longue.

"Unless you want to eat in your bikini," Teddy replied. He smiled lasciviously, exposing his perfect white teeth.

"I had some food in mind," she said, playfully slapping him on the leg. "Anyway, we'd better put something on. It's already started to get cooler." She sat up on the chaise and looked at him. "And where are those drinks you mixed for us?" she asked.

"In the conservatory," he said, squatting down beside her. He leaned over and kissed her on the tip of her nose. "Ready and waiting."

"Let's get changed," she said. "It'll only take me a couple of minutes to shower off and put something on."

Teddy rose to his feet and extended a hand to her. She took it and let him pull her up, off the chaise. She picked up her rubber thongs and grabbed her towel.

Elvis immediately perked up and slowly got to his feet, then shook his wet fur furiously.

"Race you to the pool house," Valerie said. And before Teddy could answer her, she slipped from his grasp and was off, running across the gray stones of the terrace to the rose-covered pergola that decorated the front of the pool house. Elvis raced along behind her as fast as his old legs would carry him, barking joyfully.

Teddy padded along behind, watching her graceful barefooted lope appreciatively. *She's like a rare, beautiful gazelle,* he thought with satisfaction. *I couldn't have made a better choice.*

When he reached the pool house, she had already taken one of the bathrooms, its door open wide, her emerald-green bikini tossed carelessly across a sink, her towel on the tile floor. From the shower came her voice. It was almost a yodel actually, for she was bellowing a rendition of "You Ain't Nothin' But a Hound Dog." Elvis, on his haunches, his head lifted to the ceiling, sat outside the shower howling along with her.

Teddy stood still, listening to the raucous cacophony. On the way to the pool house he'd thought about joining her for a little predinner fun, but now he decided against it.

She and Elvis are enjoying themselves too much, he thought, *and besides, I want tonight to be very special for her. One night that she'll never forget.*

He walked to the bathroom at the other end of the pool house. *So I'll hold off till later.*

He pulled off his bathing trunks, feeling foolishly proud of himself for this uncharacteristic show of restraint.

This isn't like me at all, he thought. *No, siree. Because when Teddy wants it, Teddy really wants it. And when he really wants it, he gets it.*

With that thought, he stepped into the Mexican-tiled shower stall, closed the thick glass door, and twirled the water on, lathering up, excited at the prospect of the night ahead.

Valerie poured herself a martini from the silver cocktail shaker that sat perspiring on the marble-topped drinks table in the conservatory. She tossed four olives in, then a fifth for good measure. It was the gin-soaked olives that she liked best about a martini. Holding the crystal glass up to the light, she admired its sparkling radiance a moment before taking a cautious sip.

"Manna from heaven," she cooed to herself.

She walked over to one of the big, comfortable, down-filled sofas and sat, enjoying the feel of its crisp white duck against her silk pants and blouse as she sank into its luxurious softness. She set the martini glass down on the coffee table, and stretched her arms above her head, breathing deeply.

She'd had a long, hard week at the veterinary clinic, and the late afternoon swim and the hot sun, followed by a revitalizing shower, had worked their magic: She felt calm, relaxed, even a bit serene. Although she was on call at the clinic this weekend, she didn't anticipate any problems. She'd quickly scanned the patient roster before she'd left the clinic and hadn't noticed any animals that might present her with serious problems.

But you never know, she reminded herself, reaching over and picking up her drink. What she did know, and very well at that, was that you could plan endlessly, trying to anticipate every need, every problem that might arise. Then when you thought you had everything covered, a dire emergency would strike.

Well, I'm not going to think about it tonight, she told herself. *I'm going to relax and enjoy myself.*

"Aha," Teddy exclaimed when he walked into the room. "I see you've been a very naughty girl and started without me."

She looked up and saw that he'd put on spotless, perfectly ironed white linen trousers and an appropriately faded blue knit polo shirt that was the precise color of his eyes. Somehow he always managed to look perfect. Almost too perfect.

"You bet I have," Valerie said. "That cocktail shaker looked so lonely—and so seductive." She smiled up at him. "Besides, I knew you'd take forever in the shower. You always do."

He leaned down and planted a kiss on the top of her

head. "You know me too well," he said. Then he made a beeline for the drinks table, where he poured himself a martini and popped in an olive.

Teddy sauntered over to the sofa and sat down, putting an arm around her shoulders and hugging her to him. He brushed her cheek with his lips, lightly and tenderly.

"I'm so glad you could spend the weekend with me," he said. "All weekend. Just the two of us."

"Don't forget Elvis," she said, scowling at him playfully.

"Yeah," he said, "and Elvis." He looked around the room. "And where is the ugly beast?" he asked.

"He's not ugly," she replied. "He might not win any beauty contests, but, well, he's beautiful *inside*."

Teddy kissed her nose again and smiled. "I'm sure he is," he said. "And I'm glad you told me, but where is the internally beautiful beast?"

Before she could answer, he held up a hand to silence her.

"No, wait . . . let me guess," he said, placing a hand on his forehead dramatically. "I'm getting psychic vibrations. Could he be . . . ? He's . . . in the kitchen with Hattie."

Valerie laughed. "Of course he's in the kitchen with Hattie, you fool. He knows where all the good stuff is."

Teddy hugged her shoulders again, leaning over and kissing her neck. "Hmm, you smell so good," he said. "I could eat you up."

Valerie looked at him out of the corner of her eye. "Why don't we have dinner first?" she said.

"Must we?" he countered, licking her neck and ear

hungrily. Then he abruptly stopped and sat up, reaching over for his drink.

Hold off, Ted, he told himself. *Remember, you're going to make tonight very special for Val.* He took a long swallow of his martini, finishing it off, and set the glass back down. Then he rubbed his hands together and got to his feet.

"Ready for another?" he asked.

"Not yet, Teddy," Valerie said, surprised that he'd downed his so quickly.

Teddy picked up his empty glass, plucked out the olive, popped it into his mouth, then walked over to the drinks table for a refill.

Valerie eyed him speculatively. *It's not like Teddy to back off,* she thought, slightly puzzled. *I wonder what's gotten into him?*

She nervously ruffled her long strawberry-blond hair with one hand. She'd taken care dressing tonight, even though she'd finished in half the time Teddy had. She'd blow-dried her hair and let it hang loose rather than pulling it back in a ponytail or—her usual for work—a long single braid. Then she'd carefully applied a little makeup—eyeliner, mascara, a touch of blusher and lipstick. Finally, she'd donned a cream silk blouse, matching pants, and expensive leather thong sandals, completing the look with gold knot earrings, a heavy gold link necklace, and a gold link bracelet. All to please him.

If truth be told, she'd much rather have jumped out of the shower and into old jeans and a T-shirt without bothering about her hair and makeup. But Teddy had always hated it when she looked anything less than perfectly groomed and dressed, no matter the occasion.

He loved to see her turned out in a ladylike fashion. And she, in turn, hated the disapproving glances he would give her if her attire didn't meet his exacting standards. That furrowed brow, those cocked eyebrows, and those thin, grimly set lips reminded her all too much of the disapproving looks she'd suffered over the years from her mother, Marguerite. For years such looks had diminished her sense of self-worth. When she and Teddy had started dating in college, she had been surprised to see him react to her cavalier attitude toward clothing much as her mother had. She had worked hard to please him, and still did, but lately she'd found herself lapsing in this area and pleasing herself more often.

Teddy looked over at her thoughtfully, swirling his fresh martini in its crystal glass before taking a sip. "You look beautiful tonight," he said after he'd swallowed. "Absolutely beautiful."

Valerie felt all of her doubts and worries vanish as if by magic. "Thanks, Teddy," she said, and she meant it. "And you look as handsome as ever."

Hattie quietly stepped into the conservatory, Elvis at her heels, wagging his tail furiously, watching her every movement with adoring eyes.

"Dinner's ready," she said. "I can serve anytime, Teddy."

"Thanks, Hattie," he replied. "We'll be right in."

Hattie left the room, Elvis prancing along beside her, his tail wagging.

"Hattie's got a serious fan tonight," Valerie said. "I wonder what wonderful goodies she's been giving him."

"Something really special," Teddy said. "Because I came up with the menu."

Valerie looked up at him. "You did?" she exclaimed. "What's the occasion?"

"You," he said, extending his drink toward her. "Me." He took another sip of his martini. "Us."

"You're sweet, Teddy."

"I'm glad you think so," he replied. He walked over, leaned down, and kissed her forehead again. "Ready to go in to dinner?" he asked, looking into her eyes.

She nodded, returning his gaze. He seemed somehow nervous . . . but no, that wasn't precisely the word. *What, then?* she asked herself. *Just a little anxious, I guess. As if . . . as if he's hiding something. But what?*

"I'm starved," she said gaily, dispensing with her concerns. "Swimming always makes me hungry."

"Well, you've come to the right place." He offered her his free hand. "We'll be glad to do something about that."

Valerie took his hand and rose to her feet.

Teddy finished off his martini, set the glass on the coffee table, and together they went to the dining room.

The beeswax candles flickered in their Georgian silver candelabra, casting shadows onto the dining room walls. The elegant robed figures in the antique Chinese murals mysteriously appeared to come to life in the dancing light, as if to bear witness to tonight's special occasion.

Valerie sighed with pleasure, inhaling the heady perfume that wafted through the air from the huge old-fashioned roses. Hattie had stuffed full-blown reds, pinks, yellows, and creamy whites into a turn-of-the-century Tiffany silver bowl placed in the center of the table.

"You look contented," Teddy said from across the table.

Valerie looked over. His eyes glittered in the candle-light, a bit mischievously, she thought, and there was a smile on his lips. "I *am* contented," she said, returning his smile. "Supremely contented. I don't remember the last time I've eaten so much that was so good. And the dessert!" She patted her tummy in an unladylike manner and looked down at the empty Flora Danica dessert plate in front of her. "I don't believe I ate all of it."

"That's one of Hattie's specialties," Teddy said. "*Boca negra*. Killer chocolate cake with white choco-late sauce."

"It's the best chocolate cake I've ever eaten," Valerie said.

"I know," Teddy replied, grinning. "It's the bour-bon, I think. It's like the Cartier of chocolate cakes, but I won't let her make it too often. It's so good it could be addictive."

"I'd forgotten what a great cook Hattie is," Valerie said. "And the dining room looks so beautiful. The flowers and candles and everything." She waved a hand and looked around the room. "I don't think we've ever eaten in here, except for a couple of your important client dinners." She paused and looked at him. "The only thing missing is Elvis."

Teddy returned her look. "You're worried about his being out in Hattie's cottage, aren't you?"

"Nooo, Teddy," she replied, shaking her head. "I just hope she doesn't give him too many goodies."

"He'll be fine," Teddy said. "I just wanted us to be alone tonight. Besides, Hattie's crazy about him." He stared into her eyes for a moment. "She's crazy about you."

"I like her, too," Valerie replied. "And I love her cooking." She laughed but stopped abruptly when she saw that Teddy's expression had suddenly turned serious.

"Then you shouldn't be such a stranger around here, Val," he said. "You could have Hattie's cooking anytime."

"Oh, Teddy, you know how busy I am," she replied. "With the clinic and having my own place to look after . . . well, it's all I can do to go anywhere. It's different for you," she went on, "being in the city most of the week, then coming up here to relax or going up to the place in the Adirondacks to hunt and fish. I'm either on call weekends, or I have to catch up on the house and garden and a thousand other things."

Teddy got up and went around to her side of the table, pulling out a chair to sit beside her. She turned to face him, and he took her hands in his. "I could make it a lot easier for you," he said earnestly.

His eyes burned with an intense light that she'd seldom seen in them. It was similar to the terrible gleam they held when he was extremely angry about something. She began to feel slightly uncomfortable. "What . . . what are you driving at, Teddy?" she asked.

"I think you know," he said.

"I . . . I'm not certain," she sputtered.

He released her hands and stood up. She saw that there was a solemn expression on his face as he turned to the mahogany sideboard behind him and plucked something from the huge Imari bowl set in its center.

Valerie gazed at him in silence, her expression curious. Teddy was often quite formal, sometimes even stuffy, but tonight his behavior was practically ceremonial. *What's going on?* she wondered. *Because he is definitely up to something.*

He sat back down, taking one of her hands very gently and reverently. He looked into her eyes, his expression still sober. He cleared his voice. "I . . . I have something for you," he said.

"For me?" she said quietly. She felt that any show of excitement would somehow interfere with the ceremony—or whatever it was—that was taking place.

He nodded and held out his hand.

Valerie looked down at it and saw a small, black, cloth-covered box. Even in the flickering candlelight she could see that impressed into the cloth top was one word: *Bvlgari.* The jeweler who used the Roman *u.* Her breath caught in her throat, and she held it, not daring to breathe. Her mind began to race, whirling around in crazy circles. She couldn't sort out her thoughts and feelings, so overcome was she by his gesture.

"Teddy . . . Teddy . . . ," she finally stammered breathlessly. "I . . . I . . ."

"Shhh," he hushed, squeezing the hand he held. "Just take it, Val," he said. He let go of her long, slender hand and placed the box in it.

Valerie held it cupped there, still at a loss for words.

She took a deep breath and looked briefly at Teddy's serious face. Then, hands quivering, she lifted the lid off the box. She was prepared for the gleam of an expensive bauble of some sort, but inside, fitted perfectly, was another box, this one covered in black leather. *Bvlgari* was pressed into the leather as on the cloth box.

She quickly opened the leather box, unable to bear the tension any longer. She gasped when she saw the ring resting in the soft beige suede that lined the interior of the box. It twinkled back at her as if alive, its stunning canary yellow color animated by the candlelight that reflected off it.

"Oh, my . . . God," she stammered. "Oh . . . Teddy, . . . I don't know what . . ." Unbidden, tears sprang into her eyes and, like the ring, they glimmered in the light.

He was watching her intently, his eyes never leaving hers. "You only have to say one word, Val," he said. "One simple little word."

She looked at him, wanting to please him, but she found herself speechless, unable to utter the word that she knew he wanted to hear.

He threw his arms around her, tugging her to him. "Come on, Val," he urged. "Say yes. Just say yes."

Her mind was still in a whirl, and she was not sure how to react.

Teddy pulled back and looked into her eyes. "You can do it," he said, nodding his head. "You don't have to say, 'Yes, Teddy, I'll marry you.'" He laughed and chucked her under the chin with a hand. "All you have to say is yes!"

Valerie felt elated and somehow defeated at the same time. She was thrilled that a man desired her this much, and she found it difficult to believe that the man was somebody as sought-after as Teddy de Mornay. For years she had been genuinely puzzled by his attraction to her. How could she be so lucky? But at the same time, deep down inside, she realized that if she committed herself to him, she would be doing them both a disservice. Some instinct was telling her this was all wrong, despite the fact that she liked Teddy, perhaps even loved him, or once had.

Oh, God, help me, she thought. *What do I do?*

Teddy's eyes searched hers pleadingly, and she saw the earnest, loving expression there, so like a puppy's that her heart was wrenched in two.

Oh, my God. What do I say?

"Say it, Val," he repeated anxiously. "Or just nod. Yeah. That's all you have to do. Just nod!"

And she did.

She felt her head, as if with a will of its own, almost involuntarily begin to nod that yes that he was begging for. A yes that was perhaps a lie, a yes that was a defeat of her spirit.

She looked up at him, her eyes teary. She wanted to tell Teddy that she loved him, but that she wasn't certain that she was "in love" with him. The words, however, could not be summoned up from her tortured soul.

Teddy threw his arms around her again, pulling her to him passionately, kissing her neck, her ears, forehead, eyes, nose, cheeks, mouth. Then he began to lick the tears that had spilled down onto her cheeks.

"I love you, Val," he murmured. "Oh, I love you so

much. I want to make you the happiest woman alive. I want to make you *mine*."

Valerie stiffened at these last words, but she remained mute, hoping that her silence would neither offend him nor imply assent to his wishes.

When he drew back again, Teddy smiled at her radiantly. "You've made me the happiest man in the world."

She couldn't help but find his excitement infectious. "I'm . . . I'm glad, Teddy," she said, returning his smile.

"Do you like it?" he asked.

"Like it?" She looked down at the ring. "Teddy, it's the most beautiful ring I've ever seen."

"Put it on," he said. "Let's see what it looks like on."

Valerie took the ring from its nest of softest suede and held it between two fingers. Her hand trembled slightly.

"Here," Teddy said, "let me put it on your finger." He took the ring from her, and Valerie held her hand out straight, trying to keep it from shaking.

Teddy slipped the ring onto her finger, and Valerie moved her hand back and forth, watching the diamond reflect the candlelight. Despite the turmoil that she felt about committing to Teddy, she couldn't help but be mesmerized by the diamond's beauty. *It's truly magnificent,* she thought. *More than I'd ever dreamed of . . . or even wanted, for that matter.*

She moved her hand again, watching the gemstone reflect the light. *Trust Teddy to go for the unusual,* she thought. *He would have to get something extraordinary, something over the top.*

She looked up at him. "I'm practically speechless, Teddy," she said. "It really is the most beautiful ring I've ever seen."

Teddy grinned like a proud little boy. "You don't think it's vulgar?" he asked. Then he laughed.

"It is a little big," she allowed, joining in his laughter.

"If you ask me, only people who can't afford them call them vulgar," Teddy said. He stood up and leaned down, kissing her on the forehead. "Why don't we go back to the conservatory and have coffee and a brandy in there?"

She nodded. "That'd be great."

Teddy took her hand, and Valerie rose to her feet. They walked back to the conservatory, one of Teddy's powerful arms slung around her shoulders.

"I'll go get the coffee," he said. "You get comfortable."

"You spoil me, Teddy."

"I want to," he replied.

She sank back onto the downy luxury of the huge sofa, watching Teddy leave the room. She couldn't help but smile. There was a spring in his step that she recognized immediately. It was almost a cocky strut that said he was immensely pleased with himself.

She looked down at the ring on her finger, becoming entranced again as she watched it sparkle. *My God*, she thought, *this ring must have cost Teddy a fortune. I wonder if he can really afford it.*

The thought made her feel uncomfortable again. He had always kept her in the dark about his mysterious wheeling and dealing. She knew that he'd inherited money and that he had rental income here in the country, but he kept her at a distance about his job in New York City, trading stock and investing money for friends.

When she asked him, Teddy always shrugged off her questions, telling her that she'd only be bored with the details. At the same time, he'd never failed to boast about the enormous profits he had reaped on a particular day or during a particular week.

At first she'd found his secrecy intriguing—just one of the many things she had to learn about him—but lately she'd begun to think that it was vaguely suspicious that he wouldn't be more forthcoming at this point in their relationship.

She sighed. *I really don't want to think about all that right now,* she told herself.

She kicked off her sandals, then walked over to the windows that looked out on the terraces and swimming pool. She could feel the wind coming through the screens. *A storm is coming,* she thought.

Stepping through the French doors, she walked out onto the terrace and looked up at the sky. She stared at the huge, shifting cloud formations that alternately revealed, then concealed the brightness of the full moon. Gazing out toward the pool, she could see that one moment it shimmered with the moonlight and the next it was almost pitch-black.

Music, a soft and sexy jazz tune she couldn't name, drifted out through the French doors behind her. Then Teddy's strong arms encircled her from behind, and she felt his lips brushing her hair, searching out the nape of her neck.

"Hmm," he murmured, "you look so beautiful standing out here in the moonlight."

She felt herself respond to his sensuous touch. It was a kind of giving in that was pleasant, if not yet passionate. Turning in his arms, she faced him with her eyes closed and felt his lips instantly fall upon hers, kissing her with urgency. She put her arms around him and let herself go, responding to his kisses, enjoying his desire for her, taking pleasure in the knowledge that this man wanted her so much.

Teddy pulled her firmly against him, his hands moving slowly up and down her back, down to her beautifully rounded buttocks, one in each hand, massaging her gently, and pressing her against his aroused manhood.

Valerie moaned softly and put her head down on his shoulder, clinging to him.

"You're enjoying yourself," Teddy murmured.

She nodded her head on his shoulder.

"The night's still young," he said quietly. "Why don't we go have our coffee and drinks, then head upstairs? Soon."

Valerie nodded her assent again, but in actuality she was enjoying the feel of his powerful body against her own and didn't really care about anything else to drink. No, she would have preferred to go straight up to the bedroom and crawl under the covers with him, taking more pleasure in his body, in their bodies together.

Teddy drew back and took one of her hands in his, then silently led her back into the conservatory. She saw a big silver tray with china cups and saucers on the coffee table and, alongside them, two crystal balloons of brandy.

They settled down on the sofa, and Teddy handed her a cup of coffee. "I put the cream and sugar in it the way you like it."

"Thanks, Teddy." She smiled and took a sip. The coffee was exactly the way she liked it. Sweet and rich. Much better than she ever made for herself at home. She glanced at him and saw that he was looking at the ring on her finger.

"It's so beautiful," she said. "Isn't it?"

"It really is," he replied. He put his coffee down and slid an arm around her shoulders, looking into her eyes. "When do you think we ought to set the date?" he asked.

Valerie's mind was instantly set awhirl again. *Oh, no! What should I say?*

She looked down into her coffee cup as if it held the answer to his question. She certainly hadn't anticipated this, and she had given it no thought whatsoever. She knew that Teddy eventually wanted to get married and have a family, but she'd always managed to neatly tuck away any considerations of marriage with him—or anybody else, for that matter.

"Oh, Teddy," she said, struggling to keep her voice even, "tonight's been so . . . well, it's already been so much to absorb. Can't we wait to discuss it?" She smiled, and her eyes searched his. "Please?" she added.

"Sure, babe," he said, squeezing her shoulder. He smiled brightly. "We'll wait to talk about it. Anything for you." He kissed her lips. "Just not too long. Okay?"

She nodded in acquiescence. "I promise," she said. "Not too long."

"Good," he replied. He slid his arm from around her shoulders and reached over and picked up a snifter of brandy. "Ready for a nip?"

"Are you trying to ply me with booze?" she joked.

"Who, me?" he asked. "You bet I am."

"Then please do," she said. "I want to be plied. I could use a good stiff drink of that." And she meant it now.

Teddy handed her the brandy. He reached for the other snifter and held it next to hers. "To us," he said.

"To . . . us," she replied, then she took a large sip. She savored the aroma and the taste of the fiery liquid on her tongue before she swallowed. It seemed only moments before she felt a glow spread through her body, warming her and loosening her up, helping cast away the worries that preyed upon her mind.

Teddy, she noticed, had nearly drained his glass in a single swallow. He set it down and turned his attention back to her. He stared into her eyes for a long moment with the hint of a smile on his lips.

"What?" she asked.

"Nothing," he replied, slowly shaking his head. "I just love looking at you when you look like this. So . . . fresh. So radiant. So innocent."

Teddy always says the right things, she thought. *And I always respond to them.*

He took the brandy snifter from her hand and set it on the coffee table, then pulled her to him, his mouth and tongue brushing her ears and neck slowly, sensuously, before finding her mouth and kissing her deeply.

Valerie's body immediately responded to his, and she gave herself over to the erotically charged moment, returning his kiss, her hands stroking his muscular back and shoulders, her tongue dancing a carnal dance with his.

He shifted on the sofa, and she felt his hand on one of her breasts, stroking it ever so gently, then cupping it firmly as his mouth descended to the silk of her blouse and his tongue darted out and began to lick her nipple through the thin silk.

"Hmmm," Valerie moaned. "Ohhhh, Teddy." She moved her hands up and down his back, massaging him, loving the feel of the masculine strength beneath his shirt. She wanted to hurry now, to reach that magic moment when he entered her, engulfing her with his manhood, obliterating the rest of the world with it.

He raised his head and looked up at her. His face was flushed and his breathing was labored. "Ah, Val," he rasped. "This is so good. Let's go upstairs. Okay?"

"Okay," she said, and nodded.

He was off the sofa in a flash, his hand extended toward her. She took it, and they left the conservatory, her head on his shoulder, their arms around each other.

Teddy was on his knees between her widespread legs. When she opened her eyes, Valerie could see, even in the dim candlelight, that his mouth was wet and red from his enjoyment of her most secret place. She could also see his engorged manhood poised to enter her, and she shivered with anticipation.

A sudden clap of thunder so near and loud that it seemed to shake the entire house roared in their ears but didn't distract them from one another. As he plunged into her, she gasped. Her sounds of delight were drowned out by the drumming of the intense rain as it hit the windows and French doors that surrounded the room on three sides. The draperies whipped in the wind, and some of the candles were abruptly blown out by the powerful gusts, but they ignored them, so intent were they on giving one another pleasure.

He rode her and rode her, withdrawing and hesitating before plunging in again and again, each time more ruthless than the last, bringing her to a frenzy of desire and need for him, until she suddenly cried out.

Her body began to spasm as she climaxed beneath him, and Teddy became a man possessed, plunging ever more furiously until he let out a bellow, the cords in his neck standing out, his body convulsing on hers as his seed burst forth, filling her to overflowing.

He collapsed atop her, wrapping her in his arms, quickly peppering kisses on her forehead, cheeks, nose, eyes, and lips, all the while his chest heaving against her breasts as he gasped for breath. Valerie held on to him tightly, absorbed in the moment, unwilling to let it go just yet.

At last they lay on their sides, facing one another, their bodies coated with a sheen of perspiration. He was still inside her, and she enjoyed the feel of him there.

Teddy kissed her tenderly, then drew back slightly, staring into her eyes. "That was so wonderful," he whispered. "So perfect."

Val nodded. "Oh, yes," she said. "It was heaven, Teddy." She breathed a long sigh of contentment, and he pulled her closer to him.

The rain beat a steady tattoo against the windows and doors, and for the first time Teddy looked up and noticed that the wind, still gusting powerfully, had made sails out of the long, silk curtains, blowing them out into the room.

"I guess I ought to get up and close the doors and windows," Teddy said. "But I don't want to move."

She hugged him tightly. "Then don't," she said. "Stay right where you are. You feel wonderful."

He kissed her with renewed passion, running a hand up her back and then on down to her buttocks, where he stroked gently, slowly pulling her against him.

Valerie could feel his cock begin to swell inside her, filling her with its might. A moan escaped her lips, and Teddy began to move his pelvis in a lazy rhythm, enjoying the look of pleasure on her face, relishing the power he had over her. Gently he moved, and slowly, slowly, slowly, until he heard another barely audible moan of pleasure. He rolled them both over then, with his body spread out atop hers, his manhood still in her, teasing her, drawing out the—

Suddenly there was a beep, a terrible shrill-sounding beep like a car alarm.

Valerie jerked upright into a sitting position. When Teddy tried to ease her back down onto the bed, she said firmly, "No, Teddy, that's my pager. I have to—"

His mouth went over hers, determined to keep her quiet, but she shook her head from side to side. "No," she rasped. She struggled to get out from under him. "Let me up, Teddy," she cried. "Let me up, goddamn it! Now!"

Reluctantly he backed off, letting her leap free to

pick up her pager. It was obviously the service beeping her to call in. She grabbed her cell phone off the bedside table and snapped it open.

"Dr. Rochelle," she said in a professional voice.

From his position on the tangled bed, Teddy listened to her end of the conversation, looking up at her with a mixture of disappointment and disgust. Becoming increasingly frustrated and angry, he jammed a fist into a pillow, then leapt up off the bed and marched around the room, noisily slamming the French doors and windows shut. When he was finished, he stood, arms akimbo and feet planted wide apart, glaring at her. Then he turned and stomped into the bathroom, slamming that door behind him.

When her conversation with the service was finished, Valerie punched in the telephone number they'd given her. Her call was picked up on the first ring.

"Dr. Rochelle," she said.

"Dr. Rochelle," a man said, "this is Santo Ducci at Stonelair. We have a sick horse out here, and we wondered if you could come take a look."

"I'll be there in about fifteen or twenty minutes."

"Thanks a lot," the man said.

Valerie pressed the end button and quickly placed her cell phone in the big leather and canvas carryall that went everywhere with her. She walked over to the bathroom door. She hesitated a moment before tapping on it.

There was no response, and she knocked a little louder. "Teddy?" she said. "I'm really sorry, but . . . well, you know this comes with the territory." There was still no response, and she knocked again. "Teddy?"

She started to open the door when it suddenly swung open.

He stood there, still naked . . . and so handsome, she thought, a smile on his lips that exposed his perfect white teeth. "Come here," he said, holding his arms out. Before Valerie could move, he stepped forward and hugged her to him.

"I'm the one who's sorry," he whispered. "I . . . I shouldn't have reacted that way, but I wanted this to be a perfect weekend for us." He drew back and looked into her eyes. "Forgive me?" he said in a little boy voice. "Please?"

Valerie couldn't help but smile, even though she found his behavior immature and inconsiderate. She'd become inured to Teddy's little temper tantrums. He was a spoiled rich boy who couldn't tolerate not getting his way.

She planted a quick kiss on his lips. "Forget about it," she said, ruffling his hair with her fingertips. "I'm sorry, too, but I've got to go."

She rushed to the closet, where she grabbed a pair of Levis, a T-shirt, and a white lab coat. Tossing them on a chair, she rifled through a dresser until she found bra, panties, and socks. She began dressing hurriedly as Teddy stood watching her.

"What's up?" he asked. "Somebody's pooch miscarry or something?"

She thought she detected a hint of sarcasm in his voice, but she chose to ignore it. "There's an emergency out at Stonelair," she replied.

"Stonelair?" he said, his eyes widening. "You're not going out there, are you?"

"Yes," she said, grabbing a pair of sneakers from the closet floor.

"Since when did you start working for that creepy drug lord?"

"Since now," she replied, pulling on her socks.

"Je-sus, Val!" he cried, his voice angry. "Isn't that a little stupid? Maybe even a little dangerous, huh?" He stood staring at her, his body rigid, his eyes bright with intensity.

She finished tying her sneakers, then got to her feet, grabbing her carryall and slinging it over her shoulder in one swift movement.

"Look, Teddy," she said in a determined voice, "I don't know anything about the people at Stonelair, and neither do you. I just know that there's a horse out there that's in trouble, and I've got to go take care of it. It's my duty as a veterinarian."

"But-but . . . you don't even know what the hell's going on out there, Val," he sputtered. "I mean, those people could have a drug lab set up or—"

"I don't care what's going on out there," she broke in angrily. "There's a sick horse and I'm going to it. And I'm going now."

As she started for the bedroom door, Teddy rushed to her, throwing his long, muscular arms around her. "Just a quick kiss," he said, all sweetness again.

She turned to him and let him kiss her, then pulled away. "I'm in a hurry, Teddy."

"I know, I know," he said agreeably, nodding. "So go. Go." He slapped her playfully on the butt.

Valerie headed out of the bedroom and down the hallway to the staircase.

"Val?" he called as she reached the top of the stairs.

She quickly glanced back toward the bedroom door, where he stood, his tall, strong body filling the doorway.

"I'll be here waiting for you," he said, one hand shaking his penis at her.

Valerie sputtered helplessly with laughter. "Oh, *you,*" she laughed, then hurried on down the stairs and out into the dark and stormy night.

Chapter Two

Valerie drove like a woman possessed. Forgotten now was the lavish dinner and the bedroom frolic. Even the exquisite canary diamond that still sparkled on her finger went unnoticed in her haste to get to Stonelair. It was after midnight, and the summer storm was lashing the countryside.

Valerie could barely make out the road ahead of her as she raced over the curving country roads. The rain-drenched landscape was a void of total darkness, except when the terrifying streaks of lightning rent the sky, momentarily illuminating the fields and woods and the occasional house and barn in an eerie glow. The accompanying thunder came in such ferocious rolling claps that she involuntarily jumped.

"Jeez," she said aloud, "it sounds like it's coming through the roof." Suddenly she wished that Elvis was with her to keep her company. She reached over and turned on the radio. It was the next best thing, she supposed. It was set on the classical station, and strains of Schubert's piano quintet "The Trout" filled her ears. She laughed nervously, thinking that Schubert's trout would be very happy indeed in this weather.

Virtual rivers, washing off the hills, flowed across the road at points, but the big Jeep negotiated them easily. On she rolled, hunched over the steering wheel, determined to get to Stonelair as soon as possible. She'd never ministered to this particular horse before, but from what she'd heard over the cellular, it didn't sound good. And she never knew when she might be too late.

She slowed down when her headlights picked out the stone walls that surrounded the old estate. She seldom drove on this remote stretch of road, but she remembered that somewhere along here were the big iron gates. *Why would I remember that?* she wondered. *Maybe it's because these gates have always looked so forbidding. Like they really meant "Stay Out."*

"Oops!" she said aloud. "There it is." She'd just passed them on her right.

She shoved her foot on the brake, skidding slightly, then had to back up a few feet, thankful that there wasn't any traffic on the road. She swung the Jeep onto the blacktop drive that led up to the huge stone piers with their black gates. They'd told her that there would be a column with a push-button speaker in the middle of the drive, and now she saw it. She pulled over next to it, rolled down her window, and pressed the speaker button. The sleeve of her lab coat was instantly drenched, and rain lashed into the car, splattering her face and hair as well.

A man's voice asked who it was. *Who the devil are they expecting after midnight?* she thought. "Dr. Rochelle," she replied, raising her voice to be heard above the rain.

"When you come to the Y in the road," the disembodied voice said, "take the one to the left. It leads to the stables."

Then the speaker went dead, and the gates slowly began to swing open. At the same time, she saw that video cameras were mounted on the stone piers. They appeared to focus their eyes upon her like alien monsters in a sci-fi movie.

What the hell is all this security about? she wondered. Most of the horse owners hereabouts didn't have any security at all, and the handful who owned extremely valuable animals usually had nothing more than an alarm system in the stables. But then, she reminded herself, she didn't know these people. She did know that they'd paid a fortune for the vast, somewhat rundown estate, and she had heard rumors that they'd spent another fortune sprucing it up. Stonelair, a white elephant with huge taxes and impossibly large spaces to heat, had sat vacant for years until these people had come along from out of nowhere.

Ah, the follies of the extremely rich, she thought as she sped down the narrow blacktop lane toward the house. *And the paranoia!*

The road was lined on both sides with enormous evergreens—spruce, pine, and hemlock—with rhododendrons tucked in front of them next to the road. On ahead a hundred feet, she spotted the Y in the road, and when she came to it, she veered to the left as the voice had instructed her. The road apparently circled around the mansion and toward the back of the estate.

In another minute she came to a large parking area. On her left she could make out what was definitely a stone stable block. She slammed on her brakes and killed the engine. Grabbing her carryall, she jumped out of the car and hurried around to the rear. Opening the door, she took out her heavy medical bag.

She turned to dash toward the stable.

"Oh, my God!" she gasped.

A giant stood poised in her path. He had appeared from out of nowhere, without a sound, at least none that she could detect over the driving rain and wind.

"Sorry," she said, quickly recovering her composure. "I didn't hear you." She surmised that he must be a benign giant, because he held an umbrella aloft and was opening another one for her. She took it from him, glad for the shelter from the rain.

"Dr. Rochelle?" he asked.

"Yes," she replied, nodding her head.

"Santo Ducci," the man said. He didn't extend a hand to shake. "This way," he said with a slight nod of his head. Without another word he began walking toward the stable.

Valerie quickly fell in step beside him, taking sidelong glances at her decidedly odd escort. His head was completely shaved, and he had a black mustache and small goatee. In his ear was a large gold ring.

Mr. Clean, she couldn't help thinking. As they moved, his body was a study in rippling musculature. Tree trunk arms and legs to match, six-pack abs, a chest from here to yon. *Jeez, a human HumVee.* But then, she decided, she must make a rather odd picture herself: hair practically plastered to her head, wet jeans, T-shirt, and lab coat, and shoes that were already nearly soaked through.

They quickly reached the stable, and he opened a door and held it for her. Valerie stepped into a truly luxurious office. Mahogany-paneled walls, an old Tabriz rug on the floor, handsome old leather-upholstered couches and chairs, a huge mahogany table that served as a desk, and, the only giveaways that she was in the twenty-first century: a computer, printer, fax machine, and filing cabinets.

She closed her umbrella and put it in the old iron stand by the doorway. "Which way do we go?" she asked, in a hurry to get to the sick horse.

"Over this way," he answered. He led her through a door into a tack room. Its walls were covered with riding accessories: saddles, bridles, reins, breastplates and collars, jawbands, browbands, nosebands, halters, leads, and on and on, all of it, Valerie noticed, leather and brass alike, gleaming from the polish of meticulous care. From the tack room he led her through another door and out into the stable proper. Valerie calculated that there must be at least thirty stalls in the immaculately kept space, but her attention immediately switched to the air of anxiety, of instinctual nervousness, that she sensed about the stable tonight.

The storm, she thought. *The lightning and thunder have them on edge.*

Then she heard it, above the sounds of the storm and the restlessness of the other horses: the sound of an animal in acute distress. *That only increases the nervousness of the rest of them,* she thought.

Without waiting for Ducci, she quickened her pace, heading in the direction of the sound. When she reached the stall, she looked in through the barred opening in the stall door and saw the magnificent Arabian stallion, to all appearances of excellent bloodlines, lying on its side though tethered to the stall. In its pain it might do harm to itself, so they'd tied it down. She could see that the horse had been rolling in agony and was sheathed in sweat.

She set down her carryall and medical bag and started to open the door to the stall, but the giant grabbed her arm from behind.

"Wait!" he said with alarm. "You're liable to get hurt. He's an extremely high-strung animal and could be dangerous like this. Hadn't you better try to sedate him or something first?"

Valerie turned to him. "He's tethered, and I know something about what I'm doing. Just back off a little bit," she said calmly. "Let me be alone with him for a few minutes."

"I don't know . . . ," Ducci said.

"I do," Valerie replied emphatically. "I don't mean to be rude, but I know what I'm doing. If you could just wait over there"—she indicated a bench near the door to the tack room—"I'll call you if I need you."

Ducci shrugged. "Whatever you say," he said gruffly.

With him out of the way, Valerie turned her attention back to the stall. On its door was a brass plaque with the horse's name engraved on it: Storm Warning. *How appropriate,* she thought. She unlatched the stall door and stepped inside confidently but quietly. She stood staring at the magnificent creature a few moments before getting down on her knees beside him, steering clear of his hindquarters. The horse was in severe distress. Stroking his head, she began talking to him in a soft, gentle voice. Her eyes swept his body as she continued, assessing his general physical condition, seeing if he appeared to present with anything other than what she thought. After her cursory examination, she continued to stroke and talk to him for another minute before slowly getting to her feet and retrieving her medical bag and carryall.

She placed them near Storm Warning and got back down on her knees, speaking soothingly to him the whole time. Just as she opened her medical bag, there was a sudden crash of thunder and flash of lightning. The lights flickered for a moment, then went out, plunging the stable into complete darkness. The horses reacted to the violent weather with noises of their own, stomping, snorting, and whinnying.

"Dr. Rochelle?" Ducci called to her.

She stroked Storm Warning again. "Yes?" she replied.

"You okay?" he asked.

"I'm fine," she said. "Have you got a lantern or something?"

"I'll be right there," he answered.

She heard him moving about, feeling in the darkness. "There," she whispered, as her hands stroked the horse's slick, well-groomed coat. "You'll be okay, Storm Warning. We'll have you better in no time."

The minutes seemed to stretch interminably in the pitch black of the stable, but she soon heard Ducci approaching from the direction of the tack room.

"I'm on my way," he called. He appeared in the stall a moment later, lantern held high in one hand.

"Is there some place to hang that?" she asked.

He hooked it over an iron hanger in the wall. "Right there."

"Good," she said. "If you don't mind, there's a box of supplies in the back of my Jeep. It's on the left-hand side, right inside the door. Could you get it for me, and another lantern, if you've got it?"

"Right away," he replied. He sensed that she knew what she was doing and turned to go, carrying a flashlight to light his way.

In the halo of light cast by the lantern, Valerie rummaged around in her medical bag until she found what she was looking for. Then she proceeded to work on Storm Warning. First, she felt his neck, ascertaining where his jugular vein was. Then she injected him with Rompun. The sedative worked quickly, putting the horse at some ease, as well as making the rest of her work less difficult. Ducci returned and stood in the doorway with the box and another lantern.

"Is there another hanger for the lantern?" she asked without looking up.

"Right over here," he said, indicating the wall to the left of the door.

"Hang it there if you would, please," she said. "And you can set the box down next to my medical bag."

"I can hold the lantern for you."

"That won't be necessary," she replied. "I think Storm Warning and I will be better off alone."

"Whatever you say." He set the box down and hung the lantern up, then turned to leave. "You want me to wait for you?"

"It's okay," she said. "If you have something to do, go ahead."

"I'll be in the office for a minute," he said. "Need to check on things at the house."

She didn't reply but resumed her running whispers, trying to soothe the nervous animal, readying him for another injection. This one was a painkiller, Banamine, and it was injected, like the Rompun, in the jugular vein. She would wait a bit and give the sedative and painkiller time to ease the magnificent horse even more before she performed the next procedure.

The storm ended almost as quickly as it had begun. The stable fell silent as the thunder died out and the animals resettled themselves for the night. She didn't stop stroking Storm Warning or whispering her litany of soothing words until he seemed to be in less pain and somewhat lethargic. Then she retrieved the supplies she needed from the medical box and got busy again. She passed a nasogastric tube through one of his nostrils and down toward his stomach. Through the tube she poured mineral oil. It would act as a laxative, relieving the horse's painful cramps. She focused on her work in the quiet, losing track of the time. She was almost finished when suddenly the hair at the nape of her neck stood on end, and she felt a chill clutch at her heart.

Somebody's watching me, she thought.

Jerking her head up, she looked behind her into the pitch black of the stable. She could have sworn that she saw a figure suddenly step back into the darkness, but she couldn't be certain.

"Ducci?" she asked. "Is that you?"

There was no reply, and after a moment she shook her head as if to clear it and turned her attention back to the horse. *I guess the stormy night and the power failure have me spooked,* she thought. *Just like the horses.* She felt silly because ordinarily mere power failures and storms didn't affect her in the least. They were common in the country.

Maybe it's simply the situation, she thought. *My first time at Stonelair. All of the crazy rumors about the owner. And the giant, Ducci himself, though he seems harmless enough. I wonder what happened to him anyway?* Then it occurred to her that an estate like Stonelair, as lavish as it must be from the look of the stables, surely had a backup generator system.

She quickly finished her work on Storm Warning, giving him the last of the mineral oil, then easing the nasogastric tube back out of his nostril. She sat for a few minutes more, whispering to him and rubbing him with long, patient strokes. Satisfied that he was resting comfortably, she got to her feet. Taking first one lantern, then the other, she set them down outside the stall. Finally she repacked her medical bag and carryall and box of supplies.

At the end of the brick walk between the stalls, the glow of a flashlight appeared, and Ducci hurried toward her. "Sorry," he said, "I've been trying to get the backup generators going, but didn't have any luck yet."

"That's okay," she said. "I'm done here."

"What's the problem seem to be?" he asked.

"Severe colic," she replied. "I've given him a sedative and painkiller and mineral oil as a laxative. Let me know if there's no improvement overnight."

"Okay," Ducci said.

"And if you don't mind, could you help me get my

things back out to the Jeep?" Valerie asked. She shouldered her carryall and picked up her medical bag.

"No problem," he replied. He leaned down and
turned off the lanterns, then picked them up along with
the heavy box of supplies.

"Just follow me," he said, leading the way with the
flashlight.

When they reached the office, he held the door open
for her, and she saw that several candles had been lit.
But Valerie didn't linger. She headed toward the door
that led out to the parking area.

"Dr. Rochelle?" Ducci called from behind her.

She turned to face him, her eyebrows raised in a
question. "Yes?"

"Should I give you a check now or—?" he began.

"That's not necessary," she said, shaking her head.
"The clinic will send a bill. If you've got a business
card with the billing address, let me have one. I'll call
tomorrow to check up on Storm Warning, by the way."

"Great," he said. He went over to the big desk,
where he set down the lanterns, then flipped open a
small wooden box and extracted a card. He handed
it to her, and Valerie took it and tossed it into her
carryall.

"Thanks," she said.

He walked her out to the Jeep and opened the cargo
door for her. She shoved her medical bag in, then Ducci
set the box down in its corner and closed the door.

"Thanks a lot, Dr. Rochelle," he said.

"It's okay," Valerie said. "Keep an eye on Storm
Warning, but I think he'll be fine."

She went around to the door on the driver's side,

tossed her carryall in, then climbed in after it. As she glanced down toward the stable, a light caught her eye, visible through the outside stall doors. It moved slowly from the end near the tack room, down to the middle of the stable, and stopped in the area where Storm Warning was housed.

Weird, she thought. *Maybe Ducci and I weren't alone in there.*

She started the Jeep and nodded at Ducci, who stood watching her leave. Going back down the drive the way she'd come in, she wondered if that had been Stonelair's new occupant who'd been going to visit the horse.

But why so mysterious? she asked herself. *For that matter, why didn't he come down and introduce himself to me? Why wasn't he hovering around, like most horse owners would, while I was working on Storm Warning?* She decided she didn't have a particularly high opinion of an owner who would have an underling deal with a sick animal and not participate in its treatment himself.

Her headlights shone off the huge gates that guarded the entrance to the estate, and before she could wonder how to open them, they began to slowly glide apart as the car approached.

"Open sesame!" she said aloud. She drove through and on toward the country lane that passed the entrance to Stonelair.

What a weird place, she thought as she pulled out onto the road. Mr. Clean, the giant who'd give anybody the creeps. The storm and then the darkness. The feeling that she was being watched.

She reached over to twirl on the radio. "I could use some music after that," she said. "Maybe some loud rock and roll." *Anything,* she thought, *to shake away this creepy feeling.*

The man had watched Santo take her to the office. Then he'd stepped out of the empty stall across from Storm Warning's and gone across the brick walk to the sick horse's stall. He'd stood staring into it, unable to see the horse in the darkness. When he'd heard them leave the office and go to her car, he'd gone to the office and gotten one of the lanterns, lighting it and returning to Storm Warning's stall.

He opened the door and hung up the lantern. Then, much as he'd heard her do, he got down on his knees and whispered soothingly to the enormous animal, stroking him lovingly all the while. He'd always treated his animals with such affection—who didn't?—but he'd never seen anyone with her ability to calm an animal. Certainly not a high-strung horse like Storm Warning.

It's as if she could really communicate with the animal, he told himself. *Well, that's not so unusual, is it? But it's almost like she's got some kind of weird magic touch.* Then he smiled. *Maybe it's that whopping big sparkler of a ring she was wearing,* he thought. It had picked up the lantern light and flashed it all around the stables. "Maybe that whopper has healing powers," he whispered to Storm Warning.

Chapter Three

Valerie turned off the highway and began the drive up to the veterinarian clinic, perched on top of a hill, overlooking summer fields of green and verdant woods. It was a cool morning, and a mist still hovered over the ground. The grass was soaking wet with dew, but she knew that the mist would soon burn off, and the ground would be quickly dried by a scorcher of a summer day.

She pulled into her customary parking spot in the back of the clinic and killed the engine. She was tired for a Monday morning, and that did not sit well with her. She was usually bright-eyed and bushy-tailed when she went into the clinic, eager to get to work. But not today.

It wasn't because she'd been on call this weekend. There'd been only the one emergency at Stonelair and five or six telephone consultations on Sunday, an easy weekend. It was spending the weekend with Teddy that had been exhausting, she decided. And not because of their vigorous physical activities, either. No, it was the emotional toll that dealing with Teddy had taken out of her that had left her feeling wrung out, limp, and ineffectual. That and her own weakness in handling the situation. She had come to realize that she and she alone was responsible for her actions, and she felt that she had failed herself this weekend. In spades.

"Elvis," she said, turning to look at the mutt in the passenger seat, "I've got to snap out of it. I've got a busy week ahead, and I've got to be on my toes." Elvis turned and looked at her, wagging his tail sluggishly.

Valerie smiled and patted him, then put her car keys in her carryall and got out of the Jeep. She held the door open, allowing Elvis to jump out behind her. Letting herself in by the staff door, she headed down the hallway toward the reception area, where the door to her office was located. Elvis bounced along beside her, exhilarated as usual by being here in one of his favorite domains.

When she stepped into the reception area, the chatter she'd heard in the hallway suddenly stopped, and there was complete silence as four heads turned to stare at her: Daphne Collins and Charles Bradford, fellow vets, and Tami Reeves and Annie Wolsky, who doubled as secretaries and receptionists.

"Well, well, well," said Charles Bradford, who was also the owner of the clinic, in a hostile voice, finally breaking the silence, "we hear you've been out to the infamous Stonelair."

Valerie nodded in response.

"So it's true?" Daphne chimed in. "Our little Valerie has met the mysterious Mr. Conrad."

Valerie smiled brightly even though she was puzzled by Daphne's obvious sarcasm. It was an unusual tone for the very pretty, very blond Daphne to take with her. Valerie had always liked her and assumed that the feeling was mutual. They weren't best friends, but their relationship had been amicable from the start.

"Yes," she replied evenly, "I had to go out to Stonelair Saturday night. A horse—"

"What was he like?" interrupted Charles in a clipped, imperious manner.

"Oh, yes, Val," Daphne said, "tell us all about him." She ran her fingers through her hair in a nervous gesture and shifted her weight on her feet. She appeared to be waiting anxiously to hear what Valerie had to say.

"This Arabian stallion—" Valerie began.

"*No*-body cares about the horse, Val," Daphne said. "Tell us about Conrad!"

Everyone laughed, including the dapper Dr. Charles Bradford, who seldom ventured so enthusiastic a response.

"I didn't meet him," Valerie replied.

"What?" the three women cried in unison.

Valerie noticed that even Charles appeared to be perplexed by her response. He took off his glasses and began to clean them on a handkerchief, as if his hearing had been affected by dirty lenses.

"Sorry," she said. She smiled and shrugged apologetically.

"Damn," Daphne swore. "You mean you didn't even get a glimpse of Conrad himself?"

"No," Valerie said. "Some guy who works for him met me at the stable, and I never saw him."

"Was it the big muscley one we hear so much about?" Daphne asked.

Valerie nodded, looking at her. "Yes," she said. "He looks sort of like Mr. Clean."

"You didn't see anybody else?" Charles asked. "Nobody at all?"

"No," Valerie answered, shaking her head. "He was the only person around."

"What was he like?" Daphne asked. "Is he . . . well, I've heard he's really kind of creepy."

"He was strictly business," Valerie replied. "I didn't really get to know him. You know, I was dealing with the horse, and—"

"Oh, hell," Daphne said. "You're worthless, Val. No useful information at all."

The telephone rang, and Tami picked up. "Animal Clinic," she said in her pleasant professional voice. She listened for a moment, then said: "Hold, please."

She looked up at Valerie and held the telephone out over the top of the reception counter, a triumphant gleam in her eyes. Everyone looked over at her.

"It's for you, Dr. Rochelle," Tami said. "It's Mr. Santo Ducci at Stonelair. Line one."

"I'll take it here," Valerie said. She reached for the receiver at once rather than retreating to the privacy of her office to take the call. She wondered if Storm Warning might have taken a turn for the worse.

"Dr. Rochelle," she said.

"Good morning, Dr. Rochelle," the giant said. "This is Santo Ducci at Stonelair."

"Yes, Mr. Ducci," she replied. "Is there a problem with Storm Warning? Is he okay?"

"He's doing great," Ducci said. "Really great. There's no problem there."

"Good," she said, relieved.

"The reason I called," Ducci continued, "is that Mr. Conrad would like for you to take care of all the animals here at Stonelair. I mean you personally."

Suddenly Valerie noticed the four pairs of eyes on her. Now she wished that she'd taken the call in her office. "I appreciate that, Mr. Ducci," she said, "but that's not clinic policy. Generally speaking, we have a share-and-share-alike rule here. It depends on who's on duty. We do make exceptions, but I'd have to discuss it with the other veterinarians."

"I see," he said. "Well, I'm sure Mr. Conrad would make it worth your time if you agreed to see to his animals personally," Ducci went on. "He likes the way you handled Storm Warning, and there are a lot of animals out here to take care of."

Valerie could see that Ducci—or Conrad—was not to be easily rebuffed. "I'll see what I can do, Mr. Ducci."

"I'd appreciate that," he said. "I mean, surely the other vets there would understand if somebody wanted your services."

"I'll have to discuss it with my colleagues and get back to you," Valerie said.

"Good," Ducci said. "We'll be waiting to hear from you."

"Okay."

"And thanks again, Doc."

"You're welcome," Valerie said. When she was certain he'd hung up, she handed the receiver back over the reception counter to Tami. "Thanks, Tami."

Valerie saw the questioning looks from everyone in

the reception area. Charles Bradford broke the silence once again. "That's the guy who works for Conrad, I take it?"

Valerie nodded.

"So, what did he want?" he asked, his cold gray eyes boring into hers.

Valerie hesitated before answering, then plunged ahead. "He said they'd like for me to take care of the animals out at Stonelair," she said.

"You mean you personally?" Daphne said. "Not the clinic?"

"That's what he said."

"He must've liked your looks," Charles Bradford snapped, his tone burning with scorn. He slapped a medical chart against his thigh and strode out of the reception area toward his office, his slightly long gray hair flipping up in the breeze he created as he walked.

Valerie felt her face flush with embarrassment.

"What's wrong, Val?" Daphne asked, seeing the look on Valerie's face. "Did Charles hit a sore spot?" Without waiting for an answer, she turned and, like Charles, headed for her office.

Annie suddenly looked very busy behind the reception counter, but Tami gave Valerie a look of understanding and concern.

Valerie felt like screaming, but instead, ears burning with indignation, she quickly got a cup of coffee from the communal coffeemaker, then went to her office, Elvis trailing along behind her. She closed the door, and Elvis immediately went to his bed under her desk, where he curled up to nap. She heaved her carryall onto the desktop, then sat down heavily.

She had become accustomed to Charles's behavior, but she couldn't fathom this sudden sarcasm in Daphne. *Jeez!* she thought. *How much longer can I take this crap?* She knew that Charles was miffed because time and again clients asked for her to see to their animals rather than anyone else at the clinic. And time and again, she'd had to endure Charles's resentful, jealous remarks.

Charles had singlehandedly established the clinic and built it up into the very successful practice that it had become. Valerie realized that he had a right to feel proud of his accomplishments, but did he have the right to be so demeaning toward others? He relished his role as the boss and treated her as a Johnny-come-lately underling who should always defer to him. Perhaps he felt threatened by her in some way, particularly by her popularity with patients. He had always been the "face" of the clinic, and he wanted to keep it that way.

Daphne was another matter. She had moved up from the south only three years ago, her arrival surrounded with rumors of a torrid affair gone bad. Valerie had never learned if there was any truth to these stories, but they had gradually died down anyway and were replaced by gossip about the obvious sexual interest that Charles had in Daphne. She had quickly become the clinic's most valued employee since Charles was determined to get in her pants. As Valerie and Daphne became friendly, she'd had several opportunities to see Daphne fend off Charles's advances. She naturally assumed that Daphne had no feelings for Charles and was perhaps still stinging from the wounds of her last relationship. But she didn't really know. For as friendly as they became, Daphne never revealed much of her personal life. Theirs was an easy friendship that had grown over the past three years. Or at least that's what Valerie had thought. Today made her wonder.

"Shit, shit, shit!" she said aloud. To have to take abuse from Daphne as well as Charles was too much. *When is this ever going to end?* she thought. But she knew the answer to that question, in theory at least: *When I have my own clinic and I'm my own boss, that's when.*

There was a knock at the door, then it opened before she could answer.

"Here," Tami said, her hand extended. "You forgot your schedule for today."

"Thanks, Tami." Valerie took the proffered sheet of paper.

"You're welcome," Tami said, eyeing her curiously before closing the office door.

Valerie took a sip of coffee and looked down at the schedule, but she didn't really see it. *I can't concentrate,* she thought miserably. She realized that her defenses were at a low point this morning and that the catty remarks had bothered her more than usual. Suddenly she felt almost overwhelmed by worry and fear and had a powerful urge to cry, but she was determined not to.

I'm not going to let them get the best of me, she thought.

It had all started with Teddy this weekend—her worries and fears—with his proposal and her own stupid response. Now it was only getting worse, and here at work, which she'd always thought of as a sort of haven.

Her vision of working in a veterinarian clinic, caring for animals, had always been one of a peaceable kingdom where concern for animals was of paramount importance. She hadn't envisioned the office politics, the games of one-upmanship. She had never dreamed of the sometimes callous attitude that doctors and staff displayed toward the animals and their owners. Nor had she imagined that it would take her years to pay off the tens of thousands of dollars she owned in loans that she'd taken out to get through school.

Elvis growled in his sleep, and she reached down and stroked him gently. *I've got to snap out of it,* she thought. *Self-pity will get me nowhere fast.* She picked up the daily schedule and took a sip of her coffee. She could see that it was going to be a busy day, and she was glad of that. It would keep her mind off of her troubles. The telephone rang, and she idly picked up the receiver, still perusing the schedule.

"Hello," she said.

"Valerie, dear," the cultured, dulcet voice of her mother intoned.

"Hi, Mother," she said, wishing now that she'd told Tami to screen her calls—and feeling guilty about having such a thought.

"How was your weekend, dear?" her mother asked.

Damn! Valerie thought. *I wonder if Teddy's already talked to her, and she knows about the ring.* "It was okay," she replied mildly.

"That's all?" her mother asked pointedly. "Okay?"

"Yes," Valerie replied. She decided she would not let her mother push her around this morning.

"I see," Marguerite de la Rochelle said. She paused momentarily, then continued. "I phoned because I want you and Teddy to come to dinner tonight."

"But today's Monday, Mother," Valerie said. "Teddy's gone back to—" Then she remembered that Teddy was taking the week off. He was staying out in the country.

"I should think you would know better than that," Marguerite said with reproach. "I spoke to him early this morning. He's staying at Apple Hill all week, and he'll be here for dinner."

Valerie's heart sank. *They're ganging up on me,* she thought. *The two of them are in cahoots as usual.* "I wish you'd discussed this with me first," she said. "I have a very busy day and need to get a lot of things done at home tonight."

"I'm sure that whatever it is you have to do at your little home can wait," Marguerite said disparagingly. "I'll expect you around eight, dear."

Before Valerie could answer, her mother had hung up. *Shit,* she thought as she replaced the receiver in its cradle. *Why do I let her do this to me? And why does she always make me feel like a naughty child who is guilty of something? Why does she always make fun of my little house? The house I've worked so hard to buy?*

She wanted to scream for the second time that morning, but restrained herself, gritting her teeth. *I'd like to choke them both,* she thought. *Teddy and my mother!* She could already envision tonight's dinner. First, Marguerite would have to see the ring and swoon and coo to Teddy about it. Then Teddy and Marguerite would laugh and talk amiably, like old lovers, gossiping about mutual friends and acquaintances, the latest antics among the bluebloods in Manhattan and here in the country, and finally coming to focus all of their considerable energies on *her*.

Pressuring her into setting a date. Pressuring her into putting her house on the market and moving in with Teddy. Pressuring her to accept Teddy's offer to build her a clinic of her own and pay off her loans. Pressuring her into giving up nearly all the independence and self-reliance that she'd worked so long and hard to achieve. Soon enough, they'd be pressuring her into having babies and working part-time or giving up her work altogether.

And never once taking into account her own thoughts and feelings on anything. Never once giving her any credit for having an opinion, discounting out of hand any that she might express. It was as if she didn't matter in all of the elaborate plans they'd worked out for her.

Some things never change, she realized. Growing up, Valerie had been an outsider even in her own family. Marguerite was a vain and beautiful woman, obsessed with her own physical appearance and, equally as important, the image that the de la Rochelle family presented to the world. She was still incensed that Valerie had chosen to drop the "de la" from her name and go simply by Rochelle, failing to understand that Valerie had done it for simplicity's sake. Valerie de la Rochelle was a mouthful for some of her clients, and actually created a sort of barrier between her and others. Besides, she thought, we're no longer living in the Dark Ages when such distinctions came about and might have actually meant something.

Her mother, however, didn't see it that way at all. The de la Rochelle family could be nothing less than perfection at all times—in looks, behavior, and manners. They were also to be perceived as having healthy, happy—perfect!—relationships with one another and the coterie of rich, old-money families that made up their social circle.

In this and nearly every other respect, Valerie had been a miserable disappointment to her mother—and her father, for that matter. While he'd been alive, he'd been in league with Marguerite just as Teddy was now. Armand de la Rochelle had always dressed well, behaved well, and played the role of the wealthy gentleman heir to the fortune he'd inherited—and had managed to increase by his marriage to the equally rich Marguerite de Coligny.

Like Marguerite, Armand had been obsessed by appearances, and until the end, people had been fooled into believing that the world of the de la Rochelles was perfect in every way. Beautiful, tasteful, elegant, to the manor born.

She had loved her father dearly and missed him still, but she couldn't fool herself into believing that it had been reciprocated. He'd been as disappointed in her as her mother, with many of the very same complaints.

"Why must you keep your nose buried in that book, Valerie, dear?"

"Why don't you play with the other young people, Valerie, dear?"

"Why must you devote yourself to those filthy animals, Valerie, dear?"

"Why must you be all elbows and knees? So unattractive, so *ugly*, Valerie, dear?"

She could hear their voices as if it were yesterday. Both of them, Mother and Father, denigrating her from the time she was old enough to understand what they were saying to her. Perhaps they hadn't meant to be cruel; perhaps they had been challenging her to be her best. Whatever the case, the result had been to make her retreat into herself, to shy away from a world that also thought she was a gangly, awkward, four-eyed bookworm.

Virtually friendless and scorned by her beautiful parents, she had eventually found solace in animals. From an early age she had made friends of her pets, confiding in them, playing with them, telling them her joys and sorrows, her deepest secrets, caring for them in a way that others found eccentric. As she'd grown older, she'd begun to nurse her pets and any other sick or injured animal she came upon. Birds, dogs, cats, even a racoon and a chicken.

She had discovered that she could communicate with her pets on a level that most people would consider amazing—or, more likely, frightening. She'd kept this knowledge to herself, knowing that her family would disapprove anyway. She had decided early on that she wanted to be a veterinarian, a profession that would draw an equally unenthusiastic response from the powers that be.

She was expected to go to the "right" schools, blossom into a beautiful debutante, and eventually marry the "right" man. If she must work, she must do something genteel. Charity committee work, board directorships, perhaps something in the art or publishing worlds, if not too commercial, might fill the bill.

Valerie had gone to the "right" schools. Just before Armand died, she had even been presented to society in a New York City debutante ball. All to please her parents.

It was about this time that Valerie began to blossom. The gangly, awkward girl who'd been all knees and elbows with no breasts to speak of was gradually turning into a swan. Suddenly young men began to pay attention to her, but Valerie, who'd spent her childhood and youth alone, didn't really know how to cope with the attention. She had no use for small talk, was terrible at the social niceties, and really preferred the company of her menagerie, who understood her as she understood them.

When the question of college came up, Marguerite, newly bereaved, insisted that Valerie attend one of the Seven Sisters or, preferably, go to an exclusive finishing school in Switzerland. Valerie, however, had defied her mother for the first time in her life, choosing instead to go to Cornell and prepare for veterinarian school.

"Then you'll pay for it yourself," Marguerite had said. "You could be in Switzerland learning the proper way to be a wife and mother and a social figure of importance. Besides which, you would inevitably meet young ladies of your class and an appropriate young man to marry. But Cornell! I won't give you a penny for such nonsense."

"I'll find a way," Valerie had responded.

And she had, working part-time and taking out student loans, year after year. She never once asked her mother for anything, and her mother never volunteered it. Nor had Marguerite deigned to come to her graduation ceremonies.

Now, sitting in her office, Valerie imagined that her mother would be very pleased if she knew how miserable she was this morning. She caught herself laughing suddenly, amused by the situation. *Well,* she thought, *I'm not going to give her a reason to gloat. No way! I've succeeded in doing what I set out to do. And if I stick it out, I know I can do the rest.*

An image of Storm Warning abruptly came into her mind. She could see the stallion, panicked at first, rolling in his stall, covered with sweat, scared for his life. And later, after her gentle care, she could see the trusting look in his eyes. She could still sense the bond that had been formed between them, and it made her feel good.

Then she remembered the shadowy figure she'd seen while she'd been working on Storm Warning. Was it Conrad? she wondered. And, if so, why the secrecy? For that matter, why hadn't a single person hereabouts laid eyes on the mystery man since he'd bought and renovated Stonelair?

She felt a sudden twinge in her stomach, an uncomfortable feeling that she couldn't quite describe. All thoughts of tonight's dinner and unpleasant office politics were swept away, and she felt a new sense of uneasiness that she couldn't explain. It was something about Stonelair, of that she was certain, but what was it that had her so spooked?

Chapter Four

Wyndhym Ashley Conrad III slowly paced back and forth across the library's faded Portuguese needlepoint rug, a mug of coffee in one hand and an unlit cigarette in the other. A black baseball cap partially hid his long, slightly curly raven-black hair and all but obscured the thoughtful expression in his velvety dark brown eyes. The sleeves on his long-sleeved black T-shirt were rolled up above his elbows, revealing strong, muscular forearms and powerful-looking hands. Matching sweatpants, cinched tightly against the flat plane of his stomach, hung loosely on his muscular legs.

As he paced, four enormous Irish wolfhounds watched his every move. Two of them, both gray, were ensconced on tufted antique leather sofas that faced one another in front of the French limestone fireplace mantel. The other two, one brindle and the other brown, had arrayed themselves on the rug near the hearth. On their alert faces were looks of equal parts devotion and curiosity.

Wyn, finally weary of his aimless strides, sprawled on the cracked leather of an ancient Georgian wing chair and looked over at Santo Ducci, who was talking on the telephone behind Wyn's desk, a Louis XV *bureau plat*. He took a sip of his coffee and grimaced. It was already cold.

He tossed his unlit cigarette into a crystal ashtray and got back up, walking over to an ornate gilded console and draining the coffee mug in an orchid plant on the marble top. Then he walked to the minibar that was concealed behind a jib door near the fireplace and poured himself a fresh cup of coffee from the coffeemaker there. He retraced his steps, sipping the hot black coffee as he went, but before he could sit back down, Santo quietly hung up the telephone and looked over at him.

"That was the vet, right?" Wyn asked.

Santo shook his head. "No," he replied. The sun, which streamed through the French doors behind him, shone off the top of his shaved head.

"No?" Wyn said irritably. He glared at Santo, but the giant couldn't read the look in Wyn's eyes because of the long shadow cast by his baseball cap. "Didn't I tell you to call her first thing this morning?"

"And I did," Santo said mildly. He gazed at his boss dispassionately, his hugely muscled arms folded across his chest, his feathers completely unruffled by Wyn's irritation. "That was somebody else," he added.

"Oh," Wyn said, frowning. "Well then, tell me, Santo. What the hell did the vet say?"

"They share and share alike," Santo said. "She said it was usually against clinic policy."

"Against clinic policy?" Wyn stormed. "That's a crock of shit."

Santo held his hands out, gesturing at Wyn to hold on a minute. "Chill out," he said calmly. "She said she'll discuss it with the other vets and get back to me. It's a possibility."

"I never heard of anything so stupid," Wyn groused.

"I told you, she said they have a share-and-share-alike policy," Santo countered.

"What the hell is that supposed to mean?"

"It's simple. You don't normally get to choose a particular vet," Santo said. "You get whoever's on duty."

"That's ridiculous," Wyn spat. "This isn't a third-world country."

"Maybe not," Santo said, "but that's the usual policy."

"Damn!" Wyn sat down in the big wing chair and slammed his mug of coffee on the table next to it. Coffee sloshed out onto the table's highly polished walnut surface, but he ignored it. "Find out who owns the fucking clinic," he demanded, casting a scowl in Santo's direction.

"That's what I just did."

"And?" Wyn asked impatiently.

Santo looked down at some notes he'd scratched out on a pad. "A guy named Charles Bradford—he's one of the other vets," he said. "Owns it lock, stock, and barrel. Rochelle is just a salaried employee."

Wyn looked disgruntled. "Aw, shit," he said.

"Look," Santo said, trying to placate his unhappy boss, "don't get yourself so worked up. I bet it'll work out. She said she'd discuss it with the other docs, so she must be interested, Wyn. Right? She wouldn't bother talking to them if she wasn't. She'd have just said no." He looked at Wyn for some indication that he was satisfied. *Jeez,* he thought, *the guy's acting like a spoiled rich kid that has to have it his way, or else. What's worse, lately he's been carrying on like a genuine nutcase.* Santo was patient, however, because he figured that with all of Wyn's worries, he'd be pretty much a basket case himself.

Wyn finally nodded. "I guess you're right," he agreed. He looked thoughtful for a moment, then added: "Call her back and tell her that, if she does it, there'll be a bonus in it for her. A bonus that the others don't need to know about."

"If you say so."

"I say so," Wyn said emphatically.

But before Santo could pick up the telephone, it rang, and he answered it. "Stonelair," he said.

He listened for a minute, then said: "I'll have to put you on hold for a moment."

He punched the hold button and looked over at Wyn. "It's Arielle."

Wyn shook his head. "I'm not available," he said. "But put her on the speaker so I can listen."

Santo punched the hold button again, then the speaker button, after which he replaced the receiver in its cradle. "I'm sorry, Arielle," he said. "He can't come to the phone right now."

"You're lying to me, Santo." Her disembodied voice filled the room, its smokiness tinged with anger. The Irish wolfhounds pricked up their ears at the sound of their former mistress's voice.

"No, Arielle," he replied, "I'm not lying."

"You bastard!" she cried nastily. "You sound like you're in a garbage can. You put me on the fucking speaker so that shit can listen."

Santo looked over at Wyn, whose lips formed a smile.

"Let me speak to him," Arielle shouted.

"I told you, Arielle," Santo said in his most patient voice, "he can't come to the telephone now."

There was an audible sigh of resignation from the speaker. Then in calm and measured tones, Arielle said, "Tell him that his monthly support check hasn't arrived yet, and it's overdue. As you well know. I called Goldman's office, and his secretary said they haven't received it yet."

"I'll pass the word along," Santo said.

"You do that," Arielle replied, a bit more vinegar in her voice. "And while you're at it, tell him that they told me he hasn't sent back the signed divorce papers yet."

"I don't know about that," Santo said.

"I just bet you don't," she snapped. Then she sighed loudly again, as if suddenly realizing that she must take a different tack. Being demanding and unpleasant was getting her nowhere with Santo, and certainly wouldn't with Wyn, that she well knew. Thus, the hint of the helpless, little-girl plea that crept into her voice.

"Oh, Santo, please," she said rather sweetly. "You've got to help me. You're the *only* person who can. I don't know what I'm going to do. First the monthly support check's late, and now I find out he hasn't signed the divorce papers yet."

"I'll see what I can do," Santo said.

"Yes, please, Santo," she begged. "You know they won't release the final settlement check until he's signed everything, and I really need it. I mean, Christ, until the measly support check comes"—a sob that might arguably have been genuine caught in her throat— "it's all I can do to eat!"

Wyn almost laughed aloud when he heard this, but restrained himself. He knew that she was fairly certain he was listening, but he wanted to keep her guessing. If nothing else, it compounded her misery, and that gave him no end of pleasure.

"I'm sick and tired of the whole mess," Arielle went on. "I just want it over with, and I thought he did, too. It's time we both got on with our lives, you know? Even all the therapists say so. This isn't doing either one of us any good."

"I hear what you're saying," Santo said. He looked over at Wyn again and saw a twisted smile on his lips. *He's really enjoying this,* Santo thought. *Sick fucker.* He cleared his voice. "I'll do what I can, Arielle."

"Please do, Santo," she whined. "I mean, I always thought we were friends, you and me, and I really need your help." Her voice choked up again.

Was it real? Wyn wondered with amusement. *Or had her acting abilities improved?*

"Oh, Jesus!" she managed to cry. "If you only knew! They started to turn off the electricity today. It's that bad."

"I told you, Arielle," he said, "I'll do what I can. I promise you that."

"Well . . . thanks, Santo," she whimpered girlishly. "Talk to you later. Ciao."

They heard her hang up, and Santo reached over and turned off the speaker. The room was once again silent but for the collective breathing of the dogs. It was momentary, however.

"Of all the women I had back in those days," Wyn said ruefully, "I had to go and pick Arielle. What a joke." He began to laugh. It was a laugh that began somewhere deep down within him, gradually swelling up and out, filling the room with a roar. It was an evil sound, this laugh, and Santo turned and stared at his boss as did the wolfhounds.

He looks like a man possessed, Santo thought, almost mesmerized by Wyn's gleeful laugh. *Possessed by a demon straight from hell.* Sometimes lately, he'd begun to think that Wyn really had gone off the deep end.

Santo stared out through the French doors toward the swimming pool in the distance. He didn't want to be a witness to a scene that was, to his mind, sick, even perverse. It made him feel somehow unclean and stirred something deep down inside him, something frightening and inexplicable in his own nature that he'd yet to face.

When Wyn had at last exhausted his well of laughter, he got to his feet and padded over to a big Sicilian rococo gilt console. On its marble top were dozens of bottles—liquor, wine, seltzer, tonic, mixers, soda, and mineral water—a sterling ice bucket, and crystal glasses of every kind. He picked up a large crystal glass, plopped a few ice cubes in with tongs, and poured himself a glass of mineral water. He took a slice of lime from an ornate silver bowl and squeezed it into the drink, then tossed it in. Taking a crisp linen cocktail napkin from the stack that was replenished daily by Gerda, his Austrian housekeeper and cook, he nestled the glass in it, then turned to look at Santo. He took a sip of his water, staring at the giant's back across the room.

"You don't like it, do you, Santo?"

"Like what?" Santo said without turning around.

"This divorce business," Wyn said. "Making sure the monthly support checks are late and all that."

"It's none of my business."

"Then make it your business," Wyn said. "Tell me what you think."

Santo turned around and looked over at his boss. He could hardly make out Wyn's face at all beneath the cap. "Well, if I were you," he said, "number one, I'd send her monthly support check out. I could overnight it, you know. Number two," he went on, "I think you ought to go ahead and sign the papers and get this whole thing over with. You're spending a fortune on the lawyers as it is, and there's no advantage in dragging it out any longer."

"Oh, yes, there is," Wyn said with merriment.

"What?"

"It makes the bitch that much more miserable," Wyn said.

Santo sighed and rolled his eyes. "Well . . . yes," he agreed. "But—"

"Shut up, Santo," Wyn said. He took a long, leisurely swallow of the mineral water. "I'll sign the papers when I get good and ready. She's just in a hurry because she wants the settlement check."

He walked over to the table beside the wing chair and picked up the unlit cigarette from the ashtray, then stuck it in his mouth. "*And* she's in a hurry for the settlement check not only because she's a greedy little bitch but because she wants to tie the knot with that South American dude with the big equipment."

Santo sat down in the chair behind Wyn's desk. "Are you just pissed off and trying to punish her because she's found somebody she wants to marry?" he asked.

Wyn looked at him. "Maybe." He nodded. "That and a lot of other things."

"I still think you ought to let it go," Santo said. "It'd be the best thing for both of you. Get the whole thing over with. Besides, you know she's going to marry him no matter what."

"Maybe," Wyn agreed. "But I want to watch them squirm a little while longer." He smiled widely, a smile that even Santo could see from across the room. "It'll be interesting to see if her stud decides to stick around or vamoose for richer territory."

"Maybe they're really in love," Santo suggested.

"Aw, Jesus, Santo," Wyn said with exasperation. "They're both like sharks on the prowl, seeing what they can finagle out of each other. Sometimes I think you're as stupid as you are ugly. *Love!*" He barked a laugh. "Sex and money make the world go around," he said, pointing a finger at Santo. "Love's got nothing to do with it, my friend. And don't you forget it."

Santo stared at him, then cleared his throat. "I'm not ugly."

"Yeah, well, I didn't mean that," Wyn said. "What I meant was . . . menacing. You look menacing."

Santo smiled. "Menacing," he said, as if tasting the word on his tongue. "I like that. Yeah, I can deal with that. Menacing."

"I would hope so," Wyn said. "It's one of the reasons you work for me." He got to his feet and stretched. "What time is it?"

Santo looked at the gold Rolex on his wrist, a gift from Wyn. "About ten."

"It's time," Wyn said.

Santo nodded. "I'll be right back." He rose to his feet and strode in a ripple of muscles out of the library.

Wyn walked over to one of the French doors and stood gazing out at the pool, thoughts of Arielle swirling in his head. Paddy, one of the wolfhounds, bounded off the couch and edged up to his side, nuzzling him. Wyn idly stroked the massive dog's head.

"She may be a beauty, Paddy," he said thoughtfully, "but she's also a bitch. And she's got it coming to her . . . anything I dish out. She's got it coming to her."

Santo returned to the library. In one hand he gripped a black leather bag that he placed on the desk. He opened it and extracted a bottle of rubbing alcohol and a paper packet containing a cotton swab. Setting them aside, he delved back into the bag and withdrew a glass, rubber-topped medicine bottle and a still-packaged disposable syringe and needle.

From the French doors, Wyn turned and watched as Santo tore the wrapper off the syringe, then inserted the needle in the rubber-topped glass container. The syringe filled with a colorless fluid. When Santo was finished, he looked over at Wyn.

Wyn walked to the desk, loosened his sweatpants,

and pulled down his jockstrap. He put both hands on the desk and bent over, exposing his bare buttocks to the air. He jerked involuntarily as the cold alcohol hit his ass, then gradually relaxed. He didn't tense up when he felt a prick of pain as the needle plunged in. He waited a moment, the breath caught in his throat, and there it was. That almost instantaneous—he was always amazed that it only took mere seconds—feeling that washed over him as the drug's powerful effect began to work on his body.

As he straightened up, he could feel himself already begin to drift. He bent down and pulled up his jock-strap and sweatpants. Then he turned around, his eyes blinking slowly as they swept the magnificence of the mahogany-paneled library. Santo came to his side, and a faint smile touched Wyn's lips.

He began walking, slowly and deliberately, toward the spiral stairs that led up to the balcony, which ran around three walls of the library. When he reached the balcony, he went through a hidden jib door built into the balcony bookcases, and on down a hallway to his bedroom. Santo was right behind him, shadowing his every step, following him to the bedroom, to make certain he got there.

Even before they reached the darkness of his inner sanctum, Wyn felt himself begin to float, detaching from this place as if he were a balloon let loose to drift in the sky. Floating above it all up to a better place, a place with no pain, a place with no harsh realities. Floating, floating.

Chapter Five

Teddy de Mornay was comfortably sprawled in the office desk chair at Apple Hill Farm, his feet propped up on the desk. There was a glint of mischief in his eyes as he hung up the telephone, and he smiled widely when Lydia Parsons, his part-time secretary, click-clacked into the office on zebra-print stiletto heels.

"Hey, Lydia," he said. "How are you this morning?"

Lydia Parsons, her hair dyed a flaming red and set in huge swirls that looked as if they'd been fixed in place with cement, returned his smile, revealing big, yellowing teeth. "I'm fine, Teddy," she said. Her eyes narrowed as she looked down at his feet on the desk. "I see you've been out riding this morning."

"Yep," he replied, knocking his cowboy boots together.

"What's the big occasion?" she asked, knowing he despised horses.

"Oh, you know Val," he replied. "She claims old

Kaiser doesn't get enough exercise and says I ought to ride him more."

"Aha," Lydia exclaimed. "So you're trying to impress your honey, doing all these things you hate to do."

"Huh," Teddy grunted noncommittally, although trying to please Valerie was exactly what he'd been doing. He'd gotten up early this morning, put on worn cowboy boots and old Levi's, and taken a short ride up into the hills. It had been beautiful, and he'd hated every single minute of it.

"Bet you two had fun this weekend," Lydia said with a lewd wink.

"That, too."

"Good," she said. "Because you've got a busy week ahead of you."

"What's up?" he asked.

She walked over to her desk and picked up a clipboard. "Let's see," she began. "Today we've got the pool cleaners. No big deal. The nursery guys are coming to do some general garden maintenance and see about that big maple that was struck by lightning. Then the painter's supposed to be here to do an estimate on painting the guest house, but that's Sammy Burke—" she looked over at him meaningfully—"so you never know if the son of a bitch will show up. He might be on a bender."

Teddy laughed.

She looked down at the clipboard again. "Then there's a stack of paperwork to sign, a bunch of checks to get out, some money transfers to take care of . . ."

"Never mind," Teddy said testily. He reached over

and unceremoniously jerked the clipboard out of her hands, failing to notice the bright purple nail polish with little gold stars she'd had applied at the mall beauty parlor over the weekend.

Lydia stared at him, one hand on a hip, as he perused the clipboard briefly, then tossed it on the desk.

"Damn," he said. "There's a lot to do. And I've got to have dinner with Mrs de la Rochelle to boot."

"Well . . . ," Lydia said, brushing imaginary lint off of her leopard-print blouse, "there's nothing here that I can't handle by myself, Teddy. Except for signing some of the paperwork. You could do that later or tomorrow. You don't have to stick around."

Teddy looked off into the distance, then back up at Lydia, really seeing her for the first time this morning. *She looks like a circus clown,* he thought uncharitably. *All that makeup: blue eyeshadow, red, red rouge, purplish lipstick. Big red hair. And those clothes! Leopard blouse with tiger skirt. Lots of cheap costume jewelry. Zebra-print stiletto heels with little leopard bows. She's sixty going on sixteen.*

He kept his thoughts to himself, however, because Lydia Parsons was an ace secretary, a great organizer, knew everybody in the area, and was fearless. She could get almost anything she wanted out of anybody. Plus, she was utterly devoted to him, and, he was certain, would hop into the old sack with him at a moment's notice. Not that he wanted her. God, no.

"Do you think you could hold down the fort for the next couple of hours?" he asked at last. "Just till after lunch, say?"

Lydia laughed good-naturedly, bending over his

desk, exposing a couple of inches of cleavage. "Sure," she said. "It's done." She eyed him fondly—and conspiratorially. "You never could keep that thing in your pants, could you, Teddy?"

He shrugged. "Why should I?"

"Never was a truer word spoken," she countered with a cackle.

He got to his feet, leaned down, and planted a noisy kiss on Lydia's cheek. "You're an angel from heaven," he said, tapping her on her ample butt.

"And you're the devil from hell," she retorted. "But I love you anyway."

"See you in a bit," he said, already heading out to his car.

"Yeah," she said. "See you." She watched through the window as he hopped into his silver Jaguar convertible and fired it up. The top was down, and as he drove off, his blond hair was tossed about in the wind.

Jeez, she thought, *he is a vision. I wouldn't mind a little of that myself.* But she knew better than to pursue it because she and Teddy had a good thing going as it was. Strictly business. And sometimes, Lydia had decided wisely, that was the best way to keep things. *Besides,* she thought, a smile of wicked pleasure on her purple lips, *I've got Randy, and he's more than enough for one woman to handle. Twenty-three years old and just full of energy!*

Teddy's Jaguar spewed gravel as he pulled out of the drive and onto the highway. It was only five or six miles down the road to the little clapboard cottage that Tiffani Grant leased from him—at a greatly reduced rent—but he was in a hurry to get there. Monday was her day off work, and he didn't spend many Mondays in the country.

When he'd called her after his horseback ride, she'd picked up after several rings, sleep still in her voice. He could just see her, still in bed, bleached blond hair disheveled, a sexy nightie or, better yet, nothing at all on, a sheet draped over those big breasts, curled up in a big warm bed waiting for him. Teddy could feel a rise in his pants just thinking about it, and stepped on the gas.

When he neared the dirt road that led to the old cottage, he began to brake, then made the right turn off the highway and sped the hundred feet or so to the house, the car leaving a dust cloud in its wake. Circling around in the back to park, he drove across the lawn and pulled in close to the house where his car wouldn't be visible from the highway. Even though he owned the property, he didn't want anybody to see his car parked there for too long a time.

No need to give any of the old biddies around here an excuse to talk, he thought. *They all think I'm a perfect gentleman with real class. One of the few city people who treats the locals with the respect they deserve.* He laughed aloud. If they only knew! He loved fooling them, and he loved the sneaking around. That was part of the fun for him, because he had a real taste for the illicit. In fact, he had never really enjoyed sex much unless it involved some kind of subterfuge.

He hopped out of the car and bounded up the wooden steps to the back door, knocking on it a couple of times with his knuckles. When she didn't respond immediately, he tried the knob. *Damn!* he thought. *It's locked.* But before he could dash around to the front, he could hear Tiffani hurrying through the kitchen, headed to the door.

After fumbling with locks, she opened the door a crack and looked up at him. "Teddy," she said, smiling lasciviously.

He pushed his way in, then turned around and pulled her to him. She had a big pink towel wrapped around her voluptuous body, and her long, bleach-streaked hair was still wet from the shower.

"Hey, Tiff," he said, his hands already on her buttocks, pushing her hard against him. His mouth was on her neck then, kissing and licking and nibbling.

"Wait, Teddy," she said, trying to wriggle out of his grasp. "Just a minute."

He lifted his head and looked at her. "What is it, babe?" he said.

She smiled again, then slammed the door shut behind her and jerked off the towel. It fell to the floor in a heap.

Teddy stared at her body, his eyes sweeping her up and down, widening at the sight of her large creamy breasts with their raspberry nipples, lingering momentarily on her firm creamy thighs, fixing themselves hungrily on the completely shaved honeypot that lay between them. He groaned aloud, then threw himself against her, his hands everywhere at once.

Tiffani giggled gleefully and struggled against him. "Come on, Teddy," she gasped. "Not here. Let's go into the bedroom."

He followed her across the kitchen's worn linoleum,

through the little dining room and living room, and down a hallway to one of the two bedrooms, getting out of his his polo shirt as they went. In the bedroom, he quickly pulled off his cowboy boots and tossed them on the floor, then loosened his belt and took off his jeans, throwing them on top of the boots.

Tiffani watched him, taking delight in his long, lean torso and his well-defined musculature. He was so unlike most of the men she knew. Teddy was so clean and blond and hard, in shape but not a steroid freak either. Most of the men she'd been with in the last few years—and there'd been too many to count—had been former football players gone to fat; hairy, dirty bikers with big beer bellies; or rangy, raw, or clumsy farm boys or tradesmen who didn't really give her much pleasure. There'd been more than a few of the local bodybuilders, and she liked their bodies, for sure. But they seemed more pleased with themselves than any-thing she could offer them. With most all the men, Tiffani often reflected, it had been the old in and out, slam, bam, thank you, ma'am. Except most of them had omitted the thank-you. She could count the real good lovers—the ones who wanted to give her pleasure as well as get it—on one hand.

Teddy was so different. She watched, entranced, when he started to take off his jockey shorts, but quickly stopped him with a hand and a knowing look and went down on her knees in front of him. She slowly began pulling his shorts down with her long, pink-lacquered fingernails, looking up at him reveren-tially for a moment, then straight ahead at the prize between his legs.

As it sprang free, her tongue darted out and began licking his cock slowly, delicately, and lovingly, all the while gradually easing his jockey shorts down to the floor. He stepped out of them and put his hands on her head, guiding it onto his engorged phallus. Tiffani took it, going down as far as she possibly could, then began to suck on it furiously.

"Ahhhh," Teddy groaned, thrusting himself at her, "Tiff, you're going to make me come."

She eased her mouth away and stood up facing him. Teddy reached over and took a breast in each of his hands and began stroking them, thrumming her nipples with his thumbs. Tiffani gasped and pushed up against him, reaching down for his cock. He slid one hand down between her thighs and began stroking her soft shaved mound, excited by its nakedness, then slowly put a finger in her, feeling her wetness.

Tiffani trembled and whimpered. "Oh, please, Teddy," she begged. "Please."

Unable to wait any longer, he pushed her onto the bed and mounted her, her legs spread wide to welcome him. They were both in a frenzy of desire, and Teddy began thrusting away like a man possessed, Tiffani grinding against him with all her might. It was over almost as quickly as it had begun, Teddy bellowing as he heaved against her in release, and Tiffani squirming wildly against him, squealing ecstatically, kicking her legs as she contracted with one climax after another.

He collapsed on top of her, then rolled off onto his back, the two of them gasping for breath. When she could speak, Tiffani rolled to her side and kissed his cheek. "Can you stay a while?" she asked.

"An hour or so," he said. Then he looked at her. "Why?" he asked. "You got something special in mind?"

Tiffani giggled. "Maybe," she said. She sat up in bed and threw her legs over the side, her back to him. She reached over to the bedside cabinet and opened a drawer, rummaging around inside it. When she turned back around, she held up a small glass vial of white powder. A tiny metal spoon was attached to the top of it.

"Lookee what I've got," she said, wiggling her hand.

Teddy's eyes were riveted to the vial of white powder. "Wow, baby," he said, sitting up. "You won the lottery or what?"

Tiffani's brown eyes gleamed with mischief. "Something like that."

"Come on," he said. "Where'd you get it? I know that's not any of my stuff."

She spread out on the bed, and he stared down at her. "A little birdie," she said teasingly.

"Aw, Tiff," he cajoled. "Where?"

"You know that bar where I used to work?" she said.

He nodded. It was a local joint that catered to a crowd of hard partyers, mostly in their twenties to forties, a lot of them divorced and on the make, most all of them hourly workers.

"Well, I was in there the other night, just having a drink. You know. Anyway, this guy I used to know—he was a regular customer when I worked there—he gave it to me."

"You mean he just *gave* it to you?" he asked incredulously.

She stared at him a moment. "Why not?" she asked.

"We're friends, sort of. You're not jealous, are you, Teddy?"

"No," he said, dropping onto the bed beside her. "That's stupid. Why would I be jealous?"

"Oh, I don't know," she said coyly. "You just don't look very happy suddenly."

"You're crazy, Tiff," he said. "But it doesn't make sense, does it. This guy just *gives* you a couple of hundred bucks worth of coke? Don't tell me he doesn't want something for it."

"If that's what you're thinking," she said, "you're wrong. He's just being nice to me 'cause I used to fix him up with girls. Besides, he's always got lots of coke 'cause he's a dealer."

Teddy's eyes sparkled with glee, then he laughed. "You know some interesting characters, Tiff."

"I guess so," she said. She sat up and unscrewed the bottle cap, then spooned out some coke, carefully holding it steady. "Want some?"

Teddy sat up on one elbow and, when she had the spoon under his nose, took a deep snort, a finger closing one nostril while he sucked the precious powder up the other. The taste was terrible, medicinal, but he knew the effect would be highly pleasant.

He lay back and watched as Tiffani snorted some, then replaced the cap on the bottle. She slid out of bed and turned to him. "I'll be right back," she said.

He watched her walk toward the bathroom. *Amazing body,* he thought. *Straight from heaven.* She never ceased to arouse him, even though she wasn't exactly the brightest woman he knew. She was pretty dense actually. But what the hell?

Tiffani was great for sex. Loved a little kink, too. She was like forbidden fruit, now that he thought about it: from the wrong side of the tracks, too much makeup, too much hair, cheap sexy clothes. Completely unsuitable for somebody like him and just his cup of tea. A lot like Lydia must have been forty years ago, except Lydia was smart. Beyond that . . . well, she was only amusing in bed, but that's all he wanted her for.

Tiffani came back into the bedroom, her large breasts bobbing against her rib cage. She slid onto the bed and put an arm across his chest. "You're so quiet," she said. "You tired, baby?"

"Had a rough weekend."

"Ah," she said. "Did that horse doctor fuck your brains out?"

"No," he said, irritated that she would bring Valerie into the conversation. "She had an early night yesterday because she was up nearly all night Saturday. At your boss's place, as a matter of fact."

She lifted her head and looked down at him. "You're kidding, really?"

"Really," he said.

"What did she say about him?"

"Nothing," he replied. "She didn't even see him. Just that muscle freak who works for him."

"God," she said, shivering involuntarily, "that guy's so weird. He scares me half to death. But the whole place scares me."

"Why?" Teddy asked without any real curiosity. "That sounds pretty stupid to me."

"It's not stupid!" Tiffani replied. "I've been working there part-time ever since they bought that place.

Conrad bought it three years ago, and he's lived there for a year. And you know what? I still haven't seen him, the owner, except maybe if you count one time when I think I saw him at the window, staring outside."

"What did he look like?" Teddy asked idly. He could feel the cocaine begin to work its magic.

"Who knows?" Tiffani said. "All I saw was a man standing there. Not Santo 'cause I could tell if it'd been him." She lay back on the pillow again and slowly ran a finger down Teddy's chest.

"And you know what else?"

"What?" he asked, indulging her.

"I've never even been in that house. I've never been anywhere but the office in the stable," she said. "That creepy Santo runs the place like some kind of Nazi. I never see anybody but him and that awful old man Helmut. Sometimes his wife."

"Who's that?" Teddy asked.

"Helmut Reinhardt," she said. "He and his spooky wife, Gerda, live in a little house on the estate. They moved in when Conrad bought the place. At least I guess they did."

She ran her fingers through Teddy's hair. "Helmut, he's like a handyman, and his old lady's the cook and housekeeper. They're both real quiet, like the walking dead or something. Real zombies."

"Yeah," Teddy said, "but so what?"

"Think about it, Teddy," she said passionately. "You've got Santo, who's like some kind of weirdo giant freak with his shaved head and earrings and muscles and tattoos. You've got Conrad, who might as well be a ghost. Then you've got the old zombie couple, Gerda and Helmut. You're not there, so you don't see how creepy it is."

She paused and looked at him with a pouty expression. "But you know what the worst thing is? They don't give me the time of day. Any of them. It's like I'm garbage or something as far as they're concerned."

"You shouldn't pay any attention to them, Tiff," he said, taking her hand and moving it down to his crotch. "Conrad probably has them under his thumb. Probably doesn't like for the help to get to know each other too well. He's just another paranoid rich jerk," Teddy went on, easing a hand between her thighs.

"Everybody says you're rich, too, Teddy," she said.

"Huh? I do all right." He frowned. "I'm sure not rich like that creep. But then I'm not into drugs or the Mafia or whatever his game is."

"I just don't understand why he's so secretive," she countered, now stroking Teddy's cock firmly.

"Probably doesn't want you to see all those hot chicks he's got tied up down in the cellar," he said, grinning at her. "All of them just waiting to fulfill his every command."

Tiffani laughed. "God, I wouldn't doubt it," she said. "But I think that's what *you'd* like." She squeezed his penis.

"Hey," he said, "watch it! That's not replaceable, you know."

Tiffani laughed again. "But seriously, Teddy, it gives me the heebie-jeebies just to think about it. All that money. I've never seen so much come in and go out of a place in my life. It's hard to imagine being that rich.

And the horses! Some of them worth a fortune. But you know what?"

"What?" Teddy rasped, completely losing interest in the conversation as she aroused him.

"I've never even seen him ride one," she said. "I've never seen anybody ride one."

"Probably can't," Teddy said, working a finger inside her. "They're just a hobby or something. Anyway, who needs him and his horses?" he said. "Look what we've got here."

She looked down between his legs and giggled. "Boy, are you so right, Teddy."

"I think we can make you forget all about Conrad and the freaks out there, Tiff," he said in a whisper. He pulled her to him and began kissing her ardently, his hand working between her thighs. "I love that shave job, babe," he whispered. "Really turns me on."

"I'm so glad you did it," she said. "It's turning me on, too."

"It's a beginning."

"Oh, yeah?" she said, pushing harder against him, totally immersed in the moment, thoughts of Stonelair already out of her mind. "Oh, Teddy," she cooed, "you make me feel so good. You excite me so much."

"That's what it's all about, babe," he said, shoving himself up inside her.

"Oh, God," she moaned, "I'm so lucky. How'd I ever get so lucky?"

Chapter Six

The summer sun was still bright when Valerie drove up the long, twisting gravel lane that led to her mother's house, a rambling Italianate Victorian. The house was perfectly sited in a heavily wooded copse atop a hill that sloped gently down to lush meadows and a meandering stream. The Berkshires, clothed in their summer greenery, were visible from its eastern windows, and the Catskills, on the far side of the Hudson River, rose regally to meet the eye from the west.

This evening, its majesty seemed more depressing to Valerie than usual. *Maybe it's just that I'm not in a very good mood,* she thought, dreading the dinner she was about to have with her mother and Teddy.

She drove around to the parking area in back of the house and pulled in next to Teddy's silvery Jaguar. *So,* she thought, *he's already here, no doubt enjoying himself immensely, telling Mother every detail of last weekend that she doesn't already know.* Valerie wasn't surprised, although she couldn't help being miffed, because Teddy and her mother had long since formed a mutual admiration society. They seemed to genuinely enjoy one another's company.

Valerie quickly checked her reflection in the rearview mirror, patting down her unruly hair. It was pulled back into its customary long braid, the end of which fell across one shoulder onto her breast, but the top and sides had managed to create a frizzy halo about her face as usual.

"Ah, well," she said to her reflection, "you'll just have to do. Even if Teddy and Mother would like to see you coiffed to perfection with a real ladylike 'do."

She swung out of the Jeep and began brushing dog hair off the black linen pants and blouse she'd changed into. It had been her hope that the outfit would match, and thus conceal, Elvis's hair, which invariably managed to attach itself to everything she owned. No such luck, she noted. Elvis, whom she'd left at home in deference to her mother's wishes, was decidedly blacker and shinier than the black linen she wore.

Oh, well, she thought. *This too will have to do. Love me or leave me!*

She heard familiar voices in the garden and walked over to the iron gate that led into it and peered inside. Teddy, dapper as usual in a dark blue blazer, crisp white linen trousers, and a light blue shirt with a daring apricot-colored tie, and Marguerite, a vision of loveliness in a cream suit with emerald trim and an emerald blouse, were strolling toward her, arm in arm, their voices animated in conversation. Teddy's hair, she noticed, was sunny blond perfection, and Marguerite's, a stunning silvery white, was fixed in an elegant French twist. Neither of them had a hair out of place.

Of course, she thought with wry amusement.

Suddenly Teddy looked up. Seeing her, he began waving and calling to her. She waved back.

"We'll be in shortly," she heard her mother call. "Get yourself a drink."

"Okay," Valerie called back, nodding. She turned and walked to the big screened-in back porch and on through it into the kitchen.

"Well, look who's finally here," Effie said, wiping her hands on a towel. She tapped a dark cheek with a finger. "Right here," the tiny, white-haired woman said.

Valerie leaned over and kissed her on the cheek where she'd indicated. "You look great, Effie," she said, straightening up. "And whatever you're cooking up in here smells terrific."

"It's a surprise," Effie said, "so don't ask. I'm just glad you and Teddy came to dinner. It gives me a chance to do some real cooking. Your mother eats like a bird, so I hardly get to do much."

"I guess she's on one of her diets," Valerie said.

"She's always on a diet," Effie said grumpily. "One more disgusting than the next. It's a wonder she doesn't make herself sick, she's so skinny."

"Some things never change," Valerie said, and, she reflected, they really didn't. Effie had complained for as long as she could remember about Marguerite's eating habits, among many other things, but had remained devoted to her nevertheless. "I'm going to get a drink, Effie. Do you want me to mix something up for you?"

Effie grinned. "Thanks, Val," she replied, "but I already had a little nip of gin."

"Aha!" Valerie said. "I should've known, but I won't tell." Effie's nips of gin were a deeply guarded secret between Valerie and the old woman, a secret that everyone knew about.

"You better not," Effie replied, "or I'll tell Teddy some of your secrets."

"Blackmail!" Valerie cried with a laugh. "I'll see you in a bit," she said, heading out the kitchen door to the butler's pantry.

Scanning the bottles there, she quickly decided on a vodka and tonic, with lots of vodka. She didn't often drink anything other than wine, but tonight, she thought, a little fortifying medication was in order. *My mother by herself is excuse enough,* she told herself, *but Mother and Teddy conspiring together ought to make drinking straight out of the bottle permissible.*

Taking her drink, she began to roam the big quiet house, going from room to room, sipping as she went. Her eyes swept over the antiques with their beautiful silk, velvet, and leather upholstery. She scanned the walls, hung with luxurious silks from Lyons or the finest hand-blocked papers from Zuber in Rixheim. She glimpsed the elegant chandeliers of crystal and ormolu that hung suspended from the ceilings of nearly every room, and eyed the paintings that decorated the walls. Family portraits from France, Denmark, England, and America were rivaled by fine landscapes from all over Europe; plus drawings and watercolors, some of them nearly five hundred years old, hung chockablock in virtually every room.

Like the art, bibelots and treasures of all kinds covered almost every surface. Chinese and Japanese porcelains, Meissen and Sèvres, ormolu mounted vases, flower arrangements made of semiprecious stones and gold, photographs in fantastically carved silver or gilt frames.

The house was an Aladdin's den that would make an auctioneer's pulse race, she'd often thought. Many of the treasures had come from the big apartment in New York City that they'd sold after her father died. Memories of her childhood—both in the formal city apartment and here in the more casual atmosphere of the country—always swept over her when she came here. It was almost as if her entire past were contained in this one house.

Perhaps, she thought, *that's why I stay away from here as much as possible.*

A familiar sadness began to pervade her usually bright spirits, infusing her with a sense that all of this material beauty was part of a world gone by, a lifestyle that had all but ceased to exist, and a way of life that she had once been part of but never really belonged to. Even the familiarity with every object her eye rested upon did not dispel the feeling that she was an interloper.

In one of the drawing rooms she lingered over a favorite drawing, a Berthe Morisot of a field. Then she picked up an old black-and-white photograph of her father on horseback. He looked so handsome in his riding habit, she thought as she replaced it on the table. She meandered on into the music room and lightly stroked the ivory keys on the antique

Bösendorfer, the same piano on which she'd learned to play. She climbed the curving stairs and went down the hallway to her old bedroom, where she sat on the lacy canopied bed that had once been hers. Looking at the antique dressing table, its surface still cluttered with crystal bottles of different scents and a monogrammed silver dressing set, she remembered the countless times she'd sat before its mirror, trying to make herself into the woman that her mother wanted her to be. To no avail.

No, she thought idly. *I was never the girl she wanted and haven't become the woman she wanted me to be. But then, I never really felt that I belonged here or that I was even an important part of life here.*

There had been a time when she would have given anything to fit in with these people and what most thought was their fabulous lifestyle. She'd really struggled to be the daughter her mother and father wanted her to be.

But no more. *I don't want to live like them. I want to live my own life, the way I want to live it. I want to be me.*

It sounded so simple, she thought, but she'd found it very difficult to break the bonds. It had been hard to see the disappointment on her parents' faces, to hear the recrimination in their voices, to deal with the constant pressures that they exerted on her. But despite all the battles, she was finally living her life in a way that she found fulfilling.

Her thoughts were interrupted by the tinkling of her mother's laughter and the sound of Teddy's doting voice. She took a sip of her drink and sighed. *Might as well go face the music,* she decided. She retraced her steps downstairs.

Teddy and Marguerite were standing in the marble-floored entrance hall, drinks in hand, and looked up at her as she came down the stairs.

"Hi, you two," Valerie said cheerfully.

"Hello, dear," Marguerite said, her eyes sweeping appraisingly over her daughter's appearance. She offered up a cheek for a kiss.

"It's good to see you, Mother," Valerie said.

"I'm glad you could fit me into your busy schedule," Marguerite said with a light laugh.

Valerie didn't reply, but kept a smile fixed on her face.

"Hi," Teddy said, brushing her lips with his, then putting an arm around her shoulders and hugging her to him. "We've been out looking at the garden," he said unnecessarily. "It's incredible what your mother does practically by herself."

"Oh, Teddy," Marguerite said, "you don't have to humor me. I know it's a disaster, but what can one do?" She spied Effie out of the corner of her eye. "Oh, look," she said, "Effie's ready to serve. Shall we go in?"

"Let's," Teddy said, offering Marguerite his arm. She took it, and he winked at Valerie. "Can you manage?" he asked.

"It's twenty or thirty feet, but I think I can manage it," Valerie joked.

Darkness had descended outside, and in Marguerite's dining room the silver and crystal sparkled in the candlelight. They had finished Effie's delicious feast of chilled avocado and cucumber soup, tiny stuffed Cornish game hens grilled with a ginger and plum sauce, fresh asparagus drizzled with Hollandaise sauce, wild rice with Portobelo mushrooms, and a salad of micro-arugula, endive, radicchio, and baby oak with a balsamic vinaigrette. She had just served the dessert, homemade ginger ice cream topped with fresh organically grown strawberries and raspberries smothered in a syrupy kirsch sauce.

"Thanks, Effie," Teddy said, "this looks delicious. Everything was really wonderful."

"Thank you, sir," Effie replied as she headed back into the kitchen.

"She never ceases to amaze me," Valerie said appreciatively. "I don't know how she does it. Cooking and cleaning and—"

"She *is* good," Marguerite interjected, "but I'm trying to teach her to rely less on sauces. They're so awfully rich, don't you think?" She glanced at Teddy speculatively, and he didn't disappoint her.

"Everything was very rich," he readily agreed. "You certainly couldn't eat like this all the time."

"Indeed not," Marguerite said. "It would spell certain ruin for both your health and your figure. And as for her cleaning, Val, dear"—Marguerite looked at her daughter pointedly and shrugged—"well, she barely hits the high spots with a feather duster anymore. I do think it's awfully sweet of you to be so loyal to her, but I sometimes think that Effie is taking advantage of me."

"Oh, Mother," Valerie burst out in barely concealed astonishment. "Effie's devoted herself to you for over forty years. I hardly think that if she slows down a little bit at her age, you should call that taking advantage of you."

Marguerite haughtily ignored her daughter's outburst entirely. She turned her attention back to Teddy. "The wine was divine," she said, "and perfect with this meal."

"Why, thank you, Marguerite," he said. "I have a fairly good cellar now, but it'll take a long time and a lot more money to get it where I want it. The Puligny Montrachet was a . . ."

Valerie withdrew into herself, eating the ice cream and berries and watching the easy exchanges between her mother and Teddy. *He's just her type,* she thought somewhat resentfully. *Handsome, rich, and charming to boot.* But equally as important was that Teddy came from the same background and class that they did. Her marriage to him would be considered an alliance between two descendants of the same gloriously aristocratic French Huguenot heritage, and any foibles he might have would be overlooked by her mother because of that illustrious background. Her father, she knew, would agree wholeheartedly about Teddy. Valerie, while not disrespecting her lineage, held it in no particular regard. It seemed so remote in time and meaning to her that she really never gave it a thought.

It's no wonder she and Teddy get along so well, Valerie thought, nibbling on the kirsch-soaked berries. *He's as much of a snob about his lineage as she is. Too bad Mother's not younger.*

She saw Marguerite adjust one of the cabochon emeralds at her ears and regarded her more closely.

Despite the resentments she harbored toward her mother, Valerie had to admit that Marguerite Louise de Coligny de la Rochelle was a woman every bit as formidable as her name implied. Even though she was sixty-five years old, she had a flawless and creamy, if subtly lined, complexion. She had prominent, elegant cheekbones, a high forehead, a straight nose, and wide lips that were just full enough. Her silvery hair, even white teeth, trim figure, and immaculate grooming made her seem almost ageless.

Her vanity about her appearance had always astounded Valerie. Her mother spent hours at the dressmaker's, choosing fabrics and being fitted, as she had all of her clothes custom made. They were usually faithful and expensive copies of Chanel and other great designers. Then she spent hours with the hairdresser, the pedicurist, the manicurist, and untold time at home grooming, grooming, grooming. She went to bed slathered virtually from head to toe in some lotion or other, and never permitted the bright sun to touch her skin.

Yet Marguerite had told Valerie she would never submit to the surgeon's knife or dye her hair. She considered women who did beneath her, contemptible really, slaves to unintelligent and ill-formed notions about beauty. These poor women, willing victims, she averred, were products of the brash, tacky, and utterly tasteless view of beauty promulgated by an aesthetically impoverished mass media.

"Valerie, my dear!"

Marguerite's cultured voice interrupted her reverie. She found her mother staring at her quizzically.

"I'm sorry," Valerie said. "I missed what you were saying."

"You haven't been paying any attention to us, dear," Marguerite said in a chiding manner. The emerald on the finger she pointed accusingly at Valerie glinted in the light. "How like you. We were discussing Teddy's business, Val. Something I should think you would take an interest in. He's been having a wonderful year with the stock market."

"Oh," Valerie said, "that's great, Teddy." She wondered why he never discussed his business with her.

Teddy smiled indulgently, as if Valerie couldn't possibly be capable of comprehending the complexities of this business-related conversation.

"You're so clever, Teddy," Marguerite enthused, "and I think you're to be congratulated."

"Well, trading definitely has its ups and downs," Teddy replied. "But I *have* had an extraordinarily good run recently. Of course, the way the market's been lately, Marguerite, who wouldn't?"

"Yes," she allowed, "but not everyone knows how to take advantage of it the way you do, Teddy. I guess bloodlines always tell, don't they? It's all in the genes."

Teddy laughed. "Maybe," he said. "But I doubt if I'll ever be the investment guru my father was."

Marguerite tinkled laughter. "Well, my dear, I think your father would be very proud of you."

"Well, thank you," Teddy said with an amiability that he didn't feel. He really didn't know or care what the late, great Theodore de Mornay would have thought. He'd hated the son of a bitch while he was alive and had grown to like him no more in death. The same with his mother, Claudine, who'd been nothing more than an apparition to him, coming and going in ball gowns, jewels, and expensive perfumes before spending the last of her fifty-odd years a virtual prisoner in her own bedroom, addicted to prescription drugs and alcohol.

"I wish Dockering Wainwright did so well by me," Marguerite said, worrying the emeralds at her neck with long slender fingers. She looked over at Valerie. The significance of the look was not lost on her daughter.

Valerie cleared her throat and placed a smile on her lips. "Dock's been handling your affairs forever, Mother," she said, "and he seems to have done a fine job. Dad always thought so," she added. She looked at Teddy. "That's not to say you wouldn't, Teddy, but Dad always had Dock do it . . . and, well . . ."

"I wouldn't think of encroaching on the great Dockering Wainwright's territory," Teddy quickly interrupted. "I'm sure he's a great investment advisor."

"Nevertheless," Marguerite said, "he certainly doesn't seem to get *your* results, Teddy. If you ask me, he's half asleep at the wheel."

"I think Dock's on top of things," Valerie said. "He may be old-fashioned and conservative, certainly he's not a risk taker, but he's astute and dependable nonetheless."

"Is he?" Marguerite asked. "I may be an old woman who knows very little about these things," she continued in an overweeningly self-deprecating manner, "but it seems to me that my little portfolio has hardly grown in value at all. Needless to say, it naturally follows that my dividends haven't either. And in a market that everybody knows is going great guns. Why, half the real estate sold around here is for cash! Total asking price, if not more. It's all these smart young men like Teddy from New York." She paused and looked directly at her daughter.

"Maybe you're right, Mother," Valerie conceded, "but I've never heard a complaint against Dock." She looked directly at her mother then. "Anyway, it's really not for me to decide who handles your affairs, is it?"

"No," Marguerite said, "it certainly is not." Her focus shifted back to Teddy again. "I think it's high time I gave old Dock a little goose," she said. "I suppose we all get a little complacent at times, don't we?"

"It's easy to do," Teddy said. "Especially when it's not your own money you're handling. Or if you don't have some sort of special interest in your client's welfare."

"Well said, Teddy," Marguerite pronounced. "I'll get on the telephone to Dock tomorrow, then give you a call to let you know what he has to say for himself. If that's okay with you, that is."

"Of course, Marguerite," Teddy replied. "I think it's a sound idea."

"Good, that's settled, then," Marguerite said. She took a sip of water, the huge emerald on her finger catching the light again, then set the glass down and turned the full wattage of her gaze on Valerie. "Valerie, my dear," she said, "I think there's something you haven't told me."

"Told you?" Valerie knew right away what her mother was talking about, but she decided to play dumb. She knew it would antagonize Marguerite if she didn't give her the satisfaction of an immediate answer. She also knew that she was being petty, but she decided to make her mother weasel the answer out of her. That would punish her and Teddy for discussing the engagement ring behind her back. "What's that, Mother?" she asked. "What haven't I told you?"

Marguerite's eyes took on a steely expression, but it was fleeting and quickly replaced by a laugh of amusement. "Valerie, my dear," she said, "you've been working far too hard with those filthy beasts. I can't think what else would make you forget something so important."

Teddy cleared his throat and smiled. "Val," he said, "she might be referring to a little something that happened over the weekend. Remember?"

Valerie decided to quit playing her little game. "Oh!" she cried. "How could I!" She looked at Teddy, who smiled endearingly at her. "Oh, Teddy, I'm sorry," she said. "I feel like such an idiot."

"Don't worry about it," he said good-naturedly.

Valerie glanced over at her mother. "Teddy and I . . . we . . . he gave me an engagement ring last weekend," she finally managed. She couldn't bring herself to say, We're engaged.

"Splendid," Marguerite pronounced, as if surprised. "Absolutely splendid." She reached over and touched her daughter's hand. "I'm so pleased for you," she said. Then she reached over and patted Teddy's hand. "Both of you. It's wonderful news."

Valerie nodded. "I'm glad you're happy, Mother," she said in a quiet voice.

"You must show me your ring, Val, dear," Marguerite said.

"Uh, well," Valerie sputtered, feeling herself blush hotly. "Oh, I . . . I forgot to put it on."

"You what!" Marguerite exclaimed. She stared at her daughter in disbelief.

"Oh, Val," Teddy groaned. "I noticed you weren't wearing it, but I thought that surely you had it tucked away in your handbag or someplace to surprise your mother."

"I'm sorry," Valerie murmured. "I was in such a rush to change clothes and get here after work, and besides"—she shrugged and smiled—"I'm just not used to it yet."

"No harm done," Teddy said in a forgiving voice.

Valerie turned to her mother. "It's really beautiful, Mother," she said. "And huge! You'll love it. I promise to come by with it one day this week after work."

"I do hope so," Marguerite said, not adding that Teddy had shown her the ring the day he'd bought it. "Teddy's made such an effort on your behalf, and I should think you'd be terribly happy with so generous a gift."

"I . . . I've just been so busy and everything," Valerie said. "I was on call at the clinic this weekend, and there was an emergency. And—"

"That clinic," Marguerite said with a frown of distaste. "It's always that clinic. I knew it. You spend far too much time there. And what sort of emergency could possibly make you forget you'd become engaged?" She looked at her daughter questioningly.

"Stonelair," Teddy said grimly, not giving Valerie

the opportunity to answer for herself. "The mystery man."

"Oh, dear, *no*," Marguerite said, visibly shaken. "Don't tell me you've been out to that dreadful place, Val, dear. I've been told on the best authority that he's some sort of drug baron or something. Is it true?"

Valerie shrugged. "Who knows?" she replied. "I was taking care of a sick horse. I didn't even meet the man." She paused, then added jocularly: "But I didn't see mountains of drugs or guns or anything."

No one laughed.

"Well," Marguerite said in her most indignant voice, "it seems to me it would almost have to be drugs or something equally disgusting to support a place like that. Not even the young Wall Street tycoons that are buying everything in sight around here could afford that place." She paused, looking at her daughter significantly. "Besides," she continued, "nobody of any importance knows him as far as *I* know. And he's so secretive that I'm certain something evil is going on out there."

"I don't know anything about any of the gossip you've heard," Valerie countered defiantly, "but they've asked me to take care of all their animals. Personally."

"Oh, dear," Marguerite said, her eyes widening in alarm.

"You're surely not thinking of taking them up on their offer," Teddy said.

Valerie didn't answer him at once.

"Well, you're not, are you?" he prodded.

"I don't know yet," Valerie replied. But it was at that precise moment that she made up her mind to accept Conrad's offer and become Stonelair's exclusive veterinarian. She would make certain to discuss it with the clinic staff tomorrow.

"You don't know yet?" Marguerite parroted. "I must say I'm surprised by your cavalier attitude. I shouldn't think you would even entertain the notion." Her voice and demeanor were disdainful in the extreme. "He must be some sort of horribly evil Mafioso or some such thing. Why, I'm told that the beastly man has turned down every invitation that's been extended to him."

"What's so evil about that?" Valerie asked. "I mean, how does that make him a drug lord or Mafioso? Maybe he just doesn't like to mingle."

"Well, it makes him antisocial if nothing else," Marguerite said. "Which is highly suspicious, if you ask me."

"I haven't seen the place," Teddy interjected, "but I've talked to a couple of local guys who've been in there to do work. From what they say, the guy's spent millions on the place. Brought all the labor from down south, Florida or someplace. He sure seems to have bottomless pockets. I know that I couldn't even begin to do what he's done to that place."

Valerie had been watching Teddy, and she couldn't help but detect the somewhat cocky manner he assumed when he felt bested. Nor did she miss the distinct note of resentment in his voice. *He's jealous of Conrad,* she realized. *Jealous of his money, if nothing else.*

"Well, enough said about such an unsavory and frightening subject," Marguerite announced. "Let's have coffee on the porch, shall we? It's lovely out." She smiled at them both.

"Just what the doctor ordered," Teddy said.

Marguerite rose, and Teddy followed suit, taking her arm to lead her out to the screened-in porch. Valerie trailed along behind them. Effie had already lit candles on the porch, and it looked invitingly casual after the formality of the dinner. Teddy saw Marguerite to her chair, and Valerie spread out on a big, comfortable, old wicker sofa.

"I'll be right back, ladies," Teddy said, excusing himself to the bathroom.

The instant he was out of earshot, Marguerite turned her gaze on Valerie. Even in the dim, flickering light of candles, Valerie could see her mother's look of determination.

"I hope you're giving Teddy the attention he so richly deserves," Marguerite said. "I must say, you certainly seem somewhat lackadaisical about your engagement."

"I've just been very busy, Mother," Valerie answered defensively.

"Busy! That tiresome excuse!" Marguerite leaned toward her daughter. "You must not forget that Teddy can give you everything any young woman could ever want. He has money, Val, and what's more, he's very good at making more. And it doesn't hurt that he's also extremely popular. Everybody adores him."

"Or fears him," Valerie said.

"What?" Marguerite looked shocked. "You're being fanciful. Ridiculous. Why would anyone fear Teddy?"

"Well," Valerie said, "from what I hear, he's not so popular with some of his tenants, Mother."

"Perhaps they don't pay their rent on time," she countered. "Anyway, how could you possibly concern yourself with what some tenant would say?"

"They're people, too," Valerie said quietly.

"Humpf!" Marguerite dismissed her daughter's remark and straightened her shoulders for another assault. "And how could you forget to wear your engagement ring, Val? That's positively insulting. Teddy tells me that you won't set a date for the wedding yet. What in heaven's name is wrong with you?"

"Nothing's wrong with me," Valerie said with rising anger. "I'm just not ready yet."

Her mother's eyes caught hers once again. "It's inevitable, Valerie, dear," she said with a quiet forcefulness. "There's nobody else, and Teddy is ideal. Certainly more of a man than I would've ever dreamed it possible for you to attract."

Valerie swallowed, determined not to lose her temper, but she couldn't allow her mother's last remark to pass. *That was the old Valerie,* she told herself. *The Valerie who would sit and take whatever her mother felt like dishing out.*

"Why do you always have to put me down?" she asked.

Marguerite was taken aback for a moment, then plunged on. "Well, face it, Val, dear," she said, "you were never a great beauty. Now that you're older, you do have a certain . . . appeal, I must admit. But you didn't have that growing up. Besides which, you were always a little . . . strange . . . a little peculiar. That hasn't changed."

She smiled at Valerie, a smile that a stranger might

assume was sweetness itself, but that Valerie knew to be
filled with scornful disdain. "You certainly weren't very
social," Marguerite went on, "with your nose always in
a book. Or playing with your precious pets instead of
other children."

Valerie digested her mother's diatribe in silence,
wounded by the dispassionate way in which she
described a shy little girl starved for love. *Despite all of
my resolutions to the contrary*, she thought, *I still want
this woman's approval and love. And no matter how
independent I tell myself I am, I still let her hurt me.*

She finally cleared her throat and replied. "If you'll
remember, Mother," Valerie said, "there weren't a lot
of girls you'd let me play with. You didn't think that
most of the ones I tried to make friends with were good
enough."

"One has to protect a child from the . . . less desirable elements in society, Valerie," Marguerite replied.
"And you seemed drawn to that element."

"Then when I got older," Valerie said, "you always
made me feel like I wasn't pretty enough or clever
enough. You always made me want to run and hide
from other girls—and boys—my age because you
thought they were so much brighter and better-looking
than me."

"They usually were," Marguerite said firmly. "I
pointed them out as examples for you to follow. Don't
you see, Val? I was trying to get you to make something
better of yourself. But no, you couldn't be bothered
with your hair and clothes, could you? You couldn't be
bothered with making yourself attractive to suitable
young men. Thank *God* Teddy came along. And thank

God you'd become a more presentable young lady by then and outgrown some of your silly shyness and backwardness. At least Teddy could see the possibilities."

Valerie was growing increasingly furious but decided to hold her tongue. She knew that any further argument with her mother would be an exercise in futility.

"Ah," Marguerite exclaimed with delight, "here comes our handsome young man now. I was just talking about what a wonder you are, Teddy."

"Me?" he asked in an amused voice. He stood by Valerie, waiting for her to make room for him on the wicker couch, then sat down next to her and took one of her hands in his. "I hope your daughter feels the same way," he said.

Valerie looked at him and smiled. "I think I'll keep you guessing," she replied. But deep down inside, she was beginning to feel as if Teddy was anything but the wonder her mother thought he was, and she wanted nothing more than to get up and go home to Elvis.

They sipped their coffee, chatting a while longer, until Teddy pointedly looked at his watch. "It's getting late," he said, "and I'm afraid we've kept you up past your bedtime, Marguerite."

"Not at all," she said. "I've enjoyed every minute of it."

"Well, I've got a very early morning," Valerie said, "and I'd better get going."

"I forgot," Teddy said. "Being up here all week loafing around, I tend to forget that you have a job to go to."

"It's too bad you couldn't arrange to be off this week, Val dear," Marguerite said.

Valerie rose to her feet and stifled a yawn. "It was impossible, Mother," she said. "Things are too busy at the clinic."

Teddy got to his feet and put an arm around Valerie's shoulders. "We can see ourselves out, Marguerite," he said. "Keep your seat."

"Thank you, Teddy," she said, "but I think I'll go on in now."

He removed his arm from Valerie's shoulder and extended Marguerite a hand. She rose and offered a cheek for him to kiss.

"I'm so glad you could come," she said. "And I'm thrilled with the news."

"Thanks, Marguerite," Teddy said.

"Good night, Mother." Valerie kissed her cheek. "Dinner was delicious."

"I'm glad you enjoyed it, dear," she said. "And I hope to see more of you both."

They walked to the porch door, which led out to the parking area, and Marguerite patted Teddy on the back. "We'll speak soon," she said.

"Yes," he said. "I hope so."

For a moment, Marguerite watched as they walked out toward their cars, then she snuffed out the candles and went inside.

In the parking area, Teddy turned and put his arms around Valerie, then kissed her deeply, running his hands up and down her back. She drew back and looked up at him. "I'd better run, Teddy," she said. "It's late, and I'd better get home."

"What?" he said testily. "I thought you'd spend the night with me."

"I can't, Teddy," she said. "I've got to take Elvis out."

"Then why don't you go home, take the ugly mutt out, and then come on over to my place?" he cajoled, brushing her neck with his lips.

"Not tonight, Teddy," she said. "I've got a very early morning and a really busy day ahead."

He continued nuzzling her neck. "Come on," he whispered. "We'll have a real good time, Val. We could fuck all night long."

"Teddy!" she said. "I just told you that I have to get up very early, and I have a long, hard day ahead of me."

"Call in sick," he said, his hands pressing her buttocks to his groin.

"No can do," she said. "I mean it."

"Aw, Val," he whined, "come on. You can do it. Let the dogs and cats and horses take care of themselves. Just this once."

"No, Teddy," she said firmly, trying to wriggle away from his arms. "I've got a job to do. Now, let me go. I've got to go take care of Elvis."

Teddy finally let her loose. "Then go," he said. "Go take care of your fucking mutt."

She looked at him challengingly. "I will," she said. She opened the door to her Jeep and climbed in, closing the door after her. She fired up the engine and gazed at him, standing alone next to his Jaguar. He looked like a little boy who hadn't got his way, as he increasingly did these days.

Well, too bad, she thought. *Nobody who calls Elvis a fucking mutt and doesn't apologize is going to get to sleep with me.*

She started down the long gravel lane to the highway and home to Elvis.

"Bitch!" Teddy snapped under his breath as he watched her taillights disappear. Then he got in his car and headed straight for Tiffani's, hoping that she would be home. *If not,* he thought, *I'll find somebody else. No problem.*

Chapter Seven

Arielle Conrad's high-heel, magenta leather mules, festooned at the toe with a bouquet of lemon-yellow flowers, click-clacked against the purple bougainvillea-draped coral stone and marble loggia that adorned the rear façade of her palatial Palm Beach mansion. The Atlantic Ocean, its breakers rhythmic and muted, slapped lazily against the pristine beach just beyond the walled-in perfection of the lawn, and the steady offshore breeze was refreshing in the summer night's steamy torpor.

Arielle, however, took no solace from her grand estate with its manicured gardens. Tonight, the luxurious trappings of her life seemed to her no more than a stage set for a tragedy. A Boodles gin with tonic in one hand and a thin brown cigarillo in the other, she paced restlessly from one end of the columned loggia to the other, pausing occasionally to run long, tanned fingers with magenta-lacquered nails through her platinum-streaked hair.

Catching sight of her reflection in an enormous

mother-of-pearl-framed mirror, she saw how tousled her hair was. The candlelight was flattering, and she was pleased with what she saw. Her long hair had that sexy just-had-a-roll-in-the-hay look that so many women spend small fortunes to achieve but that for Arielle seemed just another of her many desirable, if not altogether natural, assets. Her face was perfectly made up, as usual. Her heavily mascaraed eyes were thinly lined with black and shadowed with a honey hue accentuating the shards of amber that streaked through the topaz brown of her irises. A terra-cotta blusher accentuated her high, prominent cheekbones, and glossy magenta lipstick adorned her full, sensuous, and cosmetically enhanced lips. Bee-stung lips, she thought, and sexy as hell, with a come-hither look.

She turned from the mirror and resumed her nervous pacing, puffing on her cigarillo, secure in the knowledge that, if nothing else, she looked appropriately beguiling. Then one of her heels caught on the weathered marble, and she lurched forward, just managing to catch herself before she fell to the hard stone.

Shit! she thought, looking down at herself. *Just my fucking luck.* She'd slopped gin and tonic onto the sheer orange silk blouse that she wore unbuttoned to the waist, where it was tied in a lavish knot. Somehow, she'd managed to miss all that lovely exposed flesh.

I must be getting a little drunk, she thought. *No, not drunk,* she amended. *Just getting a buzz on.* She quickly click-clacked to the big marble table where trays of liquor and mixers stood in attendance. Putting down her drink and cigarillo, she grabbed a napkin, dabbed it with club soda, and began brushing her blouse vigorously.

There, she thought after a few furious strokes, *that's better*. She tossed the napkin onto the table, picked up her drink and cigarillo, and went over to a chaise longue, where she spread out, kicking off her mules and making herself comfortable. She picked up the latest issue of French *Vogue* and idly flipped through its glossy pages, but lost interest after a few minutes and tossed it to the marble floor with a sigh.

Where is the son of a bitch? she wondered, taking a sip of her drink. *He should've been here for dinner ages ago.* She took a long draw off her cigarillo. *Now, of all times, he's decided to disappear on me. Maybe I should call the club.*

She smashed out her cigarillo in the ashtray at her side, then pulled another one from the pack that lay there, lighting it with her gold Cartier lighter. *Yes*, she decided, *that's what I'll do. I'll call the club.* She was reaching for the cell phone on the table when she heard his distinctive heavy boot heels on the marble. She looked up as he sauntered toward her from the French doors that led out from the drawing room. He was still in his polo gear and looked sweaty and dusty.

"Lolo!" she cried, sitting up. "I've been worried sick about you. Where the hell have you been?"

Lolo's darkly tanned face lit up at the sight of her. Then his dark brown eyes became concerned when he heard the distress in her voice. "What is it, Arielle?" he asked in his heavily accented English, rushing to her, the sound of his heels resounding off the loggia's stone floor and walls.

"What is it?" She glared up at him malevolently. "You're late!" she cried. "And just when I need you, Lolo!"

"I'm on Spanish time," the handsome young man joked, his teeth sparkling white against his dark skin. He put one hand on each side of her face and leaned down and kissed her lips. "You know how Argentinians are."

She grimaced at his attempt at humor. "Why're you so late?" she asked, patting the chaise longue next to her and scooting over to give him room to sit down. She leaned back again, looking up at him.

He eased his muscular body down next to hers, and shrugged his massive shoulders. "I was out at the polo grounds till dusk," he said. "Like I told you I would be." He leaned over and kissed her lips, a hand moving to one of her easily accessible breasts, taking great pleasure in the feeling of her nipple as it began to harden under his touch. After a moment, he sighed with satisfaction and sat back up. "Then Palmer Johnson wanted me to look at some new polo ponies of his, so I went over to his place—"

"Oh, fuck Palmer Johnson," she said.

"Arielle," he said softly, looking into her eyes, "don't take your anger out on me. I've done nothing wrong. I'm just a little late. Whatever it is that bugs you—"

She sat up and threw her arms around his neck, hugging him to her tightly, relishing the feel of his hard, sweaty body next to hers. "Oh, it's not you, Lolo," she said contritely. "You're right. I'm sorry. It's that horrible Wyn." Her eyes became flinty with hate. "I could kill him, Lolo. I really could."

Lolo heaved a sigh. "What's the asshole done now?"

"It's the same old story," Arielle said, removing her arms from around his neck. "He hasn't signed the damned papers yet, and he knows good and well I can hardly make ends meet on that stupid temporary allowance the court decided on."

"Did it come today?" he asked casually. "The check, I mean?"

"No," she said, gritting her teeth.

"Jesus!" Lolo spat. "I'd like to go to New York and kill the son of a bitch myself. And I mean it, Arielle."

"I wish you would," Arielle countered, assessing him, wondering if he really did mean it. "That would solve all of our problems."

She paused and took a sip of her drink. It certainly wasn't the first time she'd thought about killing Wyn. "If I thought you could get away with it," she said, "I'd ask you to do it. I wish I could do it myself. I hate him." She tapped a fist against Lolo's chest. "I hate him, hate him, *hate* him!"

Lolo took her fist in his hand and brought it to his lips, kissing it. "You know, Arielle, he's stalling just to torture you," Lolo said. "To torture both of us."

"Yes, I know," she replied. "But knowing that doesn't help, does it? The torture just goes on and on."

"He'll sign soon," Lolo said. "He has to. Don't worry." He put a finger under her chin and lifted it, looking into her eyes. "Then all of our troubles will be over. We'll have everything we need. Everything. You'll see." He leaned down and began planting kisses on her beautiful face, first her forehead, then her nose, eyes, each cheek, and chin.

Arielle responded to his tenderness, her lips and tongue brushing over his neck, his ears, and face, until their lips met. They hungrily began kissing, their hands roaming over one another's bodies. Lolo gently pushed her back down against the chaise and drew himself up next to her, grinding his loins against her perfect body, moaning aloud at the feel of her sweet, soft femininity against him.

Arielle ran her hand over his chest and down to his thigh, then around to his hard bubble butt, reveling in his masculine odor, his sweaty riding gear, the dusty skin-tight polo jodhpurs and boots. "You're soaked," she murmured, almost shuddering with desire.

Lolo drew back. "Maybe I'd better go shower and change," he said, knowing that she wouldn't want him to.

"No, don't. I like you like this."

He laughed softly. "And I like you like this." He ran a hand inside her blouse again, rubbing a nipple between thumb and finger.

"Ummm," Arielle murmured. "That feels soooo good."

Lolo brushed his lips against hers. "Let's make this last a while," he whispered. "Let me get us both a drink? Huh?"

"Ummm . . . ," she murmured again, pulling him to her. "I think that's a great idea." Then she gradually released him. "Let me do it for you," she said, looking into his eyes. "I want to make a drink for my Lolo."

She swung her legs off the chaise and got to her feet, then slipped into her mules and click-clacked to the marble drinks table, casting a kittenish smile at him over her shoulder. She got two clean glasses, put ice cubes into them, then poured in healthy portions of Boodles. Finally, she added a tiny splash of tonic and a squeeze of lemon to each.

She walked back over to the chaise, putting a little extra swing in her step. "Here," she said, smiling. "Just the way you like it."

Lolo's eyes traveled up and down her body before he took the proffered drink. He held it up and Arielle clinked hers against it. "*Salud,*" he said.

"*Salud,*" she echoed, then took a sip of her drink and let out a breathy sigh.

"Suddenly you don't sound very cheerful," Lolo said, running a hand up her leg.

Arielle slumped down onto the chaise and stared into her glass. Lolo was right. She didn't feel very cheerful. Thoughts of Wyn and the nasty divorce had crept back into her consciousness, like an irritating itch that wouldn't go away. There'd been a time, back in the beginning of their marriage, when she'd thought she was the luckiest woman alive. With all the women Wyn had—and there'd been a lot—he'd chosen her above all the rest. She'd never forget the blonde that was determined to have him, then left brokenhearted when Arielle had won out. *What a bitch she was,* Arielle thought. She'd taken a special pleasure in seeing that one leave, crushed by the weight of what she'd lost. But the triumph Arielle had felt then gave her little comfort now.

Lolo set down his drink and slid an arm around her shoulders. "Come here to me," he said, pulling her toward him. "Don't look so sad, Arielle," he said. "Your Lolo is here for you."

His lips brushed up her neck, and he began nibbling her ears. "I know he's a real prick," he said in a near whisper, "and he's messing everything up now. But it won't be long before the lawyers will tell him he can't stall anymore."

Arielle took a long sip of her drink, then sighed again as she set it down. "I know," she said, "but in the meantime it really is making things difficult. I can hardly afford to pay the help, and I can't afford to entertain. Thank God I can charge everything at the shops and the club."

He pressed a finger to her lips. "Shhh," he whispered. "Don't think about it now, Arielle." He began gently kneading her neck and back.

"That feels so good, Lolo," she said with the hint of a smile. "I've been so . . . tense about all of this. I mean, what the hell are we even doing here tonight? We shouldn't even be here."

"What do you mean?" he asked.

"It's summer," she said. "We should be having fun in Southampton or Europe or at least the place up in the Adirondacks. Anywhere but here in the summertime. Nobody's in Palm Beach in the summer."

He took both of her hands in his, kissing them tenderly. "At least we're together, Arielle."

"Thank God for that," she said. "If it weren't for you, I don't know what I'd do."

"I wish I could do more," Lolo said, looking into her eyes. "But you know they don't pay me that much for riding. If I had my own money and a stable it would be different—"

"No, no, no!" Arielle said earnestly. "That's not

what I mean, Lolo. I don't expect financial help from you. That's the last thing in the world I would expect. I know that Palmer Johnson's just like Wyn and all the rest of the rich bastards that play polo. They practically starve their star players." She looked into his dark eyes. "Like you," she said, "the best of them all."

He grinned, his white teeth flashing. "Well," he said, "one of the best anyway."

"I think you're the best," she said with pride in her voice, "but it's your being here that's even more important. It's what keeps me going from one day to the next."

His face became serious. "You really do feel bad tonight, don't you, Arielle?" he said. "Much worse than usual." He reached over for his drink and took a sip, waiting for her to speak, knowing that she needed to talk a while.

She sighed again. "I never would have imagined that my life would go this way. I wouldn't have believed— not in a million years!—that Wyn could be so cruel and spiteful and selfish. He wasn't like most rich men I knew. Money was never an issue. He wasn't a tightwad like most of them, you know? God knows, we threw it around like there was no tomorrow."

She reached over and shook a cigarillo from the pack on the table, and Lolo picked up her lighter and held its flame for her. "Thanks," she said, exhaling a streamer of blow.

"Go on," he said. "Tell me what's on your pretty mind."

"Well," she said. "That was one thing I liked about Wyn. He didn't really care about all that money and let me spend whatever I wanted to. That's what it's for, he always said. He's got so much he doesn't know what the hell to do with it." She took another drag off of her cigarillo and looked at Lolo, her eyes suddenly flashing anger. "But, Jesus, has the son of a bitch ever changed his tune. And there's no reason on earth he should be so horrible and mean."

"It'll all be over soon," Lolo said, not knowing what else to say. "Maybe . . . maybe I could get some kind of job or—"

"No way!" Arielle said. "No fucking way!" Then she laughed. "I can just see that. No more clubs, no parties. No trips. Early to bed, early to rise. No, Lolo." She poked his chest with a finger. "You and I weren't meant to live like that. That's for all the losers out there." She reached over and stroked his handsome face with her hand. She felt much better now, having talked about her woes. "Somehow we'll make out," she said. "At least I have you all to myself. And it's fun to see you drive all the horny divorcées around here mad with jealousy." She kissed his nose.

Lolo grinned. "You make the men a little crazy yourself," he said. "I think every man in Palm Beach wants you, Arielle."

She tossed her head and laughed. "You think so?" she asked.

"You know it," he replied. He reached over then and pulled her to him. "And that includes me," he added. He began kissing her roughly, passionately, and hungrily, his hands exploring her body. Serious talk was over, and it was time for some serious play.

Arielle responded immediately, the fires of her desire

rekindled by the feel of him against her. She ran her hands over his hard-muscled shoulders and arms, down his tight stomach, and slid one between his thighs, feeling the tumescence straining at his jodhpurs. She moaned with pleasure as Lolo began licking her breasts with his tongue, teasing her nipples between his teeth. She gasped aloud when she felt his hand between her thighs, fingering her wetness.

In one furious movement, Lolo jerked her shorts and panties down and off her legs and unzipped his jodhpurs, releasing his throbbing manhood. He mounted her then, entering her up to the hilt suddenly and quickly, and began pumping away at her.

Oh, God, Arielle thought in an ecstatic swoon, her entire body shuddering against his. *Just when I thought it was all over for me, the man of my dreams comes waltzing into my life. And what a man he is! Not like that beast, Wyn Conrad.*

Chapter Eight

Colette!" Valerie exclaimed, looking up from her desk, where she was filling in a chart. "It's good to see you." Elvis, who was in his bed, wagged his tail furiously.

Colette Richards, Valerie's elderly neighbor, swept into the office, her exotic perfume preceding her. She snatched off her sunglasses, and Valerie could see that her bright blue eyes were wide with alarm.

"Oh, Val, darling!" Colette cried, her voice at once whispery and throaty. "I'm *so* glad to see you, too. You've no idea, my darling." She spied Elvis in his bed and blew kisses in his direction.

Valerie rose to her feet and gave Colette a kiss on the cheek, then motioned her to a chair. "Here, Colette, sit down," she said. "Is it my imagination, or are you upset?"

They both sat down, Colette putting a large, expensive-looking straw tote with leather handles in her lap, then placing her arthritic hands, which were bedecked as always with huge jeweled rings, delicately across the top.

"Oh, Val, darling," the old woman gasped, "where to begin?"

Colette's habitual manner was so dramatic, Valerie thought, that she wasn't especially distressed by the elegant and arty woman's histrionics. Then it suddenly occurred to her that Colette didn't have Puff Puppy curled across an arm, yapping and snarling and otherwise making a nuisance of himself. How odd, she thought. Colette took the petite snow-white Maltese everywhere with her, as if he were a fashion accessory.

"Colette," she asked, "where's that little scoundrel, Puff Puppy?"

"At home, darling," Colette replied.

"Then what's the matter?" Valerie asked. "I saw your name on the list and assumed that something was wrong with him."

"Oh, Val, darling," Colette said, tears springing into her large eyes. Valerie grabbed the box of Kleenex she kept on the desk for distressed pet owners and pulled out a couple. "Thank you, darling," Colette said. "I'm sorry to be such a blubbering old nuisance, but it's . . . it's Hayden!" Tears began to roll down her rouged and powdered cheeks.

Valerie quickly grabbed more Kleenex and handed them to her, then got to her feet and put a hand on Colette's shoulder, stroking her gently. "Who's Hayden?" she asked softly.

She blew her nose with the Kleenex. "Oh, Val, darling," she said, looking up at her with watery eyes. "I didn't tell you?"

"No, Colette," Valerie replied.

Colette looked momentarily perplexed, then patted Valerie's hand. "Oh, do sit down, darling. And thank you for your moral support. I need all of it I can get these days." She dabbed at her tears with a fresh Kleenex.

Valerie sat back down in her chair and looked over at her old friend. She was clad all in white today, white artist's smock, white pants, even white shoes, and wore several strands of large pearls at her throat with matching bracelet and earrings. On her head was a huge straw sun hat. One glance was enough to see that the woman had been a stunning beauty in her youth, and she still had about her an air of youthfulness and vitality that belied her advanced age. Absorbed by everything around her, she found life endlessly wondrous and exciting. She was also coquettish and accustomed to having attention lavished on her. Her white hair, always perfectly coiffed, appeared to be in slight disarray beneath the sun hat, and makeup was now streaked down her cheeks.

"I simply can't believe I haven't told you about him before, but then I haven't seen much of you lately." She caught her breath before continuing. "Hayden, my darling, is right here with me, and it's high time you met." She opened the straw tote on her lap and carefully lifted out a tiny bundle.

A towel? Valerie thought. *What in the world?*

Colette delicately held the bundle in one hand and opened the towel with the other. "This is Hayden," she announced, holding her hands out for Valerie to see.

Valerie got out of her chair and stepped over for a

closer look at the tiny creature Colette cuddled in her hands. "Oh, my God, Colette," she exclaimed, "he's tiny. And so precious." She slowly extended a hand toward the creature and stroked his coat of quills, very lightly with a single finger. He made a ball of himself and trembled all over, his eyes blinking suspiciously.

"He's an African pygmy hedgehog," Colette said. "Isn't he divine?"

"Oh, he's adorable," Valerie said, stroking him some more. "What does Puff Puppy think of him?"

"Puff Puppy adores him," Colette replied, "but I'm afraid the feeling isn't mutual. I can see that he likes you, though," she went on. "I can hardly believe it. Normally he has a fit if anybody touches him but me."

"Well, he doesn't seem too happy with me," Valerie replied. "May I hold him?"

Colette held her hands out, and Valerie took him into hers, careful not to drop him or let him escape. "Where on earth did you get the name?" Val asked.

"Why, he's named after Sterling Hayden, the actor, of course," Colette said, her eyes wide and her eyebrows arching in surprise. "The love of my life that man was, though I never knew him personally. Soooo romantic, you know. So handsome. Sun-bronzed. A sailor. A real adventurer. Not like these men nowadays who spend fortunes playing at being adventurous. You know the sort. Always have a safety net. Not so, Hayden. He sailed the seven seas. Oh, Val, my darling, he was of a dying breed. Sooo sexy!"

Valerie laughed. She didn't find it surprising that Colette Richards, who she knew was in the neighborhood of eighty, was still consumed by romantic notions at her age. She was a woman with quite a past.

"Well, what seems to be the problem with our little adventurer here?" Valerie asked.

"I'm not certain," Colette said worriedly, "but he hasn't been himself lately. Not at all. He has a lovely cage with a heating pad to sleep on—they love heat, you see—and I play with him every night before my bedtime. They're nocturnal, you know, and after we play for a while, he gets on his wheel and spins, spins, spins! He adores the pocket of my bathrobe and my smocks, so I carry him around the house with me."

"Has he been eating properly?" Valerie asked.

"Funny you should ask, Val," she said. "Now that I think about it, Hayden went off his food a few days ago, so I make him this delicious turkey soup that I found out they like."

"Did he like it?" Valerie asked.

"Adores it," Colette cried. "Gobbles it right up. Broth, turkey, vegetables, and all."

Valerie carefully turned him over, examining Hayden's tiny body. He was no more than five inches long. She delicately felt along his entire body. It wasn't an easy task, considering his quills. After studying his eyes for a long time, she carefully opened his mouth and searched there for any clues. She was just about to abandon her examination when she stopped.

"What?" Colette asked.

"Look, Colette," Valerie said quietly. "I think we've found the culprit."

Colette held a wrinkled hand to her heart. "Oh, dear, Val. What?" she gasped in a whisper.

"His teeth," Valerie replied.

"His *teeth*?" Colette exclaimed.

"Yes," Valerie answered, nodding her head. "I'm fairly certain that I can see the beginnings of gum disease."

"Oh, darling Val," Colette exclaimed. "What are we to do?"

"We'll have to clean his teeth," Valerie responded, still absorbed in studying the creature's tiny mouth.

"Clean his teeth? Imagine!" Colette said. "But can you do that, Val? I mean, how—"

"I'll have to administer anesthesia," she said, "but it can be done. I'll have to be very careful adjusting the dosage."

"Oh, my goodness," Colette said. "Val, darling, you're a marvel."

"In the meantime, we'll have to start him on a course of antibiotics," Valerie said.

"Antibiotics," Colette echoed. "And when can you do the cleaning?" she asked.

"The sooner the better," Valerie replied. "Let me look at the schedule. I definitely want to do it in the next few days."

"Oh, Hayden," Colette cooed. She reached over and stroked him with her fingers.

"Here," Valerie said, "take him for a minute while I check my schedule." She gently transferred him from her hands to Colette's.

Valerie looked at her date book, then rose to her feet. "I'll be right back, Colette," she said. "I'd better check at the desk and see what's scheduled on the clinic book."

She returned quickly and stood observing Colette and Hayden. "Friday it is, Hayden," she said. "You'll have to have him here around seven o'clock."

Colette looked up. "In the morning?" she asked.

Valerie nodded.

"Oh, Hayden," she said, looking at the tiny hedgehog, "we'll have to have an unusually early night, won't we, darling? And we're both such night owls." She carefully bundled him back up in his towel and placed the bundle in her tote, closing the leather strap over the top. "Thank you, Val, darling. I don't know what we'd do without you."

"It's my job," Valerie said in her self-effacing manner.

"Ha!" Colette exclaimed. Then in a near whisper she added. "If only your colleagues cared half as much as you, the world would be a *far* better place. I wish my own doctor cared as much as you do, but I'm old so I don't matter. One foot in the grave, you know . . ."

Valerie laughed and patted her on the back. "Not quite yet, I don't think."

Colette turned and started out with Hayden. "Anyway, dear, we'll be here bright and early Friday morning. In the meantime, don't be such a stranger. I've missed our little talks lately."

"Me, too," Valerie said. "I've just been so busy."

"I know, darling," Colette said with a wink. "Teddy's been away on weekends, so you've been catching up in the garden and around the house."

"Yes," Valerie said. "Anyway, I'll see you Friday,

and maybe we'll be able to visit beforehand." She held the door open for her.

"Ta-ta," Colette said, and she swept through the lobby area on her impossibly high heels, trailing heavy perfume in her wake, waggling the fingers of one hand at Annie and Tami, who were seated behind the reception desk. At the front door she stopped and blew kisses at Valerie, who'd stepped into the reception area.

Valerie waved, and Colette headed out the front door.

When she was gone, Annie looked over at Valerie. "I don't know how you put up with that crazy old bat," she said.

"She's not crazy, Annie," Valerie said in Colette's defense. "And she's not an old bat, as you so unkindly put it. She's just different, that's all."

"Could've fooled me," Annie said, giggling.

"Dr. Rochelle," Tami piped up from behind the reception desk, "you've got a call on line three."

"Who is it?" Valerie asked.

"It's somebody at Stonelair Farm," Tami replied. "You want to take it or have them call back?"

"I'll take it now," Valerie said. She retraced her steps to her office and closed the door, then looked down at Elvis, who was snoring quietly. She punched line three on her telephone. "Dr. Rochelle."

"Dr. Rochelle," the man's voice said, "this is Santo Ducci at Stonelair."

"Yes, Mr. Ducci," she said. "What can I do for you?"

"All of our dogs—four Irish wolfhounds—need checkups, and their Lyme disease vaccinations," he said. "Plus, there's the cat. The sooner the better because they're behind schedule. We were hoping you could make a house call. It's sort of a problem to bring in four big Irish wolfhounds, you know."

"I understand," she said. And she did. Irish wolfhounds were like small ponies. It wasn't at all uncommon in the country to make house calls for big animals. That's why she usually spent half her days on the road, ministering to everything from horses to llamas.

"Hold on just a minute, Mr. Ducci," she said, "and I'll see what's scheduled and exactly when I'm scheduled to do house calls. They may send somebody else, you know."

"Either you do it," Ducci said, "or skip it."

Valerie was stunned by his bluntness, then said, "I'll see what I can do, Mr. Ducci."

She put him on hold and pushed the button for reception, where Tami picked up. "Tami, can I fit in a house call either this afternoon or tomorrow afternoon? Say, an hour at the most?"

"Let me see," Tami said.

Valerie waited patiently while Tami looked at the schedule.

"You can do it today between three-thirty and four-thirty, but you'll have to be back before four-thirty for sure for clinic appointments," she said.

"Great," Valerie said. "Put me down for a house call at Stonelair Farm."

"Gotcha," Tami said, hanging up.

Valerie punched Ducci's line. "Mr. Ducci," she said.

"Yes," he replied somewhat gruffly.

"I'll be there at three-thirty."

"Thanks," he said, his voice all politeness now, "that's great."

"How many dogs did you say there are?" she asked.

"Four," he replied, "and a cat."

"Okay," she said.

"By the way, Dr. Rochelle," Ducci said, "you never did get back to us about taking care of our animals."

Valerie felt a pang of guilt for not having returned his call, but she'd been putting it off. She'd dreaded discussing it with Charles.

"I assume you still haven't discussed it with the owner," Ducci continued, "since you said somebody else might be coming out here. You know, we've been waiting to hear from you. We have a lot of animals, and their health is very important to us."

"I understand, and I'm sorry about that," she replied. "I promise you that I'll discuss it with my colleagues as soon as possible."

"I'd think that the clinic would be glad for the business you'd be bringing in," Ducci said with unerring logic.

"I suppose you're right," Valerie said, "but I'll still have to discuss this with them. I'll try to speak to them today and get back to you, either this afternoon when I see you at Stonelair or sometime tomorrow."

"Good," Ducci said. "We'd appreciate that."

"Okay, then," Valerie said. "I'll see you at three-thirty. Good-bye."

Santo Ducci didn't respond because he'd already hung up. "Thanks to you, too," Valerie said, replacing the receiver in its cradle.

She glanced at her watch. It was noon already. Where had the time gone? It seemed as if she'd just gotten there. *Well,* she thought, looking back over her morning, *I guess it's no wonder.* First, there'd been a slightly premature birth at Breezy Hills Farm very early this morning. A beautiful foal. Then there'd been a llama with a leg injury at Maplecrest. She'd also seen a horse with parasites at Silver Fox, and a horse with gastric ulcers at Streamside. Two dogs and one cat here at the clinic. Fairly routine stuff. Then Colette with Hayden.

And now I'm supposed to be perfection itself and meet Teddy for lunch at his place, she thought wearily.

She sat there for a moment, reflecting. It'd been nearly a month since he'd given her the ring and gone back to New York City, and he hadn't been up here on the weekends. He'd had important dinner parties with big-shot clients in the Hamptons the previous weekend, but he'd called her frequently. Now he had come up for part of the week to relax—just when she was at her busiest.

Funny enough, she thought, *I really didn't miss Teddy the last month, and I really would just as soon not see him for lunch today.* But she'd promised him, and she wasn't one to go back on a promise.

She rose to her feet and stretched, then took off her lab coat and hung it up. Elvis immediately roused himself from his bed and yawned, knowing that it was lunchtime. "Give me a minute, Elvis," she said, reaching down and giving him a few strokes.

She grabbed her shoulder bag and went into the bathroom and flipped on the light. Looking into the mirror, she applied fresh pale pink lipstick, then a little blusher. She was so tanned from being out in the sun working in her garden that she hardly needed any makeup. Her hair, in its single long plait, was rolled into a knot at the nape of her neck.

Take it down or leave it? she asked her reflection. She knew that Teddy didn't like her practical work look, especially her hair, but she decided to leave it exactly as it was. She had to return to work, after all, and Teddy would simply have to learn to like it. That or quit complaining about it. She flipped off the light and went back into her office. "Let's go, Elvis," she said, and stooped down and put his leash on.

Daphne Collins was in the reception area, tapping a chart against the desk. "Hi, Val," she said with a smile on her face. "I hear that Colette was here."

"Yes," Valerie replied. "Her African pygmy hedgehog."

"Oh, really!" Daphne replied. "I wish I'd seen her and the hedgehog. She's so wonderful. I bet it was as adorable as she is. What will she think of next?"

"There's no telling," Valerie replied. "By the way, have you got a minute?" she asked. "I need to have a quick word with you and Charles.".

"I'm getting ready to go to lunch," Daphne replied, "but I can give you a minute, if Charles isn't busy." She turned to Annie. "Does Charles have a patient?" she asked.

"No," Annie replied. "He's in his office."

"Let's go," Daphne said, already heading down the hallway to Charles's office.

Valerie followed her with Elvis, and when they

reached the door to his office, Daphne knocked and went on in without waiting for a response.

Charles looked up from the desk. In his gray eyes there was an expectant expression.

"Val needs a word with both of us," Daphne said.

"What is it?" Charles asked.

"The people at Stonelair want me to take care of their animals," Valerie replied.

"You mean you exclusively?" Daphne asked.

Valerie nodded.

The news did not sit well with Daphne. She turned to try to hide the disgruntled expression on her face, but Valerie didn't miss it.

Charles took off his glasses and looked at Valerie. "You know we don't generally operate that way," he said. "Except under special circumstances."

"Of course," Valerie said, "but they're pressuring me to ask about it, so—"

"This has happened time and again," Daphne said abruptly, her voice tinged with anger. "I don't know why you don't recommend one of us so that the workload is more spread out."

"I made it clear that we have a share-and-share-alike policy," Valerie said, "but they don't like that. They want to see one vet consistently, and since they've met me . . . well, they want me to handle it. There are a lot of animals out there, and it would generate a lot of income for the clinic."

Daphne stared at her, her brows knit crossly, but Charles barked a laugh. "You must've made quite an impression on the Mafia guys out there," he said. "What did you do for them, Val?"

She decided to ignore his remark, but could feel her face blushing heatedly. *Well, I am not going to stand here and be insulted,* she thought.

"Yes or no?" she finally said, her voice steely with determination.

"What do you think, Daphne?" Charles asked.

"I don't like it," Daphne replied. "She knows—"

"If I don't agree to do it," Valerie interjected, "Stonelair will take its business elsewhere. They won't use this clinic at all."

Daphne's mouth opened in a silent gasp, then snapped shut. She crossed her arms over her chest and looked at Charles. "Well, it would generate a lot of income," she said. "Like Val said, there're a lot of animals out there. Think about it, Charles."

As if taking a cue from her, Charles looked thoughtful for a moment. "I suppose so," he finally said. Then he smiled. "It's not a bad idea at all, come to think of it. Valerie here would be taking care of their animals, and we wouldn't have to deal with the slimy people." Charles nodded. "I think you're right, Daphne," he said. "But there'd have to be a couple of conditions."

"What?" Valerie asked, keeping strictly to business.

"We'd have to triage emergency situations," he said. "You wouldn't be able to drop everyone else for those people, you understand. You'd still have your usual duties."

"Of course," Val said.

"So if more than one emergency arises at a time," he went on, "you'll have to make a decision about which is more urgent and see to it first. And it may not be theirs."

"Yes," Valerie said, becoming impatient since he was stating the obvious.

"And don't forget," Daphne added, "if you're away for some reason, on vacation or whatever, then they'll have to agree to use one of us. Isn't that right, Charles?"

He nodded. "Absolutely."

"I understand," Valerie said. "Is that all?" she asked.

Charles looked at Daphne, and a silent signal seemed to pass between them.

"I believe so," Charles said.

"Thanks," Valerie said. "Let's go, Elvis." She turned on her heel and left the office quickly, then heard the door slam with a loud bang when she got farther down the hall.

Jeez, she thought, *the sooner I get my own practice the better. I can't take this crap much longer. They are jealous, plain and simple, and want to put me through hell.*

In the reception area, Tami called to her.

"What is it, Tami?" she asked.

"If we're not too busy here this afternoon," Tami said, "I wondered if I could go with you out to Stonelair and help."

"I don't mind at all," Valerie said with a smile, "if Daphne and Charles agree to it."

"It would be sort of special to me," Tami said.

"Why's that, Tami?" Valerie asked.

"Well, you know, when I was little we lived out in the woods near there," Tami said, "so my brother and I used to play there a lot."

"At Stonelair?" Valerie asked, surprised.

Tami nodded. "There wasn't anybody but a care-taker, and Jimmy and I knew how to get in and out of the place through the fences in the backwoods. We even got in and out of the house without anybody ever knowing it."

Valerie laughed. "Then you're the only person I know who's ever been there," she said. "Talk to Daphne and Charles and see what they say. I'll be glad for you to come along, even though it wouldn't be much of a learning experience for you. It's just vacci-nations and stuff like that."

"That's okay," Tami said. "I'd just like to see the place again."

"Well, if you can't come this time," Valerie said, "there'll be others, because I'm going to be taking care of all the animals out there."

"Great!" Tami said.

"I'd better run," Valerie said. "I've got a lunch appointment."

"Teddy?" Tami asked, smiling.

"Yes," Valerie replied, already heading to the door.

"Have fun," Tami called after her.

"I'll try," Valerie said.

She hurried out to her car, and began to wonder what she'd gotten herself into with this Stonelair deal. *Stonelair,* she thought. *A truly forbidding place.* And why did this Conrad guy insist on her? She didn't think she'd ever actually felt so pressured into handling a person's animals before. And certainly not for a person she'd yet to meet or see. *I guess the mysterious Mr. Conrad thinks he's too important to take care of mun-dane affairs himself.*

Suddenly she began to wonder about all the rumors that swirled around Conrad and the goings-on at Stonelair and if there was any truth to them. *But so what if they are true?* she thought. *I'm only the vet. How could they hurt me?*

Chapter Nine

At Apple Hill Farm, Valerie and Teddy sat under the protection of a large market umbrella out by the sun-drenched pool. Hattie had set the big weathered teak table for lunch, which she was serving. No fool, Elvis was stationed between Valerie and Teddy, ideally positioned to beg. At his most charming, his eyes shone with gleeful greed, and his tongue was stuck out, making his mouth look as if it were spread in a giant smile. His blue-black tail swept the stone terrace at regular intervals, anticipation in every swipe.

"Thanks, Hattie," Valerie said, "this looks delicious."

"You're welcome," Hattie replied. "Do you want me to take Elvis inside with me?" she asked tentatively. "I can give him a little something in the kitchen."

"Well . . . ," Valerie stalled, reluctant to say yes, for she knew that Hattie would let him have anything he wanted—and a lot of it. "I think he'll be all right out here, Hattie."

"Oh, come on, Val," Teddy prodded. "Let him live

a little. It's not often he gets to eat really good food."

Valerie laughed. "Is that a reflection on my culinary abilities, Mr. de Mornay?"

Teddy smiled. "I know how you feed him at home," he said. "Yourself, too. Shall we just call it exceedingly healthy?"

"Oh, okay," Valerie conceded with a growl. "Elvis," she said, looking down at her attentive treasure, "you go with Hattie. Have a party."

"Let's go, Elvis," Hattie said, beckoning to him as she started toward the house.

He immediately sprang to her side, knowing what was in store for him.

Valerie watched them leave, convinced that Hattie and Teddy prearranged these little trysts to get Elvis out of the way. It worried her, because Teddy didn't seem to really like having Elvis around. Oh, he did a good job of pretending, she supposed, extending his generosity to Elvis as he did almost anyone around, but she sometimes wondered if Teddy actually liked animals—any animals—at all. He didn't have any pets, and poor Kaiser, his horse, went largely ignored.

Teddy picked up the chilled bottle of Pouilly Fuissé that was sweating in its silver wine coaster and was about to pour some into Valerie's wineglass, but she quickly put her hand over it. "Unh-unh. Not for me, Teddy," she said. "I've got a long day ahead of me yet."

"Christ, Val," he groused. "Just a glass?"

"No," she said firmly. "I'll stick with the mineral water."

"What? You afraid you'll butcher a poodle or something?" he joked.

"Not funny, Teddy," she replied. "What if your doctor had a couple of drinks before . . . say . . ."

"Okay!" He laughed. "Let's don't go there."

"Thought you might see it my way," she said.

"Well, cheers, anyway," he said amiably, lifting his glass.

"Cheers," she echoed, lifting her glass of water and clinking it against his wineglass. "This looks yummy," she said, gazing down at her plate.

"Hattie loves to cook for you," Teddy said, forking up a large bite of lobster salad.

Valerie buttered a cheddar-scallion biscuit, one of Hattie's specialities. "I'd forgotten about these scrumptious little goodies," she said before taking a bite.

Teddy smiled, taking pleasure in her delight. "I'll have to live on rabbit food when I get back to the city," he said. "Between the food here and the food out in the Hamptons the last few weekends, it's going to be time for lettuce, lettuce, and more lettuce."

"Maybe so," Valerie said, "but you're really lucky to have Hattie. She's not only a treasure around the house, but she clearly adores you like a favorite son."

"She could be your treasure, too," Teddy said.

Valerie's fork paused midway to her mouth, but then she continued eating, deciding not to respond to that remark.

Teddy continued to watch her as he took a sip of wine. "Just think, Val," he continued. "Hattie would do all the cooking and cleaning. Lydia would run the office, pay all the bills, hire all the workmen and everything. You wouldn't have to do a thing because it would all be done for you. You'd just have to show up." He took another sip of wine. "You'd be the queen of Apple Hill."

Valerie felt her stomach lurch. *The queen of Apple Hill?* she thought. *That is so ridiculous. I'm a veterinarian, for God's sake.*

"The queen of Apple Hill, huh?" she said with amusement. "I don't think I'd look too good in a crown."

With that, Teddy launched into the joys that her future life at Apple Hill would entail, reiterating what he'd just said, but embellishing with great detail the host of benefits she would enjoy being the mistress of such a perfect estate.

She tuned him out almost entirely, picking at her food. She knew exactly where this conversation—or monologue, she corrected—was headed, and she didn't like it. She didn't need this pressure from Teddy. Not now.

She expelled a silent sigh, pretending to listen to him, while at the same time she began to feel an unpleasant sensation of guilt. *I swear,* she thought, *he learned his techniques at my mother's knee.*

She realized that, in effect, she'd been leading Teddy on for a long time now, unwilling to discuss her feelings with him, letting their relationship just coast along as if there were nothing wrong.

When they'd first started dating in college, she was so thrilled with his pursuit of her that she'd genuinely confused her feelings for him with true love. As they gradually became an item, their relationship was prodded along by their families and friends, who viewed them as an appropriate match. Later on, while he'd worked on his MBA and she'd gone to veterinary school, their relationship had continued long-distance.

There'd been the occasional boozy weekend and holiday parties that had been exciting and fun for her, opening up a whole new world of sophisticated acquaintances. Teddy was extremely popular and good-looking, and her acceptance by his friends had helped give her more confidence in herself. She had also blossomed physically, that gangly, gawky body maturing into an enviable tall and elegant beauty. She had gradually begun to see that there were myriad possibilities for her out there. Possibilities other than Teddy de Mornay.

She took a sip of her mineral water, then dabbed at her lips with a napkin, catching pieces of his monologue, all of it a familiar rehash of conversations past. She looked over at him with a fixed smile on her face, but her mind ranged elsewhere, analyzing their fractured relationship, even as he talked of permanently sealing it, cementing them into a marriage that everyone seemed to think was inevitable.

Since college, she thought, this sense of inevitability had only increased. For the last four years while building up her practice, they'd spent most every weekend together—always at his place, even though she now had hers—and everyone assumed that marriage was the next step.

She'd thought the same thing for a period of time, but she had become increasingly disenchanted with the idea as her love for Teddy—whatever kind of love it might be called—had diminished with time. She couldn't place the blame—at least not entirely—on Teddy himself. He hadn't really changed all that much. Over the years she definitely had begun to recognize behavioral patterns that she hadn't detected at first but that had always been there. Teddy, she'd come to realize, was a great charmer, a great actor.

Finally, she put her fork down and looked across at him, waiting for a pause. When it came, she quickly took advantage. "Teddy," she said in an even voice, "we've been over this, time and again. And I still feel the same way. I can't help it." She shrugged. "I want to wait a while."

He attempted a smile, but his eyes weren't smiling. As he poured more wine into his glass, she continued. "You know that I appreciate everything that you've offered me. I really do. But I've also explained to you repeatedly that what I have to concentrate on now is building up my clientele and starting a practice of my own. Plus I want to get out of debt. I've still got huge student loans to pay off, and now I've got a mortgage. I just—"

"Oh, Val, for Christ's sake," he said, disgruntled. "Sometimes I think you actually forget who you are. You're a de la Rochelle. You're descended from French aristocracy. Even your very name, Valerie, is on the list of names approved by the French court, and don't you ever forget it."

She looked at him in disbelief. He was sounding increasingly like her snobbish mother.

"You shouldn't even be thinking about mundane things like that," he went on. "You know I'd pay off your crummy student loans for you. And when we get married, you could sell that little house you bought. That'd take care of the mortgage. Hell, Val, you could sell the house now. Move in here." He glared at her for an intense moment. "You didn't have to buy it to begin with, you know."

"Oh, yes, I did," she countered. "We talked about that, and I told you that I wanted to try living on my own for a while." She sighed audibly. "Don't you see? I want to be able to stand on my own two feet, Teddy. And I don't feel like I'm ready to get married until I can do that. I want to wait a little while longer and—"

"You told me Christmas," he said emphatically. There was a smile on his lips, but there was no missing the edge in his voice.

Valerie's face burned with the truth of his words. "I think I said probably, didn't I?" she said, in a futile attempt at levity.

He didn't laugh but continued staring at her with the expression of a petulant child.

Christmas, she remembered, had seemed so far away at the beginning of the year when she'd told him she thought she'd be ready to settle down by next Christmas. Now, of course, summer would soon be over, and she'd accepted his engagement ring.

"You're right," she said, "I did say that, and I meant it at the time. But—"

"But what, Val?" he said angrily. "You're not putting me off again, are you? What's the big deal about getting married anyway?" He held a hand out and starting counting off points on his fingers. "You spend nearly every weekend with me." One finger down. "All of our holidays." Two fingers down. "We see each other, maybe get to eat lunch or dinner together, practically every day if I'm up here during the week."

Three fingers down. "We're like a married couple now, for Christ's sake." Four fingers down.

If we are indeed like a married couple now, and if this is what marriage is like, she thought, *then I don't want any part of it—ever.*

She said: "You're right again, Teddy. It's just . . . I don't know . . ."

Teddy realized he was pushing too hard. He reached across the table and took one of her hands in his. "Oh, God, Val. I'm sorry," he said contritely. His familiar harsh stare had become that familiar puppy's beseeching plea. "I . . . I guess I just love you so much that waiting is . . . well, it's really such hell."

"I'm sorry, too, Teddy," she said softly but firmly. "You know that I really have feelings for you. Right now I just feel as if I'm being pushed from all directions."

Teddy quickly nodded in agreement. "You're right, Val. Don't worry about it. "Now, let's eat," he said, digging into his lobster salad with renewed gusto.

Valerie picked up her fork and began eating again. The salad was delicious, but she'd almost completely lost her appetite.

"Did you have a busy morning?" Teddy asked after taking a large sip of wine.

Valerie nodded. "Yes. A very busy morning. All the usual, and Colette, too."

"Colette!" he exclaimed. "Oh, God, what's her problem?"

"She has a pet African pygmy hedgehog that's having trouble," Valerie said. "So we're going to fix him up."

"I can't figure her out," Teddy said. "She's smart as a whip, sophisticated, all that, and loaded to the gills with money. But"—he thumped a hand on the table—"she won't let me handle her portfolio."

"You asked her?" Val said, surprised to hear this news.

"More than once," Teddy said. "But she won't give an inch. Says she's quite happy with her present money managers. I can't figure it," he said. "She's known my family forever, but she just refuses to see reason and switch."

"I didn't know," Valerie replied. "She hasn't mentioned anything to me at all."

"If she does," he said, "let me know, will you?"

"Sure," Valerie said, thinking that she probably wouldn't.

"You have a busy afternoon coming up?" he asked.

"The usual late-afternoon office appointments, plus I've got to go out to Stonelair."

"Stonelair?" he said with alarm. "Again?"

"He's got four Irish wolfhounds," she said, "and they all need the Lyme vaccine plus heartworm medication and checkups. And there's a cat."

"So why are you going out there?" he asked. "Why doesn't he bring them into the clinic?"

"Teddy!" she exclaimed. "It would take a horse trailer to bring them in. They're Irish wolfhounds. You know, practically ponies."

"Well, I hope you know what you're doing," Teddy said ominously. "Getting mixed up with weirdos like that."

"There was nothing weird the night I saw the

horse," Valerie said defensively. "I think all this talk is just that. Talk."

"There's usually a reason for it," Teddy said. "And from what I've heard, things are really strange out there."

"You sound like my mother," she said.

"Maybe so," Teddy said, "but your mother's got very good instincts, I think. And she smells a rat." He sat looking at her for a moment. "By the way," he asked, "did she give old Dock Wainwright a call?"

"I don't have any idea," Valerie said, looking at him curiously. "Why?" she asked, although she thought she already knew the answer to that question.

Teddy shrugged nonchalantly. "Just wondered," he replied, swirling the remains of his wine around in the glass. "She talked about it at dinner that night. Remember?" He looked over at her. "Old Dock's twiddling his thumbs. Just letting her account sit there gathering dust. He probably nods off reading financial reports."

"So now you want to get your hands on my mother's money," Valerie said teasingly.

He gazed at her seriously, ignoring her joking tone. "Well," he began, "I don't see why not, Val. Your mother certainly seemed interested in my handling it. She knows what the market's like, and she knows Dock's not doing anything for her. The way he invests money, it probably doesn't even keep up with the rate of inflation."

For a long time now, she'd wondered when Teddy would approach her mother about handling her money. For some reason she couldn't put her finger on—

perhaps, it was simply an instinct—she didn't like the idea of Teddy becoming involved in her mother's finances. She couldn't shake the feeling that it would be a mistake, even though she realized that she was probably being irrational.

I guess I'm being silly, she thought. After all, Teddy was supposed to be a great moneymaker, wasn't he? And he certainly did live like one. The lavish bachelor pad in New York City, the meticulously restored showplace up here, the new Jaguar for himself and a truck for the farm every year. A gazillion-dollar wardrobe. Those expensive weekends in the Hamptons.

Suddenly she realized that Teddy had asked her a question.

"What?" she asked.

"You're not listening to me," Teddy said. "You're already thinking about all those poor dogs you've got to neuter."

"Oh, stop with the dumb vet jokes," she said with good humor.

"I was just asking if you had any idea how much money she's got invested with Dock," he said.

"I don't know anything about that," Valerie replied, surprised that he'd asked something that personal. Teddy was aggressive, but usually a lot more subtle than this. "That's strictly *her* business," she added, "and she doesn't talk to me about it." She looked down at her wristwatch. "Anyway, I'd better get going," she said.

"Don't you want dessert?" Teddy asked. "It's just some fruit, but—"

"Too many donuts at the office this morning," Valerie glibly fibbed, already getting to her feet.

Teddy followed suit and walked around the table to her. He slid an arm around her waist and gave her a kiss on the cheek. "I'm glad you came," he said. "I've missed you the last few weekends."

Valerie smiled and nodded. "I . . . I'd better hurry and go get Elvis," she said.

"I'll go with you," he said.

They strolled up to the house in silence, but when they reached the door, Teddy turned and stared into her eyes.

She looked at him with an expectant smile.

"You're not wearing your engagement ring," he said softly. "Why, Val?"

She felt a blush rise to her face. "Teddy," she said, "think about it for a minute. I don't think it's a good idea to wear it to work. At least not my work. I mean, it's not the kind of thing you wear to help give birth to a foal, is it? Or set a llama's broken leg? I don't think you want to see it covered up with blood, do you?"

"Well . . . no," he said, "but you could've had it handy for lunch."

"I'm not about to carry around a ring like that and take it on and off," Valerie replied. "I'd lose it in no time. Or have it stolen."

"You're probably right," he agreed.

"I know I am," Valerie said. "Besides, it's so big, I'd never be able to fit my surgical gloves over it."

Teddy laughed. "You may have a point there, too," he conceded as he opened the door. "You going to be able to come over tonight?" he asked as she headed into the conservatory. "I'm going back to New York tomorrow, you know."

Valerie kept walking toward the kitchen. "I really shouldn't, Teddy," she said. "I've got a lot to do when I get home tonight."

"But—" Teddy began, then he immediately thought better of trying to persuade her to spend the night. *Pressure*, he remembered. *Lay off, Teddy, old boy. You don't want to chase her away now.*

"But what?" she asked.

"Nothing," he replied. "I was thinking out loud. About all the work Lydia's got lined up for me in the office."

"See?" she said. "You've got a lot to do, too, so I don't have to feel guilty."

In the kitchen, Elvis happily greeted them, reluctantly leaving Hattie to prance proudly alongside Valerie back out to the car. Teddy watched as she opened the door for Elvis, then started to get in herself.

"Aren't you forgetting something?" he asked.

Valerie turned and looked at him.

He held his arms out, and she went into them, letting him embrace her. He gave her a quick kiss and let her go. "I know you're in a rush to get back," he said. "I'll give you a call tonight, okay?"

"Sure," Valerie replied. "Talk to you tonight." She got in the Jeep, Teddy closing the door after her. She started the engine and backed out of the parking area, turning around to head down the drive. She waved as she left, and Teddy stood in the driveway waving back until she was out of sight.

Oh, Lord, she thought. *Why is it becoming more and more of a trial to see Teddy? And why, oh why, don't I feel like a woman who's supposed to be getting*

*married to the perfect man at Christmastime? Why
don't I have the courage to do what I know I must
eventually do?*

Lydia had gone out to lunch, and in the privacy of
his office, Teddy picked up the telephone and punched
out the number. The machine picked up after the fourth
ring.

"Hi, this is Tiffani," her disembodied voice answered.
"I'm not here right now, so leave your number and a
message. Oh, and wait for the beep. Thanks." Her voice
sounded perky and sexy, he thought. Just like her.

After the beep, he said, "Hey, babe, it's Teddy. I got
hot just listening to your voice. What about me coming
over there after you get off work? We could have a real
good time. I've got a little candy for you, babe. Give me
a call when you get in."

He replaced the receiver in its cradle and smiled,
thinking about Tiffani, that voluptuous body of hers,
the things they could do. He knew she'd call back. *She's
really into me,* he thought. *Really gets off on it.* Besides,
she wasn't about to turn down the chance to snort a
little nose candy.

Chapter Ten

Valerie drove the Jeep toward the big iron gates at Stonelair, stopping at the post in the middle of the drive to push the intercom button.

"Who is it?" a voice asked. *The not so jolly bald giant,* she thought.

"Dr. Rochelle," she answered.

"When you get to the split in the drive, veer to the right," the voice said. "To the house."

"Okay," she said, noting once again that video cameras, mounted on the stone piers to which the gates were attached, swiveled toward the Jeep. Must be motion sensitive, she thought. She had the urge to wave at them and stick her tongue out, but decided that would look pretty silly on the monitors. Not very professional, either.

The gates swung open, and she drove through, anxious to see Stonelair in the daylight for the first time. On her last visit in the darkness and driving rain, she'd seen virtually nothing but the stable compound. The mile-long drive was beautifully landscaped, bordered on both sides by giant old conifers, with ancient maples and oaks behind them. Rhododendrons, mountain laurel, and azaleas were massed along the edge of the drive and banked around the bases of the big trees. They were long past their blooming stage, but it must be spectacular in the spring, she thought. The place was like a beautifully kept park.

She came to the split in the road and veered to the right, following Ducci's instructions. When she finally came within sight of the house itself, her first glimpse was of massive chimneys and a slate roof reaching to the sky above the treetops. As she rounded a bend in the road, the house itself came into full view. She slowed down and looked at it with awe.

My God, she thought, *it's a small château!* Built of limestone, it loomed in the near-distance like a great fortress, albeit an elegant one. She'd heard about it all of her life and seen very old photographs of it, but nothing had conveyed the monumental reality of the house.

She knew that it had been built by one of the great robber barons before the turn of the century, a railroad tycoon, as she remembered. Then it had descended to one family member after another, none of them staying there for more than a month or two a year. Sometime back in the early sixties the family had boarded it up, their fortune largely squandered over the course of the last century, until finally they'd sold it to Conrad.

The drive led into a courtyard in the center of which was a large fountain, its bronze horses spouting sprays of water. She drove up to the wide stone terrace that led to the front door. Killing the engine, she got out, grabbing her large carryall, then went around to the back of the Jeep, where she retrieved her medical bag from the cargo compartment.

Valerie looked over as one of the massive wooden doors across the terrace opened. Santo Ducci, giant that he was, didn't quite fill it. He quickly strode across the terrace toward her, his entire body seeming to ripple as he approached.

"Here," he said as he reached her, "let me take that for you."

"No need to," Valerie said, looking up at him with a smile. "I'm used to it."

"Have it your way," he said, shrugging.

He led her across the terrace and into the entrance hall, where their shoes echoed loudly on the stone floors. Valerie glimpsed a limestone fireplace and neoclassical *boiseries* on the walls. Over the ornately carved *boiseries* hung old oil paintings, their picture lamps casting little pools of light in the dimness. She caught only a fleeting glace at them before Ducci gestured her to the left and down a long gallery, its lefthand wall hung with more paintings and the right punctuated with French doors, which led out onto another stone terrace that gave onto acres of manicured lawn.

They finally arrived at a set of double doors, and Ducci stopped, gesturing for her to enter. "The dogs are in here," he said, "and probably the cat." He smiled.

"The cat may be on the prowl, huh?" she said.

"You never know," he replied, "but she hangs out with the dogs a lot."

Valerie stepped just inside the doors and found herself looking into a library, a cavernous double-height room with a balcony running partway around it. Bookshelves lined the walls both beneath and above the balcony, and a spiral staircase led up to the balcony's walkway. On one wall was a huge fireplace similar to the one in the entrance hall, and another wall was set with French doors that gave onto the stone terrace she'd seen from the gallery. Two matching Dutch baroque brass chandeliers were suspended from the ceiling, and the fireplace wall was hung with oil paintings, hunt scenes and horses galore and several dog portraits. Bronzes, primarily of horses, stood atop bookcases and on the shelves, and needlepoint carpets covered the floor. Despite its grandeur, the room had an air of being truly lived in.

She stepped on into the room and was surprised—and delighted—to see that amid this incredible luxury four giant Irish wolfhounds lounged in various positions, two on the rug looking out toward the lawn and two spread out on old leather couches in front of the fireplace. That explained some of the room's lived-in feeling, she surmised.

The moment they became aware of her, all four sprang to their feet, bounding over to greet her. She immediately set down her bags and began stroking their somewhat wiry coats, talking to the giant beasts all the while, her face beaming with joy at their sheer size and friendliness.

"Oh, they're beautiful," she exclaimed.

"Thanks," Santo said. "They're a handful sometimes."

"I bet you are," she said to the dogs, trying to divide her attention equally among the four.

"What are their names?" she asked Santo.

"Paddy, Katy, Sheila, and Seamus," Santo replied.

Valerie couldn't help laughing. "So they're Irish through and through," she said.

He nodded. "Yeah," he said. "We got them when they were pups. From a breeder in Castleknock, outside Dublin. Flew them over here."

"I can see why," she said. "They're such great beauties. Which is which?" she asked.

"Paddy and Katy are the grays," Santo replied, "Shelia's the brown, and Seamus is the brindle."

Valerie continued letting the dogs get a good scent of her, stroking them and crooning all the while until suddenly she caught a movement out of the corner of her eye. She looked up. An enormous cat, a fat, long-hair calico, was not so much walking down the steps from the balcony, Valerie thought, as descending them grandly, her every step measured and regal.

"Ooooh," she cooed, "and who do we have here?" The cat strode toward Valerie, her feet practically invisible beneath her fat, furry body, and continued through the veritable thicket of dogs' legs, rubbing herself up against Valerie when she finally arrived at her feet. She was totally comfortable with the dogs, ignoring their friendly sniffs and licks at her. Valerie leaned down and stroked her silky fur, noticing her huge green eyes.

"That's Mina," Santo said.

"Oh, Mina, you are a beautiful lady," Valerie said. "Quite the *madame,* aren't you? And you look like you have a lot of Maine coon in you."

"We think so, but we're not sure," Santo said. "Wyn—Mr. Conrad—got her at the pound several years ago."

"She's certainly brave with these dogs," Valerie said.

"She's fearless," he replied. "She had a Mexican standoff with a six-foot-long snake once. I don't think she's due any shots, but you can check her chart. I have all their medical charts here."

Valerie looked up at him in surprise. "They usually send them to us," she said.

Santo looked stony-faced. "I had them sent to Mr. Conrad overnight so you'd have them today. You can take them with you when you leave."

I guess Mr. Conrad gets whatever he wants, she thought. "That's great," she said. "Could I take a look at them?"

"Sure," he said. "They're over here." He walked over to an enormous French *bureau plat,* and she picked up her bags and followed him, the dogs and cat trailing behind her.

Santo indicated the pile of charts on the desk, then placed them on a corner, where they were easily within her reach.

Valerie set her bags down and studied the charts for a while, then neatly placed them in a stack on the desk's old burgundy leather surface and looked up at him.

"You're right about Mina," she said. "She's up-to-date on everything." She turned around, looking at the dogs. "So it's just you guys," she said. Then turning back to Santo, she asked: "Okay if I set up here?"

"Sure," he replied. "Whatever's best for you."

Valerie set her leather medical bag on the desk,

opened it, and started pulling out supplies: four syringes, already filled with fluid, swabs and alcohol, and several boxes of medication.

"I'll help hold them for you," Santo said, starting to straddle Paddy's huge body with his own.

"No," Valerie said. "Just leave them be. That won't be necessary."

"Uh, I beg to differ," Santo said. "I think you're going to be a very sorry lady if you don't let me help you out here."

She shook her head. "No," she said emphatically. "Trust me on this."

Santo saw that she meant what she said, just as she had down at the stables some weeks ago, and reluctantly backed off. "Okay," he said, "but I think you're making a mistake."

Valerie paid no attention to him as she picked up an alcohol-soaked swab, looking over at the pack of tail-waggers. "Okay, who's first?"

The dogs looked at her expectantly.

"Aha," she said, "I think Katy wants to be first. You know the old rule, don't you, Katy? Ladies first."

She began stroking Katy's neck, talking to her softly and reassuringly, all the while rubbing the alcohol-soaked pad on the back of the neck where she wanted to give her the injection. After a moment, she put down the pad, picked up the syringe, and then deftly plunged it in. Katy looked around, but her attention was diverted by Valerie's constant crooning.

Santo watched as she repeated the process with the three remaining dogs without experiencing any difficulty whatsoever. When she was finished, he shook his head. "I don't believe it," he said, "not a single complaint."

Valerie smiled and continued petting the animals. "You're all good boys and girls, aren't you?" she said. "Okay, now we'll have our first heartworm pill. That's nothing. It tastes like a real treat."

She opened one of the boxes on the desk and tore off four of the large chewable pills. "They should have one of these a month," she told Santo, opening the blister packs one by one. "Here's a magnetized calendar you can put on the refrigerator or wherever to keep track of when they should have them. You can mark down today's date and go from there."

"Thanks," he said, taking it from her.

When she was done, she gave each of the dogs one of the pills, and all four returned to their favorite spots to chew them.

With a tiny meow, Mina jumped up on the chair at the desk, then onto the desk itself. "Oh-ho," Valerie said, "are we jealous?" She stroked the big cat, then looked at her more closely. "Oh, Mina," she said. "You have a tiny tick on your chin."

"What?" Santo said, looking at the cat.

"Yes," Valerie said. "See right there, just below her lower lip? A tick."

"I hadn't seen it," Santo said, apologetic.

"Well, it's easy to miss," Valerie said. "It's barely begun to feed. I'll just get rid of it." She reached over a thumb and finger, prepared to pinch off the tick.

"Don't do that!" a voice boomed out authoritatively from somewhere above her.

Valerie jerked around, looking up, but she didn't see

anybody. She did see all four of the Irish wolfhounds spring from their various positions and go bounding toward the spiral steps that led up to the balcony.

"You'll either have to put her under or heavily sedate her to do it," the voice continued, its volume now lower, but still commanding.

Valerie's eyes followed the dogs to the spiral stairs, where she finally spotted a figure standing up on the balcony at the opposite end of the room. There her eyes rested, trying to make out the distant figure, his body silhouetted against the sunlight pouring in through the window behind him. He appeared to be very tall and lean. His polo shirt revealed powerfully built arms, a neck thickly corded with muscle, and hinted at an imposing chest. Other than that, she could tell almost nothing about him because he was wearing a baseball cap pulled low over his face, casting it in shadow.

The elusive Mr. Conrad? she asked herself. *Obviously,* she decided. *Who else around here would issue orders from on high?*

"I think I can take care of the problem," she finally replied in an even tone.

"Then I don't think you know the animal," he said challengingly.

"And I don't think you know me," she retorted without thinking.

"You're right about that," he said, "but I know Mina extremely well."

She flushed in anger and embarrassment. Who the hell did he think he was, questioning her abilities like this? First the man all but begs her to come out here and treat his animals, and now he insults her about those very abilities he is willing to pay for.

"Mr. Conrad," she said, making an effort to control the irritation in her voice, "if you *are* Mr. Conrad, I think I know what I'm doing. And I don't think I need your help."

There was the sound of Santo catching his breath, then dead silence in the vast room. It was finally broken by a chuckle coming from the balcony.

"It's your hand," the voice finally said. "Bloody it if you will."

Valerie heard the amusement in his voice, and wasn't certain whether to be further insulted or somewhat placated. She wished she could see his face so that she could read the expression on it, but the man didn't move from his spot. His face was still in complete shadow.

"But don't tell me I didn't warn you," he continued. Then he paused a moment before saying: "And, by the way, I *am* Conrad. Wyn Conrad."

Valerie still felt flustered, but replied cooly, "And I'm Dr. Rochelle." *Not Valerie Rochelle to you,* she thought.

"Pleased to meet you, Doc, I'm sure," he said.

"And now I'd better get about my business, if you don't mind, Mr. Conrad," she said.

"Don't let me stop you, Doc," he replied.

Valerie turned back to Mina then, stroking and caressing her gently.

"You'd better hold her tight," Santo said.

But Valerie ignored his advice and continued stroking the huge cat. Then, using her thumb and finger, she reached down and, in the blink of an eyelid, grasped the tick and removed it with apparent ease.

Mina didn't even react to the procedure, but simply continued her contented purr, obviously enjoying Valerie's gentle strokes on her back. Out of the corner of her eye, however, Valerie had seen Santo flinch, then relax. She couldn't help but feel satisfied with herself, perhaps even a bit smug. She had accomplished the simple deed Santo and Conrad seemed to believe was impossible without risk of bodily injury.

"I never saw anything like it," Santo exclaimed in wonder. "I . . . I don't believe it. She won't let anybody touch a tick on her. Not even a burr." He looked up at the balcony, where Conrad still posed, though he had stepped forward a pace to get a better view. "Did you see that?" Santo asked.

"I saw it," Conrad said. He sounded a little disgruntled.

"She looks awfully well groomed for a cat that won't let anybody take a burr or tick off her," Valerie said with irrefutable logic.

"Well," Santo said, "she lets Wyn—Mr. Conrad—brush her. In fact, she goes to him every day after lunch to be groomed, and she won't let anybody else groom her. I mean *nobody*."

So the mighty Mr. Conrad stoops so low as to groom a cat, Valerie thought. *I'd like to see that.*

"But," Santo continued, "and this is a big but, she won't even let him pull off ticks or burrs."

She smiled and gave Mina a final stroke. "Well, I guess I'm finished here," she said, pleased. "So I'll be on my way. I'll get their charts updated and filed, so you'll get notices about vaccinations and so on from now on. Let me know if you need anything else."

"Thanks a lot," Santo said. Then he picked up the animals' medical records and put them in a large padded envelope. "I think everything's here."

"Thanks, Mr. Ducci," she said, taking them from him.

"Santo, please."

Valerie nodded slightly. "Santo, then."

"And by the way, I sent copies of the medical records for all the horses over to your office this afternoon," he said.

"Great," she replied, disposing of the syringes in a special plastic carrying case she'd brought. This little case she would have to put in the biohazard garbage back at the clinic, from where it would be picked up, along with all the other biohazardous materials, and sent to Canada for disposal. She closed her leather bag with a snap, shouldered her carryall, and turned to leave.

She glanced up toward the balcony, and Conrad quickly retreated a step backward. "Nice to meet you, Mr. Conrad," she said gaily.

He nodded from his distant perch. "You too, Doc," he said, then he did an about-face and disappeared down a hallway.

"Do you want a check now?" Santo asked.

"The office will bill you."

"Okay," he said. Santo indicated the door they'd used to enter the huge room. She followed him back through the long gallery to the grand entrance hall. She noticed a few of the paintings appeared to be by

George Stubbs, arguably the greatest painter of horses, and several that she was certain had been painted by Alfred Munnings.

Suddenly she stopped, drawn by a tiny, postage-stamp-size drawing of a horse's head. She stood, entranced, studying the remarkable image. It was exquisite, rendered in charcoal, and signed by Stephano della Bella. She shook her head in wonder.

"Mr. Conrad's an art collector, I gather?" she casually said to Santo, who had stopped with her.

Santo nodded. "Sort of," he replied. "He inherited a lot of the stuff and now and then he'll pick something up to add to it. Like the drawing you just looked at. He got that himself."

"It's truly beautiful," Valerie said.

"He thought so."

They reached the front door, and Santo opened it. "Thanks again, Dr. Rochelle," he said. "I've got to hand it to you. You did a good job."

Valerie smiled. "You're welcome," she said, accepting the compliment with ease. "If there are any problems, let me know."

"Will do," he said.

She walked across the stone terrace and down the wide steps to the driveway and her Jeep. She stowed her medical bag in the rear compartment, then went around to the front door, opened it, and climbed in with her carryall bag.

Santo waved from the doorway as she pulled out, and she waved back. Slowly going back down the long drive, she was rounding a curve, then almost slammed on the brakes to bring the Jeep to a stop. She took a deep breath. *Shit!* she swore. She was certain she'd glimpsed a figure about to step out into the drive. But no. The figure—not an apparition, she told herself— rushed behind a stand of hemlocks.

She felt goose bumps rise on her flesh, and her heart began to race. She almost pulled the car over to relax a minute, but then she thought better of it.

I'm getting out of this weird place, she thought, *as fast as possible.*

She gunned the engine and swiftly arrived at the entrance gates, where she was buzzed through automatically. On the highway at last, she pulled over for a moment and took a few more deep breaths. *What's going on in that place?* she wondered. *And why is Conrad like some kind of ghost? Staying up on the balcony, watching me from a distance?*

She checked for traffic, then pulled back out onto the road. *I don't think I'll be going back there,* she told herself. *It just makes me feel too uneasy.* Despite her laughing at all the silly rumors, she had to admit that the atmosphere was somehow . . . eerie.

On the other hand, she told herself, the animals were well adjusted and happy. *Conrad must love them,* she thought. *But,* she asked herself, *what can I really make of what I know?* He had appeared to be quite an impressive specimen from what she could see. She wished she could have seen his face, seen if it matched the rest of his body. She had to admit that his insulting sergeant-major behavior and then his amusement at her obvious anger should have been a real turnoff. Men like that were generally for the birds as far as she was concerned. But for some reason she couldn't put her finger on, she couldn't shake her curiosity about him.

Suddenly she realized that she wanted to know more about him. She had become intrigued by the old place and its owner. Despite just deciding that she didn't want to return, she realized that she couldn't wait until the next time she was called back.

Chapter Eleven

Arielle's head jerked wildly from side to side as Lolo thrust away at her, sweat flying off his body, his grunts like those of a rutting animal. Then she screamed, her nails sinking into his back, as she felt him release a flood tide inside her, his body in an arc of rigid muscle atop her, his bellow of spent passion almost like a wail of pain.

He fell on top of her, and flushed and panting, they threw their arms around one another, their sweat-soaked torsos meeting as they peppered each other with kisses. They lay gasping for breath amid a tangled mass of Egyptian cotton sheets, discarded silk lingerie, and polo gear ripe from the practice field. On the table next to the bed were half-empty gin and tonics.

The air was pungent with the aromas of her Caron perfume, the lavender water her sheets were laundered in, and the sandalwood-scented powder that she lavished on her body. Intermingled with the sweet scents of her boudoir was the sweaty leather of his polo boots and knee pads, and the faintest hint that remained of the spicy vetiver cologne he'd used much earlier in the day. But overpowering all of these scents was the indisputable smell of their sex.

"Oh, my God, Lolo," Arielle gasped in a breathy voice, "that was fantastic stuff." She barked a short laugh and hugged his hard muscularity. "*You're* fantastic stuff."

Lolo stroked the perfect length of her nose with his fingertip and smiled, his teeth gleaming against his darkly tanned flesh. "I think I'm beginning to love everything in Palm Beach," Lolo said, a hand stroking her buttocks.

"Well, I hope not everything," Arielle said. "Maybe just me."

"Yeah," he said. "Just you." He reached over to the bedside table for a package of Arielle's cigarillos and her gold lighter. Sitting up in the bed slightly, he took two of the long, thin cigarillos out, placing both of them in his mouth. He lit them and handed Arielle one.

She took the cigarillo and sat up next to him. "Thanks," she said, kissing his cheek.

He draped an arm around her shoulders and held her close, proprietarily, but he smoked in silence, blowing lazy plumes of gray fog toward the ceiling, staring off in the distance.

Arielle watched him, aware of his unusual silence and his thoughtful expression. Normally they were chatty after sex, oftentimes sharing their dreams for the future they wanted to build together, the future they would have after the divorce was finalized and the settlement was paid.

"You're awfully quiet, Lolo," she finally said,

unable to bear his distance any longer. His silence frightened her.

Still, he smoked silently, not responding to her remark. The lazy whorls of smoke streamed toward the ceiling, shifting about in the breeze coming in off the ocean.

"Come on," Arielle cajoled, her voice rising with concern. "What is it? Why the silence? Something's wrong, isn't it?" She stubbed out her cigarillo in the ashtray, grinding it hard against the crystal with nervous fingers.

He shrugged and sighed loudly, exhaling smoke at the same time. Then he looked into her eyes and smiled wanly. "I'm sorry, Arielle," he said. "It's just that . . ." He sighed again, and all of the energy seemed to seep out of his body with its sad, defeated sound.

"Come on," she said with alarm. "You can tell me, Lolo. You know that. You can tell me *anything*."

"Well," he finally said, averting his eyes from hers and looking off into the distance, "it's just that"—he flashed a look at her—"I don't have the money for the car payment on my Ferrari this month."

She looked at him in confusion. "You mean the fucking thing's not paid for?" she cried in horror. "I can't believe this." She slapped the bed with both of her fists, and her pretty face contorted in a mask of fury.

Lolo had known she was going to be outraged, but there was no avoiding the issue. Not if he wanted to keep the car. A few more days and the fiery red Ferrari would be hauled off right out from under him.

Finally, he ground out his cigarillo and turned to look into her eyes again. "I'm sorry, Arielle," he said. "I should've told you before. I just didn't want you to worry about it."

His expression was so genuinely contrite that Arielle melted. "Oh, darling Lolo," she said softly, placing her hands on his cheeks. "Nothing you could do would worry me." She leaned toward him and kissed his lips, then sat back and looked at him lovingly.

He tried to smile, but the effort was too much. He looked down at the bed hopelessly.

"Tell me how this happened," she said, stroking his cheek with a long magenta-lacquered fingernail. "I thought you paid for the Ferrari when Palmer gave you the bonus for signing up to play for his polo team."

Lolo shook his head slightly, then his downcast eyes rose to meet hers. "No," he said. "I made a down payment with part of it," he said, "and they let me finance the rest."

Arielle slumped despite herself. Jesus, she thought, *what's this going to cost? And where the hell did the rest of the money go?* "What happened to the rest of the money, Lolo?" she asked calmly, trying not to sound distressed.

"It's all gone," he said.

"All of it?" she replied in astonishment.

He nodded.

"But . . . but what the hell did you do with it?" she asked, her voice becoming strident in spite of herself.

"I had to pay some bills," he said sheepishly. "You know. Clothes and stuff."

"What?" She looked at him in amazement. "Clothes and stuff? Jesus, I've charged a fortune in clothes for you. In every fucking shop in Palm Beach! What the hell could you've bought that took that kind of money?"

He looked at her with a sulky expression. "Shit, Arielle," he said irritatedly, "you know what custom-made polo gear costs? One pair of new boots over two thousand—"

"Why the hell didn't you get Palmer to cover those costs?" she snapped angrily. "You're playing for him, for Christ's sake!"

"You know I can't ask that of him," he replied, the irritation gone from his voice and a softness replacing it. "I'm expected to have all of that or get it with my bonus."

She looked at him, studying his face, his splendid torso, and those hard-muscled, inviting arms. She knew that his machismo would prevent him from admitting to Palmer—or any other man—that he couldn't afford new polo boots, or anything else for that matter. Hell, she thought, he could hardly afford a polo shirt, but he would never let on. She also knew that this wasn't unusual in the rich and rarefied world of polo. Like many South American players, Lolo was one of those penniless, uneducated guys who'd learned to play on the *estancias* of the very rich, then been recruited by wealthy American team owners who brought them north and kept them on a very tight rein.

"I understand," she finally said, nodding her head. And she did, too. Lolo wanted it *all,* just like she did, and he wanted it *now,* not tomorrow or the next day, also like her.

She ran her fingers through her disheveled hair, then reached over and idly began running them through

Lolo's. He was looking at her expectantly, but she was silent, lost in thought, twirling his damp black curls around her fingers. Then she leaned in and placed her smeared, collagen-enhanced lips against his.

"I'm sorry, Lolo," she said. "I really didn't know. I just assumed—"

"You think I do nothing to contribute," he said. "That I just use you."

"Oh, no," she cried in a pleading voice. "That's not true. You make me so happy. Oh, my God, I don't know what I'd do without you." She leaned over and kissed his lips again. "Please. Let's don't argue, Lolo. I'm sorry. I just wasn't thinking. Please forgive me."

Lolo remained silent for a moment, his eyes averted from hers, then he turned his gaze to her. "Okay," he said, nodding. "But that still doesn't solve the problem of the Ferrari."

"No," she said with a sigh, "it doesn't." She swiveled around and lay back against the pillows, staring at the ceiling thoughtfully for a minute. "I guess I could pawn some jewelry," she finally said.

"No!" Lolo said. "I won't let you do that, Arielle."

"I don't mind," she replied, stroking his face. "Not for you, Lolo. It'll only be for a little while. Till that shit Wyn comes through with my money."

"It always goes back to him," Lolo replied. "The stingy bastard."

"Yes," she said, nodding her head. "It always goes back to him." Her features suddenly screwed up into an ugly, angry mask. "God, how I hate him!" she cried furiously. "He's the cause of all our problems. If it weren't for him—" She slammed a fist against the bed.

Lolo grabbed her arm and pulled it to him, kissing her hand, trying to placate her. "Don't worry," he cooed. "It won't be much longer. Maybe I can hold off the car dealer long enough." Then he looked into her eyes. "I've been thinking about something," he said.

She looked at him with curiosity, her eyes brightening. "What?"

"If you like," Lolo said, "when we go up to Saratoga, I could go and see Wyn and try to talk some sense to him."

She jerked up. "I'd forgotten about Saratoga," she exclaimed. She ignored him for a moment, her eyes seemingly focused on the Venetian mirror atop her dressing table, as if its baroque beauty held the answer to all of their problems.

"What?" Lolo asked, tugging at her arm. "What is it, Arielle? I can tell you're thinking of something important."

"I'm just thinking," she replied. Then she slowly turned to him. "Yes, maybe seeing him in Saratoga is a good idea," she said.

"I would like that very much," he said. "We could have a man-to-man talk."

"I'm sure that Bibi and Joe Whitman will fly up in their jet," she said excitedly. "We could hitch a ride with them. Or the Connollys. Even if I can't stand that bitch Peggy Connolly." Her eyes began to brighten even more, and she rubbed her hands together.

Lolo watched the transformation in her demeanor, and his eyes began to widen. "What—what do you have in mind, Arielle?" he asked quietly.

"Oh, I don't know," she replied cagily.

"Arielle," he said. "I know that crazy look." He tugged at her arm again. "What are you thinking of doing?"

She turned to him and smiled widely. "Me?" she asked innocently. "Why would you think I would be up to something?"

"Come on," he cajoled. "What have you got on your pretty mind? What are you thinking of doing?"

Her eyes glittered with an intense flame that seemed to Lolo to be a mixture of excitement, wrath, and perhaps a little madness, and it frightened him, for he knew that Arielle was capable of doing really crazy things.

"It's not what *I'll* do," she said evenly, staring into his dark eyes steadily. "It's what *you'll* do, Lolo." She jabbed his muscular chest with a painted fingernail.

He stared at her curiously for a moment, then sat up beside her. "Wait a minute," he said. "Tell me what you have in mind."

She smiled secretively, then lay back on the pillows and stretched out on the bed. "Let's have another drink," she said, her hands reaching down between his thighs to stroke his much-talked-about equipment. "And have some more fun." She stroked him gently, pleased to see that her hands could excite him as they did. "Then we'll talk about it."

Lolo expelled a deep breath, his eyes running up and down the length of her magnificent body. All thoughts of his Ferrari and Saratoga were swept out of his mind as if by magic, his body surging with renewed desire.

He smiled and began stroking her breasts, slowly

and gently, then more urgently as he felt her rise to his touch. "Ah, what a future we'll have, Arielle," he whispered as he fell on top of her.

If you only knew, she thought. *If you only knew.*

Chapter Twelve

Dusk was settling and Wyn Conrad walked alone toward Stonelair's stable block. *It's a perfect late summer evening,* he thought.

He approached a bend in the path and heard footsteps and soft-pitched voices nearby. *Helmut and Gerda Reinhardt,* he thought, *taking an evening walk.* He rounded the corner, and there they were, walking briskly along the path that led from their cottage to the parking area at the stables. Gerda had changed out of her customary uniform and was wearing a big flowery print blouse and shorts. Helmut wore baggy shorts and a pale short-sleeve shirt. Both of them wore sandals. They were holding hands like teenagers, he observed, though they were well into their sixties.

"Ah, good evening, Mr. Conrad," Gerda called to him, her English, like her husband's, heavily accented with the inflections of her native German.

"Mr. Conrad," Helmut said, nodding respectfully.

After all these years, Wyn thought, *they still insist on being so formal, so Old World in manner.* He'd asked them repeatedly to address him by his first name, but he'd long since learned it would never happen. They considered themselves employees, and he was their boss. Apparently, never the twain would meet.

"Hi, Gerda," Wyn said, "Helmut. Taking a walk?"

"We're going to a movie," Gerda said.

"Have you got my medication?" Helmut asked his wife.

"*Ja*, Helmut," she responded. She lifted an arm. "Right here in my *Beutel*." She held up a small vinyl bag with drawstrings. It looked almost as old as she did. "The cell phone, too, Mr. Conrad," she said, nodding at Wyn. "We always have it with us in case you need us, just like you've told us."

Wyn smiled. "You two have a good time."

"I'm sure we will," Gerda said.

"We'd better hurry," Helmut added, "or we're going to miss the beginning."

"See you later," Wyn said.

He watched them hurry on toward the lighted parking area, feeling a twinge of envy. They were a taciturn, thrifty, and childless couple with little if any sense of humor, and they seemed to get little joy from life, at least that he could see. He was surprised that they were allowing themselves a trip to the movies. But, he realized, they were also exceedingly hardworking and loyal to him. They were also devoted to one another and had been for over forty years, something of a record among the people he knew.

He shot a last glance in the direction of the parking lot, where they were already driving out in their old Volkswagen, then resumed his walk, trying to shake the sense of loneliness that had come over him. Gazing out in the direction of the surrounding forest, toward a clearing to the north, he noticed that Santo's cottage was in darkness, except for a dim porch light. He'd probably gone into town to the gym to work out as he sometimes did, even though there was a well-equipped gym here. Or maybe, Wyn thought, he'd gone out to a bar in one of the nearby towns. He wasn't really certain how Santo spent his free time, other than working out, but he imagined that he went out seeking company. Santo might appear to be nothing more than a muscle-bound steroid freak, practically inhuman to strangers, but Wyn knew that he must grow tired of the monotonous days and nights of virtual imprisonment at Stonelair. He never discussed it with him—in fact, he'd never given Santo's personal life much thought—but he trusted him implicitly. He'd stayed by his side through thick and thin for the last decade, never asking questions, never making demands, and always doing as he was told. Loyal, like the Reinhardts, he thought dismally, but then that was part of what they were all paid for, wasn't it?

He reached the stable office and flipped on the lights, then went on through to the tack room. He flipped on the lights there, revealing all the mementos of polo seasons past, artfully arranged on the pine-paneled walls: crossed mallets, team photographs, and trophies. He walked over and looked at an old framed polo shirt of his, hunter green, the letters and numbers in white. On the sleeve was his number, 1, and on the chest the TC logo, for Team Conrad. The shirt was ripped nearly to shreds and was stained a dull brown all over. Dried blood.

He averted his gaze and looked at some of the team photographs. A few of the familiar ones from the more recent years were missing because Santo had carefully edited out those that had Arielle posing with the team as well as those in which Lolo appeared with Team Conrad or the opposition. His eyes swept over some of the photographs briefly: the Paris Open at the Polo Club of Paris at Bagatelle, the Prince of Wales Trophy at the Royal County of Berkshire Polo Club, the Royal Windsor Cup, and the Queen's Cup, all in England, shots from Greenwich, Houston, Sante Fe, Santa Barbara, Wellington, Saratoga, and on and on. In most of them he was soaked with sweat, splattered with turf, and smiling with utter joy.

Those days are over, he thought bitterly. The loneliness that had descended on him earlier only became more acute. Any magic these mementos might have held for him turned to nothing more than a terrible reminder of the drastic changes in his life. *There's no one to share the beauty of the summer night with,* he thought sadly, *but then there's nobody who could stomach living with what I've become.*

He looked longingly at the saddles and tack, all of it polished and displayed, ready for immediate use. He remembered the feeling of the air on his face and the exhilarating sense of freedom when he rode. *Damn,* he thought, *I'm sick of being bored, sick of being cooped up, sick of all of my problems. And I'm the only person who can do anything about it.*

With that he turned and strode over to the dressing room, flung the door open, and flipped on the light. He sat down and took off his sneakers, then stood up and pulled off his Levi's. *This is crazy,* he thought giddily, *but I'm going to ride. It's been far too long.*

He quickly slid into riding jodhpurs before he could change his mind, then grabbed boot hooks and a pair of the custom-made riding boots that had been gathering dust. He sat down and slid the boot hooks through their loops and pulled them on, then stood back up to ease his feet completely into the boots.

Suddenly a woozy feeling overcame him, and he sat down again for a moment to wait for it to pass. *It must be that last shot,* he thought. He took several deep breaths and wiped away the beads of sweat that had popped out on his brow. *I really must be crazy,* he decided. *In my condition, with all the drugs in my system—*

He wouldn't think about that now. No, he was going to do this no matter the consequences. He got back to his feet and snatched the first helmet he saw, put it on, and went back out to the tack room, where he grabbed a bridle, reins, and girth off wall hooks, then took an English saddle and quilted saddle pad off a rest.

In his weakened condition the saddle was heavy, but he manhandled it through the door to the horse stalls, eased it down on the bench there, and flipped on the light. He would saddle up Demon. It had been too long since he'd been on the old hellion. He began walking down the length of the stalls, peering in at the horses, stopping to talk to them and stroke their necks, something he used to do on a daily basis, but lately had neglected.

He took his time, lingering at one stall after the

other, until he finally reached Demon. He eyed the magnificent Arabian admiringly, then began stroking him as he had the others, talking to him in almost a whisper. Demon had been his favorite for a long time now, and he couldn't wait to saddle him up.

He had started to open the stall door when a sudden noise made him stand still and listen. After a few seconds of hearing nothing more than the usual sounds of the stable at night, he reached for the stall door again. And heard the strange noise again.

What the hell? he wondered. He stood listening once more. He walked down past Demon's stall, being as quiet as he could in his riding boots, and heard the sound again, unmistakably to his right this time.

He looked into the stall from which the sound had emanated. His eyes grew wide with alarm and then growing disbelief and horror as he stared at the horse that stood staring back at him from within the stall. It was a horse that Santo had purchased only a few days ago, Layla by name, and she was in acute distress, of that there could be no mistaking. The sounds had been her whinnies of pain.

Opening the stall door, he stepped in for a closer look. Her nose was bleeding profusely, and her legs were horribly swollen, as was her neck. Then he noticed something else. Her coat was covered with a wet, slick-looking secretion. *I've never seen anything like this in my life,* he thought. *What the hell could it be?*

He went down on one knee to get a closer look at her swollen legs. They were white, and he could clearly see where she was hemorrhaging beneath the skin. He felt her swollen throat. It was as if she had the mumps.

His mind began to race, and his heart was sick, for he knew the horse must be in great pain. He stroked her neck for a moment, then backed out of the stall and closed the door.

Gone were all thoughts of riding tonight as he ran toward the office telephone. He would have to call the vet immediately to see to Layla. Then it occurred to him that he was alone here at Stonelair. Santo was gone. The Reinhardts were gone.

It's okay, though, he thought. *They'll have their cell phones. I'll call Santo first and get him back here as quickly as possible. Then he can handle the vet.* He reached the office and lunged toward the telephone there. He picked it up and punched in Santo's number. It began to ring.

Darkness was descending, and Valerie had spread out on a chaise longue on the screened-in porch at the back of her house. Elvis was curled up on the floor beside her, sleeping soundly. She idly gazed out at the pale moon's reflection on the small pond in the garden. *It's such a perfect late summer night,* she thought.

Her eyes shifted to the approach to the pond and the flower beds bordering the stone steps that led down to it. The whites and silvers of the moon garden she had planted were beginning to reflect the moon's light, as the pond reflected the moon itself. She'd worked hard planting it, not quite believing that it would be as effective as Colette had sworn it would be. She'd been delighted to discover that Colette had not only been right, but that it held a magic she would never have anticipated. It was like looking at a particularly

complicated painting, mysterious and secretive, not
wanting to give up all of its details, compelling one to
delve deeper to discover what lay hidden in its combination of darkness and light.

She squeezed herself with her arms, aware of the
fact that she felt somewhat lonely, despite the beauty of
the night. She didn't have to be alone tonight. Teddy
had called to tell her that he was coming up and was
going to stay over a couple of nights since he couldn't
be here over the weekend. He had to spend another
weekend with important clients, this time in
Connecticut. He'd wanted her to come over and stay
with him, but she'd begged off.

Frogs, along with unseen creatures of all sorts, had
begun singing their nightly chorale, but she took little
comfort from their cacophony. She had to admit that
company would be nice, human company preferably,
but was determined that she wouldn't let her loneliness drive her to Teddy.

Suddenly she heard a noise around at the side of the
house. Elvis scrambled to his feet and barked. For a
moment she was alarmed. Then she realized that it was
simply the creaking of the hinge on the front garden gate.

Colette, she thought. With the exception of her
mother and Teddy—both of whom would call first—
Colette was the only person who would come around
that way rather than ring the doorbell at the front first.
Elvis had quit barking and stood wagging his tail at the
door that led onto the porch. Valerie smiled somewhat
ruefully. *I'm going to have company after all,* she
thought.

"Val, darling?" Colette's near whisper was like an

exotic sigh carried by the late summer breeze. "Are you there?"

"I'm here, Colette," she replied. "On the porch."

"Am I a bother?" the older woman asked.

"You know better than that, Colette."

From out of the darkness, the older woman's snowy hair appeared, and Valerie watched as she took deliberate little steps on the stone path that led to the porch.

"Wait, Colette," she said. "Let me turn on the light for you."

"No, no, my darling," Colette said. "Don't break the spell. It's so lovely like this. So romantic."

Valerie rose to her feet and went out onto the path and took Colette's arm. "Here," she said. "Let me lead the way at least."

On the porch, Colette settled herself in a chair, petting Elvis while Valerie lit several candles on the dining table.

"Would you like a glass of wine?" Valerie asked.

"Oh, lovely, darling," Colette said. "My grandfather, a doctor, always said a glass before bedtime was just the ticket."

"I'll be right back," Valerie said.

She stepped through the open French doors into the kitchen and got a crystal wineglass out of a cabinet, then retrieved a bottle of chilled white wine out of the refrigerator. She set Colette's glass on the table next to her chair, then filled the glass.

"Oh, Val," Colette enthused, "you are a saint for putting up with an old ninny like me."

Valerie laughed. "Don't be silly," she said. "You know you're welcome here anytime, Colette."

Valerie refreshed her own glass of wine and sat back down. She took a sip, staring at one of the candles, ringed by moths, its honeysuckle scent pleasant in her nostrils. She felt Colette's eyes on her, but didn't break the silence.

Colette lifted her goblet delicately by the stem, swirled the wine in the glass, then took a tiny sip. "Delicious," she pronounced, setting the glass back down. "Heavenly on the palate."

Valerie turned to her slowly and smiled. "It is, isn't it?" she agreed. "Teddy gave it to me." She paused a moment, her gaze shifting back to the candle. "He knows so much about wine," she continued, "and always makes such good choices. He doesn't trust me to." She laughed lightly, but there was no humor in it.

"Teddy does have excellent taste," Colette said, "but that's not everything, is it?"

Valerie looked at her, and Colette cocked her brow. Valerie laughed again, but it was genuine this time, full of mirth. "You're a pistol, Colette," she said.

"And you're unhappy," the older woman said, picking up her wineglass again. The large rings on her fingers flashed brilliantly in the candlelight.

Valerie started to reply, but clammed up instead, watching Colette sip the wine, thinking about what she'd said. A lot of people thought of Colette as a supercilious woman, capricious to a fault, eccentric in her ways, and spoiled by money, and Valerie realized that all of that was undeniably true. It was not all that Colette was, however, and Valerie would never underestimate her friend. For among her other assets, Colette was extremely observant, worldly wise, and had a wealth of experiences and knowledge. *In fact,* Valerie thought, *she's probably the sharpest person I know.*

Much of Colette's eccentricity, Valerie had decided, was part of a pose that the old woman had long ago perfected, a protective pose that she had developed to keep the world at arm's length. On the surface, Colette appeared to be carefree and fun-loving, a bit zany and daring, and she was all of those things. But she'd also been wounded by life and chose to keep her disappointments to herself.

Valerie decided not to brush off Colette's remark, and at last asked, "Why do you say that, Colette?"

Colette turned sharp eyes on her. "It's simple, Val. I don't see the blush on the peach that ought to be there when one is deeply in love," she replied. "You're not excited by Teddy. That much is clear. To me at least."

Valerie felt her face burn with embarrassment. *Is it that obvious?* she wondered. She looked off into the distance, then cleared her throat and turned to Colette. "I . . . I guess you're right," she said in a small voice. "I've been seeing Teddy so long that I guess he's . . ." She stopped and searched for words.

"Teddy's become a habit," Colette supplied. "And why not? He's handsome and has charm. He has money and connections. He's well-bred, and . . . he's a dreadful bore. At least, to you. And, I daresay, to me as well."

Valerie erupted into laughter.

Colette smiled. "Am I on the mark, darling?"

Valerie nodded her head and ran her fingers through her hair. "I guess you are, Colette," she said. She looked over at her friend. "Oh, hell," she said with a laugh, "you've hit the nail on the head, as usual."

Colette nodded knowingly, her eyes still on Valerie.

Valerie took a sip of her wine, then set the glass down. "But I don't know what to do about it," she said with a sigh. "I feel so damn guilty. We've gone together for so long, and he's so determined. And so is Mother, of course."

She paused and her eyes took on a faraway look before continuing.

"I used to think that I was really in love with Teddy. He is good-looking and sweet and considerate, most of the time at least. All those things you said." She smiled ruefully at Colette. "But I'm beginning to realize that he was really the first man that paid any attention to me. I guess I felt so grateful that I thought I was in love."

Colette reached an arm over and brushed Valerie's cheek with her fingertips. "These things happen, Val darling, and they're unfortunate and sad. But you mustn't allow it to drag you down and make you unhappy. If you really think it's over with Teddy—and it certainly sounds as if that's the case to me—then the thing for you to do is end it." She sliced a hand through the air. "Like that!" she exclaimed. "Cut the cord. If you don't, the pain—yours and his—will go on and on. You're just prolonging the inevitable. Don't you see?"

Valerie shifted uncomfortably in her chair. She knew very well that Colette's words were true, but they were difficult to hear nevertheless. It was a problem she simply didn't want to face.

"I just . . . I guess I'm just a chicken," Valerie said at

last. She looked over at Colette. "I don't want to have to deal with this. I'm . . . I'm . . . scared, Colette. Especially since I accepted his engagement ring."

"Oh, darling," the older woman sighed, reaching over and squeezing Valerie's hand in hers. "I understand that perfectly, and I'm so sorry. I know I come on like a virago sometimes, but I *am* thinking of you. I hate to see you unhappy, and you haven't been happy with Teddy for quite a long time, I think."

Valerie nodded.

"The only cure for your problem is being honest. With yourself. And Teddy. A tall order, I know, but the sooner the better, I say." She looked at Valerie steadily, those large blue eyes glistening in the candlelight.

"You've got everything going for you, Val," she went on. "Everything. You have an unusual beauty. You have a wonderful career. You have a marvelous personality, and even with all your assets, you manage to be down-to-earth. You're a good person, Val, a very good person. And they're hard to find."

Valerie shifted in her chair again. She appreciated the compliments, but sometimes she still had a difficult time accepting them as the truth about herself.

"And," Colette said with emphasis, "someone, someday soon, I expect, will come along for you. A man better suited to you. I'm sure of it."

Valerie looked at her. "Do you . . . do you really believe that, Colette?" she asked.

Colette nodded dramatically. "Absolutely," she said. "Someone whom you'll be happy with." She paused and sipped her wine. "Oh, realistically speaking, we all have to make concessions at times. We have to compromise, Val, don't we? But that doesn't mean you have to align yourself with a man who makes you unhappy, even if he has a lot of good qualities. Think about five years down the road. Ten. If you're unhappy with Teddy now, think of years of it."

"Oh, Colette," Valerie groaned. "I know you're right, dammit."

"And I refuse to believe that a man won't come along who'll help make your life more joyous," Colette said.

"You make me feel so much better," Valerie said. "And . . . a little bit less afraid, too."

"Remember, darling," Colette said, "Teddy may be a man, and a strong and forceful one at that, but what's he going to do?" She shrugged expansively. "He has no ironclad hold over you. You're not married, after all, and this sort of thing happens all the time. So I expect he'll fuss about for a while, lick his wounds a bit, then get on with his life. There'll undoubtedly be harsh words because of his disappointment, some unpleasantness to deal with, but that won't last long. You'll see."

Valerie stared out toward the moonlight on the pond and the silvery flowers surrounding it. Its beauty held her attention for but a moment. For all of Colette's well-intentioned efforts to make her feel better and to give her courage, her last words had had a chilling effect.

Over the years she had come to realize that Teddy was a much needier man than she would ever have expected, and that from this neediness sprang a desire to control and manipulate everything—and every-body—around him, including Valerie herself. And that's where his ruthlessness came into play. For he ruthlessly pursued what he wanted—she could see that now—and would stop at almost nothing to get it. Woe be to anything or anybody who got in his way.

She suddenly wrapped her arms around herself and shivered slightly.

Does that include me? she wondered. *Will Teddy refuse to let me go?*

She quailed inwardly at the thought. She was glad, however, that she and Colette had had this conversation. For if nothing else, the realization that had been gradually asserting itself in her consciousness—that she didn't love Teddy and didn't want to marry him—had become crystal clear. She knew now that she must talk to Teddy as soon as possible. Colette had given her the courage to act on her feelings.

Still, a pervasive sense of dread made her uncomfortable with this knowledge. She would have to handle Teddy with kid gloves, of that she was certain.

"You're awfully quiet, Val," Colette said. "Have I disturbed you terribly with my unsolicited advice?"

"Oh, no, Colette," she replied. "I'm really grateful to you for being honest with me." She reached over and squeezed her friend's hand. "You've made me feel more sure of my own feelings. Thank you."

Colette smiled tenderly. "I love you, Val. You know that."

"I know," she replied, "and I love you. I've sometimes wished that you'd been my mother."

Colette sputtered with laughter. "As much as I love you, I would never, not in a million years, want to compete with Marguerite for that honor."

Valerie laughed with her. "How's Hayden doing, by the way?"

"Ah, he's doing beautifully," Colette exclaimed. "I just made him a new batch of turkey soup. I make a lot, then freeze it in ice trays and microwave a cube for him. He's positively addicted to it. He turns up his piggy nose at mealworms, which is what all his hedgehog friends love. I suppose Hayden's an iconoclast, which doesn't surprise me in the least. Do you want to say hello?"

"What?" Valerie asked. "You have him with you?"

"Of course, darling," she replied. "He's right here in Mummy's pocket." With one hand she reached down into one of the large pockets in her smock and carefully lifted Hayden out, holding him for Valerie to see.

"He loves my pocket," Colette said. "So he travels about the house with me."

Valerie reached over and carefully stroked the pygmy hedgehog's quills, surprised once again at their sharpness. He quivered for a moment, but then settled down as he seemed to recognize her through his excellent sense of smell.

Elvis stirred on the floor when he heard that particular cooing sound of Valerie's voice.

"Oh, ho," Valerie said. "Maybe we'd better put Hayden back in your pocket before Elvis gets too interested."

"I do let Puff Puppy have a little sniff," Colette said, "but I can't honestly say that Hayden really enjoys it half as much Puff Puppy does. Perhaps I should tuck him back in." She carefully replaced Hayden in her smock pocket, then stroked him for a while with a single finger. "It's odd, isn't it," Colette said, "the things that can give us pleasure?"

Valerie nodded in agreement. "It never ceases to amaze me. Especially in the animal—"

The telephone on the table rang loudly, its shrill man-made sound slightly unnerving them both in the quiet.

"I have to get that," Valerie said. "It could be the service calling."

"Of course, darling," Colette said. She picked up her wineglass and took a sip.

Valerie lifted up the receiver. "Hello?" she said.

"Dr. Rochelle?" a familiar voice asked.

"Yes?" she replied.

"It's Dotty at the service. Sorry to bother you, but there's been an emergency call from a place called Stonelair."

Valerie felt an involuntary chill go up her spine. *Uh-oh. Can I handle a call out there tonight?* she wondered. *But of course, I can,* she told herself.

"What seems to be the problem, Dotty?"

"Something with a horse," the operator answered. "I didn't get it all. Something about swelling and bleeding. The man sounded very upset, and I do mean very upset."

"You don't remember anything else?" Valerie asked.

"Sorry, Dr. Rochelle," she replied. "He was talking so fast I just couldn't get it all."

"Okay, Dotty," Valerie said. "And thanks a lot. If he calls back, tell him I'm on my way."

"Will do," the woman said and hung up the phone.

Valerie let out a sigh and turned to Colette. "I've got to go out to Stonelair on an emergency," she said.

Colette's eyes registered alarm. "Nothing serious, I hope?"

"I'm not sure at this point," Valerie said. "Whoever called the emergency in was very distressed, and Dotty didn't get all the details. Anyway, it's a horse, so I'd better get cracking."

"Indeed, darling," Colette said. "Hayden and I will vanish in the bat of an eyelid."

"Why don't you sit and finish your wine?" Valerie said. "You know you don't have to leave just because I am."

"Well, perhaps we will sit a tad longer and keep Elvis company," she said. "Then we'll toddle along home."

"Be right back," Valerie said. "I have to get some things." She dashed through the open French doors and into the kitchen, then on into the hallway, where she grabbed a clean lab coat from out of the closet. Then she sat down and quickly laced on a pair of sneakers. There, she thought. That will do it. She already had on jeans and an old T-shirt, so none of her good clothing was in danger of being ruined, and there was always that possibility when going on an emergency call. She grabbed her carryall and dashed back out to the porch.

"Ready?" Colette asked.

"Ready," Valerie replied. "But you and Hayden stay as long as you want," she added. "Elvis will love the company."

"Fine," Colette said. "Off you go."

Valerie dashed through the screen door, down the steps, and around to the gate that led to the front yard and her car.

Colette heard her start the Jeep and spew gravel as she pulled out of the driveway, rushing off to help a horse in some sort of distress. She took another sip of her wine and reached down and gave Elvis a few strokes. "Valerie will be back soon, Elvis," she said. She looked at her watch then and saw that it wasn't that late, around ten-thirty, if her eyes served her correctly.

The telephone shrilled again, and Colette stared at it. *Should I answer it?* she wondered. She reached over and picked up the receiver. *What's to lose?* she thought.

"Hello," she said. "Dr. Rochelle's residence."

"Who's this?" a man's voice demanded.

Colette did not appreciate the edge she heard in the words. "This is Colette Richards, Dr. Rochelle's neighbor."

"Oh, you."

Colette listened and heard nothing but heavy breathing.

Then the man spoke again. "Where's Val?" he demanded.

"She's on an emergency call," Colette replied, thinking that she recognized the voice now.

"Jesus!" the man exclaimed. "She's always on an emergency."

"Is that you, Teddy?" Colette ventured.

"Yes," he said, his voice almost a snarl.

"Oh, how nice to speak to you," she said. "I haven't seen you in forever, it seems."

"I've been busy," he said imperiously. "Very busy. What's the big emergency tonight?"

"Stonelair," Colette said. "There's an unfortunate horse in distress of some sort."

"Stonelair!" Teddy almost shouted. "I told her not to go out to that damn place. That guy's some kind of mobster or something."

"I think Valerie is old enough to take care of herself, Teddy," Colette said calmly. "This is a professional call, and she is highly trained to handle it."

"Yes, well, maybe so," he snapped, "but she's not trained to handle trash like Conrad."

"Oh, I think you underestimate our Valerie, Teddy," Colette said. "I think she's capable of handling a lot more than you can imagine, and I think she should be respected for it."

"What the fuck do you know?" Teddy spat.

Colette was shocked by his language. *He's been drinking,* she thought. *Or using some sort of drug.* Whatever it was, he was quite obviously in an altered state. His words were rushed, clipped, and at the same time breathy. He certainly wasn't the ever-charming and proper young man with the perfect manners everybody seemed to love. *Why am I not surprised?* she asked herself.

"I think I know Val," she finally said. "And furthermore, I don't think you know her very well at all." Colette clapped a hand over her mouth after her last statement and rolled her eyes. *Oh, dear,* she thought. *Now, I've gone and done it. But I don't care. The little weasel deserves it.*

"You don't know what you're talking about," Teddy said. "Are you drunk or something?"

"Not yet," Colette said in an amused voice.

"Just crazy," Teddy said.

"Maybe," Colette said, "for having this ridiculous conversation with you."

"You . . . you . . . never mind," Teddy spat. "You'll be sorry." Then he slammed the telephone in her ear.

Colette carefully replaced the receiver in its cradle. For a moment she felt a bit giddy. *I guess I got that brat's goat,* she thought. *And a brat he most certainly is.*

Colette took a long swallow of wine and set the glass back down. *I'm going to have to find out as much as I can about Teddy and what's going on with him. Yes, I need to stay on top of this if I'm going to be of any help to Val. And help, I'm afraid, she's definitely going to need.*

Chapter Thirteen

Valerie clipped along the dark highway at a steady pace, driving fast but not recklessly, her mind torn between the conversation she'd had with Colette and the emergency call she was on. When she reached the gates to Stonelair, she pulled over to the intercom post and slammed on the brakes. She reached out the open window and pushed the intercom button.

"Dr. Rochelle?" the man's voice asked. It was not Santo, of that she was certain. Was it Conrad himself?

"Yes," she replied.

"Through the gates and down to the stables, where the driveway veers off to the left," the man said. "I'll be there."

"Okay," she said.

The gates began opening at once, and when they had fully opened, she sped past the big stone piers and on down the drive until she could see the well-lit parking courtyard in the stable area. Racing to it, she pulled over and parked the Jeep. She gathered up her big canvas carryall and her heavy medical bag.

No one had come out to greet her, so she headed toward the office where she'd been the first time she was here. She could see that lights were burning in there and in the stables, too. When she reached the office door, it was open, and she went on in. There was no one about.

How strange, she thought, *especially with an emergency going on.* Often in an emergency situation, the whole family and staff, if there was one, would be on hand, letting her know what had happened, offering to help. But there was an unearthly quiet here, as if nothing were amiss at all.

"Mr. Ducci?" she called.

There was nothing but silence.

"Mr. Ducci?" she called again, louder this time.

Still there was no response.

She walked on through to the tack room, where the lights were burning brightly, but there was nobody in there either. *Must be in the stable,* she thought. The main overhead lights in the stable weren't turned on, but she could see that the lanterns on the outside of each stall were lit, as was the small overhead in one of the stalls down toward the end of the stable. But she could see no one about in there, either.

"Mr. Ducci?" she called out again.

"He's not here, Doc." A man's voice, Conrad's obviously, answered from somewhere farther down the length of the stable. "You're going to have to deal with me."

"Gladly," Valerie responded. "But who are you, and where are you?" She knew who it was, of course, but couldn't resist making him tell her.

"It's Conrad," the voice replied, oddly quiet and noncombative, "and I'm down here at the tenth stall on your right. Where the light's on."

"I'm on my way," she said, and began walking down the length of the stable. When she got to the tenth stall, she set her medical bag down, then her carryall, and stepped into the stall.

"Oh, God," she whispered, looking at the horse that stood before her, tethered to the stall. The first thing that caught her eye was the horse's profusely bleeding nose. She very carefully felt its neck. It was quite obviously swollen, as if the horse had the mumps. She stroked all around the horse's neck, studying it.

As she took her hands away, she looked down at them in consternation. They were covered with a secretion from the horse's coat, the likes of which she'd never seen. She wiped them off on her lab coat, wondering what on earth was going on.

She looked down and noticed the horse's forelegs. "Ahhhh . . . no," she whispered to herself. She bent down on a knee for a closer look, then scooted around to examine all of the horse's legs. They were enormously swollen, and because they were white, she could clearly see hemorrhaging through the skin, up and down the length of the legs. Touching them delicately, she could feel the same secretion here as on the neck. She wiped her hand on her lab coat again and stood back up, a puzzled look on her face.

She reached out and stroked the horse's body in various places. The secretion was everywhere, oozing from its pores. She stood back, her eyes still searching its body for clues. *What is going on?*

Only then did she become aware of Conrad, leaning against the wall in a darkened corner of the stall, his arms crossed and his head down. He was in riding gear, even with his helmet still on, she noticed, its visor casting his face in darkness. All she could make out distinctly were his riding boots, the light reflecting off of their highly polished leather. She was startled, so intent had she been on examining the horse that she'd forgotten all about him. Now, his silence in the darkened corner perplexed her even further.

"I didn't see you," she said.

"I've just been watching," he said quietly. And he had been, appreciating her sensitivity to the animal and its condition. Marveling at her composure in the light of the horror story that the horse presented. Perhaps it was to be expected, he thought. She was a professional, after all, accustomed to the blood and guts that her work sometimes entailed.

"Well, we've got a real problem here," she said.

"I know we do," he replied. "I was going out for a ride and heard Layla here making some strange whinnying noises. The blood in her nose, I guess. So I called your office."

"You found her like this?" Valerie asked, discomfited that she could see him only in shadow.

"Exactly like this, Doc," he replied.

"Okay," she said, thinking, still puzzled by the horse's condition. "What do you know about this horse's history?" she asked.

"Nothing," he said. "Santo bought her for himself about a week ago from some people at a farm near Saratoga."

"Do you have her medical records?" Valerie asked.

"Uh . . . jeez," he said. "I really don't know. I'm sure Santo must've gotten them, but I don't really know anything about it."

"Is he here?" she asked.

"No," Conrad said somewhat testily, "and I haven't been able to get him on his cell phone. I don't know where the hell he is or why he isn't picking up."

"I really need to see this horse's records," she said, "or at least get some idea of its history. I know you keep copies of medical records here," she went on, "because Santo told me you did since he does some of the vaccinating himself. Where would the medical records be?"

"In the office," he replied.

"Could you please show me?" she asked.

"Well, I . . . I could tell you where they might be," he said hesitantly.

"Oh, come on, Mr. Conrad," she said angrily, irritated by his manner. "Layla is a very sick horse, and if you give a damn about your animals, you'll get those medical records for me. Or take me in there, and *I'll* help look for them. The answer to her problem may be in those records, and I've got to find out what's going on with her before it's too late."

Wyn glowered at the stall's straw-covered floor. He hadn't given the horse's medical records any thought because he'd been in such a panic trying to get Santo or the Reinhardts on the telephone. When he couldn't get anybody, he'd finally decided he'd have to handle the problem himself. He couldn't under any circumstances let the horse suffer. But now—this. What the hell was he going to do?

"Come on, Mr. Conrad!" Valerie cajoled. "The sooner we get those records, the closer I'll be to solving Layla's problems. You don't want her to die, do you?"

"No!" he said emphatically. "Aw, shit! Let's go get the records."

What is his problem? Valerie asked herself. *You'd think I was asking him to give me all his gold.* She stepped back out of the stall and turned toward the office, waiting for him to join her.

Wyn shoved himself out of the darkened corner, stalked around Layla and out the open stall doorway, then rushed past her in a blur. "Follow me," he said without further preamble.

Valerie was taken aback by his abrupt behavior, but she followed along behind him, wondering what on earth could make a man so disagreeable and rude.

When she reached the tack room, he had already passed through it, presumably, and had switched off the lights on his way. *What a creep,* she thought. *Is he one of those filthy-rich misers who resents every kilowatt of electricity burned?*

She entered the office and saw that he'd turned off most of the lights in here, too, leaving only a small banker's lamp lit on the desk. His back was turned to her, and he was bent over a file cabinet searching through folders, virtually in the dark. *Well,* she thought, *he can search in the dark if he wants to, but not me.* She reached over and flipped on the wall switch, flooding the room in light from the ceiling fixtures.

Conrad jerked up and turned around.

Valerie started to tell him that she needed the light, even if he didn't. Then she glanced over at him and instantly started to scream.

BOOK TWO

The Beast

Chapter Fourteen

In the split second before he did an about-face, hiding his head away from the harsh overhead lights, she understood everything. His aversion to the outside world, his desire for complete privacy, and his unwillingness to interact with a stranger. *No wonder he has Ducci act as his go-between,* she thought.

Her initial horror dissipated, and she felt sorry for him. She wanted to reach out and enfold him in her arms and tell him that it was okay. But she couldn't do that, of course, for she would only antagonize him. Some instinct told her that he was not a man who wanted to be pitied, that he was in fact a man who despised pity.

Her mind reeled with what she should say now that she had learned his secret, and the only conclusion she could come to was to behave as naturally as possible. She swallowed hard, took a deep breath, and spoke. "Do you want to search for the file alone?" she asked, giving him an opportunity to be by himself, away from her outsider's eyes.

"No," he said after a moment's hesitation. "It's . . . okay, Doc. You've got a job to do. I guess you need the operating room lights."

She heard a note of irony in his voice. Apparently he had a sense of humor, even if macabre, about his situation.

"All right," she said, "you want to show me where to look?"

"Sure, Doc," he said. "Why not?" He slid a filing cabinet drawer open, then gestured toward it. "Ought to be in there," he said. "Help yourself. I'll be right here if you've got any questions." He sat down in a chair over in a corner, his head turned slightly sideways.

Valerie quickly thumbed through the files to get an idea of how they were arranged. It was the simplest system possible, using each animal's name for a file folder, arranged in alphabetical order. It looked like the four dogs, the cat, and a number of horses were there, no more than twenty-five or thirty files. She searched for Layla's file, and found it exactly where it should be. She pulled the file out and began looking it over in silence.

She saw that Santo Ducci had bought the horse only a week previously from a couple named Hurley. It listed their address and telephone number. Then she saw that Santo had vaccinated the horse himself only yesterday. It was the usual vaccination against multiple horse diseases, except rabies. Nothing unusual there at all. An owner was permitted to vaccinate against everything except rabies. She stood puzzling over the record, forgetting about Conrad, who remained silent.

There was nothing in the record that could explain the horse's condition. Then suddenly it occurred to her that the problem might lie in that fact itself: there was nothing indicating any past vaccinations or diseases or conditions.

Valerie put the file down. "I've got to call the previous owners," she said, thinking out loud.

"What seems to be the problem?" Wyn asked.

Valerie turned and looked at him, still preoccupied with thoughts of the horse. Her initial fright at his appearance had become almost like a distant memory as she'd become caught up in the mysterious nature of the horse's plight.

"I don't know," she said frankly, "but there's no history in her file. So what I need to do is get in touch with the previous owners. They may have the key to her problem."

"How so?" he asked, intrigued.

"I'm not sure," she replied, shrugging her shoulders, "but the file contains absolutely nothing to go on except for the vaccinations."

"It's strange," he said.

"What?" she asked.

"That Santo would've bought a horse like that," he replied. "I mean, without a lineage, let alone without any records at all."

"I guess it is," she agreed, "especially when you consider the other horses. They all have impeccable bloodlines." She picked up the file and flipped it open. "It's getting late, but I'm going to try to call these people, the Hurleys, anyway. If I wake them up, so be it. I need to find out everything I can about this horse."

She looked down at the telephone and saw that there were several lines, then glanced over at him. "Do I have to dial anything special on this telephone or just punch in the number?" she asked.

He came over toward the desk and peered down at the telephone. "Just dial the number," he said. "A button is already pushed for an outside line."

She looked at the file again, then keyed in the telephone number, all the while aware of the fact that Conrad was gradually becoming more comfortable in her presence. *Maybe he realizes that I don't think he's some kind of a monster,* she thought, *even if the initial shock* was *disconcerting.*

The telephone rang several times but was finally picked up. "Hello?" It was a woman's voice, sleepy and annoyed.

"Is this Mrs. Hurley?" Valerie asked.

"Yes," she replied. "Who's this?"

"This is Dr. Valerie Rochelle," she answered, "and I'm over at Stonelair examining a horse, Layla, that Mr. Santo Ducci purchased from you last week."

"What's wrong with it?" the woman asked. "There wasn't anything the matter with her when he bought her. I wouldn't sell a man a sick horse."

"No, of course not," Valerie said. "I didn't mean that. Anyway, I'm not really certain what's wrong with her, and that's why I'm calling you." She was making an effort to choose her words carefully. She might alarm the woman, especially if the horse hadn't been properly cared for, and then she would not find out anything.

"Mr. Ducci failed to get any medical records for the horse at all," she went on, trying to shift the onus to

Santo, "and I thought you might be able to fill me in on her history."

"I'll tell you whatever I can," Mrs. Hurley said. There was the sound of relief in her voice now that she realized she wasn't being accused of anything.

"Has Layla ever had any diseases or conditions that I should know about?" Valerie asked.

"Well . . ." The woman seemed to be thinking. "I can't think of—oh, wait a minute. I do remember something now. She got colicky on us once, but it wasn't anything serious. That was sometime back. I don't remember exactly when."

"Can you think of anything else?" Valerie persisted. "It's really important. She's got a badly swollen neck and her legs are, too, and—"

"A swollen neck?" the woman broke in.

"Yes," Valerie said. "Why?"

"I just remembered," the woman said. "She was the one that had strangle. Her neck was all swollen up then. She had abcesses in her throat."

"You're certain about that?" Valerie asked excitedly.

"Sure," the woman said. "Had to call the vet."

"Who saw her?" Valerie asked. "Which vet?"

"Old Dr. Kramer," Mrs. Hurley said. "It was right before he retired."

"Thank you, Mrs. Hurley," Valerie said. "I'll try to get hold of him. You've been a great help."

"I hope so," the woman said. "She was healthy as could be when that man bought her."

"I know," Valerie said, "and we want to get her back in good health. Thanks again. I'd better hurry and get hold of Dr. Kramer. Good night."

" 'Night," Mrs. Hurley said.

Valerie replaced the receiver in its cradle. Conrad was looking at her expectantly. He'd been listening to her every word, guessing at the other end of the conversation, but had remained silent, letting her handle the situation.

"From the sound of things, you're on to something," he said. "What'd she have to say?"

"I've got to call Dr. Kramer before I'm sure," Valerie said, "but I think I may know what's going on. Mrs. Hurley says that Layla had strangle sometime before Dr. Kramer retired. If that's the case, then we've got our culprit."

Wyn nodded knowingly. "Because if the horse has had strangle and Santo vaccinated it against strangle disease . . ."

"Then the vaccination is what's caused the problem," Valerie finished for him. "The strangle vaccine would set off a chain reaction in the horse's system, causing the swelling and hemorrhaging."

Strangle itself wasn't rare, Valerie knew. She'd seen it many times. It was caused by a bacterium, *Streptococcus equi*, which caused abcesses in a horse's neck. Layla's condition, however, was entirely new to her. She'd never seen a horse that had been vaccinated for the disease *after* it had already had the disease. Apparently, this was what had happened. Santo hadn't known the horse had once had the disease and gave it the vaccination.

"I've got to call Dr. Kramer," she said to Conrad. "Just to confirm that Layla's had strangle."

Conrad nodded. "You want some coffee?"

"That would be great," Valerie replied. "If it's not too much trouble."

"Not at all," he said. "There's everything we need right here. I can do that while you're on the telephone."

Valerie watched as he went over to the bookcases that lined one wall of the office and opened two narrow doors of "books," leather book spines that had been glued to the doors, making them appear to be part of the bookshelves. The open doors revealed a minibar, complete with a small refrigerator, microwave, coffemaker, sink, and cabinetry.

He started making coffee while Valerie held for information. She jotted down Dr. Kramer's telephone number when she got it, then dialed in his number. He surprised her by picking up on the first ring.

"Hello?" he said.

"Dr. Kramer," she said, "it's Valerie Rochelle."

"Hello, my dear," the veterinarian replied. "How're you doing, or need I ask if you're calling an old man like me at this time of night? An emergency, eh?"

She laughed. "You hit the nail on the head."

She related the problems with Layla and her conversation with Mrs. Hurley. Dr. Kramer confirmed what Mrs. Hurley had told her. "It was right before I retired," he said. "Last October. So I imagine with the vaccination, antibodies are racing around in that horse's system, creating havoc."

"Exactly," Valerie said.

"Well," Kramer said, "I won't insult you by asking if you know how to handle it because I know better."

"Yes," Valerie said, "I know what to do, but I do appreciate your help. Thanks a lot."

"Anytime, Val," he replied. " 'Night."

"Good night," she said.

She hung up the telephone again and turned to Wyn.

"Dr. Kramer confirmed what Mrs. Hurley told me," she said to him.

He looked up from the minibar. "So how do you proceed from here?" he asked.

"Massive doses of IV antibiotics and steroids," she replied. "And keep our fingers crossed." She smiled.

He returned her smile. "It'll only be a minute till the coffee's made."

"Great," she said. "I'm going to run back to the stall and see what I've got with me in the way of medication."

"How do you like your coffee?" he asked.

"Two sugars and a little cream," she replied on her way into the tack room.

"It'll be waiting," he said.

When she left the room, he poured their coffees, stirred in her sugar and cream, then set hers on the desk and sat down with his. He took a sip. It was hot and strong and tasted especially good tonight. *In fact,* he thought, *it's been a long time since anything has tasted this good*. But he knew why. It was because Valerie Rochelle had so quickly recovered from her shock. So she couldn't be that horrified by what she saw.

Valerie came through the tack room door, her carry-all in hand. "Well," she said, "it looks like I'm going to have to make a run to the clinic."

"Why don't you have some coffee first?" he offered, indicating the cup on the desk.

She sat down on the desk chair, dropped her

carryall, and took a sip of the coffee. "Aw," she said, "this is perfect. Thanks."

"Just what the doctor ordered," he joked.

She smiled. "Exactly," she replied. "A horse doctor, anyway."

They sipped their coffee in silence for a minute before Wyn broke it. "Do you think Layla's going to be okay?" he asked.

"I can't promise anything, Mr. Conrad," she said without hesitation.

"Hey," he said. "Back up there a minute. It's Wyn to you, please."

Valerie felt herself redden slightly with a blush that she hoped he didn't see. "Okay," she said, "Wyn it is. And I'm Val, all right?"

He nodded. "Val," he said, drawing it out as if testing the word on his palate. Then he smiled. "Sorry to interrupt you," he said. "Go on."

"Well, I think Layla stands a very good chance if I get her on the antibiotics and steroids right away." She looked thoughtful for a moment, then asked: "I guess Mr. Ducci, Santo, is going to be upset. Is he very attached to her?"

Wyn shook his head. "I don't really know," he said. "I knew he'd picked up a horse for a bargain, but we never did get a chance to discuss it. He's gone out tonight, so I won't get the full story till later or tomorrow." He took a sip of coffee, then looked her square in the eye.

"You know what surprises me the most about you, especially being a doctor of sorts, is that you've shown the restraint not to ask what happened to me."

Valerie didn't know how to respond to his comment.

"Don't you want to know?" he asked.

"I want to know what you want to tell me," she said.

He nodded. "Good answer."

"But before you tell me what you want to, *if* you want to, I'd better run to the clinic and pick up that medication," she said.

"Of course," he said.

"Want to come along?" she asked.

"No," he said emphatically, shaking his head. "I'll stay here with the horse."

She rose to her feet and picked up her carryall, then went to the door. "I'll hurry," she said.

Chapter Fifteen

Santo stood, his back leaning slightly against the bar, his legs spread wide apart, his huge arms across his massive chest, a beer clenched in one meaty paw. Even in the dim light, his shaved head shone, his gold earrings twinkled, and his tattoos—bands of barbed wire around his right biceps and chains around the left—were real attention-getters, rippling with even the slightest movement of the powerful muscles in his arms. His T-shirt revealed only a hint, but a tantalizing one, he thought, of the tribal tattoos that decorated his shoulders, chest, and back.

He knew he wasn't flattering himself to think that he'd attracted a lot of attention in the bar. *The women have been coming on to me ever since I walked through the door,* he thought.

He took a long swallow of his beer, emptying it, then turned and put the bottle on the mahogany bar. The place was packed, but the bartender immediately caught his eye and came his way. Santo shoved his empty bottle of Heineken toward the bartender and threw a five on the counter. The bartender nodded wordlessly, retrieved another bottle from the cooler, opened it, and placed it in front of Santo with a fresh napkin.

Santo turned back around, facing out toward the crowd in the bar again. Everybody seemed to be having a great time, but he knew better. Many of them were just as lonely as he was, of that he was certain, eagle-eyed and on the make.

Nothing like a night of hot sex, he thought, *to drive that lone wolf feeling away.*

He was definitely feeling it tonight. Working for Wyn had been a lot easier in Palm Beach. The town, while so very proper, immaculately clean, and morally upright on its surface, had a filthy underbelly. There was a lot of money there, and a lot of idle people.

He missed it, and although he understood why Wyn had done it, he wished that his boss had never decided to make the move up here to the hinterlands. He missed the glamour, the flash, the constant stream of parties and clubbing, and that whole underclass of servants like himself who often had very interesting lives of their own, intertwining as they did with the rich and power-ful. He missed Arielle with her incessant teasing, her unreasonable demands, and her spoiled bitchiness. She'd been a real pain at times, but she flirted with him constantly.

Damn, he thought, *if only all this mess with Wyn and then the divorce hadn't happened.* He knew he could've gotten another job in Palm Beach like the one he had now. It would've taken all of about fifteen min-utes with his experience. But there was one drawback to that, and it was a major drawback. Wyn Conrad had written him into his will—for his faithful service, he'd told him—for sticking with him through thick and thin. Now the son of a bitch had him hooked like a fish on a line.

What was he going to do? Walk away and give it up? No way. When Wyn kicked, Santo would be able to buy a little condo down on Lake Worth or someplace close by. He'd be set for life. He didn't know how long that would be, but the way things were going, Wyn might kick at any time. He might OD on drugs. Stoned as he got, he might fall down the stairs or drown in the swimming pool. He might even off himself. He wouldn't put it past him or blame him if he did. Wyn was a very unhappy man, and living up here, the way he did, it was hell. *Shit,* he thought, *I might even accidentally give him too much one day. Or not be there to drag his ass out of the pool. Or pick him up off the floor.*

He smiled to himself. He might be a fairly well-off man sooner than he'd thought. In the meantime, he had to do something to keep his sanity intact, to stay cool and bide his time.

The blonde he'd been talking to earlier sidled up to him. "Got a light?"

Santo shook his head. "Matches at the bar though," he said. He twisted around and snagged a book of them, then turned back around and struck a match.

The blonde looked at him, then took Santo's big hand, stuck the cigarette into the flame, lighting the cigarette, eyes never leaving his.

She was a real exception to the rule up here. *This*

number could even pass muster in the dens of iniquity down in Palm Beach, he thought. Up here, he hardly saw a soul, except for Wyn, the Reinhardts, and Tiffani, the girl who helped out in the office.

"You said you had a place to go, right?" Santo asked.

"Yeah, I got a place. Not too far away, either," the blonde said.

"Why don't we take a ride?" Santo said.

"Let's split."

The blonde took his great bear paw and led the way out, through a throng of watchful eyes, some of them registering surprise, many of them envious.

In the parking lot she put an arm around his waist, and he let himself be guided toward what must be her car. When they reached it, the blonde turned to him. "Get in."

"Shouldn't I follow you?" Santo asked.

"No. You ride with me," she said. "I'll bring you back to get your car."

Santo nodded. "Okay."

The blonde unlocked a big Range Rover with a remote and opened the passenger side door.

"Nice car," Santo said. "You must be loaded." *Like I'm going to be someday before too long.*

The Reinhardts had returned from the movie, and they both became terribly upset and embarrassed when Wyn, alone in the stable, had asked them why they hadn't answered his telephone call.

"*Ach, Gott in Himmel!*" Gerda had cried, her hands flying to her face. "The cell phone was in my *Beutel.*"

She brandished the ancient vinyl drawstring bag that she carried with her everywhere. "I left it in the car when we went into the theater."

Wyn calmly assured them that it was okay, but he made it clear that he didn't want it to happen again. Tonight, he'd told them, it so happened that he hadn't needed their help after all. The future might be another story.

They walked on to their cottage, Wyn listening to their argumentative voices carrying on the wind.

Shortly afterward he heard Valerie drive in, and they headed for Layla's stall immediately. Finally, after Valerie reexamined the horse and started her on massive doses of antibiotics and steroids, Valerie and Wyn sat down in the stable office. He offered her a glass of wine from the minifridge, and she accepted.

"I can't believe I'm doing this," Valerie said with a laugh.

He smiled. "I'm glad you are."

"But I've got to be up early in the morning," she said. "I've got a lot to do."

"Stay for a glass," Wyn cajoled. "I haven't gotten to talk to anybody on the outside in a long time." Then he laughed. "I don't think I've ever gotten to talk to anybody like you, for that matter."

"What's that supposed to mean?" Valerie asked, her voice one of mock anger. "I'm some kind of freak or something?"

"No," he said. "You're different, and in a most delightful way, but you most definitely are not a freak." He paused and looked down into his glass, then back up at her. "I'm the freak. I've been one ever since I was in a polo accident and got dragged across the field."

Valerie shook her head and then, unbelievably, she let out a short laugh.

"What?" he asked, intrigued with her reaction. He'd expected sympathy, assurance, pity, anything but a laugh.

"No, Wyn," she said, finding it easier to use his first name now, "you're not a freak at all. You're just a very unlucky polo player who let a polo pony practically plow a field with him. And now you look a little bit like the creature from the black lagoon."

"Creature from the black lagoon, huh?" he responded, smiling now. "That bad, eh?"

She nodded. "Only uglier."

"You . . . you . . . ," he began, but then he laughed and didn't finish.

Valerie laughed again, too, then became more serious. "At first I didn't know quite what to think," she said honestly. "With that black mask covering all the bandages on your face, it looked almost like you were wearing some kind of gruesome S&M mask like you see in the movies. All I could see were your eyes and your mouth peeking out."

"Very spooky, I know," he said.

"Very spooky," she agreed. "I think you should dispense with the mask, Wyn. Black, I might add, was a bad choice of colors for it."

"Maybe I should go for something flesh colored?"

"Maybe," she said. "Or just get rid of it. The bandages couldn't look worse."

"Maybe you're right," he said.

"Anyway, then I noticed the scar tissue on your neck and arms and hands. I thought maybe you'd been in a horrible fire or something. To top everything off, there was your secrecy and your gruff attitude. I guess I was prepared for the worst."

"Gruff attitude, you say?" he said grumpily.

"For sure," she replied. "You haven't exactly been the most polite and charming customer up to now."

"Can you blame me?" he asked. "My so-called friends don't want anything to do with me, even a lot of the longtime ones. They think I'm some kind of monster now. Hell, even my wife couldn't stand being around me. She didn't want to have to look at me."

"Can't say as I blame her," Valerie joked.

He smiled. "You're a tough broad, aren't you? You don't pity me at all, do you?"

She shook her head. "I think what happened was horrible," she said, "but with time and operations you'll be good as new. Maybe not as handsome as you look in those polo pictures I saw in the tack room, but I think you'll be fairly presentable. At least in appearance."

"What does that mean?" he asked. " 'At least in appearance.' "

"I think you could work on your manners a little bit," she said. "Maybe not come on to people like some kind of authoritarian dictator or something."

"Well, you haven't seen the way people react to me," he said seriously. "I freak them out. They stare at the bandages or the mask, if I'm wearing it. They stare at my arms and neck and hands. It makes me feel like . . . well, it makes me feel like Quasimodo or somebody. Like something in a sideshow at the circus. And I'm serious when I say my best 'friends' abandoned ship after this happened."

"That's terrible," she said sympathetically, "but I don't doubt it. Most people don't want to face the possibility of what could happen to them. Just look at Christopher Reeve. A lot of people wish he wouldn't make personal appearances. He's too painful for them to look at. Part of it's because of their own fears, I think, and part of it is because it's really not a pretty sight."

The expression in his eyes was understandably glum, but he didn't say anything.

"The bright side," Valerie went on, "and there really is one, is that with a few more operations, as painful, time-consuming, and tedious as they may be, you're going to have a lot of your old self back."

"That's what the doctors in New York told me after the last operation," he said. "But I don't know, Val, I really don't. It's so slow and painful. Sometimes I feel like giving up, you know? Sometimes it doesn't seem like it's worth it. I mean, even when all these great doctors are finished, I'm still going to look like one big skin graft. My face. My neck and arms and hands. Some of my chest and thighs. When I fell, that polo pony dragged me from one end of the field to the other, and after it was all over I'd lost nearly all the skin on the front of my body. *Down to the bone, Val.* They couldn't even suture me up in most places because there wasn't anything to suture." He grimaced with the memory. "My nose . . ." he began.

"You'll have a nose," she said. "It's amazing what

they can do nowadays, and it sounds like you've got the best surgeons money can buy."

He hung his head, staring down into his glass again. "I know you're right," he finally said. "It's just so damn hard to have to accept the fact that I'm never going to look like I used to. To have to deal with walking around with scar tissue and grafts for the rest of my life."

"Yes," she said softly. "It's not going to be easy to accept that. In a way it's like aging, Wyn. We have to come to accept what our bodies inevitably become because none of us, no matter how hard we fight it, will remain the great-looking eighteen-year-old kids we once were."

He looked at her. "You really are one tough cookie," he said.

She reached out and touched his hand, and he jerked slightly. "And so are you," she said, patting it. "You're too much of a man to let this defeat you."

From a dark corner of the parking area, someone had been watching and waiting, biding time. Now, after seeing them part company, the watcher felt blood boil in heated veins. From outside, the interloper had listened to part of their conversation, catching bits and pieces of it, easily filling in what couldn't be heard. Then witnessed their sweet, reluctant parting at her Jeep.

Still as a statue, a white-hot anger raging inside, the interloper saw Wyn make his way toward the house. Quickly processing this new development, wondering how it might change things, having to figure a new person into the equation so carefully worked out, well, it was infuriating and scary, and the interloper didn't like it at all.

No! I don't like this business one bit, and I might just have to see what I can do about it. Fists clenched into tight balls. Goddammit! Nobody's going to fuck up my chances! Nothing and nobody's going to come between me and what I want. I've worked too hard to get it!

When Wyn finally disappeared into the house, the interloper quickly darted down a path toward the woods, mind already spinning with possible solutions to this problem. It was a problem that needed to be nipped in the bud.

Chapter Sixteen

Teddy poured himself a few fingers of vodka, paused a moment and looked into the glass, then drank it straight down. He shivered from the taste and fire of it and quickly chased it with a glass of water. "There," he said aloud, almost gagging, "that's better."

He crossed to one of the big couches and sat down. A smile came to his lips. On a small mirror on the coffee table were the two long, thin lines of cocaine he'd cut, along with the sterling silver straw a friend in New York City had given him. Although he was alone in the conservatory at Apple Hill, he instinctively looked around him before picking up the straw. Bending down, he snorted up both lines, one up his right nostril, the other up his left.

Dropping the straw, he sank back into the downy comfort of the couch and took a few deep snorts of air, making sure he got all the coke up there. Then he let his mind drift, relaxing after a busy day and grueling dinner. *Whoa,* he thought after only a few mintues. *This is powerful stuff.* Seemingly of their own accord, his feet had begun tapping on the floor and his fingers were beating an erratic tattoo on an invisible drum.

He looked over at the telephone, then glanced at his watch. Tiffani surely would be home soon, he thought, and he could hardly wait. The evening had been a terrible bore. He'd called Linda and Barry Miller, clients of his who lived up here, to discuss their stock portfolio. When he let slip that Valerie was busy and wouldn't be coming over to his place, they'd very kindly invited him to dinner. He thought the Millers were loathsome, if cultivated, nouveau riche, and he hated their endless discussions of art and music and politics and civic responsibility. He'd gone, however, and been his most charming, of course, because they'd invested a lot of money with him. And he was after them to invest a lot more.

Well, he thought, *at least I managed to insult that old witch, Colette Richards.* He laughed aloud. He really didn't care because, although she was one loaded old lady, he knew he'd never get his mitts on her money. She had blue-chip, blue-blooded money managers on three continents.

He wondered what she would tell Val about the call, but then decided he didn't really care about that either. He could always pull the wool over good, trusting, naive Val's eyes, couldn't he? Always had, he told himself.

He looked at his watch again, then reached over for the telephone. He punched in Tiffani's number.

"Hello?" she answered.

"Hey, babe," he said, "where you been? Why

didn't you call me? I've been waiting for you."

"Oh, Teddy," she cooed, "I'm so glad you called. I just listened to my messages and was getting ready to call you. I went over to Billy's. You know, the bar where I used to work."

"Yeah?" he said. "What were you doing over there?"

She giggled. "Just having a few drinks with the girls. You know, ladies' night out."

"Yeah?" he said. "Well, what about spending a little time with a man?"

She giggled again. "I'll be ready and waiting."

"I'll be over there in about fifteen minutes," he said.

"I'll be here," she replied.

Teddy went back over to the drinks table and poured himself another few fingers of vodka. *One good thing about coke,* he thought, *is that you can drink and drink and never feel drunk.* He downed the vodka, shivered as before, then quickly drank a big swallow of water. He set the glass back down on the table and retraced his steps to the coffee table. He picked up the mirror, silver straw, and the little plastic bag of cocaine, and shoved them into his trouser pocket.

He could already feel his body responding to his excitement about the night that lay ahead. Just the thought of seeing Tiffani, hearing her voice, thinking about what they'd do—he never failed to get aroused. He strode to the entrance hall, grabbed his keys off a console there, and sauntered out to the Jaguar.

Troubles? he thought, smiling with pride at his sleek machine. *What troubles? Teddy de Mornay doesn't have a worry in the world. Not tonight he doesn't.* He laughed aloud again and got in the car. *No, siree. He's got a hot date. That's what he's got.*

Arielle put the remote telephone up on the swimming pool's coral stone coping and turned around to face Lolo, her arms spread out on the coping, her breasts bobbing on the water's surface. She looked at him teasingly, her sensuous lips parting in a smile. "Guess what?" she said, flipping water at him with a finger.

"What?" he asked.

"Bibi and Joe Whitman are flying us up to Saratoga," she said. "We're invited to use their guest house as long as we want."

"Great!" Lolo responded. "When are they leaving?"

"They're already there," Arielle said. "They're sending their jet down to pick us up tomorrow."

Lolo swam over and placed an arm on each of hers, pushing his body up against hers in the water. "You know what that means, don't you?" he said.

"What? That we have to hurry and pack?" Arielle asked with a laugh.

Lolo nibbled at her neck. "You know what I mean," he said. "The jet has a nice bedroom, and we can have fun all the way to Saratoga."

Arielle laughed again. "I knew you'd be thinking about all of the really important logistics," she said. She kicked her legs out and scissored them around his ass.

"That's me, for sure," Lolo said. "Always practical." He buried his head in her breasts, licking and kissing her, underwater, then above the water's surface.

"Hmmmmm," Arielle moaned. "That feels so good, Lolo."

He came up for air and placed his lips on hers, kissing her hungrily, pushing himself against her, his desire for her precluding any further conversation.

Arielle threw her arms around his neck, pulling him against her greedy body, abandoning herself to pleasure. He was already aroused, and she gasped when she felt his manhood brush against her nakedness.

Lolo moved his right hand down between her thighs and began rubbing her there. His breath became more rapid, his desire mounting as he felt her distended readiness. Putting his arms under her knees, he lifted her legs, then entered her, and Arielle trembled all over as she felt him inside her.

Lolo began moving in and out, slowly at first, teasing her with long strokes of his engorged cock, taking his time, enjoying the little whimpers and sighs and moans that escaped her lips as he moved in and out, in and out, until he couldn't hold off any longer. He suddenly began to speed up, pumping at her with more vigor, and Arielle began to moan louder, then begged him for more, her desire for him overcoming any urge to hold back. She gave herself up to him entirely, her body starved, and began moving wildly against him as he began to thrust into her with abandon, his body demanding release.

Suddenly he groaned hoarsely and rammed into her, virtually impaling her on his throbbing cock as he heaved his juices into her in explosion after explosion. Arielle screamed when she felt his release, and her entire body spasmed against him in a monumental climax, wave after wave of contractions sending her into an orbit she had never known before. They clung to one another, gasping for breath and shuddering with pleasure, their lips meeting again in a kiss before their bodies parted.

When he could finally speak, Lolo said, "See what we have to look forward to in the jet tomorrow?"

Arielle sighed with pleasure. "Oh, yes," she breathed. "And tomorrow and tomorrow and tomorrow."

And she thought: *Yes, Lolo, my love. There'll be plenty of time for this, a whole lifetime. I'll see to that. But we have a mission, too. Only you don't know it. Not yet.*

Chapter Seventeen

Wyn poured himself a cup of coffee in the library and began pacing the floor, lost in thought, as he sipped from the steaming mug. He was still worried about Layla. It was early in the morning, not long past dawn, but he had already been down to the stables and checked on the sick horse. She appeared to be somewhat better, perhaps less swollen and not in as much distress, but he wasn't really certain.

He strode over to his desk and started to call for Santo when the giant lumbered through the library door.

"I was just getting ready to call you," Wyn said, looking over at him.

"You're up awfully early this morning," Santo said somewhat grumpily. He was hungover from his night out and would have liked a little time to himself this morning. He'd already taken some aspirin to help chase away the incessant pounding in his head, and now he needed a lot of coffee before the day's activities began.

"I want you to get on the phone and get hold of that vet," Wyn said. "Valerie Rochelle."

"Now?" Santo asked. "The place isn't even open yet, Wyn."

"Then leave a message for her," Wyn said. "I want her to take a look at Layla this morning as soon as possible."

"What's the problem with Layla?" Santo asked.

"Oh, I forgot you weren't here last night," Wyn said pointedly. "When you bought her, she'd apparently had strangle. Then you vaccinated her, and now she's having a massive reaction to the vaccination."

"Aw, jeez," Santo said, his headache suddenly getting worse. "I had no idea—"

"That's why things like lineage and medical records are so important in this business, Santo," Wyn said sharply.

"I'm sorry," Santo said, "but I had no idea. She looked—"

"Just get on the phone and get that vet here as soon as possible," Wyn interjected.

Without another word, Santo picked up the address book on the desk and flipped through it until he found the clinic's number. He picked up the telephone and dialed. When the service answered, he left a message for Dr. Rochelle to call as soon as possible regarding Layla. He hung up and shrugged. "I left a message," he said. "There's nobody in yet."

"Okay," Wyn said. "I'm going to go upstairs and get cleaned up and change clothes. When she calls, you tell her to get out here pronto. Got it?"

"Yes," Santo said, "I've got it."

He watched as Wyn climbed the spiral stairs to the hallway that led to his bedroom. *What the hell's gotten into him?* he wondered. *He's hardly worn anything but sweats for months and doesn't bother cleaning up half the time.* It did not look like a promising day at Stonelair.

Valerie parked near the stable office and, carryall and medical bag in hand, she strode to the door, hoping that Layla hadn't taken a turn for the worse.

Santo Ducci stood up when she entered the office. "Good morning," he said.

"Good morning, Santo," Valerie said. "Layla's in her stall, I take it?"

He nodded. "You can go on back."

"Thanks," Val said. She went through to the tack room, then on into the stable, walking down the length of stalls to Layla's.

When she got there, the stall door was open, and Wyn was sitting on a stool intently looking at Layla. "Hi, there," Valerie said.

He looked up. "Hi, Doc," he said, standing up.

Valerie was momentarily nonplussed. He had taken off the mask and left his bandaged face exposed. She wanted to study it closely in the light to see how serious the damage was, but she didn't say anything. *Not now,* she thought. *First things first.* Her immediate responsibility was to Layla.

"Okay," she said, "what's going on here? Has Layla taken a turn for the worse?"

"That's why I called you," he said. "I don't really know. I came down here early this morning and then again a little while ago, but I can't be sure if there's any change or not. I don't mean to be an alarmist, but I want your opinion."

"I don't think you're being an alarmist," Valerie said. "She was in acute distress last night. Let me just have a good look." First she examined Layla's neck, then she got down on all fours and studied each of her legs in turn, gingerly feeling for swelling and looking for signs of hemorrhaging.

When she was finished, she stood back up and looked at Wyn. "You know what?"

"What?" Wyn asked.

"It's working," Valerie said happily. "The swelling has already gone down considerably and the hemorrhaging has stopped completely. I think she's going to pull through with flying colors."

Wyn breathed a sigh of relief. "Thank God," he said. "I was making myself crazy trying to decide, but I honestly couldn't tell whether there was any difference this morning or not."

"It's not an easy call in such a short period of time," Valerie replied, "but I'm more than satisfied with her progress overnight. She'll pull through."

"Thanks, Doc," Wyn said. "I really appreciate you coming all the way out here."

"That's what I'm here for," Valerie said.

"Well, as long as you are here," Wyn said, "could I offer you a quick cup of coffee or something?"

Valerie didn't even take the time to think about it, though she had a busy schedule today. "Sure," she said. "I'd like that."

"Why don't we go up to the house?" Wyn suggested.

"Okay."

*

They sat on a big couch in the library, the four Irish wolfhounds lounging on the floor around them. Sunlight streamed through the French doors, and Valerie could see his face clearly now. He wore a bandage across his forehead, a large one across his nose, and one eye was completely bandaged over.

"You look a lot better without the mask," she said quietly.

"Do you mean that?" he asked.

She nodded. "Definitely." She paused a moment, then asked, "Do you mind if I take a closer look?"

"No, I don't mind," Wyn said, surprising himself.

Valerie set her mug on the coffee table, then scooted across the couch. She examined his face closely, lightly brushing her fingertips across the exposed skin. "Very light scarring," she concluded. "Dermabrasion would take care of most of it, if you wanted to bother. Personally, I wouldn't even bother with that."

"Are you serious?" he asked.

"Absolutely," she said, nodding her head. "May I look at the bandaged areas?"

"Go ahead," he said, deciding to trust her. "You've gone this far."

Valerie lifted one end of the forehead bandage, looked at the wound beneath it, then carefully secured the bandage again. She followed suit with the other bandages, making certain they were properly replaced. When she was finished, she sat staring at his face for a while.

"What is it?" Wyn asked. "What do you think?"

"You're healing remarkably well," she said, "and I don't think there's going to be much evidence that you ever had an accident. Very minor scarring, if any."

"You don't have to try to let me down easy, Doc," he said. "I can take the truth."

"That's exactly what I'm giving you," she said seriously. "Oh, your nose may look like you've been in a fight or something, but other than that . . ." She shrugged. "Your looks are hardly going to have changed. I might add that you've got great plastic surgeons."

He sat in silence, digesting her words. "You really do mean that, don't you?" he finally said.

"I think that it's not half as bad as *you* think," she said, carefully choosing her words. She reached over and touched his hand. "I think that there are other, more serious scars you've got to deal with, and they're making these seem a lot worse than they are."

He looked down at her hand on his and sighed heavily. "Maybe you're right, Doc," he said softly. He looked up at her. "Maybe you're right."

Wyn showed Valerie to her car, watching until the Jeep had disappeared from view. He walked back to the library and sat down at his desk, where he booted up the computer. *It's time I e-mailed the men out West,* he thought. *See what's going on. Stay on top of things.*

Santo stood at one of the French doors, staring at his boss. He noticed that Wyn wasn't wearing the mask or his customary baseball cap and that his hair was carefully combed. Then he took in the clean knit polo shirt, the crisp chinos, and shiny loafers.

Something's definitely going on, Santo thought. *Something I don't think I like.*

He stepped into the room and approached the desk.

"Want to go over today's schedule now?" he asked Wyn.

"Sure," Wyn said. "It'd be a good idea before I start my E-mails."

"I'll go get your meds first," Santo said, starting for the spiral staircase.

"Santo," Wyn called to him.

Santo turned around and looked at him. "Yes?"

"I don't want the shots anymore," Wyn said.

"You—?"

"You heard me," Wyn said. "No more shots. You can get rid of the stuff."

Santo stood, rooted to the spot. *Is it that damn vet?* he wondered. *Could she be causing all these changes? Could some bitch like her waltz in here and waltz away with everything, Wyn included?*

He had some serious thinking to do, some very serious thinking. About his future. Wyn's future. And Valerie Rochelle's.

Chapter Eighteen

Marguerite gave Effie strict instructions. She was to serve lunch on the screened-in porch as she normally would, then disappear for the duration of the afternoon. She was not to serve dessert, nor was she to clear the table. Marguerite would see to these things herself.

"I don't understand," Effie protested, unaccustomed to any variation in her work routine. "I always serve the dessert and clean up afterward. Why are you—?"

"Shush!" Marguerite commanded, a long slender hand held straight up in the air. Her eyebrows were arched, and her emerald eyes glistened with intensity. "You are not to question me, Effie. You are to do as I say. As soon as you've served lunch, leave. Go into the village and shop or go have a drink somewhere."

"A drink! But—" Effie started to protest.

"Oh, do come off it," Marguerite exclaimed. "I know you swill gin half the day, and I really don't care. But I do want you gone this afternoon. I don't care where you go, just go!"

Effie would do as she was told, though she pouted in

the kitchen until Teddy had swept in to say hello when he arrived for lunch. "Oh, I'm so glad you're here," she told him, looking him up and down with pleasure. He was wearing a jacket and tie, an outfit most would consider overkill for a lunch in the country, but not Marguerite de la Rochelle or Teddy. "You look nice," Effie said.

"And you look worried," Teddy replied. "What's going on?"

"I don't know what's gotten into her," Effie said, nodding her head toward the parlor where Marguerite was, "but she sure could use some cheering up or something today."

"Why?" Teddy asked. "She seemed fine when we spoke on the telephone."

"I don't know why," Effie said, "but I'll tell you one thing. She's been acting strange ever since that fancy-pants cousin of hers, Mr. James de Biron, got here day before yesterday. And today, she's being meaner than a snake to me. She's making me clear out till after you leave."

"Oh, well, Effie," Teddy said reassuringly, "you know she doesn't mean any harm. Whatever it is, she'll get over it. Maybe she's just a little nervous because her cousin's visiting from France."

"Humpf!" Effie said. "I don't wonder. He may be real good-looking and always have a big smile ready, but if you ask me he's a snake in the grass. And he's not even French. He just lives there. Imagine her wanting me out of here."

Now Teddy understood perfectly well why Marguerite had banished Effie from the premises. She didn't want Effie to be privy to what she'd planned to discuss with him and Jamie de Biron. There was always the chance that Effie would overhear something, and Marguerite knew that Effie would go straight to Valerie with the information.

Marguerite, Teddy, and Jamie convened on the big screened-in porch. She always had summer lunches here rather than at a table in the garden because her beautiful skin was shielded from the sun's damaging rays and they were protected from the plethora of bothersome insects.

Soon they were enjoying the warmth of the summer heat and the remnants of dessert, sliced mango topped with a mango and papaya sorbet.

Teddy put his spoon down and smiled. "That was delicious, Marguerite," he said, "but then your food always is."

"Marguerite's always done everything perfectly," Jamie added, smiling at his cousin. Like Teddy, he was dressed casually but elegantly in a navy blue blazer with gold buttons, white trousers, and a blue-and-white striped shirt with a yellow tie. His very blond hair was short, almost in a military cut, and contrasted sharply with his darkly tanned skin. It was obvious that he was in excellent physical shape.

"Thank you both," she replied. "I'm so glad you could be here with us today, Teddy, so that you could meet Jamie and we could have our little discussion in privacy." She paused and delicately sipped her mineral water, then looked directly into Teddy's eyes. "But you mustn't forget that not a single word of this is to reach Val's ears."

"There's no danger of that, Marguerite," he replied. "I think—no, I know—that we're of a single mind on this. You and I know what's best for Val, even if she sometimes doesn't, and in this case it's best that she doesn't know anything."

"Exactly," Marguerite said. "I think you and I will get along very well, Teddy. We always have, and I see no reason why that shouldn't continue. We do see eye to eye. Certainly about my daughter." She shifted her gaze to Jamie. "And you've known her practically all of your life, Jamie, so it goes without saying that you understand why I'm doing what I am."

Jamie set down his wineglass and nodded. He had consumed several glasses of wine over lunch, Teddy had noticed, but it didn't seem to have affected him in the least. "You don't have to explain a thing to me, Marguerite," Jamie said. "I know exactly how Val is— always has been—and the only difference I see is that she's become more . . . independent, I guess is the word . . . in the last few years. Somewhat out of control, I would say."

He looked over at Teddy and smiled warmly. "I think you're perfect for Val, by the way, Teddy," he said. "And I'm so glad the two of you are going to get married. She needs somebody practical, with two feet planted firmly on the ground. Marguerite can tell you that I love Val dearly, but Val's never had any respect for her heritage or family, and she's always dilly-dallied with . . . well, *outsiders,* if you know what I mean."

"Never was a truer word spoken," Marguerite said, "and that's one reason I'm delighted that the two of you could meet. I think that the three of us together can make certain that everything of Armand's and mine will be taken care of properly. I don't have to tell you that I've become increasingly concerned about Val's behavior lately. She's getting more independent, as you so aptly put it, Jamie. She's even become somewhat distant and headstrong. Quite frankly, I'm worried that when I'm gone, she'll take everything that Armand and I worked so hard to keep and auction it all off, then give the proceeds to an animal shelter or something."

"I don't think you have to worry about that now," Teddy said, his square chin jutting out authoritatively. "Between Jamie and myself, we can handle whatever might come up. And don't forget, Marguerite," he added, "I will be her husband."

Jamie laughed. "You can whip her into shape," he said.

"Easier said than done, I'm afraid," Marguerite said seriously. "This eccentric streak of hers runs awfully deep. I don't know where it came from, but it's there, and it's powerful." She looked over at Teddy. "You'll draw up the paperwork soon, Teddy?" she asked.

"I'll have it done tomorrow," he said. "When I go home, I'll get my secretary on it right away. I'll give you a call tomorrow when it's all ready. If you like, I can run it over here, or you and Jamie can come over to my place for a drink and sign everything while you're there. Whichever you prefer."

"Wonderful," Marguerite said enthusiastically. "Why *don't* we do the signing at Apple Hill? I would love for Jamie to see what you've done with it, Teddy."

She turned to her cousin. "He's done an absolutely marvelous job of renovating the place. It's in perfect taste, and I think you would love it."

"I'm game," Jamie said.

"Good," Teddy said. "Why don't you plan on coming over about five o'clock? I'll make sure everything's ready by then. There will be loose ends to tie up with Dock Wainwright, but we can get most everything done right away. In the meantime, I hate to eat and run, Marguerite, but I'd better get back there so all the paperwork can get started." He picked up the folder of papers to the right of his place setting.

"That's fine," Marguerite said. "The sooner, the better." She rose to her feet, and the men followed suit. "We'll see you promptly at five, Teddy."

She turned to lead them out to the parking area. Jamie held the door for her and Teddy, then followed them out.

Teddy got into his Jaguar and started the engine.

"You didn't leave all the papers, did you, Teddy?" Marguerite asked.

Teddy lifted the folder off the seat next to him. "I've got everything, Marguerite," he said, "so don't worry about a thing."

"Good," she said.

Teddy roared off, and Marguerite turned to Jamie and took his arm. "Let's stroll for a moment in the garden, Jamie," she said.

They went through the nearby gate and down the path, summer blooms spilling out of their beds onto it from both sides. The warm air was filled with butterflies and sweet scents.

"What do you think of him, Jamie?" Marguerite asked.

"He's absolutely appropriate," Jamie replied without hesitation. "He's one of us. Our kind."

"Yes," Marguerite agreed. "He is indeed."

They strolled on in silence for a while, admiring the garden.

"Are they in love?" Jamie asked.

"Love!" Marguerite exclaimed. Her green eyes widened, and she shrugged her thin shoulders. "What a silly question, Jamie."

He laughed lightly. "I was just curious," he said. "It's been known to happen, you know. Mostly among the lower orders."

"Oh, I think there's been an attraction of sorts," Marguerite conceded. "In the beginning anyway, as there so often is, but I think that initial attraction has worn off for both of them. For Val more so than Teddy, surprisingly."

"Oh?" Jamie said. "Do you think she's interested in someone else?"

"No, no, no! It's nothing like that at all. I don't think she has much interest in men. Just animals."

"What about him?" Jamie asked. "You say he's still attracted to her."

"I think he's more interested in marriage than she is," Marguerite said. "I don't know that he's particularly interested in her physically. Oh, they spend a lot of weekends together, but neither of them seems all that . . . sexually charged, shall we say . . . over the other."

"Well, it sounds ideal," Jamie said. "If she gets bored, she has her animals."

"Exactly," Marguerite said, squeezing his arm. "I'm so glad you feel that way. I only wish Val knew how fortunate she is to have us taking care of her this way, but she can't know anything about our plans. It's too bad really that she doesn't know all the trouble we go to on her behalf." She looked up at him, her expression almost wistful. "It's really too bad that she doesn't know how much we love her."

Lydia was typing at the computer when Teddy came through the office door. She paused and looked up at him severely. "You've got several messages," she said, "and some of them need to be answered ASAP, Teddy. And I do mean ASAP. Like a couple of banks and a couple of brokers in New York City?"

"Don't worry about it, Lydia," he replied, smiling. "I'll get to them."

She was surprised by his nonchalant response to her urgent message. "You look like the cat that caught the canary," she finally said, a speculative smile hovering at the edges of her lips. "Must've been some lunch with that hateful old bitch, Mrs. de la Rochelle."

She was fishing for information, and Teddy knew it. He decided to let her suffer a few minutes. "I've got to make some telephone calls, Lydia," he said. "Then we'll get to those messages of yours."

She scowled. He wasn't going to be forthcoming about lunch. "Sure, Teddy," she said, her voice clipped. "Whatever you say." She looked back down at the keyboard and began typing very quickly, hitting the keys with an extra punch to try to irritate him.

Teddy ignored her and sat down at his desk. He

flipped through the Rolodex until he saw the number he wanted, then picked up the telephone and dialed it. He waited for someone to answer, feeling especially self-satisfied. On the third ring, a secretary picked up.

"Dockering Wainwright's office," she said.

"Hi," he said jauntily. "This is Teddy de Mornay. I need to speak to Dock Wainwright right away."

"I'll see if he's in," the secretary said.

"It concerns Marguerite de la Rochelle," Teddy added.

"Yes, sir," the secretary said. "Just a moment."

Teddy waited patiently, although he was anxious to speak with Dock Wainwright. He could hardly wait to hear what the old man would have to say.

"Dockering Wainwright here," the older man's voice intoned. "How are you, Teddy?"

"I'm fine," Teddy replied. "And you?"

"At my age," Wainwright said, "I have no reason to complain."

"That's great," Teddy said.

"What can I do for you, Teddy?" the older man asked. "You say this has something to do with Marguerite de la Rochelle?"

"Yes," Teddy said. "I've just come from a luncheon meeting with her and her cousin, James de Biron."

"Ah, yes," Wainwright said. "I see."

"Marguerite, and Jamie, and I," Teddy went on slowly, drawing out his news, "had a long discussion at lunch about the de la Rochelle estate."

"That so?" Wainwright replied, clearly wishing that Teddy would get to the point.

"Marguerite," Teddy said, "has decided to give me

control of all of her investment accounts." There, he'd dropped his bomb on the old man.

"I see," Dockering Wainwright replied calmly. He cleared his throat. "Her entire portfolio?"

"Yes," Teddy replied almost gleefully. "All of it."

"I see," Wainwright repeated.

"I've got the paperwork here," Teddy said, "powers of attorney and such, and I'll have it sent over to you just as soon as everything is ready."

"Yes," Wainwright said. "I'll have to have a signed statement from Mrs de la Rochelle to that effect, of course."

"I've got it right here," Teddy said smugly. "It'll be with the paperwork I send over." He paused, then added: "She wants you to send a check over to me as soon as possible, with any commissions due you deducted, of course."

"Certainly," Wainwright said stiffly. "I'll get on it as soon as I receive the necessary paperwork."

"Thanks a lot," Teddy said. "You can expect a messenger in the morning."

"Yes, well, . . . good luck with it, Teddy," Wainwright said, forcing cheer into his voice.

"Thanks," Teddy said. He wanted to tell the old man he didn't need his good wishes and started to hang up, but thought better of it. *Never burn bridges,* he told himself. *You never know when you might need them, and Dock Wainwright, old as he was, might be very useful in the future. The near future, anyway.*

"I hope there'll be no animosity on your part," Teddy said. "I think the only reason Marguerite's doing this is because Val and I are going to get married."

"Well, that's wonderful news," Wainwright said. "I hope you're both very happy."

"Thanks," Teddy responded. "I'll be talking to you."

"Good-bye, then," Wainwright said. "And please give my regards to Val."

"I will," Teddy replied. "Bye." He replaced the receiver in its cradle, then looked up. Lydia had stopped typing and was looking at him with a curious expression.

"What is it?" he asked.

"We're just full of news today, aren't we?" she said.

"Yes," he answered. Then he opened the file of paperwork he'd brought back with him from Marguerite's. He withdrew an envelope and opened it, staring down at the papers in his hand. "Tomorrow morning," he said, "stop on your way in and deposit these in the bank." He got up and handed the checks over to Lydia.

She looked down at them, and her eyes lit up brightly. "Je-sus!" she said. "I thought old Dock Wainwright had all their money."

"These are just quarterly dividend checks," he said. "They'll be coming straight to me in the future."

"My God," Lydia cried, "I didn't know they had that much money. De Mornay Investments is going to have a lot to play with."

"No," Teddy said. "Deposit them in my personal account."

"But-but these—" she began.

"Never mind, Lydia," he said firmly. "Deposit them in my personal account for the time being."

"If you say so," Lydia said with a frown.

"I say so," Teddy said.

"But how am I supposed to enter these on the books, Teddy?" she asked.

"I'll handle that," he said. *And I will, too,* he thought. *Marguerite de la Rochelle and Jamie de Biron aren't going to miss a dividend check right away. Especially not with the switch over from Dock. Besides,* he thought, *I'll be replacing them before they even receive statements from my investment company. There's nothing wrong with my making use of them for my personal needs for a short time, is there? It wasn't my fault if the technology stocks bottomed out, was it? In the meantime, this money will more than take care of my margin calls. It'll shut up the banks and the brokers.*

"Now then," he said, looking at Lydia. "What are these so-called urgent messages you've got for me?"

Chapter Nineteen

"Mrs. McDougall," Valerie said, "I don't think you have anything to worry about. Lexi is doing very well."

"I don't know that I agree with you," Mrs. McDougall said, "but we shall see." She picked up the tiny mixed-breed dog and held him in her arms.

"If you have any problems, let me know," Valerie said.

"Of course," Mrs. McDougall said.

Valerie held the door open for her, then followed the tall, thin woman out into the reception area. She waved good-bye to her and went on into her office to fill out Lexi's record. *There's really nothing wrong with Lexi,* she thought as she scribbled her examination notes. *It's Mrs. McDougall who needs the doctor. And a good and patient psychiatrist at that.* The woman had been bringing the dog in for three years, together with a laundry list of ailments that no one at the clinic had been able to discern. Lexi was perfectly healthy, if a bit neurotic, but that was to be expected in an animal that was smothered with so much attention.

Valerie finished her notes, then went out to the reception area to give them to Tami to file.

"Here you go, Tami," she said. "Lexi's file."

"Thank you," Tami said, taking the file from her. "The dog with all the phantom ailments, right? What is it this week?"

"It's a limp," Valerie said. "For about the twentieth time."

Tami rolled her eyes and laughed.

The telephone rang, and Annie picked it up. "Hold on a moment," Valerie heard her say. Then Annie looked up at her. "Val, it's for you. Mr. Conrad at Stonelair on line three."

"I'll take it in my office," Valerie said. She turned and went back to her office, unaware of the curious eyes that followed her.

She sat down at her desk, pushed the button, and picked up the receiver. "Hi, Wyn," she said. "What can I do for you?"

"I was wondering if you could have another look at Layla," Wyn said. "This afternoon, if possible."

Again today? Valerie thought, but she said, "Sure. Let me check my schedule. Can you hold on a minute?"

"Okay, Doc," Wyn said.

Valerie pressed the hold button and sat in puzzled thought. *I don't think Layla really needs a follow-up visit today,* she decided, *but Wyn Conrad obviously does.* She realized that she'd opened the door to friendship and felt as if she must follow through. More than that, she discovered that she wanted to.

She quickly checked her schedule, then got Wyn back on the line. "How about around six o'clock?" she said. "That's when I finish up here today."

"That'd be great," Wyn said. "I'll see you then."

"Okay," Valerie said. She hung up the receiver, still curious about the call, wondering if her instincts were on the mark. There wasn't time to think about it now, however, because she had a busy afternoon ahead of her.

Valerie parked and walked toward the stable office and saw that no one was behind the big desk. *I guess he's with Layla,* she thought. She went through the tack room, then on out into the stables. Down the row of stalls ahead of her, she saw Wyn, standing with two horses saddled and bridled, ready to ride. As she approached him, she saw him grin.

"What's this?" she asked.

"I thought we'd take a ride," he said.

"But I thought you wanted—" she began.

"Layla's doing great," he said, "but I thought the two of us could use a little recreation. How about it?"

Valerie couldn't help but smile. "I think it's a great idea," she replied, "and I sure am glad I'm wearing pants and sneakers."

"This is Dixie," Wyn said. "She has a lot of spirit, but she behaves herself."

Valerie set down her carryall and medical bag and stroked the beautiful Arabian's neck. "She's a real looker," she said.

"And this is Demon," Wyn said.

"Appropriately named, I take it?"

Wyn nodded. "But I can handle him." He held Dixie's reins out to her. "Ready?"

"Yes," Valerie replied. She took Dixie's reins and mounted the horse with ease, then watched as Wyn mounted Demon.

Together they rode out of the stable's open doors and toward a trail that led through Stonelair's lush meadows and on through the heavily wooded forest in the distance. When they reached the meadow, Wyn began a trot, and Valerie kept pace, enjoying the sun and wind and the feel of Dixie beneath her.

Wyn would catch her eye from time to time to make certain that she was okay. "You're a good rider," he called to her.

"You're not so bad yourself," she called back. *He's a terrific rider,* she thought. He sat a horse beautifully, in full command of himself and the handsome Arabian. *His body may be scarred but he has complete confidence on horseback.*

Wyn began a canter, moving slightly ahead of her, and Valerie followed suit as before, picking up speed, glad for the faster pace, and the opportunity to watch Wyn and Demon move. *They move as one,* she thought, *with a fluid grace seldom seen in riders, even competent, fully experienced ones.*

She caught up with him, but he put Demon into a full gallop, turning to grin at her as they headed straight toward the woods. She gave Dixie a kick, and off she went after him, determined to catch up with him again and blissful in her element.

Just as she drew up alongside him, Wyn reined in Demon and began a trot as they approached the forest trail. Valerie quickly did likewise, and they rode together along the path in the dappled sunlight.

When they finally returned to the stable, she had no idea how long they'd been riding, but she hadn't enjoyed herself so much in as long as she could remember. After they dismounted, Helmut Reinhardt appeared from within the stable and took the horses' reins.

"Helmut," Wyn said, "this is Valerie Rochelle, our vet."

Helmut Reinhardt nodded and practically clicked his heels together in an Old World manner. "I'm very pleased to meet you," he said in thickly accented English.

"I'm happy to meet you, too," Valerie said and watched as he disappeared into the stable with the horses. "That was wonderful," she said to Wyn.

"I'm glad you enjoyed it, Doc," he said. He hesitated, then added, "How about a drink or something before you go? Or do you have plans?"

"No," she replied. "That'd be great."

They sat on one of the couches in the library, sipping champagne that he had opened. The wolfhounds were sprawled about the room, all of them asleep. Valerie and Wyn talked enthusiastically about horses and their love for riding, sharing experiences and laughing together, unaware of the time. It was not until darkness approached and Wyn had to get up and turn on lamps that they realized they'd been sitting together for hours.

He returned to the couch and sat looking at her with an expression of complete happiness on his face. She returned his gaze, and her heart swelled with pleasure. She couldn't remember when she'd felt this happy, this . . . excited by someone.

He drew closer to her and said, "What are you thinking about?"

"I . . . I was thinking about what a great time I had," she said.

"I did, too," he said. "I . . . I didn't even think it was possible."

"I didn't either," she said. She reached over and touched his hand. "I didn't know it could be like this."

He grasped her hand in his, enjoying its feminine, yet strong, feel against his. *Oh, God!* he wondered. *Can this really be happening to me?* Then he thought: *To us?* He began to stroke her hand gently, reluctant to let it go.

Valerie felt her body tremble slightly at his touch, at the connection between them. She didn't know how to describe it. It was almost as if some chemical reaction had taken place between them, as if some force were operating over them without their control. It was frightening, this feeling and her knowledge of it, but simultaneously it thrilled her to the very core of her being.

She'd never felt this way before. Not with Teddy, not with anyone. *Was it merely sexual?* she asked herself. *Or was it something more?* She didn't know, but she suddenly realized that she was willing to explore it, to take a chance, to risk whatever may come to get to know this man better.

Wyn seemed mesmerized by her hand, stroking it, staring down at it, slightly embarrassed to look into her eyes, for fear that he would see mere indulgence there or, worse, rejection. But look up at her he finally did, unable to resist. His heart surged with a newfound joy when at last he witnessed the look of tenderness, perhaps even the disquiet of love or lust, in those emerald eyes. Hers was not a gaze of pity, nor was it mere empathy. It was much, much more, of that he was certain.

He set down his champagne glass and brought her hand to his lips and kissed it, barely brushing it with his mouth, all the while searching her eyes for meaning. He was not disappointed, for Valerie's lips quivered slightly at his kiss and her eyes watched him fearlessly, unblinkingly, and, he thought, a bit proudly.

When he released her hand at last, Valerie let out a deep breath. Her heart was racing, and she could feel her pulse beating a steady tattoo. She wanted to say something, but needed to recover her equilibrium first. It was as if she were under a magic spell and couldn't quite get out of its grasp.

"I want to see you again, Doc," he said softly. "Soon."

She nodded slightly and her lips parted. "Yes," she barely breathed. "Oh, yes."

After a few moments of staring into one another's eyes, she shook her head and sighed pleasantly, almost wistfully. "I'd better go," she said. "I really do have a big day tomorrow."

"I know," he said, "but I wish you didn't have to. I wish . . . well, I wish you didn't have to leave at all."

She nodded again, knowingly, understanding what he wanted, what they both wanted. She drew herself up and reluctantly relinquished the magic of the moment for the reality of what lay ahead.

"Walk me to the car?" she asked.

"You bet," he said.

They rose simultaneously, and Valerie retrieved her carryall and medical bag. Together they walked out to the Jeep, and she got the keys out of her carryall. She started to open the door, and, from behind her, his arms enfolded her in a tender hug.

She felt as if she could stay in his arms forever, just like that, and be happy, but she had to leave now or she didn't think she ever would. She turned to him and kissed his lips quickly, then turned again to the car.

"I really have to go," she said. "While I still can."

He grinned. "I'm glad you feel that way, too," he said.

She got in the Jeep and started it, then sat looking at him.

"I'll call you, okay?" he asked.

"Yes," she said.

"Tomorrow okay?"

Not soon enough, she thought. "Yes," she replied.

" 'Night, Doc." He touched his fingers to his lips and touched hers with his fingertips.

" 'Night, Wyn," she said.

She put the car in gear, pulled out of the parking area, and turned to drive down the long lane, already eager for tomorrow to come, already hungry for his touch, knowing in her heart of hearts that this was right and true and pure.

Wyn stood watching her taillights disappear down the lane, then began walking up to the house, his mind consumed with Valerie. He could hardly believe the evening that had passed, and felt the urge to shout his joy from the rooftops. But he walked on in silence, looking forward to tomorrow for the first time in many, many months. He couldn't help but grin. He'd never thought he would be able to think of such things again, not in the condition he was in. He'd never thought he would even *want* to think of such things, not after his miserable experience with Arielle.

Valerie Rochelle, he thought. *What an amazing woman.*

Chapter Twenty

There, Noah," Valerie said, giving the elderly husky a firm stroke, "I think you're as good as new." She looked up at Eddie Lowell. "He really is in great shape," she said.

Eddie smiled, his darkly tanned face a mass of leathery wrinkles. "You're like Wonder Woman, Val," he said. "I never would've believed a pacemaker would make such a difference. I didn't think he was going to last out the year, and now he's practically like a young pup again."

"Just like you," Valerie said.

"Oh-ho," he laughed. "I wish! Try telling Jonathan that. I can hardly keep up with him."

She looked at Eddie, somewhat surprised that the forty-something antiques dealer had mentioned his twenty-something boyfriend in what virtually amounted to an intimate manner.

"Maybe that's what keeps you so young, Eddie," she said. "Having a younger partner, I mean. You never seem to age at all."

"Well, you're sweet to say that, Val," he said, "but sometimes I feel like old Noah here did. Maybe a pacemaker would do the trick for me, too."

"I don't think so, Eddie," she quipped. "You'd have to have a heart first."

He laughed at her joke. "You're right," he said, "but I wouldn't be a successful antiques dealer if I did."

Valerie leaned over and gave him a peck on the cheek. "I know your heart's made out of pure gold, and you know I'm crazy about you," she said.

"And I'm crazy about you, Val," he said, beaming. "Are you coming by for that drink tonight?"

"Yes, I am," she said. "Fancy dress, right?"

"Oh, sure," he said. "As fancy as blue jeans or khakis get. Well now, I'd better get out of here and let you do your work."

She handed him Noah's leash. "I'll see you about six-thirty," she said, giving the dog another stroke.

"Good," he said, starting for the door. "Oh, and feel free to bring Teddy." Then he added, "If you want to, that is."

"Thanks, Eddie," Valerie replied, "but I think he's busy tonight, so I'll come alone."

"Okay," he said. "See you later."

She held the door to the examining room open for him and watched as he left. She quickly made some notes on Noah's chart, then left the examining room and went out to the reception desk. "Noah's chart for filing," she told Tami, handing it over the desk to her.

"Thanks, Val," Tami said.

Daphne rounded the corner from her office. "Was

that Mr. Lowell with Noah I saw leaving?" she asked.

"Yes," Valerie said.

"I remember the last time I saw Noah," Daphne said. "He was really sick. He looks like a whole new dog, doesn't he?"

"He sure does," Val replied.

"Mr. Lowell must be so happy," she said. She looked at Val with a quizzical expression. "You seem to be very good friends with him."

"I've known him for a long time," Val replied.

"You're lucky," Daphne said. "You have so many nice friends like him."

"I am lucky to have Eddie for a friend," Val agreed. "I guess you can't have too many, Daphne."

"You know when I went over to his place on an emergency," Daphne went on, "I was amazed by the house. All those paintings and things. It was really beautiful. He must be rich."

"I don't know about that," Val said with a laugh, "but it is beautiful."

The telephone rang and Tami picked up the receiver. "Good morning," she said. "Animal clinic."

Valerie started for her office but turned back when Tami called out to her. "What is it?" she asked.

"I have Mr. Conrad at Stonelair on line two," she said. "He wants to speak to you."

"Thanks," Valerie said, feeling her heart begin to flutter. She had been hoping he'd actually call.

Daphne watched Valerie rush to her office, then turned and went back down the corridor to her own.

Valerie closed the door behind her and took a deep breath. She told herself that her reaction was absurd.

I'm not a teenager, she thought. *What's happening to me?*

She went to her desk and heard Elvis's tail begin to thump against the kneehole's worn wood. "Hey, sweetie," she said, leaning down to give him a few strokes. Elvis gave her hand a lick, then settled back down to his nap. She pushed the button for line two and picked up the receiver.

"Valerie Rochelle," she said.

"Hey there," his deep voice replied. "It's Wyn Conrad. How are you?"

"I'm fine," she replied automatically. "Busy as usual."

"I was just wondering," he began slowly, "if maybe . . . well, if you'd maybe like to have dinner with me?"

His voice sounded hesitant, she thought, almost as if he were a kid asking a girl on a first date.

"I would like that very much," she said.

"Great," he said. "I thought about seven-thirty, eight o'clock. How's that sound to you?"

"Let's make it eight. I have to make a stop on the way."

"Okay," he said. "I'll see you about eight."

"I'll be there."

She hung up, then slumped down in the chair at her desk. *I can't believe this,* she thought, feeling a little bewildered. *Mr. Wyn Conrad has actually asked me to dinner. I wonder if he . . .* No, she told herself, *quit thinking that way. You can't presume anything, Val. Maybe you misread him last night. Maybe he wants to see you to set the record straight. You don't have any idea whatsoever what he has on his mind.*

Still, she couldn't help but smile. He wanted to see her.

The telephone on her desk jangled loudly, and she jumped, so lost in thought was she. She picked it up. "Valerie Rochelle," she said.

"You've got another call from your other male admirer," Tami said. "Teddy this time. On line three."

"Thanks, Tami," she said, slightly annoyed at the secretary's tone. She hung up the receiver for a moment and stared at it. *What does Teddy want?* she wondered. *And what do I tell him if he asks to see me tonight?* Then she remembered Colette's advice: *Tell him the truth, sooner rather than later.* She felt her stomach begin to flutter unpleasantly. *I can't do that now. Not on the telephone,* she told herself, rationalizing. *I'll have to play it by ear.*

She picked up the receiver. "Hi," she said cheerily.

"What took you so long?" Teddy asked in exasperation. "I've been on hold."

"That's a nice greeting, Teddy," she said. "I *am* at work, you know."

"Sorry," he said, backing down. "I didn't mean to sound grumpy."

You sure have sounded grumpy an awful lot lately, she thought. "It's okay," she said.

"I guess I've just been awfully busy, and I've had a really rough week," Teddy went on quickly. "You know what?"

"What?" she asked.

"Some of my clients are being a real pain in the ass," he said, the words tumbling out in a rush. "Interests rates are going up, the market's pretty volatile, the god-damn soothsayers are predicting everything from Armageddon to a fantastic bull market without end, and I'm caught in the middle of it all."

"Lots of nervous clients, I guess," she replied.

"God, Val," he said, "you wouldn't believe it. These are people who've never lost a dime in the market. They've never seen anything but prosperity, and when something goes wrong, bam! It's like they lay everything on me. I'm some kind of monster or something."

"I'm sorry, Teddy," she said. *He sounds so wired,* she thought. She'd never heard him sound quite this troubled before, and she was puzzled. He'd always seemed to take the swings of the market in stride and to handle his clients with ease, laughing off their nervous reactions, never taking anything personally. "It must be very difficult for you."

"Yes," he said. "It is. Anyway, I decided not to go away this weekend. I couldn't take a whole weekend of Ned and Edyth Chamberlain. They're so fucking stuffy, you know?" He couldn't tell her that he was working double-time on her mother's behalf, nor was he going to tell her that he was entertaining her mother and her cousin Jamie.

"I've never met them," she said.

"Oh, I forgot," he replied. "Anyway, so what time are you coming over?"

"Coming over?" she said. "I-I made other plans. You'd told me you weren't going to be here."

"Other plans?" he exclaimed. "What do you mean, 'other plans'?"

Valerie couldn't help but feel irritated. Why was it he expected her to be at his beck and call on weekends? At least those weekends when it was convenient for him to see her? "I meant exactly what I said," she said firmly. "You said you'd come up early because you couldn't be here over the weekend. I made other plans."

"Then change them," he said.

She felt like exploding, but she forced herself to keep her voice even. "No," she said. "I've made other plans, and I don't want to change them. I don't like hurting people's feelings."

"What about my feelings," he said angrily.

"Teddy," she said, with more than a hint of exasperation in her voice, "you weren't going to be here. Remember?"

"And what other people?" he snapped, ignoring her. "Where're you going? What're these big plans of yours?"

"I don't like being cross-examined," she said testily.

She could hear him heave a big sigh. "I-I'm sorry, Val," he said, his voice calmer, though still distressed. "I just really had a bad week, that's all."

"I'm sorry, too," she said, "but I'm not responsible for your bad week, and I don't want it taken out on me."

"Please forgive me," he said. "I didn't mean to be so . . . demanding." He paused for a moment, then said, "I guess it's best this way anyhow. I need to get some sleep. Really rest up from all the pressure."

"It sounds like it," she said. "Maybe an early night would do you some good."

"Maybe so," he agreed. "I haven't been getting much sleep lately. Why don't you come over after you've been . . . well, wherever it is you're going?"

"I don't think so, Teddy," she replied.

"Ah, come on, Val," he said. "Just you and me. Late tonight. It'd be like having a late date."

"No, Teddy," she said. "I told you I've already got plans, and I don't want to change them. Besides, I'm on call this weekend, so I'd better have an early night."

"You're always on call," he groused.

"No, Teddy, I'm not," she said. *He sounds like a petulant child,* she thought. "You know very well that we take turns at the clinic."

"You said you had plans," he argued. "So you can do something else, but you can't see me?"

"Look, Teddy, I don't want to argue about this. You told me you weren't going to be here this weekend, and I made plans. It's as simple as that. Why can't you live with it?"

"Where are you going?" he asked heatedly.

Valerie really didn't want to tell him. He wasn't fond of Eddie and Jonathan, and she didn't want to have to listen to his asinine comments about them. And telling him she was going to have dinner with Wyn Conrad made her feel queasy. He would probably explode. Then it occurred to her, as it had repeatedly over the last few weeks, that Teddy had a right to know what she was doing. After all, they were engaged, for the time being at least.

Once again, she reminded herself of Colette's encouraging words, then drew a deep breath and plunged right in with the truth. "I'm going over to Eddie and Jonathan's for a drink," she said. "Then I'm going to dinner at Stonelair." There, the truth was out.

"You're what!" he exclaimed in astonishment.

"Do I really have to repeat myself, Teddy?"

"I can't believe my ears," he snarled. "I mean, I can believe you're going over to Eddie's. For some reason, you've always liked that old fag, but—"

"Stop right there," she said furiously. "Don't you ever belittle him like that again. You sound like some stupid twelve-year-old boy posturing in the locker room. Eddie's never been anything but nice to you, and he's been a real friend to me."

"Ah, come on, Val," he said, a bit contritely. "You know I didn't mean any harm. I don't mind Eddie."

"That's certainly not the way you sound," she said.

"Yeah, well, what I can't believe is that you'd go out to that weirdo's at Stonelair."

"I don't care what you believe," she snapped, still angry. "I've made plans, and they're not subject to your approval. Neither are the people I choose to see."

There was silence for a moment as Teddy digested her remark. Valerie felt as if all her senses were heightened, and she could feel her skin tingle. *The heat of the argument,* she decided. *And telling Teddy what I actually feel. Funny, now I really* don't *feel so bad. Maybe Colette was right. Maybe I should be honest more often.*

"I don't know what's happening to us, Val," Teddy finally said, his voice soft and hurt.

"I think we'd better continue this conversation another time," she said. "I'm too angry to talk to you."

"Well, I think we'd better continue it now," Teddy countered, "because I'm getting really worried."

"No," Valerie said, "not now." He was already trying to put her on the defensive, and she wasn't going to have it. "We'll talk tomorrow, Teddy."

"Val, I don't think—" he began.

"We'll talk tomorrow," she repeated. "Good-bye, Teddy."

"Val—"

She quietly replaced the receiver in its cradle, then, elbows on the desk, she held her head in her hands. *What have I done?* she thought. For a brief moment, she thought that she should pick up the phone and call Teddy back. *I should apologize and assure him that I'll spend time with him tomorrow.* Then she remembered his remark about Eddie, and her anger returned. *No way,* she decided. *If he's miserable, it's not my fault. He deserves it for being so thoughtless and nasty.*

The telephone on her desk jangled again, and she picked up the receiver. "Yes?" she said.

"Mrs. Sutherland is here with Happy," Annie said, a note of glee in her voice.

"I'll be right out," Val replied. *Just my luck,* she thought. *That vicious old Mrs. Sutherland with her equally vicious little Happy, a yapper and a biter and a whiner. He was just like his mistress.* She rose to her feet and took Happy's chart from the pile of today's patients on her desk. Elvis's tail thumped against the kneehole again. Leaning down, she gave him a few strokes. "Oh, Elvis," she said, "today's got to get better. It can't get worse."

Arielle pulled the chintz drapery panel aside and gazed out the window of the guest house toward the swimming pool and tennis court in the distance. No sign of life about, except for a groundskeeper who was trimming hedges. Her eyes wandered to the mansion itself as she slowly sipped champagne from a crystal flute. "Oh, look, Lolo," she said. "Bibi and Joe are back. I thought I heard the car."

Lolo stepped up behind her and craned his neck over her shoulder toward the window, following her gaze. He spotted the familiar figures he'd often seen in Palm Beach, walking toward the terrace at the rear of their pristine white mansion. "They're not coming out here," he said, stating the obvious.

"No," she said. "The chauffeur said they would expect us for cocktails at six o'clock, so I guess until then we should stay out here. Bibi's a real stickler for protocol."

She felt Lolo's arms encircle her waist and his warm breath on her neck. "Good," he said. "We can have a little fun before dinner."

She let the drapery fall back into place and turned in his arms, facing him. She set her champagne glass down on a table. "Let's move away from the window," she said. "I'd hate for that old dragon lady to see us in our underwear."

"She can't see us from there," he said, nuzzling her neck with his lips.

"She'll probably have binoculars trained on the windows at all hours," Arielle said.

Lolo chuckled. "That's *loco*, Arielle," he said, snapping the waist of her flesh-colored bikini panties.

"Believe me," Arielle retorted, "Bibi's just *loco* enough to do it. She's probably even got this guest house bugged."

Lolo drew back and looked at her with genuine

concern. "Do you really think she would do a thing like that?"

Arielle shrugged. "Who knows?" she replied. "I wouldn't put it past her. I do know that she puts up a good front, acting real prim and proper, but underneath all her stupid old-lady Chanel suits, she's really a horny old cow. Joe probably hasn't been able to get it up in years."

Lolo laughed. "*You're loco*, Arielle," he said, pulling her body up against his, relishing the feel of her silk panties and bra and firm tanned flesh against him.

"Maybe," she said, "but I'm sure not stuck with an old stuffed shirt like Joe Whitman." She pressed her pelvis against his crotch, then brushed her lips lightly across his. "Why don't we have some more champagne?" she said softly.

Lolo kissed her, then loosened his arms from around her. "That's a good idea," he said. "I'll get it." He picked up her glass, then walked over to the elegantly draped table, where his champagne flute sat nearly empty next to the sweating wine cooler.

Arielle padded over to the big sofa, sat down, and drew her legs up onto the floral chintz, watching Lolo pour their drinks. She yawned and stretched her arms. It had been a long day after a very late and raucous night of lovemaking, but she'd managed to nap aboard the Whitman's Gulfstream V. The trip had gone without a hitch, and Larry, the Whitmans' chauffeur, had been at the airport to meet them in Bibi's dark green Rolls Royce Phantom V.

"Mr. and Mrs. Whitman had to go out," Larry had

explained, "and apologize for not being here to greet you. They will expect you at six o'clock for cocktails and then dinner."

When they'd reached Bibi and Joe's monstrous old house in Saratoga, Mildred, the housekeeper, had greeted them and shown them to the guest house, where a bottle of chilled champagne awaited them. The guest house was filled to overflowing with bowls and vases stuffed with beautiful flowers, roses mostly, and a cornucopia of fresh fruit sat in the center of the dining table. The kitchen was well stocked with an assortment of gourmet treats to satisfy any appetite: cheeses, patés, caviar, various cuts of prepared meat and fowl, and mineral water, mixers, sodas, and liquor galore.

Bibi, she reflected, was legendary for her exquisite taste and lavish entertaining, and deservedly so. Too bad Arielle didn't really like her or old Joe, but even the dragon lady and the stuffed shirt couldn't dampen her excitement at being here in Saratoga.

I'm only a stone's throw from Wyn, she thought, *and I can already smell all that lovely money.*

Lolo stood over her, a glass of champagne extended in her direction. She smiled and took it from him. "Thanks, Lolo," she said, moving her legs and patting the sofa with a hand.

He sat down next to her, then lifted her long, slender legs and placed them over his own. "What are you thinking about, my *loco* Arielle?" he asked, running a hand up one of her legs toward her thigh.

"Hmmm," she breathed, taking a sip of the champagne, then setting the crystal flute down on the marble-topped coffee table. She looked at him, smiled mysteriously, and withdrew a cigarillo from the pack on the table.

Lolo reached for her gold cigarette lighter and lit the cigarillo for her, looking into her eyes. Then he took one for himself and lit it. "You're up to something, Arielle," he said. "What is it?"

She took a long draw on her cigarillo. "Ooooh, just an idea," she said teasingly, smoke trailing from her nostrils.

"What?" he asked, running his hand back up her thigh again, his dark eyes searching hers.

"I thought . . . I thought we might pay a call on Wyn," she said. "I mean . . . we're so close and all." She stared at him, her eyes gleaming with mischief.

His hand suddenly stopped moving, and his eyes bored into hers. "You're joking, aren't you?" he said, already knowing that she was deadly serious. "I told you that I would talk to him, man to man, but it's crazy for both of us to try to see him. He'd never see you, so I wouldn't get to him, either."

She had the merest hint of a smile on her lips. "Maybe you're right, but I'm not joking. I've never been more serious."

"But-but what are you thinking?" he stuttered. "What kind of plan do you have? This is really stupid, Arielle. Don't you see?"

Her eyes never left his as she slowly shook her head. "Nooo," she said softly, "I don't. In fact, I think it might be one of the smartest things I've ever done." She languidly tapped her cigarillo in the ashtray.

Lolo became agitated. "Arielle," he said, "what the

hell have you got in mind? You know he doesn't want you there. It's crazy."

"He won't even know we've been there," she said, looking into Lolo's eyes. "If things work out the way I want them to." She smashed her cigarillo out in the ashtray, then reached toward him with her arms. "Come here," she said, sliding one of her legs around his back, the other still across his lap.

He set his champagne down and put out his cigarillo, looking at her anxiously. "I don't know, Arielle," he said slowly, shaking his black curls.

"Come here," she repeated, reaching for him.

He leaned toward her, letting her hook an arm around his neck, her legs scissored around his torso. Her other arm slid down to his crotch, and she eased her hand beneath his jockey shorts, encircling the growing tumescence there. "Kiss me, Lolo," she said. "Kiss me hard."

Teddy sat behind his desk in the office at Apple Hill, his feet propped up on its surface. He finished looking over the paperwork Lydia had left for him and flung it down unceremoniously onto his desk. He heaved an audible sigh of relief. The ups and downs of the last few days had almost gotten the best of him, that and having to be on perfect behavior with Marguerite and Jamie.

He knew that the nose candy had helped fuel the ups and had probably been responsible for the depth of the lows, but, hell, he didn't know how else to keep going. Between running his investment company, satisfying clients, trying to keep Val happy, and making certain that he and Tiffani had time for a little fun on the side—well, it had all begun to wear him down as never before.

But everything's in order now, he told himself grimly. He'd had a handful of investors who'd recently withdrawn all of their money from his investment service—thanks to the volatility in the marketplace—and he'd had to perform a number of intricate and time-consuming maneuvers to make certain that they were all fully recompensed.

Now at least those bastards are all out of my hair, he thought. There was no satisfaction in it for him, however. He'd been controlling a quarter of a billion dollars last week—chump change as far as a lot of high-flying Wall Street guys were concerned, but a tidy sum for him to work with—investing it for a small group of very rich clients. This week he found himself left with less than fifty million dollars, money entrusted to him by those investors who'd stuck with him despite recent losses in the market.

Thank God, Marguerite de la Rochelle and James de Biron hopped on board when they did, he thought for the umpteenth time. *And thank God Dock Wainwright came through with the paperwork and checks overnight.* Between himself, Lydia, and Dock, everything had been set up. He was in full control of Marguerite's stock portfolio now, and had a good chunk of Jamie's to boot. He'd needed all the capital he could get his hands on to repay all those investors who'd abandoned ship. Now he just had to make certain that when the time came, he could show Marguerite and Jamie that their money was not only intact but making a nice hefty profit under his brilliant and watchful eye.

I'll be able to do it, he told himself convincingly. *I've played the market successfully in the past, and I can do it again. I just need the chance to hit the right stock at the right time, and . . . voilà! I'm not only back in business but back in the black. I'll just have to be very careful dealing with Marguerite and Jamie.*

He knew they both appeared on the surface to be unconcerned with money, as if it were something dirty for others to deal with, but he also knew that beneath their sophisticated and aristocratic exteriors, they wouldn't hesitate to sacrifice him to the authorities if they detected the least impropriety on his part.

His thoughts turned to Valerie and the telephone conversation they'd had a little while ago. He considered telling Marguerite what had transpired. He knew that she was capable of instilling in Valerie a sense of duty and responsibility, if not outright fear, and he knew that she was his ally. She would certainly be mad to hear that Valerie had so offhandedly given her fiancé the brush-off.

He reached down and pulled open the bottom right-hand drawer in his desk and picked up the little box he had put there. He set it down on the desk and extracted the plastic bag of white powder and the silver straw. He ignored the mirror and razor blade as he had ever since he reached the country. Instead, he opened the bag, stuck one end of the straw in the powder and the other in his nostril. He inhaled deeply and held his breath for a long moment, then repeated the process with his other nostril. When he finished, he leaned back in his chair, enjoying the enhanced feeling of well-being that the drug rapidly induced.

He looked at the telephone, thinking that he would place that call to Marguerite, then decided to wait and talk to her when she and Jamie came over to sign paperwork. That might prove to be interesting, he thought, because Jamie de Biron was an enigma to him, and he needed to get to know him better. After all, the better he knew him, the better he'd know how to control him.

Whoa! Suddenly he realized the coke had really hit, and he felt almost as if his body had begun to vibrate with life.

I'll try to get hold of Tiffani, he thought. *Make sure we can get together tonight. He was off the hook with Val, so he might as well make the best of his time.*

He dialed her number and waited. After the fourth ring the machine kicked in. *Shit!* he thought. After the message beep, he said, "Hey, babe, it's Teddy. Call me as soon as you get in. Let's party tonight. I've got lots of toys to play with."

Slamming the receiver in its cradle, he frowned. *Where the fuck is she?* he wondered. *First Val, now Tiff. She's probably already out at that local dump of a bar with redneck friends.*

And now I've got to get ready to play host to Marguerite and Jamie, he thought. *Put my best foot forward.* But he knew they wouldn't be here long, probably no more than a couple of hours at the most. Tiffani probably wouldn't get his message until late. That left him at least a couple of hours alone.

Suddenly he decided what he would do with those two hours or so. He laughed aloud, then got to his feet and picked up the box on the desk, tucking it under his arm, grinning from ear to ear. *First I'll take a shower,* he thought, walking toward the office door. *Then change clothes for Marguerite and Jamie. Be my most charming self for them. When they've gone, I'll have a little bite of whatever it is Hattie's left in the kitchen for me. If I feel hungry. Then I'll get busy. I know what'll put the fear of God in Val for sure. And it'll serve her right, too. Serve them all right.*

Chapter Twenty-One

A table for two had been set on the stone terrace just outside the big library. In its center was a small bowl filled with daisies and other colorful wild flowers, and to either side of it, big glass hurricanes held candles that flickered romantically as the night darkened. The table was set with a colorful cotton Provençal cloth and simple pottery dishes with attractive but plain glassware and silver.

The table looked summery and beautiful, Val thought, yet casual and not too precious. Thank heaven it didn't look as if everything had belonged to some long-departed royal or immensely rich robber baron. She appreciated its simplicity all the more because of the grandeur of the house itself. She hadn't known what to expect, of course, but was hoping that the dinner wouldn't be as formal as what one might expect in such a mansion.

She'd been surprised not to be greeted by Santo Ducci, or see him at all. Wyn had answered the door himself, dressed in khakis, a crisp black linen shirt, and

Top-Siders. She'd been doubly surprised when he'd mixed their drinks himself—a vodka and tonic for her, a scotch and water for him—then served the dinner without anyone assisting him, other than Val herself.

In the kitchen, he'd confessed that Gerda, Mrs. Reinhardt, had put together the simple fare: a delectable whole cold poached salmon with a creamy dill sauce; an unusual but delicious potato salad with bits of corn, tarragon, and lobster in it; fresh chilled asparagus in a balsamic vinaigrette; and tomatoes, right out of the garden, topped with a locally made buffalo mozzarella and garden-fresh basil, lightly drizzled with a heavenly tasting cold-pressed extra virgin olive oil.

Wyn had opened a bottle of delicious white burgundy that went perfectly with the meal. "It's an Antonin Rodet Château de Rully, '98," he'd said. "I think it'll go okay. I haven't really familiarized myself with the wine cellar here yet."

"It's delicious," Val had told him after having a taste.

Now she sat sipping at the wine on the candlelit terrace, enjoying the beauty of the late summer night. She was alone, surrounded by darkness, waiting for Wyn while he made the long trek to the kitchen to bring dessert. She'd insisted on helping, but he'd told her to sit still and digest a bit before he came back with the promised dessert: homemade vanilla ice cream with chocolate sauce.

A light breeze ruffled her hair slightly. She'd worn it loose tonight, with a lightweight cream cotton sweater and cream nylon clam-diggers with cream thong sandals, all of it casual but well-cut with a hint of the glamour that Armani knows how to do. Little diamonds glinted in her ears, and a pearl necklace—her paternal grandmother's—hung around her neck. At her wrist was her "dress" watch, a gold Cartier Santos that her father had given her many years before. She seldom wore it, not wanting to subject it to the wear and tear her work would inevitably cause.

When she'd arrived at Eddie and Jonathan's earlier, Colette had been there, and the three of them had all but applauded her appearance, giving her ego a tremendous boost. Their timing couldn't have been better, because her afternoon and early evening hadn't gone well. It was as if the telephone call from Teddy had left her with an unpleasant aftertaste that she hadn't quite been able to overcome, but she'd made an effort to dress for tonight—if not formal, at least elegant and sexy.

Her efforts had paid off, she thought. Eddie, Jonathan, and Colette had practically swooned over her appearance and had immediately demanded to know what the special occasion was. When she'd told them she was going over to Stonelair for dinner, they'd all been intrigued and delighted and had quizzed her without any show of restraint. She'd told them about taking care of the animals at Stonelair and meeting Wyn, and when they'd asked her about his mysterious aloofness, she'd told them that he was recuperating from a polo accident. She didn't go into any detail, however, because she felt that she would be encroaching on Wyn's privacy.

"What about the money?" Jonathan had asked. "Do you think he's really some kind of drug lord or Mafioso or something?"

"That's ridiculous, Jonathan," Colette had snapped, glaring at him. "The man has too much good taste for that sort of thing. He'd never have bought Stonelair otherwise, and he certainly wouldn't have asked our Val to dinner. No, this is bound to be a man of discrimination. Why else would he be interested in Val?"

They'd all laughed at her remark, but Valerie had had to tell them that she knew nothing about the source of his wealth. "All I know is that he apparently lived very grandly in Palm Beach," she'd said, "because I saw a lot of polo pictures in the tack room."

"There!" Colette had exclaimed. "That proves my point. If he were really a gangster, he certainly wouldn't be playing polo in Palm Beach." Then she'd turned to Val and winked at her. "Val, darling," she'd said. "You remember our little conversation about your future? When we discussed Teddy and men in general?"

Valerie had nodded, certain of what was coming next. "Of course I remember it, Colette," she'd replied.

Colette had smiled brightly and knowingly, as if they shared a secret. "I think I already see a touch of the bloom on those lovely cheeks of yours."

Val had blushed, then laughed merrily, but she hadn't disagreed with Colette.

When she'd gotten out of the Jeep at Stonelair's front door, Wyn had opened it himself, before she could even ring the bell.

"Well, well, well," he'd said, looking her up and down. "No blood-smeared lab coat. I almost didn't recognize you."

"You're almost unrecognizable yourself," she'd replied.

"How's that?" he'd asked, looking puzzled.

"You're wearing a smile," she'd said. "I didn't know you had one in your wardrobe."

"*Touché, madame,*" he'd said, bowing slightly. He'd swung the door open wide and walked her to the library, where all four of the dogs and Mina, the cat, had greeted her.

Later, while they were eating, he'd complimented her appearance again, more directly and sincerely, if in a teasing manner. "You really do look beautiful tonight," he'd said, "especially considering how I usually see you."

"If that's a compliment," she said, "I'll accept it, and return it." She looked over at him. "You look better without the big nose and eye bandages. Almost human, in fact."

"*Almost* human?" he'd said.

"Well, maybe I'm stretching things a bit," she'd joked, "but I think I detect a faint resemblance to a human being. The eye patch is much more becoming than that huge bandage, and you look much better. You're cleaning up nicely."

Now, as she reflected about the last couple of hours in his company, she couldn't suppress the smile that came unbidden to her lips.

"Penny for your thoughts," Wyn said, coming through one of the French doors with a tray in his hands.

"Cheap, aren't you?" she said.

He smiled. "You're an expensive woman. How about a quarter?"

"I'll take it," she said. "But . . . oh, I wasn't thinking

about anything really," she went on. "It's just so nice out tonight, and I'm enjoying myself."

"You didn't expect to?" he said, setting the tray down.

"No, it's not that," she said. "I guess I didn't know what to expect, and as it turns out, I don't know when I've had such a good time."

"Do you mean that?" he asked, taking a plate off the tray and putting it in her place.

"Yes," she said, nodding. "I'd almost forgotten what it's like to . . . well, just have a good time without any complications."

He sat down and looked into her eyes. "I feel exactly the same way," he said. "It's been like being let loose from jail for me. In more ways than one. It's not just that you know about my accident and the injuries and all that. It's more than that, Val."

She felt her heart quicken a beat and could feel the heat of her blood rush from her chest up to her face. "I-I think I know what you mean," she said.

He reached over and put one of his hands over hers, where it lay on the table, and held it there tenderly, then gave it a squeeze. She almost shuddered at his touch, so electrifying was it.

"We'd better eat this ice cream before it melts," Wyn said, grinning as he removed his hand.

"It looks yummy," she said, picking up her spoon.

"Gerda makes it," he said, "in one of those electric ice cream machines, and she makes the chocolate sauce, too."

Valerie took the spoon out of her mouth. "This is fantastic," she said, still savoring its taste on her palate.

"I'm glad to see that you have a good appetite," he said. "I like to see that in a woman."

"Maybe so," she said, "but I don't think you'd like to see the results of a woman eating like this all the time."

He laughed. "I guess you're right about that, but I really do like your digging in. My ex, or soon-to-be ex, ate like a bird. And that was when she really let herself live."

Val looked over at him. "Always diet-obsessed?"

He nodded. "Percentage of body fat was a chief topic of conversation in her set, and a pound either way would make her absolutely crazy. But I think the number one topic of conversation was plastic surgeons. Who did the best breasts, the best lipo, the best . . . well, you get the picture." He looked off into the distance, then back at her. "She was crazy anyway," he added.

Valerie hesitated before responding. Ex-wives were dangerous territory, she thought, and despite her natural curiosity, this was definitely not an area of his life that she wanted to pry into. But he did seem to want to talk about her. After all, he'd brought her up.

"What's she really like?" she asked, deciding to venture into the topic. "I know she isn't really crazy or you wouldn't have married her. I mean, bad crazy as opposed to a little bit crazy, which can be good, I think."

"She was always a little bit crazy. Good crazy, as you so aptly put it," he said. "But she started getting a little too crazy for my tastes. She came from a family near West Palm Beach that didn't have much. They weren't poor, but they couldn't afford luxuries. She's very beautiful and sexy and pretty damn smart and saw what Palm Beach had to offer—as opposed to West Palm."

"Upwardly mobile, I take it?" Val said.

"With a vengeance," he replied. "And I actually appreciated that in her. Nothing wrong with wanting to make a better place for yourself in this world, is there?"

"Absolutely not," she agreed, nodding.

"Anyhow," he continued, "she got a job as a secretary in Palm Beach, met an older rich guy from New York with a condo there, and ended up marrying him. Two years later, he had a massive heart attack, and she inherited almost everything."

"Is that when you came into the picture?" Val asked.

"It was around then," he said. "She had some money and started dating, mostly proper-type rich divorced men, then started giving a little money to charities so she'd get invited to their parties. She was also throwing parties at her condo for a wilder set and hanging out in clubs, that kind of thing. I was living pretty much like her. You know, quite the ladies' man, really wild, going from one woman to the next, sowing wild oats left and right. Anyway, some friends of mine introduced us at a party, and I liked her right off the bat. It wasn't just that she was beautiful. She was like a free spirit, you know? Not stuffy and preppy like so many of those rich Palm Beach women. She was sort of a renegade, a breath of fresh air. I found out she'd almost run through nearly every cent of poor old Sydney Goodman's money by the time I met her." He laughed.

"What was she going to do then?" Val asked, genuinely intrigued.

"She didn't have the vaguest idea," he said, shaking his head slightly. "She told me that she was sure something would work out somehow. And if it didn't? She wasn't afraid. Of anything. At least not then."

"That's a gutsy lady all right," Valerie said. "Most women crave security. I guess most everyone does. Money-wise and mate-wise."

"Yes," he agreed, "and her being different was definitely one of the things that attracted me to her. But things began to change after a couple of years of marriage."

"Did familiarity breed contempt?" she asked. "Or am I being nosy?"

"Not at all," he said. "Arielle got used to a lot real fast, if you know what I mean. I loved spoiling her, but then after a while, she just didn't seem to be able to get enough no matter what it was."

"Material girl, huh?" Valerie said with a smile.

"That too with a vengeance," he said. "Plus, I think that while I was off playing polo or taking care of business, she got bored and started to hang out with a party crowd that dabbled in drugs. She stopped going to charity flings and that kind of thing, and spent all of her time with this really wild set. And I mean wild. Mostly bored Eurotrash with lots of cash, and their hangers-on."

"She must not have known what to do with herself," Valerie said. "It sounds like she didn't have any real interests and was bored."

"I guess so," he agreed. "The first year we were

married she traveled with me a lot to polo matches and even went on business trips. She really seemed to enjoy some of the polo trips. There was usually a lot of socializing, big parties, meeting people, and all that. The business trips were a bore for her, I know. I mean, looking at mines and mining equipment isn't much of anybody's idea of a good time. It's a filthy, stinking business. But for a while there, we went everywhere together." He paused and looked over at her. "Then she completely lost interest in me. In every way."

Valerie stared at him for a moment before replying. "You're still hurt, aren't you. I mean by her losing interest in your life . . . and you."

He nodded. "I have to admit that I am, Doc," he said, looking over at her with a tight smile. "She had already starting ignoring me before the accident, but it didn't help that she wouldn't have anything to do with me after the accident. And I do mean anything."

"I see," Valerie said. Obviously, Arielle, who had already lost any affection she might have had for him, couldn't cope with him after the accident. If she was as obsessed with looks as he said, then his injuries would've only made sex with him all the more unendurable.

"Why don't we have a little brandy?" he said, changing the subject.

"Just a smidgen for me," she replied. "I have to drive home tonight. Remember?"

"Yes," he said, "but I was hoping I could get you good and drunk and then keep you here all weekend and take advantage of you." He smiled.

"I'm on call at the clinic," she said, "so I'll have to let you do that some other time."

They both laughed.

"Want to have that drink in the library?" he asked. "The dogs have been so good about not bothering us tonight, I think we should reward them with our company."

"That's fine with me."

He got to his feet and came around to her chair, easing it back for her as she stood. Then he put an arm around her waist and led her into the library.

From their various positions, the dogs bounded to their feet and rushed over for attention as the two of them entered the room. While Wyn went to the drinks table and poured them each a snifter of brandy, Valerie alternated petting the four huge dogs until she'd shown them all an equal amount of affection. They finally returned to their napping spots satisfied and settled down.

"My God," she said, "they're all such pussycats."

"They are with you," he said, "but they're not that way with just anybody."

He brought her the brandy and indicated a seat on one of the big leather Chesterfield couches. "Oh, wait a minute," he said. "On second thought, maybe we'd better not sit there. You'll get dog hair all over your clothes."

"Oh, that's ridiculous, Wyn," she said. "I live in dog hair. Remember?"

"If you're sure," he said.

"I'm sure." She sat down on the couch, and he followed suit, leaving a little distance between them. He slipped off his Top-Siders and put his feet up on the coffee table.

"Make yourself comfy," he said.

"I am," she replied.

"But you've got your shoes on."

"Well, there is that," she said, slipping her sandals off and putting her feet up on the big marble coffee table, too. She wiggled her toes. "Now," she said, "I really am comfy."

"I knew it," he said. "I bet your mother and father could hardly keep shoes on you when you were little."

"That's right," she said, laughing. "And I guess I haven't changed all that much."

"Cheers," he said, holding up his brandy snifter.

"Cheers," she repeated.

They clinked glasses, looking into one another's eyes.

"This is a wonderful room," she said, breaking eye contact and looking around.

"I practically live in this room," he said, "and so do the dogs, as you've noticed. I eat and read and do all my telephoning in here. I even do all of my computer work in here," he said, indicating the laptop on the antique French *bureau plat*.

"What kind of computer work?" she asked.

"Stuff related to the mines mostly," he said. "Keeping track of production, sales, things like that, and of course I'm constantly e-mailing management."

"So you're into mining," she said.

He nodded. "My grandfather started the mines, then left them to my dad. When he died, I took over and started expanding into related areas. Chemicals and stuff. I'd worked there in the summers since I was fifteen anyhow, so I knew quite a bit about the business."

"And your mother?" she asked. "Is your mother still alive?"

He shook his head. "No," he said, "she lived about two years after Dad died. She was so lonely without him. They'd been a real team, you know? She didn't seem to want to live after he died."

"I'm sorry," she said.

"It's okay," he said. "It's been a few years."

"So you're left running everything on your own?"

He nodded. "The last few years I've been able to do nearly everything from home, but I go out west four or five times a year and stay a few days. It puts a face on the boss for the new people, and there's nothing like an up-close and personal inspection to make sure things are under control." He grinned.

"I bet you're a tough boss," she said.

"I am," he said without hesitation. "But I'm also fair, and I reward my employees accordingly. They also know that there's not a job there that I haven't personally done, so they know I'm not just some rich guy living off their labor. I've worked alongside some of them." He paused and looked at her. "That's enough about me," he said. "What about you?"

"What about me?" she said teasingly.

"I bet you had a coming-out party and went to one of the Seven Sisters," he said, "and your father set you up in a nice practice."

She laughed, almost sputtering brandy.

"What's so funny?" he asked.

"Your—your presumptions."

"I'm not wrong, am I?"

She nodded. "Yes and no," she said. "I did have a

coming-out party. That part you got right. But I didn't really get into it. I wasn't part of that scene at all. In fact, I wore a borrowed dress, and I didn't go to a single party but the ball itself."

"You were doing what Mommy and Daddy wanted you to do, I bet," he said.

"Exactly," she said. "It was easier than arguing with them. As for school, I worked my way through Cornell."

"You're kidding," he said, a look of surprise on his face.

"No," she replied. "I worked in a bookstore, worked as a waitress, a dog walker, baby-sat, house-sat, all kinds of things. And I borrowed money. Lots of money. Student loans. Which I am still paying off." She laughed, and he laughed with her. "Sometimes I think I'll be in debt the rest of my life."

"Could have fooled me," he said. "You had a coming-out and all that, but your parents didn't pay your way through school?"

"No," she said. "My mother insisted on my going to a finishing school in Switzerland or maybe doing literature or French at one of the Seven Sisters. But I wouldn't do it. I wanted to be a veterinarian. So she said I'd have to pay for it myself."

"You're kidding," he said.

"Nope," she said, shaking her head. "But I don't think she actually thought I'd go off on my own like that, and I think she was just waiting for me to come running home."

He smiled. "Well, good for you," he said. "That shows a lot of spunk."

She shrugged. "I just knew what I wanted," she said, "and I was going to get it come hell or high water."

"What do your parents think about it now?" he asked.

"My father died before I went to college," she replied. "My mother . . . well, she still doesn't like it. She has this Old World idea that I should be married to someone from the same background and living the life of leisure. You know, like one of the ladies who lunch in New York. The charity circuit and all that. The way she lived until my father died."

"You'd wither up and die in that atmosphere," he said unhesitatingly.

She nodded. "I know," she said, "but try telling my mother that."

"It seems to me she ought to be really proud of you," he said. "I would be. I *am.*"

Valerie laughed. "For what?" she asked.

"I've watched you in action," he said, "and I think you're a top-notch vet. And person."

Valerie felt herself blush again. "Thanks," she said. "I appreciate that."

"Now," he said, "tell me about whoever it is that's lucky enough to be engaged to you."

"Wha—?" She stared at him dumbstruck, unable to finish her sentence.

Slowly, somewhat reluctantly, the shadowy figure lowered the binoculars and let them hang loose on their neck strap. Fingers quickly rubbed tired eyes.

Watching them had been almost mesmerizing, as if observing some sort of forbidden ritual or an especially tantalizing pornographic video, not that there had been anything in the least bit lewd or lurid in their behavior. No, they had behaved in an exemplary fashion.

It's the invasion of privacy. That's why it feels so strange. Invading their privacy, watching them on their own turf, without their knowing anything about it. It's a real kick, though. A real sick kick.

Watching even the most mundane of activities could be fascinating if observed in this way, the interloper supposed, but that was not what this was about. No, this had a purpose, and an important one at that. In fact, seeing them together had driven home the fact that the situation held a lot more potential for danger than previously thought.

The way they'd chatted during dinner, all cozy and relaxed and laughing, with some serious-looking moments thrown in for good measure. The way he'd held her chair for her to sit down, then the way he'd slid it back for her to get up. The way he'd put a hand over one of hers during dinner, then the way he'd put an arm around her waist when they went inside together.

Now they sat together on the couch, their bare feet propped up on the coffee table like they were sweethearts, their bodies close together, nearly touching while they chatted on and on into the night.

Imagine their talk! Earnestly telling one another all about their lives, their histories, past and present, getting to know one another—all the ridiculous flotsam and jetsam about where they came from and who they were—before they made that inevitable leap into the old sack and onto each other's bodies.

It was enough to make you puke.

Spitting on the ground as if to expel a bad taste, then looking at the glow-in-the-dark watch, the figure in the shadows saw that it was a little after eleven. It was getting late, and there was work to do. It was getting to be time to do it.

"Who-who told you about that?" she finally stuttered, her mind spinning with a million questions at once.

"Nobody," he said, looking at her with a superior expression.

"What do you mean nobody?" she asked. "How could you possibly know about that?"

"It's simple," he said, breaking into a laugh.

Damn him, she thought. *He's playing with me and enjoying it.* "Tell me," she said. "What's so simple?"

"Remember the first time you came out here?" he asked.

She nodded. "Of course, I do," she replied. "Storm Warning had colic. Why?"

"I saw you that night," he said, suddenly somewhat sheepish. "I was watching you out in the stable. In the dark, so you couldn't see me."

"I see," she said with a nod, remembering the eerie sensation she'd had that night of being watched.

"I couldn't help but notice that you were wearing a real humdinger of a ring," he went on. "It practically lit up the stall when the lantern light hit it. And it sure did look like an engagement ring, at least to me, Doc."

She swallowed. It was true, she thought. That was the night that she had accepted the ring from Teddy, and she'd been wearing it when she came over to see about the horse. It was so new that she'd forgotten she was wearing it when she'd ministered to Storm Warning. Otherwise, she'd have taken it off to keep from getting it dirty.

She gazed over at him and nodded. "Guilty as charged," she said, smiling tightly.

"So you are engaged," he said, the look on his face undeniably one of disappointment.

"You . . . might say that," she replied.

"What's that supposed to mean?" he asked. "Maybe you are, maybe you aren't?"

Was she imagining it, or did she detect a hint of hope in his voice? "Well . . ." She looked up at the ceiling and shrugged. "Where do I begin?"

"The beginning's a good place, so they say," he replied, reaching over and taking her hand.

She looked down at his hand in hers and realized that it felt natural, comfortable . . . and wonderful. She looked back up at him. "I've been going with the same guy for a long time," she said. "Since college. Everybody's always expected us to get married sooner or later. Including me." She sighed heavily, then continued. "Anyhow, to make a long story short, he gave me the ring that night. The night I came over to see about Storm Warning."

His eyes were glued to hers. "But I haven't seen you wear it since then," he said.

"You're . . . you're awfully observant," she said with a short laugh.

"I'm awfully interested," he said, smiling.

She was silent for a moment, and he prodded her with another question.

"So are you still engaged or what?" he asked. "You don't seem like an engaged woman to me."

She shrugged again, then said, "I guess you could say that officially we're still engaged."

"Officially," he repeated.

She nodded.

"In other words," he said, "you haven't . . ." His words trailed off into silence.

"In other words," she said, supplying words for him, "I haven't told him that I don't want to marry him."

"Aha," he said softly, a smile on his lips. "This is getting very interesting." He paused, then said, "So when are you going to tell him that it's a no-go situation?"

"I don't know," Valerie groaned. "It's . . . it's so difficult to do, and I'm such a chicken that I keep putting it off. But I know that I've got to do it sooner or later."

"Do it sooner," he said.

She looked at him with widened eyes. "What-what are you saying?"

"You heard me," he said. "And I think you know exactly what I mean."

"You . . ." She couldn't bring herself to express what she thought he might mean.

"I want you free," he said. "For me."

Valerie's body jerked, as if she'd been shocked by a bolt of electricity. She felt her heart begin to pump violently, and a pulse beat hard against her eardrum. She couldn't quite catch her breath, and she didn't trust herself to speak. It was a moment of truth.

He's in love with me, she realized, *and I am in love with him.*

Before she could respond, he reached toward her and pulled her to him. She acquiesced, easing into the warmth of his arms happily, as if she were going home to a place she belonged. He kissed her, and she felt a thrill rush through her body, even as her hands felt the soft naturalness of his dark hair and the alien scratchiness of the gauze bandages that were wrapped around part of it.

To think that anyone could ever be afraid of this man, she thought. *To think that he has sparked dark rumors as no one else around here ever has. And to think that he loves me.*

She kissed him passionately, forgetting all else, giving herself up to this moment. It was an unforgettable moment in time, occupying some unique and magical realm all its own.

When he finally drew back, he smiled at her and his eyes searched hers for any indication of what she was thinking and feeling. She returned his smile unhesitatingly, then whispered to him, "It'll definitely be sooner than later."

Chapter Twenty-Two

Valerie rolled over in bed and glanced at the clock on the bedside table. *Six-thirty! What the hell?* she wondered. The telephone had been ringing relentlessly, and she'd tried to no avail to block out its awful early morning cacophony in her tender ears. Then suddenly she remembered she was on call at the clinic, and she quickly reached over, grabbing the receiver.

"Hello?" she said, trying to clear the sleep from her voice.

"Valerie?" The cultured voice was clipped, imperious, and demanding all at once, immediately putting her on alert.

"Mother?" she asked. "What-what is it? Is something wrong?"

"Wrong?" Marguerite de la Rochelle repeated. "Certainly not. Not with me at least."

"Oh," Valerie said. "It's just so early . . . I thought maybe . . . well, I didn't know. You don't usually call this early on a weekend morning."

"I want you to come to breakfast," Marguerite said. It was an order, not a request.

"Breakfast?" Valerie said. "But . . . I-I've really got a lot to do around the house, and—"

"Breakfast will be served promptly at nine o'clock," Marguerite interjected, "and I want you here. There are some things we need to discuss. Your cousin Jamie is here, as you know, and you've made no effort to see him."

"I haven't been avoiding Jamie at all," she said in self-defense. "I was planning on having him over or coming out there to see him. You know I've been busy at the clinic, Mother, and I just haven't got around to it yet."

"No, indeed, you have not," Marguerite said. "You have no time for family, do you, Valerie? So this morning is ideal, isn't it? This *is* the weekend, and you're not working, so we can have a lovely breakfast."

"I'm on call at the clinic," Valerie said, "so I—"

"Damn that clinic!" Marguerite exclaimed angrily. "I think you can spare the time for breakfast with your mother and your cousin. Some sick dog will simply have to wait. Nine o'clock!"

Before Valerie could respond, there was a loud and resounding bang in her ear as her mother hung up on her. She looked at the receiver in her hand for a moment, then put it down. She sighed, wondering what on earth had brought this on. Then suddenly she began to laugh aloud.

Elvis, who was spread out on the floor at the foot of the bed, began to wag his tail furiously, excited by the sound of her laughter. She looked down at him, the laughter still rising in her throat, shaking her body and lifting her spirits. "Oh, Elvis," she said when she could finally speak, "she is not going to make me upset today. Nothing could upset me today." She hugged herself with her arms, thrilled with the memory of last night. Of Wyn Conrad.

Elvis looked up at her with what she was certain was a bright smile on his face, his tail still thumping against the floor.

She slid her legs over the side of the bed and rose to her feet, stretching her arms and back and shoulders, lifting herself up on her toes, reaching toward the ceiling. "No, siree, Elvis," she said. "Marguerite de la Rochelle is not going to get my goat today, no matter what."

She dashed into the bathroom, performed her morning ablutions, and padded into the kitchen on bare feet, still in the huge T-shirt she had worn in place of pajamas, Elvis trailing along behind her. She quickly filled his water bowl and fed him his breakfast—the usual dry food with a little of the tuna fish he loved mixed in—then she ground beans and got the coffeemaker going. She let Elvis out when he was finished, then rushed back into the bathroom and quickly showered. Afterward, wrapped in a bathrobe, she poured herself a mug of coffee and wandered out onto the screened-in porch to drink it.

The morning promised to be a beautiful one, and she regretted that she wouldn't be spending it out in the garden, puttering around, prettifying here and there.

She sipped her coffee, wishing that Colette would come tiptoeing into the garden with Hayden so that they could have a good gossip. She could hardly wait to tell her what had happened last night, but she would have to put it off until later in the day. It was too early to call Colette now. She finished her coffee and went back inside. She peered at the kitchen clock. Nearly eight o'clock already. She'd better start getting ready to face breakfast with Jamie and her mother.

She went back into the bathroom and put on a touch of mascara and eyeliner, then daubed lightly at her cheeks with the merest hint of blusher. Next, she carefully applied a little lipstick, a gingery color that she liked with her strawberry blond hair and green eyes. Finally, she brushed at her hair vigorously and then let it fall naturally into place. She stood back and examined herself in the mirror.

Not half bad, she thought, even though she knew that no matter what she did it wouldn't be enough to satisfy her mother. *No,* she thought, *Mother will manage to find fault somehow or other, and she'll let me know about it.* She smiled at her reflection.

Well, this morning, Marguerite, your criticism will fall on deaf ears, she told herself. *Because nothing, absolutely nothing, is going to take the shine off my day.* Then she remembered perfume and quickly spritzed herself with some of the Femme on the vanity.

Rushing back into her bedroom, she shrugged out of her bathrobe, slipped on her bra and panties, and rummaged in her closet. *Where the devil is my green silk tee?* she wondered. She liked it because it was a close match to her eyes. She opened and closed several dresser drawers, thinking that she'd folded it and put it in one of them. No luck.

She went back to the closet and rummaged some more. Still no luck. *Oh, well,* she thought, *just find something and put it on.* She grabbed a navy blue short-sleeved tee, silk like the green one, and quickly put it on, then donned a pair of cream clam-diggers almost identical to the ones she'd worn last night. She slipped into her cream thong sandals and went back out to the kitchen, where she grabbed her shoulder bag. *Ready,* she thought. *All except for Elvis.*

She went out to the screened-in porch and called to him, and he came prancing toward her from some-where down near the pond. She opened the door and let him in. "Elvis," she said, "I'm going out to see Mother so I'm leaving you here." She leaned down and gave him several strokes. "I'm sorry to do this to you, but you and Mother both will like it a lot better this way."

She locked the porch door and left the kitchen one open for him. That way he could enjoy the porch or stay in the house, whichever he wanted. She glanced out toward the garden longingly, then turned and headed to the front door. *I really don't want to do this, but nothing can wipe the smile off my face today.*

Twenty minutes later, she pulled into the parking area behind her mother's house, and her face immedi-ately fell.

Teddy's silver Jaguar.

Oh, no, she thought. *Why didn't she tell me? And what is he doing here this morning anyway?* But it didn't take an Einstein to figure out exactly why Teddy was here. Marguerite had asked him, of course, and

most likely she'd arranged this breakfast *after* Teddy
and her mother had had a little talk last night about her
unwillingness to cancel her plans to be with him.

It would be just like Teddy to have called Mother,
she thought. *Trying to get her help to keep me in line.
Well, it's not going to work, folks.*

She stepped into the screened-in porch, where she
noticed the table had been set for breakfast, then went
on into the kitchen. Effie was bent over the oven door,
sliding out a pan of croissants. When she heard Valerie,
she turned around and smiled widely.

"I'm so glad to see you," she said, putting the pan
down on the center island.

Valerie gave her a kiss and a hug. "You look great,
Effie."

"You don't have to flatter me," the old woman
replied, "but I'm glad you do." She stared at Valerie for
a moment, then her eyes narrowed into slits. "You!"
she said, pointing a finger at her. "You're the one who
looks great, Val. You're glowing from head to toe."

Valerie smiled. "Do you really think so?"

"You know you are," Effie said. She looked at
Valerie with an expression of curiosity. "Tell Effie what
you've been up to," she said. "Because I know that
look, and it means something awful good's going on."

"Oh, Effie," Valerie replied, "I don't know what
you're talking about."

"Come on," the old woman said, cajoling her. "You
can tell me, young lady."

Valerie leaned down and kissed her cheek again. "I'll
tell you all about it later on," she said. "When you and
I can have some privacy."

"Promise?" Effie said, looking at her with widened eyes.

"Promise," Valerie answered.

Effie beamed. "I knew it!" she said. "I just knew it!"

"Where's Mother?" Valerie asked.

"She and the boys are out at the old swimming pool," she said. "I'm surprised you didn't see them."

"The swimming pool?" Valerie said. "What in the world are they doing out there?"

Effie shrugged. "Who knows?" she replied. "Since that cousin of yours has been here, he and your mother've been whispering around like a couple of conspirators. Like they were planning a murder. And they don't tell me anything."

Valerie frowned, then relaxed her features. "Well, it's probably nothing, Effie," she said. "They're probably just talking about old family secrets or something. Skeletons in the ancestral closet, that sort of thing."

"Humpf!" Effie said. "That wouldn't be anything new to me."

They heard the sound of approaching voices and turned toward the door. "We'll talk later," Valerie said, then walked out to the porch to greet everyone.

Her mother looked at her, her features set in a mask of amiability that didn't fool Valerie for a second. "Good morning, dear," she said, holding her cheek up for a kiss.

"Good morning," Valerie said, kissing the proffered cheek. "And Jamie! It's so good to see you."

Jamie hugged her and air-kissed each cheek in the European fashion. "You look great," he said.

"You look terrific yourself," she replied. "I see

you've been working out a lot. I think the South of France agrees with you."

She felt Teddy's arm slide across her shoulder. "Good morning," he said, kissing her cheek.

"Good morning, Teddy," she said without looking at him.

Effie appeared from the kitchen, laden with a tray on which sat a pot of fresh coffee, surrounded by baskets and platters of food.

"Oh, I see Effie's got everything ready," Marguerite said. "Let's sit, shall we?"

Jamie held her chair for her, and Marguerite took her place at the head of the table, while Teddy held Valerie's chair for her. She sat down, feeling a slight sense of dread despite pumping herself up before arriving here.

Effie set the tray down and put out the food, then poured coffee for everyone. There were scrambled eggs, bacon and sausage, croissants and biscuits, fruit, and various condiments. Marguerite began helping herself, then passed the food around, and everyone began eating with gusto.

"This is so good," Valerie enthused. "It's been a while since I've had one of Effie's great breakfasts."

"You should try it more often, dear," Marguerite said, looking at her daughter pointedly. "Effie makes breakfast every morning, as you know."

Teddy laughed. "I bet Val has more food in the house for Elvis than she does for herself."

Valerie felt her face flush, but she decided not to say anything. *Let them think what they will. Nothing anybody can say or do today is going to hurt me,* she reminded herself.

"Marguerite has always known how to do everything perfectly," Jamie offered. "Whether for man or beast."

Breakfast continued with small talk centered primarily on the garden and then the swimming pool, which Valerie discovered her mother had for some reason decided to completely remodel. Even though she was curious about this turn of events, she didn't ask any questions and contributed very little in the way of talk, deciding to listen and then make as quick an exit as possible. Suddenly, however, she became the center of attention.

"Val, dear," her mother said in what Valerie recognized as her most condescending tone of voice, "I'm so glad you could come this morning. I think it's high time we discussed your wedding. Your cousin Jamie and Teddy and I have discussed it at length, and we've decided that it should be as soon as possible. You won't have to do a thing. We'll take care of everything for you."

Valerie listened to her mother with disbelieving ears. Yet she knew that there was nothing wrong with her hearing, and she also knew that her mother meant every single word she was saying. She started to interrupt more than once, but restrained herself, deciding to hear her out, for the time being at least.

"You know," Marguerite went on, "you and Teddy have been seeing each other for years now, living together for all practical purposes, so we think it's time you finally made it official. I'm certain that if your father were alive, he would feel the same way. Neither of us ever really approved of young people living together before marriage, but we always knew that you and Teddy would eventually marry." She looked at Valerie questioningly. She seemed genuinely surprised by her daughter's continued silence.

"I see," Valerie finally offered in a neutral voice, taking a sip of her coffee.

"Oh, good. I'm glad you do," Marguerite continued. "We've also decided that a big church affair and reception should be dispensed with at this point. A waste of time and money, really, and you both have such busy lives. Teddy with his career, and you with your little job. So unnecessary, don't you agree?" She looked at her daughter with lifted brows.

"Absolutely," Valerie answered.

"Wonderful," Marguerite said, clapping her hands together lightly. "We'll have an intimate family ceremony here at home as soon as possible. Effie can make a nice wedding luncheon or something. It's so fortunate that your cousin Jamie is here for it. He can give you away, don't you think?"

Valerie knew that she couldn't listen to much more of her mother's talk without exploding. Her mind was already reeling with the appropriate obscenities, but she didn't really want to use them. That these people would presume to plan her life for her was enraging, but that it should all be done behind her back was adding insult to injury.

Who or what do they think I am? she asked herself. *Some pawn in a chess game they're playing? Have I always been so . . . so spineless to their demands that they think they can actually railroad me into this marriage?*

Marguerite was staring at her, her emerald eyes glittering intensely, a smile on her lips, waiting for the expected response from her daughter. After a moment, Valerie noticed, she actually began to tap perfectly manicured fingernails against the tablecloth in her impatience. Then she saw that both Teddy and Jamie were watching her as well.

Like evil blond twins, she thought. *Only Jamie's more built-up and has shorter hair.*

Finally, she set her coffee cup down on the table and took a deep breath. She looked directly into her mother's eyes. "There will be no wedding, Mother," she said quietly but forcefully.

"Don't be absurd," Marguerite replied, laughing lightly. It was as if she'd heard the words but gave them no credence. She looked at Teddy and Jamie and shrugged eloquently.

"I'm not being absurd, Mother," Valerie said.

"What on earth can you mean?" Marguerite asked, the laughter gone from her voice now.

"Just what I said," Valerie replied. "There will be no wedding. Because I'm not getting married."

"Val, dear, don't—" her mother began.

"I'm sorry to have to say this in front of other people, Teddy," Valerie said, turning to look at him, "but I'm not going to marry you."

For a moment, there was a stunned silence around the table as the words actually sank in. Valerie noticed Effie in the doorway to the kitchen, a smile on her lips. Then Jamie broke the silence with a bark of a laugh.

"Oh, Val," he said, "you were always so . . . so different. I just love it. You're such a jokester."

"I'm *not* joking, Jamie," she said, turning her gaze on him.

"Val, I think we should discuss this in private," Teddy said, reaching for her hand.

She brushed his hand away. "There's nothing to discuss," she said softly.

She reached for her carryall on the floor beside her and rummaged around inside it for a minute, finally extracting the black box stamped *Bvlgari*. She put it down on the table and slid it across the tablecloth toward Teddy.

"I hadn't planned on doing it this way, Teddy," she said, "but I don't have much choice, do I? You've planned all of this without consulting me, and I'm left with little choice but to return your ring and call it off before you plan anything else behind my back."

"But we—" Teddy began, his voice angry and bewildered at once.

"You ungrateful child!" Marguerite exclaimed, interrupting Teddy, her voice quavering with rage. "How dare you go against my wishes! And what a terrible lack of manners! I can't believe you're my daughter! My own flesh and blood! To do such a thing to such a wonderful young man without taking him aside for privacy."

"Don't preach to me about manners," Valerie said in a barely controlled anger. "You and Teddy didn't have the decency to take *me* aside to discuss my wedding with me, did you, Mother? No! You invited me over here, thinking that your plans—and Teddy's—were a *fait accompli*. That I would do anything you asked me to."

Marguerite stared at Valerie as if she thought her daughter had gone mad.

"Well, surprise, surprise," Valerie said, scooting her chair back and rising to her feet. "I'm not doing what you want this time!" She reached down for her bag and slung it across her shoulder. Turning to Teddy, she said, "I really didn't want it to end in such a shabby way, Teddy, and for that I'm truly sorry. But your plotting behind my back was a little bit shabby, too, you must admit." She looked at Jamie and her mother. "Now, if you'll all please excuse me, I'll be going."

She walked to the door, but when she reached it, a voice stopped her.

"Val, dear?" her mother said.

"Yes?" she replied without turning around.

"The two of us will discuss this later."

"No, Mother," Valerie responded, turning to face her mother, her voice full of the determination she felt, "we will not discuss this later. Or ever again, for that matter."

She opened the door and hurriedly walked to her Jeep. She got in the car, fired up the engine, and pulled out of the parking area, heading down the long drive that led away from her mother's stately home atop the hill.

By the time she reached the highway, her eyes were nearly blinded by tears. Tears of shame and humiliation. Tears of relief. But most of all, tears of joy.

She opened the front door, and Elvis virtually danced before her, his toenails clicking on the entrance hall's wooden floor. "Oh, Elvis," she said, "I'm so glad to see you." She went down on her knees and hugged him. "You're so lucky you weren't with me, but now we can start the whole day over again. It can only get better, old boy."

She walked back to the kitchen, Elvis following her. She dropped her carryall on the center island and looked at the clock. A little after ten. She had a powerful urge to call Wyn at once to tell him the news, but she decided she wanted to calm down a bit first and digest the turn of events herself. She still felt unnerved from the scene at her mother's, and she didn't want to come across to Wyn as some sort of hysterical basket case.

Maybe I'll call Colette, she thought, *and we can have a cup of coffee and talk. I need to gather my wits about me, and that should do the trick.*

She started to pick up the telephone, and it rang just as she reached for it. *Maybe it's Wyn,* she thought excitedly. She grabbed the receiver.

"Hello," she said.

"Val, it's-it's Eddie," her old friend said in a strangely choked voice.

"Hi, Eddie. What is it?" she said, her antennae on full alert. "You don't sound like yourself." He was definitely upset about something.

"It's . . . it's Noah." He managed to get the words out before his voice collapsed into heart-wrenching sobs.

"Eddie, listen to me," Valerie said. "Try to tell me what the problem is."

"He-he-he's . . . d-d-dead," Eddie sobbed.

Dead? But that isn't possible, she thought. *He checked out perfectly okay only a few days ago.*

"Please, Eddie," she said, "tell me exactly what's going on."

Eddie took a few breaths and managed to control his sobs. "I let him out to do his business about ten or ten-thirty last night," he said, "and I left one of the French doors in the back open for him like I always do. This morning he wasn't in his bed like he usually is, so I thought he was outside. I went out and called him and called him. When he didn't come, Jonathan and I went out looking for him. I thought maybe he'd cornered a chipmunk or something and just wasn't paying any attention."

His voice choked up again, and Valerie waited patiently while he calmed down. "We-we found him down near the creek," Eddie continued. "Dead."

"You're sure he's not just injured, Eddie?" she asked.

"He's been murdered!" Eddie cried. "Somebody deliberately killed him!"

"Murdered?" she asked incredulously.

"I'm positive," he declared, indignant. "Somebody murdered Noah!"

"I'm coming straight over," she said.

"Oh, would you, Val?" he said, weepy again.

"I'll be there in five minutes," she said. She hung up the receiver and grabbed her carryall, then headed to the front door.

"I'll be back soon, Elvis," she said, leaning down and giving him a few fast strokes. "You guard the house."

She dashed out to the Jeep and hopped in, heading to Eddie's as quickly as possible.

Eddie and Jonathan were both standing outside their beautifully restored Greek Revival house waiting for her when she arrived. They had obviously been crying, their red and swollen eyes testament to their grief. She hugged them both, her heart aching for them, then immediately got down to business.

"Okay," she said. "Show me."

"It's this way," Jonathan said, pointing down toward the creek that bordered the property. "You want to wait here, Eddie?" he asked. "I can take Val."

"Oh, no," Eddie said. "I'm coming, too."

They walked through the lushly planted garden and then through the parklike grounds toward the rocky creek, Jonathan leading the way, Val taking Eddie's hand in hers.

"We didn't move him," Eddie said, "because I wanted you to see him first, Val. I don't know whether to call the police or what."

"We'll have a look," she said.

"From a distance, he looks like he's spread out just like he's asleep," Eddie told her, "and when I saw him like that, that's what I tried to tell myself. That he was just sleeping. But when I got closer to him, I could see that he definitely wasn't asleep."

They neared the creek, and Jonathan came to a standstill ahead of them. Val could see his shoulders begin to shake and a hand go up to his mouth. She and Eddie drew up to his side.

Noah certainly didn't look asleep, she thought. He

looked very dead—and as if he'd died in terrible agony. Eddie really had been trying to fool himself at first. The handsome dog was on his back, his forelegs stiffly drawn back and slightly curled. His eyes looked huge, and his mouth was drawn back in a terrible rictus of death.

She went down on both knees and started to examine his body, but her eyes were drawn to a hideous, fly-infested, bloody-looking mass on the ground near Noah.

A chunk of meat, she thought, bile rising in her throat. *It must have been a roast or something.* Her eyes began to tear, but she quickly wiped them and tried to focus on Noah's lifeless body. She examined him, noticing that his eyes were widely dilated. *Poison, probably,* she thought. She turned to Jonathan.

"Have you got a freezer bag or any kind of plastic bag I could use?"

"Sure," he said. "I'll go get it."

"Thanks, Jonathan," she said.

"I'll be right back," he said, and he dashed off toward the house.

"He's been poisoned, hasn't he?" Eddie asked.

She stood back up and nodded. "Yes, Eddie," she said. "It certainly looks that way."

"Val, look at this," Eddie said. "The invisible fencing runs just along here." He was drawing a line along the property with an outstretched finger, then pointed to the bridge that crossed the big creek bordering his property. "Whoever did it probably came down the path from the bridge, then walked along the creek, and threw the meat over the invisible fencing to this side."

He looked at her, studying her face to see what she thought of this scenario.

Valerie nodded. "It makes sense, Eddie," she said.

"Noah never crossed the invisible fencing, or at least he hadn't for years," Eddie said. "Two or three shocks when he was younger, and he stayed inside it."

"So somebody would've had to toss the meat over here to this side of the fencing to get him to eat it," Valerie said. "But who would do a thing like that? And why?"

Eddie stared into her eyes. "The most important question is, who would've done it that also knew where the fencing ran?"

Val gazed at him with an expression of curiosity. "Of course, whoever threw the meat to Noah didn't necessarily know about the fence at all. But if what you're saying is true, Eddie, it would probably be somebody who knows you pretty well."

"Exactly," he said, nodding his head.

"Do you have somebody in mind?" she asked. "Is there anybody you can think of that didn't like Noah for some reason? Or . . . you?"

Eddie looked at the ground. "I keep asking myself the same thing, Val," he replied, "but I keep coming up with zilch. Some of the local guys park up near the bridge and come down here to fish, and Noah would sometimes bark at them. But he always stayed on this side of the invisible fencing. He never bit anybody or anything." He shrugged. "I just don't know, Val," he said. "Nobody ever complained to me or anything, and I can't think of anybody who has a grudge against me."

Jonathan returned with a large freezer bag. "Will this do, Val?" he asked.

"Perfect," she said. She took the plastic bag from him, then went back down on her knees. She took several Kleenex out of her carryall, then picked up the chunk of meat with them and put it in the bag, along with the Kleenex. She fingered the Ziploc bag shut and rose to her feet.

"I'll have the lab analyze this," she said, "but I'm pretty sure we all know that there's some kind of poison in the meat." She looked at them. "I'm just so sorry," she added.

"Thanks for coming over, Val," Eddie said.

"You'll let us know what they find out?" Jonathan asked.

"Yes," she said. "I'll call you as soon as I find out anything. I'll put a rush on it, and it'll be sometime this coming week. In the meantime, what do you want to do about Noah?"

"I don't know if there's a law against it or not," Eddie said, "and I don't give a damn if there is. We're going to bury him here on the property. Down near the gazebo."

"I can help you," Val offered.

"No, Val," Jonathan said. "That's okay. We can do it."

"I'll be glad to help," she said.

"No, you've done enough," Eddie said. "Jonathan and I'll do it."

"Do you want to call the police?" she asked. "I can wait for them to come."

"I don't think so," Eddie said, a defeated sound in his voice. "We don't have a thing to go on, do we?"

"Just the fact that he was probably poisoned," she said. "And I'll know with what in a few days."

"I don't think they'll be able to accomplish anything," Eddie said. "I can't imagine who would do anything like this, so I couldn't be any help to them."

"Have you thought of anybody, Jonathan?" she asked. "Or any reason?"

"No," he said. "I can't think of anybody. Maybe not everybody's crazy about us, but I can't think of anybody who actually hates us this much. I think it's got to be some kind of nutcase. That's all I can figure."

"I guess you're right," she agreed. "It's just so hard to imagine. Anyway, I'll drop this by the clinic, but I'll be back home in a hour or so at the most. If you need anything, anything at all, let me know."

"Thanks, Val," Eddie said. "You're a champ." He kissed her cheek, and they hugged again.

She hugged Jonathan next. "I'll get on my way," she said.

"We'll walk you to the car," Eddie offered.

"No," she said, turning to leave. "That's okay. You two do what you have to do. I'm fine."

She walked through the grounds, on through the verdant garden, and then into the courtyard parking area. *I wish I really was fine,* she thought, shaking her head. But something about Noah's death—Noah's *murder,* she reminded herself—disturbed her deeply. Something she couldn't put her finger on.

Who on earth would do such a thing? she asked herself. *Perhaps Jonathan was right. Maybe it was some nutcase. A random act of violence. But why go to so much trouble? Buying the poison and the meat;*

*parking at a distance so as not to be seen or heard;
taking the path down from the bridge along the creek
in the darkness of night? And what about the invisible
fencing, if that was actually a factor? Some nutcase
knew about that?*

She got in the car and started it, headed to the clinic
to put the meat-filled bag in the freezer there. A shudder went up her spine. *This is so malicious,* she
thought. *Why would anyone deliberately kill a dog?*

Chapter Twenty-Three

"Are you sure you'd rather not have dinner with us?" Bibi Whitman asked. "It's not a large party, just twenty or so." She took a sip of her vodka martini, then set it down on the table next to the white wicker chair on which she was perched. She sat erectly, one leg crossed carefully over the other, one low-heeled spectator pump planted firmly on the stone terrace.

"You're very kind, Bibi," Lolo said, "but I think after I get out of this polo gear and get cleaned up, we'll take a nap and go out for a hamburger or something. Make it an early night."

"Well, it's no wonder," she said, looking at him understandingly. "You must be exhausted. You played like a demon, Lolo. I bet every owner there wishes you were on his team. In fact, I bet you get some nice offers after the way you played today."

Lolo grinned. "Well, thanks, Bibi," he said.

"Are you sure that Joe's okay?" Arielle asked.

"Oh, yes, Arielle," Bibi said. She trilled laughter. "It's just age, dear. He tries to do too much. You know how men are. He'll be fine after a little rest."

"Oh, good," Arielle said, "I was worried about him." Arielle smiled at the older woman sweetly. *It's no wonder the old goat's half dead,* she thought. *A dinner party every single night, a luncheon every day, mimosa-soaked breakfasts, and scotch-laced teas—it's enough to kill a man half his age. On top of which he has to put up with the dragon lady.*

Arielle took a cigarillo from the pack on the coffee table, and Lolo lit it for her. "Thanks, Lolo," she said.

Bibi and Lolo began talking about the polo practice session, analyzing it play by play, and Arielle planted a smile on her face and tuned out, bored by the conversation. She'd decided she hated polo, but she liked the men who played it.

She watched her hostess with fascination, convinced that Bibi was flirting with Lolo, who seemed to be enjoying it enormously. It was all Arielle could do to keep from giggling aloud, the idea was so ridiculous. Bibi's chestnut-dyed hair looked as if it had been set with mayonnaise, and her perfectly made-up face could only be described as horsey at best. Her couture-tailored suit with matching everything only made her look older than she was.

She's somewhere north of sixty, and she looks like somebody's maid playing dress-up, Arielle thought unkindly.

She took a long drag off of her cigarillo and heaved an inaudible sigh along with a plume of smoke. It didn't matter one iota how old or ugly the warhorse was, she thought. Bibi came from big bucks, older and cleaner and better-connected than most, and she could have looked like a walrus. The society columnists would always kowtow, referring to her as a great beauty and legendary hostess and style-maker extraordinaire.

Not like me, Arielle thought enviously. *I've had to work for every dress, every piece of jewelry, every god-damn cent.*

"Well, I'd better go see to the details for dinner," she heard Bibi saying, "but you two young lovers do what-ever you want. Stay out here and enjoy the terrace as long as you like, take a swim . . . whatever." She smiled meaningfully.

"Thanks for a wonderful day," Lolo said. "I look forward to the match tomorrow."

Arielle came to attention. "Tell Joe I hope he feels better," she said.

"I will, dear," Bibi said. "Oh, and don't forget. The keys are in that little Jeep. The dark green one. Help yourselves. Come and go as you like."

"Thanks, Bibi," Arielle said. "You're a lifesaver."

"Don't mention it," Bibi said. She rose to her feet, and Lolo followed suit.

"We'll see you in the morning," he said.

"Ta-ta," she said, disappearing through an open door into the house.

Arielle stood up and stretched. "Let's go," she said.

"Finished with your drink?" Lolo asked.

"We can have another one in the guest house," Arielle said.

They strolled arm-in-arm through the lushly planted gardens toward the immaculate cottage that served as a guest house. "I think Bibi's taken a real liking to you, Lolo," Arielle said, her stiletto-heeled Jimmy Choo san-dals click-clacking noisily on the stone path.

Lolo laughed. "You must be kidding."

"I saw the way she was looking at you," Arielle said teasingly. "I've been wondering why she's always so nice to me, and I thought it was just because I'm getting a big settlement out of Wyn." She pinched Lolo's ass. "But now I know that's not the only reason. She likes to look at you, and I don't blame her."

"You're crazy," he said, slipping his arm around her shoulder and kissing her cheek. Then he looked at her with a serious expression. "You know, I do think one reason she's so nice to us is because you're divorcing Wyn. Joe was sort of the undisputed king of the polo world until Wyn came along and got all the attention."

She laughed. "Joe hasn't played polo in a hundred years," she said. "I bet he hasn't been on a horse in fifty."

"Yes, but he owned winning teams," Lolo said, "and Wyn's teams came along and started beating his."

Arielle looked surprised. "I hadn't really thought about that," she admitted. "I guess you could be right. Bibi's a competitive old coot, and she wouldn't like to think her husband's team was losing."

"That's right," he said.

"So it's not just your body she's interested in?" Arielle teased.

"No," he said. "I don't think so." He leaned down and kissed her cheek again.

"That's better," Arielle said.

"And it'll get a whole lot better than that," Lolo said with a lewd look.

"Promise?" she replied.

"Have I ever failed you?"

"No," she said. "Not yet."

Arielle, her head on Lolo's shoulder, ran a fingernail down his muscular chest, on down past his six-pack abs, and into the dampness of the curly black mat at the base of his torso. She squeezed his heroic toy. "That was better than ever," she said. "I think playing polo makes you horny."

Lolo laughed. "I don't have a thing for horses, if that's what you mean."

"No," she said, "it's not what I meant. I think you're like old Bibi. You get a charge out of the competition . . . and the danger."

"Maybe," he said hesitantly, looking at her with curiosity. "I never really thought about it, but I guess I do."

"You like a challenge," she said. "Don't you?"

"I . . . usually do," Lolo replied, knowing she was leading up to something but uncertain as to exactly what it was.

"I know you do," she said, a fingernail trailing down his biceps and onto his forearm. She took his hand in hers. "Lolo, you've got to help me with something," she said. "Maybe something challenging." She looked up at him.

"What?" he asked. Then he frowned. "Jesus, Arielle. Don't tell me. You've still obsessed with this crazy idea of going to Wyn's. Right?"

She nodded. "Not exactly," she said. "I called Santo yesterday, and we—"

"You what?" he exclaimed, sitting up.

"I called Santo," she said, sitting up next to him,

"and we had a *very* interesting conversation. I'm supposed to meet him tonight."

"I don't believe this," Lolo said, looking away from her. "The lawyers have told you to lay off and mind your own business. To wait. And you won't pay any attention to them."

"Lolo," she said cajolingly, "listen to me. You know and I know that Wyn's so rich he can drag this out in court forever. Do you want to starve in the meantime?"

"No," he said, his dark eyes fiery. "But I don't like the idea of you messing with Wyn. Or that creep Santo."

"Oh, I can handle Santo. He's just a big pussycat," she said. "At least with me. And there's no danger involved. I just want you there when I talk to him . . . as a witness."

"But what are you going to talk about?" he asked, exasperated. "How the hell can Santo help you?"

"That's exactly what we're going to talk about," she said. "How we can help each other."

"I don't like this, Arielle," he said, a hard look in his eyes. "I don't like it one single little bit."

She cupped his chin in her hand and turned his face to hers. "You're not scared, are you, Lolo?"

He stiffened. "Of course I'm not scared."

"Then, please," she said. "For me?" She stared into his eyes pleadingly. "I've asked for so little from you, and I love you so much. Don't you love me?"

His features melted immediately, and he wrapped his arms around her. "Oh, you know I do, Arielle," he said. "I love you very much."

"Then you'll go with me tonight?"

He sighed. "I think my plan to talk to Wyn man to man was a better idea, but I'll go," he said. "I don't like it, but I'll go."

"Oh, thank you, Lolo," she said, peppering his face with kisses. "You won't regret it. I promise."

"I hope not," he said thoughtfully.

Colette hung up the telephone and sighed. "Oh, Hayden," she said, brushing a finger across the tiny hedgehog's quills, "poor darling Val. We must go to her at once." She made kissing noises in his direction, then carefully placed him in the pocket of one of the big linen smocks she habitually wore around the house. She traipsed into the bathroom, flipped on the light switch, and looked at herself in the mirror. "Dear, dear, Hayden," she said. "We mustn't let anyone see Mummy looking like this."

She picked up a little case of blusher on the vanity and brushed at her cheekbones extravagantly. "Too much is not enough, Hayden," she whispered. "Not at my age." With a final flourish she finished, then snapped the case shut and picked up the tube of pale pink lipstick. She expertly applied it, then blotted her lips. "There," she said. "Mummy's almost ready. Just a bit more mascara." She picked up the bottle and unscrewed the top, pulling out the brush, then flicking at her eyelashes quickly. "Now," she said. "All better." She flipped off the light, closing the bathroom door behind her.

"Oh, Puff Puppy," she said. "There you are. I almost tripped over you." She leaned down and stroked the Maltese, then straightened back up. "Mummy must go next door. You be an angel, and I'll give you something special when I get back." She blew kisses in his direction.

Through the kitchen she hurried, then stopping near the back door, she grabbed one of the big straw hats on a coatrack there. She put it on, adjusted it just so, and rushed on through the doorway, out the porch door, and through her garden to the gate that led into Valerie's.

"Oh, darling, there you are," she exclaimed, seeing Valerie and Elvis walking toward her. "Kiss, kiss, Elvis," she said, bending over to give him a pat on the head.

"Oh, Colette, I'm so glad you could come over," Valerie said. "Do you have Hayden in there?"

"Yes, of course, I do, darling," Colette replied. "But do let's hug. Only carefully."

They embraced, then Colette stood back and looked up at Valerie. "I think we both needed a nice hug today."

Valerie nodded. "It's been one of those days."

"You must tell me all about it," Colette said. "I've already talked to Eddie, of course, and cried my eyes out. Poor, sweet Noah. It's such a tragedy."

They settled themselves on Valerie's screened-in porch with iced tea, and Valerie told her about the scene at Eddie's.

"What kind of monster would do such a thing?" Colette asked worriedly after she'd heard the complete story.

"I don't know," Valerie replied, "but it gives me the creeps."

"Me too, darling. I'm not letting Puff Puppy out in the garden without me," Colette said. "And Hayden will be with me at all times. I don't suppose it was anything, but I thought I heard someone or something outside late last night. I started to call you, then saw that your car was still gone, so I didn't."

"You heard someone?" Valerie asked, looking at her. "You're sure?"

Colette shook her head. "No, I'm not the least bit sure," she said. "I didn't see a thing, so I guess it was just an animal of some sort." She shrugged. "A racoon trying to get in the garbage or something like that probably, but never mind that. I'm dying to hear what happened this morning at your mother's." She paused and looked at Valerie conspiratorially. "And last night at Stonelair, of course."

Valerie laughed. "I'll tell all," she said, "but I think I'll get this morning over with first."

She told Colette everything that had transpired at Marguerite's. She realized, even as she told Colette the story, that it was already beginning to seem like a distant memory because of the terrible scene at Eddie's that followed it.

"This is almost too much for one person to bear in a single day," Colette said sympathetically. "It's horrible, of course, the way Marguerite treats you, the way she's always treated you, but there is one marvelous thing to come of it." She turned her beautiful blue eyes on Valerie and smiled. "It gave you the perfect opening to give Teddy the old boot to the backside."

"There is that," Valerie agreed. "It certainly wasn't what I had in mind, but what could I do?"

"Exactly what you did do," Colette said. She seemed lost in thought for a moment, then added, "I don't like Teddy, frankly, and I never did. He always seemed too good to be true, and a lot of things that seem that way are. But I hope he doesn't take it badly."

"Teddy's been really moody and irritable lately. Even nasty at times. I guess it's just work and me being too busy to see him, but I don't know. It's really sort of worrisome. And Mother, well, you know her. I don't think either of them is going to take it lying down."

"No," Colette said, "come to think of it, I'm sure you're right. I think that underneath all those lovely manners they're both real fighters who'll fight for the sake of fighting. But imagine! Those two in cahoots like that! And that stinking cousin of yours in on it, too. Well, they deserve each other, is all I can say."

Valerie smiled. "Somehow I don't think they'll find much comfort in each other."

"Ha! Cold comfort at best," Colette said. She took a sip of her tea, then looked over at Valerie. "How do you feel about it now, darling?" she asked. "Do you have regrets?"

Valerie shook her head. "None whatsoever," she replied. "I wish it hadn't happened the way it did, but I didn't plan it that way."

"Do you think you're going to be terribly lonely and blue?" Colette asked. "Any port in a storm and all that?"

"No," Val said, looking off toward the pond in the distance. "I don't think I'm going to be lonely at all." She turned and looked at her friend and couldn't help the smile that hovered on her lips.

Colette's mouth, too, slowly spread in a smile and her eyes brightened considerably. "Well, well, well!" she finally said. "I don't believe it. But I do! Yes, I do believe it." She clapped her hands together. "Is it the mystery man at Stonelair, Val?" she asked eagerly. "Who is he, or shouldn't I ask? You don't have to tell me a thing, but I'm dying to know."

Valerie was silent for a minute, then quietly said, "Yes, it's Wyn Conrad at Stonelair."

Colette's eyes widened enormously. "You-you don't mean it?" She clapped her hands together again. "It is the mystery man. This is better than I could've ever imagined. You must tell me all about it."

Valerie took a sip of her iced tea, then set the glass down. "I've been taking care of the animals out at Stonelair."

Colette nodded but remained silent, waiting for more.

"Well, when I first met him," Valerie went on, "I didn't get a good impression. In fact, he seemed like an imperious smart-ass. Then he told me about the polo accident and all, and since then, well . . . I've found out he's anything but the man I thought he was at first." She turned and looked over at Colette. "I feel like I've known him all my life."

Colette smiled dreamily. "Like an old shoe?" she said.

"Something like that," Valerie replied. "The first time we actually talked—not the first time when we just met each other—I think sparks began to fly between us. No, I *know* they did. Then last night at dinner, we got to know each other a lot better. It's just . . . fabulous." She looked at Colette again and shrugged. "So, there you are."

"I'm so thrilled for you, Val," Colette said. "This really is the best news, and the timing! Well, it couldn't be better, could it? It's almost as if it were planned this way."

"It is odd, isn't it?" Val agreed. "It almost makes you believe in some kind of fate."

Colette took a sip of her tea and sighed wistfully. "What's he like?" she asked. "I know he must be wonderful, or you wouldn't feel the way you do. And I know he must like animals or he wouldn't have them. But can you give me an inkling?"

"He's . . . oh, it's so hard to explain," she said. She decided she would confide everything in Colette, knowing that she could trust her discretion. "He had that terrible accident playing polo, like I told you, and it's going to take a long time for him to recover—in more ways than one. His looks have been affected by skin grafts and plastic surgery, and he's got to have a lot more."

"Oh, dear," Colette said. "Will he be permanently scarred?"

Valerie nodded. "Yes," she said, "and that's terrible, of course. But I think the worst damage it's done is to his ego. His pride. You can imagine. In places, his skin looks like a burn victim's. Most of that's hidden, but some of it does show. He'll have to live with it the rest of his life. There's no escaping it."

"Perhaps with time," Colette said, "he'll learn to cope with it, and perhaps . . . perhaps you can help him?"

Valerie felt herself blush slightly. "I hope so, Colette," she said. "He's still a very handsome man. Just a little rough around the edges, I guess you'd say. That's one of the reasons he came up to Stonelair. To get away from the world and have a place to recover."

"So that's it," Colette said. "Something so innocent, so harmless. And all this talk about drug lords and the Mafia and such."

Valerie laughed. "It really seems ridiculous once you get to know him." She went on to tell Colette everything she knew about Wyn Conrad, and about their dinner the night before.

When she'd finished, Colette said, "It's when wonderful things like this happen, Val, that I begin to suspect there might be a benevolent creator. That there might really be some great plan. It seems much more than a mere coincidence." She reached over and squeezed Valerie's hand in hers. "I'm so happy for you."

"Thanks, Col—" Valerie began. The telephone rang on the table next to her. "I'd better get that," she said apologetically as she picked up the receiver. "I'm on call at the clinic."

"Of course, darling," Colette said.

"Hello," Valerie said.

"Val?"

Her heart skipped a beat at the sound of his voice, and she suddenly wished she were alone. *Thank God for portables,* she thought, getting up out of her chair. "Wait just a second," she said. She pressed the hold button.

"Colette, I'll be right back," she said.

Colette smiled knowingly. "Should I go?"

"No," Valerie said. "I'll just be a minute." She stepped through the door into the kitchen, then went on down the hallway to the living room, where she curled up in a chair. She pushed the hold button again.

"Hi," she said. "Sorry about that, but my neighbor's here and I wanted to have some privacy."

"That's okay," he said. "How are you doing today?"

"I'm all right," she said. "Actually, it was sort of hectic this morning. A friend's dog was poisoned, and I had to go over there and check that out."

"Poisoned?" he said. "That's horrible."

"Yes," she said. "It really was terrible, and I can't figure it out. Sometimes that sort of thing happens because of real grudges or revenge, but there doesn't seem to be any reason for this. The owner's a friend of mine, so it was really awful."

"I'm sorry," he said. He paused a moment, then added, "Maybe I can help make you feel a little bit better?"

She felt her heart leap with joy. *So this is what it's like,* she thought. *This . . . this wonderful feeling is what I've been missing with Teddy.*

"And exactly how do you propose to do that?"

"I can think of several things," he replied with a chuckle, "but I was thinking about a little dinner again tonight. For two."

"Think you can wine and dine me and win me over, huh?" she joked.

"I am sincerely going to give it my best try."

"Spoken like a true male chauvinist pig," she said. "So comforting."

"I thought so," he said. "I am putting up my best front for you."

"I'd hate to see your worst."

"How about if I show it to you after dinner then?"

"Sounds heavenly," she replied.

"About eight o'clock okay?"

"Perfect. I'll wear my new see-through Versace."

"We don't want to scare the horses," he said.

"You're one to talk," she said.

He was silent for a beat, then roared with laughter. "You're a mean and hateful and spiteful woman, and I can't wait to see you."

"Same here."

He hung up, and she sat there staring at the living room walls, not really seeing anything. She didn't think she'd ever felt so buoyant, so happy, so alive and full of hope for the future. She went back out to the porch, where she rejoined Colette.

"The look on your face says you have a date," Colette ventured.

Valerie nodded. "Yes." She sighed happily.

Colette reached over and patted her on the arm. "God bless you, Val," she said. "I suppose Hayden and I should run along home and let you spend your time getting—"

The telephone rang again, and Valerie looked over at Colette and shrugged. "What can I say?" she said. "I'm popular."

She picked up the receiver. "Hello?" she said.

"Val, I want to talk to you." It was Teddy, and he sounded like a sergeant major giving orders.

"Not now, Teddy," she said. "Colette's here, and we're busy."

"What do you mean you're busy?" he snapped. "What's that old bitch ever done but powder her nose?"

Valerie was stunned speechless by the vehemence in his voice. "I don't have to listen to this," she finally replied. "I'll be glad to talk to you when you're not feeling quite so offensive." She quietly replaced the receiver in its cradle and turned to look at Colette.

"Oh-ho," Colette said. "He's not playing nice-nice."

"No," Valerie replied. "Definitely not."

"Oh, dear," Colette sympathized. "If there's anything I can do, darling, you just say the word, and I'll gladly do it."

"I think Teddy and I'll just have to have a little talk," Valerie said. "After what happened this morning, I don't feel like I really owe him any explanations, but I guess I ought to try to smooth over some of his ruffled feathers."

"Well, you were friends for years, so it would be a shame for it to end really badly," Colette agreed. "But don't you dare let him browbeat you, Val."

Valerie shook her head. "No, Colette," she said, "don't you worry about that. I'm not going to let that happen. I'm really sick to death of being told what to do by him—and my mother. I'd like to be friends with both of them, but I'm really up to my ears with their ordering me around."

"That's the spirit!" Colette said. "I knew you had it in you."

"I guess you knew it better than I did," Valerie said, looking over at her friend.

"Well, you know it now," Colette said. "You've

been very brave in the past, defying your parents to do what you really wanted to do, but still, you've been under their thumbs for such a long time—well, Teddy's and your mother's—that it's wonderful to see you sprouting wings."

"Speaking of which, I'm surprised Mother hasn't already called," Valerie said.

"Oh, she will," Colette said, nodding. "Knowing Marguerite, she's simply busy plotting away at her war table, drawing up new battle plans."

Valerie laughed. "You know her so well."

"Well enough to know she's not yet begun to fight," Colette said. "Unfortunately." She opened the pocket of her smock and peered in. "I thought I felt Hayden stirring about, but I see he's sound asleep. I suppose I ought to take him home and put him to bed."

"He's got to have his rest, so he can play on his wheel all night," Valerie said.

"Oh, yes," Colette said. "They're completely nocturnal creatures, and that's nice for me because you know how nocturnal I am. Hayden keeps me company in the wee hours when I read or write letters or watch television. Puff Puppy sleeps away like a smart doggy should." She looked at her wristwatch. "Anyway, darling, I'd really better go. I know you want to get all beautified for tonight."

She eased herself out of the chair, then adjusted her big straw hat. Valerie rose to her feet to show her out.

"Darling," Colette said, "I'm so thrilled for you I can't find the words." She kissed Valerie on both cheeks. "I know you'll have a wonderful evening."

"I know so, too," Valerie said, "and don't worry, I'll keep you posted."

"Oh, I hope you do," Colette said. "It's so exciting." She leaned down and stroked Elvis. "Bye-bye, sweet boy," she said. Elvis thumped his tail in response.

Valerie held the porch door open for her, and Colette left, waving as she negotiated the stone path, the sweet scent of her perfume trailing behind her. *Thank God for Colette,* Valerie thought. *I couldn't ask for a better friend.*

She filled Elvis's water bowl, added some dry meal to his food bowl, and decided to take a long, leisurely bath. After making herself a light lunch, she had worked for a long time in the garden, weeding and deadheading mostly, before she had finally decided to call Colette to come over. Now she could feel her muscles, tired and sore.

Maybe I'll take a bubble bath, she thought. Then she laughed aloud. *This is really fun. This gleeful anticipation of the evening. Now I finally know what all those other women over the years were talking about before their big dates.*

Outside, the car cruised by again, slowly, but not so slowly as to look too suspicious to anyone who happened to notice it. Not that there was anyone about to see anything. There were only the two houses on this country lane. Then suddenly there *was* somebody.

The driver sped up slightly, but not before seeing Colette come through the garden gate that led to Valerie's and noticing her take something from the pocket of her smock, holding it up to her face, and making as if to kiss it before replacing it in her pocket.

What the hell? the driver wondered. *Does she think a creepy little thing like that even knows who she is? She must be crazy, the old coot, but at least she never saw me.*

Chapter Twenty-Four

They had dined together on the candlelighted terrace again tonight, but Gerda Reinhardt hadn't had a hand in preparing the food. With some assistance from Valerie in the mansion's big kitchen, the two of them had done everything together, sipping a dry white wine as they worked. Valerie gathered up the condiments—ketchup, mustard, mayonnaise, and pickle relish—then sliced tomatoes and onions and cheese and washed lettuce, while Wyn piled charcoal in the grill outside and lit a fire, then made big patties out of the hamburger meat and peeled and sliced potatoes for French fries.

"I'm not going to deep-fry these," Wyn said, "if you don't mind."

"What are you going to do with them?" she asked.

"Spray them with Pam, then put them in the oven," he replied. "I swear they're almost as good as the real thing."

"It sounds good," she said, "and healthier, too. I guess we should make *some* concessions to healthy eating, shouldn't we?"

"Well," he said, "a little here and a little there. I don't obsess about it."

"Good," she said, "because I don't think I could stand it if you did."

He laughed. "That's what I like about you," he said. "A woman who speaks her mind."

"If I don't," Valerie replied, "nobody's going to do it for me."

Out on the terrace, they enjoyed their hamburgers and French fries, and had fresh peaches for dessert. Then they sprawled out in the library with the four dogs and the cat, who'd decided to pay a visit. They were sipping coffee laced with a dollop of brandy.

"That was really perfect," Valerie said. "I love simple food."

"I do, too," he said. "I didn't realize how much I liked it until I went to one too many fancy parties in Palm Beach. All the hostesses try to outshine each other with delicacies and exotic ingredients."

"I think that trend has even hit the provinces," Valerie said.

"I finally decided I had pretty simple tastes," Wyn went on. "Not just meat and potatoes, but fish and fowl and veggies, too, only not played with so much. You know what I mean?"

Valerie nodded. "It's become almost like an obsession with some people, and I'm worn out with it. At first I thought it was funny, but I'm really tired of going to restaurants with micro this and baby that and infused the other." She stopped and looked at him. "And I'm really sick of the pyramids."

"Oh, yeah," he said, laughing. "Now everything on

your plate has to be arranged in a pyramid. Whether it's an entree or dessert or whatever. I'm glad you noticed that, too."

"I guess it's just another fad," she said. "Something else will come along soon—maybe trapezoids?—but I'll still love hamburgers and French fries."

"You're my kind of girl," he said, looking into her eyes.

"You think so?" she asked.

He nodded. "I know so." He took a sip of his coffee, then said, "Which brings me to a ticklish subject."

"What's that?" she asked. "My feet?"

He grinned. "No," he said. "That's later." Then his face became serious. "Did you talk to that fiancé of yours yet?"

"As a matter of fact, I did. By default actually," she replied, her eyes sparkling with liveliness. She had hardly been able to restrain herself from telling him what had happened this morning, but had wanted to wait for the right moment. Now, she decided, was definitely it. "You're not going to believe it."

"Try me," he replied.

She repeated for him the events at breakfast that morning at her mother's. When she was finished telling the story, she looked over at him and said, "So you see, Mr. Conrad, I'm a free woman."

His dark eyes were boring into hers intently. "I don't know when I've ever heard better news," he said. "And I mean that, Val."

He slid an arm around her shoulders and pulled her closer to him on the couch. Then he tenderly kissed her on the cheek. "I've never meant anything more," he said. "You sparked my interest the very first time I saw you, then, well . . . you set off fireworks inside me. I didn't know it could ever be like this."

"I know exactly what you mean," she replied. "I-I've been . . . experiencing the very same thing. I guess . . . I don't know what to call it, but . . ." Her words trailed off into silence.

He kissed her cheek again, then whispered, "I think it's safe to say it's what they call love, Val."

She almost shivered with the thrill of hearing the word. It was a thrill mixed with fear, for she knew that with love came commitment and compromise, and having to give up a degree of the independence she'd fought so hard for. But she also knew that for this man she could overcome any fears. Every fiber in her being told her he was right for her, there was no mistaking it, that he was the one.

It is love, she thought, *plain and simple.* There was nothing else to call what she was feeling for him, or he her, if what he said was true.

"You can say it, Val," he whispered. "I will."

She felt his arm tighten around her, and she looked up into his dark eyes.

"I love you, Val," he said. "It may be crazy, but I know I really do love you."

She felt her face flush with heat, and she nodded slightly. "I'm-I'm in love with you, too, Wyn," she said softly.

"There," he said. "That wasn't so difficult, was it? We're in love with each other." He hugged her closer still, then kissed her lips gently, staring into her eyes.

Valerie returned his kiss, hungry for him as she had

never been for Teddy or anyone else. She put her arms around him, gingerly stroking his back, wanting to hold on to him with all her might, but afraid that she'd hurt some tender spot on his body unknowingly.

He seemed to sense her cautious restraint and leaned back and looked at her, a smile on his lips. "I'm not glass," he said. "I won't break."

"I-I'm just not sure how delicate you are," she said.

"Me?" he said. "I'm tough as leather, young lady, and don't you forget it." He smiled again. "Well . . . except maybe for my face right now."

"Aha!" she said teasingly. "So you've got a soft spot."

"For you," he said, "I've definitely got a soft spot."

He gently drew her to him again, and she felt herself melt into his arms. They began kissing once more, their hands exploring one another's bodies, their passion blossoming into urgency. Valerie forgot her concerns for any pain she might cause him and enjoyed the feel of his body, stroking him as he stroked her, wanting to get to know every inch of this man. She'd never felt the desire to merge with another as she did now. To become one with him.

When at last they parted, they were breathless.

"You look so beautiful, Val," he gasped. "You're glowing."

She suddenly realized she'd never seen his entire face at once without any bandages, except in the photographs hanging in the stable's tack room. "I'm glad I can see more of you," she said. "More of your face, I mean. I think that you glow, too."

"You're sure you like the way I look?" he asked.

"I love the way you look," she replied. "Besides, I wouldn't care if you looked like Freddy Krueger."

"You're certain about that?" he asked seriously.

She stared into his eyes. "Wyn, that's not the case, so it doesn't matter. You were handsome before, and you're handsome now."

He looked at her for a moment. "I'm still going to need some more operations," he said. "It'll take a long time. Do you think you could handle that?"

She playfully slapped him on the arm. "I'm a vet, remember?" she said. "Give me credit for knowing something about these things and being able to deal with them."

"Yeah," he agreed, "but you might enjoy leaving all that at work when you come home at night. You might get tired of coming home to more of it."

She shook her head. "Never," she said with fiery determination in her voice. "Not for a single minute. Not if I come home to you."

"You're very brave," he said. "Or very stupid." Then he grinned. "But I know you're not stupid."

"I'm neither," she said. "I'm in love."

He kissed her lips gently. "And I'm in love." He drew back and gazed at her steadily. "You know how I first knew?" he asked.

"When you saw me in my lab coat?" she joked.

He shook his head. "It was the stethoscope."

They both laughed, then he said, "I was certain when I stopped taking the shots."

"The shots?" she asked.

He nodded. "I was taking a lot of pain medication." He paused a moment, his eyes cast down, choosing his words carefully. "I think . . . I know . . . that I was overdoing it. I was lonely and depressed. And I felt like some kind of freak. The painkillers took me away from it all." He looked back at her. "Then you came along." He took her hands in his. "You changed everything, Val," he said. "You made me want to live again. To feel life again. Even if some of it is unpleasant and painful."

With his words, Valerie's heart surged with love and, she had to admit, a measure of pride. To think that she could have that sort of effect on a man was empowering.

"I was at a turning point in my life," she said, "or low point, I guess. I knew that I wasn't in love with Teddy, but in all honesty, Wyn, I was actually tempted to go through with the marriage anyway. It seemed easier than arguing, and I didn't want to be alone forever. I don't think anybody does. Then, guess what?"

"What?" he asked.

"You came along from out of the blue," she replied, looking at him and smiling. "The last thing I ever imagined."

"The old white knight or Prince Charming, huh?" he said.

"Well . . . ," she said, "more like Frankenstein."

He grabbed her and held her as she laughed. "You mean, mean woman." He kissed her passionately, almost roughly, wrapping his arms around her tightly. Within moments, they were breathlessly kissing, stroking, massaging, delving, probing, and exploring.

They finally parted, and it was Wyn who spoke first.

"I-I don't know . . . how you—how you feel . . . about waiting," he stuttered, looking into her eyes, "but it's making me crazy already. I want to make love to you, Val."

"I may be a free woman," she said laughingly, still breathless, "but-but . . . you're still a married man, Mr. Conrad."

"You won't hold that against me, will you, Doc?" he asked.

"I might," she said. "I think I really should know what's going on in that quarter."

"You're right," he said. "It's only fair. After all, you've told me all about your ex." He paused. "Arielle and I are getting a divorce, you know, but we haven't arrived at a final settlement yet."

Valerie nodded. "And?" she said, coaxing him.

"And I'm playing hardball because I'm really pissed off with her," he admitted.

"I see," she said. "I would've suspected as much from you."

"You already know me pretty well."

"I think so," she said. "You're a wronged man, and mean as a snake."

He nodded. "You bet. I could get it over with quickly," he said. "All it would take is one little phone call to the lawyer, but I've been torturing her. Deliberately."

"Of course, just what I would've guessed. But!"

"But what?"

"Does it make any sense to go on torturing Mrs. Conrad if you want there to be a new Mrs. Conrad?"

"Are you proposing to me, Doc?" he asked, smiling.

"Darn right, I am," she said. "So you've got to unload some of your riches on the first Mrs. Conrad and tell her good-bye. Besides," she went on, "I think it'll improve your disposition considerably when she's out of your hair—and I'll have you all to myself."

"You think so?"

"I do," she replied.

"Well, Doc," he said, "I think you've got a point, but are you sure you want me to make an honest woman out of you?"

"I don't think either one of us wants to live life any other way. Honest living is the only way to go."

He sat grinning at her like a boy. "I'm going to call the lawyer tomorrow," he said, "and tell him to get it over with ASAP. Give the woman what she's asking for and get rid of her once and for all."

She stared at him through slitted eyes. "Honest injun?"

"Scout's honor," he said, holding a hand up.

"Cut your finger and sign it in blood?" she asked.

"For you, Doc, I would," he replied. "But somehow I don't think you're so mean you'll make me lose blood over this." He fell on her body again, tickling her until she shrieked, then he began kissing her until they were both moaning with passion.

The parking lot out behind the bar was dark, the only light coming from distant streetlamps. The roar of the dance music playing on the bar's powerful stereo system was reduced to a muffled bass beat out here, momentarily amplified when a parting customer flung open the door and came out the back way.

Inside the car, the three people sat deeply engrossed in discussion, their conversation abruptly ceasing altogether when the occasional patron passed close by.

"You're crazy," the huge bulk in the front seat said in a quiet but intense voice. He stared straight ahead, as if he wasn't addressing the two people in the backseat, as if they didn't even exist. The light outside reflected off the smooth back of his shaved head.

"No, I'm not crazy," the female in the backseat said. "It's a cinch. When you shoot him up with the painkiller, you give him too much, then the poor guy falls down the stairs or something. It's simple."

"You mean I throw him down the steps," the giant said.

"Exactly," the woman replied. "Make sure his neck is broken or something. I'll give you fifty grand."

"Oh, Jesus," the man in the backseat said, almost under his breath. "I don't believe I'm hearing this."

The woman turned to him, her eyes glittering angrily. "You have a better idea?" she said. "Maybe *you* want to do it for fifty grand? Is that it? What if I give you a gun? I've got one at the house, you know. I brought it with me. Will you go in there and do it? Earn your keep?"

"Shit." The man sighed, turning away from her and staring out the window, his face almost pressed up against the glass. "You've had too much to drink. You don't mean what you're saying."

"Yes, I do," the woman said. "I mean every word. I'll pay fifty grand up front, then fifty when it's done. I'd do it myself except I'd be suspect number one, and I'd have hell even getting in there."

"I'd be number one," the bulk in the front seat said. "I'm there nearly twenty-four hours a day, and I'm in the will."

"That's crap," the woman said. "Make it look like an accident, like I said. Tell the cops how he shoots himself up sometimes. Wanders around the house at night. Just make sure he's dead, then go on out to your cottage and go to bed. Those stupid fools the Reinhardts wouldn't know any different. Besides, everybody knows you've been totally devoted to him for years."

"One major problem," the giant retorted.

"What?" the woman asked.

"Since he's been seeing that vet, he's quit shooting up, unless he's doing it himself."

"That doesn't matter," the woman said, "he's got needle marks on his ass, right?"

The bulk nodded.

"So who's to know he quit?" she asked.

"You make it sound so easy," the man in the back-seat said.

"It is," she said. "So why don't you give it a try if he won't? He could get you inside and back out again without any problem." She looked toward the front. "Right?"

The bulk nodded again. "I could do it."

"No way," the man in the backseat said. "No fucking way. I'm not going to have anything to do with this."

"Not even for me?" the woman asked, thrusting a clenched fist against her breast.

"No," the man said.

"And a hundred grand all your own?" she said tauntingly.

The man shook his black curls. "No," he said. "Don't ask me again. That's final. No!"

She looked toward the front again. "You've got to do it then," she said to the hulking presence at the steering wheel. "You've got to!"

The bulk sighed, then said, "I'll have to think about it. Think about how to do it. Maybe."

Tiffani frowned. "Why were you so late anyway, Teddy?"

"I just had a bunch of business stuff to do," he replied. He put the silver straw up his nose, then bent over the line of cocaine she'd cut for him, and took a snort up one nostril, then repeated the process with the other. He sniffed several times, making certain he'd gotten it all up into his nose, then looked at her and smiled. "Forgive me?"

"I forgive you," she said. "How can I be mad at a man with such good nose candy?" She giggled. She felt great. They'd already snorted several lines, made love, and had a long talk about something Teddy wanted her to help him with. *Imagine,* she thought. *Me, poor little Tiffani being able to help the rich Mr de Mornay.* Only she wasn't so sure she wanted to get involved with this little project. *I've got to make sure there's plenty in this for me,* she decided.

"What're you thinking about?" Teddy asked her, putting a finger under her chin and turning her face to him. "You look like you're in another world, Tiff."

"Oh, I don't know, Teddy," she replied, shaking her

long, copious curls. "I just . . . well, I mean, your idea sounds too dangerous to me. I don't even know my way around Stonelair except in the stable complex. It's, like, I drive there, park, go inside to the stable office and work, and that's it. Besides, that creep Santo's always there, and you never know when old man Reinhardt's going to come wandering in."

Teddy took a sip of the wine he'd brought over to Tiffani's, then set the glass down. "The stable complex would be enough for right now," he said, looking at Tiffani.

She stared back at him. "The stable?" she said quizzically. "But why the stable?"

He had to tell Tiffani that he was planning a surprise for Wyn Conrad and Valerie, but he didn't want her to know exactly what he had in mind. He'd have to keep her in the dark to some extent, or he'd never get her cooperation. Tiffani may have the hots for him, he realized, but he had the feeling that she'd only stick her neck out so far.

"Because," he finally said, "what I want to do can be done in the stables when nobody else is around." He slid a hand across her naked breasts, then ran his fingers up and down her torso gently, finally maneuvering it down between her thighs, where it rested on her warm mound.

He could feel the new line of coke kicking in, and he felt powerful, indestructible. "You don't have to worry about a thing, Tiff," he said. "It's a piece of cake. And I'll take good care of you for helping out."

"Hmmmm," Tiffani moaned. "You feel so good."

"You'll help me, won't you, Tiff?" he asked, leaning

over and licking at a nipple with his tongue. "Please, Tiff."

"Ahhhhh, Teddy," she moaned.

His fingers began to work between her ample thighs, delving into her wetness, while his tongue flicked out at her nipples between words. "Please, Tiff," he said. "For me."

"But-but I don't know what you want me to do, Teddy," she said in a gasp. Her body began to quiver with delight, and she didn't want him to stop. Ever.

"It's no big deal," he said, momentarily taking his mouth off a nipple. "Nobody'll get hurt."

"You-you sure?"

"I'm sure," he said, removing his hand and sitting up.

"Oh, no, Teddy," she immediately complained. "That felt so good."

He got on his knees between her legs and spread them wide apart with his hands. "It's going to feel even better, Tiff," he said. "I want you to feel better than you ever have." His head plunged between her thighs, and his tongue replaced his fingers there.

Tiffany began to roll her head from side to side, moaning loudly, her legs alternately stiffening and spasming, her hands pushing down on the back of his head. "Ohhhh, Teddddy," she cried. "You-you're going to make me—"

His tongue plunged into her relentlessly. Then he suddenly withdrew and sat up again.

"Nooooo, Teddy," Tiffani groaned. "That was so—"

Paying no attention to her complaints, Teddy grabbed her knees with his hands, spread them wide and, without any further preamble, he plunged into her hard, up to the hilt of his fully engorged manhood.

Tiffani gasped and nearly levitated off the bed before she began to spasm again and again, her cries of pleasure and flowing juices driving him ever harder and faster, until he was bucking like a cowboy, and with a roar like a bull and a final plunge he exploded inside of her, his entire body jerking wildly.

He collapsed atop her, and the two of them lay spent, exhausted for the moment. It was a long time before Teddy rolled off her, pulling her with him so that he stayed inside her. He stroked her damp hair and looked into her eyes. "You'll do it," he whispered. "Won't you, Tiff? For me? Please?"

She nodded slowly. "If you promise me nobody'll get hurt," she said.

"You bet," Teddy said, grinning. *Nobody will get hurt, you stupid bitch*, he thought, *but that doesn't mean nothing will.* "Nobody'll get hurt, I promise."

She smiled. "And you promise we'll keep doing this, Teddy."

"Believe me, baby, I want to do this as much as you do," he said. *At least until something better comes along*, he thought. She was already getting tiresome, he'd decided. It was time to move on soon, explore new territory.

He took her in his arms and kissed her passionately, his tongue plunging between her lips, his cock stirring to life again inside of her. Tiffani responded immediately, grinding herself against him and moaning with pleasure.

Teddy's going to be mine, she thought. *All mine,*

and nobody else's. I just know it. I'm going to be the rich Mrs Teddy de Mornay.

It was late at night, but the shadowy figure didn't want to get too close to the house because the dogs might get alarmed. It wasn't necessary anyway. Not with such great binoculars. The lovey-dovey couple was sprawled out on a big Chesterfield couch in the library with the lights on. It was as if nothing or nobody in the world could harm them.

Ha!

While they made love to one another in that magnificent room, they were in a world of their own, protected from prying eyes.

Or so they thought.

They'd undressed one another, taking their precious time, seeming to savor every single minute of it. Tenderly caressing each other, running hands all over each other, nibbling, licking, and kissing.

How sweet and gentle they were.

Then, rutting like animals, devouring one another like starved, lovesick dogs. Moaning and groaning in ecstasy, no doubt, while they pawed and clawed at each other in a frenzy of carnal delight. Then resting, breathless, but unable to keep their hands off of each other after their great mutual and explosive climax. In sync, those two. Whispering sweet nothings to each other for sure, yapping about how great it was, and oh, yeah, professing their undying love.

We'll see about that.

Then going at it again. Like a horse at stud and a mare that had never had it before. Disgusting, really.

They're nothing but animals. Dirty, filthy animals.

A shudder went through the watching figure. *And me? I've got nothing. Never had anything or anybody. Not like them. But I'm going to have to fix that one way or the other. I'll have to fix them.*

Chapter Twenty-Five

Colette awoke to sunlight streaming through her bedroom windows. *It's late,* she thought idly, sitting up in bed and rubbing her eyes. She looked over at the clock on the draped table at her bedside. *My goodness, ten o'clock.* Puff Puppy stirred at her feet, and she leaned down to pet him.

"Good morning, Puff Puppy," she said. "Your mummy overslept, and you didn't wake me, you naughty boy."

She slid her legs over the side of the bed and into damask-patterned silk slippers, then stood up, shrugged into a silk robe, and went into her bathroom. She quickly performed her morning ritual, gave her hair a few strokes with a brush, and dismissed her appearance in the mirror with one lifted eyebrow. "Later, alligator," she said to her reflection. "Yes, I'll fix you up later."

She snapped off the light and made her way to the kitchen, Puff Puppy following slowly along behind her. She opened the kitchen door, padded out onto the screened-in porch, and opened the screen door for Puff Puppy. "There, darling," she cooed. "Do your business for Mummy. I'll have your breakfast waiting when you get back."

She watched as Puff Puppy went out into the garden, sniffing here and there, and headed for one of his favorite spots. It was a patch of ferns that hid him entirely from sight, giving him a sense of privacy, she supposed. *He's awfully sluggish this morning,* she thought. *I wonder if something's wrong with him. He doesn't seem himself. I'll have to watch him,* she decided, *and if he continues behaving this way, I'll have to make an appointment with Val.*

Forgetting her promise to herself not to let Puff Puppy out of her sight, she returned to the kitchen and filled his water bowl with fresh water, then filled his food bowl with a mixture of dry food and leftover bits of chicken she'd deboned for him. That done, she ground coffee beans and filled the coffeemaker with water and aromatic coffee.

She heard Puff Puppy at the screen door and padded back out onto the porch and let him in. "Were you successful, darling?" she asked the quiet and still slug-gish dog.

Puff Puppy made a beeline for his bed in the kitchen. He slumped down and immediately closed his eyes.

"Oh, dear me," Colette said worriedly. "If you're not yourself by noontime, I'm calling Val."

She poured herself a cup of the freshly brewed coffee, then mixed in a tiny spoonful of sugar substitute and a generous portion of nonfat milk.

Coffee cup in hand, she walked over to Hayden's big

wire cage, which was entirely covered with a heavy blue cotton cloth that blocked out all light. That way the nocturnal creature wasn't bothered by the kitchen's bright daylight. She lifted the cloth and peeked in. "Hayden, darling," she cooed. "Did you have fun last night? Spinning away on your little wheel?"

She didn't see Hayden or any movement indicating that he was there. He was hidden by toys perhaps, or burrowed deeply under his blanket. African pygmy hedgehogs couldn't stand cold, and Hayden always slept on a heating pad burrowed under a little blanket. Colette straightened up and worriedly removed the cloth from over his cage entirely, putting it down on a chair.

"Hayden?" she called again. "Are you there, darling boy?" There was still no movement, so she opened the cage's door and carefully grasped his blanket, looking under it. Nothing. She took the blanket out and moved her fingers gingerly about the cage, searching in vain for the missing creature.

"Hayden? Hayden!" she began to cry. "Where are you, darling?"

She removed her hand from the cage and closed the door. *How on earth?* she asked herself in a panic. *I'm certain I had the cage door secured when I went to-bed last night. Or did I?*

Then another thought occurred to her. *Oh, dear! Maybe Hayden's loose in the house somewhere,* she worried. *He's very enterprising and may have ventured out of his cage.* She'd often let him out at night and let him explore the kitchen, so it wasn't altogether strange territory for him. But the kitchen door was open to the porch. She rushed over to it and looked about the screened-in porch. No sign of Hayden there.

She closed the kitchen door firmly and began searching the baseboards around the room. *He always seemed partial to the baseboards,* she thought, exploring the perimeter of the room. She looked and looked, but there was no sign of Hayden.

With a sigh, she turned to the notepad she kept on the kitchen counter to look at the list she'd started yesterday. All the things she had to do, the groceries and other items that she had to shop for.

Iced tea, she remembered. She had intended to make a big pitcher to have on hand for herself and Val, if she happened by later today. It was a green tea jazzed up with a delicious, rather rare kind of honey. She put the to-do list down and decided to get busy.

She retrieved a big glass pitcher on the ancient Welsh dresser, then going to the side-by-side refrigerator-freezer, she held the heavy pitcher in one hand and opened the freezer compartment with the other. She always filled the pitcher to the brim with ice cubes to start. Reaching her hand into the pile of ice that the ice-maker had churned out, she took a handful from the reservoir and put it in the pitcher. She took another handful and placed it in, then reached in for another.

"*Merde!*" she cried aloud. She must have nicked her hand on a sharp piece of ice. She removed her hand with the offending ice from the ice-maker's big reservoir and started to toss it in the pitcher, looking down at it first to make certain she hadn't gotten blood on it from her hand.

Suddenly her eyes grew enormous, and she dropped

the pitcher of ice to the floor, where it shattered into dozens of pieces at her feet. Puff Puppy barked in alarm, but she didn't hear him. Her mouth widened into a blood-curdling scream of shock and fear and horror, and she dropped the piece of ice in her hand— *no, not ice!* she told herself—to the floor, where it landed amidst the broken glass and ice cubes.

Colette stepped back, the scream still rising from deep within her. Looking down at the floor, her screams turned to wails of anguish, then into sobs of utter despair. She clutched the lapels of her bathrobe as if hanging on to them would somehow protect her from whatever evil had done this. Tears began to pour from her old eyes, running down her face in rivulets of sorrow.

On the floor, atop the broken glass and ice, lay Hayden, frozen to death, his quills as hard and sharp as knives, his beautiful gray color frosted pale, his tiny dark eyes open in a look of eternal horror.

Colette covered her own eyes and continued to sob, choking on her sorrow, until she could finally make her way to the kitchen table, where she sat down heavily in a chair, the tears still flowing.

Who could do something so demonic? And why, oh, why? She had no answers to her questions, but they continued to roar at her.

She had no idea how long it was before she quietly rose to her feet and methodically took a tea towel from the kitchen counter, then picked up Hayden's lifeless little body and wrapped it in the towel. She placed the bundle in his cage and closed the door. Then, retrieving a broom and dust pan from a closet, she cleaned up the broken glass and ice. *Puff Puppy mustn't hurt himself,* she thought.

That accomplished, she picked up the Maltese, clutching him to her as if she were still on automatic pilot, and went out onto the screened-in porch and sat down, staring off into the garden. She had to call Val at the clinic, but she felt so dispirited that she decided to wait a while. Nothing Val could do would bring Hayden back. She would spend some time alone with Puff Puppy, trying to come to terms with the evil that she'd been forced to confront.

Valerie had just finished her morning rounds of the local horse farms and had gotten out of her dirty coveralls and boots and changed into a fresh lab coat and sneakers. She was washing up, getting ready for the rest of her day, when Tami rushed into her office.

"Val," she gasped, "it's your mother. She says it's an emergency."

Val's eyes widened in alarm. She turned off the water at the sink in the little bathroom. "An emergency?" she asked, stepping into her office. "What is it?"

"I don't know," Tami said, "but she seems to be in an awful state. She's on line three, okay?"

"Thanks, Tami," Valerie said. "Tell her I'll be right there."

"Will do."

Valerie quickly buttoned up her lab coat, then approached her desk with trepidation. *What could the emergency be?* she asked herself, wondering if there really was an emergency at all.

Seated at her desk, she pressed the button for line

three and picked up the receiver. "Hello, Mother," she said as calmly as she could. "Tami tells me there's an emergency. What's going on?"

"I must talk to you at once, Val," her mother said in a voice that was uncustomarily anxious. "Before you cut me off, I must tell you that it's of the utmost importance."

"What is it, Mother?" Valerie asked.

"I thought you were going to marry Teddy," her mother began, "and—"

"I don't want to discuss that, Mother," Valerie said in no uncertain terms.

"That's not what I want to discuss, either," her mother hurriedly said. "*Please,* Val, hear me out for a minute before you rush to judgment. It's vitally important."

What on earth? Valerie wondered. "Okay," she said, "I'm listening."

"What I'm trying to say," her mother continued, "is that because I thought you were going to marry Teddy, I signed a power of attorney and turned over my entire stock portfolio for him to manage. I—"

"You what?" Valerie asked, not quite believing her ears.

"You heard me correctly," Marguerite replied with a heavy sigh. "Because I thought you were marrying him, I turned everything over to Teddy to manage. I took it all away from Dock Wainwright."

"I can't believe you did that," Valerie said. "Dock Wainwright has always handled the family's affairs. And quite conservatively, like Dad wanted him to, I might add. You know as well as I do that Teddy trades in dangerous territory. Maybe he's had success. I don't really know anything about it, but I do know that Dock always seemed to take very good care of you and Dad."

"Be that as it may," Marguerite said, "I've done what I've done, and now I'm . . . well, frankly, I'm a little disturbed. I don't think I would be if I knew you were marrying—"

"I said I don't want to discuss that," Valerie said with fire in her voice. "If you've made a decision you regret, I'm not taking the blame for it. And if you're trying to talk me into marrying him just because you've invested with him, then you might as well stop right there. There is not a chance in hell I'll marry Teddy."

"I'm well aware of that," Marguerite said, "although I don't think you have to use such harsh language to get your point across. In any case, that's not what I'm trying to do. I'm certainly not trying to convince you to marry him because I've invested with him." She sighed.

"Okay," Valerie said. "Then what is it? What can I do?"

"I'm telling you because I'm beginning to worry about the whole thing," Marguerite said. "I've just had a talk with Suzy Brooks. She and Harry have taken their account away from Teddy, she told me." Marguerite paused as if gathering the courage to go on.

"I guess people do that all the time," Valerie said. "I mean, you just did it with Dock Wainwright."

"Yes," Marguerite said, sighing again, "but in any

case, Suzy said that Teddy had been handling a substantial amount of money for them, several million dollars, in fact. She said that everything had gone swimmingly for a while, but that lately their statements had been arriving late or not at all."

"You mean they hadn't been getting anything from him?" Valerie asked. "Are you sure?"

"Absolutely," Marguerite said. "Suzy would never have made this up. She said that when they asked Teddy about it, he assured them it was all due to some sort of new accounting procedure they were switching over to in the office. Anyway, to make a long story short, they finally decided to bail out, and it's taken them months to recover their money from him. They practically had to threaten to file a lawsuit against him to get him to pay up."

"I see," Valerie said, genuinely alarmed now.

"Not only that," Marguerite continued, "but when they got their final statement and check, all sorts of highly debatable charges had been made to their account, reducing it by several thousand dollars."

"Oh, my God," Valerie moaned. "Are they going to try to do something about it?"

"They haven't come to a decision," Marguerite replied. "But I have. I want my money to go straight back to Dock Wainwright and as quickly as possible. I was going to try and get Jamie working on it this morning, but I can't find him."

"What do you mean you can't find him?" Valerie asked. "Where does he go?"

"I . . . I don't really know," Marguerite confessed. "He has friends nearby, I know."

"Look, Mother," she said. "I'm sure it'll be just fine. He's only had your money a very short time, right?"

"Yes," Marguerite said, "but I can't help worrying after Suzy's call. I thought I was doing the right thing, and having Jamie as a sort of watchdog over everything, well, how could I go wrong?"

"Jamie as a watchdog?" Valerie asked. "What do you mean? How's he involved?"

"He was transferring some money to Teddy as well," Marguerite replied. "And Jamie knows a thing or two about money management, so I signed papers giving Jamie the power to make decisions regarding stock trades and such. He is supposed to be consulted before Teddy makes any final decisions regarding changes in the portfolio. That sort of thing. But I haven't been able to reach Jamie. He's visiting friends in Saratoga, I believe."

It gets more Byzantine by the minute, Valerie thought, but didn't say. "In that case," Val said, "everything ought to be all right, Mother. If Teddy can't do anything without Jamie, then you should be okay until a transfer back to Dock is made."

"I hope so," Marguerite said. "I just don't know. Teddy is certainly an underhanded schemer."

Pot calls kettle black, Valerie thought. Did it never occur to her mother that if those two would scheme with her, they might very well scheme *against* her?

"I don't know how I can help you," Valerie said, "but if there's anything I can do, say the word."

"I was hoping that you might be able to talk to Teddy, and tell him I've changed my mind," she said. "Tell him it's because your father would be terribly disappointed to know that I'd transferred control to someone other than Dock. I certainly don't want Teddy to think that I'm suspicious of him. It might offend him. I want this done in a very civilized way."

The way you planned my wedding, Valerie couldn't help thinking. "Well," she said, "I don't think there's a chance that I'll get to talk to Teddy before you do, but if he calls I'll broach the subject."

"That would be awfully helpful, Val, dear," she said. "I've already talked to Dock Wainwright, by the way, and told him that I want the money transferred back to his firm. So he said he would get the paperwork ready at his office, and he's waiting to hear from Teddy. He's already left word with Teddy's secretary."

"Okay," Valerie said. "Is there anything else?"

"No," Marguerite said, then she added, "but it wouldn't hurt if you'd be nice to Teddy, only until this is over, I mean, so that it works out smoothly."

Valerie wanted to scream, but instead she said, "Of course, Mother. I'll be nice to Teddy. For your sake."

"It's for your own as well," Marguerite pointed out. "After all, Val, dear, you are my sole heir."

"I'll do my best," Valerie said. "Now, I'd better get off the phone because I've got a very busy day."

"Yes," Marguerite said. "I won't keep you. Goodbye, then."

"Bye, Mother," Valerie said and hung up the telephone.

She put her head in her hands and massaged her forehead as if to wipe away the worries that her mother's telephone call had brought on. *Life is never simple,* she told herself, *but can't there be days with little reprieves?* She lifted her head again and looked down at Elvis, spread out in his bed beneath the desk.

"Elvis," she said. "We need a vacation. Just the two of us." Elvis wagged his tail in response. "Wait. Not so fast. On second thought," she said, "make that the three of us. You, me, and Wyn. Oh, scratch that! What am I thinking? Make that . . . what? The eight of us. You, me, Wyn, the four wolfhounds, and Mina, the cat. How does that sound, Elvis? A vacation for eight. Maybe on some nice quiet, sunny island with no telephones or faxes, no pagers or cell phones, no E-mail, no TV. Just us animals."

She leaned down and gave him a few strokes, then straightened back up. "I like the idea, Elvis," she said. "I like it a lot, and I think you will, too."

Wyn paced in the library, the dogs watching him idly, the cat perched in regal solitude on a high-backed baroque chair. He had already called Dexter Willingham IV, his lawyer in Palm Beach, and had a long discussion with him about finalizing the divorce.

Willingham had been relieved because, although he could have billed for many more hours if the case had been dragged out, he was utterly sick and tired of Arielle Conrad and her screaming tantrums. She had even approached him at a grand charity function, pointing her finger and shouting obscenities at him in front of dozens of white-tied and ball-gowned grandees in one of Palm Beach's finest ballrooms. He had spoken to Myron Goldman, Arielle's lawyer, a number of times about the situation, but Goldman seemed incapable of controlling his client.

The whole process could be virtually over by the end of the week if all went well. Neither Wyn nor Willingham anticipated any problem in instantly resolving the case. However, the telephone hadn't rung in the last hour, and Wyn was beginning to get nervous.

What if Arielle had changed her mind about something, and decided to throw some final wrench into the process? She might hold out for more when she discovered that he was ready to settle.

Santo walked into the room on virtually silent feet, and Wyn caught sight of him out of the corner of his eye. "Where've you been, Santo?" he asked. "I haven't seen you all morning."

"I overslept," Santo said honestly. "I know that if you need me, all you have to do is call the cottage, so I guess my usual mental alarm clock just didn't go off this morning. I'm sort of under the weather."

"You have the flu or something?" Wyn asked.

"No," Santo replied. "Just . . . like a little cold or something."

"I happened to notice that you've been out late a lot recently," Wyn said with a smile. "You found somebody up here that's hot to trot?"

Santo averted his eyes, then turned his gaze to Wyn. "Aw, not really," he said. "Just been working out a lot. Gone to a couple of bars with some of the guys from the gym. You know, just shooting the shit."

The telephone rang, and Santo hurriedly picked up the receiver. "Stonelair," he said.

He listened for a moment. "Please hold," he said. He turned to Wyn. "It's Dexter Willingham for you," he said.

"I'll take it," Wyn replied, sighing with relief. He took the receiver from Santo. "Hey, Dex," he said. "What's going on? I was beginning to get a little worried."

"I've spoken to Myron Goldman," Willingham said, "and he foresees no difficulty bringing this to a very quick close. The only problem at this point is that he can't seem to locate Arielle."

"What do you mean, he can't locate Arielle?" Wyn asked.

"Exactly what I said," Willingham answered. "She's not at home. In fact, no one picks up at all. He said he'd made some phone calls, but so far he's had no luck. He'll get back to me as soon as he's spoken with her."

"Aw, shit," Wyn said in exasperation. "This could take forever, knowing Arielle."

"Or it could take an hour, Wyn," the lawyer replied reasonably. "She could simply be at the hairdresser or out shopping. Who knows? We'll probably find her in very short order."

"I hope so," Wyn said, "because I want to get this over with."

"I understand, Wyn," Willingham said, "and I'm glad you've reached that decision. However, our hands are tied until we've located Arielle."

"I realize that," Wyn said with a sigh. "I think I'll make some calls myself, Dex, and you let me know the minute you hear anything."

"Will do," the lawyer said. He chuckled then. "Don't worry about it, Wyn, if she's in Palm Beach, we'll find her in the next hour or so. You know how small this town really is."

"That's for sure," Wyn replied. "Okay, Dex. I'll talk to you later."

Wyn hung up the receiver and stared off toward the pool for a few moments, wondering where he should call first to try to locate Arielle.

"Trouble?" Santo asked, looking over at his boss.

Wyn turned to him. "They can't find Arielle, and we need to get hold of her right away. Wouldn't you know it? I decided to go ahead and get this divorce business over with, and what happens? Arielle suddenly does a disappearing act."

Santo stared at Wyn, his mind thrown into a maelstrom of conflicting thoughts. *Should I tell him that I know where Arielle is? No,* he immediately decided, *because then Wyn would wonder how I know, and I certainly don't want Wyn to know that I've met with her behind his back.* And what about Arielle's little plot? He'd have to get hold of her as soon as possible to let her know what was going on. That would put a stop to it. Or would it? He really didn't know.

"What's wrong with you?" Wyn asked. "This is what you've wanted me to do, and now that I've done it, you don't have anything to say?"

"Sorry," Santo said, clearing his throat. "I was just wondering where she might be. This is good news, though. I think it's the smartest thing you've done in a long time."

Wyn nodded. "Well," he said, "I guess you could say that Val, you know, the vet, had something to do with it." He smiled, almost sheepishly.

"What do you mean?" Santo asked, trying to act as if he didn't have any idea that there might be a

budding relationship between his boss and the veterinarian.

"Oh, come on, Santo," Wyn replied. "You know
I've been seeing her."

Santo nodded. "Yeah, I knew that, but I just thought
it was, like, real casual."

Wyn looked at him with a serious expression. "It's
more than that, Santo," he said. "Much more."

"Well," Santo said, "I guess congratulations are in
order, huh?"

"Maybe," Wyn said. "Anyway, I'm going to get on
the telephone and see if I can help dig up Arielle. If you
think of anything, let me know."

"I will," Santo said. "I'm going down to the stable,
check on things there, but I'll give a call if anything
comes to mind."

"See you later," Wyn said.

Santo turned and left the room, trying not to hurry,
heading down to the stable where he would try to get
hold of Arielle in privacy.

Wyn watched him leave. *What's going on with him?*
he wondered. *He hasn't been acting like himself lately.*

Chapter Twenty-Six

Tiffani jerked and missed a key on the computer's keyboard. *Damn!* she thought. *The creepy bastard's done it again. Scared the life out of me. Except this time, I'm already nearly jumping out of my skin.* She quickly planted a big smile on her fuchsia-painted lips and turned around, thrusting her large breasts out and giving her long, curly hair a big swing, a habit she'd developed, certain that men found it irresistible.

"Hi, Santo," she said, forcing cheer into her voice. "How are you?" She was chewing gum and popped it.

Santo returned her smile with the mere semblance of one and that was an effort. "Okay, Tiff," he replied. "You doing all right?"

"Yeah," she said. "I've got tons of typing to do. A lot of checks to get ready for signing and stuff." She paused for a moment, considering her next move. "Are you going to be working in here today?"

Santo shook his head. "That's why I came by," he said. "I've got a lot of stuff to do, too, and I wondered if you could hold the fort down today."

"Sure!" she said gaily, almost shuddering with relief. *How good can my luck get?* she thought. "I'd be glad to. I'm way behind on paperwork, so I'll be right here except to maybe run out and get a sandwich or something later on."

"That's cool," he said. "Oh, yeah, if Mr. Conrad calls down here for me, tell him I'll call him right back. Okay? Then you give me a buzz at my cottage. I'm going to be working over there."

"Yeah, I'll do it for sure," she said, thinking that he was acting pretty odd. The creepy giant never left his post, and while she was working at the stable that usually seemed to be his post. Maybe the boss had him doing something else? Maybe he and the boss had a fight?

Oh, well, who cares, she decided. *He'll be out of the way, and that's the best news I've had all day. I'll just have to watch out for old man Reinhardt, but that shouldn't be much trouble. He's always in a world of his own. Never even speaks to me, just nods. I'll be able to help Teddy out, and nobody will ever know the difference. Except Teddy. My Teddy.*

"See you later," Santo said, then went back out the door.

"Yeah, sure," Tiffani said. "See you." When she was certain that he was gone, she picked up the telephone receiver and dialed a number.

In the privacy of his cottage, Santo quickly punched in the number on his cell phone. Once. Twice. Three times. Four. *Nada. Fuck.* He was about to press the end button when she answered.

"Hello?"

"It's Santo," he said. "Maybe it's time we had a little talk."

"I was hoping you would see it my way," Arielle said.

"I'm not sure I do," Santo replied, "but I want to discuss it. Something's come up."

"What do you mean?" she asked.

"Wyn's going to settle," Santo said. "He's already contacted your lawyers about it, but they haven't been able to reach you."

"I guess his little girlfriend brought on this sudden change of heart," Arielle said.

"Yeah."

"So now that he's found somebody he wants," she went on, "he's finally willing to get rid of me."

"You could say that."

"Listen, Santo," she said, "could you get away from there now? I want to talk to you in private."

"What about Lolo?"

"He's over at the polo grounds. He might be back soon so we'd have to meet someplace."

"You mean you don't want him involved?" Santo asked.

"No way," Arielle said. "He can't handle it. I'm very disappointed in him. I thought he was more of a man." She paused, then added, "Like you."

"What've you got in mind?" Santo enjoyed her obvious flirting.

"We'll talk about it when I see you," she replied. "Can you get away?"

"Sure."

"I know a place between Saratoga Springs and Albany," she said. "We'd have privacy there. Nobody in the world we know would see either one of us."

Santo listened as she gave him the name and address of a motel. "I can be there in less than an hour," he said.

"Good," Arielle said. "I knew I could count on your help, Santo."

"I don't know," he said, "but I'm willing to discuss it."

"See you in an hour," she said and hung up.

Santo depressed the end button on his cell phone and flipped it shut. He felt life stir in his groin and smiled as he headed out to the garage.

Valerie had just finished examining George and Jesse, two Labrador retrievers, and giving them Lyme disease vaccinations. She was filling in their charts and sipping coffee when the telephone jangled.

"Yes?" she said, still focused on a chart.

"Val," Tami said teasingly, "guess who's holding on line four?"

"I don't have any idea," Valerie replied. "Is it friend or foe?"

"Oh, it's definitely friend," Tami said conspiratorially. "In fact, I would say it's probably a whole lot more than that."

Tami hung up, and Valerie pressed the line four button. "What can I do for you, Mr. Conrad?" she asked.

"Ask not what you can do for me, Doc," Wyn retorted, "but what I can do for you."

"The possibilities are infinite, I'm sure," she said

with a laugh, "but did you have something specific in mind?"

"Indeed, I did," he replied. "I want to wine and dine you again tonight at my humble abode, then see what happens from there. If you're not already bored with my company, that is."

"I'm certainly not bored with your company, Mr. Conrad," she replied, "but why don't you come over to *my* humble abode for a change and let me show off my culinary skills?"

"Because I have something special in mind," he said, "and I think we ought to do it here at Stonelair. Besides, I'd like to cook for you since I know you'll be tired after a long day at the office."

"Why, thank you, Mr. Conrad," she replied.

"How about eight?" he asked.

"I think I can fit that into my schedule," she said.

"I'll see you then."

"Okay, bye." She hung up the phone and squeezed herself with her arms. "This is what they call dreamy, Elvis," she said, looking down at him. "I hope you've felt it at least once in your life. Dreamy, dreamy—"

The telephone jangled again, and she reached over and picked it up. "Yes?"

"Val," Tami said in an alarmed voice, "it's Colette on line two, and she's absolutely hysterical. It's something about Hayden, that African pygmy hedgehog of hers."

"I'll get it," Valerie said. She immediately pressed the line two button. "Colette, what's going on?" she asked.

"V-V-Val, darling," Colette managed to say, "someone's m-m-murdered Hayden!"

"Give me ten minutes to get there, Colette," Valerie replied.

"You're a darling," Colette said.

Valerie pushed the button for Daphne's line. "Daphne," she said, when she'd picked up, "I have an emergency that may take about an hour. Could you cover for me?"

"What's the emergency?" Daphne asked.

"Colette Richards's African pygmy hedgehog," Valerie replied.

"Oh, no," Daphne said. "Of course I'll cover for you. I hope it's nothing serious."

"I'm not really certain," Valerie said noncommittally. "I'll leave the charts with Tami."

"Sure, Val," Daphne said. "Let me know what happens."

Valerie hung up, gathered up her charts and carryall, put Elvis on his leash, and rushed out to reception to leave the patient charts with Tami.

Santo knocked on the motel room door, and it was opened at once by Arielle.

"Come on in," she said, swinging the door wide.

Santo stepped into the room and noticed that she was dressed in a filmy blouse that left little to the imagination and a micromini skirt that barely covered her silk bikini panties. Bottles of vodka and tonic sat open on a bedside table, along with two glasses. One of them wore Arielle's plum lipstick.

She saw him looking at the bottles. "Want to wet your whistle?" she asked.

"I better not," Santo replied. "I don't have much time. I've got to get back to Stonelair."

"Oh, come on, Santo," she cajoled, running a fin-gertip down his chest, "as big a man as you are, one itsy-bitsy drink won't do you any harm. Besides, I hate to drink alone."

Santo shrugged. "Okay," he said, "just one."

Arielle padded over to the bedside table on bare feet and poured a generous portion of vodka into a glass and added a splash of tonic. She handed it to him, then picked up her own.

"Cheers," she said, tapping her glass against his.

Santo nodded and took a sip of the drink.

"Let's get comfortable," she said, spreading out on the bed and patting the cover next to her.

"We need to talk," Santo said, eyeing her hungrily.

"So we'll talk," she said. "Here." She patted the bed a second time.

Santo shrugged his massive shoulders again and strode over to the bed and sat down facing her on the spot she'd indicated.

She looked into his eyes and ran a fingertip down his chest once more. "Tell me, Santo," she said softly, "what's on your mind?"

"It's like I told you on the telephone," he said, "Wyn's decided to settle, so you can drop all your plans to get rid of him. But . . ."

His voice trailed off into silence, and he took another swallow of vodka and tonic.

"But," Arielle said, "we both know that I'm worth more with him dead. Isn't that right?"

Santo nodded slowly.

"If I accept a settlement," she went on, running a hand up and down his powerful biceps, "I'd be getting a fraction of his worth. But if he suddenly dies and a settlement hasn't been arrived at, I'm still legally his wife . . . And if he marries again, he might change his will, leaving you out in the cold." She lifted her micromini skirt and smoothed out an imaginary wrinkle in her black silk panties.

Santo watched her with unabashed lust in his eyes. She'd always flirted with him, but they'd never actually made it. Things were different now, though. They weren't under Wyn's watchful eyes, and besides, she and Wyn were going to be divorced or . . . Wyn was going to be dead.

"We would have to move fast," Arielle said, unbuttoning her sheer blouse down to the waist. "Before the lawyers track me down and offer me a deal."

Santo nodded, but his eyes were riveted to the perfect breasts that were revealed right in front of him, within his touch.

"I know you could pull it off, Santo," she said seductively. "And I would go there with you to help if need be." She took a sip of her drink. "Just think, we could go off together."

"That would certainly look suspicious," he said.

"I mean eventually," Arielle said. "After it's all over, and I've got his money."

"What about Lolo?" he asked, his hand beginning to rub her naked thigh.

"Lolo," she said nastily. "What a joke. He's not half the man you are, Santo. He doesn't deserve a woman like me. Especially with all the money I'm going to have. And don't worry, he'd be terrified to talk. Even if he knew anything."

She reached up and ran a finger down his thick neck and back up to his lips, rubbing them, then trying to penetrate them.

Santo caught her wrist in his hand. "We need to work this out. Plan on exactly what we'll do—tonight," he said.

"And we will," she said. "But let's have some fun first, why don't we?"

Santo loosened his grip on her wrist. "You were always a little crazy, Arielle," he said.

"So were you," she said, reaching between his muscular thighs and stroking the erection that was visibly pressing against his pants.

"I'm in a real hurry," Santo said. He set his drink down and took hers out of her hand and placed it next to his. He stared into her eyes for a mere instant before his massive torso was on top of her.

"Yeah," he whispered, "we'll work out the details later."

Chapter Twenty-Seven

Colette sat at the kitchen table, a soggy linen handkerchief wadded in her wrinkled hand. Her eyes were red-rimmed and swollen from the fitful tears that still came.

Valerie was leaning back against the center island, looking over at her with a deeply saddened heart. Colette looked her age today, she thought, and her normally optimistic and extravagant demeanor was subdued. Valerie cleared her voice. "Colette, I know it's difficult to make decisions now, and I don't want to seem insensitive and crass. But I have to know what you want to do with him."

Colette looked up at her. "Oh, darling," she said, "you could never be insensitive or crass. I . . . I think I'll bury him in the garden and put a little marker there. That way we can visit him. What do you think?"

"I think that's a very good idea," Valerie replied. "I'll help you do it."

"No, Val," Colette replied. "You don't have to do that. I'm quite capable. I'll find a little box and wrap him up and put him in it, then do it myself."

"You're sure?" Valerie asked. "I don't mind at all, you know. I loved Hayden, too."

"I know, darling," she said, "but I think maybe I'd better do this alone. Just me and Hayden, maybe Puff Puppy if he'll behave himself." She heaved a melancholy sigh. "I'll wait until after the police have been here and gone. I should've called them a long time ago, but I simply couldn't face having them here. I appreciate your doing it, Val."

"I'm glad you let me call them," Valerie said. "This is getting to be really scary, especially when you think that somebody actually came into your house to do it."

Colette shivered anew. "Oh, the very thought," she cried. "I feel so . . . violated, Val darling, I can't begin to tell you."

"Well, I think that this was clearly a premeditated act," Valerie said. "But I don't think that whoever did it was after you."

Colette looked at her again. "You don't think so, really? It's just like with Eddie, isn't it? The same person, I would venture. Whoever murdered poor Noah knew exactly when and where and how. The same with Hayden." Her voice broke, and she paused a moment before continuing. "It's awful to think that someone would take out their hate on innocent animals, no matter who or what has angered them."

Valerie strode over and put an arm on Colette's shoulder, patting her tenderly. "I have a feeling, Colette," she said, "that you and Eddie may not be the targets at all."

Colette looked up at her, her watery blue eyes questioning. "Then who, Val?" she asked.

Valerie went around and sat down at the table opposite her. "It sounds crazy, I guess," she said, "but Hayden and Noah were my patients, and you and Eddie are my friends. Neither you nor Eddie can think of anybody that might have a grudge against you." She paused and looked Colette in the eye. "But I know of at least one person who has one against me."

Colette's eyes widened in alarm, and her hand flew to her breast. "Oh, Val, darling," she cried. "You can't think . . . but . . ."

Valerie nodded.

"Oh, it's too dreadful," Colette said. "Teddy surely couldn't do anything this repugnant."

"I don't really know what he's capable of," Valerie responded, "but I'm seriously thinking about it. I don't know who else both has a grudge against me and knows who my patients and friends are."

"Will you tell the police?" Colette asked.

"I don't honestly know," Valerie said. She sighed wearily. "I certainly don't want to, but we have to get to the bottom of this, Colette. If Teddy didn't have anything to do with these crimes, then he shouldn't have any problem proving it. At the same time, of course, I hate to put him through police questioning if he's innocent. Imagine how that'll make him feel."

"It's so hard to know what to do," Colette said. "I wonder what's keeping the police anyway?"

"They shouldn't be much longer," Valerie said.

Valerie's cell phone rang and startled them both.

"I guess I'm a little jumpy," Colette said.

"It's no wonder," Valerie replied, slipping the cell phone off her belt and flipping it open. "I'll just be a minute," she apologized.

Valerie pushed the talk button. "Valerie Rochelle," she said. As she listened, she slowly turned away so that Colette couldn't see her face. She didn't want her friend to catch the increasingly worried expression there.

"Doesn't sound good," she finally said, trying desperately to control her reaction to Wyn's news. She didn't want to disturb Colette unnecessarily. Colette had received enough terrible news today.

"Hold on for a minute, Wyn," she said. "I'm over at my friend Colette's, and I need to speak to her for just a moment." She pressed the hold button.

"Colette," she said, "there's an emergency out at Stonelair. Something's wrong with a horse. Will you be all right if I leave you alone until the police get here?"

"Of course, Val," Colette said. "You must go tend to the horse. There's not a thing more you can do for Hayden. Or me."

Valerie pressed the hold button again. "Wyn," she said, "I'll come right out there."

She pushed the end button, then snapped the phone shut and slipped it back on her belt. "I'm sorry, Colette," she said. "Are you sure you can handle the police?"

"Of course I can," Colette responded. "I may be old, but I'm not a fool."

"I didn't mean to imply that you were," Valerie said.

"I know you didn't, darling," Colette said. "I'm just a bit touchy, I suppose. Forgive me." She paused a moment, then went on. "And Val, I don't think I'll say anything to the police about Teddy. What do you think? Perhaps I should just tell them that you have some ideas that they should discuss with you. Is that all right?"

"I think that's perfect, Colette," she replied. "I hate to leave you now, but I'd better run."

"I'll be fine," Colette said. "Now run along. You've got work to do. Oh, and why not leave Elvis here with me? He and Puff Puppy can keep each other company. They get along so beautifully."

"You're sure?" Valerie asked.

"Certainly," Colette said.

They brushed cheeks, and Valerie shouldered her bag. She leaned down and gave Elvis a pat. "See you later, Elvis," she said. Then she rushed out to her Jeep.

Chapter Twenty-Eight

Lydia looked up from her desk when Teddy walked into the office. "Thank God, you're here," she exclaimed. "The telephone's been ringing off the hook, and let me tell you, boss, there are some people who want to talk to you real bad. And pronto isn't fast enough. Catch my drift?"

"Hello to you, too, Lydia," he said with a smirk on his face. He went over to his desk and sat down in his chair, then began rifling nervously through paperwork stacked there.

She turned to face him, hair aflame with fresh carrot-red dye, eyes flashing brightly with purple shadow and black liner. "Listen, Teddy," she said earnestly, "I'm dead serious. The shit's starting to hit the fan. Or I should say *fans*, to be more precise. I don't know exactly what's going on, but I've got a damn good idea, boss. And I'm telling you, you'd better get your ass in gear and start making some mighty sweet phone calls. They're going to be asking for your pretty blond head on a nice big platter."

"You think I don't know that, Lydia," he said angrily. "I don't need you telling me what to do. I've got enough on my mind as it is."

"Humpf!" she went on, "I've had to listen to old Dock Wainwright all day long. Marguerite de la Rochelle and her nasty-mouthed cousin, Jamie de Biron, want their money back. Plus a half dozen other clients. And I mean they want it *now*. No wonder you're like a damn cat on a hot tin roof. I am, too."

Teddy looked at her furiously.

"I'm telling you, Teddy," she exclaimed, shaking a tangerine fingernail at him. "You're in trouble this time. The brokers are climbing out of the woodwork, calling by the bushel load. Wanting *their* money. Something to do with your margins, little buddy. Like maybe something to do with all that trading you did on credit and now they want their money. All that money you've gone and lost!"

"Shut up, Lydia," he cried. "I get the message, loud and clear."

She stared at him for a minute before replying. "All right," she said angrily, "but I can't take this much longer, Teddy. Seriously. I don't like being part of a sinking ship. And that's what this is. It's the fucking Titanic, and I think I'm going to have to get in one of the lifeboats."

"Then do whatever the fuck you want," he shouted. "I don't fucking need you."

"That's all you've got to say?" she cried, rising imperiously to her feet. "I've devoted myself to you for the last six years, Teddy de Mornay. Always going to bat for you, lying for you, cheating for you, and sometimes cleaning up your damn messes so nobody'd know the real you. And that's all you have to say?"

"Just get out, if you're going," he snapped nastily.

Lydia stomped one leopard-patterned stiletto heel on the floor with rage, then turned and got her pocketbook out of a desk drawer. She paused dramatically at the door and glared at Teddy.

He returned her look. "Get out, Lydia," he spat. "Go get that hot young stud you're so crazy about and get him to fuck your brains out. I'm sick of trailer trash around here anyway."

She looked momentarily stunned. "I may live in a trailer, *Mr* de Mornay," she said between gritted teeth, "but you're the trash." She turned and left, slamming the door behind her with a resounding bang.

Teddy snatched up his message slips and stared at them for a moment. He swiveled in his desk chair wih agitation, then started to lift the telephone receiver.

It rang before he could pick it up, and he waited for the machine to click in so he could screen the call. When his message was finally over, he heard Tiffani and immediately answered.

"Hey, babe," he said.

"Teddy, we've got to talk."

"We're talking, aren't we?" he said with frustration.

"No, I mean in person, Teddy," she replied. "It's really important."

"Come on, Tiff," he said huffily. "I'm very busy right now, and besides, we have a big date late tonight. Remember? A really special date. A special little party, just the two of us."

"I know, Teddy," she said seriously, "but I need to

talk to you right away. In person. I-I can't discuss it over the phone."

"Goddamn. Can't it wait till tonight?" he complained. "I'm really tied up here."

"Teddy," she said in exasperation, "I have to talk to you *now*. At my place."

She sounded as if she might burst into tears. *What the hell now?* he wondered. Everything was beginning to go sour. But the game wasn't over yet, and he had to protect his little investment in Tiff.

"Shit, Tiff," he said, "I've got to do some really important stuff here. Make some calls and all."

"You'll understand once we talk."

He sighed. "Fuck it. I'll be over in a few minutes."

He replaced the receiver in its cradle and sighed again. "Shit," he said aloud. "I knew it was time to unload her." He got up to leave, then sat back down. *One more call to make,* he thought. *Do a little potential damage control.* He picked up the receiver and dialed the number.

She answered on the third ring. "Hello?"

"Marguerite," he said. "It's Teddy."

He thought he heard a sharp intake of breath before she replied. "Well, hello, Teddy. How are you?"

"I'm fine," he replied. "I thought I might stop by later and take you out for drinks and dinner. I'd like to talk to you."

There was a long pause, then Marguerite said, "I think that would be lovely, Teddy, but why not have drinks and dinner here. It would be so much nicer than a restaurant, don't you think?"

"Great," he said. "I have some errands to run.

What if I come on over when I'm finished?"

"Perfect," she said. "It'll be such a pleasure to see you, Teddy."

He hung up the receiver, then headed out to the Jaguar.

That takes care of one bitch, he thought. *Now to go take care of another one. Tiffani. What's wrong with her anyway?* he wondered. *Just when I'm about to get her out of my hair once and for all, she has a problem. Another problem. Just what I need. Oh, well,* he consoled himself as he fired up the Jaguar's engine, *I'll be through with the bimbo tonight. Yeah, late tonight after I'm finished with her, I'll tell her good-bye forever. Then evict her from the cottage.*

Valerie stomped on the brakes at the gates to Stonelair and reached out and pushed the intercom button in one swift movement.

"Val?" It was Wyn's voice, not Santo Ducci's.

"Yes," she replied.

"Down at the stable," his disembodied voice said.

The gates immediately started opening, and she inched the car forward until she could finally race between them and on down the lane that led to the stable. She pulled into the parking area, braked with a screech, and cut off the engine.

She jumped out of the Jeep and grabbed her gear. She could already hear noise coming from the stables. The horses, whatever might be the matter, sounded very disturbed. She saw Wyn coming toward her. His face was still partially bandaged, but his body language did enough to convey his worry.

"Hey," he called to her, "slow down. I don't want you to kill yourself."

"I'm okay," she said, approaching him now. "I've never had an accident."

"And I don't want you to start now," he said. He kissed her lips and put an arm around her shoulders.

She was thrilled by his touch and couldn't ignore it, despite the fact that she was intent on getting to the stable and the horses. She smiled up at him. "I'm glad to see you even if the circumstances aren't the best."

"Likewise, Doc," he replied. "Why don't you let me carry that bag for you?"

"No, it's okay," she said. "I'm used to it, Wyn."

"Okay," he said.

"Is Santo with the horses?" she asked.

"He is now," Wyn replied.

"Uh-oh," she said. "Do I detect a note of anger in your voice?"

"Well, a little," he admitted. "I was up in the library and thought I heard noise from the stables. I called down there, and nobody picked up. Nobody! The Reinhardts had gone into town to do some shopping, that I knew. The girl who works part-time here had just left, I guess, because it was quitting time for her, but Santo should've been down there and he wasn't."

They reached the door to the office in the stable complex and went in.

"Anyhow," Wyn continued, "I called his cottage over and over. He wasn't there. Finally, he picked up and came running down here and saw that all hell had broken lose. That's when I called your office. That girl Tami gave me your cell phone number."

They went through the tack room and on into the stables, and Valerie was shocked by the state of panic among the horses. She turned to Wyn. "Does one of them seem to be more affected by whatever it is than the rest?" she asked.

"They're all spooked, some of them more than others," he said. "But they're all acting so crazy it's hard for me to tell. I guess I overreacted a little when I saw what was happening."

Santo appeared from the other end of the stable, walking toward them. Even from a distance, Valerie could see that he looked very worried.

He nodded to her as he drew up to them.

"Hi, Santo," she said.

"Hi," he replied, then looked away, shamefaced.

Valerie went to the first stall, set down her carryall and medical kit, then approached the barred door. The horse, Clever Cookie, was highly agitated, rearing and snorting and twitching, his eyes enormous with fear. It was almost as if there were a fire in the stable, she thought.

"There hasn't been any smoke they could smell?" she asked.

"No," Wyn said. "None at all."

"Any loud or strange noises?"

"Nope," Wyn said, shaking his head. "I've been here, and I would've heard it, too."

Valerie looked back into the stall. "Hey, Clever Cookie," she cooed through the opening. "Hey, buddy, what's troubling you?" She reached one of her hands past the bars to let the horse smell it, but Clever Cookie didn't even make an effort to approach her. He was totally spooked by something. She noticed the electrical conduit running through the stall.

She turned back around. "Wyn," she asked, "does the electrical conduit run through all the stalls?"

He nodded. "Yes," he said, "why?"

"Is it possible," she said, feeling that she was grasping at straws, "that there's a short or something running through that line, and the horses could've been shocked?"

"I don't think so, Val," Wyn replied. "The lights are on those lines, and there's nothing wrong with them." He turned to Santo. "Just to be sure, Santo, why don't you throw the circuit breakers for this building?"

Santo nodded and set off toward the office, where the circuit breakers were.

"I guess we can give it a few minutes and see if there's any change in their behavior," Wyn said.

"It's a long shot," she said, "but this is really strange. I've never seen anything like it, except where there's smoke."

"Me either," Wyn said.

"I'm going to walk past all the stalls," Valerie said, "and try to spot the horse that's the least spooked."

She began going from stall to stall, Wyn following along with her, looking into each one, watching each horse for a minute.

Suddenly the lights went out, and they both flinched. They stopped in their tracks but recovered quickly.

"That was pretty crazy, knowing that it was coming," Valerie said.

"This whole situation is pretty crazy," he said.

There was sufficient daylight coming in from outside, so they continued walking down the length of the stalls, looking in on each horse. When they arrived at Demon's stall, they both noticed that the immense stallion was definitely agitated, but he seemed relatively calm compared to most of the other horses. Wyn began talking to him quietly and reached in, trying to stroke his neck. Demon seemed to want the attention, but he was reluctant.

Wyn turned to Valerie. "Do you think the lights have been off long enough?" he asked. "Should they've calmed down in this length of time if it had to do with a shock or something?"

Valerie looked at him and shrugged. "I don't know," she said, "but I would think so. It's been several minutes, and you're here with them. They know you and trust you, so I would think that if that were the problem they would've calmed down by now. But there hasn't been any change, has there?"

"No," he said. "I'll go tell Santo to turn the power back on. Be right back." He dashed off in the direction of the office.

Valerie went back to Clever Cookie's stall to retrieve her carryall and medical bag, then walked back down to Demon. She would begin her work with him.

Wyn and Santo returned from the office, hurrying to where she stood.

"What're you doing?" Wyn asked.

"I'm going to need you and Santo to help me tether Demon to the stall," Valerie said. "I've got to get blood from one of the horses for toxicology. Quite frankly, I don't know what else to do. Demon seems to be the least disturbed, so I think he's our best bet."

Wyn and Santo both approached the stall. Wyn opened the door slowly, and he and Santo eased themselves inside. In a flash, Wyn caught Demon's bridle, and before the horse managed to rear away, Santo clipped on a rein and snapped it to a ring in the stall wall.

They backed away as the big horse tried to rear. "Demon," Wyn whispered. "It's okay, boy. It's okay." He stroked Demon several times, trying to calm him. Santo left the stall, stepping outside and watching.

Valerie had retrieved a syringe from her medical bag and slipped into the stall with Wyn.

"You sure you want to do this, Val?" Wyn asked quietly without turning around. He continued stroking Demon.

"I have to get some blood," she said, "and I've done it many a time. I'll just stay clear of his hindquarters." She sidled up next to Wyn and began her rhythmic cooing to calm the agitated horse. She reached up and began stroking Demon's neck, locating the jugular vein. She concentrated on stroking him there, then, when he seemed somewhat distracted by their strokes and whispers, she quickly plunged the syringe into the vein and began drawing blood.

Demon reacted instantly, shifting his feet and trying to rear, but she managed to get enough blood for toxicology, then gingerly backed out of the stall.

Wyn joined her after a moment. "You're a brave woman, Doc," he said.

"It's my job," she said, taking the needle off the syringe and leaning down to put it in the special container in her medical bag. She straightened back up.

"I'm going to call the clinic to come pick this up for immediate testing," she said. "I think it would be best if I stayed here for a while and watched them. See if I can get any inkling of what's going on."

She slipped the cell phone off her belt, flipped it open, and dialed. "Tami, it's Val. I need somebody over at Stonelair right away. I've got a blood sample that needs a toxicology screen ASAP, and I mean ASAP."

She listened a minute, then said, "Oh, great. I'd forgotten that you know where this place is. Tell Daphne I want you to pick it up. Somebody will be waiting with the blood at the front gate. Got that?"

She listened for a moment longer, then pressed the end button, snapped the phone shut, and replaced it on her belt. "Santo, do you mind waiting up at the gate with this for me? It'll probably take Tami about fifteen or twenty minutes to get here, so you don't have to leave quite yet." She held up the vial of blood.

"Sure," he said, nodding. He took it from her.

"I want to take a look at the others," she said, and started slowly walking down the length of the stalls again, first one side, then the other. Every single one of the horses was still in some state of panic.

"It's just like you said," she remarked, turning to Wyn. "Some of them are more acutely affected than others, but they're all spooked. I've never seen anything quite like it." She looked thoughtful for a moment. "Was anybody in here with them this afternoon?" she asked.

"Not as far as I know," Wyn replied. He turned and looked over at Santo, who stood near Layla's stall, seemingly distracted.

"Santo," he said, "do you know if anybody was in here with the horses this afternoon?"

Santo shrugged. "Tiff was here at work," he said. "I saw her in the office around lunchtime, I guess. I told her I wasn't feeling so hot and was going to go take a few Tylenol and go spread out. She said she had a lot of paperwork to do and would call me if anything came up. Said she might go get a sandwich or something."

"So you weren't here all afternoon?" Wyn asked.

"No," Santo said. "I told you, I—"

"It's okay, Santo," Wyn said. "You can't help it if you were sick." He sighed. "So she was the only person around, right?"

Santo nodded. "Yes. The Reinhardts had gone into town, so she was alone."

"After they pick up the blood at the gate, why don't you go give her a call, Santo?" Wyn said. "See if she knows anything."

"Okay," he said. "I guess I'd better get up to the gate now." Santo turned and walked toward the door to the tack room.

When he had left, Wyn turned to Valerie. "I don't know what's wrong with him, but he sure isn't acting like himself."

"How do you mean?" she asked.

"I can't put my finger on it," he replied.

"It's probably nothing. Circumstances being what they are, you're probably reading too much into his behavior."

"Maybe you're right, Doc," he said. "You're a very sensible woman."

They continued checking on the horses, and Valerie remained perplexed by their behavior. She'd never felt quite so defeated. Nothing in her training had prepared her for anything like this. She hated to let Wyn down, and she felt almost sick at the prospect of not being able to help the horses.

Wyn took her hand and squeezed it. It was as if, she thought as she turned to look at him, he could sense her feelings.

"It'll be okay, Doc," he said, smiling.

"I hope so," she replied, a worried look on her face.

They walked on, arriving at the last stall, pausing to look in on the horse there, then turned and started back up the way they'd come. Suddenly, Valerie stopped dead in her tracks and jerked on Wyn's hand.

"Look!" she said in a near whisper.

"What?" he asked, turning to face her.

"Oh, my God, Wyn!" she exclaimed, leaning down to the floor to pick up a small object just outside one of the stalls.

Valerie held a gel capsule between two fingers. It was just like medication would come in, and inside she discovered a fine white powder.

"Can you think of a pill that any of the horses might be taking that looks like this?" she asked Wyn.

He shook his head. "No," he said. "I'd have to check with Santo, but I can't think of a thing." He looked at it closely. "Isn't it a lot smaller than most horse pills?" he asked.

"Exactly," she said. "And I can't think of anything that we'd use that resembles this. Let me go up to the gate and give this to Santo to give Tami. We can run it through toxicology, too. I bet it'll be the same thing that shows up in Demon's blood."

"I'll go with you," he said.

"You can wait here," she replied.

He shook his head. "No, I want to keep you in my sight."

Chapter Twenty-Nine

Teddy sat down on Tiffani's big bed, where she was spread out, her eyes teary, her expression troubled. Her long curly hair, the product of much untalented cutting, dyeing, bleaching, and styling—what color *is* it? he wondered—was fanned out around her head.

He took one of her hands in his and held it, looking down at the thin gold and silver junk rings she wore on every finger. The fuchsia polish on her fake nails was chipped, and the gold-tone and silver-tone bangle bracelets at her wrists were bent and scratched from wear.

Every time he'd made a move on her, she'd shaken her head from side to side and whined. "Not yet, Teddy," she'd say. "Not yet. We have to talk."

"So let's talk, babe," he'd said, but so far she'd hardly said a word.

He was quickly losing his patience with her. *Shit,* he thought, *this is ridiculous.* He'd already snorted a few lines of coke. It was time to get busy. He had to get her to start talking.

"I'm worried about you," he said. "Won't you tell me what's wrong?"

"Well," she began slowly, finally responding to his apparent concern, "there's something we need to talk about."

"Okay," he said, sliding an arm around her shoulder.

"Well," she said, looking down into her lap, then back up at him, "you told me that those pills you gave me wouldn't hurt anybody. Those pills you told me to give the horses."

Teddy was silent for a moment, wondering what further absurdity she would present him with now. "That's right," he said. "They wouldn't hurt anybody."

"Well," she said, "I was having second thoughts. That's why I asked you to come over. And then Santo called me at home, saying the whole place was in an uproar." She paused. "They're analyzing blood and one of the pills I dropped."

Teddy stared at her openmouthed. "You dropped a pill?" he said.

She nodded. "Yeah, but it wouldn't matter, Teddy," she replied, "because they're analyzing the blood anyway. Santo said there are millions of dollars in horses there, and they're calling in the police. He said I was in big trouble because I was the only person there."

"That's bullshit," Teddy snapped. "They can't prove you did a thing."

"I know that," she said. "I can tell them that I went out to get a sandwich for lunch, which I did, and anybody could have come in and done it." She looked at

Teddy, a hard glint in her eyes. "Or . . . I could tell them that you gave me the pills to give to the horses because you wanted to get even with your vet friend for going out with Mr. Conrad."

Teddy looked over at her and saw that look in her eyes, and he knew that she was telling the truth. *She would do it,* he thought. *The bitch would implicate me just so she wouldn't go down alone, even after all I've done for her.*

Then he had a sudden inspiration. *Nobody's ever seen us together,* he thought. *Nobody has any idea that we even know each other. Unless . . .*

"Tiff," he said calmly, "you didn't tell anybody else about the stable business, did you?"

She shook her head. "No, Teddy," she replied. "Do you think I'm crazy?"

He smiled. "Smart girl."

"But some of my girlfriends know I've been hanging out with you. I've told them all about you and me."

The smile faded from his face, and he looked crestfallen. *Is she lying?* he wondered. But then he realized that of course she wasn't lying. She'd probably been bragging to her friends all summer. Telling them about how she was screwing her rich landlord, Teddy de Mornay. Getting a rent reduction *and* free dope.

How the fuck do I clean up this mess? he asked himself. He made a decision. He'd tell her not to worry, that he'd fix everything and come back later as planned. *After my meeting with Marguerite,* he thought, *I'll come over, ready to party. Maybe bring a little something extra special, make sure greedy Tiff gets her share and then some. She was my tenant,* he'd tell the cops, *but I have no idea why she'd poison any horses. Pretty girl, too. Damn shame about her overdosing like that . . .*

It was going on seven o'clock, and Val and Wyn had agreed that they'd have dinner later, after their long vigil at the stables. The horses had largely calmed down, but a few were still spooked. Their agitation, of course, only served to disquiet those that had calmed down. It might be hours yet, depending on what they had in their systems, before they were all back to normal.

Val had called the police to report what had happened, and they had paid a brief call, looking around the stables and questioning both Val and Wyn. She had told them about Noah's almost certain poisoning, Hayden's death, and assured them she would let them know as soon as she had a report on the blood work and capsule. She'd reluctantly told them that the only person she knew who had a grudge against her was Teddy de Mornay.

Santo had given them Tiffani's name and address, and they were supposed to question her as well as Teddy. Finally, after the police had left, Val had agreed to go home and change and check on Elvis, then come back for dinner. Santo and the Reinhardts would be at Stonelair tonight, Wyn had told her, so if there was any problem, there would be help at least.

She'd finished taking a quick bath, made up her face, brushed her hair, and was rummaging through her closet, exasperated because she couldn't figure out *what to wear*. She stood back and looked at her closet, considering the possibilities that presented themselves and cursing herself for not taking the time to do more clothes shopping when she was in New York City.

Wyn had told her that tonight was going to be a special dinner, so she wanted to look special.

She began pushing hangers apart, quickly scanning what hung on them, then moving on. Then an old djellaba that she'd picked up on a trip to Tangier years ago jumped out at her. She'd forgotten all about it. She pulled it out of the closet and held it up.

Perfect, she thought with a smile. *And Wyn will get a kick out of it. Wait till I tell him about bargaining for it in the Medina.* Ankle length, it was made of a white gauzy fabric that was embroidered with real gold thread around the neck, on the long sleeves, the hem, and down the bodice. It unbuttoned practically to the waist with little frog closures of gold.

She slipped it on over her head, then buttoned the bottom three or four buttons, and turned in front of the mirror. *Really perfect,* she thought, delighting in the rediscovery of the Moroccan garment. *It's summery and sexy and exotic and dressy, but casual, too.*

Now, if she could find the little gold sandals that she'd worn with it, she'd be all set. She delved back into the closet, searching the floor, under piles of shoes of all kinds, and *voilà.* There they were, needing a dusting off, but none the worse for wear.

She took them into the kitchen and wiped them with a damp paper towel, then dried them with another one. She tried them on, and they still fit. *Well,* she thought, *at least something's working out right today.*

She looked at the clock on the kitchen wall. Just

time enough, if she hurried. She checked to make sure Elvis had enough water and food, then grabbed her carryall and keys. She checked the back door to make certain it was locked, then headed for the front, Elvis following along behind her.

At the door, she leaned down and petted Elvis. "I'll be late, old boy," she said, "so you can have a nice nap." She looked into his eyes. "And I promise that you'll meet the new man in my life and all of his animals, too, very soon." She hugged him, then got up and left, making sure she'd locked the door behind her.

She fired up the Jeep and pulled out of her driveway, wondering what Wyn was up to. *What's so special about tonight?* she wondered. *Was he having someone else over?* Probably not, because he didn't see anyone else, at least not that she knew of. But he'd told her to dress up more than usual. *Why?* She couldn't think of a thing. *Was it just a matter of the food?* Maybe.

She sped down the road, eager to get to Stonelair. Excited to find out what Wyn would think was special.

Darkness had fallen, and the odd couple in the big car was speeding down the road, headed toward Stonelair. At the wheel was Santo, in Stonelair's Range Rover. When they arrived, should anybody be about, which was highly unlikely, they would think nothing of seeing him driving in alone. His passenger would simply slide to the floor until the car was safely parked in the garage at his cottage.

He'd hardly ever used the garage, usually walking over from the parking area at the stables, but tonight he'd even brought the remote for the garage door. *Open sesame,* he thought. *Then close and conceal.*

Sitting next to him in the front was Arielle. She was chain-smoking cigarillos, occasionally taking a sip from a little silver flask in her pocketbook. She had come dressed in her extraordinarily sexy way, perhaps adding a little extra pizzaz on Santo's account. The snakeskin micromini, the sheer blouse unbuttoned to the waist, thus exposing her perfect breasts, the stilettos. The effect of her outfit was not lost on him. It was as provocative now as it had been earlier in the day. He knew that Arielle was a shark, of course, but she was the sexiest shark he'd ever come across. Maybe they really would be a great team.

"We're just about there," he told her.

"So now I do my disappearing act, right?" Arielle said.

He nodded. "Slide all the way down onto the floor and keep your head down. We don't want the video cams to pick you up."

Arielle took a quick swig of vodka from her flask, then slid to the floor of the Range Rover. She tucked her head down but managed to take a couple of drags off her cigarillo before handing it to Santo to put out.

"It'll only be for a few minutes," he said, reaching over and stroking the top of her head. "Just don't get up until I give the clear."

"Don't worry," she said. "I'm fine."

The road leading to the estate appeared ahead, and Santo flipped the turn signal and began to brake. He made the turn, and the gates to Stonelair loomed in front of him. He pulled over to the security post and punched in the code. The video cams were like evil eyes tonight, but he didn't care. They couldn't pick up Arielle.

The gates opened, and he drove swiftly past them. "We're in," he said to Arielle, "but don't get up yet. Not until we're in my garage."

Arielle shifted on the floor. "Not soon enough," she complained. "This is really cramping my style."

"I'll work all the knots out later," he said.

"I bet you will," she replied, "and I can hardly wait."

Chapter Thirty

Teddy sped along the country road in his silver Jaguar, the cocaine still racing through his bloodstream. He didn't dread his talk with Marguerite. Not now. He was on a high and felt like he could conquer the world. *What's a little chat with Marguerite?* he thought. *Nothing. Nada. Zilch.* He'd always been able to sweet-talk her, hadn't he?

Tonight would be no different. He and Marguerite were two of a kind. She'd always been crazy about him, so determined for him to be her son-in-law. *Maybe,* he thought, *maybe I'll be a whole lot more to her than that. After all, she's still a damn good-looking woman, and I'm just her kind of man.*

Yeah, he thought, turning onto the road that led up to her house, *I bet I can sweet-talk her straight into bed and right out of trouble.*

Marguerite sat at the head of the magnificently laid dinner table, with Jamie at the foot and Teddy to her right. The food was simple, but beautifully served and delicious. There was a fresh salad of mixed greens, poached salmon with a dill and lemon sauce, tiny new potatoes, and haricots vert. Teddy, however, had picked at his food, moving it around his plate, as if by doing so it would disappear, and he would seem to have eaten.

The coke had suppressed his appetite, and the surprising presence of Jamie had done nothing to stimulate it.

"I'm so glad you came by, Teddy dear," Marguerite said. "We do need to talk."

Teddy nodded.

Jamie looked over at Teddy. "We've asked that our money be returned to Dockering Wainwright, you know."

"Yes, I know," Teddy said, "and that's why I wanted to talk to Marguerite. I really think you're jumping the gun. Both of you. If only you'll give me a chance to—"

"You've had your chance," Jamie said.

"Yes, indeed," Marguerite added. She pointed a bejeweled finger at Teddy. "I want to know what's happened to my money."

"Marguerite, I can explain if—" Teddy began.

"You do that, Teddy," Jamie snapped. "Explain what's happened to Marguerite's money. And mine. And make it quick."

Teddy had forsaken any pretense of eating and put down his fork and knife. He sat in his chair uneasily, crashing from the cocaine high, his stomach churning, sweat beading his face and neck, his world crumbling down around him. He thought he might be sick.

"Tell us, Teddy," Jamie insisted. "Tell us this minute. If you can explain, then explain away. We're waiting."

Teddy feigned a smile, sickly though it was, and tried to rally. His world as he knew it depended on convincing these people that they would not only get their money back but make more. Greed was the key, he knew. "As you know, there have been some market fluctuations recently," he began, "especially in the high-tech sector—"

"Yes, yes," Jamie said angrily. "Every idiot who watches CNBC knows that."

"Well, because of these fluctuations," Teddy said, deciding to give them a grain of truth, hoping that would appease them, "I've had to move money from one account to another. You understand, just to cover temporary losses. And—"

"Where is our money!" Jamie thundered.

"Yes," Marguerite chimed in, "quit this ridiculous prevaricating, Teddy. Tell us what we want to know."

Teddy glared at them both, angry now. He wasn't accustomed to being yelled at. Not by anyone. "I don't have to sit here and take this," he said between gritted teeth. "Who do you think you are—"

There was the rustle of movement behind him, and Teddy saw Marguerite and Jamie look in that direction. He turned, following their eyes, and saw Dockering Wainwright standing directly in back of him with policemen at his side.

"Teddy," Dock said, "I'm sorry to do this, but you might as well leave with these gentlemen peace-fully. Save yourself any embarrassment in front of Marguerite and Jamie."

"What the hell are you talking about, Dock?"

"I think you know the answer to that," Dock said.

"We've had a long chat with Lydia Parsons, your secretary. Former secretary, excuse me. These gentlemen are here to arrest you."

"Arrest me?" Teddy shouted. "You're crazy. For what?" He jumped to his feet, china, silver, and crystal clattering as he knocked against the table. He started toward the door.

The policemen moved in quickly, each taking an arm and restraining him before he could leave the room. Teddy struggled in their grasp, but it was useless. The coke high that had made him feel omnipotent was gone, and in its place was a staggering powerlessness.

"You'll be charged with misappropriation of funds, young man," Dock said, "and I'm sorry to say you'll be charged with securities fraud and God alone knows what else." He cleared his throat, then said, "If you gentlemen don't mind, would you read him his rights outside so that Mrs. de la Rochelle doesn't have to witness such a scene?"

The police cuffed Teddy and began walking him out of the room. "You'll pay for this, Dock," Teddy said. "You too, Marguerite. All of you will pay."

When they were gone, Dock turned to Marguerite. "I'm happy to say that I think we've managed to save most if not all of your money, my dear." He looked at Jamie. "Yours, too, Jamie. Teddy didn't have it long enough to do any real damage."

Marguerite rose and strode over to the old man. She took one of his hands in hers. "Thank you, Dock," she said, "and forgive me for deserting you. I was very foolish."

"I think your daughter has pretty good instincts, Marguerite," he said. "You might do well to listen to her in the future."

They sat in a small conservatory surrounded by a veritable forest. Huge potted palms interspersed with ferns of several different kinds, orchids, many of which were in colorful bloom, gardenia bushes, camellias, lemon and orange trees—the variety and beauty was endless, Valerie thought. As if their perfume wasn't enough, a bitter orange incense burned in hidden corners, infusing the room with a heady and exotic aroma that she found irresistible.

Some of the glass in the conservatory windows was actually cut Bohemian crystal in blues and reds and whites, and overhead was a crystal chandelier lit with thirty-six burning tapers. The light was subdued but dazzled nevertheless, reflecting off the windows, the chandelier, and the table's Venetian glassware, silver, and exquisite china.

The marble floors were covered with a multitude of Turkish kilims, some running over others. Even the table had been draped with a richly colored kilim that looked unbelievably beautiful.

Tonight is special, all right, she told herself. She didn't think she'd ever eaten in such magnificent surroundings, and the combination of the opulent with the earthy only made its appeal seem that much more luxurious and exotic.

"I don't believe it," Wyn had said when he greeted her at the door. "You're wearing a djellaba. It's perfect for tonight. Perfect!"

"Are you just saying that?" she'd asked. "Or trying to make me feel better about my crazy wardrobe?"

"No, Val," he'd said, "I really mean it. You'll see why."

And now, of course, she did. He'd planned a sort of Arabian Nights dinner in the conservatory, which felt almost like eating in a luxurious pasha's garden. The rugs and the incense and the flowers and plants and the food itself had made the evening a feast for all the senses. They'd had a lamb dish and couscous and unidentifiable tiny fried fish, and delicious sweet cakes of all kinds, many saturated with honey and nuts.

Wyn had gone to fetch some brandy, because they'd decided to have a drink in here before going to the library. The room was hard to leave, its beauty so enticing. They would wait until the candles had burned a little lower, then move on to the library, where Val was certain further delights of a different nature awaited her.

Wyn stepped into the conservatory, the brandies in hand. He looked so extraordinary, she thought, dressed in a wildly colored silk smoking jacket. It was made of several different stripes of silk, individually sewn together, with velvet lapels and cuffs. He'd laughed about it and told her that his mother had bought it for him in Paris years ago. But she could tell that he loved it.

He handed her a brandy, then sat down at the table next to her. "Cheers," he said.

"Cheers," Val said, and they clinked glasses, then took sips of the fiery liquid.

"Now," Wyn said, "there's just one more little thing to make this evening special, and I think the time has come."

She looked into his eyes. "I think the evening has already been so special that I don't know if I could stand anything else."

"Somehow, I think you'll be able to appreciate this one more thing." He slipped his hand into the pocket of his jacket and pulled out a box.

Valerie's eyes grew wide. She couldn't help but be reminded of the night only a short time ago when Teddy had given her the ring, but she didn't want thoughts of that night to intrude, to ruin the exquisite pleasure—and love—that she had found with Wyn.

He took one of her hands and placed the box in it. "This is for you," he said. "I hope you like it."

She looked down at the box, then opened it without hesitation. She drew in her breath, stunned by the ring that sat winking up at her.

"Oh, Wyn," she said, "I've never seen anything so beautiful in my life! I mean it. It's the most beautiful ring I've ever seen."

She took it out of the box without being told to and slipped it on her finger. It fitted perfectly.

Wyn was grinning from ear to ear, watching her every expression, listening to her every word, enjoying the sight of her taking it out of the box and putting it on.

She leaned over and placed her hands on his shoulders, then kissed him on the lips. "Thank you, Wyn," she said. "I love you."

"I love you, too," he said tenderly.

They kissed a moment longer, then he drew back. "Let me see it on you," he said.

She held the ring up proudly, twisting her finger this way and that. "It matches my eyes perfectly."

"That's what I hoped," he said, "and believe me, it took a lot of calling around and sending pictures back and forth before I found what I hoped would be just the right diamond for you."

"Diamond?" she said. "You mean it's not an emerald?"

He shook his head. "No, it's a green diamond."

"I didn't even know there was such a thing," she said in wonder, looking at the stone anew.

"Well, Doc," he said, "stick with me and you might learn a thing or two." He looked into her eyes, and she held his gaze. He leaned down and kissed her lips, his arms encircling her in their warmth.

Valerie almost sighed aloud with happiness. The feel of his lips on hers and those powerful arms drawing her to him sent a quiver of excitement up her spine. *I could stay like this forever,* she thought as she returned his kisses. *In his arms, against his warm body, feeling so completely loved by the man I love.*

Wyn drew back. "Come with me," he said softly, gently leading her toward a velvet upholstered chaise nestled among the conservatory's profuse greenery. There, surrounded by the intoxicating perfume of exotic blooms, he eased her down onto the chaise, then removed his smoking jacket and lay beside her. He took her into his arms again, drawing her next to him, his hands stroking her lovingly, his lips seeking out hers once more.

Valerie reveled in the feel of his hard and determined maleness against her own soft and yielding flesh, and his distinct and tantalizing masculine odor aroused her more than the scent of a thousand flowers. As his lips lingered on hers, she began to stroke him slowly and tenderly, wanting their exquisite togetherness to last forever.

His lips moved to her neck, where he kissed her reverently before trailing down to the barely exposed cleavage between her breasts. As he inhaled her sweet femininity, Valerie felt her heart swell with pleasure and passion and love for this man whose every touch increased her desire for him.

Wyn lifted his head and looked into her eyes. "Let's undress," he said.

She nodded, a smile of anticipation hovering on her lips.

He stood and held out a hand to her. She took it and let him pull her to her feet. Within mere moments he had taken off her clothes and laid them across a chair, then she removed his and placed them atop her own. They stood before one another, their eyes taking delight in one another's magnificent nakedness.

Wyn began brushing his fingertips across her shoulders, down her arms, then in circles around her creamy breasts. Valerie gasped and drew nearer to him, almost as if she needed to support herself against him, but in reality unable to bear their separation any longer. She stroked his powerful shoulders and chest, then brought her hands down onto his buttocks, savoring their hard roundness. She felt Wyn's hot breath on her neck and his maleness assert itself against her.

He took her hand and eased her back down onto the chaise, positioning himself over her, poised as if to enter her. But he waited, his eyes lingering on hers before his tongue swept over her breasts and flicked at her nipples, arousing each one in turn. Valerie reached for his throbbing manhood, her fingertips brushing lightly down it and then encircling it with her hand. Wyn gasped, then lowered himself atop her body, pressing his hungry lips to hers once again, urgent now despite his wish to hold off.

Valerie wrapped her arms around him as he entered her, slowly, tenderly, relishing her enveloping warmth and the sweetness of her juices. Her desire for him almost overwhelmed her as she felt his manhood inside her, filling her up. She began to move against him, her body craving glorious release. But Wyn continued to move gently, restraining himself, drawing out their mutual pleasure for as long as possible.

Valerie tried to check her own urgency, concentrating on the ecstasy of each moment, trying not to rush the inevitable. But with his deep, slow thrusts, her body suddenly began to convulse with climax after climax, engulfing her in a pleasure and happiness such as she'd never known, and, crying out, she clasped him to her with all her might.

Wyn's passion for her was instantly heightened by her powerful contractions, and he drew back, hesitated a moment, then in a final mighty plunge found release. His entire body spasmed atop her as he let out a joyful groan.

He collapsed onto her, panting as she did, but peppering her face with kisses, his hands all over her at once. "I . . . love . . . you, Val," he said breathlessly. "I love you . . . so much."

"And . . . and I love you," she replied, holding him tightly.

They lay silent for a while, letting their breathing return to normal before Wyn finally eased off of her and lay at her side, an arm draped around her shoulders.

"Did I tell you that I love you?" he asked, squeezing her shoulders.

"Yes," she said. "But you can say it as often as you like . . . if I can."

"You're permitted," he said, nibbling on her ear. "And encouraged."

"I love you, Wyn."

"Ah, Doc," he whispered, kissing her gently, "I can't believe how lucky I am."

He hugged her, then drew back and looked into her eyes. "Think we ought to repair to the library, as they say?"

"I think we'd better do it quickly or we'll never get there."

"You're right," he said and laughed.

They rose to their feet, then Wyn reached for the long candle snuffer and slowly began extinguishing all the candles before they dressed and left the magnificence of the conservatory.

Valerie looked around the room, wanting to remember its every detail before it was completely darkened. *This has been the most special night of my life,* she thought. *And it happened here, in this wonderful, magical room, a moment in time I'll never forget.*

"The Reinhardts didn't notice anything," Santo said. "Their lights are out, so they're in bed. They always go to bed really early."

"I remember," Arielle said. "The screwballs are almost never up after the sun goes down."

They sat on the couch in his cottage, drinks on the coffee table in front of them.

"So nobody will know we've come in?" Arielle asked.

Santo nodded. "It's highly unlikely that Wyn and the vet would've noticed, and even so, it would just be me, driving down to my cottage."

"What's this business about the video cameras you were telling me about?" Arielle asked.

"It's very simple," Santo said. "The cameras saw me leave earlier to pick you up. They saw me come back in alone because you were hidden. They're going to see me leave alone again because you'll be hiding, after Wyn's dead. Then they'll see me come back in alone later. I can make it look like I was gone during the time of the murder by replacing the videotape that shows me coming back the first time and leaving the second time. I'd have to fiddle with the timers, make the tape look continuous, because the time is printed on them. I could wipe out everything but my trip to pick you up and make out like I'd spent the night away. I've got a girl lined up who'll let me spend the night, and she could be a witness that I was there all night."

He paused and took a sip of his drink. "There are several options, depending on how I want to play it."

"It's sounds complicated to me," Arielle said. "You'd have to be here to fix the timers and change the videotapes."

He nodded. "Yeah," he agreed. "That's why I'm

leaning toward ripping the damn cams out when we leave. We'll just take them with us and get rid of them. Then tomorrow I cruise in after being out on a hot date all night. Shocked as shit by what's happened while I was gone."

"I like it," Arielle said. "It's not as complicated." She took a long drag on a cigarillo and blew a streamer of smoke toward the ceiling. Then she turned and looked at Santo. "And how are you going to do it?"

"I'll show you," he said. He got to his feet and went back into the bedroom, then reappeared with a dirty-looking white towel in his hand. He sat down next to her and pulled the towel back to reveal a gun, dark and oily and menacing.

"This is a Smith & Wesson Mark 22," he said, "With a silencer. It's called a Hush Puppy."

"A Hush Puppy," Arielle said mirthfully. She reached for it, but Santo grabbed her hand.

"It's loaded," he said, "and we don't want any mistakes."

"Don't you trust me?" she asked.

"Yes," he said, "but accidents happen."

Arielle looked miffed and took a swallow of her drink, then set the glass down. "When's this going to happen?" she asked.

"Every time she's out here," he said, "they end up in the library. Wyn virtually lives in that room, and it has several sets of French doors. So I'll wait until a little later, when I think they've had time to finish dinner and get to the library. Then I'll mosey up there and wait outside for the right moment. Too bad he told his doctors about stopping the injections. That would have been much easier. This way, there are two of them to worry about."

"I want to watch," Arielle said.

"We discussed that at the motel," he said. "You're here in case I get hurt. You can get us out of here. I've got to be able to get the videocams, but you'd have to drive."

"Santo," she cried, "what if you get hit and knocked out or something? What then? I won't be able to move you, and you won't be able to get the cameras."

"We've been through all that, Arielle," he said. "It isn't going to happen. They'll be like sitting ducks in there, and I'll be outside. I'm an expert shot. Plus, the timing's perfect. It will look like whoever poisoned the horses did them in. It's a win-win situation."

She still looked worried.

"If anything happened to me, which is extremely doubtful," he went on, "you get in the Range Rover and drive like hell out of here. Cover your head with a towel or something going through the gates, then get Lolo to help you ditch the car."

She smashed the cigarillo out in an ashtray. "I would still like to watch," she said. "Watch Wyn and his new girlfriend go down."

"You've got to be here," he said emphatically. "Ready to leave. It's really important." He put a massive arm around her shoulders and pulled her to him. "Come on, Arielle," he said, "you're getting what you always wanted. All of Wyn's money. And me."

She kissed him hard on the lips. "You're right, Santo," she said. "It'll work out perfectly, and I'll get everything I want."

*

Wyn and Valerie walked to the library arm in arm and were greeted, as usual, by the Irish wolfhounds, who leapt up from their various positions and bounded over for licks and pets.

Valerie began her routine of petting and stroking and cooing to the dogs, trying to divide her attention among them equally, only making certain tonight that their large tongues laved her new diamond in the process.

"See that?" she said, looking up at Wyn. "They know this is a new ring, and they have to put their special good luck licks on it."

He looked at her with an affectionate grin. "You think of everything, don't you?"

"I try to," she said.

"I'm going to put on some music," Wyn said. "Any requests?"

"No," she said, "I'll let you choose."

The dogs settled down, and Valerie wandered about the room, looking at the books, paintings, and bronzes, picking up bibelots, examining them, then putting them back down again. She noticed several leather boxes on a bookshelf, their tops propped open to display the fantastically embellished guns nestled in specially fitted satin-covered niches. She took one out and looked at it closely. It was decorated with elaborately carved gold, silver, and bronze. She'd never seen anything like it, except in pictures in some of her father's old auction catalogs.

"Watch it," Wyn said from across the room, where he was rifling through CDs that were stacked next to the CD player. "Some of those are loaded," he said.

"They're really beautiful."

"They were my father's," he said. "Some of them are Purdy's, Holland and Holland, different makers. You wouldn't believe what they go for nowadays."

"Have you ever used them?" she asked, placing the gun back in its niche.

"Sure," he said. "Growing up, Dad would take me out to shoot. It was target practice, though. He didn't get into hunting at all, and neither did I."

"I bet you were a good marksman," she said.

"Not as good as Dad was," he said, "but pretty fair." He put a CD in the player and pressed the play button.

Suddenly the room was flooded with melodious instrumental chords. "Whoa!" he said. "That's a little loud." He adjusted the sound, then picked up his brandy snifter and went over to a wall switch, where he turned off the big chandeliers, leaving only the painting lights, a desk lamp, and a couple of table lamps burning. He sat down on one of the big Chesterfield couches, watching her.

"What is it?" she asked. "The music, I mean." She picked up another of the elaborately carved guns and looked at it closely.

"Spanish Renaissance music," he replied. "From the fifteen hundreds. I like to listen to it in this room sometimes."

"It's very . . . haunting," she said. "Beautiful." She replaced the gun in its case, then went to the couch and sat down beside him. She held her hand up in front of them, looking at it with a smile of satisfaction on her face. "Like this," she said. "Beautiful." She leaned over and kissed him.

Wyn set his brandy snifter down and embraced her,

and they began to kiss in earnest, their lips and tongues exploring, their hands traveling the terrain of one another's bodies. In moments that seemed somehow outside of time or place, they became lost in each other, suspended within a paradise that was of their own making and for them alone. They reached a point of breathlessness, as if from a fever brought on by their desire.

Valerie drew back reluctantly and looked into his eyes. "I-I'll be rignt back," she said, almost in a whisper. "I want to freshen up."

"Hurry," he said. "I'll be waiting."

She rose and leaned down, kissing the top of his head. Then she padded across the needlepoint rug and through a passageway between bookshelves, on her way to the nearest bathroom, anxious to return to his waiting arms.

The lone figure, dressed in black, had watched Valerie and Wyn through the conservatory's big glass windows, cursing the Bohemian glass inserts that were difficult to see through. Watched, fascinated, as Wyn gave her a ring, and she slipped it on. Watched as they went at it like horny teenagers. Then moved with them as they inevitably migrated to the big library, watching through binoculars from beyond the terrace as she wandered about the room and he messed with the CDs. Watched as she fiddled with antique guns. Watched in disgust as they made out on the couch.

Then watched as Valerie got to her feet and left the library.

Now! It's time!

Bending down and scurrying across the terrace practically on all fours, the black-clad figure rushed through the open French doors and stood up.

Then:

Pop!

Pop!

Pop!

Pop!

All four dogs slumped, the powerful tranquilizer darts immediately knocking them out.

Wyn, standing at the CD player, thought he heard a strange cracking sound above the music. He turned around and stared in horror at the black-clad figure.

"Daphne—?" he began.

Phump! The Heckler & Koch P9S made a muffled explosive sound, barely detectable above the music, thanks to the pistol's Qualatech silencer.

He jerked back, his eyes enormous, then down he went, blood spraying from his head.

Valerie came down the hallway and entered the room just as Wyn fell. From between the bookcases, she looked across the huge room, and her mouth opened in terror. But she clamped it shut before any sound could come out, then dropped down to a crouch and scuttled to the bookcase where the gun cases were. She pulled out the first one her shaking hand could find, then stood up, ready to fire.

Running up to the terrace, he saw someone standing in front of the open French doors. He grinned. *A piece of cake,* he thought. *First her, then him.*

As he fired he heard the gunshots. His Smith &

Wesson Mark 22 had a silencer. *What the hell?* He
didn't know, but he saw the body drop. *Got the vet.
Now I've got to get him.* He stepped forward to look
for Conrad, but didn't see him. *Where is he?* Then he
saw Wyn's body sprawled on the floor. *What's going
on?* But he didn't have time to figure it out. *Those gunshots—got to get out of here.*

Valerie stood with the heavily ornamented pistol in
her hand, quivering from head to toe. The shots she'd
fired had made her ears ring. Even from this distance,
she could see that Wyn was dead. His body lay inert,
sprawled on the floor in front of the big walnut cabinet
that housed the CD player. His eyes were wide open,
and there was no sign of life in him.

She walked over to the other body. The person she
was certain she'd murdered. She looked down.

My God. Daphne Collins.

Why? she asked herself, staring at the body. *We were
friends, weren't we?*

She looked around then, almost in an otherworldly
daze.

Blood.

It was everywhere.

Valerie stood over the body—Daphne's body, she
reminded herself—looking down at it with utter dis-
passion. Daphne's eyes, usually so bright with curiosity,
were now stone-cold. Dead, they looked. Her lips,
normally ready with a smile, were drawn into a thin,
colorless, and unfamiliar line. Her blond hair hung
about her face in Medusa-like snakes, the tendrils
matted and dirty.

After an eternal minute, Valerie stepped closer, then knelt beside the body, noticing the blood that stained the dark needlepoint rug. A Jell-O-like pool of it had fanned out in a small kidney shape on the oak floor where the head rested. Its taint suddenly assailed her nostrils with its unmistakable metallic odor. But she was accustomed to it and didn't recoil or tremble or feel the urge to faint or vomit. Her composure remained intact.

Reaching out a hand, she took one of Daphne's blood-smeared hands in her own. She held it there for two full minutes, feeling for a pulse. She didn't detect one, but then she hadn't expected to. She'd seen death countless times in her thirty years and knew that what she was doing was unnecessary. But she kept feeling for a pulse, nonetheless, concentrating all of her efforts on the procedure, as if by feeling hard enough she could produce the heartbeat she was certain she wouldn't hear. After a few more moments she gently replaced the hand on the rug and got to her feet.

There was no doubt that Daphne was dead.

Dead, she thought without emotion. She had gone completely numb and felt like a zombie operating on remote control. The stone-cold expression on her face didn't change with this awful knowledge. There was no quiver of fear or horror or sadness about her lips. No tears of remorse or grief sprang to her eyes. Anybody happening upon the macabre tableau would think her an ice maiden, seeing her features thus composed.

She walked over to the *bureau plat* and reached down and picked up the receiver, then dialed the number with a steady hand. When a voice answered at the other end, she replied in a cool, even voice.

"This is Dr. Valerie Rochelle," she said. "I just murdered someone."

Chapter Thirty-One

Santo ran quickly to his cottage and hurried in. Arielle jumped up from the couch where she was sitting, her eyes huge with fright.

"What *happened?*" she gasped. "I heard shots!"

"I'm not really sure," Santo replied. "Something went wrong."

"Oh, *Jesus*!" Arielle exclaimed. "Hadn't we better get out of here?"

"We're going to haul ass," Santo said. "We've got to beat the cops." He withdrew the Hush Puppy from his waistband and studied it closely.

"What about the Reinhardts?" she asked.

"Their lights are still out," Santo said. "I don't think they heard anything." He looked back down at the gun, then shoved it back in his waistband. "There's nothing wrong with this silencer as far as I can tell," he said, still baffled by the turn of events.

"If the silencer works," Arielle asked, "then who fired the shots?"

"I don't know," Santo said. "I didn't see anything much except her taking a hit." He wasn't going to tell

Arielle that he'd seen Wyn sprawled on the floor in a pool of blood, but that he hadn't shot him. He'd explain that later.

"It had to be the silencer—" Arielle began.

"Come on," he said. "We're haven't got time to stand around here talking. We're getting out of here. You were supposed to have the car ready."

Arielle grabbed her flask off the coffee table, then rushed into the kitchen and looked at the liquor bottles on the counter, finally selecting a bottle of Stoli.

"Hurry," Santo growled. He was already past her, through the laundry room, and going into the garage.

Arielle rushed after him, vodka bottle in hand.

Santo fired up the big Range Rover, then opened the garage door using the remote. He backed out into the drive, turned onto the road that led to the stables and on out to the gates.

We're out of here, he thought, *on our way to freedom.*

Shit! The video cameras. Almost forgot them. I'll just dismount them when we get to the gate, and take them with us. Then show up tomorrow morning, like I planned.

He gave the Range Rover gas, anxious to get to the gates and out of this place.

Valerie stood looking over toward Wyn's body. Her icy façade, a defensive response to the horrible reality she'd witnessed and been a part of, began to crack. She'd been on automatic pilot, hardly aware of what she'd been doing. Fixated on Daphne, Wyn's death had barely registered.

Now she began to shake uncontrollably, and bile rose up in her throat. She thought she was going to throw up and started for the bathroom. She stopped suddenly near the bookcases when she heard a loud moan. *From over near the CD player*, she thought, *I'm sure of it*. A chill went up her spine, but she turned around and looked back into the big room.

Her heart began to race. She rushed to the spot where she had seen Wyn's body and stopped in her tracks. For a moment she thought she would faint. His body wasn't there. She saw the blood on the rug leading toward his desk, and then she saw him, crawling with all his might toward the telephone.

"Wyn!" she cried, running to him. She reached him and got down onto her knees, tears already streaming from her eyes, flowing down her cheeks in rivulets. Her body shook with both relief and joy.

He moaned again, louder this time, and moved his head, trying to look up at her. "Hey, Doc," he breathed. "Got shot."

"I know you did," she cried, still shaking all over. "I know you did."

"Doc," he said, "open . . . open that drawer." With a crooked finger, he indicated a small drawer in the *bureau plat*.

Valerie opened it immediately. "What, Wyn?" she asked. "What is it?"

"See . . . see that row of buttons?"

"Yes," she said, "I see it."

"Push the one marked 'Front Gates,'" he said. "Push it hard."

Valerie did as she was told, depressing the button

with all her might, then she turned back to him.

He started to say something else but only a groan escaped his lips.

"Shhh," she said. "I've already called the police. They should be here any minute with an ambulance. I thought you were dead, Wyn. You looked dead, and there was so much blood."

His eyes were still open, and there was a hint of a grin on his lips. "It's . . . it's nothing, Doc,"

Valerie didn't know whether to believe him or not, but she could plainly see the track of the bullet along the side of his head. It looked like a scalp wound, only she didn't want to take any chances.

"Wyn," she said, "lie perfectly still." Maybe she could do something for him. Maybe she could stop the flow of blood, for he was still bleeding. It was all over the rug. "Just stay where you are. I'll be right back."

"Don't leave me, Doc," he said.

"I'll be right back," she said. "I'm just getting some scissors off your desk."

Her eyes scanned the top of the desk until she saw scissors in a malachite cup. Grabbing them, she ran back over to him and started cutting the gauzy hem of her djellaba away.

"The dogs," he muttered.

"They must've been shot with tranquilizer darts," she said. "I'll take the darts out, but they won't come around for a while yet. They should be just fine."

"Good," he gasped.

The Range Rover pulled to a stop at the front gates, and Santo pushed on the remote to open them. When

they didn't at first open, he pushed on the remote
again. Still they didn't move.

What now? he wondered.

He opened the car door and jumped out, holding the
remote pointed directly at the gates. Still they didn't
budge. *What's going on?*

He ran toward the gates, constantly pressing the
remote to no avail. When he reached them, he grabbed
hold of them, one iron bar in each of his hands, pulling
with all his might. Nothing. They didn't budge an inch.
"Jesus!" he swore aloud.

"What's the matter?" Arielle cried from the car.

"The remote won't open the gates," Santo called
back to her.

"What do you mean it won't open them?" she
cried.

"Just what I said, you stupid bitch," Santo yelled.

He ran back to the Range Rover and got in the
driver's seat. "Listen," he said, "hold on tight. We're
going to have to ram the car through the gates. I don't
know any other way to open them."

Santo backed up the Range Rover, aimed directly
toward the point at which the two gates connected,
then stomped on the gas. The car launched into the
gates at breakneck speed, and there was an earsplitting
grind of metal against metal that practically drowned
out Arielle's scream.

The gates didn't give.

"Shut the fuck up, Arielle," Santo roared. He
backed the car up again, farther back up the lane this
time, then stomped on the gas again.

The big car roared forward and hit the gates at

about thirty miles an hour. The shattering sound of the impact was even louder than before.

Santo, his seat belt firmly secured, was fine, but Arielle was thrown first backward, then forward, and almost went into the windshield. Santo started to back up a third time. At that moment, he heard the screeching sirens of police cars and ambulances, and saw their flashing red and blue lights as they raced down the road. From overhead, the sound of a helicopter's churning rotors was deafening, and its powerful search floodlights swept the entire scene, rendering the night surreal. The police cars and ambulances appeared on the opposite side of the gates, which suddenly began to part.

Santo flung the car door open and started to run, but before he got twenty feet he was tackled by two policemen who manhandled his wrists behind his back and slapped cuffs on him.

Two other policemen rushed to Arielle's side of the Range Rover and jerked open the door. She began screaming and crying all at once, blindly kicking and flinging her arms at them, but she was pulled out of the car and cuffed before she could inflict any bodily harm.

"You're both coming into the station," a big officer grunted as he strolled up, taking in the scene. "Get 'em out of here."

The library had become crowded with policemen and EMS personnel. Wyn was on a stretcher now, and they were about to carry him out to the ambulance.

"Thank God," Valerie said. She turned to the policeman standing next to her. Cawley, his name tag said.

"I've got to go with him, Officer Cawley," she said frantically. "I've got to."

"You placed the call, right?" he said.

"Yes," she replied.

The officer retrieved the Purdy pistol that Valerie had used to shoot Daphne. "Is this it?" he asked, showing her the weapon.

Wyn lifted his head from the stretcher.

"You couldn't have killed her with that, Val," Wyn said. "It's loaded with blanks. Nearly all of them are." He looked toward Cawley and winced in pain. "Check it out, officer," he said. "You'll find blanks in that gun and nearly all the others."

Cawley looked down at it, then back up at her. "Let her go to the hospital," he said.

Chapter Thirty-Two

Wyn and Valerie dismounted and led their horses into the stable yard, where Helmut Reinhardt took the reins from them. He would put the horses in their stalls. Then, hand in hand, they started up the stone path that led to the house. Winter was around the corner, and it was already cold and gray. They could see smoke rising skyward from the library's great chimney.

Their faces and ears were red from the cold wind, but they were oblivious to any discomfort. Under their riding jackets, they both wore heavy sweaters, and in any case, they were too happy to allow the weather to interfere with their time together.

When they reached the library, they greeted the Irish wolfhounds and Elvis, who had become a steadfast friend and member of the pack within two days. They shrugged out of their jackets and took off their gloves, but left their boots on for the time being. They would wait until they had warmed up to change into something more comfortable.

Wyn went to the drinks table and poured them both a snifter of brandy. He turned to her and handed her one, then lifted his. "Cheers, Mrs. Conrad," he said.

"Cheers, Mr. Conrad," she replied. They had married two weeks before in the conservatory at Stonelair. Valerie and Wyn had invited Marguerite, who had been impressed by the splendors of Stonelair and had determined that Wyn might be worthy of a de la Rochelle, although she had disapproved of the presence of all the animals at the wedding.

They clinked glasses, then sat down on one of the big Chesterfield couches. "That was a wonderful ride," Wyn said.

"Yes, it was," she agreed. "How does your head feel? Any aches? Pains?"

"It's okay," he said. "Funny, now that it's quit bothering me, I forget about it." He looked over at her. "It was a close call, wasn't it?"

"Very close," Valerie said.

"I knew there was a reason I stopped seeing Daphne Collins," he said seriously. "She was pretty and smart and desirable. I guess we went out together for a few months, around the time I met Arielle, but I began to think that Daphne was irrationally possessive. Maybe even a little obsessed with me."

"She was obsessed all right," Valerie said.

"Yes, but I had no idea she'd actually moved up here after I bought Stonelair," Wyn said. "And to think, once she found out about us, how she started killing your patients to get back at you. It's so crazy how our affair meant so little to me but everything to her."

Valerie patted his shoulder. "It's not your fault,

Wyn," she said. "You were simply the object of her obsession. You didn't have any control over that."

"I know," he said, "and that's what Colette keeps telling me."

"Colette?" Valerie said. "Have you talked to her?"

"I forgot to tell you that she called today," he said. "She's really excited."

"What did she have to say?"

"Let me see," he said. "There was a lot."

They both laughed. Colette had taken to Wyn like a fish to water, and the feeling seemed to be mutual. Right now she was looking after Val's cottage, until she decided whether to sell it.

"She's got a new African pygmy hedgehog," he said. "Named it Spike."

"Oh, that's wonderful," Valerie said. "It means she's getting over Hayden's death, a little bit anyway."

"Eddie and Jonathan gave it to her for a present," Wyn said. "Isn't that great?"

"It is," Val agreed. "And just like them."

"It gave me an idea, but I wanted to ask you about it first."

"What?" she asked.

"I thought it might be nice if we give Eddie and Jonathan a husky pup to replace Noah," he said. "What do you think?"

"I think it's terrific, Wyn," she said, "but first let me feel them out about it, without letting on. You know, to see if they're ready."

"That's a good idea," he said. "They may not be, and I'd hate to put them in the position of feeling like they had to take it."

Valerie looked at him and felt her heart absolutely surge with love. *How could I be so lucky?* she asked herself for the thousandth time. *To have such a wonderful, loving, and thoughtful man to love me?*

"Colette was excited about you setting up your own practice, too," Wyn said, "and told me to congratulate you. The bad news—or I guess sad news—from Colette," he went on, "is that they've indicted Tiffani Grant for poisoning the horses and for possession of an illegal drug. The amphetamine she used. Really nasty highly concentrated stuff. I've forgotten the specific charges, but I'm sure Colette will fill you in."

He gave her a sidelong glance. He knew that she'd been devastated to learn that Teddy had been seeing Tiffani. She'd wanted to believe that Teddy loved her in some way or other, but she now believed that he'd always used her and never really loved her at all. She'd begun to question her own judgment, and Wyn had done everything in his power to help her overcome her feelings of inadequacy and self-doubt.

"What do you think will happen to her?" Valerie asked.

Wyn shook his head. "It's a hard call," he replied. "Claims she didn't know what it was. I think a lot of it depends on the jury, what they believe. She may get off pretty light, considering."

Valerie didn't respond immediately, but sat thoughtfully looking off into space. "And Teddy?" she finally asked. "Any news there yet?"

"He's been indicted on a number of charges, but the investigation continues, Colette said. Misappropriating clients' money, breaking all kinds of SEC rules. Jesus. A lot of stuff. Apparently that secretary of his—"

"Lydia?" Valerie asked.

"Yes, I think that was her name," he replied. "Anyway, she's a material witness and word is she's a good one. It's lucky she stepped forward when she did, or all of your mother's money, and your cousin's, might have gone up in smoke."

"I'm glad they didn't lose anything," Valerie said.

"The big losers in this whole mess were Teddy and Tiffani and Santo and Arielle," he said. "Santo would've gotten a nice retirement package from me, but instead he's going to be pumping iron in a prison gym for killing Daphne. Ditto Arielle. She'd have gotten a huge financial settlement, instead of jail time if she hadn't gotten so greedy."

"You're right," she said. "I can only feel pity for them."

He looked over at her and took one of her hands in his. "Val," he said, "I've got to say that I've never respected or loved anybody in my life like you."

She laughed. "Why are you saying that now?"

"Because you just reminded me of it," he said. "Wishing your mother well even though she's been so unkind to you. Inviting her to the wedding like you did. A lot of people, most people probably, would've turned their backs on her."

"I couldn't do that," she said.

"No," he said, "I know you couldn't." He hugged her to him then. "What say we get out of this riding gear now, and go upstairs for a little romp in the hay?"

"Are you up to that, Mr. Conrad?" she asked.

"You bet I am, Mrs. Conrad," he replied.

"It seems," she said, looking up into his dark eyes, "you know me awfully well."

"And I love what I know," he said, leaning down to kiss her.